SPERRY
SYMPOSIUM
CLASSICS

The New Testament

SPERRY SYMPOSIUM CLASSICS

The NEW TESTAMENT

EDITED BY
FRANK F. JUDD JR.
AND GAYE STRATHEARN

B Y U

DESERET
BOOK

SALT LAKE CITY, UTAH

Copublished by the Religious Studies Center, Brigham Young University, Provo, Utah, and Deseret Book Company, Salt Lake City, Utah.

Library of Congress Cataloging-in-Publication Data

Sperry Symposium (Brigham Young University)
Sperry Symposium classics : the New Testament / edited by Frank F. Judd, Jr. and Gaye Strathearn.
  p.   cm.
Includes index.
ISBN-10 1-59038-628-0 (hardbound : alk. paper)
ISBN-13 978-1-59038-628-6 (hardbound : alk. paper)
  1. Bible. N.T.—Criticism, interpretation, etc.—Congresses. 2. Jesus Christ—Mormon interpretations—Congresses. 3. Church of Jesus Christ of Latter-day Saints—Doctrines—Congresses. 4. Mormon Church—Doctrines—Congresses.
I. Judd, Frank F. II. Strathearn, Gaye. III. Title.
  BS2361.3.S64 2006
  225.6—dc22
2006014558

Printed in the United States of America
Worzalla Publishing Co., Stevens Point, WI

10   9   8   7   6   5   4   3   2   1

CONTENTS

INTRODUCTION

In his essay contained in this volume, Elder John K. Carmack writes, "We accept the New Testament as scripture—that is, as authoritative and inspired. We use it all the time, we cite it as authority, and we read and study it at home and in our Church instructional sessions. . . . We believe that indeed all of the books of the New Testament are inspired. For thousands of years, people have felt something basic, special, and authoritative in the New Testament. We have that same feeling today as Latter-day Saints."

This volume contains a selection of essays on the New Testament that were presented by General Authorities and religious educators during the Sidney B. Sperry Symposium series. We have included essays that cover a wide range of topics from the four Gospels, Acts, the Epistles, and Revelation. Some essays deal with broad themes, such as "The Four Gospels as Testimonies," by S. Kent Brown; "The Love of God," by Matthew O. Richardson; or "Walking in Newness of Life: Doctrinal Themes of the Apostle Paul," by Robert L. Millet. Other essays focus on more specific aspects of the New Testament, such as "Sanctification and Justification Are Just and True," by Elder Gerald N. Lund, or "The Jerusalem Council," by Robert J. Matthews. In addition, we have included two articles that are of particular significance for Latter-day Saints: "The Book of Mormon as an Interpretive Guide to the New Testament," by Dennis L. Largey, and "New Testament Prophecies of Apostasy," by Kent P. Jackson. Throughout it all, our intent has been the same as John's and Paul's: "These are written, that ye might believe that Jesus is the Christ, the Son of God; and that believing ye might have life through his name" (John 20:31), and, "For I determined not to know any thing among you, save Jesus Christ, and him crucified" (1 Corinthians 2:2).

The selecting and preparing of these essays has been a labor of love because we love the New Testament and its teachings. Speaking of the Bible, the Prophet Joseph taught, "He who reads it oftenest will like it best"

(*Teachings of the Prophet Joseph Smith,* comp. Joseph Fielding Smith [Salt Lake City: Deseret Book, 1976], 56). Of course, no supplement can or should replace the original text, and this is particularly true for our study of the New Testament. It is our hope that readers will view this volume as a worthy supplement for their ongoing study of the New Testament.

CHAPTER ONE

"A SURETY OF A BETTER TESTAMENT"

PRESIDENT JAMES E. FAUST

My calling places upon me a responsibility to witness concerning the reality of the Savior and His mission. I hope that my assignment with the BYU Jerusalem Center and the Holy Land will be a helpful background against which to discuss some phase of the life and ministry of the Lord Jesus Christ.

I take my text from the Apostle Paul's Epistle to the Hebrews: "By so much was Jesus made a surety of a better testament" (Hebrews 7:22). What is a "surety"? We find in turning to the dictionary that *surety* is "the state of being sure"; it is an undertaking or a pledge. It also refers to "one who has become legally liable for the debt, default, or failure in duty of another."[1] Do not the Savior and His mission have claim upon all these meanings?

What is a testament? The primary meaning of *testament* is a "covenant with God." It is also holy scripture, a will, a witness, a tangible proof, an expression of conviction.[2] So the Savior as a surety is a guarantor of a better covenant with God.

We all know that moving from the Old Testament to the New Testament is moving from the rigid formality of the letter of the law to the spirit of the law. It is a better testament because the intent of a person alone becomes part of the rightness or wrongness of human action. So our intent to do evil or our desire to do good will be a free-standing element of consideration of our actions. We are told we will be judged in part by

President James E. Faust is Second Counselor in the First Presidency.

1

the intent of our hearts (see D&C 88:109). An example of being convicted by free-standing intent is found in Matthew: "Ye have heard that it was said by them of old time, Thou shalt not commit adultery: But I say unto you, That whosoever looketh on a woman to lust after her hath committed adultery with her already in his heart" (Matthew 5:27–28).

This New Testament is harder doctrine. In the old English common law, a formality and rigidity developed in the administration of the law to the point where, for justice to be obtained, the law of equity developed. One of my favorite maxims about equity is, "Equity does what ought to be done." The New Testament goes further. In a large measure we will be judged not only by what we have done but by what we should have done in a given situation.

Much of the spirit of the New Testament is found in the Sermon on the Mount. The New Testament requires a reconciliation of differences. "Therefore if thou bring thy gift to the altar, and there rememberest that thy brother hath ought against thee; leave there thy gift before the altar, and go thy way; first be reconciled to thy brother, and then come and offer thy gift" (Matthew 5:23–24).

In the New Testament, swearing becomes completely prohibited: "Again, ye have heard that it hath been said by them of old time, Thou shalt not forswear thyself, but shalt perform unto the Lord thine oaths: But I say unto you, Swear not at all; neither by heaven; for it is God's throne: Nor by the earth; for it is his footstool: neither by Jerusalem; for it is the city of the great King. Neither shalt thou swear by thy head, because thou canst not make one hair white or black. But let your communication be, Yea, yea; Nay, nay: for whatsoever is more than these cometh of evil" (Matthew 5:33–37).

Then follows more of the difficult doctrine of the New Testament:

> But I say unto you, That ye resist not evil: but whosoever shall smite thee on thy right cheek, turn to him the other also.
>
> And if any man will sue thee at the law, and take away thy coat, let him have thy cloke also.
>
> And whosoever shall compel thee to go a mile, go with him twain.
>
> Give to him that asketh thee, and from him that would borrow of thee turn not thou away.
>
> Ye have heard that it hath been said, Thou shalt love thy neighbour, and hate thine enemy.
>
> But I say unto you, Love your enemies, bless them that curse you,

do good to them that hate you, and pray for them which despitefully use you, and persecute you. (Matthew 5:39–44)

The New Testament suggests a new form and content of prayer. It is profoundly simple and uncomplicated:

And when thou prayest, thou shalt not be as the hypocrites are: for they love to pray standing in the synagogues and in the corners of the streets, that they may be seen of men. Verily I say unto you, They have their reward.

But thou, when thou prayest, enter into thy closet, and when thou hast shut the door, pray to thy Father which is in secret; and thy Father which seeth in secret shall reward thee openly.

But when ye pray, use not vain repetitions, as the heathen do: for they think that they shall be heard for their much speaking.

Be not ye therefore like unto them: for your Father knoweth what things ye have need of, before ye ask him.

After this manner therefore pray ye: Our Father which art in heaven, Hallowed be thy name.

Thy kingdom come. Thy will be done in earth, as it is in heaven.

Give us this day our daily bread.

And forgive us our debts, as we forgive our debtors.

And lead us not into temptation, but deliver us from evil: For thine is the kingdom, and the power, and the glory, for ever. Amen. (Matthew 6:5–13)

The New Testament suggests that the doing of our good works ought to be in secret: "But when thou doest alms, let not thy left hand know what thy right hand doeth: That thine alms may be in secret: and thy Father which seeth in secret himself shall reward thee openly" (Matthew 6:3–4).

But the greatest challenge, the hardest doctrine, is also found in the Sermon on the Mount: "Be ye therefore perfect, even as your Father which is in heaven is perfect" (Matthew 5:48).

The Savior as "the mediator of the new testament" (Hebrews 9:15) introduced a higher law of marriage:

And the Pharisees came to him, and asked him, Is it lawful for a man to put away his wife? tempting him.

And he answered and said unto them, What did Moses command you?

And they said, Moses suffered to write a bill of divorcement, and to put her away.

And Jesus answered and said unto them, For the hardness of your heart he wrote you this precept.

But from the beginning of the creation God made them male and female.

For this cause shall a man leave his father and mother, and cleave to his wife;

And they twain shall be one flesh: so then they are no more twain, but one flesh.

What therefore God hath joined together, let not man put asunder. (Mark 10:2–9)

The challenge of Jesus was to replace the rigid technical "thou shalt not" of the law of Moses that the spiritually immature children of Israel needed with the spirit of the "better testament." How was that to be done? Time was short. He had only three years. How should He begin? Obviously He must begin with the Apostles and the small group of disciples around Him who would have the responsibility to carry on the work after His death. President J. Reuben Clark Jr., a counselor in the First Presidency, describes this challenge as follows: "This task involved the overturning, the virtual outlawing, of the centuries-old Mosaic law of the Jews, and the substitution therefore of the Gospel of Christ."[3]

It was not easy for even the Apostles to understand, of whom doubting Thomas is a good example. Thomas had been with the Savior when the Savior, on several occasions, foretold of His death and Resurrection. Yet when Thomas was told that the resurrected Christ lived, he said, "Except I shall see in his hands the print of the nails, and put my finger into the print of the nails, and thrust my hand into his side, I will not believe" (John 20:25). Perhaps Thomas can be forgiven because so great an event had never happened before.

What about Peter's conversion to the great principle that the gospel of Jesus Christ is for everyone? He had been an eyewitness, as he stated, that "we have not followed cunningly devised fables, when we make known unto you the power and coming of our Lord Jesus Christ, but were eyewitnesses of his majesty" (2 Peter 1:16). To what had Peter been an eyewitness? He had been an eyewitness to everything in the Savior's ministry. He had seen the Savior welcome the Samaritans, who were loathed by the Jews, following the encounter with the Samaritan at the well of Jacob (see

John 4). Peter had seen a vision and heard the voice of the Lord, saying, "What God hath cleansed, that call not thou common" (Acts 10:15). Finally, fully converted and receiving a spiritual confirmation, Peter opened his mouth and said, "Of a truth I perceive that God is no respecter of persons: but in every nation he that feareth him, and worketh righteousness, is accepted with him" (Acts 10:34–35).

It is strengthening to review the testimonies of the Apostles that Jesus is, in fact, the Christ. These testimonies are also a surety of a better testament. The first recorded testimony of the divinity of the Savior is the occasion of Jesus walking on the water, which is most fully recorded in Matthew 14:24–33:

> But the ship was now in the midst of the sea, tossed with waves: for the wind was contrary.
>
> And in the fourth watch of the night Jesus went unto them, walking on the sea.
>
> And when the disciples saw him walking on the sea, they were troubled, saying, It is a spirit; and they cried out for fear.
>
> But straightway Jesus spake unto them, saying, Be of good cheer; it is I; be not afraid.
>
> And Peter answered him and said, Lord, if it be thou, bid me come unto thee on the water.
>
> And he said, Come. And when Peter was come down out of the ship, he walked on the water, to go to Jesus.
>
> But when he saw the wind boisterous, he was afraid; and beginning to sink, he cried, saying, Lord, save me.
>
> And immediately Jesus stretched forth his hand, and caught him, and said unto him, O thou of little faith, wherefore didst thou doubt?
>
> And when they were come into the ship, the wind ceased.
>
> Then they that were in the ship came and worshipped him, saying, Of a truth thou art the Son of God.

The second is that of Peter. The fullest account appears in Matthew, with which we are all familiar:

> When Jesus came into the coasts of Cæsarea Philippi, he asked his disciples, saying, Whom do men say that I the Son of man am?
>
> And they said, Some say that thou art John the Baptist: some, Elias; and others, Jeremias, or one of the prophets.
>
> He saith unto them, But whom say ye that I am?

And Simon Peter answered and said, Thou art the Christ, the Son of the living God.

And Jesus answered and said unto him, Blessed art thou, Simon Bar-jona: for flesh and blood hath not revealed it unto thee, but my Father which is in heaven.

And I say also unto thee, That thou art Peter, and upon this rock I will build my church; and the gates of hell shall not prevail against it. (Matthew 16:13–18)

The third instance again involves Peter. After the great sermon on the Bread of Life, in which the Savior made clear to those who had been fed by the loaves and the fishes that He and His doctrine were the Bread of Life, John records: "From that time many of his disciples went back, and walked no more with him. Then said Jesus unto the twelve, Will ye also go away? Then Simon Peter answered him, Lord, to whom shall we go? thou hast the words of eternal life. And we believe and are sure that thou art that Christ, the Son of the living God" (John 6:66–69).

The testimony of the divinity of the Savior given by God the Father and heard by Peter, James, and John is recorded in connection with the happenings on the Mount of Transfiguration. The accounts of Matthew, Mark, and Luke all tell of the appearance of Moses and Elias talking to the Savior. Matthew records:

Then answered Peter, and said unto Jesus, Lord, it is good for us to be here: if thou wilt, let us make here three tabernacles; one for thee, and one for Moses, and one for Elias.

While he yet spake, behold, a bright cloud overshadowed them: and behold a voice out of the cloud, which said, This is my beloved Son, in whom I am well pleased; hear ye him.

And when the disciples heard it, they fell on their face, and were sore afraid.

And Jesus came and touched them, and said, Arise, and be not afraid.

And when they had lifted up their eyes, they saw no man, save Jesus only.

And as they came down from the mountain, Jesus charged them, saying, Tell the vision to no man, until the Son of man be risen again from the dead.

And his disciples asked him, saying, Why then say the scribes that Elias must first come?

And Jesus answered and said unto them, Elias truly shall first come, and restore all things.

But I say unto you, That Elias is come already, and they knew him not, but have done unto him whatsoever they listed. Likewise shall also the Son of man suffer of them.

Then the disciples understood that he spake unto them of John the Baptist. (Matthew 17:4–13)

We are grateful for these profound statements of the "eyewitnesses of his majesty" (2 Peter 1:16). They form part of the footings of our faith. But the miracles performed by the Savior and the testimonies of those who saw and heard were far from convincing to everyone, perhaps because a testimony is such a personal, spiritual conviction.

The New Testament is a surety of a better testament because so much is left to the intent of the heart and of the mind. The refinement of the soul is part of the reinforcing steel of a personal testimony. If there is no witness in the heart and in the mind, there can be no testimony. The Sermon on the Mount produces deep, spiritual reinforcing that moves us to higher spiritual attainment.

I leave with you my blessing. May the Lord watch over you and strengthen you. I invoke a blessing upon the institutions sponsoring the Sperry Symposium to be powerful in instructing faith and witness and testimony. And I witness to you in the authority of the holy apostleship of the divinity of the calling and mission of the Savior and of the Restoration of the gospel by Joseph Smith. To this I bear witness and testimony in the name of the Lord Jesus Christ, amen.

NOTES

1. *Merriam-Webster's New Collegiate Dictionary,* 11th ed., s.v. "surety."
2. *Merriam-Webster's New Collegiate Dictionary,* s.v. "testament."
3. J. Reuben Clark Jr., *Why the King James Version* (Salt Lake City: Deseret Book, 1979), 51.

CHAPTER TWO

THE NEW TESTAMENT AND THE LATTER-DAY SAINTS

ELDER JOHN K. CARMACK

Have you ever read something you or someone close to you prepared decades ago and have been struck by the feeling that it is still sound, useful, and fundamentally true? Perhaps you have had the opposite and more common experience of reading something you or someone else wrote that once excited and moved you but now you find that the impact you originally felt is no longer there and, in fact, the writing strikes you as cynical, or shallow, or lacking in basic soundness, or no longer relevant.

For instance, how long has it been since you picked up the Constitution of the United States and read it? If you do this, you may think it improbable for fifty-five men and women currently representing our states to produce a document equal in brevity and good sense and as solidly rooted in timeless principles as did those who gathered in Philadelphia that hot summer of 1787.

When I read the New Testament, a compilation of letters and treatises written by men associated with the Savior some two thousand years ago, I asked myself if any small group of men today could write a series of letters and religious documents equal in wisdom and inspiration to those comprising the New Testament canon. If they tried, do you think what they produced would end up being used and revered by millions of people for two thousand years?

Now to raise some more general but related questions, are some ideas more important than others? Is there a center of things? Are some

Elder John K. Carmack is an emeritus member of the Seventy and managing director of the Perpetual Education Fund.

principles, doctrines, and ideas of infinitely greater value and more basic than others? Is that which is written today by our best minds likely to be of greater value than that which was written by the best available authors one or two millennia ago? If modern man is thousands of years further along than New Testament authors, would our best written thoughts not be of infinitely more value than those of our ancestors in Palestine who wrote the documents comprising the New Testament? If man has had significant upward progress in the last two thousand years, does the New Testament have *any* relevance today? I shall address a few of these questions.

Is the New Testament Authoritative and Relevant Today?

One addressing a church group will often ask, "Did you bring your scriptures?" To most in the world this question means, "Did you bring your Holy Bible?" To the Latter-day Saint it means, "Did you bring your Bible and your triple combination that contains the Book of Mormon, the Doctrine and Covenants, and the Pearl of Great Price?" One of the most revered of the books of scripture is the New Testament portion of the Bible. It is not only that these "holy men of God spake as they were moved by the Holy Ghost" (2 Peter 1:21)[1] but that these New Testament authors wrote their messages. Then what they wrote became, in process of time, accepted by the Church as especially authoritative, binding, and inspired, as well as useful for doctrine and instruction in the Church. On the other hand, much, even most, of what others spoke and wrote in the past, though useful and instructive, does not quite have that authoritative status in Church literature. For example, there is available to the student a large amount of ancient literature dating to biblical days, including the writings of the apostolic Fathers and others, which are not accepted generally as scripture, although they are useful to scholars.

We accept the New Testament as scripture—that is, as authoritative and inspired. We use it all the time, we cite it as authority, and we read and study it at home and in our Church instructional sessions. We clearly prefer the King James Version of the New Testament,[2] but we are not adamant about that. Any responsibly prepared version could be used and might be helpful to us. It is the doctrine and the teachings in their historical setting that are useful and authoritative to Latter-day Saints.

Unlike some students of ancient history and scripture who reject any suggestion of influence from a divine source in the writing of scripture,

following the notion that nothing is worth much if it cannot be established by analytical and scientific means, faithful Latter-day Saints accept
without such qualification the influence of the Holy Spirit and heavenly
messengers in the lives of men, including those who wrote the scriptures.
We believe that Matthew did write what is known as "The Gospel
According to St. Matthew" and that indeed all of the books of the New
Testament are inspired. For thousands of years, people have felt something
basic, special, and authoritative in the New Testament. We have that same
feeling today as Latter-day Saints. I will try to identify a few reasons for our
feeling together with some differences in our approach to using the New
Testament.

A RATIONAL APPROACH TO THE NEW TESTAMENT

It would not shake our faith if it were proven that someone other than
the ascribed author penned one or more of the books of the New
Testament. We doubt that evidence will ever be found of this, but Latter-
day Saints are realists who believe that "truth is knowledge of things as
they are, and as they were, and as they are to come" (D&C 93:24). We do
not reject truth in favor of fairy tales.

The essence of our practical approach to truth can be gathered from this
statement by Brigham Young: "Were you to ask me how it was that I
embraced 'Mormonism,' I should answer, for the simple reason that it
embraces all truth in heaven and on earth, in the earth, under the earth,
and in hell, if there be any truth there. There is no truth outside of it; there
is no good outside of it; there is nothing holy and honorable outside of it;
for, wherever these principles are found among all the creations of God,
the Gospel of Jesus Christ, and his order and Priesthood, embrace them."[3]
Whatever is found to be true of the New Testament, therefore, becomes
ipso facto a part of the religion and belief of the Latter-day Saints.

It is interesting and useful to read the conclusions of Paul Johnson, a
noted scholar, concerning the authenticity of the books of the New
Testament. He concluded, "The earliest Christian document is Paul's first
Epistle to the Thessalonians, which can plausibly be dated to about AD 51.
Paul was writing in the fifties and early sixties; his authentic epistles
(Romans, 1 and 2 Corinthians, Galatians, Philippians, 1 Thessalonians and
Philemon) are in an evidential sense straightforward written documents;
there is no oral tradition behind them and the editing process is

minimal—indeed some of them may have been circulated or 'published' in edited form even during Paul's lifetime."[4]

If such an assertion of fact concerning the authenticity of books of the New Testament as that made by Johnson should prove to be correct, which is possible although we accept all of the New Testament as authentic, it would not change the faith of the Latter-day Saints but would add to their factual knowledge of how the New Testament came into being as a book. Latter-day Saints would be quick to recognize that if those few books that Johnson listed as surely authentic were the only authentic books of the New Testament, they would be sufficient to clearly establish early Christian teachings on crucial doctrines such as the fatherhood of God; the divine mission of His Son Jesus Christ; His identity as a separate and distinct, though closely related, personage; the principles of love, repentance, and faith in the Lord Jesus Christ as basic doctrines; the important role of the Holy Ghost; the Crucifixion, death, and Resurrection of Christ; and the salvational aspects of the Atonement of Christ in the lives of those who believe and practice the principles of the gospel of Jesus Christ. Even the doctrine of the Second Coming of Christ is established in those epistles that Johnson clearly labeled as authentic and historic.

In summary, we believe in the historicity of the New Testament and in the divinely inspired nature of these writings. We rise above dogmatism, however, because we believe only what is ultimately true about these writings. The Book of Mormon adds emphasis to our rational viewpoint when it quotes Jacob's teaching that the Spirit "speaketh of things as they really are, and of things as they really will be" (Jacob 4:13).

A SPECIAL ENDORSEMENT OF THE NEW TESTAMENT

We have a special endorsement of the New Testament from an unexpected source—section 20 of the Doctrine and Covenants. The endorsement began, oddly enough, with a reference to the Book of Mormon and a statement that the book is true because it was confirmed to certain witnesses by the administration of angels, who disclosed to the world that the Book of Mormon was true. Then switching gears, and in point for our discussion of the New Testament, section 20 states that one of the key reasons for bringing forth another sacred and inspired book was to prove "to the world that the holy scriptures are true" (D&C 20:11).

It is obvious from the context of the quoted section of the Doctrine and Covenants that the term "holy scriptures" used in the section means the

Bible, including, of course, the New Testament. Latter-day Saints, therefore, have an unexpected ringing endorsement of the New Testament in the coming forth of the Book of Mormon and its clearly established authenticity by witnesses to whom angels appeared and who publicly endorse every published copy of the Book of Mormon by their printed testimony. By accepting the Book of Mormon as authentic, a person automatically accepts the divine authenticity of the New Testament. Indeed, one of the principle reasons for the necessity of another book of ancient scripture being found, translated, and published is to establish the divinity of the New Testament for a world largely turned to secular thinking, which has separated Christians from the central role formerly played in their lives by the New Testament. Section 20 of the Doctrine and Covenants provides the person who accepts it as sacred scripture the means of identifying things of enduring value in religion and life.

RELIGION AND REAL HISTORY

To Latter-day Saints, New Testament religious history is real, meaning that the events written and described in it actually happened. We believe there was a man named Jesus who hung on a cross on a hill called Calvary that actually existed and in fact still does exist. Special and deeply spiritual experiences occurred in a garden on the Mount of Olives called Gethsemane. These were real events in real time. They are not stories or parables that form part of a doubtful and largely symbolic literature for the purpose of establishing a set of ideas making up a philosophy called "Christianity."

We believe firmly that real events on earth are, have been, and will again be directly connected with our Heavenly Father, His Son Jesus Christ, and by inspiration to man through the Holy Spirit. We also believe that there have been and are on earth virtuous and inspired men called prophets.

When we speak of religious history, we add to places sacred to Christians, such as Galilee and Golgotha, places in our own age where special revelatory experiences with heavenly influences came to virtuous and inspired men such as Joseph Smith, Brigham Young, and Gordon B. Hinckley, to name only three. Places such as Nauvoo, Liberty Jail, and the farm of Joseph Smith Sr. are not only real but are sacred just as Bethlehem is sacred. One can visit these places to learn more about man's relationship to God. We believe that God does influence man's course on earth by revelation to those living virtuous lives who ask and seek.

Understanding this view of the New Testament helps one better understand the beliefs espoused by the members of The Church of Jesus Christ of Latter-day Saints. It is a tangible and historical religion but not a superstitious or dogmatic one. These things either happened or they didn't happen. If they happened, as Church members believe, they indicate that God loves and interacts directly with men and women. The ultimate implication is, of course, that God informs man how he should live and act to receive salvation. And that gets us to the heart of things.

"As Far as It Is Translated Correctly"

An oft-quoted qualification to Church members' belief in the Bible is the article of faith stating, "We believe the Bible to be the word of God as far as it is translated correctly" (Articles of Faith 1:8). This statement implies that translation errors were possible, even probable, in the Bible. To some Christians, it is blasphemous to imply that there could be errors in God's word. Latter-day Saints believe that errors are possible. This belief is consistent with what I have already said about the history of the New Testament. And even more to the point, the Book of Mormon contains language which indicates that "plain and precious things" have been removed from the Bible (see 1 Nephi 13:40).

Another way of understanding this idea is the obvious and consistent fact that the authors of the Bible were real people, often humble people of limited literary education, who were involved in and reported real events. In turn, other men copied these writings by hand. Reporting and copying errors were inevitable in such circumstances, even when those men were inspired and virtuous people operating with excellent intentions. A book made of such writings is more believable, tangible, and real to us than one created perfectly and delivered by Deity to men who had no part in creating it. Working through humble and often less-educated men seems to be God's *modus operandi*.

What Do We Believe about Christ?

Let us now turn to a crucial question—what do Latter-day Saints believe about Christ? Remember, as Paul Johnson confidently asserts, "Christianity is essentially a historical religion. It bases its claims on the historical facts it asserts."[5] And, examining the scanty but firmly established evidence, he concludes that "there can, at least, be absolutely no doubt about his [Christ's] historical existence."[6] He then reminds us of the few, but sufficient, references to Christ in well-authenticated historical documents. He includes the references to Jesus in *Antiquities* by Josephus (published about AD 93), another reference to Christ by Tacitus in his *Annals* concerning events in AD 64, and another reference to Christ by Pliny the Younger, written in AD 112. Thus firm evidence clearly establishes that a person named Jesus Christ actually lived. We believe that.

As for the authenticity of the Gospels, though it may be true—as many scholars of the New Testament assert—that these manuscripts are based originally on oral teachings which were not written until well after Paul's letters were written, we are confident that the four Gospels are based on actual writings by Matthew and John, who were Jesus' Apostles, and by Mark and Luke, disciples and missionaries of Jesus. There may also have been early source documents by unknown authors and witnesses. These Gospels are not biographical manuscripts but rather a statement of the doctrine and teachings of Christ in the context of His life and brief ministry. But these authors were eyewitnesses of many of the events described, and their writings bear marks of authority and authenticity. Although, as is true with almost all other books as old as those in the Bible, we do not have originals of the books of the New Testament. After a lifetime of studying the New Testament as a written document, eminent scholar Frederic Kenyon has concluded, "It is reassuring at the end to find that the general result of all these discoveries and all this study is to strengthen the proof of the authenticity of the Scriptures, and our conviction that we have in our hands, in substantial integrity, the veritable Word of God."[7]

He adds in a later publication, "The interval then between the dates of original composition and the earliest extant evidence becomes so small as to be in fact negligible, and the last foundation for any doubt that the Scriptures have come down to us substantially as they were written has now been removed. Both the *authenticity* and the *general integrity* of the books of the New Testament may be regarded as finally established."[8]

We believe that Kenyon was essentially correct in those conclusions. Doubt cast on the New Testament by higher criticism and the fact of not having available originals of the books is almost completely overcome for us by the strong evidence that what we have was directly descended from authentic documents and that, although mistakes, deletions, and insertions probably occurred in the documents by those who reproduced them by hand, they are basically what they purport to be.

We also have another authenticating witness. The Book of Mormon account of Christ's visit to America and His teachings to those living there at Christ's Crucifixion amounts to another Gospel. That the Book of Mormon account so closely parallels and confirms the substance of the New Testament account is evidence to those of us accepting the Book of Mormon, "that the holy scriptures [meaning the Bible] are true" (D&C 20:11).

Thus, the Christ a person meets in Matthew, Mark, Luke, John, Acts, and the Epistles of the New Testament is basically the Christ in whom Latter-day Saints literally believe. His teachings, His divine Sonship, His Atonement, and His Resurrection are for us established historical facts. The Prophet Joseph Smith did a thorough work, considering his limited tools, in revising the New Testament and restoring concepts lost in it so that the "key of knowledge, the fulness of the scriptures" (JST, Luke 11:52c) could be available to man.

One may ask, why has the Joseph Smith Translation not been made more generally available to Church members if Joseph Smith and Sidney Rigdon corrected errors and recaptured meanings therein? One answer to that excellent question is that through extensive footnotes, cross-references, and excerpts in the appendix, most of the significant additions and corrections by Joseph Smith are now available using the 1979 edition of the King James Version of the Holy Bible published by The Church of Jesus Christ of Latter-day Saints. With the cross-referencing, footnoting, and other integrating of the Bible, the Book of Mormon, the Doctrine and Covenants, and the Pearl of Great Price, the Church has made available to diligent students a coherent fulness of the standard works.

Christ is revealed in those four standard works in great detail, especially in regard to His teachings and divine mission. What Latter-day Saints believe about Christ is found therein. More scriptural explanations and references are available to the careful student than have ever before been available to mankind. As an example of this enhanced availability, a quick look at the Topical Guide included in the Church's 1979 publication will reveal many pages of scriptural references to Christ from a number of different conceptual bases.

In addition to personal revelation through the Holy Ghost, the real key to understanding Christ is in studying Him in the New Testament and then expanding that knowledge by adding what inspired men have known of Him in the Old Testament, the Pearl of Great Price, the Book of Mormon, and the Doctrine and Covenants. Thus, for example, Jacob of the Book of Mormon, writing in about 500 BC, explained that he wrote "for this intent . . . that they may know that we knew of Christ, and we had a hope of his glory many hundred years before his coming; and not only we ourselves had a hope of his glory, but also all the holy prophets which were before us" (Jacob 4:4). This adds a breathtaking dimension to our knowledge of Christ totally unknown to those bereft of the additional books of scriptures available to us.

So not only do we have a strong belief in the Christ of the New Testament, but we have a much expanded global and dispensational view of Christ through "the fulness of the scriptures." Our view is not that of the fundamentalist that sees the New Testament as the *only* source of knowledge of Christ and as a *perfect* document from God. It does not bother us to find, for example, varying accounts of Christ's visit to Paul on the road to Damascus (see Acts 9:7; 22:9). We expect that there will be a need for further reconciliation, expansion, and even correction of these New Testament documents precisely because they are real, historic writings. This does not in any way diminish their inspired nature. God continually reveals His will to man, and therefore we have an expanding, ever-increasing body of revelation rather than a closed, sterile, or perfect canon. The expanding body of revelation, however, does not change fundamental verities.

WHAT USE DID JOSEPH SMITH MAKE OF THE NEW TESTAMENT?

For his part, Joseph Smith made constant use of the New Testament. Not only was he inspired at an early age by a passage of the New Testament found in James 1:5–6 to seek inspiration from God, but the role of the New Testament in Joseph's life continued and expanded. His lengthy sermons to the Saints during the zenith of his prophetic career in Nauvoo were peppered with New Testament passages. His mastery of the scriptures was phenomenal. Our understanding is that Joseph almost always spoke extemporaneously without notes, writing few if any talks for delivery to the Church. On one occasion he was working on a rare prepared talk with his scribe Robert B. Thompson. Thompson subsequently read the talk Joseph dictated in general conference on October 5, 1840. The subject of that address was "Treatise on Priesthood." This description of the process of preparation by Howard Coray, one of Joseph's clerks, is interesting.

> One morning, I went as usual, into the Office to go to work: I found Joseph sitting on one side of a table and Robert B. Thompson on the opposite side, and the understanding I got was that they were examining or hunting in the manuscript of the new translation of the Bible for something on Priesthood, which Joseph wished to present, or have read to the people the next Conference: Well, they could not find what they wanted and Joseph said to Thompson "put the manuscript [to] one side, and take some paper and I will tell you what to write." Bro. Thompson took some foolscap paper that was at his elbow and made himself ready for the business. I was seated probably 6 or 8 feet on Joseph's left side, so that I could look almost squarely into Joseph's left eye—I mean the side of his eye. Well, the Spirit of God descended upon him, and a measure of it upon me, insomuch that I could fully realize that God, or the Holy Ghost, was talking through him. I never, neither before or since, have felt as I did on that occasion. I felt so small and humble I could have freely kissed his feet.[9]

On that occasion, although he had no Bible at hand, Joseph accurately cited and dictated fourteen scriptural passages. Only twice did he not remember the chapter and verse of a passage but quoted it accurately anyway.[10] Joseph Smith summed up his own view of the Bible as follows: "I believe the Bible as it read when it came from the pen of the original writers. Ignorant translators, careless transcribers, or designing and corrupt priests have committed many errors."[11]

CENTRAL IDEAS AND DOCTRINES AND THE NEW TESTAMENT

As implied in the introduction, some ideas are more important than others. Some are central to the guidance of man into a righteous life, and some are on the periphery. Christ's teachings are without any question central to the gospel in all ages and that is true for the era of restoration commenced through Joseph Smith. Elder Bruce R. McConkie summarized his thoughts on the subject as follows: "Nothing in the entire plan of salvation compares in any way in importance with that most transcendent of all events, the atoning sacrifice of our Lord. It is the most important single thing that has ever occurred in the entire history of created things;

it is the rock foundation upon which the gospel and all other things rest. Indeed, all 'things which pertain to our religion are only appendages to it.'"[12]

To return to an introductory idea, we do not subscribe to the notion that man is a purely physical animal, evolving slowly upward to a higher form so that the latest generation of men and women is higher in ability and intelligence than were men living in earlier eras. Our view of man as an intelligent and knowledgeable being is dispensational. At times the truths of the gospel are more generally available with greater intensity among men than at other times. In other words, the availability of gospel light fades and flickers to dimmer brightness at times and then is reestablished and grows brighter again.

We believe that men, as Richard Weaver observed, constantly need to "return to center" and thus recapture days in which truth is held in high value and when men are driven more nearly by ideas that properly position them vis-à-vis God. Weaver sees that "there is a center of things, and . . . every feature of modern disintegration is a flight from this [center of things] toward periphery."[13] Of course, our notion and Weaver's is the ancient and much maligned one that there are eternal verities that can be lost by concentrating on peripheral things and by too much specialization and fragmentation. For us there is a center of things as revealed in the New Testament, and that center is Christ. Knowledge of Christ is also discovered anew and expanded in the restoration of His gospel through Joseph Smith.

BOOK OF MORMON EMPHASIS BRINGS US TO CENTER

In my view, the reason President Benson and President Hinckley have emphasized again and again a return to the Book of Mormon is that the book is the restorational vehicle for the return to center accomplished by reestablishing, in a document not changed by time and interpretation, the primacy of the New Testament Christ. Thus the Book of Mormon brings us back to the center of things once again. When we drift toward the periphery, we leave the center and are in danger of wandering in treacherous byways. The prophet Mormon aptly taught in the Book of Mormon: "This [meaning the Book of Mormon] is written for the intent that ye may believe that [meaning the Bible]; and if ye believe that ye will believe this also" (Mormon 7:9). Had there been no drift from the central doctrines of the New Testament, there would have been no need for the Book of

Mormon to bring us back to the basics. But there was clearly a fateful flight from the solid central doctrines needed by man.

The consequence of leaving the center is spiritual wandering. Man drifts easily from the central truth that he is a divine son of God to the variant view that man is just another beast wandering on earth in a society in which child abuse, selfishness and war, unbridled sexual pleasure without family responsibility, immorality of all kinds, egotism, lack of interest in one's daily work, and pride exist. The Book of Mormon teaches that if such a drift downward by mankind is unchecked, civilization will eventually decline and be destroyed by hatred, bloodshed, and war. We seem to be teetering on the edge. Only a return to the center of things, as taught in the New Testament and authenticated by the Book of Mormon, can save this generation.

As pessimistic as it may sound, that is our view of the state of civilization in an era in which men leave the New Testament Christ and the eternal verities of the center to man's uninspired and vain philosophies that exist on the periphery. Secularism, founded on the ideas of men that scoff at God and His teachings, has had its day, and such philosophies clearly lack the ability to ennoble, inspire, and exalt men. When God and His dealings with man are thoroughly debunked, what takes the place of that core concept in men's lives? What inspires men to do well and serve each other?

A Word about the New Testament and the Constitution

Actually, the New Testament influence is more pervasive in our lives than we will ever know. Its teachings have deeply influenced the lives of countless great men and women and shaped institutions. As an example of this influence, although it is beyond the scope of these remarks to undertake a detailed analysis of the underlying concepts of the United States Constitution and trace them to the New Testament, I want to say a word or two about the Constitution because I wrote this in the bicentennial year for that noble document. What I say should be looked at more as an intuition of a situation (to borrow a phrase from Weaver) than a careful analysis.

In general, those most responsible for drafting the Constitution were men schooled in theology and religion in the colleges and churches of their day. In both church and school, the New Testament was always a primary text. Thus, since the men who wrote the Constitution were schooled in the scriptures, the influence was undoubtedly there. For example, James Madison of Virginia, who is often called the father of the Constitution, was a brilliant, well-educated man who began his schooling under a Christian minister and completed it with a college education heavily influenced by the Christian religion. He, with contributions from many (and notably James Wilson of Pennsylvania), was the man most responsible for the final form of our Constitution. The preparation of Madison for this historic task seems to have revolved around religion and political theory, the primary educational interests of many of our founding fathers.

My intuition of the situation is that New Testament principles were well known to all of the delegates of the Constitutional Convention and had a profound influence on what they thought and wrote, irrespective of their religious persuasion. In addition, of course, they had available almost all of the writings of the day on the theories of government and politics.

These men accomplished a miracle. In the concluding paragraph of *The Federalist*—a series of eighty-five essays defending the Constitution that were published to assist the ratification of that document by authors Alexander Hamilton, James Madison, and John Jay—Hamilton wrote: "The establishment of a Constitution, in time of profound peace, by the voluntary consent of a whole people, is a prodigy to the completion of which I look forward with trembling anxiety."[14] These participants sensed the greatness of the achievement of which they were a part. Washington wrote to Lafayette these words about the completion of the Constitution: "It appears to me, then, little short of a miracle, that the Delegates from so many different states . . . in their manner, circumstances, and prejudices, should write in forming a system of national Government, so little liable to well founded objections."[15]

The underlying principles of the Constitution are not the creation of our founders. Those principles always existed and are eternal. The miracle is that these fifty-five men were able to come together that hot, muggy summer and agree on a Constitution establishing a form of government incorporating those principles and then persuade the states to adopt the Constitution. I will touch on an example or two illustrating the influence of the New Testament on what these men agreed to.[16] The Lord made it clear by revelation to Joseph Smith that the Constitution was inspired of God (see D&C 98:5–7; 101:77–78; 109:54)—that it was based on principles which were not new but which had their source in God. Many of those principles can be found in the New Testament.

First, the New Testament teaches that men are children of God and are thus heirs of His attributes and destiny (see John 10:34–36; 1 John 3:1–3; Revelation 3:21). This noble and far-reaching view of man can be seen everywhere in the Constitution. Its very idea is that men have the intelligence to participate in the process of governing themselves. As observed in essay forty-nine of *The Federalist,* "The people are the only legitimate fountain of power, and it is from them that the constitutional charter . . . is derived."[17]

Second, the New Testament also teaches the reality of evil and the temptations of selfishness, power, and greed that men face in striving to govern themselves (see Matthew 4:1–10). Thus the Constitution incorporates a system of checks and balances on those elected or appointed to positions of power in recognition of man's natural tendencies. Further, and also in point, the powers granted by the people to those governing were carefully limited in scope. Again, as an illustration that this point had not escaped the Founding Fathers, we read the following in *The Federalist:* "Men, upon too many occasions, do not give their own understandings fair play: but, yielding to some untoward bias, they entangle themselves in words and confound themselves in subtleties."[18]

Third, in the New Testament, we find an account of Christian converts defying the corrupt and well-established religious order in Israel, seizing the inherent right to preach and proclaim the gospel, speaking freely of their faith, even though that faith was built on a set of religious principles despised and misunderstood by those in power. The ideas of Gamaliel, Paul's teacher and a member of the Sanhedrin, are interesting and seem almost to be from the colonial America era. He advised his fellow council members in these words: "Refrain from these men, and let them alone: for if this counsel or this work be of men, it will come to nought: But if it be of God, ye cannot overthrow it; lest haply ye be found even to fight against God" (Acts 5:38–39). This kind of thinking also found its way into the Constitution. The first ten amendments to the Constitution, adopted almost as a part of the original Constitution and called as a block "The Bill of Rights," begin with the well-known guarantees of freedom of speech, the right to a free press, and not only freedom of religion, but the guarantee against a state-established religion. The New Testament ideas in favor of religious freedom are therefore clearly incorporated in the Constitution.

My intuition of the situation is that the New Testament had both a direct and indirect influence on the men who drafted the United States

Constitution and that it influenced the form of government established by that document. The underlying principles of the Constitution were from a place near the center of things. That such basic principles were involved seemed to be recognized by Hamilton when he observed: "In disquisitions of every kind, there are certain primary truths, or first principles, upon which all subsequent reasonings must depend. These contain an internal evidence which, antecedent to all reflection or combination, commands the assent of the mind. Where it produces not this effect, it must proceed either from some defect or disorder in the organs of perception, or from the influence of some strong interest, or passion, or prejudice."[19]

In this quotation we find evidence that a clear thinker has noticed man's tendency to leave the center and move to the periphery unless brought back to basic ideas or truths. The New Testament, especially as restored to its center place through the Book of Mormon, brings us back home to that center. Perhaps, as Weaver observed: "It has been well said that the chief trouble with the contemporary generation is that it has not read the minutes of the last meeting."[20] Maybe those minutes of the last meeting are in the New Testament.

It is not enough, however, to have a great Constitution. As people drift into the periphery and lose sight of the center of things, we are in danger of losing the moral force and righteousness necessary to retain the benefits of our government created by that inspired and excellent document. The more we recede from the inspired precepts of the New Testament, the more danger there is that we shall lose what we have so long enjoyed. As the New Testament teaches, we are children of a loving God and are capable of growth and development beyond our wildest imagination if we do not lose the way and drift away from our spiritual roots in Christ.

OUR ACCEPTANCE OF THE WHOLE NEW TESTAMENT

In conclusion, it is important to add that our acceptance of the New Testament includes all parts of it, insofar as correctly translated. We accept and follow the principles of Christ found in the four Gospels; Acts; Paul's epistles; the epistles of Peter, James, John, Jude; the book of Hebrews; and the book of Revelation. We don't apologize for or ignore James's appeal for good works or Paul's emphasis on grace. There is a unity and a harmony in the view of the Latter-day Saints concerning the New Testament.

Our Church's early history places us in a position to understand and empathize with the early Christian Saints. As they experienced, we believe that angels played a part in the restoration of the gospel in the nineteenth century, and we also had a seminal founding person who experienced extreme persecution and martyrdom. We have the leadership of Apostles, the unprecedented program of missionaries who have experienced and continue to experience hardships and persecution, and a form of Church government similar to that of the New Testament Church. The doctrine of the Church also conforms closely to that found in the earlier Church. Temple worship and ordinances have played a major role in both societies.

SUMMARY

First, the New Testament is historical and real to The Church of Jesus Christ of Latter-day Saints. We believe it to be basically accurate, fairly complete, and in the greater measure true.

Second, we have extensively supplemented it and have reestablished its authority with the Book of Mormon: Another Testament of Jesus Christ. With the help of that book, modern inspiration and revelation, and with careful scholarship, we have a fulness of the scriptures not known to others which sheds great light on the New Testament and illuminates its doctrines and teachings.

Third, the New Testament was a central and guiding document in the ministry of Joseph Smith.

Fourth, moving away from the central theme of Christ and His doctrine, including His Atonement, Resurrection, baptism, and so forth, is a dangerous move to the periphery of ideas leaving society bankrupt of those special truths which can save and preserve mankind.

Fifth, the New Testament has had a more pervasive influence upon men and institutions than we can ever discover. One example of an important document influenced by it is the United States Constitution.

Finally, we accept, use, and love all of the New Testament. It plays a central role in the gospel plan.

My personal witness is that the New Testament is basically historically authentic. I have always loved the New Testament. It has the ring of truth, is not only profitable for instruction but binding as canonized scripture, and it establishes the basic doctrines of the gospel of Jesus Christ in beauty and power. Through the inspiration of the Holy Ghost, I have had experiences that entitle and obligate me to bear a special witness, not only of the New Testament but of the Lord and Savior who is revealed in it. I do so with full understanding of the words I have chosen. In the holy name of Jesus Christ, amen.

NOTES

1. Peter's reference was to the Old Testament scriptures, but the principle also applies equally to New Testament scriptures.

2. See J. Reuben Clark Jr., *Why The King James Version* (Salt Lake City: Deseret Book, 1952), for an interesting and scholarly exposition of how various versions of the New Testament came to be published and the author's opinion of their relative value.

3. Brigham Young, in *Journal of Discourses* (London: Latter-day Saints' Book Depot, 1854–86), 11:213.

4. Paul Johnson, *A History of Christianity* (New York: Atheneum, 1980), 23.

5. Johnson, *History of Christianity,* vii.

6. Johnson, *History of Christianity,* 21.

7. Sir Frederic G. Kenyon, *The Story of the Bible* (Chicago: University of Chicago Press, 1936), 144.

8. Sir Frederic G. Kenyon, *The Bible and Archaeology* (London: Harper & Brothers, 1940), 288–89.

9. Joseph Smith, *The Words of Joseph Smith,* comp. and ed. Andrew F. Ehat and Lyndon W. Cook (Provo, UT: Religious Studies Center, Brigham Young University, 1980), 51.

10. See Smith, *Words of Joseph Smith.*

11. Joseph Smith, *History of the Church of Jesus Christ of Latter-day Saints* (Salt Lake City: Deseret News, 1912), 6:57.

12. Bruce R. McConkie, *Mormon Doctrine,* 2d ed. (Salt Lake City: Bookcraft, 1958), 60.

13. Richard Weaver, *Ideas Have Consequences* (Chicago: University of Chicago Press, 1948), 52–53.

14. Quoted in Robert Maynard Hutchins, ed., *Great Books of the Western World* (Chicago: Encyclopædia Britannica, 1955), 43:259.

15. Letter dated February 7, 1788, quoted in Catherine Drinker Bowen, *Miracle at Philadelphia* (Boston: Little, Brown, 1966), xvii.

16. See also Dean Mannion, "The Founding Fathers and the Natural Law: A Study of the Source of Our Legal Institutions," *American Bar Association Journal* 35 (1949): 461.

17. Quoted in Hutchins, *Great Books of the Western World,* 43:159.

18. Quoted in Hutchins, *Great Books of the Western World,* 43:104.

19. Quoted in Hutchins, *Great Books of the Western World,* 43:103.

20. Weaver, *Ideas Have Consequences,* 176.

CHAPTER THREE

THE PARABLE OF THE TWO SONS: A REVELATION ABOUT GOD

ELDER JAY E. JENSEN

That Jesus revealed in part the nature of God the Father is evident through-out the four Gospels. Beginning with the experience in the temple at twelve years of age when He said, "Wist ye not that I must be about my Father's business?" (Luke 2:49) to His final statements on the cross, "Father, forgive them; for they know not what they do. . . . Father, into thy hands I commend my spirit" (Luke 23:34, 46), Jesus continually talked about, taught about, and revealed God to His hearers.

In the early part of His ministry, Jesus pointed out His relationship with His Father and some of God's characteristics and attributes.[1] Through per-sonal experience, His followers learned about God. On the Mount of Transfiguration, Peter, James, and John "were eyewitnesses of his majesty"; they "received from God the Father honour and glory"; they heard "a voice . . . from the excellent glory"; and they had "also a more sure word of prophecy" (2 Peter 1:16–19). The great Intercessory Prayer revealed the importance of knowing the Father and the Son, as well as Their oneness, teaching and commanding us to become one with Them (see John 17:3–26).

It is in the parables that Jesus taught, particularly those He taught in the latter part of His ministry, that I have found insights into the character of God.[2] The parable more commonly known as "The Prodigal Son" is unique

Elder Jay E. Jensen is a member of the First Quorum of the Seventy.

25

because of what can be learned about God the Father (see Luke 15:11–32). I prefer to call this parable "The Parable of the Two Sons: A Revelation about God."

Before studying this parable, the thought expressed by the Prophet Joseph Smith about understanding parables is essential: "I have a key by which I understand the scriptures [or parables]. I enquire, what was the question which drew out the answer, or caused Jesus to utter the parable?"[3]

The parable of the father and his two sons is given somewhere near the end of the northern Galilean ministry, shortly after the Transfiguration. The specific setting focuses on four groups: publicans and sinners, who came to hear Him, and Pharisees and scribes, who came to trap Him.[4] Their complaint was that "this man [Jesus] receiveth sinners, and eateth with them" (Luke 15:2). Why is this so? Why does He eat with them? What is our responsibility toward sinners and publicans, or those who are lost? The answer to these questions came in three parables. The first was the parable of the lost sheep—those that through their own choosing become lost because of ignorance and temporal concerns. The second was the parable of the lost coin—an object that was lost because of carelessness or neglect. In these two parables, going after and seeking diligently are the two main activities, joy in heaven being the result of finding the lost. The third parable is the one studied here and is much longer, has different characters, and is written in greater detail than the two shorter parables.[5]

THE YOUNGER SON

"A certain man had two sons" (Luke 15:11). Who is the man referred to here? Many feel that the certain man represents God the Father.[6] The evidence for this will be seen as we study the parable. "The younger of them said to his father, Father, give me the portion of goods that falleth to me. And he divided unto them his living" (v. 12). Note that Luke said "he divided unto *them*"—both sons. To give both sons their inheritance was in harmony with the law at that time.[7] "Not many days after the younger son gathered all together, and took his journey into a far country" (v. 13).

God has given each of us an inheritance—spiritually and temporally. Each of us is on a journey in life. Some are on a journey seeking an eternal companion. Some seek a degree. Others are on a journey seeking a livelihood. Most of us are on several journeys at the same time. With our inheritance in hand, we travel through life, no longer in the actual presence of God. And God has allowed us "his living" (v. 12) to journey to this "far country" (v. 13).

While on this journey, the younger son "wasted his substance with riotous living" (v. 13), perhaps spending his time with harlots (see v. 30). Some in this life, when away from home—away from father and mother—feel they are free to do what they want since they do not have to report in each night. "And when he had spent all, there arose a mighty famine [not just an ordinary famine—a mighty one] in that land; and he began to be in want. And he went and joined himself to a citizen of that country" (vv. 14–15). It is interesting that when he was in want, he sought to join someone or something. However, because of his circumstances, his choices were limited—choices he would never select if he were still basking in his inheritance. We know that in our day people go through similar experiences.

The citizen of that country "sent him into his fields to feed swine" (v. 15). George A. Buttrick notes, "Jesus' hearers would consider a swineherd's occupation the most degrading a Jew could accept. A Talmudic proverb declares: 'Cursed is the man who tends swine, and the man who teaches his son Greek wisdom!' He soon came to envy the swine the food doled out to them. He himself was not allowed even such pitiful fare. Pods of the carob tree are . . . fodder for domestic animals, but as food for men only in times of dire need."[8]

Why did the Savior choose the occupation of feeding the swine to teach His audience? To the Jews, swine were unclean. To fall that low could only illustrate with even greater power the main theme of the parable: can a swineherder—someone who occupies a base, vile, degrading position—be accepted, be forgiven, and be permitted to rejoice "in the presence of the angels of God?" (v. 10).

"And no man gave unto him" (v. 16). No parents, no family members, no friends, not even local welfare offices would offer help. If anyone had helped him at this low point of his experience, the thought expressed in the next phrase probably never would have occurred: "He came to himself."[9] What must we face to come to ourselves? For some it has been the death of a loved one, an interview with a priesthood leader, a scripture, a meeting, an inspired talk, an illness (personal or that of someone you know), or some other such experience. Such shock treatments can help us to see ourselves as we really are. To the younger son, his was a spiritual shock treatment.

At this point the young son began to talk to himself, planning ahead carefully, anticipating what to say. "How many hired servants of my father's have bread enough and to spare, and I perish with hunger! I will arise and go to my father, and will say unto him" (vv. 17–18):

1. "Father, I have sinned against heaven" (v. 18).
2. "[I have sinned] before thee" (v. 18).
3. "[I] am no more worthy to be called thy son" (v. 19).
4. "Make me as one of thy hired servants" (v. 19).

Have you ever done something wrong, something for which you are ashamed? Where do you want to go? Would you rather be alone? The younger son said he would arise and go to his father. Since he had fallen so far, so low, the only place for him to go was up—to ascend. Not only did he say he would go up, but he would go to his father. To me this is one of the most beautiful sentences in the parable: "I will arise and go to my father" (v. 18). This illustrates the truth President J. Reuben Clark spoke:

> Every human being is born with the light of faith kindled in his heart as on an altar, and that light burns and the Lord sees that it burns, during the period before we are accountable. When accountability comes then each of us determines how we shall feed and care for that light. If we shall live righteously that light will glow until it suffuses the whole body, giving to it health and strength and spiritual light as well as bodily health. If we shall live unrighteously that light will dwindle and finally almost flicker out. Yet it is my hope and my belief that the Lord never permits the light of faith wholly to be extinguished in any human heart, however faint the light may glow. The Lord has provided that there shall still be there a spark which, with teaching, with the spirit of righteousness, with love, with tenderness, with example, with living the Gospel, shall brighten and glow again, however darkened the mind may have been.[10]

That the son's faith would grow was only one important truth. Another great truth was that he would go to his father. There is a homewardness in all of us.[11] That feeling of homewardness leads us to our earthly homes as well as our heavenly home. Apparently the younger son had learned enough from his father to know that home is a sanctuary, a place of love and acceptance. The desire to return home and the confidence he would be accepted are evidences that support the thesis that the father in the story is God and, as His children, we can arise and go to Him no matter how far we have fallen. A first step of repentance is to arise and *look up* to Him for help. The Father is both *just* and *merciful*. Knowing the character of the Father inspires a confidence to return. The son did arise, and he did go to his father.

"But when he was yet a great way off, his father saw him" (v. 20). I am grateful the writer included the expression "when he was yet a great way off." It convinces me that with every dawn, a concerned father arose and looked into the distance with the hope his son would return. The father looked with anxiousness when a traveler appeared on the horizon and thought, *Could that be my son?* Do we understand the anxiousness with which our parents and leaders have watched for us? Do we understand why parents lie awake at night and worry whether children will return home pure, chaste, and in one piece? This great father knew his son well enough that when yet a great way off he recognized his son. Perhaps this is another illustration of the character of God. He recognizes the individuality of His children, even while they are yet a great way off.

"A country lad listened in an English cathedral to the reading of this story. Came the words 'But when he was yet a great way off, his father saw him, and had compassion, and ran.' . . . The lad, quite forgetful of place and people, wishing perhaps that he had that kind of home and father, shouted, 'Eh, but yon was a grand old man!'"[12]

The good father did four things: (1) he had compassion, (2) he ran to his son, (3) he embraced him, and (4) he kissed him (see v. 20). It is interesting to note that the father did not say, "Well, I see you have learned your lesson," or "I am busy right now; I will see you in a minute," or "Go on home to your mother, and I will see you after work." The apparent message is one of acceptance and forgiveness, a continuation of the theme taught in the parables of the lost sheep and the lost coin. Nothing is said, however, about a restoration of blessings, and in that an important lesson is given to us in our day.

When those who have not attended meetings regularly return to the Church, we too can have compassion and follow the custom of our culture, which is to eagerly greet them (run to them) and extend a hand of fellowship. (In certain world cultures, it is acceptable to embrace them or even to kiss them on the cheek.)

"And the son said unto him, Father, I have sinned" (v. 21). This open confession was voluntary, as opposed to an admission of guilt when confronted. It was one that came from a man who "came to himself" (v. 17).

The son voluntarily confessed to have sinned against heaven and to have sinned in his father's sight. I have seen people who recognize that one party has been offended but not that both have been offended. In working with missionaries who had committed moral transgressions in the past, I found that most realized they had broken the Lord's commandments and by so doing had offended heaven; but when asked if they realized they had offended people on earth, many said they had not understood this. If a young man offends a young lady by committing moral transgression, should he not seek her forgiveness, realizing he has sinned against her and heaven? Also, some transgressions are to be confessed "in the sight" of a judge in Israel.

"The father said to his servants" (v. 22):

1. "Bring forth the best robe" (v. 22)—reserved for special guests, a very special honor.

2. "Put a ring on his hand" (v. 22)—suggesting dignity, honor, and a recognition of family acceptance.

3. "Put . . . shoes on his feet" (v. 22)—indicating he was a son, not a slave. A mark of a slave was to go barefooted. The son had fallen to such a lowly state, but now he was restored to family status.

4. "Bring hither the fatted calf, and kill it" (v. 23)—the one reserved for special occasions. "For this my son was dead, and is alive again; he was lost, and is found. And they began to be merry" (v. 24).

We have now come to the end of what some consider to be the first half of this parable. Buttrick says, "The first (vss. 11–24) illustrates the joy with which God welcomes the repentant sinner. It is complete in itself, and teaches much the same truth as the parables of the lost sheep and the lost coin. The second (vss. 25–32) rebukes the criticism of this interpretation of the love and mercy of God that had been made by 'righteous persons that need no repentance.' . . . The second part is just as parabolic . . . as the first, and the whole is best regarded as a unity."[13]

The attributes of God revealed in this first half of the parable are:

1. He is a God of law who gives an inheritance to His children, allowing them agency to use their inheritance as they choose.

2. He is a God of compassion and mercy, accepting the repentant on conditions of sincere repentance.

3. He is an omniscient God, knowing the thoughts and intents of the repentant, and can therefore judge according to justice and mercy.

THE DUTIFUL SON

Having learned about the younger son, the attention is focused on the older son. "Now his elder son was in the field" (v. 25) performing his duty, apparently faithful in his responsibilities, caring for the inheritance his father had given him. Returning from the field, he heard music and dancing and asked a servant the meaning. The servant said, "Thy brother is come; and thy father hath killed the fatted calf, because he hath received him safe and sound. And he was angry, and would not go in" (vv. 27–28). To refuse to go was an insult. The attitude of the elder son was wrong, especially if the elder son understood the laws regarding inheritance.[14]

"Therefore came his father out, and intreated him" (v. 28). To entreat is to ask earnestly, to persuade by imploring. The fact that the father left the festivity, which he did not have to do, and entreated his son is evidence to me of the mercy and condescension of God the Father. On other occasions He has entreated His disobedient children to turn to Him: "For notwithstanding I shall lengthen out mine arm unto them from day to day, they will deny me; nevertheless, I will be merciful unto them, saith the Lord God, if they will repent and come unto me; for mine arm is lengthened out all the day long" (2 Nephi 28:32).[15] Considering the many scriptural evidences, it is not out of character for the Father to entreat His son.

The elder son listened but did not understand the message, for he responded with "Lo [implying a reproach or an attempt to put the father in his place], these many years do I serve thee, neither transgressed I at any time thy commandment" (v. 29). If the elder son had truly been as faithful as he indicated here, and if he were to maintain the right attitude, and if he were to endure to the end, he would be blessed to return to the presence of God.[16]

The elder son continued his expressions of displeasure, even accusing his brother of "devouring thy living" with harlots (v. 30). Whether the younger actually spent his time with harlots or the elder son was accusing him falsely out of jealousy and anger is not known. If the younger son were guilty of such, he must fully repent; and if the elder son were speaking out of anger and jealousy, he must also repent.

The father then reminded his son of three important truths:

1. "Son" (v. 31)—addressing him as son was a reminder of who he was.

2. "Thou art ever with me" (v. 31)—he still had all the blessings and rights of family association, even eternal associations.

3. "All that I have is thine" (v. 31)—all that the Father has to give, the entire inheritance, even eternal life, could be his.

An important message that comes from the second half of the parable (vv. 25–32) is that Jesus taught the audience, the Pharisees and the scribes, that they were like the elder son. They felt they "had it made." The Savior held out hope for them. If they would be entreated, they could enjoy the blessings of heaven. If they would accept and follow the counsel of the Father, He would say, "All that I have is thine." If they refused to accept the message, their hypocritical, self-righteous attitude (like that of the elder son) would lead to their destruction.

SUMMARY

The following are the key principles I see in the parable of the father and his two sons. First, a loving Father, following the laws He has ordained, gave inheritances to His children and allowed them agency to do with the inheritances what they chose. Second, God allows His children to experience shock treatment to help them come to themselves and see themselves as they really are. Third, sinners can and should be received by the Father and His faithful Saints. We are to have compassion for them, extend fellowship to them, embrace them, and clothe them with dignity, honor, and respect. Fourth, God, our Heavenly Father, condescends to entreat His children. Fifth, justice will be satisfied and mercy will claim both the repentant and the obedient and the faithful. No amount of repentance could restore to the younger son the actual inheritance he had wasted. He lost something that cannot be regained. If the elder son will repent of his self-righteous attitude, he can enjoy all that the Father has. If he will not repent, he will lose the rights to an eternal inheritance in the kingdom of his Father. Finally, God is all-powerful, all-knowing, compassionate, just, and merciful, and much, much more.

The Savior revealed in this parable these attributes and characteristics so that by knowing the Father and His Son and striving to become like Them, we can be inheritors of eternal life and be crowned with this same godly nature.

NOTES

1. Nine specific points of the Father–Son relationship and God's nature are outlined by John as follows (see John 5:17–30):
   a. "My Father worketh . . . and I work" (v. 17).
   b. "The Son can do nothing of himself, but what he seeth the Father do:

for what things soever he doeth, these also doeth the Son likewise" (v. 19).

c. "For the Father loveth the Son" and the Son loves the Father (v. 20).

d. The Father "sheweth [the Son] all things that himself doeth" (v. 20).

e. "The Father raiseth up the dead, and quickeneth them; even so the Son quickeneth whom he will" (v. 21).

f. "The Father judgeth no man, but hath committed all judgment unto the Son" (v. 22).

g. "The Father hath life in himself; so hath he given to the Son to have life in himself" (v. 26).

h. The Father "hath given him authority to execute judgment also, because he is the Son of man. . . . As I hear, I judge: and my judgment is just" (vv. 27, 30).

i. "I seek not mine own will, but the will of the Father which hath sent me" (v. 30).

2. Some of these later parables include that of the unmerciful servant, the wicked husbandman, the marriage of the king's son, the unjust judge, the talents, and the sheep and the goats.

3. Joseph Smith, *Teachings of the Prophet Joseph Smith,* comp. Joseph Fielding Smith (Salt Lake City: Deseret Book, 1976), 276–77.

4. Jesus may have intended to draw parallels between the four groups mentioned and the sheep, the money, and the sons. For example, the lost sheep and the lost silver could represent the sinner and the publicans, who were lost spiritually. The two sons could represent the Pharisees and scribes, who had been given inheritances and had either wasted them through riotous living (like the younger son) or immersed themselves in their traditional self-righteous shells (like the older son). In this chapter, it is more appropriate to classify all four groups as being lost, regardless of how they became such. None can enter heaven without walking the strait and narrow path, submitting to the ordinances from authorized priesthood holders.

5. Obviously there are certain guidelines and potential problems when interpreting parables. Some helpful rules are: "(*a*) Do not force a meaning on subordinate incidents. (*b*) Do not regard as parallel parables that are connected by superficial likeness of imagery. (*c*) Bear in mind that the same illustration does not always have the same significance—leaven, e.g., signifies a principle of good as well as a principle of evil. (*d*) Remember that the comparison in a parable is not complete, does not touch at every point. Thus, the characters of the unjust judge or the unjust steward or the nobleman who went into a far country—possibly referring to the infamous Archelaus—do not concern the interpretation of the parable. The parable draws a picture of life as it is, not as it ought to be, and compares certain points in this picture with heavenly doctrine.

(*e*) Observe the proper proportions of a parable, and do not make the episode more prominent than the main line of teaching" (Bible Dictionary, "Parables," 741).

6. See Bruce R. McConkie, *Doctrinal New Testament Commentary,* 3 vols. (Salt Lake City: Bookcraft, 1965–73), 1:513; J. R. Dummelow, *Commentary on the Holy Bible* (New York: Macmillan, 1936), 758; Department of Seminaries and Institutes of Religion, *Life and Teachings of Jesus and His Apostles* (Salt Lake City: The Church of Jesus Christ of Latter-day Saints, 1979), 124; Joachim Jeremias, *Rediscovering the Parables* (New York: Scribner, 1966), 101, 103.

7. "It may seem strange that such a demand should be made, and that the parent should have acceded to it. . . . It has been an immemorial custom in the east for sons to demand and receive their portion of the inheritance during their father's lifetime; and the parent, however aware of the dissipated inclinations of the child, could not legally refuse to comply with the application" (Adam Clarke, *The New Testament of Our Lord and Savior Jesus Christ* [Nashville: Abingdon, 1977], 1:457).

8. George A. Buttrick, ed., *The Interpreter's Bible,* 12 vols. (Nashville: Abingdon-Cokesbury Press, 1952–57), 8:272–73.

9. "*The Abingdon Bible Commentary* suggests that the Greek word is a medical term: when he 'came to his senses after fainting.' The idiom was in many languages before Jesus used it, but only he could give it heavenly light. Because of him it is in our language, for we say of a neighbor's black mood, 'He is not himself today.' Acts 12:11 says of Peter waking out of sleep: 'And when Peter was come to himself'" (Buttrick, *Interpreter's Bible,* 8:274).

10. J. Reuben Clark Jr., in Conference Report, October 1936, 114.

11. This homeward feeling is seen elsewhere in scripture. Following the first vision, Joseph Smith "went home" (Joseph Smith–History 1:20). The Nephites were told to "go ye unto your homes, and ponder" (3 Nephi 17:3). The healed blind man was sent home (see Mark 8:22–26).

12. Buttrick, *Interpreter's Bible,* 8:270.

13. Buttrick, *Interpreter's Bible,* 8:270.

14. "In every point of view, the anger of the old son was improper and unreasonable. He had already received his part of the inheritance, see ver. 12, and his profligate brother had received no more than what was his just dividend. Besides, what the father had acquired since that division he had a right to dispose of as he pleased, even to give it all to one son; nor did the ancient customs of the Asiatic countries permit the other children to claim any share in such property thus disposed of. The following is an institute of the GENTOO law on this subject: (Code, chap. ii. sect. 9, p. 79) 'If a father gives, by his own choice, land, houses, orchards, and the earning of his own industry, to one of his sons, the other sons shall not receive any share of it.' Besides, whatever property the father had

acquired after the above division, the son or sons, as the prodigal in the text, could have no claim at all on, according to another institute in the above Asiatic laws, see chap. ii, sect. ii, p. 85, but the father might divide it among those who remained with him: therefore is it said in the text, 'Son, thou art always with me, and all that I have is thine,' ver. 31" (Clarke, *New Testament of Our Lord and Savior Jesus Christ*, 1:459).

15. See also Isaiah 5:25; 9:12, 17, 21; 10:4. Even though the people mentioned had turned from the Lord, "his hand is stretched out still." The Lord has also entreated and will continue to entreat His children through the voices of prophets, angels, and even the elements (see D&C 43:20–28).

16. "The weeks and months of doing work which his brother had previously done, compensating for his father's inattention, receiving no compliments, and the father's preoccupation settled in on him. Perhaps he thought he should have taken his inheritance also. He would not have wasted it, but increased it. In spite of these thoughts, he had stayed at home and been a dutiful son. There was no music, no dancing for his righteous life; and yet when his younger brother returned, all of these things celebrated his coming.

    "Word came to the father that his son was outside and would not come in, 'therefore came his father out, and intreated him' (Luke 15:28). The father must have realized the oversight; he may even have apologized. The great concern for his younger son was off his mind. He remembered he had not been as complimentary to the older son as usual. He recalled the older son's more intense work to compensate—no dancing, no music, no sumptuous feasts. Hearts were too heavy for those things" (Vaughn J. Featherstone, "However Faint the Light May Glow," *Ensign*, November 1982, 72).

CHAPTER FOUR

"HE IS RISEN"

ELDER L. ALDIN PORTER

The Psalmist said, "Thy word is a lamp unto my feet, and a light unto my path" (Psalm 119:105). I love the word of the Lord—whether through the scriptures or through His living prophets. My prayer is that the Holy Spirit may attend us that we might have truth and light.

The golden chain that makes its way through the book of Acts and through the book of Revelation and throughout all of the scriptures is that Jesus is the Son of God and has been resurrected. The dominant message of the scriptures in all ages is "He is risen" (Matthew 28:6). The Prophet Joseph Smith taught, "The fundamental principles of our religion are the testimony of the Apostles and Prophets, concerning Jesus Christ, that He died, was buried, and rose again the third day, and ascended into heaven."[1]

The Apostles Peter, Thomas, Paul, and others bore personal witness of the Resurrection, and their individual testimonies highlight different aspects of this supernal event. Ultimately, the power of their words to bring about conversion in their listeners depended upon the confirming witness of the Holy Ghost, "for when a man speaketh by the power of the Holy Ghost the power of the Holy Ghost carrieth it unto the hearts of the children of men" (2 Nephi 33:1).

There is power in the witness of the spoken word. The voice has the capability to reach the heart of man in a remarkable manner. When that voice is accompanied by the Holy Spirit, there is light and truth. That light and truth is shared by the speaker as well as the listener (see D&C 50:22).

Elder L. Aldin Porter is an emeritus member of the Seventy.

Peter Testifies of the Resurrection

On the day of Pentecost, in Peter's first recorded discourse after the Ascension of the Lord, the chief Apostle referred to the prophecies of Jesus Christ and then said: "This Jesus hath God raised up, whereof we all are witnesses. . . . Therefore let all the house of Israel know assuredly, that God hath made that same Jesus, whom ye have crucified, both Lord and Christ. Now when they heard this, they were pricked in their heart, and said unto Peter and to the rest of the apostles, Men and brethren, what shall we do? Then Peter said unto them, Repent, and be baptized every one of you in the name of Jesus Christ for the remission of sins, and ye shall receive the gift of the Holy Ghost" (Acts 2:32, 36–38).

Later, Peter and John healed the man who was lame at the gates of the temple. As they entered the temple grounds, a large group came running together, greatly wondering. The people in this gathering were obviously very different from the people Peter spoke to on the day of Pentecost. Note the significant change in his instructions: "But ye denied the Holy One and the Just, and desired a murderer to be granted unto you; and killed the Prince of life, whom God hath raised from the dead; whereof we are witnesses. . . . Repent ye therefore, and be converted, that your sins may be blotted out, when the times of refreshing shall come from the presence of the Lord; and he shall send Jesus Christ, which before was preached unto you: whom the heaven must receive until the times of restitution of all things, which God hath spoken by the mouth of all his holy prophets since the world began" (Acts 3:14–15, 19–21).

This second group of listeners apparently included those who participated in calling for the Crucifixion of the Son of God, and there would be no baptism and no hope until another distant time. It is interesting that in both cases Peter made a major point of the fact that the Savior had been raised from the dead but gave a call to repentance and baptism to one group and a call to repent with far-off possibilities to the other. Each time he boldly gave a witness that God had raised Jesus from the dead. I draw attention to not only the message but the method by which it is transmitted. Peter did not argue, he did not plead, he did not cajole—he simply bore witness of the Master and His Resurrection with a power we can feel as we read the accounts. He knew the fundamental truth that the convincing power of the Holy Ghost would accompany his words.

Earlier, while Jesus lived in mortality, Simon Peter had an experience that gives background to his testimony:

When Jesus came into the coasts of Cæsarea Philippi, he asked his disciples, saying, Whom do men say that I the Son of man am?

And they said, Some say that thou art John the Baptist: some, Elias; and others, Jeremias, or one of the prophets.

He saith unto them, But whom say ye that I am?

And Simon Peter answered and said, Thou art the Christ, the Son of the living God.

And Jesus answered and said unto him, Blessed art thou, Simon Bar-jona: for flesh and blood hath not revealed it unto thee, but my Father which is in heaven.

And I say also unto thee, That thou art Peter, and upon this rock I will build my church; and the gates of hell shall not prevail against it. (Matthew 16:13–18)

The Savior could have said to Peter, "You have seen me feed the five thousand, restore sight to the blind, give hearing to the deaf, and bring life to the dead, and now you know who I am." He did not say those things. What He did say is, "Flesh and blood hath not revealed it unto thee, but my Father which is in heaven" (v. 17).

The Lord's work moves forward on personal revelation and the power of testimony. Today we testify before the world that these things are true. Our parents, teachers, priesthood and auxiliary leaders, missionaries, and apostles and prophets bear witness of the divinity of the Lord's Atonement and Resurrection. We have spiritual progress in this kingdom when our quorums, classes, and pulpits resound with the sure word of testimony. President Harold B. Lee taught this supernal truth: "More powerful than sight, more powerful than walking and talking with Him, is that witness of the Spirit. . . . When that Spirit has witnessed to our spirit, that's a revelation from Almighty God."[2]

THOMAS FEELS THE SAVIOR'S WOUNDS

From the experience Thomas had with the resurrected Christ, it appears that the Lord required the reality of His physical Resurrection to be understood by those who were to be His special witnesses. Thomas's experience occurred shortly after the Resurrection but before the Ascension, as the scriptures record:

Thomas, one of the twelve, called Didymus, was not with them when Jesus came.

The other disciples therefore said unto him, We have seen the Lord. But he said unto them, Except I shall see in his hands the print of the nails, and put my finger into the print of the nails, and thrust my hand into his side, I will not believe.

And after eight days again his disciples were within, and Thomas with them: then came Jesus, the doors being shut, and stood in the midst, and said, Peace be unto you.

Then saith he to Thomas, Reach hither thy finger, and behold my hands; and reach hither thy hand, and thrust it into my side; and be not faithless, but believing. (John 20:24–27)

There is little chance that Thomas did not believe that man survived the grave. How many times had he heard the Master teach the principles of eternity?

Elder Bruce R. McConkie provided this insight: "Thomas apparently did not understand or believe that Jesus had come forth with a literal, tangible body of flesh and bones, one that could be felt and handled, one that bore the nail marks and carried the spear wound, one that ate food and outwardly was almost akin to a mortal body. Obviously he had heard the testimony of Mary Magdalene and the other women, of Peter, and of all the apostles. It is not to be supposed that he doubted the resurrection as such, but rather the literal and corporeal nature of it. Hence his rash assertion about feeling the nail prints and thrusting his hand into the Lord's side."[3]

It was necessary that Thomas believe in the eternal nature of the spirit and also, to fulfill his apostleship, necessary that he know and testify of the physical resurrection of the body. Today the nature of the physical resurrection is often overlooked. When we testify of the certainty of physical resurrection, the Holy Spirit accompanies our words with power. If we are to enjoy the full benefits of the Holy Spirit we, through revelation, must testify of the certainty of the Lord's life, death, and Resurrection.

It is a comfort as well as a warning to understand that the resurrection is physical. Consider the comfort this knowledge brings to those who lay their children in the grave. Have you not seen the power of this faith in the faces of bereaved parents? The reality of death descends on us in stark tones as we stand at the grave of a loved one. But the reality of a literal resurrection comes with the power of certainty only the Comforter can give. In that moment, the resurrection ceases to be just an abstract doctrinal subject. Instead, this glorious certainty fills the soul with joy.

Does this knowledge not impact us when we realize that we will stand in the flesh before the judgment bar of God? The spiritual confirmation that there is a resurrection brings with it a sureness that we are dealing with life in its most certain, eternal forms. Moroni's closing words in the last chapter in the Book of Mormon have a ring of finality to them. He says, "And I exhort you to remember these things; for the time speedily cometh that ye shall know that I lie not, for ye shall see me at the bar of God; and the Lord God will say unto you: Did I not declare my words unto you, which were written by this man, like as one crying from the dead, yea, even as one speaking out of the dust?" (Moroni 10:27).

One reason the Book of Mormon is given to us in this day is so we may effectively teach and testify of the divinity of the Lord Jesus Christ and of the certainty of His Resurrection. Alma taught, "Yea, every knee shall bow, and every tongue confess before him. Yea, even at the last day, when all men shall stand to be judged of him, then shall they confess that he is God; then shall they confess, who live without God in the world, that the judgment of an everlasting punishment is just upon them; and they shall quake, and tremble, and shrink beneath the glance of his all-searching eye" (Mosiah 27:31).

Ezekiel saw the day when all must accept the Savior's position in the face of evidence which cannot be denied: "Therefore prophesy and say unto them, Thus saith the Lord God; Behold, O my people, I will open your graves, and cause you to come up out of your graves, and bring you into the land of Israel. And ye shall know that I am the Lord, when I have opened your graves, O my people, and brought you up out of your graves" (Ezekiel 37:12–13).

It will be a tragedy for those who wait for this final day to accept the Master and His sacrifice. They who "live without God in the world" will have endured so much pain and needless sorrow. For many it will be a dark and fearsome day, but surely it will not be such for those who have received the testimony of Jesus and have overcome by faith. For them it will be a day of most sublime joy.

PAUL TESTIFIES OF THE RISEN LORD

Now we come to the testimony of the Apostle Paul. This great Apostle to the Gentiles was a powerful witness of the Resurrection throughout his life. "They came to Thessalonica, where was a synagogue of the Jews: and Paul, as his manner was, went in unto them, and three sabbath days reasoned with them out of the scriptures. Opening and alleging, that Christ must needs have suffered, and risen again from the dead; and that this Jesus, whom I preach unto you, is Christ" (Acts 17:1–3).

Later at Mars' hill, Paul testified: "Forasmuch then as we are the off-spring of God, we ought not to think that the Godhead is like unto gold, or silver, or stone, graven by art and man's device. And the times of this ignorance God winked at; but now commandeth all men every where to repent: because he hath appointed a day, in the which he will judge the world in righteousness by that man whom he hath ordained; whereof he hath given assurance unto all men, in that he hath raised him from the dead" (Acts 17:29–31).

Many months passed, and Paul found himself testifying before King Agrippa: "Why should it be thought a thing incredible with you, that God should raise the dead? . . . Having therefore obtained help of God, I continue unto this day, witnessing both to small and great, saying none other things than those which the prophets and Moses did say should come: that Christ should suffer, and that he should be the first that should rise from the dead, and should shew light unto the people, and to the Gentiles" (Acts 26:8, 22–23).

Elder McConkie taught that the Apostle Paul's example is pertinent to all of us who seek to serve the Master:

> Paul testifies that Jesus is the Christ. True he quotes selected Messianic prophecies to show his witness is in harmony with what other prophets have foretold. But the burden of his message is one of announcement, of bearing record that Jesus was raised from the dead; that he was seen of witnesses who now declare the glad tidings of salvation to others. . . .
>
> It is the resurrection of Christ which proves the truth and divinity of the Christian faith. Jesus is shown to be the Son of God because he rose from the dead. The Messianic prophecies are known to apply to him because he broke the bands of death. . . . And so it is with all the Messianic prophecies; their fulfilment is known because Christ gained the victory over death.[4]

THE BOOK OF MORMON TESTIFIES OF CHRIST

The Lord, who knew the end from the beginning, revealed many years ago that we would need the Book of Mormon to carry the work forward in this dispensation:

And the Lord said unto Enoch: As I live, even so will I come in the last days, in the days of wickedness and vengeance, to fulfill the oath which I have made unto you concerning the children of Noah;

And the day shall come that the earth shall rest, but before that day the heavens shall be darkened, and a veil of darkness shall cover the earth; and the heavens shall shake, and also the earth; and great tribulations shall be among the children of men, but my people will I preserve;

And righteousness will I send down out of heaven; and truth will I send forth out of the earth, to bear testimony of mine Only Begotten; his resurrection from the dead; yea, and also the resurrection of all men; and righteousness and truth will I cause to sweep the earth as with a flood, to gather out mine elect from the four quarters of the earth. (Moses 7:60–62)

On this passage, Brother Robert Matthews commented: "Five thousand years ago the Lord revealed to the prophet Enoch what the fundamental message of the Book of Mormon would be. Neither history, culture, nor geography were mentioned. The book would testify of the Only Begotten and the resurrection. . . . Almost every prophet in the Book of Mormon makes some reference to the resurrection."[5]

The Book of Mormon's title page explicitly states that it is written "to the convincing of the Jew and Gentile that JESUS is the CHRIST, the ETERNAL GOD, manifesting himself unto all nations." Clearly He who gave us this sacred scripture has made known its divine purposes. These facts were placed in the book to draw our attention to those important doctrines the Lord wants us to understand. Therefore, the Book of Mormon is not merely the history of a people; it is the history of a message, of those who carried that message, and of the people's response to it. The testimony of Jesus permeates its pages from the title page to Moroni's final testimony.

REVELATION GUIDES THE CHURCH TODAY

This kingdom moves forward today on the power of the personal revelation that there is a Savior to this world and He is Jesus Christ. A living prophet was the instrument through which the Lord restored the priesthood with all of its power. We often underestimate the overwhelming importance of this revelatory gift.

On September 15, 1986, while serving as a mission president, I received a letter from an elder then serving as a missionary in Alabama. He and his companion had been teaching an investigator who had a genuine interest in the Church. Her minister gave her some material which purported to answer the questions of Mormonism. He titles it "The Taproot of Mormonism." I quote:

> Mormons teach that every individual can directly receive divine revelation. In fact, this is the Mormon method for distinguishing truth from error. Mormon missionaries teach non-Mormons that, in order to know whether or not the Mormon teachings are true, people should pray to God to send revelation directly and personally to them—God will send the Holy Spirit to speak directly to their heart.
>
> The importance of this concept cannot be overemphasized because it is the very means by which Mormons are convinced Mormonism is true. . . . They believe because they are convinced that God himself has personally told them Mormonism is true. This is why few Mormons will reject Mormonism simply if they are shown contradictions between the Bible and Mormonism. They conclude the Bible must be in error (it has been changed through the years, etc.). It cannot be Mormonism is wrong, because they know God has told them it is true! This is the taproot of Mormonism—the source from which all Mormonism flows. It is the foundation of the structure of Mormonism. Destroy it and Mormonism falls.

When I finished reading it, the thought came to me that "the children of this world are in their generation wiser than the children of light" (Luke 16:8). The author had rare insight.

The gentleman then went on to say: "We seek to show the validity of the following concept of revelation which we affirm is taught in the Bible: The Bible is the only revelation from God to man today. The time came when God's message was fully revealed and fully recorded in written form in the Bible. There then ceased to be a need, in God's plan, for continued direct revelation to man, so that process ceased." It is a tragedy that so many hold to the position that God no longer speaks through revelation.

MODERN WITNESSES TESTIFY OF CHRIST

Today our prophets, apostles, and other leaders testify of the risen Lord and the power of the Atonement and Resurrection. Years ago, as a new regional representative, I was on assignment to a stake conference with Elder Bruce R. McConkie. In the planning meeting Saturday afternoon with the stake presidency, he asked that he be scheduled for one hour in the evening meeting and one hour in the Sunday meeting. It was Easter weekend. Saturday evening he spoke under the influence of the Holy Spirit on the Atonement. Sunday he spoke with the same power on the Resurrection of the Lord Jesus Christ and of all men. On the way to the airport, I said to him, "Those two discourses were magnificent." Note carefully his response: "Yes, they were. It is amazing how much I learn when I speak under the influence of the Spirit of God."

I have come to know since that day that I receive more revelations while teaching and testifying of the Lord Jesus Christ, of His servant the Prophet Joseph Smith, and of the living prophets of our day than at any other time.

This great and powerful witness that we have so abundantly seen in the scriptures has fallen upon the apostles and prophets and faithful members of the Church in our day. We are blessed with prophets who have a sure and certain knowledge of these basic truths.

President Gordon B. Hinckley testified of the Resurrection, saying:

> Never had this occurred before. There had been only death without hope. Now there was life eternal. Only a God could have done this. The Resurrection of Jesus Christ was the great crowning event of His life and mission. It was the capstone of the Atonement. The sacrifice of His life for all mankind was not complete without His coming forth from the grave, with the certainty of the Resurrection for all who have walked the earth.
>
> Of all the victories in the chronicles of humanity, none is so great, none so universal in its effects, none so everlasting in its consequences as the victory of the crucified Lord, who came forth from the tomb that first Easter morning.
>
> Those who were witnesses of that event, all who saw and heard and spoke with the Risen Lord, testified of the reality of this greatest of all miracles. His followers through the centuries lived and died in proclamation of the truth of this supernal act.
>
> To all of these we add our testimony that He who died on Calvary's cross arose again in wondrous splendor as the Son of God, the Master of life and death.[6]

We have the honor and the obligation through revelation to bear witness that Jesus literally came forth from the tomb. Our teaching should be filled with this eternal fact. Ours is the joyful burden of standing as His witnesses in our day and time.

I add my testimony to those of the prophets. God has made known to me in an unmistakable way that He lives and that His Beloved Son, Jesus Christ, is the Savior of the world and was resurrected to lead all men through that incredible transformation. In the name of Jesus Christ, amen.

NOTES

1. Joseph Smith, *Teachings of the Prophet Joseph Smith,* comp. Joseph Fielding Smith (Salt Lake City: Deseret Book, 1976), 121.

2. Harold B. Lee, *Teachings of Presidents of the Church: Harold B. Lee* (Salt Lake City: The Church of Jesus Christ of Latter-day Saints, 2000), 39.

3. Bruce R. McConkie, *Doctrinal New Testament Commentary,* 3 vols. (Salt Lake City: Bookcraft, 1971), 1:860.

4. McConkie, *Doctrinal New Testament Commentary,* 2:126–27.

5. Robert J. Matthews, *Selected Writings of Robert J. Matthews* (Salt Lake City: Deseret Book, 1999), 509.

6. Gordon B. Hinckley, "Special Witnesses of Christ," *Ensign,* April 2001, 15.

CHAPTER FIVE

SANCTIFICATION AND JUSTIFICATION ARE JUST AND TRUE

ELDER GERALD N. LUND

For some reason, sanctification and justification intrigue and puzzle many Saints who sincerely seek to understand the principles and requirements of salvation. Even a cursory study of the scriptures quickly proves that these are important, indeed central, concepts to an understanding of the gospel of Jesus Christ. The terms *sanctification* and *justification* and their cognate words are used hundreds of times in the four standard works. However, as important as they are, nowhere does any scriptural writer attempt to formally define either concept. Thus, we are left to derive their meaning from how the terms are used in various contexts or from the effects which result from their application.

In some ways, an examination of the usage only adds to the puzzlement because, on the surface at least, the very scriptural record seems paradoxical, if not inconsistent. For example, a statement in the Pearl of Great Price seems very clear and straightforward. Adam was taught that "by the Spirit ye are justified, and by the blood ye are sanctified" (Moses 6:60). The blood, of course, refers to the blood of Christ offered as atonement for sin. Other scriptures refer to the idea that we are sanctified or cleansed or have sin remitted through the blood of Jesus. To wash our garments in the blood of the Lamb is a well-known scriptural phrase (see 1 Nephi 12:10; Alma 13:11). Moroni spoke of being sanctified by the shedding of the

Elder Gerald N. Lund of the Seventy is serving as Area President of the Europe West Area.

blood of Christ (see Moroni 10:33). These scriptures seem to clearly support the idea that sanctification comes by the blood of Christ. And yet in
several places the scriptures just as plainly and clearly speak of sins being
remitted and of sanctification coming through the influence of the Holy
Ghost (see 2 Nephi 31:17; Alma 5:54; 3 Nephi 27:19–20; D&C 84:23). This
seeming contradiction happens in almost the same breath when Alma
speaks about the people of Melchizedek. He notes they were "*sanctified* and
their garments were *washed white through the blood of the Lamb.* Now they
. . . [were] *sanctified by the Holy Ghost*" (Alma 13:11–12; emphasis added).
And to further confuse the issue, the Doctrine and Covenants mentions
neither the blood nor the Spirit but speaks of sanctification as being
accomplished *by law* (see D&C 88:18–35, especially 21, 34). And other
places in the Doctrine and Covenants command the Saints to *sanctify
themselves* (see D&C 43:11, 16; 88:68, 74; 133:4).

We find this same kind of multiplicity in the scriptural use of the word
justification. As noted, Adam was taught that "*by the Spirit* ye are justified"
(Moses 6:60; emphasis added). And yet again and again, the Apostle Paul
teaches that we are justified by faith (see Romans 3:28; 5:1; Galatians 2:16;
Acts 13:38–39). Still Paul agrees with the scripture in Moses and says we
are justified *by the Spirit* (see 1 Corinthians 6:11). And yet Paul specifically
states "justified *by his blood*" (Romans 5:9; emphasis added). Both Lehi and
Paul are equally specific in saying that *by the law* no person can be justified (see 2 Nephi 2:5; Romans 3:20; Galatians 2:16). But again we see the
seeming contradiction, for just a few verses before Paul emphatically states
that "*by the deeds of the law there shall no flesh be justified*" (Romans 3:20;
emphasis added). He just as emphatically states "for not the hearers of the
law are just before God, *but the doers of the law shall be justified*" (Romans
2:13; emphasis added).

It is not difficult, therefore, to understand why so many scholars,
including some Latter-day Saints, have approached the study of sanctification and justification as though it were some great mystery, some mystical process beyond the understanding of all but the most erudite or
spiritually mature. It is the position of this paper that just the opposite is
true. While the application of the two concepts into our lives may be a
great challenge, it is my firm contention that the doctrine of sanctification
and justification is profoundly plain and simple, so much so that a child of
accountable age could easily understand it and the implication it has.

In its simplicity, it answers the paradoxes and seeming inconsistencies previously described.

The primary purpose of this chapter is not to provide an exhaustive analysis of the doctrine, nor is it even to attempt a complete and definitive outline of the principles. Much, much more could and should be said about these two principles, but our purpose here will be a limited one: to provide some conceptual tools that help us better understand and apply sanctification and justification in our lives.

DEFINITIONS

As previously noted, one of the problems we face in thinking about sanctification and justification is that they are not specifically defined in the scriptures. Thus, we must study their usage in order to determine their meaning. Some of the clearest statements on the two doctrines are found in modern scripture, and they are extremely valuable. However, we can come closer to a true definition of the words when we study them in their biblical setting because there we can examine their original meaning in both Hebrew and Greek. This study can provide a basic foundation of understanding which influences our usage of the words in modern English.

Sanctification. Ask Latter-day Saints or even modern Christians what it means to sanctify something and they will almost always answer in terms of cleansing or purifying. This is not incorrect, but it does not embrace the original sense of the Hebrew root *kadash,* which means "to set apart or separate something or someone for the work of God." The concept of purity or holiness flows out of this idea of separation because to be set apart for God requires worthiness and a separation from the common or normal worldly use of things. "Perhaps the English word *sacred* represents the idea more nearly than *holy,* which is the general rendering in the A.V. The terms *sanctification* and *holiness* are now used so frequently to represent moral and spiritual qualities, that they hardly convey to the reader the idea of *position* or *relationship* as existing between God and some person or thing consecrated to Him; yet this appears to be the real meaning of the word."[1]

Kadash (and its cognate words) is applied in the Old Testament to places, from which we get a word related to *sanctified;* namely, *sanctuary.* The camp of Israel was called Kadesh Barnea, or "the Sanctuary of Barnea" (see Numbers 13:26; 32:8), and the ground surrounding the burning bush was called *kodesh* (see Exodus 3:5). The idea of sanctification as separation was also applied to days or times such as the Sabbath (see Genesis 2:3; Exodus 20:8, 11). And *kadash* could also be applied to persons (see Exodus 13:2; 28:41) or a whole group of people (see Deuteronomy 7:6).

The need for *kadash,* or sanctification, sprang from the separateness or holiness of God. As Girdlestone notes, "God Himself was regarded as holy, *i.e.,* as a Being who from His nature, position, and attributes is to be set apart and revered as distinct from all others; and Israel was to separate itself from the world and the things of the world because God was thus separated; they were to be holy, for He was holy."[2]

Kadash, in its various forms in the Old Testament (and the Greek *hagiadzo,* which corresponds to *kadash* in New Testament usage), is translated variously as "hallowed," "holy," "holiness," "purity," "sanctification," "sanctified," "sanctify," and "saint" (one who is set apart to God or one who is sanctified).

So while it is proper and correct to think of sanctification as a cleansing from impurity and the effects of sin, it is helpful to remember the idea of being *set apart* or separated from the world and all that is unclean or profane so we can establish a relationship with God, whose very nature and essence is that of holiness.

Justification. The English words *just, justify,* and *justification* are translations of the Hebrew root *tsadak* and various forms of the Greek word *dikay.* Originally, the Hebrew root signified stiffness or straightness, and out of that came its meaning of "conformance to law," meaning, of course, the law of God.[3] Thus, *tsadak* is usually translated as "righteousness" or "justness." One who has been put in a state of *tsadak* has been "justified" or is in a state of "justification." This idea of being put right differs from the concept of innocence—that is, never having been guilty of violating the law. A different Hebrew word, *nakah,* is used for that. Girdlestone notes the difference between the two words:

> *Nakah* . . . generally appears to signify proved innocence from specified charges, whether those charges are brought by God or man. The offences, if committed, were punishable; but when they have not been committed, if that innocence can be made clear, the person against whom the charge is made goes off free from blame and punishment. . . . Where Nakah is used, man is regarded as actually clear from a charge; where *Tsadak* is used, man is regarded as having

obtained deliverance from condemnation, and as being thus entitled
to a certain inheritance.[4]

The Greek is particularly interesting for our understanding of justification, since the root word is *dikay,* which means "law of justice." Thus, to be
righteous (*dikaios*) means "one is in conformance to law." The verb form
(*dikaiooh*) means "to render something as righteous, or as it ought to be."
"Righteousness" (*dikaiosunay*) is the state achieved when our lives are in
harmony with law. *Dikaiosunay* is also translated in the New Testament as
"justification." In other words, *to be righteous is to be justified and justification is to be made righteous.* This accords with Elder Bruce R. McConkie's
definition of justification:

> What then is the law of justification? It is simply this: "All
> covenants, contracts, bonds, obligations, oaths, vows, performances,
> connections, associations, or expectations" (D&C 132:7), in which
> men must abide to be saved and exalted, must be entered into and
> performed in righteousness so that the Holy Spirit can justify the
> candidate for salvation in what has been done (1 Nephi 16:2; Jacob
> 2:13–14; Alma 41:15; D&C 98; 132:1, 62). *An act that is justified by the
> Spirit is one that is sealed by the Holy Spirit of Promise, or in other words,
> ratified and approved by the Holy Ghost.* This law of justification is the
> provision the Lord has placed in the gospel to assure that no unrigh-
> teous performance will be binding on earth and in heaven, and that
> no person will add to his position or glory in the hereafter by gaining
> an unearned blessing.[5]

The Holy Spirit can only approve and ratify that which conforms to
God's law.

Thus, we can see that as we use the terms today, sanctification and justification are closely related and are in some ways synonymous.
Sanctification is to be holy or pure; justification is to be righteous. Indeed,
so closely are the two interrelated and interdependent that it is preferable
to speak of the doctrine of sanctification and justification instead of the
doctrines. Both are inherently related to God's own nature, and *both involve
relationship to Him.* That latter concept is especially important. If we are not
pure (sanctified) or if we are not righteous (justified), we cannot have a full
and complete relationship with God. Thus, the natural man is an enemy to
God (see Mosiah 3:19).

THE DILEMMA—OUR NEED FOR JUSTIFICATION

To understand the need for sanctification and justification, we must first understand the dilemma that mankind faces. This is fundamental doctrine related to the Atonement and is familiar to most readers, but it merits a quick review.

Because of His absolute holiness (separateness from all unholy things) and His perfect righteousness (adherence to the laws of godliness), God requires that any who dwell with Him meet these same standards. No unclean thing can dwell in His presence, for He is a Man of Holiness (see Moses 6:57). Or to use the terminology under discussion, to dwell with God we must be perfectly righteous (in an ultimate or perfect state of justification), and we must also be perfectly holy and pure (in an ultimate state of sanctification).

But as soon as we become accountable, we transgress the law and become carnal, sensual, and devilish, or what the scriptures call the natural man (see Mosiah 3:19; Alma 42:10; D&C 20:19–20). Thus, a tremendous breach in our relationship to God is set up.

Fallen Man	**God**
1. Carnal	1. Perfectly holy
2. Sensual	2. Perfectly righteous
3. Devilish	
4. Enemy to God	

This is true of all men since "all have sinned and come short of the glory of God" (Romans 3:23).

Theoretically, we can be justified in one of two ways: we can keep the law perfectly (be proven right), or we can have the demands of the law satisfied (be declared or made right). In almost identical wording, both Paul and Lehi taught that by the law no flesh is justified (see Romans 3:20; 2 Nephi 2:5). They were speaking in the ultimate sense of justification, and that is easily understood. Not one of us keeps the laws of God perfectly; therefore we cannot be justified (made perfectly righteous) by our own works alone. Of all men, only Christ lived a perfect life, or, to put it in Lehi's terminology, only Christ was justified by His works. The classic tragedy of the Pharisees was that they sought to justify themselves by their

works. This explains their obsessive concern about the minute requirements of the law.

Repentance is not a solution to this dilemma (remembering that for the
moment we are leaving the Atonement out of this). Repentance alone
cannot restore our broken relationship with God. In an ultimate sense,
repentance is not forward progress but only a return to the original point
of departure. This could be diagrammed as follows:

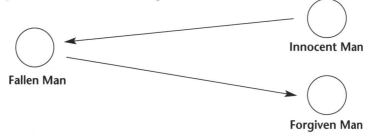

To put this another way, when we repent of sin we are only doing what
we should have been doing all along. So repentance alone cannot justify a
person. Something else is required.

Once a law has been violated, some kind of punishment must be
exacted or else justice (*tzadak*) will still have claim on the person. However,
once payment is made, justice is satisfied, and this payment can be made
either by the individual or by another person. If an individual is cited for
violation of a traffic law, the court can be satisfied in one of two ways. The
person can prove his or her innocence (justice has no claim because there
was no violation), or a fine can be paid. The court does not care whether
the money for the fine comes directly from the individual, from the person's father, or from some other source. As long as the fine is paid in the
person's behalf, the law is satisfied.

So it is with justification for sin. Since we all violate the law, justice will
not declare any one of us innocent by virtue of our behavior (justification
by works). Suffering is the price required for violation of law (see D&C
19:15–19), and in the Garden of Gethsemane Jesus suffered for all the sins
of the world. Therefore, if He chooses, Jesus can pay the price required for
us. Justice, which cares only that payment is made, is satisfied. This
explains why Paul could say that we are justified by the blood of Christ
(see Romans 5:9). Christ's atoning sacrifice made it possible for us to be
declared righteous (justified). Therefore, as the Doctrine and Covenants
states, justification is through the grace of Jesus Christ (see D&C 20:30).

OUR DILEMMA—THE NEED FOR SANCTIFICATION

Satisfaction of justice does not fully solve our relationship problem with God for, as we have seen, not only is His nature in perfect harmony with law (*tzadak,* or righteousness) but He is also perfectly holy and clean (*kadash,* or separated from all uncleanness). If we never violated the law, we would be both holy and righteous. But no one except Jesus Christ has successfully accomplished this. Violation of law makes us both *unrighteous* and *unclean,* or not holy. (In the Hebrew sense of *kadash,* we are no longer separated from the world and therefore are not holy or set apart for God's purposes.) If the demands of justice are met (if we are justified), we come back into a state of righteousness, in the sense of conformance to law. But this does not make us holy—it only makes us righteous. A rough analogy is that of a felon who goes to prison for his crime. When he is released, he has fully met the demands of the law (he is justified), but he still has the taint of being an ex-convict. He somehow must reestablish the status (or relationship) he had before his crime.

So it is with sin. Justification, being made right with God, is not sufficient. We must also be separated again from the uncleanness that resulted from sin. In other words, not only must we be justified, we must be sanctified—cleansed from the effects of sin so that we can be holy as God is. The scriptures clearly teach how the Atonement sanctifies us or cleanses us from the effects of sin. Thus, "by the blood [we] are sanctified" (Moses 6:60).

Separating sanctification and justification in this way may cause some people trouble because in our gospel understanding we tend to equate righteousness and holiness, while they are not technically the same. Righteousness (conformance to law) results in holiness (separateness or cleanness) only because the Atonement is operating, and the process of justification and sanctification takes place automatically when we meet the requirements of Christ. Perhaps this analogy will help. The price required for entry into God's presence is perfection in keeping the law. When we violate the laws of God, we forfeit any *legal claim* we had on His kingdom. Justification restores that legal claim because to be just means to be righteous or to be in conformance to law. But our sin not only causes a loss of our legal claim to the kingdom, it makes us unclean (not separated, not holy, not sanctified). Since no unclean thing can dwell in God's presence, even if we restore our legal right to the inheritance (justification), we must also be cleansed (sanctification) if we are to live with God.

THE SOLUTION—THE PROCESS OF SANCTIFICATION AND JUSTIFICATION

If we are to be like God—that is, perfectly holy and perfectly righteous (the ultimate sense of sanctification and justification)—we must inaugurate the process of sanctification and justification in our lives. However, there are two ways or senses in which the doctrine of sanctification and justification must operate for us. First, we must overcome the initial state of being a "natural man," and then we must maintain that redeemed state. In other words, we must *be made* right and holy, but we must also then *be kept* right and holy. Let us go back to our diagram of the dilemma we face and illustrate this dualism of the doctrine.

Fallen Man	Strait and narrow path >	**God**
1. Carnal		1. Perfectly holy
2. Sensual		2. Perfectly righteous
3. Devilish		
4. Enemy to God		

To be reunited with God we must *get on* the strait and narrow path, and then we must *stay on* that path until the end (see 2 Nephi 31:17–21).

Getting on the path—being made right and holy. To get on the strait and narrow path, we must be made both holy and righteous; we require sanctification and justification. We must be brought into a state of conformity to law (righteousness), and we must be separated from the uncleanness of the world (become holy). Both of these are made possible because of the atoning sacrifice (the blood) of Christ, but the actual medium or means for both sanctification and justification is the Holy Ghost. His very influence burns out the effects of sin and purges out the unholiness that comes upon us when we sin. However, we can only do so because Jesus Christ met the demands of justice and made it possible for mercy and grace to operate in our behalf. This explains why the scriptures can speak of sanctification—and likewise justification—as being by blood in one case and by the Spirit in another.

The condition for the blood of Christ being applied in our behalf is that we achieve a certain level of personal obedience to Christ's law, which involves faith, repentance, and baptism. Only then can the Holy Spirit make us right and make us holy.

Staying on the path—being kept right and holy. But the initial justification and sanctification is not enough. As the Lord warned, "There is a possibility that man may fall from grace and depart from the living God" (D&C 20:32). Or as Nephi asked, "After ye have gotten into this straight and narrow path, I would ask if all is done? I say unto you, Nay. . . . Ye must press forward with a steadfastness in Christ" (2 Nephi 31:19–20). We must continue in a state of justification (righteousness or conformance to law), which we can do because we have the Spirit to guide us in all we do, teaching us how to live perfectly (see D&C 11:12–14).

However, even with the help of the Holy Spirit we will not live a perfect life at first. We will continue to sin, though to a lesser and lesser degree until we achieve perfection. Thus, there is a continuing need for ongoing sanctification as well as justification. This seems to be what King Benjamin meant when he talked about "retaining a remission of your sins from day to day, that ye may walk guiltless before God" (Mosiah 4:26). Thus, we need to be sanctified from both former and continuing sins, and we need to be brought into conformance with law and be kept in conformity with it. This explains the dual nature of sanctification and justification. We need two things if we are ever to enter back into God's presence: we must be made right and holy, and we must be kept right and holy.

HARMONIZING THE SCRIPTURES

At the beginning of this chapter it was suggested that the primary purpose of this discussion was to provide some conceptual tools that would help a person understand the doctrine of sanctification and justification. With these tools acquired, let us now examine what appears to be contradictions or at least inconsistencies in the scriptural discussions of these two concepts. Knowing the basic meaning of the terms *sanctification* and *justification* and also knowing what role the atoning blood of Christ, combined with the Holy Spirit, plays in each quickly resolves these apparent problems.

Without the blood shed by Jesus Christ in His atoning sacrifice, there would be no hope for mankind; there would be no chance that anyone could either be made righteous or holy. Therefore, the scriptures correctly point out that both sanctification and justification are by the blood of Christ. He is the validating power that makes it all possible, and from Him come the principles which bring it about.

But the role of the Holy Ghost in applying the blood of Christ in our lives is direct and specific. It is His power and influence that actually purges out the dross, cleanses us from sin, and makes us holy. This is called the baptism of fire. Also, it is under His direction and promptings that one derives the power and knowledge to live righteously. So we can legitimately say that one is both sanctified and justified by the Spirit (see Moses 6:60; 2 Nephi 31:17; Alma 13:12; 3 Nephi 27:19–20; D&C 84:24).

Where the Doctrine and Covenants indicates that we are sanctified through and by law (see D&C 88:21, 34), it clearly specifies that the law is the law of Christ (see D&C 8:21). In other words, unless we are willing to conform to the law, including the conditions for having the Atonement applied in our behalf (such as faith, repentance, and baptism), we cannot be sanctified.

Paul's seeming contradiction (see Romans 2:13; 3:20) is easily resolved in this light. Although we cannot be justified (in the ultimate sense of being perfectly righteous) by our own efforts, in the interim sense, only those who are willing to do as the law requires can ultimately be justified. Thus, only the doers of the law will be justified. This also explains the command to sanctify ourselves (see D&C 43:11, 16). It does not suggest that we can make ourselves holy but only suggests that we must initiate the process for ourselves.

This should also answer any questions about the salvation-by-grace-or-works debate that rages in the Christian world. None of us can live perfectly enough to return to God on our own merits. We cannot be perfectly righteous (we cannot be justified), and therefore we are not perfectly holy (we are not sanctified). Only through the grace of the Father and the Son was the power provided to reclaim us from this state. On the other hand, to suggest that one's behavior (works) does not matter is a contradiction of terms, for justification (*tzadak*) means to be in conformance to law, and sanctification (*kadash*) means to be separated or set apart from sinful things. The Prophet Joseph Smith brought this more clearly to light when he corrected Romans 4:16 to read, "Therefore ye are justified of faith and works, through grace." Moroni captured this interdependence between grace and works when he said:

> Yea, come unto Christ, and be perfected in him, and deny yourselves of all ungodliness; and if ye shall deny yourselves of all ungodliness, and love God with all your might, mind and strength, then is his grace sufficient for you, that by his grace ye may be perfect in

Christ; and if by the grace of God ye are perfect in Christ, ye can in nowise deny the power of God.

And again, if ye by the grace of God are perfect in Christ, and deny not his power, then are ye sanctified in Christ by the grace of God, through the shedding of the blood of Christ, which is in the covenant of the Father unto the remission of your sins, that ye become holy, without spot. (Moroni 10:32–33)

SUMMARY

There is no need to try to make the doctrine of sanctification and justification into a mysterious, difficult doctrine. It is very simple and yet deeply profound. God's nature is that of perfect holiness and perfect righteousness. Anyone who would be like Him and dwell with Him must achieve a similar state of holiness and perfection. Through the blood of Jesus Christ and the operation of the Holy Ghost in our lives, we can be made just and holy, and then by continually looking to Christ and the Spirit we can be kept just and holy.

Without justness (*tsadak*) and holiness (*kadash*), we cannot have a full relationship with God, for uncleanness and unrighteousness are contrary to His nature. Thus, the doctrines of justification and sanctification are designed to make us more and more like God. President Brigham Young understood this when he defined virtue (another word for righteousness or justness) and sanctification in this manner:

> What I consider to be virtue, and the only principle of virtue there is, is to do the will of our Father in heaven. That is the only virtue I wish to know. I do not recognize any other virtue than to do what the Lord Almighty requires of me from day to day. In this sense virtue embraces all good; it branches out into every avenue of mortal life, passes through the ranks of the sanctified in heaven, and makes its throne in the breast of the Deity. When the Lord commands the people, let them obey. That is virtue.
>
> The same principle will embrace what is called sanctification. When the will, passions, and feelings of a person are perfectly submissive to God and His requirements, that person is sanctified. It is for my will to be swallowed up in the will of God, that will lead me into all good, and crown me ultimately with immortality and eternal lives.[6]

NOTES

1. Robert B. Girdlestone, *Synonyms of the Old Testament* (Grand Rapids, MI: Eerdmans, 1976), 175.

2. Girdlestone, *Synonyms,* 176.

3. See Girdlestone, *Synonyms,* 103.

4. Girdlestone, *Synonyms,* 171.

5. Bruce R. McConkie, *Mormon Doctrine,* 2d ed. (Salt Lake City: Bookcraft, 1976), 408; emphasis added.

6. Brigham Young, in *Journal of Discourses* (London: Latter-day Saints' Book Depot, 1854–86), 2:123.

CHAPTER SIX

THE BOOK OF MORMON AS AN INTERPRETIVE GUIDE TO THE NEW TESTAMENT

DENNIS L. LARGEY

Through President Ezra Taft Benson, the Lord caught our attention with repeated admonitions regarding the blessings of the Book of Mormon and our responsibilities toward it. In the October 1986 general conference, President Benson called God's gift of the Book of Mormon "more important than any of the inventions that have come out of the industrial and technological revolutions" and "of greater value to mankind than even the many wonderful advances . . . in modern medicine."[1] He also made the charge that "every Latter-day Saint should make the study of [the Book of Mormon] a lifetime pursuit. Otherwise he is placing his soul in jeopardy and neglecting that which could give spiritual and intellectual unity to his whole life."[2]

In a First Presidency Christmas message, President Benson said that we should know the Book of Mormon better than any other text.[3] In light of President Benson's statements and persistent charges to read the Book of Mormon, our challenge is to find where we can appropriately incorporate the message of the Book of Mormon into New Testament study. The intent is not to overshadow the first testament of Christ but to magnify it through providing inspired commentary.

Dennis L. Largey is a professor of ancient scripture at Brigham Young University.

Does the New Testament Need Book of Mormon Clarification?

The eighth article of faith of The Church of Jesus Christ of Latter-day Saints states that "we believe the Bible as far as it is translated correctly." The Prophet Joseph Smith wrote: "I believe the Bible as it read when it came from the pen of the original writers. Ignorant translators, careless transcribers, or designing and corrupt priests have committed many errors."[4]

In a vision, Nephi learned that when the biblical records would first go forth from the Jews to the Gentiles, they would be pure and would contain "the fulness of the gospel of the Lord." However, after tampering by "the great and abominable church," many plain and precious parts and also many covenants would be taken away. This deliberate effort would be to "pervert the right ways of the Lord" and "blind the eyes and harden the hearts of the children of men." Nephi then beheld that this incomplete record, missing precious parts and the plainness it once had, would cause an "exceedingly great many [to] stumble." The angel then revealed God's plan to alleviate the stumbling: Jesus would manifest Himself and minister to the seed of Nephi. The Nephites would write "many things" which would be "plain and precious," and the record would be "hid up" and come forth unto the Gentiles by the gift and power of the Lamb. The second record (the Book of Mormon) would therefore restore plain and precious gospel truths which had been taken from the first record (the Bible; see 1 Nephi 13:24–40).

Nephi's revelation has significant application for Latter-day Saints. Failure to incorporate the gospel plainness of the Book of Mormon into New Testament study is failure to understand one of the central purposes of the book's existence.

It would be impossible within the scope of this paper to explore all the doctrinal contributions and insightful expansions available to those who read the New Testament by the light of the Book of Mormon. The intent, therefore, is to explore three areas which demonstrate the power of combining these two testaments. First, we will compare and contrast a study of the gospel with and without Book of Mormon commentary. Second, we will show, through selected examples, the corrective and explanatory contribution the Book of Mormon makes on various doctrines and issues, some of which are only briefly referred to in the New Testament. Third, we will show how the Book of Mormon combines with the New Testament to confound false doctrine.

A STUDY OF GOSPEL DOCTRINE WITH BOOK OF MORMON SUPPORT

First and most important, the Bible and the Book of Mormon are testaments of Jesus Christ and the gospel He preached. The first four books of the New Testament bear the descriptive introduction: "The Gospel According to . . ." The word *gospel* is not defined in the New Testament in any detail. The resurrected Christ appeared to His Nephite disciples and in conversation with them gave us one of the most definitive statements concerning the gospel in all scripture: "Behold I have given unto you my gospel, and this is the gospel which I have given unto you—that I came into the world to do the will of my Father, because my Father sent me. And my Father sent me that I might be lifted up upon the cross; and after that I had been lifted up upon the cross, that I might draw all men unto me, that as I have been lifted up by men even so should men be lifted up by the Father, to stand before me, to be judged of their works, whether they be good or whether they be evil" (3 Nephi 27:13–14).

According to Jesus, then, the foremost elements of His gospel center in His redemptive mission in rescuing mankind from both spiritual and temporal death. The Atonement—which enables repentance, remission of sin, resurrection, and universal judgment—constitutes the core of gospel truths. As stated, parts of that core were eliminated.

Contributions to Our Understanding of the Atonement

Searching from the Gospel of Matthew to the book of Revelation, one can find some sixty passages that make *direct* reference to Jesus' sacrifice for the remission of sin. Of these passages, more than fifty refer to the Atonement or the effects of the Atonement but are not sustained with definitive explanation. In other words, no scriptural passage precedes or follows to explain the doctrine. Combining the content of New Testament scripture related to redemption from sin, we learn that justification, sanctification, propitiation, intercession, reconciliation, and mediation come through Jesus Christ who offered Himself, through the shedding of His blood, as a sacrifice for the sins of all those who believe. In contrast, the Book of Mormon expands and defines doctrine and terminology which the New Testament briefly mentions. For example, while the Apostle Paul refers to the intercessory role of Jesus in offering Himself, Abinadi adds that the Resurrection empowered Jesus to make intercession, in that He "ascended into heaven, having the bowels of mercy; . . . standing betwixt them and justice; having broken the bands of death, taken upon himself their iniquity and their transgressions, having redeemed them, and satisfied the demands of justice" (Mosiah 15:9).

While Paul stated that "Christ is the *end of the law* for righteousness to everyone that believeth" (Romans 10:4; emphasis added), Lehi explained that "by the law no flesh is justified." But the sacrifice of Christ answered the *"ends of the law,"* efficacious only for "those who have a broken heart and a contrite spirit; and unto none else can the ends of the law be answered" (2 Nephi 2:5, 7; emphasis added).

With clarity unparalleled, King Benjamin added that "his blood atoneth for the sins of those who have fallen by the transgression of Adam, who have died not knowing the will of God concerning them, or who have ignorantly sinned" (Mosiah 3:11).

While Paul taught that men are justified by the blood of Christ, which will save them from wrath, Amulek explained the doctrine of justification by teaching that the intent of Jesus' sacrifice was to initiate a plan of mercy which would overpower justice and enable men to have faith and to repent. The result of this, Amulek continued, is that mercy can satisfy justice and encircle the repentant person in the arms of safety (thus saving him or her from the wrath Paul mentioned), "while he that exercises no faith unto repentance is exposed to the whole law of the demands of justice" (Alma 34:16; see Romans 5:9).

While the Apostle John spoke of Jesus as the propitiation for our sins, Alma discussed *propitiation* using the verb *appease:* "And now, the plan of mercy could not be brought about except an atonement should be made; therefore God himself atoneth for the sins of the world, to bring about the plan of mercy, to appease the demands of justice, that God might be a perfect, just God, and a merciful God also" (Alma 42:15; see also 1 John 4:10). Interestingly, the word *justice* is not mentioned in the New Testament, nor is the word *plan,* indicating a plan of salvation.

Luke recorded that the Master sweat great drops of blood in Gethsemane (see Luke 22:44). King Benjamin added that the anguish that caused our Lord to bleed from every pore was due to His suffering for the wickedness and abominations of His people (see Mosiah 3:7). With only the New Testament as a guide, the Christian world looks predominantly to the cross for the remission of sins. Latter-day Saints, knowing the words of King Benjamin and having a further witness of the Savior's suffering recorded in the Doctrine and Covenants, believe the suffering began in the Garden of Gethsemane and was consummated on the cross (see 3 Nephi 27:13, 14).

Paul recorded that death and sin entered the world through Adam, and life through Christ (see 1 Corinthians 15:16–22). Lehi enumerated conditions before and after the Fall: the necessity of opposition, the wisdom of Adam's fall, the freedom of man to choose between two enticing forces, the role of Satan, and Jesus' role as the great Mediator (see 2 Nephi 2).

Can one understand the redemption of man without the true doctrine in relation to the Fall of man? Other than the doctrine that Adam's Fall brought death and sin and Christ brought life, a study of the Atonement from the New Testament will be in isolation from the Fall. Lehi, Jacob, Abinadi, Alma, King Benjamin, Aaron, Amulek, and Ammon all either make reference to or offer doctrine and explanation concerning the Fall while teaching about the Atonement.

The New Testament message on the Atonement is largely descriptive of Christ's atoning mission but is not descriptive of the atoning doctrine. The New Testament tells us that there *was* an atonement for sin; the Nephite record explains with clarity and depth *why* it was necessary.

The Book of Mormon passages quoted are not isolated verses but are references embedded in masterful discourses which tie the doctrines of salvation together into what Amulek terms "the great plan of the Eternal God" (Alma 34:9).

Contributions to Our Understanding of the Resurrection

The Atonement of Jesus Christ offers redemption from physical death through the Resurrection. There are over one hundred references to the Resurrection in the New Testament. Of these references, nearly eighty are in context with either prophecy before the Resurrection, apostolic witness after the Resurrection, or the storyline of the New Testament. Therefore, there are about twenty-five references we look to for doctrinal explanation.

From these verses we learn the following: (1) Jesus would rise on the third day (see John 2:19) with a body of flesh and bone (see Luke 24:36–39); (2) His Resurrection would bring the Resurrection of all men (see 1 Corinthians 15:22); (3) Jesus was raised for our justification (see Romans 4:25); (4) each will be resurrected in his own order (see 1 Corinthians 15:23); (5) Jesus' Resurrection will bring about the resurrection of the just and unjust (see Acts 24:15); (6) just as the sun, moon, and stars differ in glory, so will the resurrected bodies of men (see 1 Corinthians 15:39–42); (7) the second death will have no power over those worthy to come forth in the First Resurrection (see Revelation 20:6); and (8) the Resurrection brings a lively hope (see 1 Peter 1:3).

Almost in every case the Book of Mormon acts as a second witness to the New Testament doctrine on the Resurrection and then goes beyond to offer additional insights. For example, if one wrote down all doctrine gleaned from the New Testament on the subject of resurrection, one could then add the following information from the Book of Mormon: details concerning the resurrection of the just and the unjust (see 2 Nephi 9:10–19), the fate of the spirit were it not for an infinite atonement (see 2 Nephi 9:7–9), a definition of the resurrection of damnation (see Mosiah 16:11), specific qualifications to achieve the First Resurrection (see Mosiah 15:21–24; 18:9), the necessary relationship of resurrection to universal judgment (see 3 Nephi 27:13–18), information on the space of time between death and resurrection (see Alma 40), the inseparability of the spirit from the body after resurrection (see Alma 11:45), and a clear definition of what resurrection is (see Alma 11:44; 40:23).

Contributions to Our Understanding of the Universal Judgment

Having discussed redemption from sin and death we now come to our third element of gospel study—the universal judgment.

From New Testament passages, we learn that God will judge all men through Jesus Christ (see John 5:22; Romans 2:16), according to their works (see Revelation 22:12), on the appointed day (see Acts 17:31), and when every knee shall bow and tongue confess to God (see Romans 14:11). Those who are worthy to be on the right hand of God will have right to the tree of life; they can enter the Holy City (see Revelation 22:14) and can sit down on the throne of Christ (see Revelation 3:21). Those found on His left hand will depart into a lake of unquenchable fire to be tormented day and night forever and ever (see Revelation 20:10), which is the second death (see Revelation 20:14).

Here the Book of Mormon again offers significant insight regarding a central gospel doctrine. Information unique to the Book of Mormon includes what the souls of men will confess at the judgment bar (see Mosiah 16:1; 27:31), the fact that we will be judged not only according to our works but also according to the desires of our hearts (see Alma

41:3, 5), that mankind will be judged from scriptural records (see 2 Nephi 29:11), a definitive statement concerning the second death (see Alma 12:16–18), and that hell is *as* a lake of fire and brimstone, in that the unjust are "consigned to an awful view of their own guilt . . . , which doth cause them to shrink . . . into a *state* of misery and endless torment, from whence they can no more return" (Mosiah 3:25; see also v. 27; emphasis added).

The purpose of this comparison is not to cast any disfavor upon the New Testament but to show how the records can and should work in concert. Ezekiel prophesied that the stick of Judah and the stick of Joseph are to become one (see Ezekiel 37:15–19). We have seen them become one under one cover in our editions of the scriptures. The challenge now is to use them as one. Nephi was told by an angel that "the words of the Lamb shall be made known in the records of thy seed, as well as in the records of the twelve apostles of the Lamb; wherefore they both shall be established in one; for there is one God and one Shepherd over all the earth" (1 Nephi 13:41).

The two testaments of Christ complement each other. The messages and sermons were given to different audiences for differing reasons, thus the varying content. Elder Neal A. Maxwell said: "Imagine, for a moment, where we would be without the New Testament's matchless portrait of the Savior. . . . Granted, much doctrinal fulness came later in 'other books,' . . . but it remains for the New Testament to provide the portrait of the mortal Messiah." Elder Maxwell then went on to say, "Wonderful as the New Testament is, it is even stronger when it is joined with the 'other books' of scripture."[5]

Occasionally at lectures or forums, time is given at the end for questions and answers. Often during these sessions the most significant learning takes place. Here explanations are given, elaborations are made, and terms are defined. The New Testament constitutes some of the greatest literature known to our world, yet because of its brevity on important subjects, with the myriad misinterpretations, a question-and-answer session which elaborates concepts and defines terms would be of significant worth. The Bible contains many doctrinal statements that are pronounced but not sustained with further discussion. The Book of Mormon comes to support the Bible by providing the sustained discussion, as would a question-and-answer period. For example: "And Zeezrom began to inquire of them diligently, that he might know more concerning the kingdom of God. And he said unto Alma: *What does this mean* which Amulek hath spoken concerning the resurrection of the dead, that all shall rise from the dead, both the just and the unjust, . . . to stand before God to be judged according to their works?" (Alma 12:8; emphasis added). Alma then gave not only a description of the elements of judgment but a chronological order of events (see Alma 12:9–37).

Consider the depth of the doctrine Abinadi offered the questioning priests of Noah, recorded in Mosiah 12–17. Amulek sought to answer the Zoramites' question, "Whether the word be in the Son of God" (Alma 34:5), and by so doing restored plain and precious truth (see Alma 34). Alma's answers to the concerns of his wayward son Corianton makes available information on the spirit world, the law of restoration, and the interaction between the justice of God and the plan of mercy that are unrivaled for clarity and plainness of language (see Alma 40–42).

Perhaps Mormon, aware of the Savior's definition of the gospel (see 3 Nephi 27:13–18) and knowing the stumbling that would take place as plain and precious parts of the gospel were extracted by the great and abominable church (see 1 Nephi 13), searched the records available to him and then incorporated into his abridgment sermons that taught the gospel so plainly that no one could possibly err.

Alma invited his Zoramite listeners to "cast about [their] eyes and begin to believe in the Son of God, that he will come to redeem his people, and that he shall suffer and die to atone for their sins; and that he shall rise again from the dead, which shall bring to pass the resurrection, that all men shall stand before him, to be judged at the last and judgment day, according to their works. And now, my brethren, I desire that ye shall plant this word in your hearts, and as it beginneth to swell even so nourish it by your faith" (Alma 33:22–23).

The seed, identified by Alma as the redemptive act of Jesus Christ, permeates the pages of the Book of Mormon. It was an intentional act by the great and abominable church to take out plain and precious gospel truths (see 1 Nephi 13:27), and it was an intentional act to replace them through the Nephite record (see 1 Nephi 13:35).

CORRECTIVE AND EXPLANATORY CONTRIBUTIONS OF THE BOOK OF MORMON

Example 1: The Book of Mormon offers interpretive commentary on New Testament passages. When Jesus came to John the Baptist to be baptized,

John forbade him, saying, "I have need to be baptized of thee. . . . Jesus answering said unto him, Suffer it to be so now: for thus it becometh us to fulfil all righteousness" (Matthew 3:14–15). The New Testament student might be left puzzled inasmuch as there is no explanation offered as to what it means to fulfill all righteousness.

The prophet Nephi was blessed with a vision of the ministry of Christ. In the vision, he was shown the prophet who would baptize the Savior. Years later, in one of his final sermons, Nephi discussed the baptism of Jesus and taught his people the meaning of Jesus' words to John:

> And now, if the Lamb of God, he being holy, should have need to be baptized by water, to fulfil all righteousness, O then, how much more need have we, being unholy, to be baptized, yea, even by water!
>
> And now, I would ask you, my beloved brethren, wherein the Lamb of God did fulfil all righteousness in being baptized by water?
>
> Know ye not that he was holy? But notwithstanding he being holy, he showeth unto the children of men that, according to the flesh he humbleth himself before the Father; and witnesseth unto the Father that he would be obedient unto him in keeping his commandments. . . .
>
> And again, it showeth unto the children of men the straitness of the path, and the narrowness of the gate, by which they should enter, he having set the example before them. (2 Nephi 31:5–7, 9)

Example 2: The Book of Mormon contains clarifying words and phrases not found in the New Testament text. Matthew 5–7 contains one of the most powerful sermons ever given—the Sermon on the Mount. Jesus repeated many of the same teachings to His people in the Americas. In comparing discourses, the Book of Mormon account contains additions which clarify to whom Jesus was speaking as He taught various segments of His sermon. The Beatitudes were for those who would come to Christ. To "Blessed are the poor in spirit," the Book of Mormon adds *who come unto me,* for theirs is the kingdom of heaven" (Matthew 5:3; 3 Nephi 12:3; emphasis added). In the New Testament, the clarifying phrase "who come unto me" is omitted. It is not a blessed condition to be poor in spirit, as the Matthew account portrays; however, if one finds oneself poor in spirit, and as a solution to that condition comes to Christ, as the Book of Mormon teaches, his is the kingdom of God.

The Matthew account has Jesus telling the multitude to take no thought for their physical provisions. This seems in conflict with good sense and not in harmony with other words of the Master. In the Book of Mormon account, we read that Jesus turned from the multitude, or the general audience, before He gave these particular instructions and "looked upon the twelve whom he had chosen" (3 Nephi 13:25). The meaning then becomes clear: those who were to devote themselves to full-time service, as the presiding twelve, would have their daily needs taken care of by the Lord whom they served.

Example 3: The Book of Mormon expands upon doctrinal concepts briefly mentioned in the New Testament. The Apostle Paul described himself as "the apostle of the Gentiles" (see Romans 11:13). In his epistle to the Romans, he referred to the Gentiles as being a wild olive tree, to be grafted into the natural tree (i.e., Israel), to partake of the root. He told the Gentile audience that the natural branches were broken off because of unbelief and warned them that since "God spared not the natural branches, take heed lest he also spare not thee. . . . For I would not, brethren, that ye should be ignorant of this mystery, lest ye should be wise in your own conceits; that blindness in part is happened to Israel, until the *fulness* of the Gentiles be come in" (Romans 11:21, 25; emphasis added).

Again there is no sustained discussion concerning his reference to the fulness of the Gentiles. By way of commentary, in 1 Nephi 15:7 we read, "And they [Laman and Lemuel] said: Behold, we cannot understand the words which our father hath spoken concerning the natural branches of the olive-tree, and also concerning the Gentiles." In reply, Nephi taught:

> Behold, I say unto you, that the house of Israel was compared unto an olive-tree, by the Spirit of the Lord which was in our father; and behold are we not broken off from the house of Israel?
>
> And now, the thing which our father meaneth concerning the grafting in of the natural branches through the *fulness of the Gentiles,* is, that in the latter days, when our seed shall have dwindled in unbelief, yea, for the space of many years, and many generations after the Messiah shall be manifested in body unto the children of men, then shall the fulness of the gospel of the Messiah come unto the Gentiles, and from the Gentiles unto the remnant of our seed. (1 Nephi 15:12–13; emphasis added)

Here Nephi not only answered his brothers' questions but also gave a definitive statement of interpretation to Paul's reference. In the latter days, the fulness of the gospel would come to the Gentiles, and the Gentiles would then take it to the house of Israel. This would cure the blindness, for as Nephi further taught, "They shall be brought out of obscurity and out of darkness; and they shall know that the Lord is the Savior and their Redeemer, the Mighty One of Israel" (1 Nephi 22:12).

While the New Testament refers to the house of Israel and the Gentiles, the Book of Mormon expands upon the importance of the distinctions and shows their interrelationship in the gospel plan. For example, the Book of Mormon uses the term *gentile* 110 times. Some 64 percent of the time the context of the passage concerns Gentiles living at or after the time of the Restoration. Chief among the latter-day Gentiles was to be a man who would be named after Joseph of old (see 2 Nephi 3:15). Joseph Smith opened the dispensation of which Paul spoke to the Ephesians: "In the dispensation of the fulness of times he [will] gather together in one all things in Christ, both which are in heaven and which are on earth; even in him" (Ephesians 1:10).

Example 4: The Book of Mormon serves as a corrective lens in reading difficult passages. A good example of how the Book of Mormon helps in understanding difficult passages can be seen from a passage in Hebrews:

> For this Melchisedec, king of Salem, priest of the most high God, who met Abraham returning from the slaughter of the kings, and blessed him;
> To whom also Abraham gave a tenth part of all; first being by interpretation King of righteousness, and after that also King of Salem, which is, King of peace;
> Without father, without mother, without descent, having neither beginning of days, nor end of life; but made like unto the Son of God; abideth a priest continually. (Hebrews 7:1–3)

Here we are left with the impression that there was a man, a king, with no father, mother, genealogy, beginning, or end. In Alma 13, we have an expanded discourse on Melchizedek and the clarification that Paul was not referring to a man but to the high priesthood: "This high priesthood being after the order of his Son, which order was from the foundation of the world; or in other words, *being without beginning of days or end of years,* being prepared from eternity to all eternity, according to his foreknowledge of all things" (Alma 13:7; emphasis added).

Example 5: The Book of Mormon contributes key insights concerning the Jews who crucified Christ as well as the spiritual destiny of the Jewish nation. The Nephite prophets offer us insight into the character of those who crucified their king. Nephi said, "The world, because of their iniquity, shall judge him to be a thing of naught" (1 Nephi 19:9). Jacob taught that it was expedient that He come among the Jews, "among those who are the more wicked part of the world, . . . and there is none other nation on earth that would crucify their God." Priestcraft and iniquity would be the causal factors, that they at Jerusalem would "stiffen their necks . . . that he be crucified" (2 Nephi 10:3, 5). King Benjamin added, "They shall consider him a man, and say he hath a devil, and shall scourge him, and shall crucify him" (Mosiah 3:9).

Nephi prophesied that because the Jews would turn their hearts aside, they would "become a hiss and a byword, and be hated among all nations." The cure would be to turn their hearts back to their Messiah, and then would the covenant the Holy One made with Israel be remembered; that is, that all the people of the house of Israel would be gathered in (see 1 Nephi 19:14–16).

How would Judah return to Christ? After giving the parable of the wicked husbandmen, Jesus alluded to Psalms (see 118:22–23) as an interpretation for His listeners, which consisted of the chief priests and scribes: "The stone which the builders rejected, the same is become the head of the corner." He added, "Whosoever shall fall upon that stone shall be broken; but on whomsoever it shall fall, it will grind him to powder." After He quoted this prophecy, the chief priests and scribes "sought to lay hands on him" (Luke 20:17–19). They supposed that the parable had been spoken against them.

The Book of Mormon prophet Jacob also used these verses and related them to the Jews:

> And now I, Jacob, am led on by the Spirit unto prophesying; for I perceive by the workings of the Spirit which is in me, that by the stumbling of the Jews they will reject the stone upon which they might build and have safe foundation.
>
> But behold, according to the scriptures, this stone shall become the great, and the last, and the only sure foundation, upon which the Jews can build.
>
> And now my beloved, *how is it possible that these,* after having

rejected the sure foundation, can ever build upon it, that it may become the head of their corner? (Jacob 4:15–17; emphasis added)

In answering the question of how the Jews will return to Christ after rejecting Him, Jacob restored to us the allegory of the ancient prophet Zenos. The allegory not only concerns itself with the Jewish remnant but portrays God's dealings with all the house of Israel in gathering them after apostasy (see Jacob 5).

The Book of Mormon provides commentary on Judah's past and also its future. The Savior stated, "The fulness of my gospel shall be preached unto them; and they shall believe in me, that I am Jesus Christ, the Son of God, and shall pray unto the Father in my name" (3 Nephi 20:30–31).

THE BOOK OF MORMON CONFOUNDS FALSE DOCTRINE

The last item in this examination is yet another role the Book of Mormon plays. Joseph Smith, in his search for a true church, resorted to the admonition of James to "ask of God" (James 1:5) because the ministers in his area "understood the same passages of scripture so differently as to destroy [his] confidence in settling the question by an appeal to the Bible" (Joseph Smith–History 1:12). Without additional light, gospel truths taught in the New Testament were intermingled with the precepts of men, doctrines differed, priests contended, and confusion reigned.

Lehi, in blessing his son Joseph, restored to us a prophecy made by his progenitor Joseph who was sold into Egypt: "Wherefore, the fruit of thy loins shall write; and the fruit of the loins of Judah shall write; and that which shall be written by the fruit of the loins of Judah, shall grow together, unto the confounding of false doctrines" (2 Nephi 3:12). It was to be the combined effort of two records that would counteract the wresting of scripture.

Mormon's reading of the small plates "greatly influenced" his abridgment of the large plates.[6] He would have known the prophetic commission of combining testaments to confound false doctrine. He would also have read Nephi's vision in which Nephi beheld that the record that would proceed forth from the mouth of a Jew had been altered from its purity, causing confusion among the Gentiles (see 1 Nephi 13:29).

How would he fulfill his responsibility so that the last record (the Book of Mormon) would powerfully establish the truth of the first record (the Bible), confound false doctrine, and restore what was lost? Within the enormous library of plates, of which Mormon states he could not write a "hundredth part" (Words of Mormon 1:5), how would he know what was needed or what to include? A statement made by his son Moroni indicates a principle upon which Book of Mormon abridgers must surely have relied in their selection process. After describing the corruption of latter-day churches, Moroni spoke directly to his latter-day audience: "Behold, I speak unto you as if ye were present, and yet ye are not. But behold, Jesus Christ hath shown you unto me, and I know your doing" (Mormon 8:35).

The implication is that those responsible for the major work of compilation saw our day and, thus aided, selected what was needed based upon what they saw. With this thought in mind, it is interesting to ask ourselves why certain parts of the Book of Mormon were included. For example, why would the abridger give us Alma 31, a story about an apostate people who would go to a particular spot once a week to offer up a repetitious creedal prayer which proclaimed God to be a spirit forever? The Zoramites believed they were "elected" to be saved, while others were "elected" to be damned. The Zoramites' belief in predestination to heaven or hell predates Calvin and exposes this belief as a false doctrine.

Through story, prophecy, and sermon, the Book of Mormon denounces those who preach only for money (see Alma 1:3, 20; 2 Nephi 26:31); infant baptism (see Moroni 8); systems of religion that deny miracles, revelation, and prophecy (see 2 Nephi 28:4–6; 3 Nephi 29:5–6); systems that preach that salvation comes exclusively through obedience to the law (see Mosiah 13:27–32); being saved by grace alone and supposing that discipleship is not necessary (see 2 Nephi 25:23); and the philosophy that mercy can rob justice (see 2 Nephi 28:7–8). The Book of Mormon also offers a sober warning to those who refuse to receive additional revelation and scripture to that which they have already received (see 2 Nephi 28:27–29; 29).

SUMMARY

Numerous additional points could be made. Paul spoke of charity (see 1 Corinthians 13); Mormon gave us a formula on how to obtain it (see Moroni 7, 8). While the New Testament tells of an Apostle who would tarry until Jesus returns in His glory (see John 21:20–23), the Book of Mormon contains a whole chapter on the nature of translated beings (see 3 Nephi 28). Again this information comes to us as an answer to a question. Mormon inquired of the Lord, the Lord responded, and Mormon recorded the answer for all to be enlightened. While Paul taught about election and predestination, doctrines which cause many to stumble (see

Romans 8–9), Alma taught that men were "called and prepared from the foundation of the world according to the foreknowledge of God, on account of their exceeding faith and good works; in the first place being left to choose good or evil; therefore they having chosen good, and exercising exceedingly great faith, are called with a holy calling" (Alma 13:3).

In Acts 8, we read about Philip and his meeting with the eunuch. The Ethiopian was sitting in his chariot reading the book of Isaiah. The Spirit told Philip to approach him, and Philip responded by running to the chariot. As he heard the man read from the book of Isaiah, he asked, "Understandest thou what thou readest?" The eunuch answered, "How can I, except some man should guide me?" (Acts 8:29–31). He then asked Philip to join him. The particular passage was from Isaiah 53: "He was led as a sheep to the slaughter; and like a lamb dumb before his shearer, so opened he not his mouth: in his humiliation his judgment was taken away: and who shall declare his generation? for his life is taken from the earth. . . . Then Philip opened his mouth, and began at the same scripture and preached unto him Jesus" (Acts 8:32–33, 35).

The dialogue between Philip and the eunuch ended at this point. Philip identified the suffering servant as Jesus, but what else he said concerning this precious chapter is not told us. In Mosiah 14, Abinadi, in defense of his preaching concerning the condescension of God, quoted the entire fifty-third chapter of Isaiah to the wicked priests. Abinadi then offered an interpretation of his quote. In his commentary, he revealed who constitutes the seed of Jesus Christ and who it is that will declare his generation (see Mosiah 15:10–13).

In short, as Philip in this story was to the eunuch, the Book of Mormon prophets are to us. We have a host of men to guide us in the interpretation of the sacred scripture. To the reader of the New Testament aided by the Book of Mormon, the gospel drama unfolds prior to Matthew's declaration of the genealogy of Jesus. In approximately 550 BC, Nephi taught the doctrine of Christ and proclaimed His name as the only name whereby man can be saved (see 2 Nephi 31:21). About 124 BC, King Benjamin gave his people a new name, the name of Jesus Christ (see Mosiah 5:8–12). Jesus is the God of Israel; His doctrine was taught before His birth. The characters in the messianic drama were known hundreds of years before their mortal births. King Benjamin taught that the Creator of all things would be called Jesus Christ and that His mother's name would be Mary (see Mosiah 3:8). Nephi was told by an angel not to write a portion of his

vision concerning the end of the world because that stewardship belonged
to an Apostle whose name would be John (see 1 Nephi 14:18–22, 24–25,
27).

The scriptural story of Jesus is a two-continent story—as Mary and
Joseph were making preparations for the advent of Jesus' birth in the
manger at Bethlehem, Jesus was speaking to Nephi, giving comfort and
instruction, "Lift up your head and be of good cheer; . . . on the morrow
come I into the world, to show unto the world that I will fulfill all that
which I have caused to be spoken by the mouth of my holy prophets"
(3 Nephi 1:13). The Lord said to Nephi, "I speak the same words unto one
nation like unto another. And when the two nations shall run together the
testimony of the two nations shall run together also" (2 Nephi 29:8).

In view of what has been presented, the following suggestions are made
concerning study of the New Testament in conjunction with the Book of
Mormon. First, we should seek to fulfill President Ezra Taft Benson's directive and know the Book of Mormon better than any other text. If we do
so, we will always have available to us the magnifying and corrective lens
of the Book of Mormon as we read the Bible. Many of the plain and
precious parts of the biblical text have been restored. However, that
restoration is of no effect unless we personally restore those precious truths
in our own study. Perhaps the command and understanding Joseph Smith
had of the Bible can be attributed to the fact that he *first* translated the
Book of Mormon.

Second, when reading and studying a particular standard work, either
personally or in one of our Church classes, we should incorporate the contribution of the other standard works where appropriate. The depth of our
knowledge comes from the depth of our witness. With the Book of
Mormon, the Doctrine and Covenants, and the Pearl of Great Price, we are
three-deep in backup testimony and clarification when studying the Bible.
As teachers of the New Testament, we keep waiting witnesses on the wings
of our teaching stage to strengthen the concepts presented. Thus, the five
hundred who saw Jesus after His Resurrection in the Old World (see
1 Corinthians 15:6) are joined with twenty-five hundred who both saw,
heard, and touched the Master in the land Bountiful (see 3 Nephi 11). The
raising of Tabitha by Peter (see Acts 9:40) is joined by the raising of
Timothy by Nephi (see 3 Nephi 19:4), and so forth. Is it not common in
the work of the Lord to call forth as many witnesses as possible to prove
the truth of a righteous claim? Witnesses express themselves differently,

even though they are speaking about the same events. Some have seen more, or were present longer, or were present in a different capacity. The people in Ammonihah rejected and ridiculed Alma and his message *but became astonished* at the words of Amulek, "seeing there was *more than one witness* who testified of the things whereof they were accused" (Alma 10:12; emphasis added). It was the *second* witness that astonished the people.

Third, consider our Bible-believing brothers and sisters across the congregations of Christendom who have inherited the creeds and doctrines passed down over the centuries by those disadvantaged by the loss of revelation, prophets, and priesthood. Many doctrines of men have been incorporated with Jesus' teachings forming the various sects of our day. We should be ambassadors of the plain and precious parts of the gospel. By knowing how to use the Book of Mormon as a missionary tool, we can disperse the darkness of false doctrine and restore to our investigating friends precious truth not available from any other source.

TESTIMONY

Many who know the gospel and then become less-active do not, for the most part, join other churches. Perhaps one reason is that scripturally they know too much. Stop and think how much understanding of the gospel comes from the Restoration. It would be difficult to listen to a sermon about Jesus' "other sheep" in which the one preaching identifies the other sheep as Gentiles. It would be difficult indeed, especially knowing that the Savior visited the Nephites in America and personally said to them, "Ye are they of whom I said: Other sheep I have which are not of this fold; them also I must bring" (3 Nephi 15:21).

In a published sermon entitled *What Think Ye of Christ,* my father-in-law, B. West Belnap, told the following story: "Once I was in a far city, far from home, on Mother's Day, and I was alone. I went into a church . . . in town, as there was no Latter-day Saint Church nearby. The minister gave a very fine sermon, and in the course of his address he said, 'Adam fell that men might be, and men are that they might have joy' (2 Ne. 2:25). My ears pricked up at this. Afterward I went up to him and said, 'I'm interested in that statement 'Adam fell that men might be.' He looked at me and said, 'Are you a Mormon?' I said, 'Yes, I am.' He said, 'come with me.' He took me back to his office and pulled down a Book of Mormon and said, 'there is a lot of good stuff in here; I just don't tell them where it comes from.'"[7]

There *is* a lot of good "stuff" in the Book of Mormon, and Latter-day Saints are most fortunate to know where it comes from. Having God's gift of the Book of Mormon and knowing of its truthfulness bestows upon every member of the Church a responsibility, for, as Lehi said, "Wherefore, how great the importance to make these things known unto the inhabitants of the earth" (2 Nephi 2:8).

NOTES

1. Ezra Taft Benson, "The Book of Mormon Is the Word of God," *Ensign,* May 1975, 63.
2. Ezra Taft Benson, "The Book of Mormon—Keystone of Our Religion," *Ensign,* November 1986, 4–7.
3. First Presidency Christmas message, satellite broadcast, December 1986.
4. Joseph Smith, *Teachings of the Prophet Joseph Smith,* comp. Joseph Fielding Smith (Salt Lake City: Deseret Book, 1976), 327.
5. Neal A. Maxwell, "The New Testament—A Matchless Portrait of the Savior," *Ensign,* December 1986, 21–24.
6. Boyd K. Packer, *Let Not Your Heart Be Troubled* (Salt Lake City: Bookcraft, 1991), 276.
7. B. West Belnap, *What Think Ye of Christ?* (Provo, UT: Brigham Young University, Extension Publications, 1965), 17.

CHAPTER SEVEN

THE FOUR GOSPELS AS TESTIMONIES

S. KENT BROWN

The Gospel of John closes with the following important observation: "And there are also many other things which Jesus did, the which, if they should be written every one, I suppose that even the world itself could not contain the books that should be written. Amen" (21:25; see also 20:30–31). This passage characterizes the heart of our discussion. To see how that is so, let me begin by making a few observations about the efforts to deal with all of the Gospel accounts from the New Testament.

As is well known, a familiar approach to studying Jesus' life has been to harmonize the accounts of the four Gospels. It is natural to ask why this has been the case. One apparent reply is that, after a cursory review of the Gospels, we come to realize that each by itself does not compose a complete account of Jesus' words and deeds. Rather, these narratives have included only a portion selected from the events of Jesus' ministry. To be sure, there is frequent overlapping of materials among the Gospels. But it is equally true that many incidents are preserved by only one of the Evangelists. In the synoptic Gospels, of course, we find basically the same pattern of narrative. But in no single account do we see a complete picture. Hence, the need has arisen to seek to portray the ministry of Jesus as fully as possible by including every detail preserved by the Gospel writers. Even with this effort, we can be assured, we still do not have the entire view, an observation confirmed by John's remark quoted above. But by

S. Kent Brown is a professor of ancient scripture at Brigham Young University and current director of the BYU Foundation for Ancient Research and Mormon Studies.

drawing together a harmony of the Gospels, we do gain a clear perception of many of the faint and dark lines in the sketch of Jesus' mortal career.

The earliest effort to assemble all of the Gospel accounts into some sort of order was made by Tatian, a native of Syria. After being educated in Greek rhetoric and philosophy, he was converted to Christianity in Rome at a date between AD 150 and 160. Although he was later rejected as a heretic, Tatian compiled what is known as the *Diatessaron,* a history of Jesus woven together from the four Gospels.[1] This work enjoyed official acceptance in eastern Christianity, having been employed in the Syriac Church until the fifth century after Christ, when it was finally replaced by the four Gospels. The language in which Tatian wrote the *Diatessaron* remains disputed, although champions have been found for Greek, Syriac, and Latin. Whatever the case, the fact that Tatian's work enjoyed "official" popularity in eastern Christendom illustrates the substantial appeal that this avenue to Jesus' ministry has carried.

One can see the continuing popularity of this approach in non–Latter-day Saint circles, a fact illustrated by the significant number of reprints of A. T. Robertson's widely-used *A Harmony of the Gospels.*[2] At the base of approaches like Robertson's has lain the concern to present Jesus' ministry as completely as possible. Like others, he has done this not only by giving order to the reports but also by placing parallel incidents side by side on the page for the sake of completeness and comparison. Moreover, as Dr. Robertson noted in his preface, "A harmony cannot give all the aid that one needs, but it is the one essential book for the serious study of the life of Jesus. . . . One who has never read a harmony will be amazed at the flood of light that flashes from the parallel and progressive records of the life of Jesus Christ."[3]

Efforts to harmonize the Gospel accounts have certainly not been lacking among Latter-day Saints. One of the most significant attempts, of course, remains James E. Talmage's work, *Jesus the Christ.*[4] Although Dr. Talmage's work is by no means a harmony in any real sense, at its foundation Dr. Talmage has laid together the whole range of information available from the Gospels, interweaving all of the pieces into an order to make a complete whole. Thus, while Dr. Talmage's effort should be characterized properly as a "life of Jesus," both his braiding together of the various incidents and his placing of the Gospel stories in a chronological order do effectively what harmonies traditionally have done.

In addition to Dr. Talmage's enduring piece, other Latter-day Saint authors have contributed important works offering harmonies of the life of the Savior. After *Jesus the Christ,* the next to appear was J. Reuben Clark's *Our Lord of the Gospels.* In this work President Clark first provided a chronological framework for the Savior's ministry "based primarily upon the different missionary activities of his life,"[5] arranging "the incidents in a chronological order that seemed generally to represent the majority view of the harmonists consulted."[6] Second, he sought "to annotate these Gospel texts by reference to our own [modern] scriptures on important doctrinal matters."[7] Third, as in other modern harmonies, President Clark placed parallel accounts side by side for easier comparison. Finally, at the center stood his effort to demonstrate that the accounts of Jesus' "conception, birth, life, death, and resurrection are as factual as any in all history."[8]

David H. Yarn, professor of philosophy at BYU, recently reissued a revised synthesis of the Gospel narratives entitled *The Four Gospels as One.* In this work, Dr. Yarn has linked together the accounts of Jesus' ministry as they appear in the four Gospels but without placing parallel incidents side by side as harmonies traditionally do. As he tells us in his preface, "The major objective in this work has been to provide a single, continuous, scriptural account of the life, ministry, and mission of the Lord. In other words, here the Four Gospels are synthesized as one Gospel,"[9] much like Tatian's *Diatessaron.* In fact, his intent was "not to arrange another harmony but to make a synthesis of the Gospels."[10] His work does provide cross-references to parallel accounts as well as to appropriate passages in 3 Nephi.

Dr. Yarn's book was followed by Elder Bruce R. McConkie's *Doctrinal New Testament Commentary.* Of this three-volume set, the first consists essentially of a harmony of the four Gospels.[11] But rather than simply plow old ground, Elder McConkie regularly pointed his readers to pertinent passages from the Joseph Smith Translation that are illuminating. If we were to highlight this feature alone, it would be apparent that it represents a significant advance over earlier works. It is worth noting that he also provided extensive and helpful commentary, including relevant statements from Church leaders.

In 1976 Thomas Mumford published his *Horizontal Harmony of the Four Gospels in Parallel Columns.* The format consisted of the traditional harmonizing arrangement of the four Gospels in columns so that parallel accounts could easily be consulted, because, as he noted, "the greater message of the life of Jesus can only be seen when all four are arranged together."[12] Naturally, any incident preserved by only one of the four appears separately in its own column. Of the reason for his composition, Mumford wrote, "Since each writer has his own unique style and emphasis, any effort to truly study the life of Christ must include the complete study of all four gospels."[13] While the two parts of this statement may not necessarily go together, as we shall see below, the arrangement of Mumford's work is useful since he has provided a basic chronological framework throughout his harmony.

Eldin Ricks, professor emeritus of ancient scripture at BYU, published a book entitled *Story of the Life of Christ*.[14] He has since updated and revised this work, entitling it *King of Kings: The New Testament Story of Christ*. Like Dr. Yarn, Dr. Ricks has sought to improve on the harmonizing method of A. T. Robertson and others by providing a "single, connected narrative freed from the repetitious elements that necessarily attend the reading of the four gospels separately."[15] Throughout, he has followed the "most detailed" of the narratives when more than one Evangelist wrote about an incident. His work grows out of many years of teaching the life of Christ and has specific merit not only in the manner it presents the material but especially in its inclusion of helpful outline maps and geographical notations.

Although it is not a harmony, we should mention the most recently published treatment of the four Gospels, authored by Daniel H. Ludlow, *A Companion to Your Study of the New Testament: The Four Gospels*.[16] Dr. Ludlow's work follows the order of the New Testament Gospels: Matthew, Mark, Luke, and John. Like Elder McConkie's work, it includes statements from Latter-day Saint Church leaders and helpful references to the Joseph Smith Translation, in addition to quotations from non–Latter-day Saint sources and illuminating citations from modern scripture. Probably its greatest strength lies in the fact that it is cross-referenced to the Latter-day Saint edition of the Bible, specifically to its topical guide and Bible dictionary.

If there is any weakness in the harmonizing avenue, it will lie in the fact that occasionally the Gospel writers differed from one another both in their sequence of Jesus' ministry and in their emphasis, making it difficult both to learn the precise order of events and to remain sensitive to the nuances preserved in each record. On chronological questions, each harmonizer had to make judgments based on personal perceptions of the order of events of Jesus' ministry.[17] The obvious strengths of harmonies are that we are offered (1) a more thorough overview of Jesus' ministry than that available in any one of the Gospel accounts and (2) a broader sense of continuity and sequence among individual occurrences.

Bearing this in mind, I wish now to review what I consider a significant idea linked directly to the work of the Prophet Joseph Smith. Moreover, I want to note that the Prophet's view has influenced my approach to studying and teaching the life of the Savior. While each of the first four works of the New Testament is called a "Gospel," the Prophet changed the titles of two Gospels in the Joseph Smith Translation to "testimony." Thus we have the Testimony of Matthew and the Testimony of John.[18]

What I have just noted was not isolated. That this titular change goes back to the Lord Himself can be seen in the last verse of Doctrine and Covenants 88. There, in a discussion concerning the School of the Prophets, the Lord made reference to the ordinance of the washing of feet, noting that this was to be administered by the President of the Church "according to the pattern given in the thirteenth chapter of John's testimony concerning me" (D&C 88:141). In this revelation, received in stages during the latter part of 1832 and early 1833, it becomes clear that the Lord Himself could and did characterize the Gospel accounts as testimonies, for He specifically referred to the Gospel of John in this manner.[19]

It is worth noting here that the Prophet's insight predated by almost a full century the efforts of modern scholars to study the Gospels as highly individualized texts that reflect the point of view of each Evangelist, whatever that may have been. It has only been in recent decades that interest has focused on the Gospels as whole pieces, each with a certain integrity of its own.[20] Before that, much non–Latter-day Saint interest in the Gospels focused on the individual sayings and events of Jesus' ministry, with a consequent disregard of the fact that these brief accounts had been integral parts of a whole record.[21] To be sure, there was already a good deal of commentary literature seeking to elucidate the distinctive features of each of the Gospels.[22] But specific interest in what is now known as redaction criticism—the study of each individual Gospel as an entire composition—manifested itself only in the 1940s.[23]

The flaw submerged in the modern study of the redactional, or editorial, activity of the Evangelists consists of highlighting the compositional work of each Gospel writer with an unfortunate corresponding deemphasis on the information that concerns the Savior. This line between the two concerns, in my view, is to be balanced in favor of the latter. One must be wary of overdramatizing—say, what and how Luke wrote—at the expense of minimizing what Jesus said and did. This major pitfall—and minor chuckholes besides—impels us to place warning signals. But with all this, there is some value in such an approach. And the Prophet was the first to erect the signpost. In the first place, one is invited to treat each Gospel as possessing a certain integrity in its story of the Master. Secondly, one can come to sense how four authors—each from a different background and each needing to address a different audience—met the sacred task of writing about the Savior. Thirdly, one comes to realize that it was the concerns of the Evangelists that frequently influenced what they included in their accounts, a notion which leads us to perceive how much poorer we would have been, for example, had not Luke taken pen in hand and detailed for us the wealth of information about Jesus which he alone preserved. But more on this below.

In my own teaching, I now study with students at least one of the synoptic Gospels followed by a thorough review of the Gospel of John. There is a certain basic core of material which the synoptics share, recording similar instances in like sequence. Consequently, I have felt free to feature any one of the three in my classes. When one moves to the Gospel of John, however, one immediately encounters quite a different portrayal of the Savior, a perception that can be gained by surveying in the same course these very different but complementary views of the Savior.

Before reviewing a few cameos that may help to characterize each Gospel's witness of the Master, let me note something that derives from our common experiences as Church members. It is a true observation that different persons have varying perceptions of the same event. In instances that involve our deepest religious convictions and feelings, one has only to listen to the testimonies of people who have been to the same place, heard the same sounds, and seen the same sights. The testimonies almost always diverge in a number of ways, for what was important to one was not to another. Seemingly, the perception of each person has varied because of each one's personal inner situation at the shared moment. Consequently, to observe that the Gospel writers—possessing different backgrounds and addressing different audiences—would naturally emphasize different aspects of Jesus' ministry should not surprise us. Further, instead of coming to insist that one Gospel's view must be more trustworthy than another's, as is often assumed by modern scholars,[24] one must be willing to entertain the possibility that all taken together provide an amazingly rich tapestry of varying hues and shades. (That is what harmonies are all about.) But the integrity of each Gospel record, I submit, will produce its own special feeling for the Savior, something missed when all four are woven together. And it is this which I now wish briefly to address.

Modern scholarship generally accepts the conclusion that the Gospel of Mark was the first written.[25] While this is not beyond dispute,[26] for our purposes we can begin with this shortest record. Several features are striking. First, Mark opened his Gospel at the beginning of Jesus' ministry. For him, apparently all that had gone before was simply a preface. The main event—the one worth one's attention—began in earnest with the appearance of Jesus where John was baptizing and preaching. Mark was more interested in the words and deeds of Jesus' ministry—including His death and Resurrection—than in the Savior's origins.[27] For him, the proof apparently lay in what Jesus finally said and did, not in the signs of His wondrous birth. In this sense, Mark shows himself to be interested in the practical, hard evidence of what Jesus came to teach and to do. Secondly, as an extension of the first point, we note the high frequency of the word "immediately." Mark's inclination to use this word often, especially in his narrative connecting the incidents of Jesus' life, underscores his impression that Jesus was a person who acted decisively, always taking the initiative.[28] Third, within Mark's record of Jesus' teaching stands an undergirding plea that disciples be patient in persecution. When one becomes sensitive to it, one sees a substantial amount of Jesus' preaching concerned with enduring hard times for the sake of the kingdom.[29]

The last point which I shall mention is the so-called Messianic secret. One notes at key turns of the narrative that the disciples—even those most closely associated with Jesus—did not seem to understand Him until after His Resurrection. Simply stated, they perceived neither that He was the Messiah nor the nature of His messiahship.[30] Naturally, one asks why Mark has emphasized this in his narrative. In reply, one can surmise that Mark and his Christian readers had faced rather harsh critics who had asked, "Why was it not apparent to us that this Jesus was the promised Messiah?" Part of Mark's response, I suggest, consisted of the point, subtly made, that not even Jesus' closest associates gained full understanding until after His Resurrection.

In mild contrast to the emphasis and major themes of Mark stand the interests apparent in Matthew's Gospel. One need only recall that Matthew—himself a Jew—was writing to a Jewish audience skeptical of the claims made for Jesus by His followers.[31] To these Matthew came with a special message about his Master, a message designed to meet the criticisms of his Hellenistic Jewish readers. Like Mark, Matthew seems to have faced the question why the hearers of Jesus had not recognized Him as the Messiah. The reply, Matthew found, was on Jesus' lips at Caesarea Philippi where of His messiahship Jesus had told Peter, "Flesh and blood hath not revealed it unto thee, but my Father which is in heaven" (Matthew 16:17). To those who did not accept Jesus as the Messiah, then, the answer was that this knowledge could come only by revelation, not by having merely observed Jesus' activities or His physical characteristics. In addition, Matthew seems to have faced a second question: Why was Jesus killed? In reply, Matthew has judiciously included in his narrative several accounts of Jesus' confrontations with Jewish leaders who eventually brought about His death.[32]

A third major object of Matthew was to demonstrate that Jesus was rightfully king of the Jews. To underscore this notion, Matthew opened his book by tracing Jesus' lineage back to King David and to Abraham, in a genealogy consisting of three parts with fourteen generations each. It is highly probable that Matthew knew his Jewish readers would perceive immediately that the number fourteen represented the numerical sum of the letters of David's name in Hebrew.[33] In the same pattern of stressing Jesus' royal connections stands the confrontation with Herod that Jesus and His family escaped by fleeing to Egypt, an incident in which the usurping king recognized a legitimate heir and sought to destroy him. Another incident, shared by Matthew with the other Gospel writers, is the triumphal entry. On that occasion, of course, Jesus was hailed as the "Son of David" (Matthew 21:9), tantamount to calling Him king.[34]

The last emphasis which I shall notice here is that Jesus was to be viewed as the new lawgiver. Two elements in Matthew's record accentuate this trait. The first is the Sermon on the Mount. Note that Matthew specifically says that Jesus went "up into a mountain" (Matthew 5:1). So had Moses. But unlike Moses, who went to receive the word of God, Jesus as the lawgiver is found in the organization of the book. In five places, at the end of major teaching segments before introducing more narrative, Matthew says of Jesus' activities, "When Jesus had ended these sayings" (Matthew 7:28).[35] As others have observed, this repeated statement neatly

divides the teaching of Jesus—as preserved by Matthew—into five segments. By this means Matthew has apparently imitated the five-part
division of the law of Moses, albeit in miniature form.[36] Thus Matthew
highlighted Jesus as the lawgiver who brought the teaching that was to
replace the Mosaic code.

When one comes to the Gospel of Luke, one notices first that Luke
stressed the compassionate side of Jesus, a feature that may well have been
attractive to him because of his own experience as a physician. Luke
doubtless had seen a great deal of suffering caused by disease and accident.
The stories of Jesus' compassion must have impressed him deeply, for he
has preserved a great many.[37]

Connected with the notion of Jesus' compassion is a second observation that Luke sensed Jesus to be a man for all people. For instance, we read
of Jesus being welcomed in the rich man's palace as well as in the most
humble hovel in the village, meeting the needs of all there.[38] The additional fact that Luke chose to feature the shepherds who came at Jesus'
birth indicates his interest in the one person who attracted all people to
Himself (see Luke 2:8–18).

Third, Luke stressed that from the beginning, everyone connected both
with the family of Jesus and with the movement that He later led—
including John's family—were law-abiding people.[39] At the time of Luke's
writing, authorities of the Roman Empire did not distinguish between
Christians and Jews.[40] Luke was determined to point out that whatever
troubles Jews had caused in the Empire—and they were considerable[41]—
Christians were not to be implicated. From the very beginning, they had
always been observant, both to their religious law and to the emperor. For
Luke, Christians stood for law and order, and he gathered stories to illustrate his case from the very beginning of the Christian movement.

Fourth, as a Gentile, Luke was interested in the Gentile mission. We
recall that it is only in Luke that we read of the commissioning of the
seventy disciples. The number seventy, as I shall demonstrate below,
ultimately goes back to the table of the Gentile nations listed in Genesis
10. Jesus' calling of the seventy reflects the number of the names listed
there.[42] And as we know from modern scripture, the seventies are specifically commissioned to go to the Gentiles (see D&C 107:25).

The last accent of Luke that I shall mention concerns property and
money. Having been a physician, Luke occupied a lofty place in society
and very likely enjoyed what money could bring him. Interestingly, his

Gospel includes more stories and sayings from Jesus which concern this matter than any other account.[43] I have consequently become convinced that after his conversion, Luke inverted his values so that no longer were property and money of primary concern. Rather, his loyalty to the Lord had replaced his former interests. As he prepared to write his record, he must have been pleased to learn what Jesus had said on the matter and how closely it matched his own priorities, after conversion.

In the Gospel of John, we find a text very unlike the synoptic Gospels both in style and in tone. At its heart stands the idea that Jesus came as God's gift, a concept mentioned in various places and ways.[44] Another overarching theme is that Jesus was Jehovah. One thinks, for example, of the end of the prologue, which says that Jesus "was made flesh and dwelt among us" (John 1:14). The word "dwelt" translated means literally "to live in a tent."[45] As Jehovah had anciently dwelt in His tent among His people at the time of the Exodus, so Jesus came as the great Jehovah to tent again among His people. John further illustrated this in Jesus' discourse in which He called Himself the good shepherd (see John 10). There can be no doubt that every Jew within the sound of Jesus' voice had read or heard Ezekiel's prophecy that Jehovah Himself would become the shepherd of His people (see Ezekiel 34). Third, John stressed in obvious ways that one must be truly commissioned by the Lord in order to undertake a divine errand. He used the verb "to send" repeatedly in this sense. For instance, John the Baptist was sent from God (see John 1:6–7), whereas the priests and the Levites were sent by the Jews (see John 1:19). Jesus Himself spoke frequently of the one who sent Him,[46] implying clearly that those who carry only a human commission do not bear the same authority as those who wear the mantle of the Lord. Fourth, more openly than in any other Gospel, John bore his witness that Jesus came as the Son of God. During His mortal ministry, Jesus' own mind and heart were not clouded with doubts or questions. He knew who He was and what God expected Him to do. Finally, it has been noted by modern students that John made use of a variety of language in describing Jesus, employing both philosophical terminology and language appropriate for Hellenistic religion, in addition to phraseology at home in Jewish thought.[47] By so doing, it is naturally inferred, John was stating that no matter what we say about Jesus—or how we say it—we cannot really describe Him. In some way, He transcends our ability to describe Him with mere words. He was God. In saying more, we cannot do justice to Him.

From what I have said here all too briefly, one cannot hope to gain a full sense of the richness of the individual testimonies of the four Evangelists. But our review may offer a starting point from which we can study the solemn witness of the Master borne by each of the four writers. In his own way, each accentuated those features of Jesus' ministry which were both personally appealing and important to emphasize for his audience. Each took up the task of inscribing a history of his Lord. Each was obliged to choose what he would employ in his account. None could be entirely thorough. But they did write, they did testify, and in doing so they blessed all of our lives and made us richer.

NOTES

1. See, for instance, J. Quasten, *Patrology* (Utrecht: Spectrum, 1966), 1:220–28, especially 224–28 for bibliography.
2. A. T. Robertson, *A Harmony of the Gospels* (New York: Harper and Row, 1922). Robertson's harmony was based on the work of J. A. Broadus, *A Harmony of the Gospels in the Revised Version* (London: Hodder & Stoughton, 1893).
3. Robertson, *A Harmony of the Gospels,* viii.
4. James E. Talmage, *Jesus the Christ* (Salt Lake City: Deseret Book, 1963); this work was first issued in September 1915.
5. J. Reuben Clark Jr., *Our Lord of the Gospels* (Salt Lake City: Deseret Book, 1954), v; second printing in 1974.
6. Clark, *Our Lord of the Gospels,* vi.
7. Clark, *Our Lord of the Gospels,* vii.
8. Clark, *Our Lord of the Gospels,* viii.
9. D. H. Yarn, *The Four Gospels as One,* rev. ed. (Salt Lake City: Deseret Book, 1982), vii.
10. Yarn, *The Four Gospels as One,* viii.
11. Bruce R. McConkie, *Doctrinal New Testament Commentary,* 3 vols. (Salt Lake City: Deseret Book, 1976), 1:v.
12. Thomas M. Mumford, *Horizontal Harmony of the Four Gospels in Parallel Columns* (Salt Lake City: Deseret Book, 1976), v.
13. Mumford, *Horizontal Harmony of the Four Gospels in Parallel Columns,* v.
14. Eldin Ricks, *Story of the Life of Christ: A Harmony of the Four Gospels* (Salt Lake City: Deseret Press, 1977).
15. Eldin Ricks, *King of Kings: The New Testament Story of Christ* (Salt Lake City: Publishers Press, 1982), 7.
16. Daniel H. Ludlow, *A Companion to Your Study of the New Testament: The Four Gospels* (Salt Lake City: Deseret Book, 1982).
17. Note, for instance, the remark of D. H. Yarn, *The Four Gospels as One,* viii:

"The principle idea [was] . . . to include what in my humble judgment
appeared to be the most complete or best expressed account of events or
teachings."

18. Joseph Smith Jr., *Inspired Version: The Holy Scriptures* (Independence, MO:
Herald Publishing House, 1961), 1085, 1131, 1160, and 1207; as will be
seen, all the Gospels are renamed "testimonies" in current editions of the
Joseph Smith Translation.

19. According to the chronology of the Prophet's work on the Joseph Smith
Translation detailed by Robert J. Matthews, in *A Plainer Translation: Joseph
Smith's Translation of the Bible, A History and Commentary* (Provo, UT:
Brigham Young University Press, 1975), 36–37, Joseph Smith was work-
ing through the New Testament when Doctrine and Covenants 88 was
revealed; see also 256.

20. Luke–Acts has received significant attention in recent years. See, for
instance, the collected essays in the following two works: L. E. Keck and
J. L. Martyn, eds., *Studies in Luke–Acts* (Philadelphia: Fortress Press, 1966);
C. H. Talbert, ed., *Perspectives on Luke–Acts* (Edinburgh: T. & T. Clark,
1978).

21. The most influential publications concerning *Formegeschichte* or Form
Criticism have been M. Dibelius, *From Tradition to Gospel* (New York:
Charles Scribner's Sons, 1935), translated from the revised second
German edition of *Die Formgeschichte des Evangeliurns* (1933); and R.
Bultmann, *The History of the Synoptic Tradition* (New York: Harper and
Row, 1963), translated from the second German edition of *Die Geschichte
der synoptischen Tradition.*

22. See, for example, *The International Critical Commentary* series first published by T. & T. Clark in Edinburgh, Scotland, between 1895 and 1921.

23. The first major work was that of H. Conzelmann, *The Theology of Saint
Luke* (New York: Harper, 1961), translation of the German *Die Mitte der
Zeit* (1954); but Conzelmann's study was not the first, as N. Perrin points
out in *What Is Redaction Criticism?* (Philadelphia: Fortress Press, 1969),
21–33.

24. Among many others, see the reliance on Mark by A. Schweitzer, *The Quest
of the Historical Jesus* (New York: Macmillan, 1961), especially 330–97; N.
Perrin, *Rediscovering the Teachings of Jesus* (London: SCM Press, 1967); G.
Bornkamm, *Jesus of Nazareth* (New York: Harper & Bros., 1960).

25. Almost all standard introductions—both conservative and liberal—accept
this conclusion. See, on the one hand, W. D. Davies, *Invitation to the New
Testament* (Garden City, NY: Doubleday, 1966), 198–200; and W. G.
Kümmel, *Introduction to the New Testament* (Nashville, TN: Abingdon
Press, 1966), 35–60.

26. Consult the challenge of W. R. Farmer, *The Synoptic Problem* (New York:
Macmillan, 1964); also H. C. Thiessen, *Introduction to the New Testament*
(Grand Rapids, MI: Eerdmans, 1962), 241–45.

27. The question, of course, is whether Mark knew of Jesus' birth and youth. Nothing in the text points decisively one way or the other. If one could show clearly that Mark was written after one of the other Gospels, then we would be reasonably sure that he was aware of Jesus' earlier life but chose not to write about it. But attempts have so far remained unconvincing.

28. Mark used the word "immediately" (*eutheos*) a total of forty times, thirty-four in narrative sections and six in sayings of Jesus. We compare this figure to a total of fifteen times in the Gospel of Matthew, eight in Luke, and four in John.

29. References to persecution—both against Jesus and against his (future) disciples—in Mark can be found in the following passages: 2:6–7; 3:2, 6; 8:31, 34–37; 9:31, 42; 10:28–30, 35–40; 13:9, 13, 19–20; 14:18, 27; 15:10.

30. Notice of the so-called Messianic secret, or *Messiasgeheimnis*, was published by William Wrede in *Das Messiasgeheimnis in den Evangelien* (Gottingen: Vandenhoeck und Ruprecht, 1901). See the following examples: 3:20–22; 4:10–13, 39–41; 5:16–17, 43; 6:51–52; 7:36–37; 8:14–21, 31–33; 9:32. Wrede's radical conclusion that absolutely no one had an inkling of Jesus' messiahship until His Resurrection has often been challenged; see, for example, W. Barclay, *The First Three Gospels* (Philadelphia: Westminster Press, 1966), 183–89.

31. Matthew's ethnic origins remain a matter of dispute among the commentators. But the questions he addresses, in addition to major emphases in his record, lead me to view him as a Jew. See the observations of W. Barclay, *First Three Gospels*, 200, 211–20; and W. F. Albright and C. S. Mann, *Matthew*, in *The Anchor Bible* (Garden City, NY: Doubleday, 1971), CLXXVII–CLXXXI.

32. The most vividly portrayed confrontation between Jesus and Jewish leaders in all the Gospels occurs in Matthew 23:1–35; see also 9:11; 12:2, 24, 38–39; 15:1–9; 16:1–4; 19:3–4; 21:15–16, 23–27; 22:34–35, 41–42.

33. See, for instance, Barclay, *First Three Gospels*, 222; W. C. Allen, *The Gospel According to S. Matthew*, The International Critical Commentary, 3d ed. (Edinburgh: T. & T. Clark, 1912), 6–7; see also Albright and Mann, *Matthew*, 5; and J. C. Fenton, *Saint Matthew* (Baltimore, MD: Penguin, 1963), 40–41, 54.

34. See the comments of Barclay, *First Three Gospels*, 226–27; Albright and Mann, *Matthew*, CLI–CLVII, 252; Allen, *Gospel According to St. Matthew*, lxvi, 2; Fenton, *Saint Matthew*, 36–37, 328.

35. The five passages in which this notation closes sections of teaching and reintroduces the narrative are 7:28; 11:1; 13:53; 19:1; and 26:1.

36. The five major discourses thus framed are the Sermon on the Mount (5–7), charge to the Twelve (10), parables of the kingdom (13), discourse on personal relationships in the kingdom (18), and the last days (24–26).

See the comments of Barclay, *First Three Gospels,* 221–23; Allen, *Gospel According to St. Matthew,* lxv, 70.

37. Concerning Luke's profession, see Barclay, *First Three Gospels,* 267–69; L. Morris, *The Gospel According to St. Luke* (Grand Rapids, MI: Eerdmans, 1974), 17–18; J. A. Fitzmyer, *The Gospel According to Luke I–IX,* in *The Anchor Bible* (Garden City, NY: Doubleday, 1981), 36, 40, 51–53. One central theme appears in the saying, "For the Son of Man is come to seek and to save that which was lost" (19:10). In light of this, stories of Jesus' compassion—present or promised—can be found in Luke 4:18, 38–39, 40; 5:12–13, 24–25; 6:6–10, 19; 7:13; 8:48, 49–56; 9:13–17, 37–42; 13:11–13; 17:12–19; and 18:35–42; sayings of Jesus concerning compassionate acts are recorded in 6:27–36; 7:22; 9:56; 10:25–37; 13:34; 16:19–31; 18:2–5; and 23:34, 43.

38. Compare Luke 7:34–50. For illustrations of the universal effectiveness of Jesus' mission, consult 1:37; 2:30–32; 3:14, 38; 4:25–27, 43; 5:27–31; 6:20–23; 7:9, 29, 34; 8:1–3; 15:1–2, 11–32; 18:10–17, 27; and 19:8–10. See the remarks of Barclay, *First Three Gospels,* 284–91; G. B. Caird, *Saint Luke* (Baltimore, MD: Penguin, 1963), 36–37; Morris, *Gospel According to St. Luke,* 36–37, 40–42; Fitzmyer, *Gospel According to Luke I–IX,* 187–92.

39. Among passages in Luke which stress following law or custom are 1:6, 50, 59; 2:4–5, 21–24, 25, 39, 41, 51–52; 4:16; 5:14; 6:9, 45; 8:15, 21; 12:59; 18:20; 19:46; 22:7–8, 25–27; and 23:47.

40. This seems to be Luke's point in writing to Theophilus (see Luke 1:3; Acts 1:1), whom he addresses as if he were an official of the Roman Empire. (Compare the same term of address in Acts 23:26; 24:3; and 26:25.)

41. For example, Jews were driven from Rome for rioting in AD 49 by an edict of Claudius. Depending on the date of Luke's composition, he might have had one or both of the following two events in mind: First, in AD 64 Rome was burned and Nero blamed the Christians who had doubtless been understood simply as a Jewish sect. Second, within two years the Jewish revolt against Rome erupted in Judea in AD 66 and was not brought under control until the late summer of AD 70 when the temple went up in flames. Some have argued that Luke wrote late enough that he had these later two events in mind (see, for instance, G. B. Caird, *Saint Luke,* 13, 231).

42. The case is made not by the number 70 but by the number 72; for seventy-two names are listed in Genesis 10 in the Septuagint (Greek) account: an extra name is added in both verses 2 and 22. Early Christian scribes, knowing that the call of the seventy was linked back to Genesis 10 and assuming that Luke had made a mistake, "corrected" the text to read 72 in Luke 10:1, 17 (see the note in Morris, *Gospel According to St. Luke,* 181). Regarding Luke's interest in Gentiles, see also 2:30–32; 3:14, 38; 4:25–27; 7:9; 8:26–40 (the setting was in Gentile territory); and 24:47.

43. Sayings of Jesus which concern property and money appear in 6:24–25,

38; 12:13–30, 33–34; 14:12–14; 15:4–9; 16:1–15; 17:33; 18:22–25, 28–30; 19:8, 12–26; 20:22–25; and 21:1–4; consult Barclay, *First Three Gospels,* 286–88.

44. John 3:16; compare 1:12; 3:27, 34–35; 4:10, 14–15; 5:22, 26–27, 36; 6:27, 31–34, 37, 39, 51; 10:28–29; 11:22; 12:49; 13:3, 34; 14:16, 27; 15:16; 16:23; 17:1–2, 4, 8, 14, 22, 24; 18:11; and 19:11.

45. The Greek infinitive is *skenoun;* but see the cautioning remarks in G. Kittel and G. Friedrich, eds., *Theological Dictionary of the New Testament* (Grand Rapids, MI: Eerdmans, 1971), 7:385–89.

46. John employs the Greek verbs "to send" (*apostello* and *petnpo*) 61 times. Of these only one instance does not reflect a sense of commissioning (see 9:7); see J. Seynaeve's study, "Les verbes et dans le vocabulaire theologique de Saint Jean," *Bibliotheca Ephemeridum Theologicarum Lovaniensium* 44 (1977): 385–89.

47. One is impressed by the volume of recent studies, whether summaries or particularized studies, which focus on the seemingly unending variety of contacts between John's Gospel and the religious and philosophical milieu of the first century after Christ. Among recent specializing essays, one can consult Raymond E. Brown, "'Other Sheep Not of This Fold: The Johannine Perspective on Christian Diversity in the Late First Century," *Journal of Biblical Literature* 97 (1978): 5–22; Edwin D. Freed, "Theological Prelude to the Prologue of John's Gospel," *Scottish Journal of Theology* 32 (1979): 257–69; T. Korteweg, "The Reality of the Invisible: Some Remarks on St. John XIV 8 and Greek Philosophic Tradition," in M. J. Vermaseren, ed., *Studies in Hellenistic Religions,* E. J. Brill: Leiden (1979), 50–102; *idem,* "'You Will Seek Me and You Will Not Find Me' (John 7:34): An Apocalyptic Pattern in Johannine Theology," *Bibliotheca Ephemeridum Theologicarum Lovaniensium* 53 (1980): 349–54; Judith M. Lieu, "Gnosticism and the Gospel of John," *The Expository Times* 90 (1979): 233–37; V. C. van Unnik, "A Greek Characteristic of Prophecy in the Fourth Gospel," *Text and Interpretation, Festschrift for Matthew Black* (Cambridge: Cambridge University Press, 1979), 211–29. Although uneven in quality, recent summaries of various aspects of the theological currents apparent in the fourth Gospel include Ramond F. Collins, "The Search for Jesus: Reflexions of the Fourth Gospel," *Laval Theologique et Philosophique* 34 (1978): 27–48; Jean Giblet, "Developpements dans la theologie johannique," *Bibliotheca Ephemeridum Theologicarum Lovaniesium* 44 (1977): 45–72; David John Hawkin, "The Johannine Transposition and Johannine Theology," *Laval Theoiogique et Philosophique* 36 (1980): 89–98; James McPolin, "Studies in the Fourth Gospel—Some Contemporary Trends," *Irish Biblical Studies* 2 (1980): 3–26; Leon Morris, "The Composition of the Fourth Gospel," *Scripture, Tradition and Interpretation, Festschrift for E. F. Harrison* (Grand Rapids, MI: Eerdmans, 1978), 157–75; R. Schnackenberg, "Entwicklung und Stand der johannischen Forschung seit 1955," *Bibliotheca Ephemeridum Theoiogicarum Lovaniensium,* 44 (1977): 19–44.

CHAPTER EIGHT

MARK AND LUKE: TWO FACETS OF A DIAMOND

ROGER R. KELLER

Elder Bruce R. McConkie has made the following statement concerning the four Gospels: "It is apparent . . . that each inspired author had especial and intimate knowledge of certain circumstances not so well known to others, and that each felt impressed to emphasize different matters because of the particular people to whom he was addressing his personal gospel testimony."[1] In reality, each Gospel is like a facet of a diamond that brightens and highlights the picture of Jesus Christ that we receive. Just as a diamond would be terribly uninteresting without its facets, so also would the picture of Jesus be flat and one-dimensional without the composite picture of Him that is presented when the four Gospels are brought together. All bear witness of Jesus Christ and teach the plan of salvation but each with a slightly different cut, clarity, and color. In this light, it would have been a great loss to all generations of the Church had we not had both Mark and Luke—two facets of the gospel diamond.

JESUS CHRIST

In His three years' ministry, Jesus walked and talked with numerous people in a wide range of situations. He gave many public sermons as well as considerable private instruction to His disciples. He met in highly charged situations with the religious leaders of His day. He spoke to prince and pauper, priest and peasant, saint and sinner. No one was so exalted that Jesus was intimidated by him, nor was anyone so insignificant that

---

Roger R. Keller is a professor of Church history and doctrine at Brigham Young University.

Jesus did not have time for him or her. Women and children had a special place in His heart and ministry, something that was not common in the Judaism of His day.[2]

Jesus taught about an immense range of subjects. He dealt with the nature and purposes of God, the plan of salvation, the nature of human destiny, the morality of the kingdom, and many other issues. Much of His teaching among the crowds was done in parables, not merely to put the message in an understandable form but also to hide the message from those who were not yet spiritually prepared to comprehend it (see Matthew 13:10–15; Mark 4:10–12; Luke 8:9–10). Later, in private, He also told His disciples in clear language what the parables meant (see Matthew 13:18; Mark 4:13; Luke 8:11). Thus He chose what He would say to whom and how He would say it, depending upon the hearer's ability to understand.[3]

John tells us that in the scriptures we have far from all that Jesus said or did (see John 21:25). Yet we have that which the Lord, through the Holy Ghost, guided the Gospel writers to preserve in preparation for the fulness of times in the latter days. No one Gospel portrait of the Lord is complete in itself, but as we encounter Christ and His teachings in all the Gospels, we will come to know Him better.

MARK AND LUKE: THE AUTHORS

Neither Mark nor Luke was one of the original Twelve. Their precise relationship with Jesus is not known, although Mark may have been among the larger circle of Jesus' early followers. Tradition says that Mark was a missionary companion of Peter and that the Gospel of Mark represents in large measure Mark's account of Peter's recollections of the Lord and His ministry.[4] That seems probable. Luke is usually identified as the beloved physician and companion of Paul and was thus a bit more distant from the historical Jesus than was Mark. However, many consider him a very careful and deliberate historian who gathered all the information he could from "eyewitnesses, and ministers of the word" (Luke 1:2)[5] as he wrote his two-part work, Luke and Acts, which he dedicated to Theophilus, a person otherwise unknown to us.

Mark is traditionally said to have written his Gospel in Rome during the time of Nero's persecution of the Church. Many of the slums of Rome had been burned, an act that is probably attributable to Nero, who wanted to make room for public buildings. Nero needed a scapegoat, however, and the Christians, who were not popular anyway because of their rather "narrow" religious views, were a group that could be easily blamed. Thus the members of the Church among whom Mark worked and served were undergoing tremendous persecution and suffering greatly. Apparently Mark longed to bring a message of hope to these people in the midst of their sufferings, as well as to explain through Jesus' own words and actions why people suffer in this world when they are doing what the Lord requires of them. Thus the persecution that Peter and Mark faced in the Roman Church determined to a large degree Mark's focus on the suffering in Jesus' life and the lives of His followers.[6]

Luke was in an entirely different situation. He probably lived where there was a large Gentile community,[7] where many wanted to know whether the gospel was for them or only for the Jews. Luke himself was a Gentile (see Colossians 4:10–14).[8] He was a companion of Paul,[9] the Apostle to the Gentiles. He knew well that the gospel was for persons of all races and for all persons—male and female, rich and poor, slave and free. Thus Jesus' message about the universality of the gospel becomes the focal point of Luke's portrait of the Lord.

Both Mark and Luke accurately portray Jesus' words and deeds, but each sees different aspects of Jesus' ministry. The Lord's words are for all generations and all times, but no one Gospel could possibly contain all that Jesus said and did. Each contains a piece of the whole.

THE GOSPEL OF MARK

"And he took the blind man by the hand, and led him out of the town; and when he had spit on his eyes, and put his hands upon him, he asked him if he saw ought. And he looked up, and said, I see men as trees, walking. After that he put his hands again upon his eyes, and made him look up: and he was restored, and saw every man clearly" (Mark 8:23–26). This passage represents the central point in the Gospel according to Mark. As we come to an understanding of Jesus' true role, we then come to clarity about our own role as His disciples.

This story is unique in the Gospels. At no other time did Jesus need two attempts to heal a person. This healing occurred shortly before Jesus asked His disciples, "Whom do men say that I am?" and "Whom say ye that I am?" Peter, of course, gave his classic answer: Jesus is the Christ (Mark 8:27, 29). Jesus then told him that the Son of Man must suffer and die, and Peter immediately reacted by saying that could not happen (see Mark

8:31–32). One of Jesus' harshest replies was then immediately directed at Peter. "Get thee behind me, Satan: for thou savourest not the things that be of God, but the things that be of men" (Mark 8:33). Clearly, Peter—and perhaps we as observers—missed something. What was wrong with Peter's desire that Jesus not suffer? Everything—for Jesus came precisely *to* suffer and die![10]

"Behold, we go up to Jerusalem; and the Son of man shall be delivered unto the chief priests, and unto the scribes; and they shall condemn him to death, and shall deliver him to the Gentiles: And they shall mock him, and shall scourge him, and shall spit upon him, and shall kill him: and the third day he shall rise again. . . . For even the Son of man came not to be ministered unto, but to minister, and to give his life a ransom for many" (Mark 10:33–34, 45).

Anyone who stood in opposition to that goal did not understand the nature and purpose of Jesus' messiahship. Such a person was like the blind man who, after Jesus' partial healing of him, saw partially but unclearly. By contrast, only those who understood unequivocally that Jesus must die understood the nature of His messiahship as well as the possible consequences of their own discipleship. They would be comparable to the blind man who saw clearly after Jesus' second act of healing. Peter, however, understood only in part what the actual role of the Messiah would be and thus perceived Christ's mission only dimly. He did not yet understand that the Messiah must suffer and die. Only after Jesus' death and Resurrection would he and others finally see more clearly.

Confrontation. Peter knew and declared that Jesus was the Messiah, even though his conception of the Messiah was not predicated on the same understanding that Jesus possessed. What led Peter to this unequivocal testimony of Christ but only a partial understanding of His mission? Perhaps the answer lies in Jesus' ministry to that point. Mark shows us clearly that Jesus' ministry was characterized by conflict and confrontation from the beginning. The Spirit led Jesus out into the wilderness to be tempted by Satan (see Mark 1:12). That cosmic confrontation then became an earthly conflict as Jesus confronted demons, disease, religious leaders, and ultimately even His own disciples who did not understand the nature of His ministry.[11]

Such confusion among His disciples, however, often resulted from Jesus' own actions. He could not turn away persons in need. Thus, immediately after coming out of the wilderness, He was confronted by a man with an unclean spirit in the synagogue at Capernaum. He drove out that spirit, amazing all that were present (see Mark 1:21–27). He then went to Peter's home, where He found Peter's mother-in-law ill, and He healed her (see Mark 1:29–31). Then people brought the sick and those possessed with devils from the surrounding countryside, and Jesus healed them of their infirmities and cast out the devils (see Mark 1:32–34). The next morning, however, the disciples looked for Jesus and could not find Him. Ultimately they located Him in an isolated spot where He had gone to pray. The disciples were impressed with Jesus' healing ability and indicated to Him that many were already waiting to receive such blessings at His hand. Jesus' response to their well-intentioned request is enlightening, for He said, "Let us go into the next towns, that I may preach there also: for therefore came I forth. And he preached in their synagogues throughout all Galilee, and cast out devils" (Mark 1:38–39). Thus Jesus indicated that His healing ministry, with which all were so impressed, was really not His foremost purpose on earth. He had something more important to do, that is, proclaim the nearness of the kingdom of God (see Mark 1:14; 2:2).[12]

Even so, Jesus continued to heal and to drive out demons (see Mark 1:24, 39; 2:10; 5:2–8; 6:56; 7:26–30; 9:23–24), leading to confrontations with religious authorities, who sought ways to get rid of Him. They watched like vultures to see if He would heal on the Sabbath so that they might accuse Him of breaking the law (see Mark 2:24–28; 3:2–6). Later, He sent His disciples out to accomplish the same things He had, giving them authority to heal the sick and cast out demons (see Mark 3:14; 6:7, 13). Both the cosmic order and religious order were being shaken by Him. No wonder Peter believed Him to be the Messiah! Only the Messiah could do what Jesus did.

Tell no man. Jesus forbade the demons to proclaim who He was (see Mark 1:25, 34; 3:12), but that is understandable. He did not want demonic testimony to His messiahship. Yet the knowledge of the demons points to an interesting dichotomy. The minions of Satan recognized and knew who Jesus was, but the religious authorities did not. The scribes, Pharisees, and Sadducees wanted only to rid themselves of Him. Mark was appalled at how utterly blind they were.

A more difficult question is why Jesus commanded those whom He healed not to tell what He had done for them (see Mark 1:43; 7:36). Shouldn't people have known that the Messiah had come with compassion and "healing in his wings"? (Malachi 4:2). Yet, when people ignored

His admonition, Jesus found Himself having to go into the wilderness to get away from the crowds who wanted Him to heal their sick (see Mark 1:38, 45). None of the people, including Jesus' disciples, completely understood who He was. They assumed that He was the Messiah, which was correct; but their conception of the Messiah was of one who worked miracles, healed the sick, fed the hungry, and ultimately would cast the Romans out of Judea.[13] They were like the blind man who understood only in part. So also with Peter. Despite revelation from the Father (see Matthew 16:16–17), Peter based his intellectual understanding of Jesus as the Messiah on His miracle-working and confrontational ministry. That was not the character of Jesus' messiahship, and Jesus knew that Peter did not fully understand his own declaration, "Thou art the Christ, the Son of the living God" (Matthew 16:16). Then He told Peter not to tell anyone (see Mark 8:30).

Suffering. Jesus told Peter plainly that His messiahship required that He suffer and die (see Mark 8:31).[14] But that was not Peter's understanding of messiahship. He liked the image of the miracle-working, powerful Messiah who was not afraid to confront anyone.[15] Thus he objected (see Mark 8:32), and Jesus forcefully chastised Peter for not allowing God to readjust his preconceived notions about what the Messiah would be like.[16] From this point in Mark's Gospel, Jesus moved inexorably toward the cross, pointing out several times that His destiny was to suffer and die for humanity (see Mark 9:12, 31; 10:33–34, 45; 12:7–8; 14:7–8, 22, 24, 27). Yet it was a Gentile centurion, as he watched Jesus breathe His last breath, who first comprehended that Jesus in the midst of His suffering was truly "the Son of God" (Mark 15:39).

But if Jesus' role was to suffer, then it is highly probable that those who followed Him might have to share the same fate (see Mark 8:34–35; 10:39–40; 13:9, 12–13). Such was and is the case. Those of the early Church faced torture and death. According to tradition, Peter was crucified upside down.[17] Paul was beheaded.[18] Stephen was stoned (see Acts 7:59). James was beheaded (see Acts 12:2). Once empowered by the Holy Ghost, however, men who had run and hidden in locked rooms became giants for the faith, unafraid of death. What more powerful message could Mark have conveyed to the suffering Church in Rome than this? He told those frightened people that even the Son of God was destined to suffer because the world could not tolerate His presence, His goodness, and His message. So also the world could not tolerate those who followed Him, and His disciples would have to suffer, as Jesus had warned them during His lifetime. Evil cannot tolerate good. It will do all it can to stamp it out. But good will be conquered only momentarily, for the righteous powers of heaven, which raise men from the very depths of the grave, can never be overcome.

That, therefore, was Mark's message to Rome as he viewed Jesus' life and ministry. So also is it his message to us of the latter-day Church who are comfortable and all too often conforming to the model of the world rather than receiving in our lives the imprint of heaven. If the world is comfortable with us and we are comfortable with it, we see the mission of the Messiah only as the partially healed blind man saw. Like the disciples at Pentecost, who did not see clearly until they received their "second" healing through the bestowal of the Holy Ghost, we must also receive the understanding that we will suffer as we faithfully follow the Lord—suffer because we do not agree with the values of the world. And like the disciples who went on to endure grievous persecution, we will be fortified by this clearer vision, knowing that our suffering is linked to His. Then we will more fully comprehend what it means to know that Jesus is "the Christ, the Son of the living God" (Matthew 16:16).

THE GOSPEL OF LUKE

Like Mark, Luke saw certain aspects of Jesus' ministry as being particularly applicable to his day and situation. Of great importance to him was that the gospel be relevant for persons such as himself who were not Israelites. Luke also had a concern for those who seemed to be on the fringes of society. Was the gospel for them, too, or was it a gospel for the privileged classes? He further felt, like Mark, that it was important to explain what it meant to be a disciple. In Luke, also, one sees an emphasis on the spiritual dimension of Jesus' life, a dimension that could and should be part of the lives of all who follow Christ. The principal Lucan concerns are initially expressed in the birth narratives in chapters 1 and 2. We can trace them through the Gospel and into Acts, for Luke and Acts are really one whole. Many of the Lucan emphases find their fulfillment in the apostolic ministry.

Witness. Luke expressed at the beginning of his Gospel that his narrative should be viewed as an authoritative witness of Jesus Christ because it had its roots in the accounts of eyewitnesses and ministers of the word (see Luke 1:2). Luke demonstrated that his account was accurate because it could be traced to original witnesses who met, walked, and talked with the Lord or who were divinely informed about Him.[19] Thus Jesus' birth was heralded by appearances of Gabriel to the witnesses Zacharias (see Luke 1:11–20) and Mary (see Luke 1:26–38), while the baby in Elisabeth's womb leaped in witnessing recognition of the baby in Mary's womb (see Luke 1:41). Both Simeon (see Luke 2:25–35) and Anna (see Luke 2:36–38) received divine confirmation of Jesus' messiahship and bore testimony of Him.[20] Throughout Jesus' ministry in Galilee, people were always with Him, hearing every word He spoke and seeing every act He did (see Luke 5:1; 6:17; 7:1, 11; 8:1–4, 19, 40, 42). The same thing was true on the long trip to Jerusalem (see Luke 10:23–24; 11:29; 12:1; 14:25; 19:37).[21] Witnesses were constantly present. Finally, in choosing an Apostle to replace Judas, the remaining Apostles determined that he had to be an *eyewitness* of Jesus' entire ministry, so that he could bear authoritative *witness,* or testimony, of the historical ministry of Jesus[22] as well as to His Resurrection: "Wherefore of these men which have companied with us all the time that the Lord Jesus went in and out among us, beginning from the baptism of John, unto that same day that he was taken up from us, must one be ordained to be a witness with us of his resurrection" (Acts 1:21–22).

Eyewitnesses were the foundation upon which the testimony of the life, ministry, Atonement, and Resurrection of the Lord were to be proclaimed. One *witnessed* first by seeing, and then one *bore witness* by telling the message to all who would listen. The Gospel according to Luke reflects the eyewitness accounts of the companions of Jesus, and Acts reflects the witnessing proclamation of the disciples from Jerusalem to the center of the known world—Rome: "But ye shall receive power, after that the Holy Ghost is come upon you: and ye shall be *witnesses* unto me both in Jerusalem, and in Judea, and in Samaria, and unto the uttermost part of the earth" (Acts 1:8).

A universal gospel. Luke was a Gentile. Thus, the question of whether the gospel was limited to Israel or was for all people was important to him personally. The gospel was for everyone—rich and poor, men and women, Jew and Gentile—although some persons might have more trouble hearing and responding to it than others.

From the very beginning of the Gospel of Luke, the reader is made aware of the Lord's concern for women. In the birth narratives, women are clearly the dominant figures. Elisabeth (see Luke 1:5–7, 24), Mary (see Luke 1:26–56), and Anna (see Luke 2:36–38) play prominent roles. Zacharias and Joseph are essentially silent; Simeon is the only male, apart from Jesus

Himself, who plays an active role—namely, affirming Jesus' identity and mission. It is Mary, not Joseph, who receives Simeon's witness (see Luke 2:34). Luke alone among the synoptic[23] writers included the account of the raising to life of the son of the widow of Nain (see Luke 7:12–13), the sinful woman's anointing of Jesus (see Luke 7:37–50), the identification of some of the women who followed Jesus (see Luke 8:1–3), the account of Mary and Martha[24] (see Luke 10:38–42), the woman with a spirit of infirmity (see Luke 13:11–17), the woman searching for the lost coin (see Luke 15:8), the woman and the unjust judge (see Luke 18:2–8), Jesus' words to the women on the way to His Crucifixion (see Luke 23:27–28), and the account that the women amazed the disciples with their story of being unable to find Jesus' body (see Luke 24:22–24). Clearly, Jesus violated so many Jewish sanctions against association with women that other writers, like Mark and Matthew, may have been hesitant to include all such accounts. But Luke understood that Jesus had opened the heavens to all persons, regardless of sex, and thus he included Jesus' association with persons who were considered inferior to devout Jewish males.

While Matthew focused on Joseph's response to Mary's pregnancy, Joseph's visionary experiences, and the coming of the Magi, Luke chose to stress another element. He knew that people with little or no status in society were the first to hear the message of the Messiah's birth. Thus we have from his hand the account of the shepherds to whom the heavens were opened (see Luke 2:8–20) and who received the glad tidings—men to whom no self-respecting Jewish religious leader would probably have spoken.[25]

Once again, only Luke among the synoptic writers recorded Jesus' announcement in Nazareth that He was appointed to preach good news to the poor, the captives, the blind, and the oppressed (see Luke 4:18). Similarly, he gave us the accounts of the centurion who had the sick servant (see Luke 7:2–9), the response to John the Baptist's disciples which stressed the healing of the downtrodden and simple folk (see Luke 7:22), the parable of the good Samaritan (see Luke 10:30–37), the parable of the wedding feast (see Luke 14:12–24), the accounts of the lost coin and the lost (prodigal) son (see Luke 15:8–32), the story of the rich man and Lazarus (see Luke 16:29–31), the account of the ten lepers—the only one who returned to thank Jesus being a Samaritan (see Luke 17:11–16), the tax collector's prayer in the temple (see Luke 18:13–14), the story of Jesus eating with Zacchaeus the tax collector (see Luke 19:2–10), and Jesus' words of forgiveness to the thief on the cross (see Luke 23:41–43).

Luke knew that Jesus had thrown the door open wide to all, if they would but come to Him. None was to be excluded except those who excluded themselves.[26] Often, these were the rich.[27] Jesus warned against treasures on earth, for wealth had a way of corrupting even the best of intentions. Consequently, Luke recorded Jesus' warning against covetousness (see Luke 12:15) and against planning without considering God's purposes (see Luke 12:20–21). Similarly, Jesus charged the Pharisees with being lovers of money (see Luke 16:14–15) and pronounced the parable of the rich man and Lazarus (see Luke 16:19–31). Each of the Gospel writers recognized that Jesus intended the message of the kingdom of God for all persons, not merely for the Jews. Luke, however, emphasized that fact more clearly than the others, because it was central to his presence in the Church. He was a Gentile.

In his account, Luke shows that the gospel is not to be limited to Israel: "His mercy is on them that fear him" (Luke 1:50). It is for "those who sit in darkness and in the shadow of death" (Luke 1:79), and it is to bring peace on earth and "good will toward men" (Luke 2:14). More specifically it is for "all people" (Luke 2:10).[28] Simeon actually surprised Mary and Joseph, who already knew that Jesus was the Son of God, when he said, "Lord, now lettest thou thy servant depart in peace, according to thy word: for mine eyes have seen thy salvation, which thou hast prepared before the face of all people; a light to lighten the *Gentiles,* and the glory of thy people Israel" (Luke 2:29–32; emphasis added). Even Mary and Joseph did not comprehend the scope of Jesus' work or the full grace of God, and thus Luke recorded, "Joseph and his mother marvelled at those things which were spoken of him" (Luke 2:33).

Luke recorded the whole of the Isaiah passage (see Isaiah 40:3–5) which John the Baptist quoted, including the words, "and *all flesh* shall see the salvation of God" (Luke 3:6; emphasis added). In addition the genealogy in Luke is more universal, for it traces Jesus' lineage not merely to Abraham but to Adam and ultimately to God (see Luke 3:38).[29] Jesus created opposition in Nazareth not merely by claiming that salvation might be present in Him but by further implying that the saving gospel would go to the Gentiles because the unrighteous Jews would not receive it. He made this same point by reminding them of Elijah's being sent only to the woman of Sidon and of Elisha's cleansing only Naaman the Syrian (see Luke

4:16–30).[30] We also have solely in Luke the account of Jesus healing the centurion's slave (see Luke 7:1–10) and the note "that repentance and remission of sins should be preached in his name *among all nations,* beginning at Jerusalem" (Luke 24:47). The universality of the gospel and its special application to the Gentiles is further delineated by the entirety of Acts. There we see the gospel proceed forth to the ends of the earth.

Israel and the gospel. Where were the roots of the gospel? Luke knew that they were in Israel and the Old Testament, particularly in the words of the prophets. But knowing it was one thing; communicating it to persons who had no knowledge of the Old Testament was another. Explaining the relationship was a fairly simple matter for Matthew, because he was writing to a Jewish-Christian audience which was thoroughly familiar with the Old Testament. All he had to say was, "Now all this was done, that it might be fulfilled which was spoken of the Lord by the prophet, saying . . ." (Matthew 1:22; see also 2:5, 15, 17, 23). His readers knew exactly what he meant.

But Gentiles, to whom Luke's account is addressed, would not have that scriptural background. Luke's concern was tying the house of Israel and the Church together and showing their congruence and continuity. He does that by drawing attention to a very clear element in Jesus' ministry. To Jesus, Jerusalem and the temple were sacred places. They were also the central places of Judaism. Even Gentiles would know that. They might not know about the Jewish scriptures, but they almost certainly knew about the Jews' sacred city and their sacred temple. Thus Luke augments his and the Lord's references to the scriptures by stressing the importance that the Father and Jesus placed on Jerusalem and the temple.[31] Luke's Gospel begins in Jerusalem in the temple with Gabriel's appearance to Zacharias (see Luke 1:5–20). Jesus is brought to Jerusalem and the temple at the time of Mary's purification (see Luke 2:22). Jesus taught in the temple at age twelve (see Luke 2:46–49). He cleansed the temple (see Luke 19:45–46). He taught in the temple during His last days (see Luke 19:47; 20:1; 21:37–38), and His disciples worshiped in the temple even after Pentecost (see Luke 24:53; Acts 2:46–47; 3:1–8; 5:20; 21:26).

Could even Gentile readers miss the implication that the Church is rooted in Israel? Could they doubt that Jesus was heralded by Jewish scriptures when it was so clear that the sacred places of Judaism were also sacred to Him and His disciples? Luke hoped that this emphasis on Jerusalem and the temple would help the Gentile converts appreciate the importance of Israel and the Old Testament in preparing the way for Christ.

Prayer and the Holy Spirit. Luke also provided deep insights into Jesus' spiritual life. We see Jesus constantly at prayer in those moments when major events were about to occur.[32] In those instances where Luke parallels Mark's account, Luke alone added the observation in several instances that Jesus prayed. At Jesus' baptism, the Holy Ghost descended while Jesus *was praying* (see Luke 3:21–22). Jesus went to the wilderness to pray (see Luke 5:16). The night before He called the Twelve, He withdrew into the hills and prayed the whole night through (see Luke 6:12–13). Before He asked the disciples, "Whom say the people that I am?" He prayed (Luke 9:18). He went up the Mount of Transfiguration to pray, and while He was praying He was transfigured (see Luke 9:28–29). It was the result of Jesus' prayer that led the disciples to ask Him to teach them to pray (see Luke 11:1). He told Peter that He had prayed for him so that Satan might not have Peter (see Luke 22:31–32). And, of course, prayer was central to the experience in Gethsemane. Jesus commanded the disciples to pray, and He prayed in His agony (see Luke 22:40–46). It is in Luke alone that we find Jesus' parables about prayer—the parables of borrowing bread at midnight (see Luke 11:5–8) and of the widow and the unjust judge (see Luke 18:1–8). Thus prayer was the very lifeline between the Father and the Son. If Christ needed to pray, how much more do we need prayer!

In addition to teaching the power of prayer, Luke also highlighted the role of the Holy Ghost in the life of Jesus. Throughout the birth narrative in Luke, we see the constant work of the Holy Ghost. John was filled with the Holy Ghost, even in his mother's womb (see Luke 1:15). The Holy Ghost would "come upon" Mary (Luke 1:35). Elisabeth was filled with the Holy Ghost when Mary came to her (see Luke 1:41). Zacharias, John the Baptist's father, was filled with the Holy Ghost and prophesied of Christ (see Luke 1:67). Simeon was guided and spoke by the Holy Ghost as he likewise testified of the arrival of the Lord's salvation (see Luke 2:25–27, 30).

As with the use of prayer in Jesus' life, Luke makes it clearer than does Mark that it was the Holy Ghost who descended on Jesus at baptism (see Luke 3:22). By the power of the Spirit, Jesus was led into the wilderness for forty days, and in the power of the Spirit He returned to Galilee (see Luke 4:1, 4). Only in Luke is the passage from Isaiah 61:1 quoted: "The Spirit of the Lord is upon me, because he has anointed me to preach the gospel to the poor" (Luke 4:18). The Holy Ghost would teach and comfort Him in times of need and give additional power to His divine ministry (see Luke 12:12; see also JST, John 3:34). The Prophet Joseph Smith confirmed this unique contribution of Luke when he taught that Jesus had greater power than any man because He was the Son of God and had "the fullness of the Spirit."[33] Jesus rejoiced in the power of the Holy Ghost (see Luke 10:21). Luke also records that Christ taught that it was the Holy Ghost who would teach in time of need (see Luke 4:14) and that the Father will give the Holy Ghost to those who seek Him (see Luke 11:13).[34]

Thus the Gospel of Luke not only testifies of the role of the Holy Ghost in helping the Savior fulfill His mission but also points to the role of the Holy Ghost in leading and strengthening the Church. This significant theme begun in his Gospel received even greater emphasis by Luke in the book of Acts, where we read of the great new mission fields of the Church being blessed by the coming of the Holy Ghost (see Acts 2:4; 8:17; 10:44; 19:6).[35]

CONCLUSION

Through the eyes of Mark and Luke, we see the man Jesus, but we see aspects of His life and ministry that would have been lost to us without both of these Gospels. From Mark we learn that the disciples did not always understand the significance of Jesus and His work. They were initially attracted by the miracles and compassion of Jesus, but only after His Atonement and Resurrection did they fully understand that Jesus' messiahship involved suffering and that His disciples might well be called to walk in His footsteps, as many did. It was a poignant and timely message which the disciples in Rome, in their days of persecution, needed to hear. Mark reminds us that the Christian will never be completely at ease in the world today either. Like the blind man, only when people receive the healing clarity of vision will they understand that Jesus' suffering messiahship is inextricably bound to their own suffering discipleship.

From Luke's account, we learn that the gospel is for every person, be they Jew, Gentile, slave, free, man, woman, shepherd, or king. Nobody is left out. Israel continues to be special in its relationship to God, but the Church reaches beyond Israel to the Gentiles and others who had for a time been outside the pale of God's chosen, or elect, people. We also learn that the gospel is built upon the eyewitness reports of people who saw all that Jesus did and heard all that He said. Thus they could become true witnesses for Him—people who could tell what they have experienced and know. And finally, Luke teaches us through Jesus' example about the essential nature of prayer and the critical role of the Holy Ghost.

What beauty would have been lost had either Mark or Luke been left out of the canon! They, in conjunction with Matthew and John, enable us to have a more complete picture of our Lord and His mission than would have been available had their Gospels been omitted. A diamond truly sparkles when all its facets can be seen, and thus it is with Jesus Christ, the Lord of the Gospels.

NOTES

1. Bruce R. McConkie, *Doctrinal New Testament Commentary*, 3 vols. (Salt Lake City: Bookcraft, 1987), 1:69.

2. For a general treatment of the place of women in Jesus' day, see Joachim Jeremias, *Jerusalem in the Time of Jesus* (Philadelphia: Fortress Press, 1969), 359–76. More specifically, women were essentially to be invisible in public (M. Ab. i.5) and exempt from study of the Torah (Jeremias, *Jerusalem in the Time of Jesus*, 373). According to R. Eliezer (c. AD 90), women were not to be given a knowledge of the Torah, stating, "If any man gives his daughter a knowledge of the Law it is as though he taught her lechery" (M. Sot. iii.4). Jeremias makes the summary statement, "We have therefore the impression that Judaism in Jesus' time also had a very low opinion of women, which is usual in the Orient where she is chiefly valued for her fecundity, kept as far as possible shut away from the outer world, submissive to the power of her father or her husband, and where she is inferior to men from a religious point of view" (375). Citations of the Mishnah are from Herbert Danby, *The Mishnah* (London: Oxford University Press, 1967).

3. Latter-day Saints should understand this discussion well. Four accounts of Joseph Smith's first vision exist, but they differ in their content, mainly because Joseph related different aspects of the vision to different people dependent upon their ability to understand.

4. Vincent Taylor, *The Gospel According to St. Mark*, 2d ed. (New York: St. Martin's Press, 1966), 1–2. Taylor here recounts the tradition received from Papias, bishop of Hierapolis (c. AD 140) that Mark recorded what he had learned from Peter, although not completely in order.

5. Joseph A. Fitzmyer, *The Gospel According to Luke (I–IX)* (Garden City, NY: Doubleday, 1983), 14–18; E. Earle Ellis, ed., *The Gospel of Luke* (London: Thomas Nelson, 1966), 4–9. McConkie, *Doctrinal New Testament Commentary*, 1:69–70.

6. G. B. Caird, *Saint Luke* (Philadelphia: The Westminster Press, 1963), 13–14.

7. As Fitzmyer points out in *Gospel According to Luke,* 53–57, the exact place of composition cannot be determined.

8. In Colossians 4:10–11 Paul lists Aristarchus, Mark, and Jesus called Justus as sending greetings to the Colossians. He then says, "These are the only men *of the circumcision* among my fellow workers for the kingdom of God, and they have been a comfort to me" (RSV). Next, he lists those *not of the circumcision* who also send greetings; that is, Epaphras, *Luke,* and Demas. Clearly, Luke must be a Gentile, if in fact this Luke is the author of the Gospel of Luke.

9. Fitzmyer, *Gospel According to Luke,* 47–51.

10. Robert A. Spivey and D. Moody Smith Jr., *Anatomy of the New Testament: A Guide to Its Structure and Meaning,* 2d ed. (New York: Macmillan, 1974), 99.

11. Spivey and Smith, *Anatomy of the New Testament,* 88.

12. Spivey and Smith, *Anatomy of the New Testament,* 91–92.

13. Taylor, *Gospel According to St. Mark,* 123; see also Spivey and Smith, *Anatomy of the New Testament,* 101.

14. Taylor, *Gospel According to St. Mark,* 124–25; see also Edward J. Mally, "The Gospel According to Mark," *Jerome Biblical Commentary,* 2 vols. (Englewood Cliffs, NJ: Prentice-Hall, 1968), 2:22.

15. Spivey and Smith, *Anatomy of the New Testament,* 98.

16. McConkie, *Doctrinal New Testament Commentary,* 1:391.

17. F. V. Filson, "Peter," *The Interpreter's Dictionary of the Bible,* 4 vols. (Nashville: Abingdon Press, 1962), 3:755. Eusebius quotes Origen on this point (Euseb. Hist. 3.1.2).

18. Richard Lloyd Anderson, *Understanding Paul* (Salt Lake City: Deseret Book, 1983), 362. The tradition is recorded in Tertullian, *Scorpiace* 15 (Ante-Nicene Fathers).

19. McConkie, *Doctrinal New Testament Commentary,* 1:69–70. It should be noted here that Luke could not have interviewed all persons who were eyewitnesses. He had to depend for some of his information on persons who conveyed accurately the earlier traditions, that is, "the ministers of the word."

20. Spivey and Smith, *Anatomy of the New Testament,* 155.

21. Spivey and Smith, *Anatomy of the New Testament,* 167.

22. Spivey and Smith, *Anatomy of the New Testament,* 175.

23. The word *synoptic* basically means to see from a similar viewpoint. As one reads Matthew, Mark, and Luke the portrait of Jesus has many similarities, hence the name "synoptic."

24. Spivey and Smith, *Anatomy of the New Testament,* 167.

25. Carroll Stuhlmueller, "The Gospel According to Luke," *Jerome Biblical Commentary,* 2 vols. (Englewood Cliffs, NJ: Prentice-Hall, 1968), 2:117.

26. G. W. H. Lampe, "Luke," *Peake's Commentary on the Bible* (London: Thomas Nelson, 1962), 820.

27. Stuhlmueller, "The Gospel According to Luke," 2:117.

28. McConkie, *Doctrinal New Testament Commentary,* 1:97; Ellis, *Gospel of Luke,* 19.

29. Stuhlmueller, "The Gospel According to Luke," 2:117.

30. Spivey and Smith, *Anatomy of the New Testament,* 163.

31. Caird, *Saint Luke,* 134. John Martin Creed, *The Gospel According to St. Luke* (New York: St. Martin's Press, 1969), lxxiii.

32. Caird, *Saint Luke,* 36.

33. Joseph Smith, *Teachings of the Prophet Joseph Smith,* comp. Joseph Fielding Smith (Salt Lake City: Deseret Book, 1976), 188.

34. Fitzmyer, *Gospel According to Luke,* 228–30.

35. Fitzmyer, *Gospel According to Luke,* 231. To Latter-day Saints, Fitzmyer's comment on the relation between the Holy Ghost and the Twelve is of interest. Fitzmyer is Catholic. "Moreover, it becomes plain in Acts that the Spirit is given only when the Twelve are present or a member or delegate of the Twelve is on community. The reconstitution of the Twelve (1:15–26) is the necessary preparation for the outpouring of the Spirit (2:1–4). This also explains why, though Philip (not one of the Twelve, but one of the Seven appointed to serve tables [6:2–6]) evangelizes Samaria and baptizes there (8:5–13), Peter and John have to be sent before the people in Samaria receive the Spirit (8:17). Similarly, it is only when Paul, indirectly a delegate of the Twelve (see 11:22, 25–26; 13:2–4), arrives in Ephesus that 'some disciples' (i.e. neophyte Christians) are baptized in the name of the Lord Jesus and receive the Spirit through the laying on of Paul's hands (19:1–6)."

CHAPTER NINE

SPECIAL WITNESSES OF THE BIRTH OF CHRIST

JOSEPH FIELDING McCONKIE

Two events within holy writ exceed all others in importance—Christ's birth and His Resurrection. If it could be legitimately shown that the testimony of either was suspect, the very foundations of Christianity would be cracked. Of necessity, the Nativity story must establish the divine sonship of Christ, while the Easter story must establish His victory over death and the actuality of His Resurrection. The testimony of these two stories must stand unimpeached if the world is to be held responsible to accept Jesus of Nazareth as the promised Messiah, the Son of God, our Savior and Redeemer.

This chapter will confine itself to a brief review of the Nativity story. Attention will center on the testimony of those who in the providence of heaven were chosen to be the special witnesses of the birth of God's Son. We find within the New Testament account of Christ's birth the testimony of twelve witnesses. Each will be briefly examined. Of the four Gospel writers, only Matthew and Luke tell the story. Would that they all had, but two are sufficient to comply with the law of witnesses. Of the twelve witnesses within our two Gospel accounts, we have the testimony of heaven and earth, of man and of woman, of the wicked and of the pure, of the youthful and the aged, of the humble within society and of those who would command audience with kings. Indeed, as we shall see, our story is of all stories most perfect.

Joseph Fielding McConkie is a professor of ancient scripture at Brigham Young University.

Twelve Witnesses of Christ's Birth

Gabriel. Properly, our first New Testament witness of the birth of Christ is a messenger from the presence of God. Appropriately, he makes his initial appearance in the temple to a faithful priest of the Aaronic order, one who is performing the ritual function in behalf of his nation of burning incense on the altar within the holy place. In the performance of this duty, Zacharias represented the combined faith of Israel. His prayer was their prayer, and that prayer was for an everlasting deliverance from all their enemies at the hands of their promised Messiah. The ascending flames of incense symbolized the ascension of that united prayer. As Zacharias prayed within the holy place, so his fellow priests and all within the walls of the temple united their amens to his appeal.[1]

In response to Israel's prayer, an "angel of the Lord" appeared before Zacharias. He stood "on the right side of the altar of incense" and identified himself as Gabriel, one who stood "in the presence of God" (Luke 1:11, 19). By modern revelation we know Gabriel to be Noah, he who "stands next in authority to Adam in the Priesthood"[2] and holds the keys of "the restoration of all things." The keys held by Gabriel make of him an Elias to prepare the way before the Lord (see D&C 27:6–7). The name Gabriel, by which Noah performs his angelic duties, means "man of God," though it has been interpreted as "God is my champion," or "God has shown himself valiant."[3]

Gabriel is mentioned twice in the Old Testament; both instances are appearances to Daniel. The first was to interpret Daniel's vision of the ram and the he-goat, and the second was while Daniel prayed, confessing his sins and those of his people. In the second instance, Gabriel revealed that after seventy weeks (a symbol for an unknown period of time), Israel and Jerusalem would be restored and an atonement made for their sins. Gabriel promised that an everlasting righteousness would be accomplished in their behalf (see Daniel 8, 9).

Six months after his visit to Zacharias, Gabriel also visited Mary to announce to the beautiful virgin girl of Nazareth that she was to become the mother of God's Son (see Luke 1:26, 32). Thus the pattern of Gabriel's visits appears to be that of "fellow-servant" of the Saints, bearing messages of comfort and glad tidings.

In both Jewish and Christian traditions, Gabriel is spoken of as an archangel.[4] The Ascension of Isaiah announces "Gabriel, the angel of God, and Michael, chief of holy angels," as the two angels who were to open the sepulcher of Christ.[5] Jewish theology accords Gabriel a place second only to that of Michael, as do the Latter-day Saints.[6] We, of course, know Michael to be Adam (see D&C 27:11).

As to Luke's account of Gabriel's appearance and prophecy to Zacharias, we are compelled to say the story is perfect. How more properly could the birth of the Son of God be announced than by a heavenly Elias, one from the presence of God Himself? One who comes first to consecrate the birth of the earthly Elias who will announce the Messiah to the chosen nation. To whom ought our heavenly emissary appear? Why, to a priest, of course, for the sacerdotal office itself was a prophecy that the Son of God would yet come. What of the place? Jerusalem must be our answer. The holy city from which the word of the Lord was to go forth. Not Hebron, not the hill country of Judea where Zacharias lived. Where within the city? The answer is obvious to all: the temple, the place where God is to be sought. Most specifically, where within the temple? The holy place at the altar of incense, the symbolic place of the ascending prayers of Israel. At what time of day should this heaven-sent announcement come? At the solemn hour of public prayer, that time designated for those of faith to plead with the heavens that their Messiah be sent. And finally, what confirming sign? The striking of Zacharias dumb. What better symbol of the day when every tongue of disbelief shall be silenced?

Zacharias. Who, then, was this Zacharias to whom Gabriel appeared? He was a descendant of Abia (Hebrew, Abijah). His name meant "remembered of Jehovah."[7] He was married to a woman named Elisabeth, whose fathers, like those of Zacharias, had also been priests (see Luke 1:5). Her name was that of Aaron's wife, of whom she was a descendant (see Exodus 6:23). It means "God is my oath," or "consecrated to God."[8] Thus this noble couple, "consecrated to God" long before their births, were, in the Nativity story, to be "remembered of Jehovah," as the promise was granted to them that they at long last should become the parents of a child—a child destined to be the earthly forerunner of the Messiah. Of the parents of John the Baptist, we read, "They were both righteous before God, walking in all the commandments and ordinances of the Lord blameless" (Luke 1:6). Zacharias and Elisabeth honored the law of their fathers not only in letter but in spirit. Their righteousness entitled them to God's favor. Zacharias, who held that priesthood which entitled him to receive the ministering of angels, was worthy of, and received, that sacred privilege.

Elisabeth. As we read of John, that he would be "filled with the Holy

Ghost, even from his mother's womb," it tells us something of the purity of the temple in which his body was housed (Luke 1:15). Indeed, Elisabeth was a prophetess in her own right. None could tell the story more beautifully than Luke.

> When Elisabeth heard the salutation of Mary, the babe leaped in her womb; and Elisabeth was filled with the Holy Ghost:
>
> And she spake out with a loud voice, and said, Blessed art thou among women, and blessed is the fruit of thy womb.
>
> And whence is this to me, that the mother of my Lord should come to me?
>
> For, lo, as soon as the voice of the salutation sounded in mine ears, the babe leaped in my womb for joy.
>
> And blessed is she that believed: for there shall be a performance of those things which were told her from the Lord. (Luke 1:41–45)

John the Baptist. What a marvelous scene it must have been—John, yet within his mother's womb, filled with the Holy Ghost and leaping for joy in an unspoken testimony of the divine sonship of the unborn child that Mary carried; Elisabeth greeting her cousin Mary in the spirit of prophecy and Mary responding by that same spirit. Again we are compelled to say, how perfect! The testimony of two women: the aged Elisabeth and the youthful Mary; each bearing a child conceived under miraculous circumstances, rejoicing together.

As Christ was born the rightful heir to David's kingdom, so John was born the rightful heir of the office of Elias that he had been promised by Gabriel. Robert J. Matthews identifies that heirship in this language:

> The things of the law of Moses, especially with regard to the qualifications of the priests and their functions in the offerings of various animal sacrifices, were designed by revelation to prefigure and typify the Messiah and to bear witness of him. Heavy penalties were affixed to the performance of sacred rites and duties without the proper authority. It was, therefore, essential that when the Messiah came in person as the Lamb of God, John, the forerunner and witness of the Lamb, should be of the proper lineage to qualify for the mission. If it was necessary for a priest to be of the lineage of Aaron in order to labor with the sacrificial symbols, which were only prefigures of the Messiah, how much greater the necessity that John, the forerunner

of the Messiah in person, be of the proper priestly lineage and authority.[9]

Mary. There could be no more perfect mortal witness of Christ's divine sonship than His mother, Mary. From Gabriel she received the promise that she would conceive in her womb "the Son of the Highest" (Luke 1:32). Following that marvelous event, she testified, "He that is mighty hath done to me great things; and holy is his name" (Luke 1:49). Nephi gave us the most perfect scriptural account of this sacred event. Our eternal Father, he told us, condescended—that is, He came down from His royal court on high and in union with the beautiful virgin girl of Nazareth fathered a son "after the manner of the flesh" (1 Nephi 11:18). "And it came to pass," Nephi wrote, "that I beheld that . . . after she had been carried away in the Spirit for the space of a time the angel spake unto me, saying: Look! And I looked and beheld the virgin again, bearing a child in her arms. And the angel said unto me: Behold the Lamb of God, yea, even the Son of the Eternal Father!" (1 Nephi 11:19–21). Alma, testifying of the birth of Christ, said, "He shall be born of Mary, at Jerusalem which is the land of our forefathers, she being a virgin, a precious and chosen vessel, who shall be overshadowed and conceive by the power of the Holy Ghost, and bring forth a son, yea, even the Son of God" (Alma 7:10).

Joseph. We have no scriptural record of any words spoken by Joseph, the foster father of Jesus. Despite the lack of words, Joseph's testimony as to Christ's divine sonship is most eloquent. He was, we are told, a "just man," meaning that he lived the law of Moses with exactness and honor. We know that he dreamed dreams and entertained angels. Further, we know that as he was faithful in keeping the law of Moses, so he faithfully heeded each divine direction that was given to him. Surely his unquestioning obedience is evidence of belief. It included taking Mary, who carried another's child, as his wife and knowing "her not till she had brought forth her firstborn son," naming Him Jesus, fleeing by night with Mary and the holy child to Egypt, remaining in Egypt until directed to return, and then living in Galilee rather than in Judea upon their return (see Matthew 1:19–21, 25; 2:13–23). Each action witnessed anew Joseph's conviction that this child was indeed the Hope of Israel, the Son of God.

The Shepherds. On the eve of Christ's birth in the stable at Bethlehem, there were in the fields not far distant shepherds watching over their flocks. The fact that they were in the fields by night gives us some indication of the season of the year in which Christ was born. It was the custom among the Jews to take their sheep to the fields about the time of Passover and bring them home at the coming of the first rains—thus they would be in the fields from about April to October.[10] Of these shepherds, Elder Bruce R. McConkie has suggested:

> These were not ordinary shepherds nor ordinary flocks. The sheep there being herded—nay, not herded, but watched over, cared for with love and devotion—were destined for sacrifice on the great altar in the Lord's House, in similitude of the eternal sacrifice of Him who that wondrous night lay in a stable, perhaps among sheep of lesser destiny. And the shepherds—for whom the veil was rent: surely they were in spiritual stature like Simeon and Anna and Zacharias and Elisabeth and Joseph and the growing group of believing souls who were coming to know, by revelation, that the Lord's Christ was now on earth. As there were many widows in Israel, and only to the one in Zarephath was Elijah sent, so there were many shepherds in Palestine, but only to those who watched over the temple flocks did the herald angel come; only they heard the heavenly choir.[11]

That the testimony of one Apostle does not stand alone relative to the character of these shepherds, I cite that of another, Alma, who announced the principle that angels would declare the glad tidings of the Messiah's birth to "just and holy men" (Alma 13:26).

The special witness that these "just and holy men" bore relative to the birth of Christ was not limited to the night of the Savior's birth but was for each of them a lifetime calling. Their story was to be told to family, friends, and neighbors. It was to be told in the courts of the temple, and from there it was to find itself told among all the nations of the earth.[12] Luke tells us that after the shepherds had seen the "babe lying in a manger," they "made known abroad the saying which was told them concerning this child" (Luke 2:16–17). Such was the commission of the angel who stood before them that holy night declaring "good tidings of great joy," which were to go "to all people" (Luke 2:10).

The Heavenly Choir. When the heavens were opened to the shepherds, they first saw an angel of the Lord—we would suppose Gabriel—saying: "Fear not: for, behold, I bring you good tidings of great joy, which shall be to all people. For unto you is born this day in the city of David a Saviour, which is Christ the Lord" (Luke 2:10–11). Then "suddenly," according to the King James account, "there was with the angel a multitude of the heavenly host praising God, and saying, Glory to God in the highest, and on earth peace, good will toward men" (Luke 2:13–14).

In the telling of the Christmas story, there is an occasional objection to the idea that Christ's birth was heralded to the shepherds by a heavenly choir. This objection is on the grounds that the text of the Bible does not say their message was sung. In response, I first observe that there are responsible Bible translations that report the heavenly host "singing the praises of God";[13] second, it would be contrary to the order of worship in heaven for the host to do other than sing, as a host of scriptural texts attest;[14] and third, we have record of the appearance of heavenly choirs on other occasions of rejoicing.[15] Musical ability ranks among the talents with which one might be born and which one can take with him into the world to come. Elder McConkie frequently preached the doctrine that those with great musical talents are laboring on the other side of the veil to prepare the music and the choir that will attend the return of Christ.

As to the choir that sang to the humble shepherds of Judea, perhaps they had engagements the world over to herald the Savior's birth among the scattered remnants of Israel. "Yea, and the voice of the Lord, by the mouth of angels, doth declare it unto all nations," Alma wrote, "yea, doth declare it, that they may have glad tidings of great joy; yea, and he doth sound these glad tidings among all his people, yea, even to them that are scattered abroad upon the face of the earth; wherefore they have come unto us" (Alma 13:22).

The Christmas hymn "It Came upon the Midnight Clear" is an announcement of the very hour of the appearance of the heavenly choir to the shepherds. This hymn has as its roots a text from the Wisdom of Solomon, a part of the Old Testament Apocrypha. The passage states that the "night in its swift course was now half gone" and refers contextually to the destruction of the firstborn of the Egyptians at the time of the Exodus. This, however, has not prevented Christian writers from seeing it as a reference to the time of Christ's birth (see Wisdom of Solomon 18:14–15).

Simeon. Our attention now turns to Jerusalem and its temple. There an aged man, described by Luke as "just and devout," one who in faith had awaited the coming of the Messiah and who had received the promise of the Lord that he would not die until he had seen the Savior, was moved upon by the Holy Ghost to go to the temple. His is the first testimony within the sacred walls of the temple of which we have record that announced the birth of Christ. Appropriately, he bore the name Simeon, which means "hearing" (see Genesis 29:33). Indeed, God had heard his righteous plea, and now his prayer was to be answered.

Thus Simeon was there to greet parents and child as they entered the temple—Mary for the ritual of cleansing, and Joseph to pay the tax which redeemed the firstborn from priestly service. Simeon took the child in his arms and, praising God, said, "Lord, now lettest thou thy servant depart in peace, according to thy word: for mine eyes have seen thy salvation, which thou hast prepared before the face of the people; a light to lighten the Gentiles and the glory of thy people Israel" (Luke 2:29–32). Simeon's declaration, which came by the spirit of prophecy, reached far beyond the understanding and hope of those of his nation—for he saw the universal nature of Christ's ministry and attested that He was Savior to Jew and Gentile alike. Had his words fallen upon the ears of a Pharisee, they would have been greeted with shouts of heresy!

> Then Simeon blessed Joseph and Mary and said to Mary: "Behold, this child is set for the fall and rising again of many in Israel: and for a sign which shall be spoken against; (Yea, a sword shall pierce through thy own soul also,) that the thoughts of many hearts may be revealed." Would that we knew all else that he spoke, including the words of blessing pronounced upon the couple in whose custody the Child was placed. Always—as we shall see throughout this whole work—there was more uttered orally to those who then lived, usually far more, than was recorded and preserved for those who should thereafter hear the accounts. At least we know that Simeon foresaw that Jesus and his message would divide the house of Israel; that men would rise or fall as they accepted or rejected his words; that he was a sign or standard around which the righteous would rally; and that Mary, who now had joy in the growing life of the infant Son, would soon be pierced with the sword of sorrow as she saw him during his waning hours on the cross of Calvary.[16]

Anna. In the providence of God, the marvelous testimony of Simeon was not to stand alone. Anna, an aged widow, a devout and saintly woman who worshiped constantly in the temple with fasting and prayer both day and night, now approached the holy family. As Simeon was a prophet, so she was a prophetess, and her voice now joined his as a special witness of the birth of the Christ. Anna, whose name means "full of grace,"[17] bore testimony to all in Jerusalem who "looked for redemption" (Luke 2:38). Through the countless hours she had spent within the walls of the temple, she was undoubtedly well known to those of the holy city who also faithfully sought the coming of the Messiah. All such would hear her testimony of His birth (see Luke 2:36–38).

The wise men from the east. There has been more speculation about, and more legends created concerning, the so-called Magi who visited Joseph and Mary in their house in Bethlehem than about almost any other biblical event. There is an air of mystery here that appeals to the speculative mind, and the fictional accounts—as to who they were, whence they came, and the symbolic meaning of what they did—fill volumes.

They are presumed to be kings because of the richness of their gifts; it is said they were Gentiles, showing that all nations bowed before the new-born King; it is thought they were masters of some astrological cult that could divine great happenings from the stars. They are even named, identified, and described; their ages are given and the color of their skin; and one can, or could in times past, at least, even view their skulls, crowned with jewels, in a cathedral in Cologne [Germany]. They are thought to have dealt in magic, to be magicians of a sort, and they have become great heroes of the mystical and unknown.[18]

In the scriptural account, Matthew alone makes reference to the coming of the Wise Men. He simply says, "There came wise men from the east to Jerusalem" (Matthew 2:1). The more terse the text, it seems, the more voluminous the traditions. We do not know their number, we do not know whether they rode camels, we do not even know if they traveled together. Yet if we are to assume that the Lord will continue to follow the pattern we have seen in His choice of each of the others who have been privileged to testify of the birth of the Savior, we can safely say of them that they were devout, just, and holy; that they knew of Christ's birth by the revelation of heaven; and that they were destined to be lifetime witnesses of it. It would follow, then, as night follows day, that they came from a people of faith and would return to that people to testify of that which they had done and seen. All evidence within the story sustains such a conclusion.

This we know: the Wise Men were ignorant of the political situation in Jerusalem. Surely they would not have knowingly endangered the life of Christ by seeking His whereabouts from Herod. No one who knew Herod would have asked such a question of him. We know that they were visionary men, for they were "warned of God in a dream that they should not return to Herod" and that they should depart "into their own country another way" (Matthew 2:13). We also know from the Joseph Smith Translation of the Bible that they came seeking "the Messiah of the Jews" (JST, Matthew 3:2). "The probability is," wrote Elder McConkie, "that they were themselves Jews who lived, as millions of Jews then did, in one of the nations to the East."[19] It is hard to suppose that others would come seeking the Jewish Messiah. Though men of all nations are subject to the Light of Christ, the God of heaven commissions only those within the household of faith to be special witnesses of His Son. Admittedly, an Egyptian pharaoh dreamed dreams relative to the destiny of his nation, yet none but Joseph, the Lord's prophet, could interpret them (see Genesis 41). In like manner, Belshazzar was permitted to see the hand of the Lord as the message of his destruction was given him, yet Daniel alone could interpret it (see Daniel 5).

Who, then, were these Wise Men from the East? We can only assume that they were prophets of the true and living God, that they held the priesthood, that they knew the prophecies of Christ's birth—including prophecies now lost to us—and that they were directed by the light of heaven in their journey.

Herod. Our concluding witness is a most unlikely and reluctant one: a fiend in human body, a man who had drenched himself in the blood of the innocent, a man whose deeds were enough to cause hell itself to shudder—none other than Israel's king, Herod the Great. Herod had made his alliance with the powers of the world; his friends were Augustus, Rome, and expediency. He had massacred priests and nobles; he had decimated the Sanhedrin; he had caused the high priest, his brother-in-law, to be drowned in pretend sport before his eyes; he had ordered the strangulation of his favorite wife, the beautiful Hasmonaean princess Mariamne, though she seems to have been the only person he ever loved. Any who fell victim to his suspicions were murdered, including three sons and numerous other relatives.

Such is the irony of history that the most wicked man "ever to sit on David's throne was its occupant in the very day when he came whose throne it was, and who would in due course reign in righteousness thereon."[20] It was to this man, who personified the wickedness of the world and the corruptions of the earth, that the Wise Men from the East went and bore their testimony that Israel's rightful king and ruler had been born. Such a testimony would not have been heeded had it come from Simeon or Anna or from simple shepherds, but coming as it did from these eastern visitors, whose credentials, whatever they were, established them as men of great wisdom, it was given credence by Herod.

Of a truth, the kingdom of God will never go unopposed in the days of earth's mortality, the period of Satan's power. The question as to whether Herod really believed that Israel's king had been born is of little moment. What is of importance, that which makes the Nativity story complete, is the evidence of the anger and wrath of hell at the birth of God's Son. The glad tidings of heaven have no such effect on the prince of darkness and his murderous wrath. As Satan's chief apostle, with all the cunning of hell, he sought to destroy the Christ child. Thus the decree went forth that "all the children that were in Bethlehem, and in all the coasts thereof, from two years old and under," according to the time that Herod had inquired of the Wise Men, were to be slain (Matthew 2:16).

CONCLUSION

Of the restoration of the gospel in the meridian of time, the Apostle Paul said, "This thing was not done in a corner" (Acts 26:26). As was true of the spreading of the gospel, it was true of its most sacred historical events: the birth and Resurrection of Christ. As to the story of Christ's birth, Alma tells us that it was heralded by angels to those who were "just and holy" among all nations (see Alma 13:22, 26). To those in the Americas, Samuel had prophesied that there would be "great lights in heaven, insomuch that in the night before he cometh there shall be no darkness, insomuch that it shall appear unto man as if it was day. Therefore, there shall be one day and a night and a day, as if it were one day and there were no night" (Helaman 14:3–4). Thus that people were to witness the rising and setting of the sun without the coming of the darkness of night. Further, they were promised that a new star would arise, the likeness of which they had never seen, and that it would be attended by other signs and wonders in the heavens (see Helaman 14:5–6).

In the nation of Christ's birth, the testimony was also to go forth in ever-widening circles. Again our story finds its fulfillment among those who were blameless in keeping the commandments and ordinances of the Lord, those who were "just and devout," those who were filled with the Holy Ghost. There is no evidence that these special witnesses were randomly chosen, but rather that they were called and prepared even before the foundations of the earth were laid. As one evidence of their foreordination, we cite the perfect harmony of their names with the peculiar circumstances that called forth their testimony: Zacharias, the aged priest who obtained the promise of a son and whose name meant "remembered of Jehovah"; Elisabeth, whose name meant "consecrated to God," who was the faithful wife of Zacharias, and who was destined in her advanced years to become the mother of the Elias who would prepare the way before the Christ; Mary, the mother of the Christ child, of whom Simeon prophesied that the sword of sorrow would pierce her soul, whose name meant "she shall weep bitter tears"; Jesus, the son of Mary and the Eternal Father, whose name, which meant "Jehovah saves," was given by the angel; John, his forerunner, whose name was also announced by Gabriel, its meaning being "Jehovah is gracious"; Simeon, the aged prophet who had been promised that he would not taste of death until he had seen the Savior, whose name meant "hearing"; and Anna, the widowed prophetess whose name meant "full of grace," who would testify to the faithful of Jerusalem of the salvation that was theirs through Christ.

As the story unfolds, every appropriate element appears in its proper place, which is all the more remarkable because of its coming from two writers, each telling different parts of the story. Properly, it begins with an angelic announcement within the holy place of the temple to a priest whose prayers have ascended to heaven in behalf of his nation imploring the very event. With equal propriety, it ends with the announcement of Herod's satanic designs upon the life of the Christ child. Within the story, we see the heavens opened to priest and layman, to man and woman, to old and young, to the mighty and the humble, and we see each called to be a lifelong witness of the most beautiful of stories ever told.

For us of latter days, the Nativity story is more than a perfect witness of the birth of the Savior. In it we find the pattern by which the knowledge of God is to be restored and go forth once again among all the nations of the earth (see Joseph Smith–Matthew 1:31). How will it go forth? By special witnesses, witnesses called and prepared in the councils of heaven. Who will they be? The old and the young, women and men, the learned and the unlearned, but in it all they will be those who walk "in all the commandments and ordinances of the Lord blameless" (Luke 1:6), those who dream dreams, entertain angels, and are filled with the Holy Ghost. So it has ever been; so it must ever be.

NOTES

1. On this matter, Elder Bruce R. McConkie has written: "What prayers did Zacharias make on this occasion? Certainly not, as so many have assumed, prayers that Elisabeth should bear a son, though such in days past had been the subject of the priest's faith-filled importunings. This was not the occasion for private, but for public prayers. He was acting for and in behalf of all Israel, not for himself and Elisabeth alone. And Israel's prayer was for redemption, for deliverance from the gentile yoke, for the coming of their Messiah, for freedom from sin. The prayers of the one who burned the incense were the prelude to the sacrificial offering itself, which was made to bring the people in tune with the Infinite, through the forgiveness of sins and the cleansing of their lives. 'And the whole multitude of the people were praying without at the time of incense'— all praying, with one heart and one mind, the same things that were being expressed formally, and officially, by the one whose lot it was to sprinkle the incense in the Holy Place. The scene was thus set for the miraculous event that was to be" (*The Mortal Messiah: From Bethlehem to Calvary*, 4 vols. [Salt Lake City: Deseret Book, 1979], 1:307–8).

2. Joseph Smith, *Teachings of the Prophet Joseph Smith*, comp. Joseph Fielding Smith (Salt Lake City: Deseret Book, 1976), 157.

3. *The Interpreter's Bible*, 12 vols. (New York: Abingdon Press, 1965), 6:487.

4. William Smith, *Dictionary of the Bible*, 4 vols. (New York: Hurd and Houghton, 1868), 1:848.

5. L. LaMar Adams, *The Living Message of Isaiah* (Salt Lake City: Deseret Book, 1981), 110.

6. Jan Comay and Ronald Broanrigg, *Who's Who in the Bible*, 2 vols. (New York: Bonanza Books, 1980), 2:116.

7. Joseph Fielding McConkie, *Gospel Symbolism* (Salt Lake City: Bookcraft, 1985), 189–90.

8. McConkie, *Gospel Symbolism*, 189–90.

9. Robert J. Matthews, *A Burning Light—The Life and Ministry of John the Baptist* (Provo, UT: Brigham Young University Press, 1972), 18.

10. Adam Clark, *Clark's Commentary*, 3 vols. (Nashville: Abingdon, n.d.), 3:370.

11. McConkie, *Mortal Messiah*, 1:347.

12. McConkie, *Mortal Messiah*, 1:348.

13. See, for instance, The New English Translation and The Jerusalem Bible.

14. When the heavens were opened to Lehi, he saw "numberless concourses of angels . . . singing and praising their God" (1 Nephi 1:8). King Benjamin prayed that his spirit might "join the choirs above in singing the praises of a just God" (Mosiah 2:28). Isaiah twice records the Lord's injunction that the heavens herald the redemption in song: "Sing, O ye heavens; for the Lord hath done it; shout, ye lower parts of the earth:

break forth into singing, ye mountains, O forest, and every tree therein: for the Lord hath redeemed Jacob, and glorified him in Israel" (Isaiah 44:23; see also 49:13). Singing is an eternal part of the divine system of worship (see Job 38:7; D&C 25:12; 133:56).

15. Temple dedications would be one such illustration. For other illustrations, see Frederick W. Babbel, *To Him That Believeth* (Salt Lake City: Bookcraft, 1982), 57–58.

16. McConkie, *Mortal Messiah,* 1:354–55.

17. *Webster's Dictionary of First Names* (New York: Galahad Books, 1981), 112.

18. McConkie, *Mortal Messiah,* 1:357.

19. McConkie, *Mortal Messiah,* 1:358.

20. McConkie, *Mortal Messiah,* 1:362.

CHAPTER TEN

WE HAVE FOUND THE MESSIAH

ROBERT J. MATTHEWS

I have selected as a topic a passage from the testimony of John. They are the words of Andrew, Simon Peter's brother. On that day he had talked with Jesus, and he was so excited that the first thing he did was find his brother Peter to tell him about it. He said: "We have *found* the Messias, which is, being interpreted, the Christ" (John 1:41; emphasis added).

Although the passage does not tell in detail of the background and what these men had talked about previously, there is a clue in the way the sentence is worded to show us that finding the Messiah was important to them and must have been something they had talked about on earlier occasions.

To get the full impact of what it meant to them to find the Messiah, we need to look at the extended passage. In order to catch the force of these words, please notice the frequency of such words as *seek, find, come and see,* and *we have found.* I am going to read it from Joseph Smith's translation because it is a richer account. The setting is this: John the Baptist had taught a special delegation of the Jewish leaders that the Messiah was on the earth, among them, but that they had not recognized Him. Beginning with John 1:35, we read:

> Again, the next day after, John stood, and two of his disciples,
> And looking upon Jesus as he walked, he said, Behold the Lamb of God!
> And the two disciples heard him speak, and they followed Jesus.
> Then Jesus turned, and saw them following him, and said unto

Robert J. Matthews is a professor emeritus of ancient scripture at Brigham Young University.

them, What seek ye? They say unto him, Rabbi, (which is to say, being interpreted, Master;) Where dwellest thou?

He said unto them, Come and see. And they came and saw where he dwelt, and abode with him that day; for it was about the tenth hour.

One of the two who heard John, and followed Jesus, was Andrew, Simon Peter's brother.

He first findeth his own brother Simon, and saith unto him, We have found the Messias, which is, being interpreted, the Christ.

And he brought him to Jesus. And when Jesus beheld him, he said, Thou art Simon, the son of Jona, thou shalt be called Cephas, which is, by interpretation, a seer, or a stone. And they were fishermen. And they straightway left all, and followed Jesus.

The day following, Jesus would go forth into Galilee, and findeth Philip, and saith unto him, Follow me.

Now Philip was at Bethsaida, the city of Andrew and Peter.

Philip findeth Nathanael, and saith unto him, We have found him, of whom Moses in the law, and the prophets, did write, Jesus of Nazareth, the son of Joseph. (JST, John 1:35–45)[1]

There is an underlying awareness, almost taken for granted, that all these brethren were cognizant of the things Moses and the prophets had written about the Messiah. They placed a high value on those words of the prophets and considered it of greatest importance to find that Messiah who was so highly spoken of in the scriptures. Notice the joy, the sense of fulfillment, when a person is able to say, "We have found the Messiah."

The discovery by these brethren—Andrew, Simon, Philip, and Nathanael—reminds us of the words of the Lord to Jeremiah: "Then shall ye call upon me, and ye shall go and pray unto me, and I will hearken unto you. And ye shall seek me, and find me, when ye shall search for me with all your heart. And I will be found of you, saith the Lord" (Jeremiah 29:12–14).

This same idea has perhaps become more familiar to many of us through Felix Mendelssohn's oratorio *Elijah*, in which it is beautifully expressed this way: "If with all your heart ye truly seek me, ye shall ever surely find me, thus saith our God."

In the writings of Moses to scattered Israel, we find this promise: "But if from thence thou shalt seek the Lord thy God, thou shalt find him, if thou seek him with all thy heart and with all thy soul" (Deuteronomy

4:29). And Father Abraham, after a marvelous personal manifestation and blessing from the Lord, reflected on his great experience and wrote of it as follows: "Now, after the Lord had withdrawn from speaking to me, and withdrawn his face from me, I said in my heart: Thy servant has sought thee earnestly; now I have found thee; . . . and I will do well to hearken unto thy voice" (Abraham 2:12–13).

Let it be remembered and noted that this Messiah, this Jesus whom the fishermen of Galilee had found in *their* day and in *their* country, was the same being, the same God, whom Moses, Abraham, Elijah, Isaiah, Jeremiah, and many others had sought for and found in their day, whose name was Jehovah. Jesus, the Messiah in the New Testament, is the same being known as Jehovah in the Old Testament.

Searching for the Messiah

The hearts of righteous men and women hunger for more contact with their Savior, and to find Him is manna to the soul. To be in His favor is even more refreshing than drinking cool water in a thirsty land or finding a covering from the sun in time of heat. Knowledge and testimony of Christ are food for the hungry spirit, just as meat and potatoes are food for the hungry body.

Heaven, knowing the proper price to put on all its goods, has so arranged things that one has to seek and search in order to really *find* the Messiah. The Lord has to be searched for and found, discovered, as it were, by each person individually. Information *about* the Savior can be found almost everywhere, but there is a significant difference between knowing the Lord and only knowing *about* Him. We may learn *about* the Savior by reading or listening but must obey His commandments to *know* Him and understand much about Him. The Lord Himself has promised to unveil His face and be made known by His servants, but He has told us that it must be in His "own time," in His "own way," and according to His "own will."

I will read an excerpt from Doctrine and Covenants 88:63–68:

> Draw near unto me and I will draw near unto you; seek me dili-gently and ye shall find me; ask, and ye shall receive; knock, and it shall be opened unto you.
>
> Whatsoever ye ask the Father in my name it shall be given unto you, that is expedient for you;
>
> And if ye ask anything that is not expedient for you, it shall turn unto your condemnation.

Behold, that which you hear is as the voice of one crying in the wilderness—in the wilderness, because you cannot see him—my voice, because my voice is Spirit, my Spirit is truth; truth abideth and hath no end; and if it be in you it shall abound.

And if your eye be single to my glory, your whole bodies shall be filled with light, and there shall be no darkness in you; and that body which is filled with light comprehendeth all things.

Therefore, sanctify yourselves that your minds become single to God, and the days will come that you shall see him; for he will unveil his face unto you, and it shall be in his own time, and in his own way, and according to his own will.

We may think that because we live so long after the mortal life of the Savior what is being talked of in these verses—a personal visit by vision or divine manifestation—is considerably different than seeing Jesus on the roads and byways of Galilee or the streets of Jerusalem. But it is not entirely different. If we had lived at that time, in that place, and had seen Him in the mortal flesh, we would not have known that He was the Messiah or that He was anything more than a man unless the Holy Spirit whispered it to our own spirit. Many saw Him but knew not who He was. John the Baptist knew Him and declared plainly that He was the Messiah, the Son of God, but also explained, "There standeth one among you whom ye know not" (John 1:26). It is only by the testimony of the Spirit that anyone can recognize the difference between the Messiah and any other man. This is one of the functions of the Holy Ghost: to bear witness of the Father and the Son (see Moses 5:9). The scriptures testify of Christ, and the Holy Ghost bears record that those scriptures are true.

The lengthy passage quoted from the first chapter of John showed that two of the disciples of John the Baptist subsequently became Apostles of the Lord Jesus. These two are John, who was later known as John the Beloved or John the Revelator, and Andrew. However, other passages suggest that perhaps most, if not all, of the Twelve were tutored by John the Baptist, and that it was from him that they learned their earliest lessons about the Messiah, who had already come to earth and who actually lived in their neighborhood.

In Acts 1:21–22, we read a statement of Peter at the time of the choosing of Matthias as a new member of the Twelve. Peter says that from among the believers who had "companied with" the Apostles all the time, "beginning from the baptism of John, unto that same day that he [Jesus] was

taken up from us, must one be ordained to be a witness with us of his resurrection." This sounds significantly as if most of the Twelve had been followers of John the Baptist and from him they had learned that Jesus of
Nazareth was the Messiah. John's mission was to be a forerunner to prepare the way for the Savior and to prepare a people to receive Him. What
more effective way than for John to actively tutor and start on their way
those who later became Jesus' chief witnesses! He taught them the right
way to find the Messiah and introduced many of them first to the doctrines of the Lord and then to the Lord in person.

The Young Jesus

Let us now review from the scriptures what it is that people find when
and if they find the Messiah. The shepherds near Bethlehem, being
prompted by the angels of heaven, found the Messiah as a little babe,
"wrapped in swaddling clothes, lying in a manger" (Luke 2:12, see 8–18).
He looked like other babies in outward appearance, but because the shepherds knew who He was they worshiped Him and could hardly wait to tell
others of it.

About forty days later, when Joseph and Mary brought the infant Jesus
to the temple to fulfill the rites of purification according to the laws of
Moses, they met a righteous and devout man whose name was Simeon. To
him it had been revealed by the Holy Ghost that before his death he would
see the Messiah. He recognized the baby Jesus as the Messiah, the "Hope
of Israel," and took Him in his arms and blessed Him. This man was made
happy because by the Holy Spirit he had seen, understood, and found the
Messiah (see Luke 2:25–35).

At that same instant, Anna, a righteous woman of great age, who had
been left a widow more than eighty-four years after only seven years of
marriage, came into the room. She saw the child, knew who He was, and
gave thanks that she had seen the Messiah (see Luke 2:36–38).

The Wise Men, being led by His star—not just a star, or *the* star, but as
the scripture says—*His* star—a special star, found Jesus in a house as a
young child, for it was a year or two since His birth. He no doubt looked
like other children, but the Wise Men, being spiritually endowed and having knowledge, knew He was wonderfully different, and they brought Him
gifts and worshiped Him (see Matthew 2:1–12; JST, Matthew 3:1–12). In
the King James Version, the Wise Men came seeking him that was born to
be king, but from the Joseph Smith Translation we see an additional

dimension and learn that they were seeking not only a *king* who would *rule* but the *Messiah* who would *save*. You see, he who looks for and finds the *Messiah* is wiser even than he who only looks for and finds a king.

Later, when Jesus was twelve, He was taken to the temple in Jerusalem by His parents, according to the requirement of the law of Moses for the Passover observance. When the formalities were over, Joseph and Mary were returning to Galilee and had journeyed about a day from Jerusalem when they discovered that Jesus was not with them. I have often reflected on the fear, the sorrow, the near-panic emotions that must have surged through Joseph and Mary's souls, to have lost track of that son in such a large and crowded city as Jerusalem at the time of Passover.

Such an experience would be almost overwhelming for any of us with our natural children. Mary and Joseph would have had the same pain we would have, but more, for they had lost the very Son of God. That is worse than losing 116 pages of manuscript or almost anything else that could have happened to them. After three days of searching, they found Him. What did they really *find* when they found Him? A normal twelve-year-old boy? They found Him teaching the learned doctors of the scripture. The account given in Luke 2:46 reads as follows in the King James Version: "And . . . after three days they found him in the temple, sitting in the midst of the doctors, both hearing them, and asking them questions." I suppose that it is something to write about any time a twelve-year-old boy will sit for three days and listen to a discussion of the scriptures and even ask questions. However, that is only the lesser part of the story. The Joseph Smith Translation reads as follows: "They found him in the temple, sitting in the midst of the doctors, and they [the doctors] were hearing him, and asking him questions." With this clarification, the next verse then takes on more meaning: "And all that heard him were astonished at his understanding and answers" (v. 47). What did the learned doctors find when they "found" the Messiah in the temple courts? They found a young man who looked like other boys but with wisdom, knowledge, and more understanding of the spiritual things of life and the scriptures than they had been able to acquire through years of study and experience.

How did it happen that Jesus came by such wisdom at so early an age? When He was born, a veil was placed over His mind and His memory, the same as it has been with us, but He had the power of the Spirit, the Holy Ghost. In John 2:24–25, we read that Jesus "knew all things, and needed not that any should testify of man; for he knew what was in man" (JST,

John 2:24–25). In John 3:34, we read that the Father giveth Him the Spirit in unlimited abundance and not "by measure."

The Joseph Smith Translation adds yet another passage that allows us a glimpse of the unusual ability and personality of the Messiah as a youth and a young man. "And it came to pass that Jesus grew up with his brethren, and waxed strong, and waited upon the Lord for the time of his ministry to come. And he served under his father, and he spake not as other men, neither could he be taught; for he needed not that any man should teach him. And after many years, the hour of his ministry drew nigh" (JST, Matthew 3:24–26). We often hear it said that we do not know anything about the Savior's early life, but we can see from these passages that we do know something.

VIEWS OF THE CHRIST

Let us read from the scriptures the words of those who knew Jesus as an adult man and who found Him to be the Messiah. What did they say they found when they found the Messiah? As we have already read, they iden-tified Him as the one of whom Moses and the prophets had written. Many other people, when they saw Him and heard Him, thought He was one of the ancient prophets come back to earth again—perhaps Elijah, Jeremiah, or one of the other prophets (see Matthew 16:14). Herod, upon hearing of His miracles and wonderful works, but having never seen Him, thought He was John the Baptist risen from the dead (see Matthew 14:2).

There is not a single case in the four Gospel records that represents Jesus as impatient, critical, or unkind to people who were repentant, teachable, and willing to change their lives. He forgave transgressions and mingled with publicans and sinners on condition of their repentance. He cast out devils, healed the lame, raised the dead, fed the hungry, opened the eyes of the blind, gave hearing to the deaf, and restored the sick to health if they but had the faith that He could do it. But He was a terror to the workers of iniquity and those who were self-righteous, deceptive, or hypocritical. In dealing with the repentant, He was kind and gentle yet firm: the promised Messiah. To the proud, the haughty, and the arrogant, He was absolutely indomitable and irrepressible and a threat to their craftiness.

A few years ago, I made a list of Jesus' teaching methods as illustrated in the four Gospels and discovered that His methods were adapted to the need and the occasion. The idea for this search was first suggested to me by a former faculty member Glenn Pearson, in his master's thesis, so I am indebted to him for some of this material. I have listed twenty-three methods as follows:

Used simple exposition (Matthew 5; 6; 7; John 7:14–18).
Spoke with forthrightness and authority, not secondhand (Matthew 7:28–29).
Performed miracles (Matthew 12:9–13).
Used irony, almost sarcasm (Matthew 9:10–13; Mark 2:15–17; Luke 5:27–32; 15:1–7).
Used subtlety and wile (John 4:15–19).
Prophesied (Matthew 12:36–42; 24:3–51).
Appealed to Old Testament for precedence (Matthew 12:1–8).
Quoted from the Old Testament (John 10:34; Matthew 19:3–6; 22:31–32).
Taught with parables (Matthew 13).
Used logic (Matthew 12:24–28).
Used object lessons (Matthew 18:10; 22:16–22; Luke 5:4–10).
Asked questions (Matthew 16:13–15; Luke 24–26).
Asked questions of those who asked Him (Luke 10:25–28).
Bargained by means of questions (Matthew 21:23–27).
Used invective (Matthew 11:20–24; 23:1–39).
Used repartee (Matthew 22:15–46).
Posed a problem (Matthew 22:41–46).
Candidly corrected those who were in error (Matthew 22:29).
Used debate and argument (beyond mere discussion) (John 7–8).
Was selective in what He taught to different groups (Matthew 7:6; 10).
Refused to give signs (Matthew 12:38–40).
Changed the subject, thus avoiding the full force of the issue (Matthew 22:30–31).
Sometimes refused to say anything (Luke 23:7–11).

VIEWS OF UNBELIEVERS

But what did the Jewish *rulers* find when they encountered the Messiah? They saw Him as a threat to their way of life. They were amazed at His strength of character and endless wisdom. He had *not* gone through their training and curriculum or their schools, and yet He knew much about the scriptures and about men and many other things. Once, in what appears to be a mixture of surprise and dismay over Jesus' success as a teacher, they marveled and cried out, "How knoweth this man letters, having never learned?" Jesus answered them and said, "My doctrine is not mine, but his that sent me" (John 7:15–16). John records: "And there was much murmuring among the people concerning him: for some said, He is a good man: others said, Nay; but he deceiveth the people" (John 7:12).

Three days before His Crucifixion, Jesus spent the entire day in a vivid confrontation with the Jewish rulers. They found that in defense of truth He was superb. He was righteousness coupled with facts—an unbeatable combination. They learned the truth of Job's expression, "How forcible are right words" (Job 6:25). I will read only a portion of what the record tells us took place on that day. Just one day previously, Jesus had cast the money changers out of the temple. When He came into Jerusalem and to the temple the next morning, the chief priests and the elders approached Him as He was teaching and asked:

> By what authority doest thou these things? and who gave thee this authority?
>
> And Jesus answered and said unto them, I also will ask you one thing, which if ye tell me, I in like wise will tell you by what authority I do these things.
>
> The baptism of John, whence was it? from heaven, or of men? And they reasoned with themselves, saying, If we shall say, From heaven; he will say unto us, Why did ye not then believe him?
>
> But if we shall say, Of men: we fear the people; for all hold John as a prophet.
>
> And they answered Jesus, and said, We cannot tell. And he said unto them, Neither tell I you by what authority I do these things. (Matthew 21:23–27)

Discussion then ensued, and Jesus pointed out to them several flaws in their character, such as greed, perfidy, spiritual blindness, and such everyday things. Then the Pharisees held a meeting to see how they might entangle Him in His talk (see Matthew 22:15). "And they sent out unto him their disciples with the Herodians, saying, Master, we know that thou art true, and teachest the way of God in truth, neither carest thou for any man; for thou regardest not the person of men."

This was to be a trap. No matter which way Jesus answered, they could challenge Him about it and seek to discredit Him.

> Tell us therefore, What thinkest thou? Is it lawful to give tribute to Caesar, or not?

But Jesus perceived their wickedness, and said, Why tempt ye me, ye hypocrites?

Shew me the tribute money. And they brought unto him a penny.

And he saith unto them, Whose is this image and superscription?

They say unto him, Caesar's. Then saith he unto them, Render therefore unto Caesar the things which are Caesar's; and unto God the things that are God's.

When they had heard these words, they marvelled, and left him, and went on their way. (Matthew 22:16–22)

On the very same day the Sadducees came to Him, also to refute Him and if possible to embarrass and discredit Him publicly. They had a "hard question" to ask Him about marriage and about the Resurrection. It is important to note that the Sadducees did not believe there is any resurrection from the dead. We need to know that so we can understand that this question is not asked in good faith or with a desire to seek the truth but is in reality the setting of another trap.

The same day came to him the Sadducees, which say that there is no resurrection, and asked him,

Saying, Master, Moses said, If a man die, having no children, his brother shall marry his wife, and raise up seed unto his brother.

Now there were with us seven brethren: and the first, when he had married a wife, deceased, and, having no issue, left his wife unto his brother:

Likewise the second also, and the third, unto the seventh.

And last of all the woman died also.

Therefore in the resurrection whose wife shall she be of the seven? for they all had her.

Jesus answered and said unto them, Ye do err, not knowing the scriptures, nor the power of God.

For in the resurrection they neither marry, nor are given in marriage, but are as the angels of God in heaven.

But as touching the resurrection of the dead, have ye not read that which was spoken unto you by God, saying,

I am the God of Abraham, and the God of Isaac, and the God of Jacob? God is not the God of the dead, but of the living.

And when the multitude heard this, they were astonished at his doctrine. (Matthew 22:23–33)

This passage is usually the one that members of other faiths use to refute doctrine of eternal marriage because of the words "for in the resurrection they neither marry nor are given in marriage." A *casual* reading might lead a person to think that is a denial or a rejection by the Savior of the doctrine of eternal marriage. But a *careful* reading will show that this is one of the strongest examples in the Bible showing that Jesus plainly taught the doctrine of eternal marriage.

I had an experience that will illustrate this point. When I was a seminary teacher, playful high school students would sometimes put whisky bottles, cigarette cartons, and the like on my front porch during the night. Sometimes they put cigarettes under the windshield wipers on my car. Why did those students do those particular things? They thought it to be a clever reaction to my teaching about the Word of Wisdom in seminary class. They did not put milk cartons or soft-drink bottles—only liquor and tobacco items.

Once as an experiment, I said in class that some people feel that the eating of chocolate is contrary to the Word of Wisdom. And do you know what was under the windshield wipers the next day? A chocolate candy bar. I was not astute enough at the time, but I have often thought since that I should have told them that the love of money was the root of evil.

Now return to Jesus and the Sadducees. Since the Sadducees did not believe in resurrection anyway, and since this was a hostile audience and encounter, it is easy to see that these clever men were trying to give the Messiah a hard question about marriage and resurrection that they supposed He could not answer. Why do it on the subject of marriage in the resurrected state unless it was widely known that He had been teaching such a doctrine? They were reacting to what He had said. His answer simply was that this woman and her seven husbands had not been married by the proper power and authority, and hence there was no problem at all, since none of her marriages would be eternal. I say this passage, when read in its context, is one of the strongest evidences that Jesus taught both eternal marriage and resurrection from the dead and that everyone there knew it, but the Sadducees did not like it.

The chapter ends with one more encounter between Jesus and the Pharisees, and after they were properly rebuffed for their deliberate neglect and lack of understanding, the scripture says, "And no man was able to answer him a word, neither durst any man from that day forth ask him any more questions" (Matthew 22:46).

FINDING HIM TODAY

Now, in closing, let us ask, what do men and women find when they discover the true Messiah? Finding the Messiah is the greatest of all discoveries. If we were to discuss the most important thing about Jesus the Messiah, what would it be? If we were to go home today to our families and say, "We have found the Messiah!" what would we say about Him? What is the most important thing about Him that we could tell another person? Would it be His height or weight, the color of His hair, the style of His clothes, the tone of His voice? Everything about Jesus is important, and any true detail or concept would be worth knowing, but what would be the single most important thing to find out about Him? I could answer that with my own opinion, but let us take a clue from what the scriptures say about Him.

I think it can be summarized in John 3:16, "For God so loved the world, that he gave his only begotten Son, that whosoever believeth in him should not perish, but have everlasting life." While that is the central concept, it takes a considerable amount of study to know what that one verse means. I'll tell you what I have discovered about the Messiah that I have learned from the scriptures and the whisperings of the Holy Ghost. The greatest message about Jesus Christ is that He has conquered death—both spiritual and physical death. He is literally the light and the life of the world (see D&C 10:70).

We are given a plain discussion of the redeeming role of the Savior in the following scriptures:

From Paul: "For as in Adam all die, even so in Christ shall all be made alive" (1 Corinthians 15:22).

From Jacob:

> For it behooveth the great Creator that he suffereth himself to become subject unto man in the flesh, and die for all men, that all men might become subject unto him.
>
> For as death hath passed upon all men, to fulfill the merciful plan of the great Creator, there must needs be a power of resurrection, and the resurrection must needs come unto man by reason of the fall; and the fall came by reason of transgression; and because man became fallen they were cut off from the presence of the Lord.
>
> Wherefore, it must needs be an infinite atonement—save it should be an infinite atonement this corruption could not put on

incorruption. Wherefore, the first judgment which came upon man must needs have remained to an endless duration. And if so, this flesh must have laid down to rot and to crumble to its mother earth, to rise no more.

O the wisdom of God, his mercy and grace! For behold, if the flesh should rise no more our spirits must become subject to that angel who fell from before the presence of the Eternal God, and became the devil, to rise no more. And our spirits must have become like unto him, and we become devils, angels to a devil, to be shut out from the presence of our God, and to remain with the father of lies, in misery, like unto himself. (2 Nephi 9:5–9)

And from Nephi:

Behold, my soul delighteth in proving unto my people the truth of the coming of Christ; for, for this end hath the law of Moses been given; and all things which have been given of God from the beginning of the world, unto man, are the typifying of him.

And also my soul delighteth in the covenants of the Lord which he hath made to our fathers; yea, my soul delighteth in his grace, and in his justice, and power, and mercy in the great and eternal plan of deliverance from death.

And my soul delighteth in proving unto my people that save Christ should come all men must perish. (2 Nephi 11:4–6)

Do we understand that Jesus made payment with His blood in order for mercy to satisfy justice? No other person, no human being, could redeem us; the redemption could be made only by a God, as explained by Amulek:

Behold, I say unto you, that I do know that Christ shall come among the children of men, to take upon him the transgressions of his people, and that he shall atone for the sins of the world; for the Lord God hath spoken it.

For it is expedient that an atonement should be made; for according to the great plan of the Eternal God there must be an atonement made, or else all mankind must unavoidably perish; yea, all are hardened; yea, all are fallen and are lost, and must perish except it be through the atonement which it is expedient should be made.

For it is expedient that there should be a great and last sacrifice; yea, not a sacrifice of man, neither of beast, neither of any manner of fowl; for it shall not be a human sacrifice; but it must be an infinite and eternal sacrifice.

Now there is not any man that can sacrifice his own blood which will atone for the sins of another.

Therefore there can be nothing which is short of an infinite atonement which will suffice for the sins of the world.

Therefore, it is expedient that there should be a great and last sacrifice.

And that great and last sacrifice will be the Son of God, yea, infinite and eternal. (Alma 34:8–14)

What does this mean to us? It means that our association with the Messiah is not optional or casual. It is critical.

By the Fall of Adam, all mankind has suffered two deaths—a spiritual alienation from God and a physical death. We have all suffered the first—the alienation. We will yet, with no exceptions, suffer the physical death. We are thus dominated by death because of the fall of Adam. It is absolutely necessary that we understand that Jesus, in order to be the Messiah, had to be divine, that He had to be the literal, biological Son of God, and thus was not dominated by death and sin as is all the rest of humanity. Had He not been the Only Begotten, He could not have been able or worthy to pay the debt of the Fall of Adam and of our own individual sins. The infinite Atonement required the life and the death and the sacrifice of a God, not of a man.

The plan of salvation is equally real. Adam was a living person in time and in space. The Fall is so real that, if we knew the details, we could place on a calendar the time when he fell. Also, if we knew the details, we could mark on a map the location where he ate the forbidden fruit.

In the very same manner, the Atonement of Jesus Christ is so vital and so necessary in time and in space, that if we had the facts, we could place on a calendar the date of His birth, the date of His suffering in the Garden of Gethsemane, the date of His death, and the date of His Resurrection. In like manner we could mark on a map the place of His birth, suffering, death, and Resurrection. These are all events in time and geography. This is the Messiah I have found, and I believe this to be the greatest message in the world. It is the message of John 3:16 in its expanded form.

When that morning comes that any of us stands in perfection of body and spirit, resurrected, cleansed, and with eternal life in the presence of

God, we will then know with full meaning what we perceive only in part today when we say, "I have found the Messiah!"

NOTE

1. See Thomas A. Wayment, ed., *The Complete Joseph Smith Translation of the New Testament: A Side-by-Side Comparison with the King James Version* (Salt Lake City: Deseret Book, 2005).

CHAPTER ELEVEN

JESUS' USE OF THE PSALMS IN MATTHEW

THOMAS A. WAYMENT

One of the most remarkable aspects of Jesus' earthly ministry was His ability to teach the gospel in a way that caused even His most learned followers to reevaluate their thinking. He often taught principles and concepts that were new and exciting and that were difficult to understand and accept without the guidance of the Holy Spirit. In a culture where the Old Testament was accepted as the ultimate source of gospel learning, it is not surprising to find the Master Teacher drawing broadly on this important body of scripture, especially the book of Psalms, to facilitate His message and give credence to His teachings (see John 5:39). By looking at the ways Jesus incorporated the Psalter, or book of Psalms, into His teachings, we can gain a more profound understanding of how Jesus taught the gospel, as well as how He chose to explain His earthly ministry to the Jews.

The Sermon on the Mount contains nine relatively short sayings known as beatitudes.[1] This major discourse contains the Savior's teachings on the higher law of salvation. It has also been suggested that this sermon was a type of missionary preparation for the disciples.[2] The Beatitudes form an introduction to the body of the sermon, and they maintain a certain organizational consistency that helps to reveal their original meaning and function. In our biblical account of the Sermon on the Mount, there is some confusion regarding the Savior's audience. The event, as recorded by Matthew, indicates that the Savior went to the mountain to remove Himself from the multitude (see Matthew 5:1), yet at the end of the

Thomas A. Wayment is an associate professor of ancient scripture at Brigham Young University.

sermon the multitude is said to be astonished at what the Savior has taught (see Matthew 7:28). This confusion is eliminated, however, when we consider the account of the Savior's sermon given at the temple in Bountiful in the Book of Mormon or when we look at the changes made by the Prophet Joseph Smith in his inspired version of the biblical account. The Book of Mormon makes it clear that the sermon to the Nephites was delivered to a believing multitude, whereas some of the Savior's teachings were directed specifically to the Twelve (see 3 Nephi 12:1; 13:25). We may assume that the sermon delivered in the Holy Land had an audience similar to that in the Nephite setting. The Joseph Smith Translation indicates that parts of the Sermon on the Mount were directed to the disciples, thus helping to confirm our comparison (see JST, Matthew 6:1).[3]

As an introduction to the Sermon on the Mount, the Beatitudes summarize some of its more prevalent themes. The eight beatitudes represent an independent unit framed by the first beatitude, which promises "the kingdom of heaven" to the poor (Matthew 5:3), and the eighth beatitude, which repeats the promise of the "kingdom of heaven" (Matthew 5:10). The first seven beatitudes (vv. 3–10) are also composed in the third person plural (they), while the eighth and final beatitude (vv. 11–12), with its warning that persecutions may follow, is written in the second person plural (you). The last beatitude also shifts from the indicative "blessed are they" to the imperative "rejoice, and be exceedingly glad" (Matthew 5:11–12). The shift from the indicative to the imperative indicates a shift of emphasis and creates a distinction between the first eight beatitudes and the final beatitude. The "you" of Matthew 5:11 makes the connection explicit between the first seven beatitudes and the eighth one. The newly called disciples should begin to consider that persecution may follow those who seek to obey the commandments and purify their lives. While it may have been comforting to hear in the third person the expectations the Savior has for His people, the disciples have this expectation placed directly on their shoulders when the Savior turns to them and warns them of the perils that will follow the righteous.[4] Jesus strengthens this idea by telling His disciples to expect the same treatment and blessings that the prophets of old received. The Savior's profound reasoning on this issue is persuasive. How could these disciples reject the Savior's call to be like one of the prophets of old, even if it meant enduring suffering and persecution?

A close look at the first three beatitudes and the way the Savior uses them to teach His disciples the higher law demonstrates the characteristics that Jesus expected His disciples to emulate. It also provides an example of the Savior's ability to present new ideas, using the Old Testament as His text. The first three beatitudes, which are structured according to the pattern of Isaiah 61:1–3, incorporate a passage from Psalm 37:11.[5] Isaiah 61 provides the structure and some terminology for Matthew 5:3–5. Isaiah 61 promises good tidings to the poor (KJV, "meek") and comfort to those who mourn. The two passages, Matthew 5:3–5 and Isaiah 61:1–2, share a number of verbal similarities. The following will help to demonstrate the verbal relationship between Isaiah 61 and Matthew 5. Matthew 5:3: "Blessed are the poor in spirit [*ptochoi*]"; Isaiah 61:1: "The Lord hath anointed me to preach good tidings unto the poor [*ptochois;* KJV reads "meek"]"; Matthew 5:4: "Blessed are they that mourn [*penthountes*]: for they shall be comforted [*paraklethesonthai*]"; Isaiah 61:2: "To comfort [*parakalesai*] all that mourn [*penthountas*]"; Matthew 5:5: "Blessed are the meek: for they shall inherit the earth [*klerovomesousin ten gen*]"; Isaiah 61:7: "Therefore in their land they shall possess [*kleponomesousin ten gen*]; a double portion" [KJV reads "the double"]; Matthew 5:6: "Blessed are they which do hunger and thirst after righteousness [*dikaiosunen*]"; Isaiah 61:3, 8, 11 each use the term for righteousness (*dikaiosunes*); Matthew 5:8: "Blessed are the pure in heart [*katharoi te kardia*]"; Isaiah 61:1: "To bind up the brokenhearted [*suntetpimmenos te kardia*]."

One of the reasons the Savior referred to Isaiah 61 may be found in the opening verses of that chapter. Isaiah's prophecy lends authority to the Savior's message, and it forms a remarkable parallel to the power and authority the Savior's teachings would have. Isaiah may well have had the Savior in mind when he said, "The Spirit of the Lord God is upon me; because the Lord hath anointed me to preach good tidings" (Isaiah 61:1).[6] In addition, Isaiah 61 is quoted numerous times in the New Testament with reference to Jesus.[7] Jesus Himself, when given a portion of Isaiah 61 to read in the synagogue, interpreted it as a reference to His own ministry. In his Gospel, Luke reported that this reading and interpretation caused such excitement and hostility that some of Jesus' listeners attempted to take His life. They couldn't abide His declaration that this important messianic prophecy pointed to His own ministry—that He was its literal fulfillment.[8] This passage, Isaiah 61:1–3, was interpreted by the rabbis and others as a reference to the end of the world and the redemption associated with the coming of the Messiah at that time.[9] The Qumran sectarians, the authors and compilers of the Dead Sea Scrolls, likewise understood this passage messianically and eschatologically, or as a reference to the time when the Messiah would come to redeem His people at the end of the world.[10] It is significant that the Savior used this passage of scripture, one that many Jews of His day believed had reference to the ministry of the Messiah, both at the beginning of His public ministry and as the prelude to one of the greatest sermons ever given.

In using Isaiah 61 as a preface to the Sermon on the Mount, Jesus drew on an image that was highly familiar to those who were looking for the Messiah. Jesus often incorporated the Old Testament into His teachings in a manner that was completely unexpected or contrary to popular opinion.[11] This is the case with the Sermon on the Mount. Many of the Jews were expecting a national hero who would use physical force to liberate them from their Roman captors.[12] The Jews also viewed themselves as the legitimate heirs of the covenant, the only people whom the Messiah would visit and redeem, and a nationalistic pride led many of them to despise other peoples and nations. For some, Isaiah 61 was part of this mind-set and rhetoric.[13] In this setting of national fervor and excitement, the Savior did something that would cause many Jews to reflect upon their own assumptions. Instead of playing to the Jews' nationalistic hopes and expectations and the pride they took in being the chosen people, the Savior pointed out that God blesses the meek, the poor, and the persecuted, supporting that doctrine with wording derived from Psalm 37:11: "But the meek shall inherit the earth." This psalm, which the Savior converts into a beatitude, is linked with Isaiah 61 to help the Jews understand Isaiah's true meaning. This reversal of conditions would signify a dramatic shift in thinking for many of Jesus' followers, as evidenced by Matthew's commentary: "The people were astonished at his doctrine" (Matthew 7:28).[14]

Instead of emphasizing the parallel between His own ministry and the messianic ministry described in Isaiah 61, the Lord chose to focus on the plight of the poor and brokenhearted and to indicate that it is they who will receive the kingdom of heaven. In doing so, He directed the attention of the leaders of the Jews to those whom they had typically despised.[15] Both Isaiah 61 and Psalm 37 contain the Hebrew term *'anawim*, or "meek." In both passages, the Lord promises a certain blessing to the poor or meek and defines who the poor really are. The term used for "poor" in both of these passages is the same one used to describe the meekness of Moses (see Numbers 12:3). Psalm 37 interprets this to mean those who have been pushed aside by society, criticized by the wicked, and deprived of land ownership by the wealthy (see Psalm 37:1–13). The Lord promises that this class of despised servants will be given the necessities they lack, namely the land that has been usurped by the wealthy and powerful. The Savior's use of Psalm 37 in the context of Isaiah 61 helps us see that the poor spoken of in Matthew 5:3 are different from the meek of Matthew 5:5, even though both terms derive from the same Hebrew word.[16] The King James translators attempted to accentuate this difference by translating Matthew 5:5 as "meek" and Matthew 5:3 as "poor." The subtle nuance of comparing the meek of Psalm 37 with the meek of Isaiah 61 helps us to see that the Lord had two different groups in mind.[17]

The term for "meek" in Isaiah 61 connotes slavery, bondage, and oppression by a foreign power. The meek to whom Isaiah referred have their liberty taken away; they are in prison and are brokenhearted because there seems to be no relief (see Isaiah 61:1). The meek in this context are those who suffer under the weight of the oppression this world often inflicts on those who seek to live righteously. In a way, they are subject to the demands and punishments of this world, even though they are waiting to hear the good news of the gospel promised by the Lord. In a sense, Isaiah 61 may be speaking to all those who would hear the good tidings despite being taken into bondage by the world. To this group of downtrodden and afflicted, the Savior promises the kingdom of heaven. The promise of the kingdom in Matthew 5:3 is essentially the promise of all the rights, powers, and ordinances necessary for salvation. The Prophet Joseph Smith summarizes this promise: "Whenever men can find out the will of God and find an administrator legally authorized from God, there is the kingdom of God; but where these are not, the kingdom of God is not."[18]

In contrast to the meek of Isaiah 61 are the meek of Psalm 37. These are they who, due to their meekness, have been denied privilege, standing, and honor in this world. They are persecuted because they are willing to stand up to the ways of the world and "do good" (Psalm 37:3). In this psalm, the Lord calls on the meek to trust Him even though the wicked seem to prevail. The meek are also called on to cease being angry and to let go of wrath (see Psalm 37:8). The meek of Psalm 37 are those who are trying to live in the ways of the Lord even though the unrighteous prosper and appear to be blessed. The Lord reiterates His promise that the meek shall ultimately inherit the earth as a result of their humility and patience.

The magnitude of that blessing is better understood through latter-day revelation, which teaches that the earth, in its sanctified and immortal state, will become the final resting place of the righteous (see D&C 88:17–20, 25).

The Savior's skill in teaching from the scriptures is unparalleled. We find in the Beatitudes a marvelous example of the Savior's ability to teach new concepts using familiar sources. Psalm 37 and Isaiah 61 evoked certain ideas in many of Jesus' followers and antagonists. Many among those who heard the Savior teach were astonished to learn that the very groups that society had learned to despise were those whom the Lord would ultimately bless, while those who were typically thought to be blessed would be left wanting. Using these two Old Testament passages to introduce the Sermon on the Mount, the Lord declares the entrance requirements for the kingdom of heaven. The reformulation of the old law turns its attention to those who suffer, are meek, are poor, and seek after the things of God.

PSALM 118 AND MATTHEW 21

Psalm 118 has a familiar ring to many Latter-day Saints. Phrases such as "The stone which the builders refused is become the head stone of the corner" (v. 22) and "Blessed be he that cometh in the name of the Lord" (v. 26) remind us of the Savior's mortal ministry and His final days on earth. These scriptures, and others like them, confirm that the Savior came in fulfillment of the prophecies spoken of Him by David and Old Testament prophets. This scripture in particular was used by the prophet Jacob in the Book of Mormon to explain that the Jews would reject the Messiah, be gathered again after having rejected Him, and once again become His covenant people. Jacob quoted from Psalm 118 when he described the Jews' turning away from and eventually returning to the Messiah. One might even say that Psalm 118 forms an introduction to the allegory of the olive tree (see Jacob 4:15–17).

What did the Jews at the time of Christ understand this particular scripture to say? Did they, like the Nephites, believe it referred to the mortal ministry of the Messiah and His first coming, or did they expect something entirely different? Another related question Psalm 118 raises is how the Savior used this scripture to refer to His own ministry.

There is little, if any, evidence that the Jews at the time of Christ understood that Psalm 118 referred to the initial coming of the Messiah. On the other hand, there is ample evidence that the earliest Christians regarded

Jesus Christ as the literal fulfillment of Psalm 118. One New Testament scholar has remarked that there is no evidence to suggest that the rabbis at the time of Jesus interpreted Psalm 118 as a reference to the Messiah.[19] The earliest evidence that can be adduced to support a messianic understanding of Psalm 118 dates to the late second century after Christ, when the Jews had already lost their homeland.[20] Before this time, it appears that the Jews understood the rejection of the chief cornerstone and its eventual reestablishment as a reference to their own nation and the return of the Davidic dynasty.[21] The structure of Psalm 118 lends itself, on one level, to this interpretation.

Verses 1 through 4 of Psalm 118 are a song of thanksgiving for deliverance; verses 5 through 18, a description of divine rescue; verses 19 and 20, a triumphal entry into the gates of the Lord (that is, into the temple of the Lord); verses 21 through 28, a celebration of Israel's rescue; verse 29, a final call for thanksgiving.

Psalm 118 reads as though it were written to celebrate the Lord's redeeming Israel following the persecution and suffering she had endured at the hands of her political oppressors. The celebration is centered in the temple (see v. 27) and has to do with Israel's miraculous deliverance from those who sought Israel's demise. It is no surprise, then, that many Israelites derived a certain nationalistic hope from Psalm 118. For many, it was the Lord's promise that Israel would finally be vindicated and that the stone, symbolic of Israel herself, would no longer be rejected by the world.[22]

Even though the Jews at the time of Christ may not have interpreted Psalm 118 as a reference to the Messiah, they were deeply aware of its content. According to the Mishnah, one of the earliest Pharisaic oral interpretations of the Old Testament, Psalm 118 was sung as part of the Hallel at the Feast of Tabernacles, Hanukkah, and the Feast of the Passover, where it was recited at the sacrificing of the Paschal Lamb and at the Passover Feast.[23] The context of these recitations of Psalm 118 suggests that this psalm was of significant importance to the Jews at the time of Christ. The fact that this scripture was also a Jewish hymn helps us to gain an appreciation of the extent to which its content would have become ingrained for faithful Jews at the time of Christ. If we are correct in stating that many of the Jews looked at this psalm as an indication of God's promise of deliverance, then the repeated recitation of Psalm 118 makes sense, given the Jews' concern over the loss of their nation's sovereignty.

Roman oppression caused many Jews to look to the heavens for deliverance. For many, the continued recitation of Psalm 118 reminded them that God had delivered them in the past and that He would once again establish this rejected stone.

The evidence suggesting that Psalm 118 was understood as a promise of the coming and rejection of the Messiah at the time of Christ has been very weak. Most of the evidence suggests that Jews at the time of Christ were interpreting this psalm as a promise of the reestablishment of their nation. When we turn to the early Christians, however, there is very strong evidence that the early Christians thought the rejected stone and other prophecies of Psalm 118 had reference to the Messiah. Psalm 118 is, in fact, cited or alluded to at least fifteen times in the New Testament, if we do not count the occurrences where different gospel writers have recorded the same event.[24] This evidence suggests that Psalm 118 was one of the most cited Old Testament scriptures and indeed one of the most important statements about the coming of the Messiah from any Old Testament figure. The interpretation of Psalm 118 and its relative importance goes back to the Savior Himself as He sought to explain the meaning and importance of His mortal ministry to a people who were for the most part looking for a leader who would liberate them from foreign oppression.[25]

One of the most interesting ways the Savior used Psalm 118 as a reference to His own ministry can be found in Matthew 21. This chapter begins with Jesus' entry into Jerusalem on the back of a donkey, thus fulfilling the prophecy of Zechariah (see Zechariah 9:9). According to the Gospel of Matthew, many people immediately recognized the significance of this sign, and they laid out their clothes for the Savior to ride upon. They also prepared a path for Him so that he could ride into the city triumphantly. While He entered, they recited the now famous words of Psalm 118:26: "Blessed be he that cometh in the name of the Lord." After His triumphal entry, making His whereabouts public, He immediately entered the temple and cast out the money changers. The following day He again entered the temple. On this occasion, His authority to do such things as cleanse the temple was challenged. His response, in part, includes the parable of the vineyard, wherein the lord of the vineyard prepares all that is necessary for his vineyard to flourish. He then rents it out to those who end up abusing his servants and ultimately taking the life of his son (see Matthew 21:33–40). After reciting this parable, the Savior asks His inquirers what action the lord of the vineyard should take against these wicked servants.

Matthew records their response as "He [the lord] will miserably destroy those wicked men, and will let out his vineyard unto other husbandmen" (Matthew 21:41).

Having backed His accusers into a corner, the Savior summarizes the implications of the parable of the vineyard. He begins by saying that the son of the vineyard is equated with the rejected stone of Psalm 118:22, asking, "Did ye never read in the scriptures, The stone which the builders rejected, the same is become the head of the corner: this is the Lord's doing, and it is marvellous in our eyes?" (Matthew 21:42). The Savior then gives them to understand that the Jews represent the hired servants and that the kingdom of God (the vineyard) will be taken from them and given to someone else who is worthy.[26] To appreciate fully the impact of such teachings, one must look back at the Jews' understanding of this passage. Many of them believed that this scripture, Psalm 118:22, promised the return of their nation to a position of prominence, and they believed that the Lord would ultimately deliver them. Instead, the Savior interprets this scripture to mean the very opposite—the Jews become those who have oppressed the Lord's people, and the Lord will punish them as wicked servants. Moreover, the land of their inheritance will be taken from them and given to the worthy followers of Jesus, a man whom many Jews despised. Matthew underscores the impact of this interchange by saying, "When the chief priests and Pharisees had heard his parables, *they perceived that he spake of them. But when they sought to lay hands on him, they feared the multitude*" (Matthew 21:45–46; emphasis added). These Jews became so enraged at the Savior's teachings that they wanted to take His life, but they feared that the multitude would cry out against them.[27]

SUMMARY AND CONCLUSION

It is difficult to overstate the impact the Savior's statement had on His listeners. Many in the exuberant crowd that welcomed Jesus to Jerusalem saw in that event a fulfillment of the prophecy in Psalm 118. Others, however, thought the Savior's interpretation of this passage was self-serving and blasphemous. They could not see that Jesus of Nazareth was the Messiah promised by the prophets. For His critics and enemies, He was simply a man caught up in His own pride who deserved to be put to death. Jesus' use of Psalm 118 cuts to the very core of this division. Will the followers of Jesus be able to accept Him as their Redeemer even though their prior understanding of scripture indicates that He is not what they expected? For many, as indicated by Matthew 21:8, the answer is yes.

These two examples give us an insight into the ways the Lord taught from the Old Testament during His mortal ministry. In the first example, the Savior reveals His complete mastery of scripture, though He often uses familiar scriptures in new and different ways. The Lord has revealed in our dispensation that revelation helps us know when we have erred, and that it will guide us on the strait and narrow path (see D&C 1:25). For those who were ready and willing, the Savior's message was one of profound enlightenment and intelligence. In the second example, we see the Savior boldly apply to Himself the scriptures that speak of the coming of the Messiah. For many people, these scriptures were of national importance, providing hope that when the Lord came, He would redeem His people from the oppression of the world. Instead, the Savior offered a dramatically different interpretation. In both instances, the reaction of the crowd is marked; in the first, His audience is surprised, while in the second, a portion of His audience seeks to take His life as a result of His teachings.

NOTES

1. The term *beatitude* derives from the Latin adjective *beatitudo,* meaning "happy or blessed." The Latin *beatitudo* is a translation of the Greek *makarismos,* which indicates a happy and blessed state of existence that was generally achieved only by the gods in Greek-speaking cultures. At times, this state of blessedness could be achieved by mortals after death (Hans D. Betz, *A Commentary on the Sermon on the Mount, including the Sermon on the Plain,* ed. Adele Yarbro Collins [Minneapolis: Fortress Press, 1995], 92–97).

2. Catherine Thomas, "The Sermon on the Mount: The Sacrifice of the Human Heart," in *Studies in Scripture, Volume 5: The Gospels,* ed. Kent P. Jackson and Robert L. Millet, 8 vols. (Salt Lake City: Deseret Book, 1986), 5:237.

3. W. Jeffrey Marsh, "Prophetic Enlightenment on the Sermon on the Mount," *Ensign,* January 1999, 15–16.

4. Several scholars have noted this method of drawing the disciples in and then pointing out that they may expect persecution (see W. J. Dumbrell, "The Logic of the Role of the Law in Matthew V1–20," *Novum Testamentum* 23 [1981]: 2–3; Mark Allan Powell, "Matthew's Beatitudes: Reversals and Rewards of the Kingdom," *Catholic Biblical Quarterly* 58 [1996]: 447).

5. This parallel has been consistently noted by biblical scholars for many years (see Robert A. Guelich, "The Matthean Beatitudes: 'Entrance-

Requirements' or Eschatological Blessings?" *Journal of Biblical Literature* 95 [1976]: 423–26; W. D. Davies and D. C. Allison Jr., *A Critical and Exegetical Commentary on The Gospel According to Saint Matthew,* 3 vols. [Edinburgh: T & T Clark, 1988], 1:436–38; James E. Talmage, *Jesus the Christ* [Salt Lake City: Deseret Book, 1915], 74).

6. The term *gospel,* a term used by the earliest Christians to characterize the teachings of Jesus, may derive from Isaiah 61:1. The Hebrew *basher* is translated in the LXX, or Greek translation of the Old Testament, as *euangellion.* The term can most accurately be translated as "gospel." The parallel to the servant who teaches the gospel in Isaiah 61, and to Jesus who likewise teaches the gospel, is profound. The early Christian usage of the term *gospel* or *euangellion* may indicate that they were intentionally drawing attention to Jesus' fulfillment of Isaiah 61.

7. The 27th edition of Nestle-Aland, *Novum Testamentum Graece,* lists fifteen references or allusions to Isaiah 61: Matthew 5:3,4; 11:5; Luke 1:47; 4:18; 6:20–21; 7:22; Acts 4:27; 10:38; Hebrews 13:20; Revelation 1:6; 5:10; 19:8; 21:2.

8. See James A. Sanders, "From Isaiah 61 to Luke 4," in *Luke and Scripture,* ed. James Sanders and Craig Evans (Minneapolis: Fortress Press, 1993), 14–25.

9. The Targum Pseudo-Johnathan on Numbers 25:12 indicates a move toward interpreting this passage eschatologically and messianically. James Sanders, "From Isaiah 61 to Luke 4," 48–57, discusses the history of interpretation of this passage.

10. The Qumran text 11Q13, or Melchizedek, is a Midrash on Isaiah 61:1–3 and clearly understands it eschatologically and as reference to the redemption of God's covenant people. The difference of interpretation here is that Melchizedek will act as the savior of God's people instead of the Messiah. For a translation of this passage, see Michael Wise, Martin Abegg Jr., and Edward Cook, *The Dead Sea Scrolls: A New Translation* (San Francisco: Harper, 1996), 455–57. On the meaning of this passage in general, see D. Flusser, "Blessed Are the Poor in Spirit . . . ," in *Israel Exploration Journal* 10 (1960): 1–13; Merrill P. Miller, "The Function of Isaiah 61:1–2 in 11QMelchizedek," *Journal of Biblical Literature* 88 (1969), 467–69.

11. Robert J. Matthews, *A Bible! A Bible!* (Salt Lake City: Bookcraft, 1990), 221–23.

12. Talmage, *Jesus the Christ,* 74.

13. This can be seen clearly at Qumran, where Isaiah 61 is interpreted as a vindication of God's chosen people. The translation of 11Qmelchizedek (11Q13) adequately demonstrates this idea of separation and vindication: "Therefore Melchizedek will thoroughly prosecute the vengeance required by God's statutes. Also, he will deliver all the captives from the power of Belial, and from the power of all the spirits predestined to him.

Allied with him will be all the 'righteous divine beings' (Isa. 61:3)" (Wise, Abegg, Cook, *Dead Sea Scrolls,* col. 2, 456).

14. Powell, "Matthew's Beatitudes," 460. Powell argues that the structure of the beatitudes allows them to be interpreted in two distinct groups. He calls the first four beatitudes a list of reversals while he considers the next four to be a list of rewards. Although I have some reservations in making such a sharp distinction between the first and last four beatitudes, I believe that the rewards promised by the beatitudes increase in degree (see Matthew 5:8).

15. At the time of Jesus, popular sentiment held that God had blessed the rich and punished the poor. Therefore, according to popular opinion at the time of Jesus, being righteous meant being rich (see Davies and Allison, *The Gospel According to Saint Matthew,* 442).

16. Guelich, "The Matthean Beatitudes," 426–27.

17. Joseph Smith Translation, Matthew 5:3, helps to clarify this issue by adding "who come unto me" to qualify the poor who are blessed (see also 3 Nephi 12:3).

18. Joseph Smith, *History of The Church of Jesus Christ of Latter-day Saints,* ed. B. H. Roberts, 2d ed. rev., 7 vols. (Salt Lake City: Deseret Book, 1964), 5:259.

19. J. Ross Wagner, "Psalm 118 in Luke–Acts: Tracing a Narrative Thread," in *Early Christian Interpretation of the Scriptures of Israel: Investigations and Proposals,* ed. James Sanders and Craig Evans (England: Sheffield Press, 1997), 157–61. Joachim Jeremias (*The Eucharistic Words of Jesus,* trans. Norman Perrin [Philadelphia: Fortress Press, 1966], 255–62) and Eric Werner ("'Hosanna' in the Gospels," in *Journal of Biblical Literature* 65 [1946], 97–122) argued against this position in two earlier studies. Their position, however, has been greatly diminished by the discovery and publication of the Dead Sea Scrolls, which confirm the fact that the Jews expected something other than the coming of the Messiah as the fulfillment of Psalm 118. For a discussion of the problem of dating Rabbinic sources, see Craig A. Evans, "Early Rabbinic Sources and Jesus Research," in *Society of Biblical Literature: Symposium Proceedings,* ed. E. H. Lovering (Atlanta: Scholars Press, 1995), 53–76.

20. R. Jose, *b. Pesher* 118b, cited in Wagner, "Psalm 118 in Luke-Acts," 158.

21. Mitchell Dahood, *Psalms,* vol. 16 of the Anchor Bible series (New York: Doubleday, 1970), 154–59.

22. A similar sentiment is expressed by Solomon Freehof when he equates the rejected stone of Psalm 118:22 with the nation of Israel. He cites several Rabbinic sources as evidence of this position, among whom is Ibn Ezra (*The Book of Psalms* [Cincinnati: Union of American Hebrew Congregations, 1938], 338).

23. Wagner, "Psalm 118 in Luke–Acts," 160. The Mishnah was fixed in writing around the year AD 200, under the leadership of Rabbi Judah ha-Nasi.

24. Matthew 11:3; 21:9, 42; 23:39; Mark 8:31; 11:9; 12:10–11; Luke 7:19; 9:22; 13:35; 17:25; 19:38; 20:17; John 12:13; Acts 4:11; Romans 8:31; Hebrews 13:6; 1 Peter 2:4, 7.

25. Richard T. Mead, "A Dissenting Opinion about Respect for Context in Old Testament Quotations," in *New Testament Studies* 10 (1963–64): 286–87.

26. J. Ching has suggested that the controversy represented in Matthew 21 is not based on a division between Christians and Jews but is meant to point out the division between Jesus and the Jewish hierarchy (see "No Other Name," *Japanese Journal of Religious Studies* 12 [1985]: 259).

27. This idea frames Matthew 21 and forms an inclusion. It begins with a quotation of Psalm 118:26 (see Matthew 21:9) and ends with a quotation of Psalm 118:22 (see Matthew 21:42). The belief of the multitude at the beginning of the chapter is summarized as a reason for Jesus' deliverance at the end of the chapter.

CHAPTER TWELVE

THE LOVE OF GOD

MATTHEW O. RICHARDSON

The friction between Jewish traditionalism and Hellenistic philosophy became apparent among the members of the early Christian Church. Many of the Jewish Christians professed a commitment to Jesus Christ but still felt a loyalty to Jewish law. As a result, Christ's role as the Messiah was a difficult concept for most of them to accept. Many of the Hellenistic Christians, on the other hand, were influenced by an early form of Gnosticism and found it difficult to accept the humanity of Jesus Christ. On both accounts, the identity and role of Christ was distorted. It was under such circumstances that John attempted to appeal to the faithful Saints and correct the misguided teachings of the time. It makes sense that John testified of a corporeal (physical) resurrected Jesus (see 1 John 1–2) to counter Gnostic claims of a "phantom" (nonphysical) Savior. Likewise, Christ's role in our cleansing (see 1 John 1:7), His advocacy with the Father (see 1 John 2:1–3), and His overcoming the world through rebirth (see 1 John 5:4–6) testifies that Jesus Christ is the Messiah. Not to be forgotten, however, in providing a full understanding of the identity of Jesus Christ and the gospel is love. Love, as taught in John's writings, provides necessary insight for understanding the Savior, Jesus Christ.

WHAT IS LOVE?

I do not believe it is coincidence that love becomes one of the predominant themes[1] of the disciple "whom Jesus loved," or "John the Beloved" (see John 13:2; 20:2; 21:7, 20). It is likely that because John felt he was beloved, he approached this topic in a simple yet deeply profound manner.

Matthew O. Richardson is an associate professor of Church history and doctrine at Brigham Young University.

To gain this comprehensive insight, however, we must consider all of John's writings rather than concentrate on a single verse, chapter, or book. Biblical scholars often use repeated textual analysis as a way of discovering meaning from religious texts. The process requires returning again and again to the text. That is especially helpful when studying a concept as broad as love. John's writings not only become clearer when compared with his other texts but reveal fascinating relationships as well. By returning to John's texts, we find that he unfolds the meaning of love and how it relates to the gospel of Jesus Christ.

"That Your Joy May Be Full"

In an attempt to dispel the pervading philosophies of the time, John's writings reflect his desire that we obtain not a portion of truth but a fulness thereof. This is made clear as John writes, "And these things write we unto you, that your joy may be full" (1 John 1:4). *Full*, in this context, is used to translate the Greek word *pleroo*, meaning "replete, or finished." In some interpretations, *pleroo* is described as a "filler" that rounds out imperfections, or dents, or makes something complete. Because it was John's desire to provide a means whereby our joy may be made complete or full, his approach to love is not a doctrinal decoration but a load-bearing beam.

John approaches love in its fullest sense, and those who study his writings must be willing to consider that the scriptural essence of love might be something different from what they are either used to hearing or have come to expect. If one approaches John's text with a casual, self-satisfied attitude, only varying portions of the fulness can be realized. That is not to say that we are incapable of loving or that the love John describes is beyond our grasp but merely that John's message of love is profoundly simple. It is not wrought with distractions or pomp of its own. Therein lies the danger. With such a clean doctrine, we are tempted to spruce it up a bit, add our own agendas, become satisfied with a status quo vision, or allow the views of the world to define our doctrine. When properly understood, the love described in John's works provides direction for all mankind.

"God Is Love"

John invites us to "love one another" (John 13:34; 15:12; 1 John 3:11, 23; 4:11). Most of us have accepted this invitation at one time or another in our lives and have loved someone (or at least some*thing*). But John's notion of what love is, however, does not mesh with traditional concepts. The fulness of love, according to John, is considerably narrow in comparison to the world's concept of love. "Love one another," John wrote, "for love is of God" (1 John 4:7). John continued: "He that dwelleth in love dwelleth in God, and God in him" (1 John 4:16). John connects the fulness of love not with casual emotions, affection, or even passion but with God. To ensure that he was not misunderstood, John taught in the simplest of terms that "God is love" (1 John 4:8, 16). If one desires true love, one must understand God.

Some may become nervous using God as the standard and definition of love. They may think such a standard is too restrictive or unrealistic. Some may feel that if God defines love, then romance will be replaced with benevolence and brotherly love. But when we understand John's teaching of love correctly, romantic love, brotherly love, and benevolence can be appropriate under God's divine guidance.[2] God's definition of love will, however, exclude feelings, actions, and motives that are contrary to his law. That filters out the misconceptions of love, leaving only a "pure" love. To those who feel that "God is love" is an unrealistic standard, I offer Elder Henry B. Eyring's advice: "You need not fear that using God as your standard will overwhelm you. On the contrary—God asks only that we approach him humbly, as a child."[3] As we raise our standards to meet those of our God, we not only begin to act like Him but become more like Him as well.

"WE LOVE HIM, BECAUSE HE FIRST LOVED US"

Another important consideration in understanding the meaning of love is John's statement that "herein is love, not that we loved God, but that he loved us" (1 John 4:10). Although love is intended to eventually become a reciprocal relationship, we must understand that the love of God is not contingent upon our love for Him; love begins with God, not with us. John explained that "we love him, because he first loved us" (1 John 4:19). Rather than considering these statements as a reason for us to love God, we can see that John's point is that love begins with God. Thus His love is what allows us to love not only Him but everything.

"HE THAT DWELLETH IN LOVE DWELLETH IN GOD"

John makes it clear that "he that dwelleth in love dwelleth in God, and God in him" (1 John 4:16). Because the love of God is the genesis of our ability to truly love, if we remove God for any reason we forfeit our ability to practice love in its fullest sense. For example, John taught that "if any man love the world, the love of the Father is not in him" (1 John 2:15). This is not to say that if one indulges in worldliness God will no longer love him. C. S. Lewis emphasized that "the great thing to remember is that, though our feelings come and go, His [God's] love for us does not. It is not wearied by our sins, or our indifference."[4]

Although God will always love us, John emphasized that our love of the world limits the degree to which God's Spirit is manifest in our lives. How we embrace the world, whether with unabashed acceptance or with flirtatious encounters with its subtleties, creates a boundary between us and God. James, author of the Epistle of James, queried, "Know ye not that the friendship of the world is enmity with God?" He concluded, "Whosoever therefore will be a friend of the world is the enemy of God" (James 4:4). When we entertain that which removes God from our lives, it is not His love for us that decreases but the presence of His Spirit that diminishes (see D&C 121:37). Although God still loves us, our understanding and ability to truly love is forfeited because of the loss of His Spirit. Where God is not, love in its fulness cannot be.

This forfeiture is not restricted to wicked acts alone but can include using the world to define gospel principles. President Gordon B. Hinckley spoke of those who allow the world to define love. He said: "Their expression may sound genuine, but their coin is counterfeit. Too often the love of which they speak is at best only hollow mummery."[5] In a similar tone, Elder Marvin J. Ashton warned: "Too often expediency, infatuation, stimulation, persuasion, or lust are mistaken for love. How hollow, how empty if our love is no deeper than the arousal of momentary feeling or the expression in words of what is no more lasting than the time it takes to speak them."[6] Far too many of us have fallen for counterfeits of love. When we have a skewed understanding of what love really is, we are left in a frenzy to constantly feed an ever-fading emotion, or we become frustrated, discouraged, disillusioned, or even cynical.

President Hinckley taught that "love is like the Polar Star. In a changing world, it is a constant. It is of the very essence of the gospel. It is the security of the home. It is the safeguard of community life. It is a beacon of hope in a world of distress."[7] When seeking this type of love, we must understand that the night sky is filled with myriad unfixed and moving stars—counterfeit Polar Stars—each fawning for our attention as if it were the sure guiding light. These counterfeits can provide some measure of illumination and guidance, but only one star provides the constant answer for an ever-changing world. That guiding love, as John so aptly describes, is free from the world's dilutions and wickedness and is inseparably connected with God and Jesus Christ.

"THE LOVE OF GOD"

With the connection between love and God established, we can turn our focus to John's teachings about "the love of God" (1 John 3:16). When discussing God the Father's love for us, John provides critical commentary: "For God so loved the world, that he gave his only begotten Son" (John 3:16). Here John links God's love for the world with Jesus Christ. Later, John writes, "In this was manifested the love of God toward us, because that God sent his only begotten Son into the world, that we might live through him" (1 John 4:9). According to John, the love of God manifest to us is Jesus Christ.

An earlier witness of this concept is found in the Book of Mormon. Young Nephi saw a tree, "and the beauty thereof was far beyond, yea, exceeding of all beauty; and the whiteness thereof did exceed the whiteness of the driven snow" (1 Nephi 11:8). When Nephi asked for an interpretation of what the tree is, rather than giving an immediate answer, a vision of the birth of Jesus Christ was opened to him (see 1 Nephi 11:13–20). As the vision closed, the angel proclaimed, "Behold the Lamb of God, yea, even the Son of the Eternal Father!" (1 Nephi 11:21). The angel then asked Nephi, "Knowest thou the meaning of the tree which thy father saw?" (1 Nephi 11:21). The angel seems to have been checking to see if Nephi grasped the relationship between the vision of the Savior and his inquiry concerning the interpretation of the tree. Immediately, Nephi astutely answered, "Yea, it [the tree] is the love of God, which sheddeth itself abroad in the hearts of the children of men; wherefore, it is the most desirable above all things" (1 Nephi 11:22). Both Nephi and John testified that Jesus Christ is the love of God manifest to us.

THE FATHER GAVE ALL THINGS TO THE SON

Although Christ emphasized "my Father is greater than I" (John 14:28), He did not diminish His authoritative role in manifesting the Father's love. John recorded Christ's words as "Father, I will that they also, whom thou hast given me, be with me where I am; that they may behold my glory, which thou hast given me: for thou lovedst me before the foundation of the world" (John 17:24). Christ's glory was given to Him by God because of His Father's love. John further testified that "the Father loveth the Son, and hath given all things into his hand" (John 3:35). It was through God's love that Christ became the chosen and authoritative manifestation of the Father. John said of Christ's ministry that "the Father loveth the Son, and sheweth him all things that himself doeth: and he will shew him greater works than these, that ye may marvel" (John 5:20). Christ, commissioned of the Father, manifests the fulness of the Father to all mankind. Thus Christ is a mediator or a propitiator (see 1 John 4:10). Though a mediator and a propitiator are similar, Richard D. Draper explains that propitiation goes beyond mediation by uniting two parties in friendship.[8] It is Christ, therefore, who makes it possible for us to receive the fulness of God's love. John emphasized this relationship as he taught, "I am the way, the truth, and the life: no man cometh unto the Father, but by me" (John 14:6).

"BORN OF GOD"

If we expect to obtain the fulness of God's love, we must receive it through the propitiation of Christ. John reminds us that "love is of God; and every one that loveth is born of God, and knoweth God" (1 John 4:7). To receive and exercise God's love requires us to be "born of God." To some, being born of God is receiving the realization that God is our spiritual Father and that we are His spiritual offspring. To others, being born of God involves recognizing that Christ is their Savior. It is clear that being "born of God," as spoken of by John, is more than realizing that our beginnings were with God the Father or proclaiming that Christ is our Savior.

As Jesus taught Nicodemus, He emphasized that one must be "born again" to see the kingdom of God (John 3:3). The Prophet Joseph Smith further clarified that "we must have a change of heart to see the kingdom of God."[9] John later emphasized that our ability to love ("everyone that loveth") is born of God. It is true that our ability to love stems from God, but how is the love of God born in us? We may also ponder, how love relates to changing our hearts and becoming born again. Elder Bruce R. McConkie wrote: "To be born does not mean to come into existence out of nothing, but rather to begin a new type of existence, to live again in a changed situation. Birth is the continuation of life under different circumstances."[10] John wrote that "whosoever believeth that Jesus is the Christ is born of God" (1 John 5:1). If we truly believe in Christ, we must begin a renovation. We can no longer remain the same person we once were. Those who embrace the gospel of Christ become new creatures, born into new situations, new circumstances, new expectations, a new way to approach daily experiences, and a new way to love. When we believe in Christ, we begin a new existence, a life with Christ and of Christ. Those who were unable to love in the past can be transformed and find love born in them. This type of transformation is accomplished only through Christ.

"CALLED THE SONS OF GOD"

It is interesting that John linked the love of God with not only a symbolic rebirth but a metaphorical adoption as well. John taught that the love of God necessarily leads to both a rebirth and an adoption. "Behold, what manner of love the Father hath bestowed upon us," John wrote, "that we should be called the sons of God" (1 John 3:1). This verse possesses a flavor of wonderment that God's love is so grand that mere men can be called the sons of God. To some it may seem odd that John wrote of this event with wonder. John understood that we were created by God, thus becoming, as God's creations, His "sons and daughters." But John stated that God's love was bestowed upon us so that we *should* be called sons of God.

Other prophets testify of this relationship between love, rebirth, and becoming the children of God. The prophet Moroni was emphatic about obtaining the love of God and thus becoming sons of God. He pleaded with those who would hear his message to "pray unto the Father with all the energy of heart, that ye may be filled with this love [the love of Christ, or charity], which he hath bestowed upon all who are true followers of his Son, Jesus Christ; that ye may become the sons of God" (Moroni 7:48).

Another prophet, King Benjamin, addressed the importance of understanding this adoptive process. He explained that "because of the covenant which ye have made ye shall be called the children of Christ, his sons, and his daughters; for behold, this day he hath spiritually begotten you; for ye say that your hearts are changed through faith on his name; therefore, ye are born of him and have become his sons and his daughters. And under this head ye are made free, and there is no other head whereby ye can be made free" (Mosiah 5:7–8). Benjamin testified that this adoption was made possible because of the covenant we made with God.

This adoptive process is an essential part of the rebirth taught by John. Again we return to Christ's discourse to Nicodemus. After teaching of the necessity of the rebirth of the heart, Christ told Nicodemus, "Verily, verily, I say unto thee, Except a man be born of water and of the Spirit, he cannot enter into the kingdom of God" (John 3:5). He summarized, "Marvel not that I said unto thee, Ye must be born again" (John 3:7). The Prophet Joseph Smith, when referring to these passages, taught that we must "subscribe [to] the articles of adoption to enter therein."[11] John taught that the process of being born again requires more than acknowledging Christ and His mission. It requires even more than a change of heart. It also requires subscribing to the articles of adoption—making covenants. Elder Bruce R. McConkie stated that the sons and daughters of Jesus Christ "take upon them his name in the waters of baptism and certify anew each time they partake of the sacrament that they have so done; or, more accurately, in the waters of baptism power is given them to become sons of Christ, which eventuates when they are in fact born of Spirit and become new creatures of the Holy Ghost."[12] Because the love of God is manifest through Christ, we can know God only through Christ. We can experience the fulness of God's love only by entering into a covenant relationship with Jesus Christ. By maintaining our covenantal status, we are born of God and thus become the sons and daughters of Christ.

Whether discussing rebirth or becoming children of God, Christ is always at the center of the discussion. John testified that we have received Christ and exercised the power given us by Him to become His sons (see John 1:12). Elder McConkie further clarified the connection between rebirth/adoption and Jesus Christ when he explained: "Those accountable mortals who then believe and obey the gospel are born again; they are born of the Spirit; they become alive to the things of righteousness or of the Spirit. They become members of another family, have new brothers and sisters, and a new Father. They are the sons and daughters of Jesus Christ."[13]

Although this adoption is necessary, it is not a culminating event but a part of a continual process of change. That is apparent in John's writing: "Beloved, now are we the sons of God, and it doth not yet appear what we shall be: but we know that, when he shall appear, we shall be like him; for we shall see him as he is" (1 John 3:2). The process of receiving God's love, rebirth, and becoming the children of Christ is not a one-time event but a gradual experience. In this process, we shall, as John described, become like Christ (see 1 John 3:2).

"If Ye Love Me, Keep My Commandments"

As sons and daughters of Christ, we have covenanted to keep His commandments. Jesus taught, "If ye love me, keep my commandments" (John 14:15). This implies that we will keep the commandments because we love Christ (see 1 John 5:2–3; 2 John 1:6). Though this is true, an additional aspect of obedience is presented in John's writings. Christ taught that "he that hath my commandments, and keepeth them, he it is that loveth me: and he that loveth me shall be loved of my Father, and I will love him, and will manifest myself to him" (John 14:21). When we keep the commandments, we find that Christ manifests Himself to us.

This simple concept presents an interesting situation. Many of those who keep the commandments do so because they already possess a love of Christ. They, according to the prophetic blessing, will have a manifestation of Christ. But consider these verses applied in other circumstances. What of those who have not yet come to love Christ? Are they to be obedient to God's commandments as well? C. S. Lewis felt that some people worry because they are unsure if they love God. He said concerning these people: "They are told they ought to love God. They cannot find any such feelings in themselves. What are they to do? . . . Act as if you did. Do not sit trying to manufacture feelings. Ask yourself, 'If I were sure that I loved God, what would I do?' When you have found the answer, go and do it."[14] Lewis further observed: "As soon as we do this we find one of the great secrets. When you are behaving as if you loved someone, you will presently come to love him."[15] John taught that "if any man will do his [God's] will, he shall know of the doctrine, whether it be of God, or whether I speak of myself" (John 7:17). Not only will the obedient know the divine source of the doctrine but they will grow in love toward the Master as well. Thus the cycle of love and obedience begins anew, ever deepening with each act of obedience and receipt of divine manifestation.

Our obedience maintains our covenant relationship with Christ, which facilitates the manifestation of God's love. We can feel the fulness of the Father only when our covenants with Christ are in effect. As we become more proficient in maintaining our covenant of keeping the commandments, not only do we draw ever closer to the Savior but He becomes a constant fixture in our lives. Christ taught, "If a man love me, he will keep my words: and my Father will love him, and we will come unto him, and make our abode with him" (John 14:23).

LOVE ONE ANOTHER

John reminded the disciples of Christ that mere familiarity with the Savior's message was not sufficient to obtain the full love of God. "My little children," John counseled, "let us not love in word, neither in tongue; but in deed" (1 John 3:18). President Howard W. Hunter taught: "Merely saying, accepting, believing are not enough. They are incomplete until that which they imply is translated into the dynamic action of daily living."[16] A disciple of Christ, therefore, is one who not only receives Christ's law but also seeks to follow the given counsel (see D&C 41:5). In the same manner, we find that a disciple of Christ is not only one who receives God's love and who loves God but also one who seeks to love others. Christ commanded "that he who loveth God love his brother also" (1 John 4:21). This commandment was at the heart of Christ's ministry from the beginning (see 1 John 3:11; John 15:17).

Loving others is regarded as the badge of Christianity. Christ taught that "by their fruits ye shall know them" (Matthew 7:20). The discerning fruit of discipleship was determined by whether the followers of Christ loved others. "By this shall all men know that ye are my disciples," Christ taught, "if ye have love one to another" (John 13:35).

"LOVE ONE ANOTHER; AS I HAVE LOVED YOU"

Although we have covenanted to love others, it is not enough to merely go through the motions in hopes of checking off one more requirement of discipleship. It is true that Christ admonished us to "love one another." But His commandment was not merely to learn to love others but to "love one another; as I have loved you, that ye also love one another" (John 13:34; see also John 15:12; 1 John 3:23). This pattern was familiar to Christ, for He taught that "as the Father hath loved me, so have I loved you: continue ye in my love" (John 15:9). No wonder John, who was self-described as "the disciple whom Jesus loved," wrote so much concerning loving others. Since John received Christ's love, he was in a position to love others; and he understood that he must continue in that love by loving others as Christ loved him. Elder C. Max Caldwell said: "Jesus' love was inseparably connected to and resulted from his life of serving, sacrificing, and giving in behalf of others. We cannot develop Christlike love except by practicing the process prescribed by the Master."[17]

"Greater Love Hath No Man"

As we consider the depth of the love that is God's to give, it is really quite amazing to think that it has been made available to us. The pinnacle of our understanding of the love of God is centered not only upon Christ but also upon His sacrifice (see 1 John 4:9). John taught that we "perceive . . . the love of God, because he laid down his life for us" (1 John 3:16) and that the love of God is manifested toward us, *because* God sent His Only Begotten Son into the world so "that we might live through him" (1 John 4:9). Paul taught that "if any man live in Christ, he is a new creature; old things are passed away; behold, all things are become new" (JST, 2 Corinthians 5:17).[18] The Savior's mission—His sacrifice—in some miraculous way changes not only how we live and love but also changes us. "The Atonement in some way," wrote Elder Bruce C. Hafen, "apparently through the Holy Ghost, makes possible the infusion of spiritual endowments that actually change and purify our nature, moving us toward that state of holiness or completeness we call eternal life or Godlike life. At that ultimate stage we will exhibit divine characteristics not just because we think we should but because that is the way we are."[19] It is through this change that we can find everlasting life. John reminded us that "God so loved the world, that he gave his only begotten Son, that whosoever believeth on him should not perish, but have everlasting life" (John 3:16). Jesus Christ, the love of God, provides hope of salvation. No wonder John exults, "There is no fear in love; but perfect love casteth out fear: because fear hath torment. He that feareth is not made perfect in love" (1 John 4:18).

"The Fulness"

"What manner of love the Father hath bestowed upon us?" (1 John 3:1). The writings of John clearly teach of a fulness of love: not a counterfeit love, nor a portion of love, but a fulness thereof. John taught that the full measure of love is founded in God. It is from God that all love springs forth. He taught that Jesus Christ is, in reality, the love of God, and thus we can feel of the fulness of God's love as we enter into a covenant and become born of Christ. We reciprocate God's love by keeping the commandments and loving others. It is because of the ultimate sacrifice, the fulfilling of the mission of Christ, that we are able to become new creatures and thereby love others as Christ loved us. John taught that the only way to find the love that will guide and direct our lives for peace, dispose of fear, and bring us to a fulness of joy, is to be filled with pure love—even Jesus Christ.

NOTES

1. Bruce R. McConkie, *Doctrinal New Testament Commentary,* 3 vols. (Salt Lake City: Bookcraft, 1965–73), 3:371.

2. Dr. Richard D. Draper, associate dean of Religious Education at Brigham Young University, concludes that all of the forms of love (*agape, philos,* and *eros*), when used appropriately, are necessary to achieve the highest or noblest love ("Love and Joy," unpublished manuscript).

3. Henry B. Eyring, *To Draw Closer to God* (Salt Lake City: Deseret Book, 1997), 68.

4. C. S. Lewis, *Mere Christianity* (New York: Macmillan, 1952), 102–3.

5. Gordon B. Hinckley, in Conference Report, April 1969, 61.

6. Marvin J. Ashton,"Love Takes Time," *Ensign,* November 1975, 108.

7. Gordon B. Hinckley, "Let Love Be the Lodestar of Your Life," *Ensign,* May 1989, 66.

8. Draper, "Love and Joy" (unpublished manuscript).

9. Joseph Smith, *Teachings of the Prophet Joseph Smith,* comp. Joseph Fielding Smith (Salt Lake City: Deseret Book, 1976), 328.

10. McConkie, *Doctrinal New Testament Commentary,* 2:471.

11. Smith, *Teachings,* 328.

12. McConkie, *Doctrinal New Testament Commentary,* 2:471–72.

13. McConkie, *Doctrinal New Testament Commentary,* 2:471.

14. Lewis, *Mere Christianity,* 102.

15. Lewis, *Mere Christianity,* 101.

16. Howard W. Hunter, in Conference Report, October 1967, 116.

17. C. Max Caldwell, in Conference Report, October 1992, 40.

18. See *The Holy Scriptures: Inspired Version* (Independence, MO: Herald Publishing House, 1991).

19. Bruce C. Hafen, *The Broken Heart* (Salt Lake City: Deseret Book, 1989), 18.

CHAPTER THIRTEEN

JOHN THE BELOVED: SPECIAL WITNESS OF THE ATONEMENT

KENT R. BROOKS

Every prophet who has ever lived on this earth has received the sure witness of the divinity of the Son of God. As recorded in holy scripture—ancient and modern—their testimonies declare Jesus is the Christ, the Savior and Redeemer of the world, and salvation is available only through Him. One of those prophets, John the Beloved, taught about the redeeming and enabling powers of the Atonement. His writings—the Gospel of John, 1 John, 2 John, 3 John, and the book of Revelation—compose an eyewitness account and personal testimony of Jesus the Christ.

Jesus declared, "I am come in my Father's name" (John 5:43). Jesus was foreordained by the Father, receiving the authority to act in His name and to be the Savior of the world. "As many as received him," John taught, "to them gave he power to become the sons of God" (John 1:12). In this passage, the English word *power* is used to translate the Greek word *exousia,* which literally means authority, right, or privilege. Faith in Christ and acceptance of him as Savior are prerequisites to gaining the authority or power to become the sons of God. Even though we are not literal sons of God the Father in the flesh, the great plan of happiness makes it possible for us to become as such through adoption into the family of Christ. We become coheirs with the Only Begotten to all that the Father has. No one can claim this honor without proper authority from the Savior, who received it from the Father.

Kent R. Brooks is an associate professor of Church history and doctrine at Brigham Young University.

JOHN, A SPECIAL WITNESS OF JESUS CHRIST

"We believe that a man must be called of God, by prophecy, and by the laying on of hands by those who are in authority, to preach the Gospel and administer in the ordinances thereof" (Articles of Faith 1:5). John, a fisherman by trade, was called by the Lord and given the *power*, the authority, the right, and the privilege to be one of the Twelve Apostles, or special witnesses, of Jesus Christ. Upon his call, John "immediately left [his] ship and [his] father, and followed [Jesus]" (Matthew 4:22). When one is called by proper authority and acts "in the power of the ordination wherewith he has been ordained" (D&C 79:1), his background or experience matters not, for "whom the Lord calls, the Lord qualifies."[1] Under the divine tutelage of the Savior, John was qualified as one of the "special witnesses of the name of Christ" (D&C 107:23) to "bear witness to his doctrine [and] of its effect upon mankind."[2]

What is the doctrine of Christ, of which John was to be a special witness? The doctrine of Christ is the doctrine of the Father. Jesus taught, "My doctrine is not mine, but his that sent me. If any man will do his will, he shall know of the doctrine, whether it be of God, or whether I speak of myself" (John 7:16–17). "For I came down from heaven, not to do mine own will, but the will of him that sent me" (John 6:38; see also 4:34; 5:30). The doctrine of Christ is that we come unto Him through faith, repent of our sins, receive the Holy Ghost, and endure to the end (see 2 Nephi 31:17–21; 3 Nephi 11:29–41). Jesus said, "I am the way, the truth, and the life" (John 14:6). "I am the door of the sheepfold. . . . By me if any man enter in, he shall be saved, and shall . . . find pasture" (JST, John 10:7, 9).[3] John stated his whole purpose in writing was that "ye might believe that Jesus is the Christ, the Son of God; and that believing ye might have life through his name" (John 20:31).

John wrote of the premortal Christ, the "Word" who was "with God, and the word was God," by whom "all things were made" (John 1:1, 3). He recorded the Savior's testimony that "before Abraham was, I am" (John 8:58). He was an eyewitness of the postmortal, resurrected Christ. Within the first eight days following His Resurrection, Jesus visited the Twelve on at least two occasions. His special witnesses were privileged to see and feel the nail prints in His hands and feet (see John 20:19–20, 26–29; 1 John 1:1) and were given the charge "as my Father hath sent me, even so I send you" (John 20:21). After those visits, Jesus appeared to John and other disciples at the Sea of Tiberius or the Sea of Galilee (see John 21:1–2). On numerous other occasions during His forty-day ministry, they were taught many "things pertaining to the kingdom of God" and received "many infallible proofs" of the living Christ (Acts 1:3). Later, while living in exile on the Isle of Patmos, John was personally visited by the risen Lord. To His beloved disciple, Jesus testified, "I am the first and the last: I am he that liveth, and was dead; and, behold, I am alive for evermore" (Revelation 1:17–18).

As a witness of the mortal Christ, the "only begotten of the Father," who "was made flesh, and dwelt among [men]" (John 1:14), John drew upon the powerful imagery the Savior used in His sermons to teach His doctrine. Jesus spoke of Himself as the "living water" (John 4:11), the "bread of life" (John 6:35, 48), the "light of the world" (John 8:12), and the "good shepherd" (John 10:11, 14), all of which bore witness that life and salvation are to be found only in Christ. John related the tender story of Lazarus, a disciple whom Jesus loved (see John 11:5, 36), for whom He wept (see John 11:35) and whom He raised from the dead (see John 11:43–44), a vivid testimony that Jesus is the "resurrection, and the life" (John 11:25). To give emphasis to the truth that we are saved "by grace . . . after all we can do" (2 Nephi 25:23), Jesus taught the parable of the vine and the branches, testifying, "I am the true vine. . . . Ye are the branches . . . without me ye can do nothing" (John 15:1, 5). John was the only one of the Gospel writers who preserved the metaphorical allusions to Jesus as the Living Water, the Bread of Life, the Good Shepherd, and the True Vine.

The mission of Christ was to "bring to pass the immortality and eternal life of man" (Moses 1:39) through the Atonement, the supreme act of love. It was His love for the Father (see John 14:31) and His love for all of us (see John 15:13) that moved Jesus to finish the work the Father gave Him to do (see John 17:4). In what Elder Bruce R. McConkie called "perhaps the most . . . powerful single verse of scripture ever uttered," John the Beloved testified: "For God so loved the world, that he gave his only begotten Son, that whosoever believeth in him should not perish, but have everlasting life" (John 3:16). That single verse, said Elder McConkie, "summarizes the whole plan of salvation, tying together the Father, the Son, his atoning sacrifice, that belief in him which presupposes righteous works, and ultimate eternal exaltation for the faithful."[4]

No one but Christ had the ability to atone for the sins of all mankind. John taught two reasons for this. First, the Atonement had to be performed by one who was sinless—one who had been perfectly obedient to the laws of God (see 1 John 3:5). Only the unblemished "Lamb of God" qualified (John 1:29). Second, the Atonement had to be performed by one who had power over life and death. From His mortal mother, Christ inherited the power to lay down His life; from His immortal Father, He inherited the power to take up His life again (see John 5:26). In perfect submission to the will of the Father, Jesus chose to lay down His life voluntarily (see John 10:17–18). John testified that this act of matchless love could not have been completed without the shedding of blood (see 1 John 1:7; Revelation 1:5; 5:9). Christ's sinless and voluntary self-sacrifice provided a redemptive and enabling power to all mankind.

THE REDEMPTIVE POWER OF THE ATONEMENT

The Fall of Adam brought into the world both physical death, which is the separation of the spirit from the body (see James 2:26), and spiritual death, separation from God or alienation from the things of God (see Alma 12:32). The Atonement of Christ redeems, or ransoms, us from the effects of the Fall. "Redemption," Elder Bruce R. McConkie taught, "is of two kinds: conditional and unconditional."[5]

Unconditional redemption provides two free gifts to mankind. The first unconditional gift is that all who ever have or ever will live in mortality will be redeemed from physical death through the Resurrection, because Jesus "taste[d] death for every man" (Hebrews 2:9). John recorded the Savior's own testimony that all "shall come forth; they who have done good, in the resurrection of the just; and they who have done evil, in the resurrection of the unjust" (Inspired Version, John 5:29).

Whether just or unjust, all will be raised with an immortal body, never again subject to death or the pains, sicknesses, and fatigues of the mortal body (see Alma 11:41–45). I came to appreciate that blessing as a teenager. My father suffered from the effects of diabetes, including the loss of sight in the last two years of his life. Although I experienced a great loss when he died during my senior year in high school, I felt peace knowing his spirit would one day be reunited with a perfect physical body that would be free from the physical afflictions he had suffered in this life. I rejoiced to know his passing had restored his sight and that he could see his family for the first time in more than two years. "Jesus said . . . I am come into this world, that they which see not might see" (John 9:39).

The second unconditional blessing of the Atonement is expressed in our second article of faith: "We believe that men will be punished for their own sins, and not for Adam's transgression." Although each of us is certainly influenced by the Fall of Adam (that is, we all experience pain, suffering, sickness, and death), the infinite mercy of Christ prevents us from being punished for Adam's transgression or the sins of anyone else. We may suffer because of the sins of another, but that suffering does not occur as a punishment imposed by God. For God to punish one person for the sins of another would not be just. John recorded the words of Jesus: "The Father . . . hath committed all judgment unto the Son" (John 5:22) and "my judgment is just" (John 5:30).

Redemption from physical death is unconditional, but redemption from spiritual death is not. "Conditional redemption," Elder McConkie said, "is synonymous with exaltation or eternal life. It comes by the grace of God coupled with good works and includes redemption from the effects of both the temporal and spiritual fall."[6] We alienate ourselves from God and die spiritually through sin. And because all sin, John reasoned, all have need of the Atonement (see 1 John 1:8, 10). John further explained that the Atonement provides redemption from spiritual death upon conditions of repentance and subsequent obedience and makes spiritual rebirth possible (see John 3:3–5; 8:51; 1 John 1:9; 2:29; JST, 1 John 3:9; 5:18; Revelation 2:11; 20:6). "If any man sin and repent," John testified, "we have an advocate with the Father, Jesus Christ the righteous; and he is the propitiation for our sins: and not for ours only, but also for the sins of the whole world" (JST, 1 John 2:1–2). Here the English word *advocate* is used to translate the Greek word *parakletos,* which means intercessor, helper, or comforter. If our hearts are broken, our spirits contrite, and we exercise faith unto repentance, Jesus will intercede at the Final Judgment as our advocate with the Father (see Moroni 7:28). And "no man," Jesus said, "cometh unto the Father, but by me" (John 14:6).

The word *atonement* means literally to reconcile or to set at one—one with God.[7] Jesus, who was one with the Father (see John 10:30), mediates a reconciliation between God and us whereby we are "brought again into communion with [the Father], and [are] made able to live and advance as a resurrected being in the eternal worlds."[8] By so doing, Jesus, the "author and finisher of our faith" (Hebrews 12:2), answers "the ends of the law" (2 Nephi 2:7), thus bringing about our eternal happiness, which is the "end" or the "object and design of our existence."[9]

The word *propitiation* is used to translate the Greek word *hilasmos,* which denotes an appeasing, or the means of appeasing. We are accountable for how we exercise our agency and what we do with the laws of God. According to the law of justice, if we obey the laws of God, we automatically receive the blessings associated with those laws (see D&C 82:10). In a sense, we get what we deserve. But if we violate the laws of God, we will also get what we deserve because the penalty of sin automatically follows (see D&C 130:20–21). "That," Elder Dallin H. Oaks said, "is an outcome I fear. I cannot achieve my eternal goals on the basis of what I deserve. Though I try with all my might, I am still what King Benjamin called an 'unprofitable servant' (see Mosiah 2:21). To achieve my eternal goals, I need more than I deserve. I need more than justice. . . . [I need mercy through] the atonement of Jesus Christ. . . . Mercy signifies an advantage greater than is deserved. This could come by the withholding of a deserved punishment or by the granting of an undeserved benefit. . . . If justice is exactly [the punishment] one deserves, then mercy is *more* benefit than one deserves. . . . *The Atonement* is the means by which justice is served and mercy is extended."[10]

President J. Reuben Clark Jr. said: "I believe that our Heavenly Father wants to save every one of his children. . . . I believe that in his justice and mercy he will give us the maximum reward for our acts, give us all that he can give, and in the reverse, I believe that he will impose upon us the minimum penalty which it is possible for him to impose."[11] If we accept the terms of conditional redemption, then "mercy can satisfy the demands of justice, and encircles [us] in the arms of safety" (Alma 34:16). John testified "the Lamb . . . shall feed [us], and shall lead [us] unto living fountains of waters: and God shall wipe away all tears from [our] eyes" (Revelation 7:17). If we let Him, the Good Shepherd will free us from the entanglements of sin and bring us safely back to the fold.

Conditional redemption requires that we repent fully of all our sins. The repentance that brings complete forgiveness requires suffering. President Spencer W. Kimball said: "There can be no forgiveness without real and total repentance, and there can be no repentance without punishment."[12] The unrepentant sinner must pay the full price of sin. "He that exercises no faith unto repentance," Alma said, "is exposed to the whole law of the demands of justice; therefore only unto him that has faith unto repentance is brought about the great and eternal plan of redemption" (Alma 34:16). If an unrepentant sinner is exposed to the full extent of the demands of justice, then what about the repentant sinner? Jesus said: "For behold, I, God, have suffered these things for all, that they might not suffer if they would repent; but if they would not repent they must suffer even as I" (D&C 19:16–17). Can the repentant sinner escape suffering entirely, or is he still subject to part of the demands of justice? Can the repentant sinner satisfy the demands of justice by his own suffering, by his own works of repentance?

Elder Oaks answered these questions. He said:

> Do these [verses] mean that a person who repents does not need to suffer at all because the entire punishment is borne by the Savior? [No, they mean] that the person who repents does not need to suffer "even as" the Savior suffered for that sin. Sinners who are repenting will experience some suffering, but, because of their repentance and because of the Atonement, they will not experience the full . . . extent of [suffering] the Savior [did] for that sin. . . . The suffering that impels a transgressor toward repentance is his or her own suffering. But the suffering that satisfies the demands of justice for all repented transgressions is the suffering of our Savior and Redeemer. . . . Some transgressors . . . [ask] "Why must I suffer at all? . . . Now that I have said I am sorry, why can't you just give me mercy and forget about this?" . . . The object of God's laws is to save the sinner, not simply to punish him. . . . The repentant transgressor must be changed, and the conditions of repentance, including confession and personal suffering, are essential to accomplish that change. To exempt a transgressor from those conditions would deprive him of the change necessary for his salvation.[13]

Only through Christ's suffering and Christ's grace, John testified, can we receive the "fulness" of the Father, "even immortality and eternal life" (Inspired Version, John 1:16). Lehi taught "there is no flesh that can dwell in the presence of God, save it be through the merits, and mercy, and grace of the Holy Messiah" (2 Nephi 2:8). Nephi said the fullness of the Father is available only to those who have unshaken faith in the words of Christ, who rely "wholly upon the merits of him who is mighty to save" (2 Nephi 31:19). The word *merits* is found six times in the scriptures. Five of those references are in the Book of Mormon (see 2 Nephi 2:8; 31:19; Alma 24:10; Helaman 14:13; Moroni 6:4), and one is in the Doctrine and Covenants (see D&C 3:20). All six passages refer to the merits of Christ.

We must do our part, but no matter how hard we try, no matter how fully we repent, no matter how many good works we do, we simply cannot bring about our own redemption. John recorded the words of Jesus: "As the branch cannot bear fruit of itself, except it abide in the vine; no more can ye, except ye abide in me" (John 15:4). Elder Oaks said: "Man unquestionably has impressive powers and can bring to pass great things by tireless efforts and indomitable will. But after all our obedience and good works, we cannot be saved from the effect of our sins without the grace extended by the atonement of Jesus Christ."[14]

The Enabling Power of the Atonement

In the October 1995 general conference of the Church, President Boyd K. Packer said: "[Except for] the very few who defect to perdition, there is no habit, no addiction, no rebellion, no transgression, no apostasy, no crime exempted from the promise of complete forgiveness. That is the promise of the atonement of Christ."[15] Clearly, the Atonement has the power to redeem us from sin and from the effects of the Fall. But the Atonement also has the power to enable us. To *enable* means "to make able; give power, means, or ability to; make competent."[16] The redemptive power of the Atonement makes us clean. The enabling power of the Atonement, which is activated by faith in Jesus Christ, makes us powerful, able, competent, and holy. It is the power that compensates when we do our best and still fall short. It is the power that magnifies our abilities, allowing us to achieve beyond our own natural capacity. It is the power that enables us to keep trying even when we feel like giving up. It is the power by which we are "born again" (John 3:3) and become perfect (see John 17:23).

Our goal is not just to become clean. Our goal is to become like God! We cannot do that by ourselves. C. S. Lewis said:

> When I was a child I often had [a] toothache, and I knew that if I went to my mother she would give me something which would deaden the pain for that night and let me get to sleep. But I did not go to my mother—at least, not till the pain became very bad. . . . I did not doubt she would give me the aspirin; but I knew she would also do something else. I knew she would take me to the dentist next morning. I could not get what I wanted out of her without getting something more, which I did not want. I wanted immediate relief from pain: but I could not get it without [also going to the dentist].
>
> Our Lord is like the dentist. . . . Dozens of people go to Him to be cured of some one particular sin which they are ashamed of . . . or which is obviously spoiling daily life. . . . Well, He will cure it all

right: but He will not stop there. That may be all you asked; but if you once call Him in, He will give you the full treatment. . . . "Make no mistake," He says, "if you let Me, I will make you perfect. The moment you put yourself in My hands, that is what you are in for. Nothing less, or other, than that. You have [free will], and if you choose, you can push Me away. But if you do not push Me away, understand that I am going to see this job through. . . . I will never rest, nor let you rest, until you are literally perfect—until my Father can say without reservation that He is well pleased with you, as He said He was well pleased with Me."

And yet—this is the other and equally important side of it—this Helper who will, in the long run, be satisfied with nothing less than absolute perfection, will also be delighted with the first feeble, stumbling effort you make tomorrow to do the simplest duty. As a great Christian writer (George MacDonald) pointed out . . . "God is easy to please, but hard to satisfy." . . . On the one hand, God's demand for perfection need not discourage you in the least in your present attempts to be good, or even in your present failures. Each time you fall He will pick you up again. And He knows perfectly well that your own efforts are never going to bring you anywhere near perfection. On the other hand, you must realize from the outset that the goal toward which He is beginning to guide you is absolute perfection; and no power in the whole universe, except you yourself, can prevent Him from taking you to that goal.[17]

Like the redemptive power of the Atonement, the enabling power is made possible by the grace of God. We can, by our sins, spiritually disable ourselves. But we cannot, without His help, become spiritually enabled. He is the source, the "outlet," of the power. If we accept His Atonement and let our will be swallowed up in His, we can "plug into" that unfailing source of power and strength.

John wrote of the enabling power of the Atonement. Recorded in John 15:7 are the words of the Savior: "If ye abide in me, and my words abide in you, ye shall ask what ye will, and it shall be done unto you." John bore witness that "whatsoever we ask, we receive of him, because we *keep his commandments,* and *do those things that are pleasing in his sight*" (1 John 3:22; emphasis added). "And this is the confidence that we have in him, that, if we ask any thing *according to his will,* he heareth us" (1 John 5:14; emphasis added). Those who are obedient to that counsel will truly discover "with God nothing *can* be impossible" (JST, Luke 1:37; emphasis added). There is no weakness, no bitterness, no pain, no sickness, no trouble, no habit, no hurt we cannot overcome with His help. There is no attribute of godliness we cannot develop, no righteous desire we cannot accomplish through His enabling power. The Bread of Life can supplant whatever we lack. The Living Water can bring life and nurture additional growth "after all we can do" (2 Nephi 25:23).

For example, we may feel we cannot forgive another who has hurt us, cannot love someone who seems unlovable, cannot pray for those who despitefully use us (see Matthew 5:44), cannot renew trust in one who has violated our trust, or cannot continue to try when we are weary of well-doing or feel we are not succeeding. Through faith, the enabling power can help us forgive when we cannot find forgiveness within ourselves, love when we feel no love, pray when we do not feel like praying, trust when trust seems impossible, and press forward in spite of the press of life. The enabling power of the Atonement can help us overcome all things (see D&C 63:47) because "all things are possible to him that believeth" (Mark 9:23). John said those who overcome through the enabling power of the Atonement will become "kings and priests" (Revelation 1:6; 5:10), will gain eternal life (see Revelation 2:7), will avoid the second spiritual death (see Revelation 2:11), will inherit the celestial kingdom (see Revelation 2:17), will be made rulers over many kingdoms (see Revelation 2:26–28), will retain their names in the Lamb's book of life (see Revelation 3:5), will become the sons of God (see Revelation 21:7), and will be endowed with the power, the authority, the right, and the privilege to reign forever in celestial splendor (see Revelation 22:3–5). "God shall wipe away all tears from their eyes"; he taught, "and there shall be no more death, neither sorrow, nor crying, neither shall there be any more pain: for the former things are passed away" (Revelation 21:4).

In the words of the beautiful hymn "More Holiness Give Me," we find a wonderful expression of what the enabling power can bring to us:

> More holiness give me,
> More strivings within,
> More patience in suff'ring,
> . . . More faith in my Savior,
> More sense of his care,
> More joy in his service,
> More purpose in prayer.

> More gratitude give me,
> More trust in the Lord,
> . . . More hope in his word,
> . . . More meekness in trial,
> More praise for relief.
>
> More purity give me,
> More strength to o'ercome, . . .
> More blessed and holy—
> More, Savior, like thee.[18]

President Ezra Taft Benson said that "men and women who turn their lives over to God will discover that He can make a lot more out of their lives than they can. He will deepen their joys, expand their vision, quicken their minds, strengthen their muscles, lift their spirits, multiply their blessings, increase their opportunities, comfort their souls, raise up friends, and pour out peace. Whoever will lose his life in the service of God will find eternal life."[19]

The enabling power of Christ can do all that and more. Alma prophesied: "[Jesus] shall go forth, suffering pains . . . of every kind; and . . . he will take upon him the . . . sicknesses of his people . . . and . . . their infirmities, that his bowels may be filled with mercy, according to the flesh, that he may know according to the flesh how to succor his people according to their infirmities" (Alma 7:11–12; see also Matthew 8:17).

Elder Jeffrey R. Holland noted the word *succor* literally means "'to run to.' . . . Even as he calls us to come to him and follow him, he is unfailingly running to help us."[20] Such is the love of the Good Shepherd. As John so beautifully recorded: "The sheep hear his voice: and he calleth his own sheep by name, and leadeth them out. . . . And . . . he goeth before them, and the sheep follow him: for they know his voice" (John 10:3–4). Jesus understands perfectly every feeling, every temptation, every pain, every weakness, every sickness, every infirmity, and every difficulty known to man. He knows us. He loves us. He desires to help us. And that "teacher come from God" (John 3:2) can enable us to do all things, if we will but let Him.

Elder Bruce C. Hafen of the Quorum of the Seventy spoke of the enabling power of the Atonement. He said:

> A sense of falling short or falling down is not only natural but essential to the mortal experience. . . . The Savior's victory can

compensate not only for our sins but also for our inadequacies; not only for our deliberate mistakes but also for our sins committed in ignorance, our errors of judgment, and our unavoidable imperfections. I grieve for those who . . . believe that, in the quest for eternal life, the Atonement is there only to help big-time sinners, and that they, as everyday Mormons who just have to try harder, must "make it" on their own. The truth is not that we must "make it" on our own, but that he will make us his own. . . . As we [hold to the iron rod], we are likely to find that the cold rod of iron will begin to feel . . . [like the] loving hand of one who is literally pulling us along the way. He gives us strength enough to rescue us [and] warmth enough to tell us that home is not far away. . . . Sometimes we talk about how important it is to be on the Lord's side. Perhaps we should talk more about how important it is that the Lord is on *our* side.[21]

Is it any wonder that John, the "disciple whom Jesus loved" (John 21:7, 20; 13:23; 19:26–27; 20:2), spoke so often and with so much tenderness of the love of the Savior. He said Jesus loved the Twelve "unto the end" (John 13:1). As a special witness of that love, John wrote: "[I] have seen and do testify that the Father sent the Son to be the Saviour of the world. . . . [I] have known and believed the love that God hath to [me]. God is love; . . . [and] there is no fear in love; but perfect love casteth out fear. . . . [I] love him, because he first loved [me]" (1 John 4:14, 16, 18–19). The amazing thing is not that *we* could love *Him,* a being who is perfect and who has done so much for us. No, what causes each of us to "stand all amazed" is that He was willing

> To rescue a soul so rebellious and proud as mine,
> That he should extend his great love unto such as I, . . .
>
> Oh, it is wonderful that he should care for me
> Enough to die for me!
> Oh, it is wonderful, wonderful to me![22]

The Prophet Joseph Smith taught: "Would it be possible for a man to exercise faith in God, so as to be saved, unless he had an idea that God was love? He could not; because man could not love God unless he had an idea that God was love, and if he did not love God he could not have faith in him."[23] Without God's grace, His perfect love for us, we could not be saved. Without our faith in His perfect love and our determination to love and serve Him with all our "heart, . . . might, mind, and strength" (D&C 59:5), we could not be saved. But through His perfect love, His atoning sacrifice, we can be redeemed from the Fall and be enabled to return home, back to the presence of our Heavenly Father, where, John testified, we will forever "have right to the tree of life" (Revelation 22:14), the love of God (see 1 Nephi 11:21–22), and can drink freely of "the water of life" (Revelation 22:17).

"When, at last, we are truly pointed homeward," said Elder Neal A. Maxwell, "the world's pointing fingers of scorn can better be endured. As we come to know to Whom we belong, the other forms of belonging cease to mean very much. Likewise, as Jesus begins to have a real place in our lives, we are much less concerned with losing our places in the world. When our minds really catch hold of the significance of Jesus' atonement, the world's hold on us loosens. (See Alma 36:18.)"[24]

John declared of his writings, "These are written, that ye might believe that Jesus is the Christ, the Son of God; and that believing ye might have life through his name" (John 20:31). Blessed by the testimony of this special witness, our knowledge of and our faith in the redeeming and enabling powers of the Atonement are strengthened. With gratitude we exclaim, "Oh, sweet the joy this sentence gives: 'I know that my Redeemer lives!'"[25]

NOTES

1. Thomas S. Monson, "You Make a Difference," *Ensign,* May 1988, 43.
2. David O. McKay, *Gospel Ideals* (Salt Lake City: Improvement Era, 1953), 251.
3. Joseph Smith Translation quotations not available in the Latter-day Saint edition of the Bible are from Thomas A. Wayment, ed., *The Complete Joseph Smith Translation of the Bible: A Side-by-Side Comparison with the King James Version* (Salt Lake City: Deseret Book, 2005).
4. Bruce R. McConkie, *Doctrinal New Testament Commentary, 3 vols.* (Salt Lake City: Bookcraft, 1965–73), 1:144.
5. Bruce R. McConkie, *Mormon Doctrine,* 2d ed. (Salt Lake City: Bookcraft, 1966), 623.
6. McConkie, *Mormon Doctrine,* 623.
7. Boyd K. Packer, "Atonement, Agency, Accountability," *Ensign,* May 1988, 69.
8. James E. Talmage, in Hugh B. Brown, *The Abundant Life* (Salt Lake City: Bookcraft, 1965), 315.
9. Joseph Smith, *Teachings of the Prophet Joseph Smith,* comp. Joseph Fielding Smith (Salt Lake City: Deseret Book, 1976), 255.

10. Dallin H. Oaks, "Sins, Crimes, and Atonement," address to CES religious educators, February 7, 1992 (Salt Lake City: The Church of Jesus Christ of Latter-day Saints), 2.

11. J. Reuben Clark Jr., in Conference Report, October 1953, 84.

12. Spencer W. Kimball, "To Bear the Priesthood Worthily," *Ensign*, May 1975, 78.

13. Oaks, "Sins, Crimes, and Atonement," 5–6.

14. Dallin H. Oaks, "'What Think Ye of Christ?'" *Ensign*, November 1988, 67.

15. Boyd K. Packer, "The Brilliant Morning of Forgiveness," *Ensign*, November 1995, 20.

16. *Webster's Encyclopedic Unabridged Dictionary of the English Language* (New York: Gramercy Books, 1989), s.v. "enable."

17. C. S. Lewis, "Perfection," from *The Joyful Christian* (New York: Macmillan, 1977), 77–78.

18. *Hymns* (Salt Lake City: The Church of Jesus Christ of Latter-day Saints, 1985), no. 131.

19. Ezra Taft Benson, *The Teachings of Ezra Taft Benson* (Salt Lake City: Bookcraft, 1988), 361; see also Matthew 10:39.

20. Jeffrey R. Holland, "Come unto Me," *Ensign*, April 1998, 22; see also D&C 112:13.

21. Bruce C. Hafen, *The Broken Heart* (Salt Lake City: Deseret Book, 1989), 20, 22.

22. "I Stand All Amazed," *Hymns*, no. 193.

23. Joseph Smith, comp., *Lectures on Faith* (Salt Lake City: Deseret Book, 1985), 3:47.

24. Neal A. Maxwell, "Settle This in Your Hearts," *Ensign*, November 1992, 66–67.

25. "I Know That My Redeemer Lives," *Hymns*, no. 136.

CHAPTER FOURTEEN

THE PASSION OF JESUS CHRIST

RICHARD NEITZEL HOLZAPFEL

For many years, students of the New Testament have used Gospel harmonies to study Jesus' ministry as described in the writings of Matthew, Mark, Luke, and John. A Gospel harmony, sometimes called a synopsis (from the Greek *synoptos*), endeavors to weave all the details of the Gospel tradition into a single chronological strand, one composite order, or sequence.[1] A Gospel harmony usually presents the Gospels in parallel columns such that readers see all similarities in the texts at a single glance.[2] One Latter-day Saint author argues that Gospel "harmonies are based upon the Gestalt principle that the whole of anything is greater than the sum of its parts. Since each gospel represents a part, the greater message of the life of Jesus can only be seen when all four are arranged together."[3] Although it is true that any study of Jesus' life should examine all relevant texts (in particular the four Gospels), it is not necessarily true that the Gestalt principle applies totally to a study of Jesus' life. The unwise use of a Gospel harmony—taking the four Gospels as a whole—can distort the historical setting of each story. Undoubtedly each writer preserved a separate and distinct account of Jesus' life and ministry for a good reason.

Jesus proclaimed the gospel, meaning the good news (the English word *gospel* is derived from the Anglo-Saxon *godspell*, which means "good tidings").[4] Jesus declared the gospel that the kingdom of God had come through Him, and the New Testament writers presented the good news about Jesus.[5] The title given to their work from the second century onward is significant: the Gospel *according to* Matthew, the Gospel *according to* Mark, and so on. So, although Jesus proclaimed a single gospel, the

---

Richard Neitzel Holzapfel is a professor of Church history and doctrine at Brigham Young University.

evangelists presented the life of Jesus in accordance with what they under-stood. Each writer thus gave his particular testimony, and as a result today we have four Gospels.[6]

In those Gospels we have four separate and distinct viewpoints of Jesus' suffering, betrayal, trial, and Crucifixion. The "Passion narratives" include most of the material found in Matthew 26–27, Mark 14–15, Luke 22–23, and John 12–19. Each was written at a different time for a different audience. To maintain the integrity of the story of the Passion as a whole, we must examine each narrative independent of the others, instead of making one Gospel of them. Attempting to harmonize the four accounts may lead us away from the messages and insights that each Gospel writer intended to teach. The phrase "Garden of Gethsemane" is an example of what can happen when we harmonize the Gospel narratives. The phrase "Garden of Gethsemane" does not exist anywhere in the New Testament text; rather, it is a hybrid term constructed from the "garden," in the Gospel according to John (see John 18:1) and "Gethsemane," in the Gospels according to Matthew and Mark (see Matthew 26:36; Mark 14:32). Such blending of the narratives may create concepts and historical notions that have no basis in the New Testament text itself, for, although each Gospel relates the historical events of the Passion, each has a particular tone.

The first three Gospels—Matthew, Mark, and Luke—are called the synoptic Gospels because they share similar material (the Greek word *synoptikos* means "to see the whole together, to take a comprehensive view").[7] John stands apart from the synoptic Gospels because his work has a significant amount of unique material. John's narrative contains several important discourses delivered by Jesus that are not recorded anywhere else (see John 13–17).

MATTHEW'S PASSION NARRATIVE

In Matthew, the Passion narrative (see Matthew 26:1–27:56) begins with Jesus' anointing in Bethany: "Now when Jesus was in Bethany, in the house of Simon the leper, there came unto him a woman having an alabaster box of very precious ointment, and poured it on his head, as he sat at meat. But when his disciples saw it, they had indignation, saying, To what purpose is this waste? . . . When Jesus understood it, he said unto them, Why trouble ye the woman? for she hath wrought a good work upon me. . . . For in that she hath poured this ointment on my body, she did it for my burial" (Matthew 26:6–12).

Jesus' statement "she did it for my burial" can mean only that He already knows that He will be crucified and buried without the customary anointing.[8] Then we read of Judas's betrayal (see Matthew 26:1–5); the disciples prepare for the Passover (see Matthew 26:17–19); Jesus identifies the betrayer and institutes the Lord's Supper (see Matthew 26:20–30); Jesus ends the dinner in the upper room with a Passover hymn, possibly Psalms 113–18 (see Matthew 26:30).

Following His departure from the upper room, Jesus goes to Gethsemane, where He "saith unto the disciples, Sit ye here, while I go and pray yonder" (Matthew 26:36). Having separated Himself, Jesus begins to be "sorrowful and very heavy" (Matthew 26:37). Alternative translations from the Greek for *sorrowful* and *heavy* are "distressed" and "troubled" (see footnote 37*a* in the Latter-day Saint edition of the KJV). Eventually Jesus "fell on his face" (Matthew 26:39). In Matthew's account, Jesus begins His prayer sorrowful, troubled, and prostrate but ends on His feet, resolutely facing the mob that has approached. In Matthew 26:46, Jesus commands His disciples, saying, "Rise, let us be going: behold, he is at hand that doth betray me."

Judas, the traitor, greets Jesus, "Hail, master," and then kisses Him (Matthew 26:49). By using a kiss to show who the soldiers should arrest, Judas perverts a gesture of friendship he has had with his former Master. Matthew adds "hail" to the salutation as a further example of Judas's false-heartedness. After a brief skirmish between one of the disciples and the high priest's servant, "all the disciples forsook him, and fled" (Matthew 26:56).

Jesus is betrayed by one of His own, abandoned by the remaining disciples, and in the end is accused by His own religious leaders. Deserted by His disciples and surrounded by His enemies, Jesus is taken before the Sanhedrin (see Matthew 26:57–68). They take Him finally to the Gentiles for trial, mockery, and execution. In spite of these trials, Jesus is self-possessed when He confronts the Roman governor who can decree His death.

Only Matthew informs us of the custom of releasing a prisoner at the feast, thus giving Pilate a possible escape clause. Another overtly Matthean insight is the account of Pilate's wife, who as a Gentile recognizes Jesus' innocence and seeks His release, while the Jewish leaders work the crowd to have the notorious Barabbas released and Jesus crucified. Some important manuscripts of Matthew compare Barabbas and Jesus in a unique way, for they phrase Pilate's question in 27:17 thus: "Who do you want me to release to you, Jesus Barabbas or Jesus called Christ?" Since "Barabbas" probably means "Son of the Father," it would be a fascinating irony for Pilate to have faced two accused men named Jesus, one "Son of the Father," the other "Son of God."[9] Presented with the choice between the two, the Jewish crowd seeks the release of Barabbas. Pilate then "took water, and washed his hands before the multitude" (Matthew 27:24). He "scourged Jesus, [and] delivered him to be crucified" (Matthew 27:26).

Crucifixion was an ancient and malicious form of punishment that the Romans used to kill an enemy. The first-century Jewish historian Josephus, who witnessed several crucifixions as an adviser to Titus during the siege of Jerusalem, tersely describes this form of Roman punishment as "the most wretched of deaths." He reports that a threat by the Roman besiegers to crucify a Jewish prisoner caused the garrison of Machaerus to surrender in exchange for safe conduct.[10]

The practice of crucifixion was remarkably widespread in the ancient world, not just among the Romans. But for the Romans it was a political and military punishment, inflicted primarily on the lower classes, slaves, violent criminals, and the unruly elements in rebellious provinces, not the least of which was Judea.[11] The dominant reason for its use seems to be its allegedly matchless efficacy as a deterrent. Crucifixions were, of course, carried out publicly. By publicly displaying a naked victim at a prominent place such as a crossroads, a theatre, high ground, or the place of his crime, the Romans also ensured a criminal's uttermost humiliation. Jews were particularly averse to this punishment in light of Deuteronomy 21:23, which specifically pronounced God's curse on the crucified individual.

Matthew identifies some of the participants in the actual crucifixion and gives the location as "Golgotha" (Matthew 27:33).[12] The name may have been given to a place that resembled a skull, or it may have been so named because it was a regular place of execution.

Matthew's allusions to the Old Testament underscore the emphasis laid on God's acts. One such parallel Matthew offers is the story of Judas's death. After betraying Christ, Judas "went and hanged himself" (Matthew 27:5), an echo of the story of King David. It reveals the similarity of David's own flight to the Kidron and the subsequent betrayal by Achitophel, who also hanged himself (see 2 Samuel 15:12, 14, 23; 17:23).[13]

Matthew's repeated use of the Old Testament provides a clue to his unique purpose, namely demonstrating the fulfillment of God's purposes in and through Jesus.[14] Matthew is interested in themes rather than in history; the most superficial examination of his Gospel from a purely historical point of view reveals that a disproportionate amount of attention is devoted to the Passion narrative. Thus, Old Testament quotations in the Passion narrative combined with the familiar Matthean formula "that it might be fulfilled which was spoken by the prophet" (Matthew 27:35), the Gospel of Matthew reemphasizes God's salvation proclaimed from the beginning of time. The emphasis on the Messiah is His redemption of mankind from the captivity of sin, not from military power as expected by the Jews.

MARK'S PASSION NARRATIVE

In Mark's Passion narrative (see Mark 14:1–15:47), the death plot (see Matthew 14:1ff) is followed by the anointing in Bethany (see Mark 14:3–9), Judas's betrayal (see Mark 14:10ff), the preparation of the last meal, announcement of the betrayal, and the institution of the sacrament of the Lord's Supper (see Mark 14:12–25). Jesus leaves the upper room committed to the necessity that He must suffer and die.[15] In Gethsemane, the prostrate Jesus suffers in anguish (see Mark 14:32–42). He is God's Son, yet endowed with the human will to live; He does not want to die. The name that Jesus uses in His cry to God, "Abba" (Father), heightens the pathos of this tragic scene: "He took with him Peter, James, and John, and began to be horror-stricken and desperately depressed. 'My heart is breaking with a deathlike grief,' he told them. 'Stay here and keep watch.' Then he walked forward a little way and flung himself in the ground, praying that, if it were possible, the hour might pass him by, 'Dear Father,' he said, 'all things are possible to you. Let me not have to drink this cup! Yet it is not what I want but what you want'" (Phillips Translation, Mark 14:33–36).[16]

It is the Father's will that Jesus die. His disciples, however, have not yet accepted this reality. Jesus states, "The sheep shall be scattered" (Mark 14:27). Peter characteristically denies that statement (see Mark 14:29), only to be told by the Master that he would yet deny the Lord three times (see Mark 14:30). The disciples at first stand in firm opposition to Jesus' arrest, but finally they all forsake him and flee. Mark's account emphasizes the complete abandonment of Jesus by everyone, even one unnamed follower (see Mark 14:52).

Peter's denial recorded in Mark 14:66–72 is really threefold. Peter at first pretends he does not understand what he has been asked. Next he endeavors to get away from the courtyard. Unable to leave, he then denies his status as a disciple. Peter swears an oath that he does not even know Jesus. Mark ends the scene with the statement, "And Peter recalled to mind the word that Jesus said to him, Before the cock crow twice, thou shalt deny me thrice" (Mark 14:72). Ironically, at the very moment when Jesus is mocked by the Sanhedrin's challenge to prophesy (see Mark 14:65), His prophecies are coming true. Mark's account of the first trial ends at this point, and the second trial begins.

The first trial before the Jewish Sanhedrin is the more decisive one, though from a legal perspective the Roman trial is more important. Throughout both trials, Jesus remains almost entirely silent. At the first trial, He is charged with threatening to destroy the temple at Jerusalem and committing blasphemy (see Mark 14:58, 64). In the second trial, He is accused of claiming to be "King of the Jews," a title that carries revolutionary overtones for the Romans (see Mark 15:2).

During the first trial, Caiaphas, the high priest, specifically questions Jesus about His claim to be the Savior Messiah. Jesus' affirmation gives the Jewish leaders the needed pretext to bring a charge of treason against Him. This charge would then be dealt with by Roman law and power, just as the Jewish leaders expected it to be (see Mark 14:61–62). Not only does Jesus give evidence to convict Himself under Roman law but He also gives Caiaphas grounds to convict Him of blasphemy, a capital crime under the law of Moses, as the claim of being a messiah is not.

New Testament scholar Joel Marcus argues that there must have been something different about Jesus' claim to be the Messiah: "Why should Jesus' claim to be 'the Messiah, the Son of God' [KJV, Mark 14:61: 'The Christ, the Son of the Blessed'] be considered blasphemous if 'Son of God' is merely a synonym for 'Messiah'? . . . One searches Jewish literature in vain for evidence that a simple claim to be the Messiah would incur such a charge."[17] Mark's report of the first trial indicates that Jesus' claim to be God's literal Son is more crucial and controversial for the Jewish leaders.[18] The Messiah-kingship issue is simply a ruse to get the Romans to take care of Jesus in the second trial.

Mark's presentation of the events after the second trial is a painful account, albeit succinct and unadorned. Characteristically, Mark reports the events with a few vivid words and without elaborating the detail: "And so Pilate, willing to content the people, released Barabbas unto them, and delivered Jesus, when he had scourged him, to be crucified. And the soldiers led him away into the hall, called Praetorium; and they call together the whole band. And they clothed him with purple, and platted a crown of thorns, and put it about his head, and began to salute him, Hail, King of the Jews! And they smote him on the head with a reed, and did spit upon him, and bowing their knees worshipped him" (Mark 15:15–19).

At the time of Christ, scourging (flogging) was done with a whip made of several strips of leather with pieces of metal and bone embedded near the ends. The victim was bound to a pillar and then beaten with the whip. While it is true that the Jews limited the number of stripes to a maximum of forty (thirty-nine in case of a miscount), no such limitation was recognized by the Romans. Victims often did not survive this punishment. Jesus survives, only to be executed by crucifixion.

Two incidents prior to Jesus' death are recorded by Mark in this climactic part of the Passion narrative: the mockery (see Mark 15:16–20) and the actual crucifixion (see Mark 15:21–31). Mark's story of brutality ends with the veil of the temple being "rent in twain from the top to the bottom" (Mark 15:38), a final act of disorder in a violent scene when Jesus is put to death at the hands of ruthless men agitated by a frenzied crowd incited by their leaders.

LUKE'S PASSION NARRATIVE

Luke begins his Passion narrative (see Luke 22:1–23:56) with the betrayal of Jesus by Judas, the Last Supper, and the farewell discourse (see Luke 22:7–38). The narrative continues with Jesus' arrival at the Mount of Olives, His arrest, the denial by Peter, the mocking of Jesus, the hearing before the Sanhedrin, the hearing before Pilate, Jesus' going before Herod Antipas, Jesus' walk to Golgotha, His words to the women of Jerusalem, His Crucifixion, and finally His burial (see Luke 22:39–23:56).

Luke's account is marked by delicacy and tenderness. He cannot bring himself to report some details that were too distressing: Luke does not say that Jesus was scourged nor that Judas actually kissed Jesus. Luke does, however, make us aware of the magnitude of the terrible struggle between Jesus and the powers of evil. The Passion is the last decisive struggle. Jesus comes out of it as victor through His patience—a word that is not a good rendering of the Greek *hypomone,* which suggests the attitude of the believer enduring blows in his trial as he is sustained by God.[19]

The decisive struggle occurs in "the place" at the Mount of Olives. Here in great agony, the Lord bleeds from every pore: "And he came out, and went, as he was wont, to the mount of Olives; and his disciples also followed him. And when he was at the place, he said unto them, Pray that ye enter not into temptation. And he was withdrawn from them about a stone's cast, and kneeled down, and prayed, saying, Father, if thou be willing, remove this cup from me: nevertheless not my will, but thine, be done" (Luke 22:39–42).

Then, comforted by God, Jesus emerges victorious. Now at peace, held in His Father's arms, He can be wholly reconciled to His God.

Luke uses the Greek *agonia* in 22:44 to indicate Jesus' intense anxiety over what will happen to Himself. The Greek meaning of *agonia* is the "athlete's state of mind before the contest, agony, dread."[20] As a result, Luke reports, Jesus "prayed more earnestly: and his sweat was as it were great drops of blood falling down to the ground" (Luke 22:44). Although some ancient manuscripts omit Luke 22:43–44 (see, for example, Codex Vaticanus), it was known to Justin Martyr, Irenaeus, Tatian, and Hippolytus in the second century.[21]

Events happen swiftly in Luke. Judas arrives with his newfound allies and attempts to salute Jesus. Jesus reminds Judas that it is the Son of Man whom he thus betrays. Peter, anxious to do something, smites off the ear of the high priest's servant. Jesus "touched [the servant's] ear, and healed him" (Luke 22:51). He helps His opponent, even in the midst of His own danger. The physician Luke sees Jesus as the greatest healer. Whether for friend or foe, Jesus' mission is one of reconciliation and healing.

The tearing of the veil of the temple just before Jesus' death is another Lucan feature departing from the other Gospels (see Luke 23:45).[22] After the curtain is rent, Jesus addresses God: "Father, into thy hands I commend my spirit" (Luke 23:46). This action symbolizes Jesus' communing with the Father, who may have been present in the temple, at the last moment before His death.

The cry Jesus utters on the cross is not a scream of human suffering before death; rather it is the evening prayer known to every Jew: "Into your hands I commend my spirit." Jesus, however, prefaces it with the term that marks His unparalleled intimacy with God: "Father" (Luke 23:46). Jesus dies in peace, at one with God.

The Crucifixion itself is the last violent act by men in the life of Him who promised them life after death. Yet Jesus' promise to the thief and to all of us is not one of mere survival after death but, more accurately, a glorious future beyond death (see Luke 23:43).

JOHN'S PASSION NARRATIVE

John wrote his Gospel some sixty years after Jesus' death, so he had meditated on the Passion for a long time before committing it to writing. In his Passion account (see John 12:11–19:42) John chooses the episodes that have the most significance to the faithful. He presents the Passion as the triumphal progress of Jesus towards the Father. Jesus knows that He is going to die, He knows what kind of death it will be, and He goes to it freely: "No one taketh [my life] from me, but I lay it down myself" (John 10:18). John does not separate death and exaltation in his account but sees them as inextricably intertwined. The lifting up of Jesus on the cross is also the beginning of His Ascension into the glory of God, from whence He will send the Spirit upon the world (see John 19:30). "I, if I be lifted up from the earth, will draw all men unto me," Jesus declares (John 12:32).

To draw all men to Himself is the essence of Jesus' mission, according to John's writings. He anticipates and accepts death not simply as the consequence of His prophetic calling but as His last service of love. The Passion of Christ is the climax of His ministry, which offers salvation by every action.

John's story of Jesus' Passion includes the farewell to His disciples: the foot washing at the meal, designation of the betrayer, the commandment of love, the allusion to Peter's denial, consolation for His own, the metaphor of Jesus as the true vine, a discussion of the hatred of the world, and the Intercessory Prayer (see John 13–17).

John's story continues at a special garden place where Jesus and His disciples "ofttimes resorted" (John 18:1–2). John began his Gospel by discussing the Creation narrative alluding to the first garden, where the conflict between Adam and Lucifer was played out. Now in a second garden, another conflict between the Savior and the serpent is played out: "When Jesus had spoken these words, he went forth with his disciples over the brook Cedron, where was a garden, into the which he entered, and his disciples. And Judas also, which betrayed him, knew the place: for Jesus ofttimes resorted thither with his disciples" (John 18:1–2).

For John, Judas is the tool of Satan. Earlier that evening Judas had gone off into the night, the evil night of which Jesus had warned in John 9:10 and 12:35, the night in which men stumble because they have no light.

The lanterns and torches the Jews carried on the night of the arrest could perhaps illustrate that they have rejected the light of the world and so must rely on the artificial light they carry with them.

Now Jesus, completely in control of His fate, leaves the garden to confront the malevolent host before Him: "Jesus therefore, knowing all things that should come upon him, went forth, and said unto them, Whom seek ye? They answered him, Jesus of Nazareth. Jesus saith unto them, I am he" (John 18:4–5).

Jesus' simple answer causes this large armed group of Roman soldiers and Jewish temple police to step backwards and fall to the ground (see John 18:6). The adversaries of Jesus are prostrate before His divine majesty, leaving us little doubt that John intends "I AM" as a divine name (Greek, *ego eimi*).[23] John emphasizes that Jesus, as God, has power over the forces of darkness. This statement reinforces our impression that Jesus could not have been arrested unless He permitted it. That belief is further substantiated by Jesus' statement before Pilate, "Thou couldest have no power at all against me, except it were given thee from above" (John 19:11).

After relating Jesus' trial before Annas and Caiaphas, John tells of Jesus' being brought to the "hall of judgment" to stand before the Roman governor (John 18:28). As Pilate examines Jesus, he asks the question, "What is truth?" (John 18:38). John seems intent on warning the reader that no one can avoid judgment when one stands before Jesus. The scene ends with an apotheosis: Pilate makes Jesus sit at his tribunal so he can proclaim Jesus king (see John 19:13). "Sit down" may mean that Pilate "made him [Jesus] sit down."[24] For John, Christ is the legitimate judge of men; in condemning Him, the Jewish leaders are judging themselves.

John records the place of these events explicitly, even noting the time: "It was the preparation of the Passover, and about the sixth hour" (John 19:14). Passover Eve, he says—or, since *paraskeue* acquired in Jewish Greek the special sense of "Sabbath eve," that is, Friday—could be rendered, "It was Friday of Passover Week at about twelve o'clock noon."[25]

John sees a deeper meaning in Pilate's words, just as He had seen a prophecy in Caiaphas's words (see John 11:49–51). The Roman governor exclaims, "Behold your King!" (John 19:14). Pilate implies that Jesus is the true king of the true Israel, of all the people of God who obey the voice of God. Spoken at midday on Passover Eve, we can infer that Jesus is the true Paschal Lamb about to be sacrificed at the appropriate hour of the appropriate day for the life of His people.

For John, the Jewish trial is a mockery of a prophet and the Roman trial a mockery of a king. Judas, a disciple, hands Jesus over to the Jewish leaders, the chief priest hands Jesus over to a Roman leader, and Pilate hands Jesus over to the soldiers to be crucified. While no one is completely responsible, each person or group hands Jesus over to another individual or group. Therefore, all collectively are responsible. John's Passion narrative ends with the scourging, crowning with thorns, crucifixion, the piercing of Jesus' side, and finally the removal of His body from the cross (see John 19:31–42).

CONCLUSION

Because the accounts of Matthew, Mark, Luke, and John of the Passion describe the same series of incidents, it is easy to blend all the narratives in our heads and produce for ourselves our own harmony, so that our version of the Passion story includes Matthew's earthquakes and his story of Pilate's wife and her dream; Luke's scene of agony; and John's memorable quote from Pilate, "What is truth?" In reality, the New Testament writers have actually preserved not one story but four separate versions of the same scenario. For each writer, the Passion narrative is the culmination of his entire Gospel story. Each testifies that Jesus' Passion fulfills the multiple prophecies and testimonies of the Lord.

Although we have a tendency to want one picture of Jesus' life—a single Gospel, as it were—the Gospel narratives do not make a single picture of Jesus, but four beautiful mosaics. They are the words and actions of Jesus as interpreted by authentic witnesses. We do not need to cut and paste them together to form a single picture. "[The first harmonies'] declared purpose," New Testament scholar Heinrich Greeven argues, was "to fuse parallel texts into one single text," and to do so, the compilers had to harmonize and diminish the differences or supposed contradictions between the stories.[26]

If we had four mosaics giving different representations of the same scene, it would not occur to us to say, "These mosaics are so beautiful that I do not want to lose any of them; I shall demolish them and use the enormous pile of stones to make a single mosaic that combines all four of them." Trying to combine the pieces would be an outrageous affront to the artists. Because the four Gospels are different from each other, we must study each one for itself, without demolishing it and using the debris to reconstruct a life of Jesus by making the four Gospels into one Gospel. Even though it is useful to study the Gospels with the aid of such tools as a harmony, we must remember that historical and exegetical methodology and scholarly tools can, in fact, divert our attention from the real drama and the essential issues raised by each of the Gospels. Any tool of study that prevents us from asking the eternally important questions "Whom seekest thou?" and "Lovest thou me?" (John 20:15; 21:15–17) is playing false to the very faith and mission of the Gospels themselves and the early Christians who read and heard these personal and authentic testimonies.

NOTES

1. Greek *synoptos*, "that can be seen at a glance, in full view" (H. G. Liddell and Scott, *An Intermediate Greek-English Lexicon* [Oxford: Clarendon Press, 1975], 779).

2. An excellent and accessible harmony is found in the Latter-day Saint Bible Dictionary under the subheading, "Gospel," 684–96. Two harmonies with scholarly apparatus, noncanonical material, and variant manuscript readings are Burton H. Throckmorton Jr., *Gospel Parallels: A Synopsis of the First Three Gospels* (Nashville, TN: Thomas Nelson Publishers, 1979) and Robert W. Funk, *New Gospel Parallels,* 2 vols. (Philadelphia: Fortress Press, 1985). A recent technical synopsis that also included the so-called Q Document in parallel columns is John S. Kloppenburg, *Q Parallels: Synopsis, Critical Notes, and Concordance* (Sonoma: Polebridge Press, 1988). For a discussion concerning the process of making a harmony, see David Dugan, "Theory of Synopsis Construction," *Biblica* 61 (1980). 305–29.

3. Thomas M. Mumford, *Horizontal Harmony of the Four Gospels in Parallel Columns* (Salt Lake City: Deseret Book, 1976), v.

4. Walter W. Skeat, *A Concise Etymological Dictionary of the English Language* (Oxford: Clarendon Press, 1976), 218.

5. The Greek *evangelion* (good news) was known to secular authors and was used to announce a victory or great events in the life of the emperor. For a fuller discussion of its usage, see William F. Arndt and Wilbur F. Gingrich, *A Greek-English Lexicon of the New Testament and Other Early Christian Literature* (Chicago: University of Chicago Press, 1957), 318.

6. For a recent discussion on the relationship of the Gospels to each other, see Kloppenburg, *Q Parallels,* xxi–xxxiv.

7. An overview of the authorship, dating, audience, and purpose of the individual Gospel accounts may be found in the Latter-day Saint Bible Dictionary under the subheading "Gospels," 682–83. This overview provides a sound historical context for any serious study of the Gospels.

8. For a discussion of this event, see W. F. Albright and C. S. Mann, *Matthew: A New Translation with Introduction and Commentary* (Garden City, NY: Doubleday, 1986), 314–15.

9. Bruce Metzger explains, "A majority of the Committee [Editorial Committee of the United Bible Societies' Greek New Testament] was of the opinion that the original text of Matthew had the double name in both verses (27:16–17) and that *Iesous* was deliberately suppressed in most witnesses for reverential consideration" (Bruce M. Metzger, *A Textual Commentary on the Greek New Testament* [London: United Bible Societies, 1975], 67–68).

10. Josephus, *De Bello Judaico* (Darmstadt, W. Germany: Wissenschaftliche Buchgesellfchaft, 1959), 7:202ff (the quotation comes from 203). For an English translation, see *The Jewish War,* trans. G. A. Williamson (New York: Penguin Books, 1969), 389–90.

11. For a survey of this subject, see Martin Hengel, *Crucifixion in the Ancient World and the Folly of the Message of the Cross* (Philadelphia: Fortress Press, 1977).

12. The Greek place name is the transliteration of the Aramaic *gulgulta,* which means "skull." The traditional name for the place is "Calvary," which is taken from the Latin *calvaria.* It means the same as Golgotha, but is, strictly speaking, not a biblical name (see Raymond E. Brown, Joseph A. Fitzmyer, and Roland E. Murphy, *The New Jerome Biblical Commentary* [Englewood Cliffs, NJ: Prentice Hall, 1990], 628).

13. There are several other Old Testament allusions in Matthew including the darkness from noon to 3:00 P.M. (see Matthew 27:45), which may refer to the darkness over Egypt before the first Passover, or perhaps it is a reference to Amos 8:9. Whichever it is, they both are God's act. In both cases,"the day" belongs to God and not to the forces of evil.

14. For a complete list of Old Testament quotations in Matthew, see Robert G. Bratcher, *Old Testament Quotations in the New Testament* (New York: United Bible Societies, 1984), 11.

15. Mark is generally credited with inventing the new literary genre of "the Gospel" (see discussion of this point in Frank Kermode, "Introduction to the New Testament," *Literary Guide to the Bible,* ed. Robert Alter and Frank Kermode [Cambridge, MA: Harvard University Press, 1987], 375–86).

16. J. B. Phillips, *The New Testament in Modern English* (New York: Macmillan, 1972), 100–101.

17. Joel Marcus, "Mark 14:61: 'Are You the Messiah-Son-of-God?'" *Novum Testamentum* 31 (April 1989): 127.

18. Marcus, "Mark 14:61," 140.

19. Arndt and Gingrich, *A Greek-English Lexicon of the New Testament,* 854.

20. See Max Zerwick and Mary Grosvernor, *A Grammatical Analysis of the Greek New Testament* (Rome: Biblical Institute Press, 1981), 237.

21. G. B. Caird argues, "Its omission is best explained as the work of a scribe who felt that this picture of Jesus overwhelmed with human weakness was incompatible with his own belief in the Divine Son who shared the

omnipotence of his Father" (*The Gospel of Saint Luke* [New York: Penguin Books, 1985], 243).

22. The synoptic Gospels agree on this event, but Matthew and Mark place it after Jesus' death (see Matthew 27:51 and Mark 15:38).

23. For a discussion of the use of *ego eimi* in John, see Gerhard Kittel's *Theological Dictionary of the New Testament,* 10 vols. (Grand Rapids, MI: Eerdmans, 1964), 2:352–54.

24. Robert G. Bratcher, *Marginal Notes for the New Testament* (New York: United Bible Societies, 1988), 66. For a fuller discussion of this possible reading, see Barclay M. Newman and Eugene A. Nida, *A Translator's Handbook on the Gospel of John* (New York: United Bible Societies, 1980), 581; and Zerwick and Grosvenor, *A Grammatical Analysis,* 341.

25. Arndt and Gingrich argue that for the "Jewish usage it was Friday, on which day everything had to be prepared for the Sabbath, when no work was permitted" (Arndt and Gingrich, *A Greek-English Lexicon of the New Testament,* 637).

26. Heinrich Greeven, in Albert Huck, *Synopse der drei ersten evangelien/ Synopsis of the First Three Gospels with the Addition of the Johannine Parallels* (Tubingen, W. Germany: J.C.B. Mohr [Paul Siebeck], 1981), xxxvi.

CHAPTER FIFTEEN

HE HAS RISEN: THE RESURRECTION NARRATIVES AS A WITNESS OF CORPOREAL REGENERATION

RICHARD D. DRAPER

Jewish antagonism toward the early Christians was both intense and active. Justin Martyr accused the Jews of having chosen "selected men from Jerusalem" whom they sent into all parts of the Mediterranean world to say "that a godless sect, namely the Christians, had appeared and recounting what all who know us not are wont to say against us."[1] This propagation of slander appears to have been a longstanding tradition persisting from the days of Saul down to the time when Martyr wrote, about AD 160. That Origen made the same reproach suggests the enmity persisted well into the third century.[2] Eusebius, in his *Ecclesiastical History,* corroborated Martyr's and Origen's testimonies. He stated that "we found in the writings of former days that the Jewish authorities in Jerusalem sent round apostles to the Jews everywhere announcing the emergence of a new heresy hostile to God, and that their apostles, armed with written authority, confuted the Christians everywhere."[3] Because the center of this activity was Jerusalem, all the writings likely reflected conditions before its fall.

The Jewish confutation denigrated the reputation of the Savior.

Richard D. Draper is associate dean of Religious Education at Brigham Young University.

From ancient sources, we gain some idea of the character of the propaganda used against Him:

> Jesus was born, they said, in a village, the illegitimate child of a peasant woman and soldier named Panthera. The woman was divorced by her husband who was a carpenter, for adultery. Jesus himself emigrated to Egypt, hired himself out as a labourer there, and after picking up some Egyptian magic, returned to his own country and full of conceit because of his powers proclaimed himself God. His so-called miracles were unauthenticated, his prophesies were proved false and in the end he was not helped by the Father, nor could he help himself. His disciples had taken his body and pretended that he had risen again and was Son of God.[4]

This assault struck against the historical witnesses of the Lord's divinity: the conditions of His conception, His miracles and prophecies, and, important for this study, His Resurrection. The latter was the most necessary to discredit and, fortunately for the Lord's detractors, the easiest.

THE DIFFICULTY IN ACCEPTING THE IDEA OF A PHYSICAL RESURRECTION

The Hellenistic mind-set found the idea of a resurrection strange indeed. Many Greeks or Romans would have had little difficulty believing that a god had sired a son. Their mythology abounded with stories of gods consorting with mortal women and having children by them.[5] Further, the belief in prophecy and portents was widespread.[6] Publications that commonly reported miracles and miracle mongers appeared frequently.[7] Even the idea that a mortal man could become as the gods was not difficult for many to accept.[8] There were even precedents for both men and gods dying and coming back to life.[9] But the idea that a mortal could rise from the dead and enter eternal life with a *physical body* had little precedent. Much of the Hellenistic world denied the reality of any kind of resurrection, let alone a physical one. There were those who believed that mortals had been resuscitated—even brought back from the world of spirits—but these events had occurred only in isolated incidents and merely postponed eventual death.[10] In addition, the Hellenistic cosmology found the belief in any kind of a general resurrection at the end of world history totally foreign.[11]

Accordingly, it is easy to understand the Athenian reaction to Paul when "he preached unto them Jesus, and the resurrection" (Acts 17:18).

The crowd responded by calling him "a babbler" who set forth "strange gods" (v. 18). Later he gave his "unknown god" sermon (vv. 22–31), to which the people listened intently until he got to resurrection. "And when they heard of the resurrection of the dead, some mocked: and others said, We will hear thee again of this matter" (v. 32), but in the end few accepted the witness.[12] Certainly, the idea of a resurrection found no popular response from the Greeks.

Samaritan and Jewish belief, especially the belief of the Sadducees, followed suit. There was biblical precedent for people dying and being resuscitated. Elijah had raised a boy from the dead (see 1 Kings 17:17–23), as had Elisha (see 2 Kings 4:18–37), but most people rejected the notion of a corporeal and eternal resurrection. The Pharisees were the exception to this line of thinking. Basing their interpretation of the Old Testament on the oral tradition handed down by their leaders, they made belief in a literal resurrection a point of doctrine. Indeed, most Pharisees believed that the coming Messiah would hold the key to life and that when He came He would exercise that power.[13] Because of the popularity of this sect, many Jews began to accept the idea of a corporeal resurrection; however, the belief never became universal, and a strong contingent continued to reject it.

Paul's frustration in trying to teach both Jews and Gentiles about the death and Resurrection of Christ shows in this statement: "We preach Christ crucified, unto the Jews a stumbling-block, and unto the Greeks foolishness" (1 Corinthians 1:23). Paul's statement, though centered on the Crucifixion, has direct bearing on the Jewish reaction to the Christian witness of the Resurrection of the Lord.

THE IMPORTANCE OF THE CRUCIFIXION TO JEWISH ANTAGONISTS

The Jewish rulers deliberately contrived and carefully engineered the Savior's execution. They could have stoned Him as they later did Stephen and received little more than a slap on the wrist. But stoning would not do. Their purpose was insidious and ingenious—they aspired to both discredit and shame the Lord. Their plan was inspired by a popular interpretation of Deuteronomy 21:22–23: "He that is hanged [upon a tree] is accursed of God" (cf. Galatians 3:13). The Hebrew word *qelalah,* translated "accursed," denotes something or someone delivered up to divine wrath, or dedicated to destruction.[14] God removed those under this indictment from His favor and protection and delivered them over to the powers of hell.[15]

Both the Pharisees and the Sadducees believed that a crucified person fell under that condemnation. The Jewish rulers desperately needed to discredit the belief in the Lord's divinity and specifically engineered His death so that He appeared to fall under the anathema of God. Thus the manner of the Lord's death was designed to witness that Hades, not paradise, claimed Him. Paul's statement that Jesus' Crucifixion was a stumbling block to the Jews suggests that the message which the Jewish rulers wanted to give rang loud and clear.

The witness of the Resurrection, however, subverted the Sanhedrin's carefully contrived and skillfully developed plot. The Christian proclamation of the Resurrection meant that despite appearances, God never abandoned His Son. For that reason, it is not surprising that the apostolic witness within earliest Christianity held, as an article of faith, a belief in the physical resurrection. By this doctrine, the early Christians refuted the charges of the Jewish authorities. The Lord Himself emphasized this teaching.

The Savior Taught a Corporeal Resurrection

From the outset of His ministry, the Lord made it clear that there would be a resurrection and that it would involve His physical body. Soon after beginning His ministry, Jesus cleared the temple of that which was profane. When challenged by the rulers to show some sign to demonstrate His authority, He declared: "Destroy this temple, and in three days I will raise it up. Then said the Jews, Forty and six years was this temple in building, and wilt thou rear it up in three days? But he spake of the temple of his body. When therefore he was risen from the dead, his disciples remembered that he had said this unto them; and they believed the scripture, and the word which Jesus had said" (John 2:18–22).

Only after the Savior's death did the disciples come to understand the meaning of His words. During the period in which they traveled with Him, although He introduced the subject a number of times, the disciples pondered and struggled, never comprehending the Resurrection. For instance, during His discourse on the bread of life, He "knew in himself that his disciples murmured at it, [therefore] he said unto them, Doth this offend you? What and if ye shall see the Son of man ascend up where he was before?" (John 6:61–62). If they could not accept His doctrine, they would not be prepared to accept His Resurrection.

In another public discourse, He hinted strongly at the Resurrection:

"Therefore doth my Father love me, because I lay down my life, that I might take it again. No man taketh it from me, but I lay it down of myself. I have power to lay it down, and I have power to take it again. This commandment have I received of my Father." At this many cried out: "He hath a devil, and is mad; why hear ye him?" (John 10:17–18, 20). His claims sounded at best like those of a deranged mind, at worst like one possessed of a demon.

When He attempted to prepare His closest disciples for His death and Resurrection, they did not comprehend. "He took unto him the twelve, and said unto them, Behold, we go up to Jerusalem, and all things that are written by the prophets concerning the Son of man shall be accomplished. For he shall be delivered unto the Gentiles, and shall be mocked, and spitefully entreated, and spitted on: And they shall scourge him, and put him to death: and the third day he shall rise again." His statement could not be more straightforward, yet His disciples "understood none of these things: and this saying was hid from them, neither knew they the things which were spoken" (Luke 18:31–34). Mark's version helps us understand one of the reasons why the disciples did not comprehend: "He taught his disciples, and said unto them, The Son of man is delivered into the hands of men, and they shall kill him; and after that he is killed, he shall rise the third day. But they understood not that saying, and were afraid to ask him" (Mark 9:30–32). Matthew's account suggests there was at least limited understanding: "Jesus said unto them, The Son of man shall be betrayed into the hands of men: And they shall kill him, and the third day he shall be raised again. And they were exceeding sorry" (Matthew 17:22–23).[16]

On another occasion when the Lord taught about His forthcoming death and Resurrection, Peter grasped part of the message. "From that time forth began Jesus to shew unto his disciples, how that he must go unto Jerusalem, and suffer many things of the elders and chief priests and scribes, and be killed, and be raised again the third day. Then Peter took him, and began to rebuke him, saying, Be it far from thee, Lord: this shall not be unto thee" (Matthew 16:21–22). Peter clearly understood that the Lord was to die but totally missed the idea of a resurrection.

All four Gospel narratives agree that before Christ's Resurrection the disciples did not comprehend the doctrine. They did understand that He would go to Jerusalem and die there, but they do not seem to have understood what would happen beyond that point. With such a stress in the

Gospels on this idea, it seems that there were a number of converts to primitive and early Christianity who were willing to accept Christ as the Messiah but could not accept the doctrine of the Resurrection.

THE PHYSICAL RESURRECTION REJECTED BY SOME EARLY CHRISTIANS

The Apostles continually battled against antiresurrection thinking that kept pushing its way into the Church. Paul asked the Corinthian Saints: "Now if Christ be preached that he rose from the dead, how say some among you that there is no resurrection of the dead?" (1 Corinthians 15:12). A few years later, John warned that "many deceivers are entered into the world who confess not that Jesus Christ is come in the flesh" (2 John 1:7).[17]

Paul found it necessary to cite multiple witnesses of the Resurrection to combat the growing heresy. He stated that the resurrected Lord "was seen of Cephas, then of the twelve: After that, he was seen of above five hundred brethren at once; of whom the greater part remain unto this present, but some are fallen asleep. After that, he was seen of James; then of all the apostles. And last of all he was seen of me" (1 Corinthians 15:5–8).

The apostolic Fathers, writing at the close of the first century, fought the same tendency. Ignatius bore forceful testimony to both the Smyrnaeans and the Trallians that Christ rose with a real body. "I know," he cried, "that Christ had a body after the resurrection, and I believe that he still has."[18] But such doctrine was not popular. Many of the second-century converts to Christianity were Hellenists, and more especially Platonists. They could not imagine a God contaminated by association with the flesh. Origen was one of the most vocal of these. He completely rejected the idea that Christ could have risen with a corporeal body. The Father, Son, and Holy Ghost, he insisted, live without bodies. "That being the case, bodies will be dispensed with in eternity, there being no need for them. . . . To be subject to Christ is to be subject to God, and to be subject to God is to have no need of a body."[19] Jerome, who wrote a century and a half later, reported that the debate was still raging.[20]

By the time of Augustine, the doctrine had become a major point of contention within the Christian community. "There is no article of the Christian faith," he wrote, "which has encountered such contradiction as that of the resurrection." Further, "Nothing has been attacked with the same pertinacious, contentious contradiction, in the Christian faith, as the resurrection of the flesh. On the immortality of the soul many Gentile philosophers have disputed at great length, and in many books they have left it written that the soul is immortal: when they come to the resurrection of the flesh, they doubt not indeed, but they most openly deny it, declaring it to be absolutely impossible that this earthly flesh can ascend to Heaven."[21]

Greek philosophy, especially Neoplatonism, was the main contributor to the rejection of this belief so central to the apostolic witness. Many of the Greek philosophers had a deep and abiding distrust of things of the flesh, and that distrust has continued into modern Christianity.

MANY MODERN CHRISTIANS REJECT THE IDEA OF A CORPOREAL RESURRECTION

To this day a large number of Christians reject the doctrine of the physical resurrection.[22] For example, a popular college text used in many introductory New Testament classes in the United States proclaims: "We need to keep in mind that the empty tomb was an ambiguous witness to the resurrection. It attests the absence of the body, but not necessarily the reality or presence of the risen Jesus."[23] Therefore, the reports of His appearance are more important in establishing the reality of a physical resurrection.

> [These] traditions present a varied picture insofar as they portray the mode of Jesus' resurrection. Jesus ate with the disciples—they could see and touch the marks of the nails; but he could go through closed doors and vanish from their sight. It is a misnomer to speak of the 'physical' resurrection. Paul claimed that the appearance to him was of the same nature as the appearances to Peter, the twelve, and so on (see Acts 9:1–9; 22:4–11; 26:9–18), but how could that be a physical appearance? Indeed, in the same chapter of 1 Corinthians, he describes the resurrected body as a spiritual, not a physical, body and says that flesh and blood (that is, the physical body) cannot inherit the kingdom of God (1 Corinthians 15:50; cf. 15:35–58).[24]

The authors completely ignore the statement in Luke, "Handle me and see; for a spirit hath not *flesh and bones,* as ye see me have" (24:39; emphasis added), nor do they discuss what Paul meant when he stated that the resurrected body was "spiritual."

THE SPIRITUAL BODY

Paul used the word *pneumatikos* for "spiritual" in 1 Corinthians 15:44, 46. As a rule, the term was used in reference to items revealed from heaven, such as the Mosaic law (see Romans 7:14); gifts of the Spirit (see Romans 1:11); and general blessings from God (see Ephesians 1:3). Its use connects strongly with physical things. In such cases, it referred to the inner life of man. He who was filled with the Spirit of God (the spiritual man, or *pneumatikos anthropos*) could understand the things of God, while the natural man (*psuchikos anthropos*) could not (see 1 Corinthians 2:14–15). Thus Paul contrasted the spiritual member of the Church with the uninspired person of the world. The point is that the term *spiritual* does not preclude either physical or mortal association. Paul, however, made a distinction between the resurrected and the natural, or mortal, body. He taught that the resurrected body possessed the divine spirit (*pneuma*), having given up the mortal soul (*psuchē*). But his words in no way suggest an absence of physical matter associated with the resurrected body. In fact, Paul's use of *spiritual* strongly parallels Alma's statement, "I say unto you that this mortal body is raised to an immortal body, that is from death, even from the first death unto life, that they can die no more; their spirits uniting with their bodies, never to be divided; thus the whole becoming spiritual and immortal, that they can no more see corruption" (Alma 11:45).

ALL THINGS WERE DONE "ACCORDING TO THE SCRIPTURES"

The writers of the Gospels strove to remove the anathema of the cross by bearing witness of the Resurrection. They made the Old Testament their ally, demonstrating that the Savior had died and had risen again "according to the scriptures" (1 Corinthians 15:3–4).[25] They taught that definite historical events would transpire to fulfill Old Testament prophecy before the coming end (see Matthew 24; Luke 21:22; 22:37; 24:25–27, 32). They stressed that these events were according to God's bidding; He designed the whole operation and set all things in order (see Luke 21:18; cf. 12:7). The Father had determined that the Son of man would be betrayed and suffer for all (see Luke 22:22) and then triumph through the Resurrection. Of the Gospel writers, Luke especially emphasized the latter point. He quoted the Savior, saying, "*It is written, and thus* it behoved Christ to suffer, and to rise from the dead the third day" (Luke 24:46; emphasis added). Luke underscored the divine hand directing all things with the Lord's question, "Ought not Christ to have suffered these things, and to enter into his glory?" followed by the answer, "And beginning at Moses and all the prophets, he expounded unto them in all the scriptures the things concerning himself" (Luke 24:26–27). On another occasion after the Resurrection, "he said unto them [His disciples], These are the words which I spake unto you, while I was yet with you, that all things must be fulfilled, which were written in the law of Moses, and in the prophets, and in the psalms, concerning me. Then opened he their understanding, that they might understand the scriptures" (Luke 24:44–45).

Further, not only did the prophesied events have to occur, but they also had to be witnessed, especially by the Apostles, who were then to bear testimony of their reality (see Luke 21:12–13; Mark 13:9–10). They were to share that witness only after all had been fulfilled: "Jesus charged them, saying, Tell the vision to no man, until the Son of man be risen again from the dead" (Matthew 17:9). After the Resurrection, He proclaimed, "Ye are witnesses of these things" (Luke 24:48). Therefore, the Gospel writers carefully noted that the Apostles and others constantly accompanied the Savior during the final hours before His death, at the Crucifixion, and at His subsequent appearances (see Mark 14:17; Luke 22:14; see also Acts 1:21–26). At the Crucifixion "all his acquaintance, and the women that followed him from Galilee, stood afar off, beholding these things" (Luke 23:49). Here we see the emphasis of the Gospel writers on eyewitness reports of the Crucifixion. The same is also true of His interment and postresurrection appearances.

WITNESSES TO THE INTERMENT OF THE LORD

Each Gospel writer stressed that the Savior truly died. Matthew noted that three women were present with Joseph of Arimathaea when the Lord was buried. These same witnesses carefully wrapped the body in preparation for burial and placed it in the tomb. Joseph then personally rolled a large rock over the opening, and some of the women lingered for a long time (see Matthew 27:56–61).

The next day a delegation of Jewish rulers asked Pilate for permission to set a guard around the tomb, "saying, Sir, we remember that that deceiver said, while he was yet alive, After three days I will rise again. Command therefore that the sepulchre be made sure until the third day, lest his disciples come by night, and steal him away, and say unto the people, He is risen from the dead: so the last error shall be worse than the first. Pilate said unto them, Ye have a watch: go your way, make it as sure as ye can.

So they went, and made the sepulchre sure, sealing the stone, and setting a watch" (Matthew 27:63–66). This passage clearly indicates that these men remembered well and correctly interpreted the prophecies of the Lord concerning His Resurrection.[26] Matthew's account shows us two things: first, no one could have tampered with the body nor removed it; second, the Lord did not somehow resuscitate and escape from the tomb on His own.

The accounts of both Mark and Luke parallel Matthew's version, even to the point of identifying Joseph's rolling a large stone across the entrance to the tomb after the women had witnessed "where he [the Lord] was laid" (see Mark 15:47; Luke 23:50–56).

John's account varies somewhat. He noted that before the Savior was taken from the cross, a soldier speared Jesus in the side to assure His death. Joseph procured the body from Pilate and then, with the help of Nicodemus, wound the body in spiced linen and placed it in a sepulchre "nigh at hand" (John 19:42). John did not mention the presence of any women nor Joseph's rolling a stone over the entrance to the tomb. Nonetheless, John satisfied the divine mandate for more than one witness by identifying Nicodemus as a member of the party.

Taken together, the Gospels leave no doubt that the Savior actually died and was buried. The thrust of the spear, the wrapping of the body, the sealing of the tomb, the presence of more than one person at the time of and after the burial—all attest to the actual death of the Lord.

THE EMPTY TOMB

Only two specific details connected with the Resurrection are common to all four Gospel narratives: the tomb was empty, and Mary Magdalene was either the first or among the first to see it. According to Matthew, Mary and a woman he calls "the other Mary" came to the tomb near dawn. Before their arrival, an angel had descended in glory, frightened the guards into a state of immobility, and rolled back the stone. The angel remained until the women arrived to assure them that "he is not here: for he is risen, as he said. Come, see the place where the Lord lay. And go quickly, and tell his disciples that he is risen from the dead; and, behold, he goeth before you into Galilee; there shall ye see him: lo, I have told you" (Matthew 28:1–7).

The Gospel of Mark adds additional information to the narrative. He identified the other Mary as the mother of James and stated that another woman, Salome, came with them. Finding the tomb open, the women entered and there saw "a young man sitting on the right side, clothed in a long white garment; and they were affrighted." He reassured them, saying, "Be not affrighted: Ye seek Jesus of Nazareth, which was crucified: he is risen; he is not here: behold the place where they laid him. But go your way, tell his disciples and Peter that he goeth before you into Galilee: there shall ye see him, as he said unto you" (Mark 16:5–7).[27]

Luke's account noted that three women—Mary Magdalene, Mary the mother of James, and Joanna—probably the same as Salome—along with others came to the tomb early Sunday morning to finish the burial procedures. Finding the tomb open, they went inside, "and found not the body of the Lord Jesus. And it came to pass, as they were much perplexed thereabout, behold, two men stood by them in shining garments." This frightened the women, but the angels quickly reassured them with the words "Why seek ye the living among the dead? He is not here, but is risen: remember how he spake unto you when he was yet in Galilee, saying, The Son of man must be delivered into the hands of sinful men, and be crucified, and the third day rise again" (Luke 24:3–7). These women then reported what they had seen and heard to the Apostles (Luke 24:1–10).

John's account differs the most. He said that Mary came alone to the sepulchre while it was yet dark. Having found the stone rolled away, she quickly ran to find Peter and John (see John 20:1–2). John mentioned neither any other women nor an angelic visitation. He focused on Mary's experience. Joseph Smith's translation of John 20:1 indicates that the angels were present when Mary arrived; however, she apparently did not converse with them nor recognize their angelic nature, suggesting that she arrived some moments before the other women and left too early to hear the divine witness.

At any rate, her report brought an immediate response from Peter and John. Both ran to the sepulchre. John outran Peter but stooped outside the tomb and saw the grave clothes lying therein. Peter, on the other hand, did not pause at the opening but ran into the tomb. John then followed and "saw, and believed. For as yet they knew not the scripture, that he must rise again from the dead. Then the disciples went away again unto their own home" (John 20:8–10).

With the exception of John, the disciples reacted with bewilderment to the empty tomb. According to Luke, Peter, after viewing the tomb, "departed, wondering in himself at that which was come to pass" (Luke

24:12). Even the witness of the women, who arrived soon after, did not alleviate the disciples' perplexity, for "their words seemed to them as idle tales, and they believed them not" (Luke 24:11).

Though differing somewhat in detail, each Gospel narrative insists that the physical body of the Lord was missing from the tomb. The message of the empty sepulchre is clear: the physical body of Jesus played an actual part in the Resurrection. Each account stands as an independent witness with its own details; all agree that the tomb was empty of Christ's physical body.

THE LORD'S APPEARANCE TO MARY MAGDALENE AND THE OTHER WOMEN

Not only were women the first to know of the Resurrection but they were also the first to see the risen Lord. Mary of Magdala was the first to see the Savior (see Mark 16:9–10; John 20:1). Drawn back to the tomb, the troubled Mary stood outside for a time weeping. After a few moments, she looked into the tomb and there saw divine beings, likely the same angels who had testified to the other women. Mary did not recognize them as celestial. When they inquired why she wept, she expressed her fears and left before they could respond. Within moments, the Lord Jesus Christ appeared to her. Initially, she did not recognize Him, but when He spoke her name, "she turned herself, and saith unto him, Rabboni; which is to say, Master. Jesus saith unto her, Touch me not; for I am not yet ascended to my Father: but go to my brethren, and say unto them, I ascend unto my Father, and your Father; and to my God, and your God" (John 20:16–17).

This account does not directly witness a corporeal resurrection; Mary was forbidden to embrace the Lord, "for," said He, "I am not yet ascended to my Father" (v. 17). Why she was not allowed to touch Him is not clear, but that there was no physical contact between them is certain.[28] Nevertheless, the Savior's explanation intimates that the injunction was temporary.

Shortly thereafter, He appeared to the other women who were on their way to see the disciples, "saying, All hail. And they came and held him by the feet, and worshipped him. Then said Jesus unto them, Be not afraid: go tell my brethren that they go into Galilee, and there shall they see me" (Matthew 28:9–10). The scriptures do not explain why these women were permitted to touch the Lord whereas Mary had been forbidden. The word "held" correctly translates the Greek *krateo,* showing that they did not merely touch His feet but actually held fast to them.[29] Most important, they could see and feel and hold something. The testimony of the women rested on a double foundation: divine testimony and tactile witness. They saw and heard from angels that the Lord had risen, and then they actually saw the Lord and held His feet in worship.

Even in light of these sure testimonies, the male disciples refused to believe the women. Mary's personal witness, probably given not long after the other women's story, fared no better: "And they, when they had heard that he was alive, and had been seen of her, believed not" (Mark 16:11). The writer of each Gospel affirms that the women's combined testimony did not convince the men. Throughout that Sunday morning, the men were downhearted and frightened. They didn't know what to believe. Thus their eventual conversion to the reality of the Resurrection makes their witness more credible.

THE LORD'S APPEARANCES TO HIS DISCIPLES

The first of Jesus' many postcrucifixion appearances to the early Brethren occurred Sunday afternoon. The Lord met Cleopus and an unnamed disciple walking to Emmaus but did not disclose His identity. He asked them why they were troubled, and the disciples recounted the startling events of the day, especially the empty tomb and the witness of the women, concluding with an admission of their own perplexity. "O fools and slow of heart to believe all that the prophets have spoken," exclaimed the yet unrecognized Lord. "Ought not Christ to have suffered these things, and to enter into his glory? And beginning at Moses and all the prophets, he expounded unto them in all the scriptures the things concerning himself" (Luke 24:25–27; see also 3 Nephi 23:9–14). The hearts of both disciples burned for joy as He spoke to them. Arriving at Emmaus a little before sundown, they constrained the Lord to "abide with us." He agreed and "went in to tarry with them" (Luke 24:29). Graciously, the Lord blessed and began to serve the food. As He did so, the disciples recognized Him. But before their astonished minds could formulate a question, He vanished.

The Lord may not have eaten before disappearing, although He did handle the food, for "he took bread, and blessed it, and brake, and gave to them" (Luke 24:30). The disciples knew that He was substantial, real, and alive.

The two disciples quickly returned to Jerusalem and found where the other disciples were gathered. Their story met with the same skepticism; however, as that of the sisters' earlier, "neither believed they them" (Mark 16:13). While these two witnesses were yet trying to persuade their brethren, the Lord appeared to the assembled company. This initially caused panic, but Jesus reassured them: "Why are ye troubled? and why do thoughts arise in your hearts? Behold my hands and my feet, that it is I myself: handle me, and see; for a spirit hath not flesh and bones, as ye see me have. And when he had thus spoken, he shewed them his hands and his feet. And while they yet believed not for joy, and wondered, he said unto them, Have ye here any meat? And they gave him a piece of a broiled fish, and of an honeycomb. And he took it, and did eat before them" (Luke 24:38–43).

Jesus' eating appears to have been a critical factor in convincing the disciples of the reality of the physical resurrection. Although they felt the nail prints in His hands and His feet, "they yet believed not for joy" (Luke 24:41). Only when the Savior requested something to eat did they fully believe. Perhaps they then remembered His statement from the Last Supper: "With desire I have desired to eat this passover with you before I suffer: For I say unto you, I will not any more eat thereof, until it be fulfilled in the kingdom of God" (Luke 22:15–16). The act of eating fully demonstrated that the Passover was fulfilled in Christ; moreover, He had overcome all things, including physical death.

After they believed, the Lord began to teach them "that they might understand the scriptures, and said unto them, Thus it is written, and thus it behoved Christ to suffer, and to rise from the dead the third day: and that repentance and remission of sins should be preached in his name among all nations, beginning at Jerusalem. And ye are witnesses of these things" (Luke 24:45–48). This passage reveals the Apostles' purpose: to be personal witnesses to all of the Lord's ministry and teachings, and most significantly, to the corporeal resurrection.

Here John's narrative teaches an important lesson. He explained that the Apostle Thomas was absent from the initial appearance. Although Thomas received ample testimony from the others, he still refused to believe. He reacted in the same way as the others had when they had heard the witness of the women and the two disciples from Emmaus. Nothing short of tangible proof would suffice. As Thomas said, "Except I shall see in his hands the print of the nails, and put my finger into the print of the nails, and thrust my hand into his side, I will not believe" (John 20:25).

A week later all the disciples, including Thomas, were together. Once again the Lord appeared. "Reach hither thy finger," He commanded Thomas, "and behold my hands; and reach hither thy hand, and thrust it into my side: and be not faithless, but believing" (v. 27). Thomas's reaction was immediate and sincere; he simply exclaimed: "My Lord and my God" (v. 28). Because of Thomas, we now have additional evidence of the Lord's physical resurrection.

One other lesson may be learned from this narrative. The Lord said: "Thomas, because thou hast seen me, thou hast believed: blessed are they that have not seen, and yet have believed" (v. 29). The Lord's words suggest that henceforth others would be required to believe in the Resurrection based on the testimony of the disciples, not through tangible proofs. John alone among the disciples realized the significance of the empty tomb. He had not seen the Lord, yet he believed. Jesus asked the others to follow his example.

Conclusion

Each Gospel writer suggested that the early disciples found it most difficult to accept the reality of the Resurrection. However, they also showed that through irrefutable proofs the disciples came to know the truth. Those proofs came primarily through a demonstration of the physical reality of the risen Lord. The disciples were commanded to bear witness of that reality. That is the context of the testimony of John: "That which was from the beginning, which *we have heard*, which *we have seen* with our eyes, which *we have looked upon*, and *our hands have handled*, of the Word of life" (1 John 1:1; emphasis added). Those who deny the literal resurrection do so not by misinterpreting this testimony but by rejecting it.

Notes

1. Justin Martyr, *Dialogue with Trypho*, 17.1, in *Patrologia Graeca*, 6:512–13 (hereafter cited as *P.G.*); cf. 47.4; 96.1–3; 108.2; 117.3; W. H. C. Frend, *Martyrdom and Persecution in the Early Church: A Study of a Conflict from the Maccabees to Donatus* (Grand Rapids, MI: Baker, 1965), 192.
2. *Contra Celsum*, 6.27; cf. 4.32; Frend, *Martydom and Persecution*, 192.
3. Eusebius, *In Isaiah*, 18.1 in *P.G.* 24:213A; Frend, *Martyrdom and Persecution*, 192.
4. Frend, *Martyrdom and Persecution*, 192–93. For primary text see Origen, *Contra Celsum*, 1.27, 29, 32, 41, and Justin Martyr, *Dialogue*, 108.2. For the same tactic being used at the end of the second century in Carthage, see Tertullian, *Apology*, 21.22.

For Panthera as the name of a soldier from Sidon in Phoenicia in the beginning of the first century after Christ, see A. Deissmann, *Light from the Ancient Near East*, trans. L. R. M. Strachan, 4th ed. (Grand Rapids, MI: Baker, 1978), 73–74 and fig. 8.

5. For examples from the Hellenistic culture, see Ovid, *Metamorphoses*, 1.589–94; 5.301–519.

6. See, for the Romans, Cicero, *De Divinationa*, 1.1–38; 2.64, 70; Tacitus, *Histories*, 1.3, 18, 86; 4.81; for the Jews, Josephus, *Jewish Wars*, 6.285–95.

7. For healings, see Tacitus, *Histories*, 4.81; Suetonius, *Lives of the Caesars*, "Vespasian," 7; Dio Cassius, 65.271.

8. See, for example, Ovid, *Metamorphoses*, 14.800–828.

9. Among the orientals were a number of dying and rising savior-gods: Tammuz, Bel-Marduk, Adonis, Sandan-Heracles, Attis, Osiris, the Cretan Zeus, and Dionysus, for example. But these were never really mortal and thus had no bearing on the New Testament witness.

10. A number of Greek authors (for example, Homer, *Iliad*, 24.551; Herodotus, 3.62; Aeschylus, *Agamemnon*, 1360f) simply state that resurrection is impossible. Others accepted the idea but only as an isolated miracle (for example, Plato, *Symposium*, 179c; Lucian, *De Saltatione*, 45).

11. Gerhard Kittel, ed., *Theological Dictionary of the New Testament*, trans. Geoffrey W. Bromiley (Grand Rapids, MI: Eerdmans, 1964), s.v. *anastasis*; hereafter cited as *TDNT*.

12. Apparently Paul had a little success. Luke notes that "certain men clave unto him," as well as a woman (Acts 17:34).

13. The Sadducees and Samaritans, in many instances, rejected the idea while the Pharisees accepted it (see Matthew 22:23; 6–8). For discussion, see *TDNT*, s.v. *egeiro*.

14. The LXX uses *katara*, "to curse," to translate *qelalah*. A closely related concept comes from the Greek word *anathema* and carries the idea of being separated or cut off from God. Out of this grew the idea that to be crucified was to be anathematized, or damned from the presence of God (see *TDNT*, s.v. *anatithami* and *ara*).

15. In a real way, this aptly described the condition of the Savior both in the Garden of Gethsemane and on the cross. He descended below all things, suffering the pains of damnation for all (see D&C 19:17–19; 88:6).

16. Other accounts (see Matthew 20:17–19; Mark 10:32–34) mention this teaching but do not give the disciples' reaction.

17. This phrase may have been used to offset a docetic heresy entertained by some early Christians. According to this view, the Savior only appeared to have a physical body and to suffer on the cross. Such a view disallows a corporeal resurrection.

18. Ignatius, *Epistle to the Smyrnaeans*, 3, in *P.G.*, 5:709; cf. *Epistle to the Trallians*, 9; in *P.G.*, 5:681.

19. Origen, *Peri Archon,* 2.6.2, in *P.G.,* 11:210.

20. Origen, *Peri Archon,* 2. 3, in *P.G.,* 11:188–91.

21. Augustine, *On the Psalms,* Psalm 89.32, in *Patrologia Latina,* 37:1134.

22. For examples, see R. H. Fuller, *The Formation of the Resurrection Narratives,* 2d ed. (New York: Macmillan, 1980); P. Perkins, *Resurrection: New Testament Witness and Contemporary Reflection* (Garden City, NY: Doubleday, 1948); G. O'Collins, *Jesus Risen: An Historical, Fundamental, and Systematic Examination of Christ's Resurrection* (New York: Paulists Press, 1987).

23. Robert A. Spivey, and D. Moody Smith, *Anatomy of the New Testament: A Guide to Its Structure and Meaning* (New York: Macmillan, 1988), 239.

24. Spivey and Smith, *Anatomy of the New Testament,* 239.

25. There are a number of scriptures the Lord could have used; for example, Job 19:25; Ezekiel 37:12; Hosea 13:14; Isaiah 25:8; 26:19; 53:12.

26. At the beginning of His ministry, the Savior stated to the Jewish leaders, "Destroy this temple, and in three days I will raise it up" (John 2:19; see also Mark 14:58). It would be remarkable but not impossible that they remembered this statement. Certainly the conditions under which the Lord uttered it were of a singular and noteworthy nature.

27. Joseph Smith Translation, Mark 16:3–6, corrects these verses, noting that there were two angels present and that the women entered the sepulchre and saw that it was empty before they departed.

28. The Greek verb *hapto* carries the idea of clinging, embracing, and holding—often for the purpose of reassurance and affection. The object of such an embrace is often friendship, even intimacy.

29. The Greek word *krateo* used by Matthew stands in contrast to the word *hapto* used by John noted in footnote 28. The word *krateo* means to hold, seize, grasp, and restrain. The shared meaning element is to take hold and keep hold of something or someone.

CHAPTER SIXTEEN

PAUL'S WITNESS TO THE HISTORICAL INTEGRITY OF THE GOSPELS

RICHARD LLOYD ANDERSON

The fiftieth anniversary of the Allied invasion of Normandy was observed in June 1994.[1] Venturesome survivors revisited their beaches, and the daring parachuted again, reenacting their small part of the miraculous crusade to break apart an evil dictatorship. Do able minds match bodies of such surprising tenacity? I saw no article claiming that multinational veterans had invented exploits or misstated their experiences. Though these aging warriors believed deeply in their cause, modesty rather than exaggeration was the rule in published interviews. Their recollections were surprisingly in agreement with reports republished from a vanished era. Spontaneous stories dovetailed with each other, given a commonsense allowance for many points of view in many sectors. The parts had to be harmonized to repicture the whole operation. Certainly there were discrepancies in some details of sequence—exact times, precise numbers, and so forth. But no one doubts the blend of oral and documentary history that enables us to make a quality reconstruction of the most spectacular sea-to-land attack in history.[2]

PAUL AND THE CONCEPT OF LATE GOSPELS

Such living sources might inject caution into many armchair speculations on how the Gospels were written. Christianity invaded the Roman

Richard Lloyd Anderson is a professor emeritus of ancient scripture at Brigham Young University.

Empire. Converts during Christ's life numbered in the hundreds, and scores passed on their experiences to writers of the Gospels. On their face, these narratives were written by eyewitnesses or embody memories of those who originally walked with Him in Galilee and Jerusalem. But what of the time lag? Jesus went to the cross about AD 30. Mainstream Christian scholars think the religious biographies of Christ came to their present form in about the last three decades of the first century: Mark no earlier than AD 65, Matthew and Luke around AD 80, and John AD 90 or beyond. These figures are out-and-out estimates; Christ's prophecy of Jerusalem's destruction is supposedly recorded so accurately by Matthew and Luke that their Gospels must have been written after the Roman siege in AD 70, prompting a well-informed critic to remark, "It is surprising that on such inconclusive evidence . . . there should be such widespread acceptance of a date between A.D. 75 and 85."[3] I agree with a minority that sees Luke as the third Gospel, written by the year 63. Matthew and Mark would necessarily be among the "many" who had already narrated the miraculous events of the days of Jesus (see Luke 1:1–2; Acts 1:1–2). These first full-scale Gospels would then fall between the expansion of the Church beyond Israel in the forties and the increase of urban, literate converts in the fifties. On this more compressed evaluation, fifteen to thirty years would separate the composition of the synoptic Gospels from the Crucifixion. On the more prevalent scheme, this gap would at least double.

According to ancient sources near the Apostle John, he wrote a fourth Gospel to add his recollections of events not already in the synoptic Gospels.[4] *Synoptic,* of course, refers to the first three accounts of Christ's ministry in the New Testament. Because they have interdependent characteristics, they "see together" (the Greek meaning behind *synoptic*). Paul's information about Jesus correlates mainly with the synoptic Gospels, so that relationship is under discussion here. But to return for a moment to the analogy of the Normandy invasion, there are hundreds of soldiers alive in 2006 who have memories that reach back accurately to the expedition sixty years before. Early Christian sources put the Apostle John in a similar situation, writing after other Apostles were gone.[5] So in terms of late authorship alone, John's Gospel has a minor relationship with Paul's letters. Yet in a long lifetime John would have widely shared his treasured knowledge of the Master. Some themes in John's writing have intriguing counterparts in Paul's letters and speeches, but that is a more subtle study.

How was the written history of Jesus formed between AD 30 and 90? Could His life and message have been accurately handed down through this period? The obvious solution is to read the Acts of the Apostles, which covers what the Galilean Twelve and Paul taught up to about 63. But mainstream professionals reshape Acts with the same technique they apply to the Gospels. Their theory is that both the history of the Savior and the history of the Apostles were written by later generations that inherited and enhanced faith-promoting legends. Yet in Acts, the Apostles personally testify of the divinity and doctrine of Christ right after the Resurrection.

But here the important perspective of Acts must be largely set aside for another focus—what Paul had learned of Christ's life and teachings from his conversion around AD 35 until writing his early letters fifteen or twenty years later. In other words, Paul wrote during the critical years when faith stories were supposedly replacing true history of Jesus. The convert-Apostle tells more about Christ's mission and teachings than is apparent. This field of study has been productive recently, though conduits of information from Jesus to Paul are minimized by theologically correct scholars.

My purpose is to review Paul's expressed knowledge of Christ in a fresh framework, paying attention to the difference between data and speculation that was defined by Stephen E. Robinson in profiling the work of faithful Latter-day Saint scripture scholars: "They accept and use most objective results of Bible scholarship, such as linguistics, history, and archaeology, while rejecting many of the discipline's naturalistic assumptions and its more subjective methods and theories."[6]

In the current models of the writing of the Gospels, Paul's Christian career matches the period of free growth of the stories about Jesus and the teachings attributed to Him. The Apostle to the Gentiles was converted soon after the Crucifixion and was an influential leader from about AD 38 until his death late in the reign of Nero, who took his own life in 68.[7] So Paul's life spans the three decades when the Jesus of history supposedly evolved into the Christ of faith. But to what else would this Pharisee be converted? No one was more consistent in his Christian career. His first known letters went to converts at Thessalonica and Corinth. In his first letters to those churches, he reviews how he stood before their synagogues in pure testimony that Jesus was the Christ and that he had determined to know nothing but Christ. Because every letter of Paul afterward repeats this message, the humbled Pharisee certainly made this declaration from the time of his conversion, just as described in Acts 9. If this most visible spokesman had a fixed message of the divinity of Jesus from the first decade of the Christian Church, why assume the movement was then in ferment on the subject?

THEORIES ON ORIGINS OF THE GOSPELS

Most experts claim that literary evidence proves evolving historical accounts of Jesus: "It is evident from the several decades between the times when the texts were written and the times of the events recounted in them that we have to reckon with a period during which sayings and stories were orally transmitted before being written down either in our present texts or in their sources. The principal evidence for this process of oral transmission consists in multiple versions of sayings and stories that cannot well be accounted for by simply attributing them to the use of written sources."[8]

This quotation refers to the frequent individuality of stories and teachings in Matthew, Mark, and Luke. Of course, chronology and description vary in many episodes reported by more than one Gospel. They were obviously not crafted by modern professionals who worried about minor discrepancies or proofread their quotations. Scholars today struggle with how approximations can be considered history. Yet until recent times, history was largely composed from approximations. That does not mean that we fail to have real events and many correct details. Nor are "the very words of Jesus" necessarily absent from the Gospels. Ancient collections preserve several hundred authentic letters from Roman emperors and senators and their correspondents. Many Greek and Roman historians incorporate well-copied documents in rather poor narrative. Yet today's analysts tend to overstate differences among the Gospels. For instance, a respected linguist downgrades a blending approach to the four Gospels, adding this observation about Jesus: "The one statement written about him during his lifetime, the 'title' on the cross, appears with *different* wording in each gospel (see Mark 15:26; Matt. 27:37; Luke 23:38; John 19:19)."[9] But the effect of this comment is hardly justified by the record. "The king of the Jews" is on the execution placard in every Gospel, with "Jesus" added in Matthew and "Jesus of Nazareth" added in John. The art of history normally reconstructs full events from partial reports, and summaries regularly omit details that are rounded out in more complete versions.

When two Gospels differ on the precise wording of a teaching of Jesus, some analysts pronounce the sources unreliable rather than look for their essential agreement. Even if there are major differences in context or wording, rather than labeling both records nonhistorical, one could consider the option that one account may contain fuller data whereas the other may be a freer version from an eyewitness or reporter of responsible memories. Different events with loose resemblances in two Gospels are too often labeled variants of the same episode, with an arbitrary claim that one version was radically rewritten. But responsible history interprets its sources without changing them. In the case of differing details in accounts of the same event, one should avoid imposing standards of a technical era on the reasonable integrity of another period.

Although the following quotation pertains to overstating differences between Acts and Paul's letters, the same issues apply to perfectionism in comparing the synoptic Gospels: "In historical sources from other fields such discrepancies are no surprise to the scholar, nor do they make him doubt the historical reliability of the accounts except at a few points where they directly contradict each other. But many New Testament scholars adopt a very stringent attitude when no complete agreement exists among the different accounts, regardless of the fact that perfect agreement would be suspect or proof of artificial construction."[10]

Current theories project a period when stories of Christ evolved in major substance, a process supposedly discovered through form criticism. This procedure first classifies story and teaching patterns, and then similar episodes from different Gospels are compared to determine their direction of development. For instance, Matthew fully reports Peter's testimony of Christ and also Christ's promise of authority to Peter to lead the Church (see Matthew 16:13–20). Then settings and brief summaries are compared in Mark 8 and Luke 9, with the conclusion that the fuller account displays later creative development: "It seems likely that Matthew has followed his custom of adding things, in this case, to the sayings of both Simon Peter and Jesus."[11]

As a historian of Mormon documents, I see such analysis as unsupported theory. Differences in synoptic narratives are assumed by the form critics to be evidence for evolution of the narrative, but there are good alternative explanations for synoptic diversity, such as an author's habit of brevity, his particular interests, or his decision that certain events were adequately treated in a previous Gospel. Because Jesus adapted teachings to different audiences, a shift of emphasis in another setting may have nothing to do with the growth of the "story unit." These double and triple accounts are a main focus for form criticism: "The purpose of NT FC [New Testament Form Criticism] as traditionally defined was to rediscover the origin and history of the individual units and thereby to shed some light on the history of the tradition before if took literary form, that is, to determine whether the various units are traceable to Jesus, to the early Church, or to the redactional (editorial) activity of the Gospel writers."[12]

Redaction has heavy connotations of question-begging. *Editor* in today's practice includes compiling, not just altering. But *redactor* in New Testament scholarship suggests modifying or shifting the point of the inherited story. Redaction criticism, which now supplements form criticism, is defined as "the evangelist's use, disuse, or alteration of the traditions known to him."[13] It is one thing to say that every writer reveals a personality and point of view—mind prints of the author are clear characteristics of each of the four Gospels. But the intense search for "alteration of the traditions" is regrettable. As just noted, accounts of the same event show commonality and also individuality, both of which can be explained in terms of the writer, his skills, his sources, his personal style. "They can't all be right," is essentially what we hear from form and redaction critics. Many aim for the one original account by peeling off its later developments. But that is a historical version of the either-or fallacy. Each Gospel may have had independent access to some original details, even when there is literary interdependence in the synoptic trio.

The norm in this reconstructive system is illustrated in a survey of scholarship on Jesus by Aramaic expert Joseph A. Fitzmyer, an intellectual of faith who concludes basically that Christ's portrait in the Gospels is severely overstated but early Christians were afterward led to his divinity through the Holy Spirit. Fitzmyer is used here because of his positive stance, and my evaluation is given with respect for his lifetime devotion to religious learning. Although he views the Gospels as fictionalizing the life of Jesus, he also thinks that they carry far more authentic information than do their apocryphal imitations, some of which are now touted as having equal validity to the four biblical records: "Despite the contentions of some modern scholars (H. Koester, J. D. Crossan), these apocryphal gospels are scarcely a source of real information about Jesus of Nazareth."[14]

Consistent with one point in this article, Fitzmyer finds the outline of the death and resurrection of Jesus validated by a dozen major allusions in Paul's letters.[15] So he sees the Gospels rooted in actual events but with such lush overgrowth, mainly in regard to teachings, that the proportion of fully authentic incidents is small and the proportion of reliably recorded teachings of Jesus even smaller. He reviews this wisdom as the fruit of the twentieth century, which started with form criticism and then advanced to redaction-composition criticism and other types of literary analysis. The result is a "sophisticated mode of gospel interpretation [that] was unknown in earlier centuries of the church."[16]

With other New Testament scholars, Fitzmyer speaks of three stages: Jesus teaching, traditions expanding, and gospel authors freely adapting. Basically the first century is trisected, with story development in the middle third and editorial creativity in the final third. The system breeds a puzzling certainty. One may be sure that "none of the evangelists was an eyewitness of Jesus' ministry."[17] In this view unnamed authors sorted out stage-two folk traditions and created the four Gospels "by redactional modifications and additions."[18] In doing so they relied on stories produced with a slant by the unknown middle generation: "Yet none of these disciple-preachers ever sought to reproduce with factual accuracy the words and deeds of Jesus himself; they understood those words and deeds with hindsight and adapted them to the needs of those to whom they preached."[19]

PAUL AND EYEWITNESSES

But the New Testament contains a different information model about Christ, and Paul is the first one known to state it. Because he never hints of personal experience with Jesus, the Apostle is clearly at the critics' stage two, the repeating of random stories about Jesus. In 1 Corinthians, Paul reviews the conversion of southern Greeks as he carefully argues for the Resurrection. He makes a sharp distinction between his vision and the first appearances of Christ to the Galilean Apostles and their associates, naming five occasions when the resurrected Lord was seen by them (see 1 Corinthians 15:5–7). Here Paul is really defining his mentors for the earthly Christ, as he stresses the Atonement and Resurrection: "For I delivered unto you first of all that which I also received" (1 Corinthians 15:3). Information about Christ's appearance to Peter certainly came from Peter himself, because Paul tells about spending two weeks with the chief Apostle three years after the conversion vision (see Galatians 1:18), and they counseled together at Jerusalem and Antioch afterward (see Acts 15; Galatians 2:11–14). Information about Christ's appearance to James clearly came from James, because Paul tells about visiting James not very long after the conversion vision (see Galatians 1:19), and they counseled together at Jerusalem afterward (see Acts 15; see also Acts 21:18–25). Although Paul is an intermediary, he insists he has accurately relayed first-hand testimony on the Resurrection appearances (see 1 Corinthians 15:11–15).

In 1 Corinthians, Paul refers to his first preaching in Corinth about AD 50, the midpoint of the scholars' second stage, when disciple-preachers were supposedly expanding the words and deeds of Jesus. But historical constancy is Paul's message. The Corinthians are told that Christ appeared to Peter first and afterward to the eleven Apostles, James, and "above five hundred brethren at once; of whom the greater part remain unto this present" (1 Corinthians 15:6). So Paul corrects current form critics: the original eyewitness stage existed simultaneously with their stage two. Speaking of the Galilean eleven, Paul insists that the leaders are united on the historical truth of Christ's suffering and Resurrection: "Therefore whether it were I or they, so we preach, and so ye believed" (1 Corinthians 15:11). These are not anonymous "disciple-preachers." Anyone speaking or writing at that point, or until the deaths of Peter and Paul nearly two decades later, would have had access to the testimony of those who walked with Christ and also to responsible conduits such as Paul who were scrupulously careful not to modify knowledge that came from the eyewitnesses.

This is exactly the viewpoint of the author Luke, honored in Paul's letters as a trusted companion. To remove his name from the Gospel that has his byline in the earliest manuscripts is equivalent to erasing authorship from the best Roman and Greek histories. Because later apocryphal writings falsely claimed to have been written by leading Christians, the traditional authors of many New Testament books are widely questioned today. But second-century papyrus copies exist of large sections of Matthew, Luke, and John with their names in head notes or endnotes.[20] There is also a major fragment of an important second-century list of approved books, broken at the beginning but naming Luke and John as writing the "third" and "fourth" Gospels. This list sought to clarify which books were historically authentic: "There are also many others which cannot be received in the General Church, for gall cannot be mixed with honey."[21] Luke has low New Testament visibility and is not a likely name for adding prestige to a pseudo-Gospel. Indeed, the apocryphal Gospels have obvious agendas or contents that do not integrate with events, topography, geography, and culture in the New Testament world. The four Gospels are impressive for their factual framework accompanying the life and teachings of Christ.

A book on Luke's preface (see Luke 1:1–4) would of course do it more justice than the few comments possible here. That preface contradicts redactional theory by subtracting the evolutionary second stage in forming the Gospels. First for Luke are the "eyewitnesses," the Galilean Twelve who shared events with Jesus "from the beginning." Luke's second stage is preserving the Christian epic from sources and participants. The following phrases come from Luke's preface in the New Revised Standard Version, which reflects most current translations: because the eyewitnesses "handed on to us" their knowledge of Christ's ministry, "many have undertaken to set down an orderly account." Luke then writes "after investigating everything carefully from the very first." The result is what the King James Version correctly calls "certainty" that the record of Christ is reliable (Luke 1:4).

In my view, Luke penned this preface no later than AD 63, less than a decade after 1 Corinthians. Even if Luke wrote later, this missionary companion of Paul stood in his shoes as having had contact with important witnesses of the ministry of Jesus, which is a great part of the meaning of "investigating everything carefully from the very first" (NRSV, Luke 1:3). As Paul's associate, Luke here names Paul's sources of information about Christ—observers and some early records.

Luke's preface leads away from speculative models and straight to basic biography. Paul's letters from Rome mention Luke's being there with him in the early sixties, which verifies the Acts picture of Luke's going to Rome with Paul after two years in Israel.[22] That underlines the critical insight from 1 Corinthians 15 already discussed. Prominent Apostles and brothers of the Lord mingled with converts during the middle third of the founding century. Writing 1 Corinthians about AD 57, Paul appeals to common knowledge that "other apostles" were traveling with their wives, naming Peter and "the brethren of the Lord," a term that undoubtedly includes James and Jude (see 1 Corinthians 9:5; Matthew 13:55). Peter was slain about 67; James, the Lord's brother, was slain in 62; his brother Jude wrote his letter perhaps a decade later; the originally prominent James of Zebedee was killed about 44; and responsible Christian sources report his brother John exercising apostolic supervision in Asia Minor at the end of the century.[23]

Besides those documented Apostles, other leading Christians, including relatives of the Lord and prominent women, lived to see some or all of the synoptic Gospels written. If one survived childhood in the ancient world, one's longevity would on average trail current levels by ten years or so. Yet the question of sources for the Gospels continues to be discussed in a vacuum. A recent book by Utah scholars estimates that Mark's Gospel was composed about AD 65 to 70, admits that not all "personally acquainted" with Jesus had died but muzzles anyone remaining: "A generation had passed and firsthand information was no longer available."[24]

Paul would not have written such depressing lines. From known beginnings about AD 50, his epistles have a constant theme of "get it right," with occasional appeals to Jesus. As we have already discussed, Paul basically told the Corinthians that he was reviewing Resurrection appearances that he "received" from the Galilean eleven (see 1 Corinthians 15:3–7). History from those who saw and heard is being preserved before our eyes in the Corinthian correspondence. To settle insensitivity about the sacrament, the Apostle reviews how Christ established that ordinance, with narrative and words very close to those reported by Luke and a statement of Paul's source: "For I have received of the Lord that which also I delivered unto you" (1 Corinthians 11:23). This rather full record is evidently not "received of the Lord" from direct revelation, but from the Lord through Apostles present in the upper room—the pattern of "that which I also received" from observers in the later Resurrection chapter (1 Corinthians 15:3). At a minimum, the Apostle is in contact with other Apostles and writing bits of their oral history.

In my judgment, Hebrews is from Paul and was definitely written before the destruction of the temple in AD 70.[25] Referring to the earthly teachings and trials of Jesus, this book confirms the observer-to-author process in Luke's preface. In Hebrews, the things "spoken by the Lord" came face to face from "them that heard him" (Hebrews 2:3).

Written between AD 50 and 63, Paul's epistles are a public block against changes. They refer to Christ's Davidic credentials, the Last Supper, Jewish and Roman trials, Crucifixion, burial, and Resurrection appearances. Because references to Christ's life are spontaneously given throughout the Apostle's letters, they indicate that Paul had a working knowledge of the Lord's ministry. Further, the Apostle merely refers to events rather than explaining them, expecting his readers to understand incidental references to the career of the Savior. This point is pivotal in understanding why the

Apostle does not more often name Jesus as his source. A common body of knowledge makes powerful allusions possible without the clumsy ritual of naming the Lord and designating a given teaching. Today's public writings, for example, are filled with catchphrases on human rights without naming the Constitution or the Fifth or Fourteenth Amendments. Similarly, Paul's direct references to Christ show that there is a constant between-the-lines appeal to Christ's authoritative message when the Savior's words are loosely paraphrased or even condensed as concepts. Mentioning Christ as source could indicate apostolic revelation instead of Jesus' Jewish ministry, but major doctrinal revelations were well known and openly described (see Galatians 1–2). So when Paul names the Lord for authority, the Apostle generally alerts modern readers to look for teachings given during Christ's preaching in Israel.

PAUL'S DIRECT CITATIONS OF JESUS

Paul's intent to quote or paraphrase teachings from Jesus' mortal ministry is clearer in some examples than others. More skeptical scholars subtract a half dozen of the traditional fourteen letters, but most of Paul's important references to Christ's teachings are in the earlier epistles not generally challenged: Romans, 1 Corinthians, and 1 Thessalonians. My approach, however, is documentary, relying on second-century manuscript evidence and second- and third-century acceptance of books that were later challenged. This external evidence favors Paul as author of the traditional fourteen letters. The following passages are examples of Paul's references to Jesus' teachings.

First Corinthians 15:3–7. The micro gospel of 1 Corinthians has already been discussed, with Paul's retrospect on first teaching his converts "that which I also received" about Christ's Atonement and Resurrection. By mentioning the Lord's appearance to Peter, James, and the Galilean eleven, Paul discloses major sources of information, and it is known that he had contact with them. This appeal to firsthand evidence indicates reliable oral history, though Paul might have possessed early lists of Resurrection appearances. Luke's Gospel also contains the first appearances on Paul's list—to Peter and then to the Twelve (see Luke 24:33–36). Moreover, part of "that which I also received" was "that Christ died for our sins according to the scriptures." This wording is close to Christ's own explanations in Luke on how the suffering and Resurrection fulfilled scripture (see Luke 24:26–27, 45–46). This also connects with Paul's Corinthian narrative of the Lord's words in the upper room: "My body, which is broken for you" (1 Corinthians 11:24). "Died for our sins" agrees with the synoptic account of the Last Supper (see Mark 14:24; Luke 22:20) but is closest to Matthew's wording of the cup representing Christ's blood "shed for many for the remission of sins" (Matthew 26:28). Not only does Paul testify that Church leaders agree on Christ's sacrificial Atonement, but the Apostle may be relaying the Lord's own words.

First Corinthians 11:23–25. As detailed earlier, in 1 Corinthians 11, Paul reviews Christ's actions and words in establishing the sacrament and says that these "I have received of the Lord." Because Paul's account is so particularized, he is likely presenting narration originating from the Apostles rather than from personal revelation. He is tapping the synoptic record at an early point, with Christ's words in establishing the sacrament almost identical to those appearing later in Luke's Gospel: "This is my body, which is broken for you: this do in remembrance of me. . . . This cup is the new testament in my blood" (1 Corinthians 11:24–25; see also Luke 22:19–20).

This correlation indicates that either Paul carefully memorized Christ's words or had documentation of them. Luke's preface explains that such words were obtained by his contact with those present at the Last Supper. Yet Paul wrote them down much earlier as common knowledge, "received" in the same process as the apostolic testimony of the Resurrection that Paul relayed in the same letter.

First Corinthians 7:10–11, 25. The frequent possibility that Christ's words are behind Paul's words is shown when the Apostle gives his own command but quickly clarifies that it is really the command of the Lord: "Let not the wife depart from her husband . . . and let not the husband put away his wife" (1 Corinthians 7:10–11). Between these two directives there is a caution about remarriage not necessarily from Jesus, because Paul jots ideas within ideas. As he does in the passage on the sacrament, the Apostle gives an early form of synoptic teachings. These interrelated Gospels summarize Jesus' direction on divorce, with Luke lacking a context but Matthew and Mark reporting the situation when Jesus answered the Pharisees' question on the subject. Only Matthew gives a permitted divorce initiative for males in cases of adultery, and only Mark gives a generalized rule against divorce for men and also women (see Mark 10:11–12). Paul's dual instruction from the Lord resembles the male-female warning in Mark.

Finally, Paul drops the question of divorce and addresses the problem of when to marry, about which the Apostle remarks, "I have no commandment of the Lord" (1 Corinthians 7:25). The four Gospels are also silent on this point, which underlines Paul's broad knowledge in directly citing Jesus—when the letters directly refer to Christ's teachings, we usually find the equivalent words of Jesus in the Gospels. This practice suggests that the Apostle designed his Church messages to remind Christians of a fairly defined body of information about the Lord.[26]

First Corinthians 9:14. The New Testament contains several equivalent command terms. Paul uses one of them in a long answer to faultfinding Corinthians as he insists that he has the right to be supported as a missionary but does not demand it: "Even so hath the Lord ordained that they which preach the gospel should live of the gospel" (1 Corinthians 9:14).

Paul first quoted Old Testament scripture on support of the priests and then evidently added the directions of Jesus about missionaries. These words broadly summarize the charge to the Seventy to rely on the people for food (see Luke 10:5–7) and the short form of this same instruction to the Twelve in Matthew (10:10), with only a terse suggestion in Mark (6:8).

But Paul's main argument is the authority of the apostleship (see 1 Corinthians 9:1)—he is probably appealing to knowledge that Jesus directed support for the Twelve, as indicated in Matthew, where Christ's missionary instructions close by saying that he "made an end of commanding his twelve disciples" (11:1).

First Thessalonians 4:15–5:2; 2 Thessalonians 2:1–15. "For this we say unto you by the word of the Lord" opens a series of Thessalonian parallels to Jesus' most featured discourse in the Gospels, the prophecy of the Second Coming and of extended events that would precede it. On the Mount of Olives, the original Twelve asked about the time of Christ's return. The importance of Jesus' long answer is shown by every synoptic Gospel reporting it in detail, though Matthew's version has more words and components, plus several long parables afterward that were part of the Savior's response.

Paul's first letter to the Thessalonians unwittingly fed expectations of an early second coming in explaining the accompanying resurrection. So Paul wrote again to clarify prior events. Both letters follow distinct blocks of material in Jesus' Olivet discourse. These correlations show that the introductory "by the word of the Lord" really means His known teachings. "By" correctly translates the Greek preposition *en,* usually a simple "in" in the sense of location, but the New Testament very often displays an "instrumental" meaning—here "by means of the word of the Lord." The context of dependence is so strong that the New Jerusalem Bible clarifies the idea: "We can tell you this from the Lord's own teaching" (1 Thessalonians 4:15).

A broad pattern links Matthew 24 to the Thessalonian letters. Paul's first epistle to the Thessalonians counters their confusion on personal immortality by describing what would come: "For the Lord himself shall descend from heaven . . . with the trump of God" (1 Thessalonians 4:16), which follows Matthew's version of the Olivet prophecy: "They shall see the Son of man coming in the clouds of heaven . . . with a great sound of a trumpet" (24:30–31). Although the trumpet is mentioned only in Matthew, it is part of detail shared with Mark on the angels calling forth God's "elect" from heaven and earth when Christ appears (see Matthew 24:30–31; Mark 13:26–27). Paul uses this as the essential message: "Then we which are alive and remain shall be caught up together with them in the clouds, to meet the Lord in the air" (1 Thessalonians 4:17). Paul continues by reminding the Thessalonians that discussion of "the times and the seasons" is unnecessary: "For yourselves know perfectly that the day of the Lord so cometh as a thief in the night" (1 Thessalonians 5:1–2). Though Luke has this comparison elsewhere (12:39–40), the Olivet discourse begins with questions on the time of the Coming and ends in Matthew with several parables, one of which pictures the thief coming in the most unexpected vigil (24:43–44). In each synoptic Gospel, Jesus closes the prophecy with the warning to stay awake and "watch," adding the counterexample of drunkenness in Matthew and Luke. And Paul closes his minidiscourse by these verbal reflections of "watch," adding that drunkenness is for the worldly (see 1 Thessalonians 5:4–7). The sequence of the synoptic prophecy and Paul's survey is the same. And Paul starts with "the word of the Lord" and reminds them that they already "know perfectly" how the appearance of Christ will surprise the world (1 Thessalonians 4:15; 5:2). It seems the basic Olivet discourse was available to Paul and his converts, probably in written form because of the duplicated detail and order, together with several striking words. Luke's "unawares" (21:34) is the same word in Greek as Paul's "sudden" (1 Thessalonians 5:3), though the idea is vivid in each of the triple Gospels. Significant parallels to Paul's writings appear in more than one Gospel or in Matthew alone.

Second Thessalonians settles the false expectation of Christ's quick return, and evidence of Paul's authorship follows the first letter closely.

Though Paul's follow-up letter is questioned, that debate has much to do with academic shock at the vivid picture of Satan's approaching power. To correct false enthusiasm for an immediate Second Coming, the Apostle again parallels the Olivet prophecy for major events preceding the Lord's return. Thus Paul's second letter to the Thessalonians concentrates on the era of wickedness that Jesus predicted before coming again.

Removing some important misconceptions will highlight the parallels. First, Paul's labels for the coming evil power are too spectacular for mere mortals—the high titles for the ruling "man of sin . . . , the son of perdition" (2 Thessalonians 2:3) resemble terminology for Satan at that period, and they should be seen as naming God's chief competitor behind the scenes. Second, Paul's image of the arrogant pretender in God's temple has little to do with the Jerusalem temple, which was destroyed two decades after the Apostle wrote. Paul has the temple takeover last until Christ's return, which he insists is not in the near future (see 2 Thessalonians 2:3–8). Satan aims to possess not one building but all of Christ's church, which is regularly called God's temple in Paul's letters and early Christian literature (see Ephesians 2:21).[27]

As Paul explains what must precede the Second Coming, the parallels are striking, especially in Matthew. Though conservative commentators tend to see a compressed period of evil just before the Second Coming, Christ in Matthew predicts the era of "false prophets" right after the Apostles were killed (24:9–11) and restates the point by positioning "false Christs, and false prophets" right after the first-century fall of Jerusalem (24:24). Then "iniquity shall abound" (24:12), and Paul uses the same word for the beginning of fulfillment in his day: "The mystery of iniquity doth already work" (2 Thessalonians 2:7).

So Paul follows the substance and timetable of the Olivet prophecy. With allowance for Paul's imagery, the processes are the same: "Many," Jesus said, would aspire to take His place, "saying, I am Christ; and shall deceive many" (Matthew 24:5; see also Mark 13:6; Luke 21:8). The evil one, Paul said, would aspire to take the place of God, "shewing himself that he is God" (2 Thessalonians 2:4). Paul's forthcoming "signs and lying wonders" (2 Thessalonians 2:9) match Christ's predicted "signs and wonders" from counterfeit prophets in the Olivet prophecy (Matthew 24:24; Mark 13:22).

This does not exhaust the interplay of words and ideas between Matthew 24 and the Thessalonian correspondence. They are full counterparts in event and stage, once it is seen that Paul has extracted the religious future without repeating Christ's extensive commentary on persecution, wars, and signs of His coming. These earliest known letters of the Apostle were sent about twenty years after Jesus outlined the stages between the first and the second comings. And Paul quite certainly used a full record of the prophecy corresponding to the present Matthew 24. It is even possible that Matthew's Gospel was already written and carried by certain leaders. Moreover, the Olivet discourse is not derived from Paul, for he introduced the advent theme by relying on the existing "word of the Lord."

Romans 14:14. Paul appeals for more charity for Jewish converts with rigid dietary convictions and then insists, "I know, and am persuaded by the Lord Jesus, that there is nothing unclean of itself." The Apostle adds that a thing is unclean if one thinks it is so, his explanation of the idea he attributes to the Lord. "Nothing unclean of itself" is quite close to Mark's report of the Savior's judgments on ritual purity: "There is nothing from without a man, that entering into him can defile him" (7:15). The parallel is closer in Greek, where *defile* is the verb meaning "to make unclean or common." Current translations of Romans 14:14 favor "persuaded in the Lord Jesus," though the Greek preposition *en* ("in") is regularly instrumental, meaning here "through" or "because of the Lord Jesus." In any event, Paul's idea is quite clear—reflection on Jesus' viewpoint, which is learned through Jesus' words, has convinced the Apostle that objects do not cause impurity of themselves. Paul could be brief on this sensitive subject only if it was well known that the Lord took a strong stand on overdone purification. In this central clash of opinion between Paul and defenders of the Mosaic dietary law, one of Paul's weapons was paraphrasing Jesus.

Romans 12:14–19; 14:10. In addition to the Olivet prophecy and John's discourse on the Last Supper, one very significant address should resonate in New Testament letters—the Sermon on the Mount. It has the lead location in Matthew as Jesus' declaration of Christian standards for those who became "disciples" (Matthew 5:1) by repenting and accepting "the gospel of the kingdom" (Matthew 4:23). For this purpose, restatements would be necessary for waves of converts.

The teachings in Matthew's chapters 5 through 7 are primarily found in the Sermon on the Plain in Luke 6, but other fragments appear in Luke in different settings. This arrangement leads some to assume that Matthew assembled scattered sayings of Jesus. Yet Luke is a skilled writer by ancient standards that stressed logical as much as chronological order. For the interest of the reader, he perhaps reported a concise version of this important sermon and placed some sections elsewhere by topic. Or did the Master Teacher use repetition so regularly that both views are true—an original broad manifesto of principles followed by systematic segments in various teaching moments? Christ's unsurpassed mind was perfectly capable of organizing an effective moral overview instead of leaving that task to chance.

A unified image of the Sermon on the Mount emerges through the lens of the letters, particularly Romans: "The ethical admonitions of this and other New Testament letters, whether Paul's or not, bear a marked resemblance to the ethical teaching of Christ recorded in the Gospels. They are based, in fact, on what Paul calls 'the law of Christ' (Gal. 6:2; *cf.* 1 Cor. 9:21). In particular, an impressive list of parallels can be drawn up between Romans 12:3–13:14 and the Sermon on the Mount. While none of our canonical Gospels existed at this time, the teaching of Christ recorded in them was current among the churches—certainly in oral form, and perhaps also in the form of written summaries."[28]

Paul closes his epistle to the Romans with several chapters of personal instruction instead of the briefer admonitions found in other church letters. But Romans is the one epistle sent to an important area where Paul had not preached. That explains his obvious drive to review authoritative standards with Saints who had not heard him. The closing chapters of Romans use Christ's teachings and Christ's example in several ways; the strongest of Paul's indirect allusions to Christ's teachings, the summary of the Lord's laws of love, is recorded in Romans 13:8–10.

The last part of Romans 12 corresponds to the last part of Matthew 5 with a series of admonitions on the subject of nonretaliation. Although some content also reflects Luke's Sermon on the Plain, the style of expression follows that of Jesus as reported by Matthew. Paul opens the subject with: "Bless them which persecute you: bless, and curse not" (Romans 12:14). In the longer traditional text of Matthew, the parallel is: "Bless them that curse you . . . and pray for them which . . . persecute you" (5:44), which is closer to Paul's key words than Luke's similar report, "Bless them that curse you, and pray for them which despitefully use you" (Luke 6:28). In Romans 12:17, the Apostle restates this theme, which is clearer in literal translation: "Returning evil for evil to none, providing good things before all men." "Providing good things" has a close parallel in 1 Thessalonians: "See that none render evil for evil . . . ; but ever follow that which is good, both among yourselves, and to all men" (5:15). In a word, repay those doing you evil, not with evil, but with good. Matthew has the close model for the above negative command: "Resist not evil" (Matthew 5:39); this form is lacking in Luke, though both Gospels give examples from Jesus on how to return good for evil. And other key words of Matthew's Sermon on the Mount are in this section of Romans. Paul's "live peaceably" (Romans 12:18) could also be translated "bring peace" and correlates with Jesus' beatitude for "peacemakers" (Matthew 5:9); Paul's warning against anger (see Romans 12:19) is closely related in Greek to Jesus' warning against anger (see Matthew 5:22). This subtle coloring supplements the correlations to a well-defined section of the Sermon on the Mount.

Luke and Matthew place Jesus' caution against judging near the end of their versions of this sermon. Paul uses a similar location and a form close to Christ's speech: "But why dost thou judge thy brother? or why dost thou set at nought thy brother? for we shall all stand before the judgment seat of Christ" (Romans 14:10). As already discussed, these questions are embedded in a long correction about being overcritical because of Jewish dietary rules, with Jesus cited on nothing being unclean of itself (see Romans 14:14). Here the Sermon on the Mount parallel is strongly felt: "Judge not, that ye be not judged. For with what judgment ye judge, ye shall be judged" (Matthew 7:1–2). This phrasing corresponds to Paul's dual form just quoted—caution on judging now, as well as a prophecy of future judgment. But in Luke's pattern, one technically will not be judged if he does not judge (6:37), a step away from the coming judgment found in Matthew and Romans. Moreover, Paul confronts his readers with questions in the same style as Jesus, who follows "Judge not" with cross-examination on why we see only the faults of others (see Matthew 7:3–5).

Romans 13:8–10. "Love one another: for he that loveth another hath fulfilled the law. . . . And if there be any other commandment, it is briefly comprehended in this saying, namely, Thou shalt love thy neighbour as thyself. Love worketh no ill to his neighbour: therefore love is the fulfilling of the law" (Romans 13:8–10). Though Paul does not name Christ in this passage, he reasons from the teachings of Jesus that love is the overarching precept. Paul's own evaluation of love begins and ends this pointed passage on charity: "Love is the fulfilling of the law." *Fulfilling* in Greek essentially means "completion"—love is the purpose of all revealed laws and the crowning result of obeying them. Then Paul backs up this main concept with two silent citations of Jesus. In full form, Romans 13:8–10 names five of the Ten Commandments, adding that loving one's neighbor permeates the rest.[29] The Apostle did not need to identify the Savior's use of this Old Testament imperative. Nor did he need to mention Christ behind his second supporting saying: "Love one another" was given at the Last Supper as a "new commandment" by which all would "know that ye are my disciples" (John 13:34–35).

Although John's Gospel was not yet circulated, the eleven Apostles at the Last Supper were morally obligated to share Christ's instruction on this supreme principle. This was done afterward in the letters of Peter (see 1 Peter 1:22) and John (see 1 John 3:11). But those faithful stewards no doubt declared Christ's "new commandment" to "love one another" in the churches long before Paul used those phrases in Romans. And the same is true for "love thy neighbour as thyself," Jesus' revitalized injunction from Leviticus 19:18. In Mark's Gospel, Jesus said no commandments were more important than loving God and loving neighbor (12:28–31). But Matthew reported the more profound perspective found in Romans. Jesus had concluded: "On these two commandments hang all the law and the prophets" (Matthew 22:40). Jesus did not merely list the two in top position; He said the entire law reflected or expressed them. That is Paul's meaning in explaining the second commandment: his Greek says literally that "every other commandment is summed up" in the saying to love one's neighbor as oneself. The summary of charity in the epistle to the Romans brings together Christ's two main instructions on love.

PAUL AS A HISTORIAN OF JESUS

The preceding eight examples are segments of letters, and there are several instances of Paul explicitly referring to Christ's teaching. Yet such a reference is not always required for us to be confident that Paul relies on sources from Christ. Today's writer may quote Shakespeare and squarely say so or simply quote phrases that educated people will recognize. Thus Paul's pattern of openly quoting the Lord should alert us to many silent references to Jesus' teachings that were commonly known and appear in our Gospels. On balance, Paul's mention of Jesus does not always indicate quotation. Paul may name the Lord because the Apostle speaks with

Christ's authority (see 1 Corinthians 14:37) or also because the Lord's life is a model to follow (see Romans 15:3–7).

The preceding eight examples are impressive, however, partly because they name the Lord or indicate an authoritative source and partly because they mirror Jesus' teaching with some complexity. Shared words may reflect only a common culture; however, relationships are shown not by terms alone but by shared phrases, sentence syntax, and sequence and uniqueness of idea. After that, the direction of the relationship must be assessed. And Paul answers that question several times by insisting that knowledge of Jesus has come down to him.

Recent publications show how much this subject interests religious scholars, but I have cut my own path and will simply compare another researcher's conclusions: "We have ascertained over twenty-five instances where Paul certainly or probably makes reference or allusion to a saying of Jesus. In addition, we have tabulated over forty possible echoes of a saying of Jesus. These are distributed throughout all of the Pauline letters, though 1 Corinthians and Romans contain the most. . . . Echoes of Jesus' sayings are discernible in all the major themes of Paul's theology. . . . Paul also provides hints of his knowledge of the narrative tradition of Jesus' passion, his healing ministry, his welcoming sinners, his life of poverty and humble service, his character and other aspects."[30]

In short, there is a "Gospel according to Paul" embedded in his letters. Like Luke's, it stems from contact with the Galilean "eyewitnesses" (Luke 1:2), who answered Jesus' call, marveled at His miracles, and intently listened to His public sermons and private dialogues. The historic ministry of prominent Apostles to Mediterranean lands shows both motivation and capability in communication.[31] Were they articulate enough to carry knowledge of Jesus to new areas but lacking in power to write memoirs of Him or see that such were written? Paul knew the Apostles who knew Jesus. And Paul's presentation of Jesus' life and teachings in his letters has the scope, if not the detail, of the Gospels. This Apostle's comments combine to make up an abstract of Jesus' ministry. It is unedited and forms a blueprint of the synoptic Gospels, reflecting their own stress on the final days—the sacrament as the key to the meaning of Christ's suffering, the condemnation and His Crucifixion, the reality of His Resurrection, with names of witnesses to whom He appeared. Paul's framework includes Christ's comments on Jewish practices of ritual cleanliness and on divorce as well as a fragment of Jesus' missionary instruction to the first Twelve.

And there are salient parts of the Sermon on the Mount, the laws of love, and Christ's testimony of His return in power as part of two main segments of the Olivet prophecy. For details one reads the Gospels, but Paul authenticates their overall narrative of Jesus and His basic teachings.[32]

The early "Gospel according to Paul" can be compiled as a document because the Apostle occasionally says he is reporting what Jesus said or did, furnishing written evidence that is far stronger than literary inferences behind widely accepted theories like the precise limits of assumed source "Q," the priority of Mark, or a pre-Gospel oral period circulating highly volatile stories of Jesus. But the "Gospel according to Paul" is historically sound because it is datable. Paul's paraphrases and explicit references to Christ's teachings begin as early as his correspondence is preserved—in the Thessalonian letters from about AD 50, followed by recurrent references to Jesus' ministry in 1 Corinthians about AD 57, and the parallels in Romans about AD 58. Furthermore, Paul's first inside knowledge of the Jewish Jesus came not long after conversion, a decade earlier than the Apostle's first known epistles. It is glibly said that Paul transformed the historic Jesus into the divine Christ, but that view is contradicted by Paul's own letters. The Apostle's testimony is consistent—he first learned of the resurrected Christ through the vision on the road to Damascus (see Acts 9; 1 Corinthians 9:1). This event of about AD 35 marked the beginning of a natural education about Jesus for a man of more than usual curiosity. Paul next visited Jerusalem and talked with Peter and other early disciples (see Galatians 1:18–19). Then and afterward, they taught Paul about the Last Supper (see 1 Corinthians 11:23) and about Christ's first appearances as a resurrected being (see 1 Corinthians 15:3). So Paul's letters document the churchwide knowledge of the basics of the synoptic Gospels before AD 50. In fact, all New Testament Gospels were not necessarily composed after Paul sent the epistles. Paul's letters and the Gospels produce comparable versions of what Jesus said and did. Whether information available to Paul was preserved in manuscript or in shared memory or in both does not matter much for the big picture, though many of Paul's matching patterns seem too intricate for memory alone.

MATTHEW, JAMES, AND THE BOOK OF MORMON

Matthew unexpectedly emerges in my analysis with the greatest number of specific equivalents to Paul's words of the Lord. In the New Testament lists of the Apostles, only one appears by profession, "Matthew the publican" (Matthew 10:3). His career in Galilee required multiple languages, as well as practice in accounting and making reports. Such facts are impressive when he is early named as author of a Gospel. Moreover, the writings of the Christian historian Eusebius record an amateurish but guileless investigation of what the Church knew about the writing of the Gospels while John the Apostle was still available at the end of the century. Papias, an early second-century bishop, talked to the elders of the previous generation, including John, who seems to have been the Apostle, because Papias calls him the Lord's disciple, a known title of the Apostle (see John 21:24). This bishop's goal was to learn anything handed down from Christ's Apostles, and among those attracting his interest, he names Peter, John, and Matthew.[33]

Papias said this about the publican-Apostle: "So then, Matthew compiled the oracles in the Hebrew language; but everyone interpreted them as he was able."[34] Commentaries widely discount this early reference because Matthew's Gospel seems to have been written in Greek rather than translated from Hebrew or its cousin language of Aramaic. Details cannot be discussed here, but the early Church went through a Hebrew period before reaching out to Greek-speaking converts in the eastern Mediterranean basin. These two stages are reflected accurately in the quotation from Papias—"interpreted" is the usual Greek word for "translated," apparently indicating that the many Gentile converts had difficulty reading Matthew's original record in Hebrew or Aramaic, which contained the "oracles" (singular, *logion*), a term that in the Greek New Testament means "sayings" in the sense of revealed or sacred words. Paul and Barnabas opened the era of Gentile predominance with their mission to Cyprus and central Asia Minor soon after AD 44 (see Acts 13–14). So Papias understood that Matthew kept records of Christ's ministry in a Hebrew dialect before a Greek version was composed for Gentile Christians, whose needs became intense by mid-century. Someone genuinely bilingual could start fresh and produce a Greek record without obvious Semiticisms. Most current critics discount Matthew as the writer or rewriter but on virtually ideological grounds: "The most powerful reason today for denying even the possibility of apostolic authorship is bound up with an entire array of antecedent judgments about the development of the gospel tradition, about the shape of the history of the church in the first century, about the evidence of redactional changes, and much more."[35]

Evidence of early records of Jesus is not strange to Book of Mormon readers, where the resurrected Savior said on His first appearance: "And I command you that ye shall write these sayings after I am gone" (3 Nephi 16:4). This instruction was repeated throughout His American advent: "Write the things which ye have seen and heard, save it be those which are forbidden" (3 Nephi 27:23). And much as He did in the early ministry recorded in Matthew, the American Christ descended, first proclaimed His divinity, called for repentance and baptism for entrance to "the kingdom of God," and immediately afterward gave the law of the kingdom, the American counterpart to the Sermon on the Mount. As is well known, the Book of Mormon (see 3 Nephi 12–14) correlates with Matthew's version (see Matthew 5–7), though it is independent in many verses. Sidney B. Sperry long ago warned against assuming the two are one sermon: "The text delivered to the Nephites did not in all respects follow that given in Palestine."[36]

Some, however, claim that the Book of Mormon cannot be ancient because the Sermon at the Temple (see 3 Nephi 12–14) too closely resembles the Sermon on the Mount (see Matthew 5–7), even adopting textual errors found in the King James Version. But though the Prophet Joseph Smith evidently followed his Bible when satisfied that it mirrored Christ's message to the New World, phrase-specific translation is not indicated in Joseph Smith's discourses, where he shows a broad interest in scriptural doctrine instead of textual technicalities. Indeed, many Bible translators today favor idea equivalents over literalism, as consistently illustrated by the New Jerusalem Bible or the Revised English Bible. And as already mentioned, Jesus' most important message must have been restated by Him and His disciples with minor variations during the Jewish ministry, a significant insight that Joseph Smith added to the Sermon on the Mount in his inspired version of Matthew: "Now these are the words which Jesus taught his disciples that they should say unto the people" (JST, Matthew 7:1).

Parts rephrased by the Master or His disciples would easily collect slight variations of equal authority. For instance, early Greek manuscripts and early church writers are divided between Jesus commanding no anger, the Book of Mormon reading (see 3 Nephi 12:22), or the traditional no anger "without a cause" (Matthew 5:22). Did the Savior give both forms, one a clarification of the other? Because no first-century copies of the Gospels are known, it is intellectual cheating to claim to give Christ's original words by using much later manuscript readings in Matthew.

Yet the Book of Mormon supports the structural integrity of this sermon as recorded in Matthew. Stated another way, the Sermon on the Mount in the first Gospel is a significant test of the Nephite record. If a "Matthew-editor" created a late, nonhistorical speech, as some experts suppose, one might argue that Joseph Smith copied a faulty model. But Paul's letters in the fifties are a major test. We have seen that Romans 12 reproduces the thoughts and distinctive vocabulary of a section near the close of Matthew 5; Romans 14 does the same thing with the faultfinding warnings at the beginning of Matthew 7. In addition, the Epistle of James paraphrases many more thoughts and phrases of the mountainside sermon in Matthew.

For authenticity of the letter of James, one can choose between the positive judgment of ancient Christians, who were highly sensitive about forgeries, or modern assumptions that a lack of early quotation by name throws doubt on its authorship. But the pioneer Christian historian Eusebius wrote about AD 325 and preserved documents and data from the subapostolic era. He says that the author of the New Testament letter is James, the brother of the Lord, and adds very early information on his martyrdom in AD 62.[37] A number of scholars accept this identification, are impressed with the absence of Jewish-Gentile problems, and therefore think James composed his letter before the beginning of Paul's Gentile missions in about AD 44. Thus James's extensive use of the Sermon on the Mount shows it was available in some form even before Paul wrote the epistle to the Romans. James shows strong individuality and piety, with constant use of the Old and New Testaments: "There are more parallels in this epistle than in any other New Testament book to the teaching of our Lord in the gospels."[38]

The goal of James is clarifying the righteousness that is the thrust of the Sermon on the Mount. Though not naming Jesus as his source, this quotation-oriented author heavily uses Jesus' teachings found in the synoptic Gospels. About two dozen parallels impressed W. D. Davies, and about three dozen impressed Peter Davids.[39] Two dozen parallels from their combined lists strongly reflect Jesus' teachings, based on correlations of phrasing and distinctive idea, and they follow the trend observed by Davids—James mirrors the structure of Matthew's Sermon on the Mount more than Luke's Sermon on the Plain.[40] In my calculations, the impressive verse-resemblances between James and the Gospels fall into these categories: thirteen are shared by Matthew and Luke; eight are unique to

Matthew; two are shared by Matthew and Mark; one is unique to Luke.[41] James does use some striking language found in the short sermon in Luke, but more often he follows Christ's language in Matthew. For instance, there is close quotation by James (5:12) of the Lord's command (see Matthew 5:33–37) not to make daily honesty depend on special oaths— not to swear by heaven or by earth but to make promises with a simple yes or no. And James closely reflects Christ's beatitude on the merciful receiving mercy (see Matthew 5:7), switching to negative phrasing that those showing no mercy will receive judgment instead of mercy (see James 2:13).

What emerges is the early authority of the extensive discourse in Matthew over Luke's compressed counterpart. In my calculations, twenty verses correlate in James and Matthew's Sermon on the Mount: ten in chapter 5, three in chapter 6, and seven in chapter 7.[42] So James has used representative sections of Christ's full sermon in Matthew. How much of the epistle reflects the sermon? The answer is implicit in Massey Shepherd's conclusion that James depended on Matthew "for the presentation of his themes."[43] But these views should be read with awareness that James cites little else in Matthew but the Sermon on the Mount: "The number and extent of the Matthean parallels to James . . . are impressive; for they relate to every single section of the Epistle, and to almost every major theme."[44]

Though current scholars tend to see only "the unwritten Jesus tradition" behind these correlations,[45] James uses words, distinctive thoughts, and selection from all parts of Christ's discourse. More than spontaneous memory is at work here. Scholars favor oral tradition because of the loose nature of many parallels. But casual rephrasing is also consistent with using a well-known record. Structure and particulars in James indicate he is basically following the same version of the Sermon on the Mount used in the Gospel of Matthew. This and the Romans-Matthew correlations make memory alone an unlikely tool for these agreements of language, concept, and structure. Because Paul and James independently point to a record of the sermon made before their epistles were written, credibility is added to Papias's information that Matthew kept a Jewish-language record of the "oracles," the "authoritative words" of the Lord. The Savior's thorough explanation of the moral law of His kingdom was preserved in historical systems on both hemispheres. There is great integrity in the literary structures and the doctrines within them in the Book of Mormon.

PAUL'S WITNESS IN SUMMARY

Paul's visions of Christ become an either-or trap for those who claim the Apostle paid no attention to the Lord's earthly life. But at every period of writing, the epistles speak of both the mortal ministry and the exalted Jesus. An example precedes the Savior's words on the sacrament: "Be ye followers of me, even as I also am of Christ" (1 Corinthians 11:1). Paul has just explained his empathy for others in a context of exempting Greeks from the Jewish dietary code and here makes the point that he is following the doctrinal model of his Master. Christ's example has not faded in the next sentence: "Hold to the traditions, just as I delivered them to you" (1 Corinthians 11:2; literal translation mine). Paul soon repeats "delivered" in restating his earlier public preaching about the Savior's appearances after the Resurrection: "For I delivered unto you . . . that which I also received" (1 Corinthians 15:3). Such language throughout 1 Corinthians calls up both doctrines and deeds of Jesus—in chapter 15, atonement for sin as well as resurrection of the body. And Paul insists on common preaching: "Therefore whether it were I or they, so we preach, and so ye believed" (1 Corinthians 15:11). This fifties headline reveals corporate teaching about the close of Jesus' mortal ministry—Jesus' suffering at the end and His physical return afterward.

The convert-Apostle periodically draws on general knowledge of the man of Galilee: "Now I Paul myself beseech you by the meekness and gentleness of Christ" (2 Corinthians 10:1). Moreover, the Apostle's later letters repeat the Corinthian pattern of defending doctrine by the Lord's known earthly words. Nonetheless, any survey of Paul faces modern redefinitions of which of his letters are authentic. As earlier mentioned, there is a canonical list of the Christian books recognized at about AD 170, and its partially preserved text accepts all but one of the New Testament letters attributed to Paul. This early list includes Ephesians, probably written during Paul's Roman imprisonment about AD 62, and the messages to Timothy but a few years afterward.[46] Like 1 Corinthians, Ephesians reviews what converts first heard, though Paul is more general in what seems to be an area letter. Christians had been called out of the world—they had "learned Christ" with complete directness: "Ye have heard him, and have been taught by him, as the truth is in Jesus" (Ephesians 4:21). Paul means they know Christ's teachings, because the Apostle follows with standards of putting away lust and anger that correspond to those recorded in Matthew 5 (see Ephesians 4:22, 31), and with the message, similar to that in Matthew 6, that Saints should freely forgive because God's forgiveness is freely offered them (see Ephesians 4:32). The expressed and unexpressed message of Paul's ministry is that faithfulness is measured by "wholesome words, even the words of our Lord Jesus Christ" (1 Timothy 6:3). They are always in the background and are readily brought forward when stumbling Saints need explanation or refutation.[47]

The corporate apostleship carried the burden of preserving authentic knowledge of the Lord. Paul is early, accessible, and an example of the teaching methods of his colleagues. He periodically makes Christ the teacher, giving glimpses of the Savior's ministry to inspire or solve problems. This documented process has no time slot for anonymous teachers tinkering with the real Jesus. The New Testament Church operates by administrative and doctrinal authority. Most of the Galilean Twelve yet lived in Paul's period, and when observed, they are using Christ's earthly ministry as the norm in conversion and correction, though their preserved letters are few. James essentially adapts the Sermon on the Mount. And other Apostles stress Christ's ministry, as shown by Peter's challenge to "follow his steps" (1 Peter 2:21) and John's repeated segments of the Last Supper discourse (see 1 John). While the Apostles lived, wandering preachers with wandering stories were not in control. The full origin of proto-Gospels and present ones is not known, but by using facts about Jesus that reliably came to him, Paul has inserted datable history in his letters. These show that the mid-century Church had stable and specific knowledge of Jesus' major teachings—that its testimony that Jesus was the divine Christ was already firm and founded on broad information from witnesses who walked with Him.

NOTES

1. My memories of Sidney B. Sperry reach back nearly to the end of World War II, how he went out of his way to welcome a searching student to Brigham Young University and took time for counseling and personal tutoring in Hebrew years afterward. He left a legacy of commitment to research and faith in the restored gospel.

2. See the weaving of recollections in Gerald Parshall, "Theirs But to Do and Die," *U.S. News and World Report,* May 23, 1994, 71–81.

3. Donald Guthrie, *New Testament Introduction,* 4th ed. (Downers Grove, IL: InterVarsity Press, 1990), 128–29.

4. See Eusebius, *Ecclesiastical History,* 3.24.5–8, quoting specific earlier information on this point.

5. For the dating of John's Gospel near the end of the first century, see

Richard Lloyd Anderson, "The First Presidency of the Early Church: Their Lives and Epistles," *Ensign,* August 1988, 20, and references.

6. Stephen E. Robinson, "Bible Scholarship," in *Encyclopedia of Mormonism,* ed. Daniel Ludlow, 4 vols. (New York: Macmillan, 1992), 1:112.

7. For approximate dates in Paul's life, see Richard Lloyd Anderson, *Understanding Paul* (Salt Lake City: Deseret Book, 1983), 393–97.

8. Norman R. Petersen, "Introduction to the Gospels and Acts," *Harper's Bible Commentary* (San Francisco: Harper and Row, 1988), 948.

9. Joseph A. Fitzmyer, *A Christological Catechism,* 2d ed. (New York City: Paulist Press, 1991, 15.

10. Johannes Munck, *The Acts of the Apostles, The Anchor Bible* (Garden City, NY: Doubleday, 1967), xxxiii–xxxiv.

11. Fitzmyer, *Christological Catechism,* 66.

12. Richard N. Soulen, *Handbook of Biblical Criticism,* 2d ed. (Atlanta: John Knox Press, 1981), 73.

13. Soulen, *Handbook of Biblical Criticism,* 165.

14. Fitzmyer, *Christological Catechism,* 21.

15. Fitzmyer, *Christological Catechism,* 14.

16. Fitzmyer, *Christological Catechism,* 23.

17. Fitzmyer, *Christological Catechism,* 25.

18. Fitzmyer, *Christological Catechism,* 25.

19. Fitzmyer, *Christological Catechism,* 25.

20. "The Gospel according to" is the title formula in the manuscripts noted. For data on Luke and John, see Richard Lloyd Anderson, "The Testimony of Luke," in *Studies in Scripture, Volume Five: The Gospels,* eds. Kent P. Jackson and Robert L. Millet (Salt Lake City: Deseret Book, 1986), 88. For data on Matthew, see Martin Hengel, *Studies in the Gospel of Mark* (Philadelphia: Fortress Press, 1985), 66n3.

21. Daniel J. Theron, *Evidence of Tradition* (Grand Rapids, MI: Baker Book, 1958), 111. Theron gives the full translation of the Muratorian Canon, which is well dated by reference to second-century individuals and shows Christian hostility to invented books by naming several and criticizing their heretical sources.

22. For specifics on contact with James, the Lord's brother, and others in Israel, see Anderson, "Testimony of Luke," 93–94.

23. Acts 12:1–2 gives the execution of James, John's brother, as just before the death of his persecutor, Herod Agrippa, which is dated at AD 44 in Josephus; for the stoning of James, the Lord's brother, soon after the death of the governor Festus at 62, see Eusebius, *Ecclesiastical History,* 2.23; for the deaths of Peter and Paul near the end of Nero's reign at 68, see Anderson, *Understanding Paul,* 362–65; for the historical ministry of John at the end of the century, see Irenaeus, *Against Heresies,* 3.1.1; 3.3.4, and Anderson, "First Presidency of the Early Church," 20–21.

24. Obert C. Tanner, Lewis M. Rogers, and Sterling M. McMurrin, *Toward Understanding the New Testament* (Salt Lake City: Signature Books, 1990), 31.

25. See Anderson, *Understanding Paul*, 197–201, including the photograph of the last page of Romans in the second-century collection of Paul's letters, in which Hebrews is copied between Romans and 1 Corinthians.

26. Yet no record was made of all of the Lord's words, as the close of John's Gospel says. "It is more blessed to give than to receive" (Acts 20:35) is directly attributed to the Lord by Paul, though it does not appear in the Gospels. For non-Gospel words of Jesus, early citations are far more reliable than the apocryphal collections of sayings that were compiled and colored to support deviant doctrines.

27. For fuller discussion, see Anderson, *Understanding Paul*, 85–87.

28. F. F. Bruce, *The Letter of Paul to the Romans*, 2d ed. (Grand Rapids, MI: Eerdmans, 1985), 212–13.

29. When the rich young ruler asked about requirements for salvation, Jesus quoted several of the Ten Commandments, those with social obligations. Although the three synoptic Gospels agree thus far, in Matthew Jesus adds the Leviticus 19:18 direction to love neighbor as self (see Matthew 19:18–19). Paul does the same thing in the Romans passage under discussion, another of the many ties to Matthew's Gospel.

30. Seyoon Kim, "Jesus, Sayings of," in Gerald F. Hawthorn and Ralph P. Martin, eds., *Dictionary of Paul and His Letters* (Downers Grove, IL: InterVarsity Press, 1993), 490. For the chart "Possible Echoes of Sayings of Jesus," see 481. The considerable recent bibliography on 491–92 shows that the topic of Paul's historical access to Jesus' ministry is to be taken seriously. For instance, the studies of David Wenham are listed, some of which have intriguing insights.

31. For comments on the writing environment of early Christianity, see Richard Lloyd Anderson, "Types of Christian Revelation," in Neal E. Lambert, ed., *Literature of Belief* (Provo, UT: Religious Studies Center, Brigham Young University, 1981), 64–65.

32. For the similar judgment of a scholar trained in classical sources, see F. F. Bruce, *The New Testament Documents*, 5th ed. (Grand Rapids, MI: Eerdmans, 1987), "The Importance of Paul's Evidence," 76–79.

33. Eusebius had Papias's writing and quotes the material summarized here in *Ecclesiastical History*, 3.39.1–4. Eusebius adds his own theory that Papias names two Christians named John and could not have known the Apostle. Yet Papias lived in the area and period of the Apostle.

34. Eusebius, *Ecclesiastical History*, 3.39.16. The translation is literal and agrees with my reading of the Greek text; it comes from the edition of Hugh Jackson Lawlor and John Ernest Oulton, *Eusebius* (London: SPCK, 1954), 1:101.

35. D. A. Carson, Douglas J. Moo, and Leon Morris, *An Introduction to the New Testament* (Grand Rapids, MI: Zondervan, 1992), 73.

36. Sidney B. Sperry, *Our Book of Mormon* (Salt Lake City: Stevens and Wallis, 1947), 185.

37. For this identification of Eusebius and his quotation of early history of James's martyrdom, see Anderson, "First Presidency of the Early Church," 18, 21.

38. Guthrie, *New Testament Introduction,* 729.

39. For lists of verses in James modeled on Jesus' teachings in the synoptic Gospels, see W. D. Davies, *The Setting of the Sermon on the Mount* (Cambridge: University Press, 1964), 402–3; and Peter H. Davids, *The Epistle of James, New International Greek Testament Commentary* (Grand Rapids, MI: Eerdmans, 1982), 47–48.

40. "Of the 36 parallels listed, 25 are with the Sermon on the Mount and 3 others with the Sermon on the Plain" (see Davids, *Epistle of James,* 48).

41. Matthew-Luke parallels: James 1:2 with Matthew 5:11–12 and Luke 6:23; James 1:5 with Matthew 7:7 and Luke 11:9; James 1:17 with Matthew 7:11 and Luke 11:13; James 1:22 with Matthew 7:24 and Luke 6:46–47; James 1:23 with Matthew 7:26 and Luke 6:49; James 2:5 with Matthew 5:3, 5 and Luke 6:20; James 3:12 with Matthew 7:16 and Luke 6:44–45; James 4:2 with Matthew 7:7 and Luke 11:9; James 4:9 with Matthew 5:4 and Luke 6:25; James 4:10 with Matthew 23:12 and Luke 14:11 and 18:14; James 4:11–12 with Matthew 7:1 and Luke 6:37; James 5:2 with Matthew 6:19–20 and Luke 12:33; James 5:10 with Matthew 5:11–12 and Luke 6:23.

    Unique Matthew parallels: James 1:4 with Matthew 5:48; James 2:10 with Matthew 5:19; James 2:13 with Matthew 5:7; James 3:18 with Matthew 5:9; James 4:8 with Matthew 5:8; James 4:13–14 with Matthew 6:34; James 5:9 with Matthew 5:22; James 5:12 with Matthew 5:34–37.

    Matthew-Mark parallels: James 1:6 with Matthew 21:21 and Mark 11:23–24; James 2:8 with Matthew 22:39 and Mark 12:31.

    Unique Luke parallel: James 5:1 with Luke 6:24–25.

42. See previous note for chapter numbers in Matthew.

43. Massey H. Shepherd Jr., "The Epistle of James and the Gospel of Matthew," *Journal of Biblical Literature* 75 (1956): 47.

44. Shepherd, "The Epistle of James and the Gospel of Matthew," 47.

45. Davids, *Epistle of James,* 49.

46. See Theron, *Evidence of Tradition,* 111, and note 21.

47. For an important and careful study of Paul's references to Christ's suffering, death, and resurrection, see Richard Neitzel Holzapfel, "Early Accounts of the Story," in *From the Last Supper Through the Resurrection,* ed. Richard Neitzel Holzapfel and Thomas A. Wayment (Salt Lake City: Deseret Book, 2003), 401–21.

CHAPTER SEVENTEEN

"An Hebrew of the Hebrews": Paul's Language and Thought

C. WILFRED GRIGGS

A discussion of the language and thought of the Apostle Paul would seem to be a rather straightforward matter. One of the few things upon which scholars of the New Testament agree is that Paul wrote or dictated his letters in Greek to audiences who were able to communicate in the same language. Most scholars, though not all, also believe that Paul is responsible for placing the teachings and practices of Jesus and the first disciples into a basic system of theology or doctrine upon which the later Christian Fathers built.

If we were to ask how Paul's background prepared him to accomplish these tasks, the answer would be simple for the question of language and only somewhat problematic with regard to his thought. His having been born and raised in Tarsus, a major center of Greek culture, accounted for his training in the Greek language, and his later study in Jerusalem under the great Jewish teacher and sage Gamaliel instilled in him the philosophical foundation which he later used in formulating Christian theology. Those beliefs seem so reasonable and have been published for so long that questioning them might at first appear presumptuous or at least unnecessarily contentious.

We live in a time, however, in which change is occurring in all fields of study, including ancient history. Biblical manuscripts written in various

C. Wilfred Griggs is a professor of ancient scripture at Brigham Young University.

languages and sometimes dating to early in the Christian era, the Dead Sea Scrolls and other Jewish documents from ancient Palestine and nearby areas, Christian and other religious writings from the same era and general geography, and ongoing archaeological work at many sites in the eastern Mediterranean all combine to necessitate a revaluation of such questions as the background and training of Paul. As every student of the past knows, such reconsideration in all areas of history is a continuing activity, and our understanding of the New Testament will be enhanced by increased awareness of the setting in which Jesus and the Apostles lived and fulfilled their sacred callings to preach the gospel. Recent studies of the written sources, coupled with the results of archaeological work in the eastern Mediterranean, particularly in Israel, have demonstrated that perhaps the traditional views concerning Paul's background and training have been misunderstood and misrepresented.

A brief review of the trends of scholarship concerning Paul during the past century or so will not necessarily increase our faith, but it will be instructive to show how training and scholarly bias can influence one's perspective. We can also appreciate how scholarship that is not tempered by prophetic guidance and insight can wander off into nonproductive and meaningless trivia. If we have a knowledge of eternal gospel principles and practices as restored in modern times and believe that Paul knew and preached the same gospel, a study from that perspective of the same written and archaeological materials can provide insights into that Apostle's life which will enhance our understanding of and appreciation for his ministry in the New Testament Church.

In considering the relationship of Paul to the Judaism of his day, some major tendencies have emerged during the past century or so.[1] One of the most dominant views, characterized by H. St. John Thackeray,[2] considers Paul to have been antithetical to Judaism although originally dependent upon it. Still early in the twentieth century, C. G. Montefiore attempted to minimize the differences between Paul and rabbinic Judaism by arguing that the Judaism against which Paul objected was not traditional rabbinical Judaism but rather a Judaism weakened by the influences of Hellenistic syncretism.[3] Although the distinction between Palestinian Judaism and Hellenistic Judaism (or Diaspora Judaism, as some identify it) has been appealing to some commentators, others, such as George Foot Moore, contend that Paul's criticism of Judaism was not directed at Jews to refute them because his position was inexplicable to a Jew. Rather, as

Moore puts it, Paul was writing to Gentile converts to protect them from the influence of Jewish propagandists who would try to persuade them that "observance of the law was necessary along with allegiance to Christ."[4]

In a work considered by many to be a turning point in the scholarship on Paul and Judaism, W. D. Davies denied the neat division of Judaism into separate Palestinian and Hellenistic or Diaspora components, showing the interpenetration of both without regard to geographical considerations.[5] Despite Davies's arguments that many motifs in Paul, which were often viewed as being the most Hellenistic, can in reality be paralleled in or derived from Palestinian Judaism, E. P. Sanders claims that his mentor Davies "did not, however, deal with the essential element which Montefiore found in Rabbinic literature but which is not taken into account in Paul's critique of Judaism: the doctrine of repentance and forgiveness." Sanders faults Davies for using Judaism "to identify Paul's *background,* not compare *religions.*"[6] Sanders's own work, also perceived by many to represent a watershed in Pauline scholarship, goes beyond a comparison of Pauline motifs with rabbinic statements to describe and define the religion of Paul and the religion of Judaism, which can then be contrasted with each other.

Sanders takes positions different from those of Davies, both in many of his perceptions of what constitutes first-century Judaism in Palestine and in how Paul differed from the Judaism of his day. Two of his conclusions that emphasize Paul's differences with Palestinian Judaism would be expected because of Paul's encounter with the resurrected Christ on the road to Damascus and the subsequent reordering of his religious beliefs according to the gospel which was revealed to him (see Galatians 1:12–16). Whereas Davies had stated that "Paul carried over into his interpretation of the Christian Dispensation the covenantal conceptions of Judaism,"[7] Sanders takes an opposite position: "Paul's 'pattern of religion' cannot be described as 'covenantal nomism,' and therefore Paul presents an *essentially different type of religiousness from any found in Palestinian Jewish literature.*"[8]

Despite that negative assertion, Sanders states that in many ways Paul reflects Palestinian Judaism more than Hellenistic Judaism. One example relates to defining righteousness: "The righteousness terminology is related to the righteousness terminology of Palestinian Judaism. One does not find in Paul any trace of the Greek and Hellenistic Jewish distinction between being righteous (man/man) and pious (man/God); nor is righteousness in Paul one virtue among others. Here, however, there is also a major shift; in Jewish literature to be righteous means to obey the Torah and to repent of transgression, but in Paul it means to be saved by Christ."[9]

Is it really possible to draw such distinctions between Judaism and Hellenistic culture in the first century? "The works of E. Bickerman, D. Daube, S. Lieberman, and M. Smith have abundantly established the interpenetration between Hellenism and Judaism by the first century, so that Pharisaism itself can be regarded as a hybrid."[10] Even Sanders, whose cited book focuses on Paul and Palestinian Judaism, admits the problem of identifying to what extent Hellenistic culture may have influenced the thought and language of Paul:

> Paul does not have simply a "Jewish" or a "Hellenistic" or a "Hellenistic Jewish" conception of man's plight. It appears that Paul's thought was not simply taken over from any one scheme pre-existing in the ancient world.
>
> In claiming a measure of uniqueness for Paul we should be cautious on two points. One is that we must agree with the common observation that nothing is totally unique. Indeed, with respect to man's plight, one can see relationships between what Paul thought and various other conceptions in the ancient world. What is lacking is a precise parallel which accounts exhaustively for Paul's thought, and this has partly to do with Paul's making use of so many different schemes of thought.[11]

Although some commentators drew sharp distinctions between Judaism, Hellenism, and Christianity and thus had Paul move through some version of the first two on his way to becoming the first Christian theologian, Krister Stendahl deemphasizes the formality of religion in the first century. Admitting that the vision on the road to Damascus resulted in a great change in Paul's life, Stendahl characterizes the change as more like a "call" than a "conversion" from one religion to another, for "it is obvious that Paul remains a Jew as he fulfills his role as an Apostle to the Gentiles."[12] The question Stendahl raises is not mere pedantry, for Christian missionaries of every age have had to distinguish between cultural mores that must be abandoned at conversion and those that can be retained. Furthermore, given the increasingly anti-Semitic position of many Christian churches in late antiquity, it is of more than idle interest to see whether the noted Apostle to the Gentiles himself exhibited any tendencies to turn away from or renounce Judaism.

Establishing Paul's relationship to the Judaism of his day and also establishing the relationship of Judaism to the Hellenistic world of the first century, therefore, continues to be of interest to students of the early Church. Even the confrontations between Paul and the so-called Judaizers are seen by some to be problems with other Christians rather than with Jews. Lloyd Gaston represents that position when he notes that "the opponents seem to be in every case rival Christian missionaries, and it is not at all sure either that they represent a united front, or that all of them are Jewish Christians." He further asserts: "Even if some of Paul's argumentation should be directed against individual (Christian) Jews, Judaism as such is never attacked. Paul's letters cannot be used either to derive information about Judaism or as evidence that he opposes Judaism as such."[13]

The difficulty of trying to fit Paul into one or another category of Judaism, such as Palestinian or Hellenistic (if they really are discrete and identifiable entities), is increased by statements found both in the Apostle's letters and in Luke's Acts of the Apostles. Luke quotes Paul telling the military tribune in Jerusalem that he is "a man, a Jew of Tarsus in Cilicia, a citizen of no insignificant city" (Acts 21:39),[14] supposedly placing him squarely in the context of Diaspora Judaism. Nevertheless, Luke records Paul telling the audience in the temple courtyard: "I am a Jew, and though I was born at Tarsus in Cilicia I was brought up in this city and was educated at the feet of Gamaliel according to the strict manner of our ancestral law, being zealous for God as all of you are this day" (Acts 22:3).

Paul declared the strictness of his Jewish upbringing. In beginning his speech before Agrippa II and Berenice, he said: "My manner of life from my youth, which was from the beginning among my own nation and in Jerusalem, is known by all the Jews. They have known me for a long time, and should they wish to testify, that according to the strictest party of our religion I lived as a Pharisee" (Acts 26:4–5). When Paul addressed the Jewish council of Pharisees and Sadducees, he declared that he was "a Pharisee, the son of a Pharisee" (Acts 23:6) and that he had lived in good conscience before God up to that time (see Acts 23:1), making a claim of such strict obedience to Jewish law that the high priest had someone strike (backhand) him on the mouth.

Paul did not refer to his origins outside of Palestine, and his own statements emphasized his strict adherence to Jewish law and practices before his encounter with the resurrected Christ. In Galatians, to give an example, Paul summarized his pre-Christian life: "For you have heard of my former way of life in Judaism, . . . and I progressed in Judaism beyond many of those of my same age in my race, because I was far more zealous for the traditions of my fathers" (Galatians 1:13–14).

Later, when writing to the Philippians from Rome, where he was awaiting trial, Paul again declared his earlier strict adherence to Jewish law: "Although I have confidence in the flesh. If someone else thinks he has confidence in the flesh, I have more: circumcised on the eighth day; a member of the race of Israel; of the tribe of Benjamin; an Hebrew of the Hebrews; as to the law, a Pharisee, as for zeal, one who persecuted the church; and as to uprightness according to the law, I was blameless" (Philippians 3:4–6).

Even conversion to Christianity did not cause Paul to denigrate or repudiate his Jewish origins: "Therefore, I say, has God rejected his people? Far from it! For I am also an Israelite, of the seed of Abraham, of the tribe of Benjamin. God has not cast aside his people whom he knew beforehand" (Romans 11:1–2).

If one agrees with Davies that the distinction between Palestinian, or rabbinic, and Diaspora, or Hellenistic, Judaism is not easily defended, Paul's birth in Tarsus and his education in Jerusalem would not necessarily represent a significant shift in religious orientation or training. Such an observation does not by itself clarify or explain how much exposure to Greek culture Paul experienced in his pre-Christian years or whether he was likely to have had more of such exposure in Tarsus before moving to Jerusalem than he would have encountered in Palestine. Behind that question is an even larger one for students of the New Testament: how likely was any Jew in Palestine, either from Jerusalem or the Galilee, to have significant and continuing interaction with Hellenistic culture? We might add, parenthetically, that to answer the question for Paul brings us closer to having to answer it as well for Jesus and His Apostles in the early Church.

It must be obvious by now that despite claims in both Luke's Acts and Paul's letters that Paul was raised in the strictest form of Judaism of his day, commentators have not arrived at a consensus about his relationship to the Judaism they encounter in the documentary evidence. In an assessment of the problem, Victor Furnish stated in his presidential address to the Society of Biblical Literature: "In short, the more that historical research has been able to uncover about the varieties and complexities of first-century Judaism, the more difficult it has become to put Paul in his place as a Jew." Furnish further stated that the same difficulties exist when evaluating Paul's relationship to early Christianity or the Hellenistic world in general:

> As research has taught us more about the diversity and complexity of nascent Christianity, it has become harder to put Paul in his place within it.
>
> The same is true of attempts to situate Paul more generally within the Hellenistic world. It is no longer necessary, or even plausible, to attribute the Hellenistic characteristics of Paul's letters and thought to his direct and deliberate borrowing from the philosophical schools and mystery religions. Research has shown that one must first reckon with his background in Hellenistic Judaism, and also with the time that he spent in the mixed community of Antioch. . . .
>
> Considering all of this, must one conclude that the historical Paul is still on the loose, successfully evading every effort to put him in his place in history?[15]

Given a common scholarly compulsion to identify and explain everyone and everything in terms of previously defined categories, the problem of a century of scholarship may be an attempt to force Paul into a Jewish, ecclesiastical, or Hellenistic mold established by the research of the period. It is certain that Paul did not see the gospel of Christ as fitting into such limiting categories, and as an emissary of the Lord he must, as he said, transcend the very classifications into which modern scholars have tried to place him:

> For while I am free from all men, I made myself a servant to all, in order that I might gain more of them. And I became as a Jew to the Jews, in order that I might gain Jews; as one under the law to those under the law, although I am not under the law, in order that I might gain those under the law; as one without the law to those without the law, although I am not without the law of God but am subject to the law of Christ, in order that I might gain those without the law. I became weak to those who are weak, in order that I might gain the weak; I became all things to all men, in order that I might at least save some. Now I do all things on account of the Gospel, in

order that I might become a fellow participant in it. (1 Corinthians 9:19–23)

If indeed Paul was taught the strictest (generally understood to be synonymous with the narrowest, or most parochial) form of Judaism in Jerusalem as a student of Gamaliel from his youth, how are we to explain his developed ability to express himself in the Greek language? Even though Davies makes a strong case for not making great distinctions between rabbinic, or Palestinian, Judaism and Hellenistic, or Diaspora, Judaism, few in the scholarship of the past would go so far as to argue for Greek-teaching synagogues in Jerusalem or chief rabbis whose mother tongue was Greek rather than Aramaic and whose primary scriptural source was a revised Septuagint translation rather than a Hebrew text.

Before proceeding with the question of Paul's language and education, an explanation of the rabbinate in the first half of the first century is in order. Martin Hengel trenchantly observes that "in fact before [A.D.] 70 there was still no rabbinate and no ordination of scholars who then were given the right to bear the title 'rabbi.'"[16] However, there were numerous synagogues in Jerusalem with schools and houses of learning attached to them (one later rabbinic text states that there were 480 before the Roman War[17]), and they were likely less institutionalized and more free than in the second century when the victorious Tannaites were producing the Mishnah.[18] So little is known of Gamaliel I, under whom Paul studied, that were it not for mention made of him in Josephus,[19] confusion with his famous grandson Gamaliel II might have caused scholars to dismiss him as Luke's invention. Jacob Neusner collected the traditions relating to Gamaliel I, and he notes that his task was "complicated by the existence of traditions of Gamaliel II of Yavneh, by the absence of references to Gamaliel in accounts of the debates of the contemporary Houses of Shammai and Hillel, by the end of the system of listing pairs, and most of all, by the failure of the tradents everywhere to distinguish carefully among the Gamaliels." Neusner further states that his account of this great teacher, the first of the Pharisees before AD 70 to be honored with the title Rabban and probably the most famous instructor in the Judaism of his day, "can by no means be so comprehensive and reliable as those of earlier masters."[20]

If so little can be stated with certainty regarding Gamaliel, and if the Jewish rabbinate was so ill-defined and unstructured before AD 70 as Hengel observes, what evidence can be produced to clarify the language of the biblical texts to which the young Saul would have been exposed in Jerusalem? The student of Hellenistic history will know that in the three centuries following the death of Alexander the Great, Greek culture penetrated deeply into Egyptian society, as vividly brought to light through the tens of thousands of papyri discovered in Egypt during the last century. Eastward toward India, though the evidence is less well preserved, Tarn could note that "to parts of India, perhaps to large parts, [the Greeks] came, not as conquerors, but as friends and 'saviors.'"[21] Greeks ruled in India "until well into the first century," and Greek culture is described as being firmly established in India by the second century before Christ.[22] If those regions were significantly Hellenized before the first century, should one expect less in Palestine, which is between Egypt and India and closer to Greece? Has far too much been made through the centuries about the supposed, and perhaps erroneous, dichotomy between Judaism and Hellenism? (The later church fathers labeled it the dichotomy between Athens and Jerusalem for somewhat different reasons.)

The primary meanings given in Liddell and Scott for *Hellenizein* are "to speak Greek, write or read correct Greek," and so forth.[23] A large body of material relating to Hellenistic culture in Palestine is the inscriptional evidence. For there "the triumphal progress of Greek makes an impressive showing in *inscriptions*," and "if we disregard later Nabaatean inscriptions in Transjordania and the typically Jewish tomb, ossuary and synagogue inscriptions . . . from the third century BC, we find almost exclusively Greek inscriptions in Palestine."[24] More recently, Hengel stated that about 33 percent of the nearly 250 inscriptions found in or around Jerusalem from the Second Temple period are in Greek.[25]

For a non-Jew in Hellenistic Palestine, "the principle could probably very soon be applied that anyone who could read and write also had a command of Greek."[26] Further, within Judaism, Hengel asserts, "The high priest and the financial administrator of the temple will also have had impeccable Greek-speaking and Greek-writing secretaries for their correspondence with Ptolemaic offices and the court. If one goes on to include members of the Ptolemaic garrison, officials and merchants, even the Jerusalem of the third century BC may be assumed to have had a considerable Greek-speaking minority."[27]

By the time of the Roman conquest (in the first century before Christ), we must add an influx of hundreds of thousands of Jews to Jerusalem for various festivals, most Greek-speaking, and the need for the local inhabitants to know Greek to accommodate their needs. Josephus claims that on the basis of a count taken of Passover sacrificial lambs, greater Jerusalem contained more than 2.5 million people during that celebration.[28]

Not only did the visitors to Jerusalem speak and write Greek, but in the second century before Christ, Jerusalem itself was becoming a Greek polis. According to Hengel, "the process of Hellenization in the *Jewish upper class* then entered an acute phase, the aim of which was the complete assimilation of Judaism to the Hellenistic environment. . . . Presumably Greek 'education' in Jerusalem not only led to training the ephebes in sports but also had intellectual and literary elements."[29]

All of this presupposes the existence of a Greek school in Jerusalem, with some evidence that a knowledge of Homer was part of the curriculum.[30] Some remnants of Jewish literature written in Greek in Palestine can be found in Josephus (the romance concerning the Tobiad Joseph and his sons, composed in Egypt, but perpetuated in Palestine[31]) and Eusebius (fragments of the Jewish historian Alexander Polyhistor and fragments of an anonymous Samaritan[32]). That anonymous Samaritan writer quoted in Eusebius wrote in the second century before Christ, determined to glorify Abraham and substantiate the truth of the Old Testament. In the quotations from Alexander Polyhistor in Eusebius are statements from another Jewish historian, Eupolemus, who appears to have been a Greek-educated Palestinian Jew.[33] Second Maccabees contains a summary of yet another Jewish writer, Jason of Cyrene, and, though he was trained in rhetoric outside of Palestine, it is assumed by its detail and historical vividness to have been written in Palestine soon after the Maccabean Revolt.[34]

The countermovement to the Hellenizing forces in Jerusalem that was victorious after AD 70 gave rise to the rabbinate and resulted in the suppression of the explicit Hellenization of the earlier era.[35] Once Judaism lost two of the key elements of its identity after AD 70, through the destruction of the temple and the dispossession of the Jews from their land, new identifying elements had to be found. The establishment of the Jewish canon of scripture near the end of the first century and the rise of rabbinic Judaism in the first centuries of the Christian era, as expressed in the Mishnah, the two Talmuds, and related literatures, have provided a Jewish identity that has persisted through the centuries. It has been difficult until very recently to penetrate the historical barriers resulting from the Jewish-Roman war of AD 66–70 and to see the diversity and pluralism in Judaism of the first half of the first century. Rabbinic Judaism, which defined itself at the end of the first century and suppressed the pluralism and Hellenization that characterized prewar Palestine, was the normative Judaism which scholars used in their analysis of Paul's background. With the recent archaeological discoveries in the region and the resulting studies relating to Judaism in the prewar period before the destruction of the temple, the cosmopolitan nature of Palestine in general and of Jerusalem in particular during the New Testament era is much more evident than it was previously.

Because Paul is from the earlier period, there is no reason to deny that he could have received a good education in the Greek language and culture in Jerusalem. Remembering that the primary meaning of *Hellenizein* is to speak, read, and write Greek, and not necessarily to embrace Greek history or literature, we need not assume that Paul studied Homer, Euripides, Plato, or any other authors in the traditional curriculum of the Greeks. In point of fact, awareness of those sources in Paul is usually denied.[36] Yet, given the subject matter of Paul's epistles and the epistolary style in general, any argument relating to the substance of Paul's education based on his writings in the New Testament would be like reconstructing Elder Bruce R. McConkie's law school curriculum from his book *Mormon Doctrine*. Paul's awareness of Greek literature, as suggested above, may have been considerably greater than would be displayed in his letters to Christian congregations and close friends.

To say that Paul spoke and wrote Greek as a native tongue in no way argues against his also knowing Aramaic and Hebrew. Indeed, he stated that the resurrected Lord spoke Aramaic to him in the vision he had while traveling to Damascus (see Acts 26:14), and Paul spoke in Aramaic to the crowd in the temple courtyard after his first arrest (see Acts 21:40; 22:2). There can be no doubt that he knew some Hebrew text of Old Testament writings, even if in his speeches and letters he favors a revised version of the Septuagint. One should not underestimate Paul with regard either to his Judaism or to the influence of Hellenism in his life.

Some passages in Paul's letters might be understood to acknowledge his lack of familiarity with Greek literary sources or training in rhetoric. The most famous of these are found in the Corinthian correspondence, in which Paul testified of the superiority of God's wisdom to that of man: "And when I came to you, brethren, I came not with excellency of speech or of wisdom, because I was declaring to you the mystery of God. . . . And my speech and my preaching were not given in persuasive words of wisdom, but in demonstration of the Spirit and power, in order that your faith might not be in the wisdom of men, but in the power of God" (1 Corinthians 2:1–5). In 2 Corinthians, Paul strongly defended his apostolic calling, quoting his critics who spoke condescendingly of him: "For his letters, they say, are weighty and powerful; but his bodily presence is weak and his manner of speech is contemptible" (2 Corinthians 10:10). Paul acknowledged that he was a layman in the matter of public speaking, but he denied that he was deficient in knowledge: "But although I might be unskilled in speaking, I am not unskilled in knowledge, for in every way we have made knowledge known to you in the presence of all men" (2 Corinthians 11:6). Elsewhere Paul warned against being led captive by the learning of the world, although he did not devalue the acquisition of such knowledge: "Beware lest there be one who will lead you captive through philosophy and the vain deceit according to the tradition of men, according to the rudiments of the world and not according to Christ" (Colossians 2:8).

Such disclaimers of his rhetorical skills and of the value of philosophy are not the same as saying he was ignorant of such matters. In their commentary on 1 Corinthians, William Orr and James Walther argue that Paul must have received a good Greek education, even if he didn't parade under its banner:

> It may be significant that Paul never felt moved to mention any Greek education he may have received. But the thoroughness of his instruction in contemporary Koine Greek is demonstrated by the fact that he could occasionally rise to true eloquence while using this language to express warm religious conviction and subtle points of doctrine and morals (e.g. 1 Corinthians 13, 15; Romans 8, 12; 2 Corinthians 3). It is hard to believe he could have mastered an alien language to this degree without having received considerable instruction in its literature, particularly that of the Hellenistic Greek communities, such as Alexandria or Tarsus. His description of his early life and instruction appears to include him among those Jews of the intellectual ghetto who had extensive knowledge of their own history and culture, but had completely cut themselves off from any knowledge of Greek or Roman paganism. However, the quality of the letters themselves leads us to believe that his experience somewhere and somehow enabled him to break out of this insularity.[37]

Hans Dieter Betz places 2 Corinthians 10–13 in the Socratic tradition, stating that these chapters compose an apology, or defense, written in letter form.[38] It is not necessary to assume that Paul read a Socratic apology (though he very well may have done so) to express some of the sentiments found there, for it was common for philosophers in the Socratic tradition to disavow the pretentiousness of the rhetoricians and sophists.[39] Plato has Socrates tell the jury in his trial that he will not try to emulate the professional orators: "Now they, as I say, have said little or nothing true; but you shall hear from me nothing but the truth. Not, however, men of Athens, speeches finely tricked out with words and phrases, . . . for surely it would not be fitting for one of my age to come before you like a youngster making up speeches."[40]

Socrates was seventy years old at his trial, and he had held interviews with the leading intellects of Athens,[41] which certainly exposed him to the best speakers of the day. He nevertheless denies having any knowledge of their rhetorical skills in his jury trial, a setting in which orators were famous for showing off their skills. Just as Paul will later tell the Corinthians to concentrate on truth more than on language, so Socrates speaks in his defense: "This is the first time I have come before the court, although I am seventy years old; I am therefore an utter foreigner to the manner of speech here. Hence, just as you would, of course, if I were really a foreigner, pardon me if I spoke in that dialect and that manner in which I had been brought up, so now I make this request of you, a fair one, as it seems to me, that you disregard the manner of my speech—for perhaps it might be worse and perhaps better—and observe and pay attention merely to this, whether what I say is just or not."[42]

One could debate endlessly—and uselessly—whether the obvious echoes from the Apology of Socrates on the theme of content over form found in Paul's Corinthian letters demonstrate his familiarity with the Greek literary tradition. Even if training in and exposure to the Greek literary tradition were part of Paul's educational background, he makes it abundantly clear that his apostolic calling does not require him to refer to such materials in testifying of the Savior and His gospel or in counseling Christians on how to improve their lives. Most of Paul's writings in the New Testament are composed to give advice and correction in response to specific problems. There would be little need or opportunity for the Apostle to draw upon the poetry, philosophy, or history he might have learned as a student.

As a sidelight to this discussion and with reference to the larger question of Hellenism and the New Testament, let me note that if Jerusalem had become a Hellenistic city where the common language of general discourse was Greek, the situation in the Galilee was perhaps even more likely to have been Hellenized. There was a large Gentile population in the Galilee, and Matthew, quoting Isaiah (9:1–2), referred to a large part of the region as the "Galilee of the Gentiles" (Matthew 4:15). Eric Meyers, in an article strongly critical of the degree of Hellenization claimed for Palestine by Hengel, still admitted that "there is no doubt that Greek language was widely used in Palestine by the first century, especially in daily commercial settings and in simple forms of communication."[43] Meyers does not define "simple forms of communication," except, perhaps, to note that one should not believe that a high degree of Greek literacy (presumably of Greek literature) dominated a society in which most of the people were Jews. For some time, the belief prevailed that Galilee was simply a rural region populated by farmers, fishermen, and others who were tied too closely to the land or the lake to be interested in or aware of the Hellenistic world around them. Recent and continuing excavations, however, at such sites as Caesarea Philippi, Beth-Shean, and Sepphoris (where Meyers is one of the codirectors) demonstrate a thriving Hellenistic presence in these Galilean cities. Can we truly agree with Stuart Miller and others that Jesus and His disciples avoided going into Sepphoris, some three miles from Nazareth, or Caesarea Philippi, or any of the other Hellenized cities?[44] If Jerusalem were as Hellenized as even Meyers is willing to suggest,[45] and if Jesus spent as much time in Jerusalem as the Gospels suggest, surely it was not to avoid contact with non-Jewish culture that kept Jesus from entering Galilean cities that had a strong Hellenistic influence. The argument from silence in the scriptures about visits to those cities is inadequate because the scriptures certainly do not attempt to provide a complete list of places Jesus visited. Even Jesus' statement that He was to minister only among the house of Israel (see Matthew 15:24) does not preclude his finding Israelites throughout Palestine, including places where Gentiles and Hellenized Jews might be found.

The chief purpose of this presentation is not to assert categorically that Paul studied in a Greek school or a Greek-speaking synagogue in Jerusalem, though he may well have done either or both. Neither can we assert with confidence that Jesus actually gave the Sermon on the Mount (or on the Plain) in Greek, even though he may have done that very thing, or perhaps he gave it in Aramaic on one occasion and Greek on another. The main point is that our understanding of the past is changing rapidly, and, therefore, we should distinguish between what is spiritually enduring and unchanging and what is subject to modification with new discoveries. The New Testament and early Christian landscapes appear quite different now from how they appeared half a century ago, and the dynamic forces of intercultural contacts were greater than we previously understood. That Jesus and His Apostles, including Paul, ushered in and spread abroad a dispensation of the eternal gospel in such a world should be both exciting to study and encouraging to members of the restored Church in a rather similar contemporary setting.

NOTES

1. See Ed Sanders, *Paul and Palestinian Judaism: A Comparison of Patterns of Religion* (Philadelphia: Fortress Press, 1977), 2–13.

2. Henry St. John Thackeray, *The Relation of St. Paul to Contemporary Jewish Thought* (London: Macmillan, 1900).

3. C. G. Montefiore, *Judaism and St. Paul: Two Essays* (London: Max Goschen, 1914).

4. Sanders, *Paul and Palestinian Judaism,* 6, referring to George Foot Moore, *Judaism in the First Centuries of the Christian Era: The Age of the Tannaim,* 3 vols. (Cambridge: Harvard University Press, 1927–30), 3:151.

5. W. D. Davies, *Paul and Rabbinic Judaism* (New York: Harper and Row, 1958), 1–16.

6. Sanders, *Paul and Palestinian Judaism,* 7, 10.

7. Davies, *Paul and Rabbinic Judaism,* 259–60.

8. Sanders, *Paul and Palestinian Judaism,* 543.

9. Sanders, *Paul and Palestinian Judaism,* 544.

10. W. D. Davies, "From Schweitzer to Scholem: Reflections on Sabbatai Svi," *Journal of Biblical Literature* 95, no. 4 (December 1976): 532n14.

11. Sanders, *Paul and Palestinian Judaism,* 555.

12. Krister Stendahl, *Paul among Jews and Gentiles* (Philadelphia: Fortress Press, 1976), 11.

13. Lloyd Gaston, *Paul and the Torah* (Vancouver, B.C.: University of British Columbia Press, 1987), 3, 4.

14. This and all other quotations from the New Testament are translations by the author unless otherwise noted.

15. "On Putting Paul in His Place," *Journal of Biblical Literature* 113, no. 1 (Spring 1994): 9–11.

16. Martin Hengel, *The Pre-Christian Paul* (London: SCM Press, 1991), 28.

17. Hengel, *Pre-Christian Paul,* 119n160.
18. Hengel, *Pre-Christian Paul,* 29.
19. Josephus, *The Life,* trans. H. St. J. Thackeray (Cambridge, MA: Harvard University Press, 1926), lines 190, 309; *The Jewish War,* trans. Thackeray, 4:159; *Jewish Antiquities,* trans. Thackeray, 20:213, 223.
20. Jacob Neusner, *The Rabbinic Traditions about the Pharisees before 70* (Leiden: E. J. Brill, 1971), 341; see also 341–76.
21. W. W. Tarn, *The Greeks in Bactria and India,* 3d ed. rev. (Chicago: Ares Publishers, 1984), 180.
22. G. W. Walbank, *The Hellenistic World* (Cambridge, MA: Harvard University Press, 1981), 140, 66.
23. Henry George Liddell and Robert Scott, comps., *A Greek-English Lexicon,* 9th ed. (Oxford: Oxford University Press, 1940), 536.
24. Martin Hengel, *Judaism and Hellenism: Studies in Their Encounter in Palestine During the Early Hellenistic Period,* trans. John Bowden (Philadelphia: Fortress Press, 1974), 58.
25. Hengel, *Pre-Christian Paul,* 55.
26. Hengel, *Judaism and Hellenism,* 59.
27. Hengel, *Judaism and Hellenism,* 59.
28. Josephus, *Jewish War,* 6:422ff.
29. Hengel, *Judaism and Hellenism,* 103.
30. Hengel, *Judaism and Hellenism,* 103.
31. See Josephus, *Antiquities,* 12:157–85, 224.
32. Eusebius, *Praeparatio Evangelica,* 9.17–18.
33. J. Freudenthal, *Hellenistiche Studien* (Breslau: Verlag von H. Skutsch, 1875), 82–129.
34. 2 Maccabees, passim; Hengel, *Judaism and Hellenism,* 95–99.
35. Hengel, *Judaism and Hellenism,* 103.
36. Hengel, *Pre-Christian Paul,* 38.
37. William F. Orr and James Arthur Walther, *1 Corinthians, Anchor Bible Commentary* (Garden City, NY: Doubleday, 1976), 5–6.
38. H. D. Betz, *Der Apostel Paulus und die sokratische Tradition* (Tübingen: J. C. B. Mohr, 1972), 14.
39. Betz, *Der Apostel Paulus und die sokratische Tradition,* 66.
40. Plato, *Apology* 17b-c, trans. Harold North Fowler (Cambridge, MA: Harvard University Press, 1971), 69, 71.
41. Plato, *Apology* 21e–22a.
42. Plato, *Apology* 17d–18a.
43. Eric M. Meyers, "The Challenge of Hellenism for Early Judaism and Christianity," *Biblical Archaeologist* 55, no. 2 (June 1992): 87.

44. Stuart S. Miller, "Sepphoris, the Well Remembered City," *Biblical Archaeologist* 55, no. 2 (June 1992): 74–81.

45. Meyers, "The Challenge of Hellenism for Early Judaism and Christianity," 86.

CHAPTER EIGHTEEN

THE JERUSALEM COUNCIL

ROBERT J. MATTHEWS

The fifteenth chapter of the book of Acts in the New Testament tells of a high-level council meeting in Jerusalem of the leaders of the Church. The date is not recorded, but the events leading up to the council indicate that the meeting was held in approximately AD 49 or 50. Within the short space of those sixteen or seventeen years after the death of Christ, the preaching of the gospel of Jesus Christ among non-Jewish people raised questions of doctrine and procedure that the young Church had not encountered when missionary work was done among the Jews only. Those questions made a top-level discussion necessary, for the decision would affect the Church in matters of doctrine, in missionary procedure, and in family religious observances. The council was not held in a vacuum nor was it just an academic exercise. It was the result of, and was attended by, persons having strong opinions, religious convictions, traditions, and biases. In effect, a crisis was forming in the Church.

THE NEW TESTAMENT RECORD

The complete title of the New Testament book of Acts is "The Acts of the Apostles." It is generally understood to have been written by Luke and is in reality a sequel to the book of Luke. Both the book of Luke and the book of Acts are addressed to an acquaintance named "Theophilus" (Luke 1:3; Acts 1:1). Acts refers to the book of Luke as the "former treatise" of "all that Jesus began both to do and teach" (Acts 1:1), whereas the book of Acts itself deals with the work, growth, and development of the Church after the ascension of Christ.

Robert J. Matthews is a professor emeritus of ancient scripture at Brigham Young University.

Although each member of the Twelve is mentioned at least once in Acts, the book deals initially with the ministry of Peter, James, and John and records at great length the conversion and ministry of Paul. It is a record of the "acts" not of all the Apostles but of only a few and especially of Paul. Acts is in truth a short account of the missionary outreach of the Church to the Jews in Judea, then to the Samaritans, and finally to the Gentiles throughout the Mediterranean world. Because Paul is the dominant personality in the extension of the Church among Gentiles, he becomes the dominant personality in the book of Acts from chapters 13 through 28. Likewise, fourteen of the twenty-one epistles in the New Testament were written by Paul.

Even though our present New Testament does not contain a record of it, there can be no doubt that many, if not all, of the Twelve traveled extensively in giving missionary service. Jesus commanded the Twelve to go unto all nations, teaching and baptizing them (see Matthew 28:19–20). Tradition and apocryphal sources suggest that the original Apostles were true to their commission and traveled throughout Africa, India, Mesopotamia, the Near East, and so forth, and preached the gospel of Jesus Christ.[1] Yet the New Testament that has been among Christians for the past eighteen hundred years focuses primarily on the area immediately surrounding the northern shores of the Mediterranean Sea: Greece, Turkey, and Italy, with only slight mention of Spain. It contains no record of the ministry of the Twelve in other parts of the world such as Egypt and India.

I believe there is a reasonable explanation for that narrow focus. The New Testament is a record of the work and preaching of living prophets and Apostles who went forth with priesthood authority to build up and regulate the Church of Jesus Christ in their day, the first century after Christ. Most of the writings and records of travel of those early authorized brethren have not been preserved for later generations, yet the missionary records of Paul, Peter, and John have been. Could it be that those records in particular were preserved for the benefit of the Restoration? Perhaps the Lord, knowing among what people the Restoration in the latter days would need to begin, preserved the sacred records that dealt with the establishment of the Church in southern Europe, from where it moved throughout Europe, the British Isles, and Scandinavia. There would thus be among them a scriptural base for the Restoration of the fulness of the gospel by the Prophet Joseph Smith.

Most of the settlers in early North America came from the countries of

Europe, and they brought the Bible with them. The Protestant Reformation of the sixteenth century based most of its philosophy on the writings of Paul. The Reformation was absolutely necessary as prologue to the Restoration. The Joseph Smith family, the Richards family, the Youngs, the Kimballs, Whitmers, Taylors, and other early families in the Church were of European Protestant stock. Furthermore, when missionaries of the Church went forth in the late 1830s and immediately thereafter, most of the converts came from Europe—from England, Wales, Scotland, Scandinavia, Germany, and Holland.

I believe the Lord preserved what He did in the New Testament because it was that part of the history and doctrine of the early Church that would be most useful and serviceable in establishing The Church of Jesus Christ of Latter-day Saints in the dispensation of the fulness of times. The Lord knew and designed that it should be among those people in America who were of European extraction that the Restoration in the latter days should first take root and sprout. It would then be nourished by converts from Europe. From that beginning the gospel in the latter days would spread to all other nations. It would have been a great deal more difficult than it was for The Church of Jesus Christ of Latter-day Saints to be established among people who did not have a New Testament or who had a New Testament that had not produced the Protestant Reformation.

Events Leading to the Jerusalem Council

As noted earlier, the causes that produced the Jerusalem Council did not develop in a vacuum. The need for such a council was the consequence of several doctrinal and cultural factors that had been at work among both Jews and Gentiles for centuries. It will be necessary to review the activities of the Church as recorded in Acts 1 through 15 to understand the thrust and direction of the early Church and see what led to the council itself. Following is a summation of significant events.

Jesus ascends into heaven from the Mount of Olives, having told the Twelve not to extend their ministry beyond Judea until after they receive the Holy Ghost. They will then be empowered to go to Jews, Samaritans, and the "uttermost part of the earth" (Gentiles) in that order (Acts 1:8). Because of the vacancy in the Quorum of the Twelve, Peter calls the eleven remaining Apostles together, and Matthias is chosen (see Acts 1:13–26).

One week after the ascension of Jesus to heaven, at the annual feast of Pentecost, the Holy Ghost descends on the Twelve, and they speak in tongues to people of many nations. Gathered at Jerusalem for the feast are thousands of Jews from at least fifteen nations throughout the Near and Middle East, including Rome, Greece, Turkey, Crete, Arabia, Egypt, Libya, Parthia, and Mesopotamia. These are people of the Jews' religion who have come to Jerusalem for the annual feast of Pentecost, which is held fifty days after the feast of Passover. Many thousands are present, for from among the visitors the Apostles baptize three thousand in one day (see Acts 2:41).

It is of particular importance that the record states that those who came from those fifteen nations were Jews and proselytes, which means that not all were Jewish by lineage but some were Gentile converts to Judaism (see Acts 2:10). The term *proselyte* in the New Testament always means Gentile converts to Judaism. Certainly some of the three thousand converted to the Church on the day of Pentecost would have been from among the proselytes and thus the first persons of Gentile lineage to join the Church in the meridian dispensation. Jesus had instructed the Twelve, when they were starting on their first missions more than two years before, not to go among the Gentiles or the Samaritans at that time (see Matthew 10:5). Hence, Church members up till then were exclusively Jewish. But note this important fact: even though individuals of Gentile lineage now came into the Church, they had all previously converted to Judaism, which meant complying with the practice of circumcision, eating kosher food, offering sacrifice, and honoring the Sabbath day in proper Jewish style. Although Greek, Galatian, or Roman in lineage, they were Jews in religion.

Acts 3 through 6 deals with the ministry of the Twelve among the Jews in and around Judea. The Church grows rapidly with Jewish converts. Persecution comes from the Jewish leaders. Church growth necessitates administrative adjustments, so seven men are selected to assist the Twelve, primarily in welfare duties. Among those seven are some with such Gentile-sounding names as Stephen, Parmenas, and Nicolas. Nicolas is further identified as a proselyte from Antioch (see Acts 6:5), thus affirming that he is a Gentile by lineage who first joined the Jews' religion and then was converted to Christ and the Church. Thus at least Nicolas, and possibly others among the seven, is actually of Gentile lineage but has been circumcised and practices all that pertains to the Jews' religion and the law of Moses.

Stephen, one of the seven, is accused of having taught that Jesus would destroy Jerusalem and the temple and "change the customs which Moses delivered" unto Israel (Acts 6:14). He is taken before the Sanhedrin and permitted to speak. Found guilty of blasphemy, he is stoned to death. Saul (later known as Paul) witnesses his death (see Acts 7). Stephen is the earliest on record who is reported to have said that Jesus will change the Mosaic customs.

Philip, another of the seven, baptizes many men and women in Samaria (see Acts 8). That is another extension for the Church, which to this point had not done missionary work in Samaria. Peter and John come from Jerusalem to lay their hands on the new converts and confer the Holy Ghost. The Church is thus officially established among the Samaritans, but this is only half a step away from teaching the Jews. Even though the Samaritans were genealogically Israelite mixed with other nations and thus were technically not Jews, they practiced the law of Moses and hence were circumcised, ate kosher food, offered sacrifice, and so forth. In this respect they were similar to the Jews, and the conversion of Samaritans did not challenge allegiance to the law of Moses.

Saul is converted to Jesus Christ by a personal visit in which he sees, hears, and converses with the resurrected Lord (see Acts 9). Paul proclaims his testimony of Christ in the synagogues of Damascus. For Paul to have become a follower of Jesus Christ was a great change in his life, but his conversion did not mark a doctrinal or cultural change in the Church because he was already circumcised, ate kosher food, and so forth.

Peter, having been directed by a vision and the voice of the Spirit, baptizes Cornelius and his family at Cæsarea (see Acts 10–11). Peter is shown in vision animals forbidden to be eaten under the law of Moses, and he is told to eat them. This is a sign to him from the Lord that the dietary restrictions of the law of Moses are about to end. It takes Peter a little time to get used to the idea. Cornelius is a good man, an Italian, and a soldier, but he is not a proselyte to Judaism. An angel directed him to send for Peter. Peter, having already been prepared by the Lord, is willing to baptize Cornelius.

This is the first clear case of a Gentile coming into the Church without having first complied with the law of Moses through circumcision and so forth. The conversion and baptism of Cornelius in this manner is thus a major step—a full step—in extending the Church missionary system. It is very significant that the Lord brought about this new procedure through Peter, who, as the senior Apostle of the Church, could exercise all the priesthood keys and held the proper office through which such direction from the Lord should come.

Many Jewish brethren in the Church complained to Peter about that direct process for gaining membership in the Church, but he answered their criticism with a recital of the vision, the angel, the voice of the Spirit to him, and the manifestation of the Holy Ghost to Cornelius and his family before their baptism (see Acts 11). Cornelius did not receive the gift of the Holy Ghost before baptism, for such is contrary to the order of the kingdom. What he did receive before baptism was the witness of the Holy Ghost, as the Prophet Joseph Smith explained:

> There is a difference between the Holy Ghost and the gift of the Holy Ghost. Cornelius received the Holy Ghost before he was baptized, which was the convincing power of God unto him of the truth of the Gospel, but he could not receive the gift of the Holy Ghost until after he was baptized. Had he not taken this sign or ordinance upon him, the Holy Ghost which convinced him of the truth of God, would have left him. Until he obeyed these ordinances and received the gift of the Holy Ghost, by the laying on of hands, according to the order of God, he could not have healed the sick or commanded an evil spirit to come out of a man, and it obey him.[2]

Even after the landmark conversion of Cornelius, with Peter, the Lord's anointed, directing this phase of the missionary outreach, some Jewish members of the Church refused to accept the change, and they preached the gospel to "none but unto the Jews only" (Acts 11:19). Nonetheless, the way was opened for Gentiles to come into the Church without becoming Jews first. At Antioch of Syria, a great Gentile city about three hundred miles north of Jerusalem, so many Gentiles joined the Church that the Brethren in Jerusalem sent Barnabas to Antioch to oversee the change that was taking place. Barnabas was a good diplomatic choice: he was a Levite by lineage, was reared in Cyprus (a Gentile environment) and converted to the gospel, being "a good man, and full of the Holy Ghost and of faith" (Acts 11:24; see 4:36). Upon seeing the magnitude of the Gentile conversion in Antioch, Barnabas was pleased with the direction in which the missionary work was going and sent for Saul (Paul) to assist him. Barnabas had known of Saul earlier and had introduced him to the Apostles (see Acts 9:27).

Acts 12 deals with the martyrdom of James, one of the three most senior

Apostles and the brother of John. Administrative activities are also discussed in this chapter.

At Antioch, Saul, Barnabas, and John Mark are called and set apart to missionary service. They go to Cyprus, Barnabas's native country, and then to many cities in what is now central Turkey. While at Cyprus, Saul changes his Hebrew name Saul to the Latin Paul (see Acts 13:9). This name change is very significant and decisive doctrinally and presages some cultural changes. The Brethren preach first to the Jews and then to the proselytes who come to the synagogues. They teach that the gospel of Jesus Christ is greater than the law of Moses and that the law of Moses cannot save them (see Acts 13:38–39). The Jews are furious, but many of the Gentile proselytes join the Church. Paul and Barnabas thereafter direct their chief attention to the Gentiles (see Acts 13:45–49).

Paul and Barnabas establish branches of the Church, ordain elders in each of the cities they visit, and then return to Antioch with glowing reports of their success among the Gentiles. And of course, they have baptized many Gentiles directly into the Church without benefit of the law of Moses—that is, without circumcision and so forth.

When word of the success of Paul and Barnabas reaches certain Church members in and around Jerusalem, these Judean brethren, much concerned, go to Antioch on their own, without authorization from the Twelve or any of the presiding Brethren of the Church, and declare to the Gentile Church members at Antioch that "except ye be circumcised after the manner of Moses, ye cannot be saved" (Acts 15:1). Thus the problem is apparent: Is obedience to the law of Moses with all its attendant performances required for salvation now that Jesus Christ has made the Atonement?

Let me digress a moment to explain the great emphasis on circumcision, for it may seem to us today an odd matter for early Church members to have been fighting about. Circumcision is a very old practice among mankind, even among non-Jewish peoples, but the Lord Jehovah appointed it the token of the covenant He made with Abraham (see Genesis 17). This covenant was to extend throughout Abraham's posterity, and through this covenant the blessings and promises of God's favor were to be realized throughout time and eternity. Circumcision was the badge, the sign of identification, showing that one was a believer in the true God and in the covenant. That token was continued in the law of Moses. The manner in which the word *circumcised* is used throughout the book of Acts and the Epistles is generally as a one-word representation for the entire law of Moses; hence when the Jewish members of the Church insisted that Gentiles be circumcised, they meant that the Gentiles should obey all of the law of Moses. But back to the events at Antioch.

Paul and Barnabas are contending with the brethren from Judea on this important matter, which is not simply a topic about tradition or custom but a fundamental doctrinal issue regarding the Atonement of Jesus Christ. The dissension becomes so great that it is decided such a matter can be settled officially only by the Twelve at Jerusalem. The question is three-fold:

1. Did Jesus Christ by His earthly ministry and Atonement fulfill the law of Moses with its multitudinous ordinances and performances? If so,

2. Do converts from among non-Israelite peoples have to obey the law of Moses to become baptized members of the Church of Jesus Christ? And

3. Should Church members, Jew and Gentile, have their sons circumcised as a requirement for salvation?

The settlement of this threefold question would affect how believers regarded Christ's mission, what missionary procedures were implemented, and what would be the practice of every family in the Church with respect to their sons for generations yet unborn.

THE JERUSALEM COUNCIL CONVENES

When Paul and Barnabas arrived in Jerusalem to see the Brethren, they were respectfully received, and they conveyed an account of their success among the Gentiles. There were in Jerusalem, however, many Jewish members of the Church who had been Pharisees before their conversion to Jesus Christ. They would not give up the law of Moses and insisted "that it was needful to circumcise [the Gentiles], and to command them to keep the law of Moses" (Acts 15:5). Therefore the Apostles and the elders at Jerusalem "came together for to consider this matter" (Acts 15:6).

After much disputing in the council, Peter declared the baptism of Cornelius and others by his hand. He reminded the congregation that the conversion of the Gentiles was the work of God and that God "put no difference between us and them, purifying their hearts by faith." He also stated that the "grace of the Lord Jesus Christ" would save both "us and them" (Acts 15:9, 11), affirming the truth that works are insufficient without God's grace.

After Peter's testimony, the "multitude" in the council listened as

Barnabas and Paul told of the "miracles and wonders God had wrought among the Gentiles by them" (Acts 15:12). Then James, who may have replaced the James who was slain as recounted in Acts 12 and who apparently conducted the meeting, stated as a type of official pronouncement that no greater burden than the necessary things of purity and refraining from idol worship and from eating blood should be placed on the Gentiles who wished to come into the Church. James did not specifically mention the law of Moses, and it is conspicuous by its absence, though the context of the council implies it. The council decreed that Paul and Barnabas should return to Antioch, accompanied by two men from Jerusalem, "chief men among the brethren," named Barsabas and Silas (Acts 15:22). These two could testify with Barnabas and Paul of the decision of the council. The Brethren prepared an epistle to be carried to Antioch and the surrounding area, stating the decision of the council:

> The apostles and elders and brethren send greeting unto the brethren which are of the Gentiles in Antioch and Syria and Cicilia:
>
> Forasmuch as we have heard, that certain which went out from us have troubled you with words, subverting your souls, saying, Ye must be circumcised, and keep the law: to whom we gave no such commandment:
>
> It seemed good unto us, being assembled with one accord, to send chosen men unto you with our beloved Barnabas and Paul,
>
> Men that have hazarded their lives for the name of our Lord Jesus Christ.
>
> We have sent therefore Judas and Silas, who shall also tell you the same things by mouth.
>
> For it seemeth good to the Holy Ghost, and to us, to lay upon you no greater burden than these necessary things;
>
> That ye abstain from meats offered to idols, and from blood, and from things strangled, and from fornication: from which if ye keep yourselves, ye shall do well. Fare ye well. (Acts 15:23–29)

Upon arriving in Antioch of Syria, the Brethren assembled a multitude of Church members, read the epistle, and exhorted the people, who "rejoiced" at the news (see Acts 15:30–33).

Such is the report of the proceedings of the council recorded in Acts 15. We learn from Paul's later epistle to the Galatians the significant information we would not otherwise have that Paul went up early to Jerusalem to confer privately with the Brethren to learn of their views and to make certain they agreed with what he and Barnabas had done in receiving the Gentiles, "lest by any means I should run, or had run, in vain" (Galatians 2:2). This private meeting is probably the one referred to in Acts 15:4–5, but Paul's epistle gives it a clearer focus by expressing his motive for speaking with the Brethren in private.

Another important factor we learn from this Galatian epistle is that Paul and Barnabas took Titus, a young Gentile convert probably from Antioch (see Titus 1:4) to the council. Paul may have seen in him a kind of "exhibit A," for Titus was an uncircumcised Greek who was a model of faith and virtue, strong in the Spirit. Paul could show the Jewish members of the Church in Jerusalem a living example of the grace of God given to the Gentiles without the encumbrance of the law of Moses. Paul was apparently successful, for he declares, "Neither Titus, who was with me, being a Greek, was compelled to be circumcised" (Galatians 2:3).

The Galatian epistle also helps us determine the date of the council. In chapter 1, Paul tells of his conversion to Jesus Christ; in chapter 2, he tells of going to Jerusalem with Barnabas and Titus to the council fourteen years later. We do not know when Paul joined the Church, but it could not have been less than a year or two after the Ascension of Christ. Assuming that he was baptized around AD 35 or 36 (see Galatians 1:15–19), fourteen years later would be AD 49 or 50. Paul mentions an event "three years" after his conversion, but a close reading of Galatians 1 shows that the three years were within the scope of the fourteen, not in addition to them.

THE JERUSALEM COUNCIL WAS ONLY A HALF STEP

As forward-reaching and beneficial as the decision by the Jerusalem Council was, it was only a half step forward in the progress of the Church. For one thing, the council did not decisively declare an end to the law of Moses. The announcement part of the epistle sent from the council does not use the words "law of Moses" nor declare its fulfillment or its final and absolute end as a practice in the Church. Furthermore, the epistle was addressed not to all members of the Church but only to the Gentile members in Antioch, Syria, and Cicilia. The council settled the matter of observing the law of Moses with respect to the Gentiles; it did not address the subject with respect to Jewish Church members. So far as the epistle is concerned, the Jewish members of the Church could continue to observe the ordinances of the law of Moses as a supposed requirement for salvation.

Why would the Brethren have been so ambiguous and nondeclarative? They seem to have said as little as they could about the matter. Perhaps they hoped to avoid dividing the Church and alienating the strict Jewish members. Likewise, they would not have wanted to invite persecution from nonmember Jews. James seems to have had that in mind when, after announcing the moderate decision, he said to the council, "For Moses of old time hath in every city them that preach him, being read in the synagogues every sabbath day" (Acts 15:21).

The decision of the council was favorable to Paul, Barnabas, Titus, and the Gentiles who were already in the Church and who would yet join, but it also left the Jewish members free to continue the practice of the law of Moses if they wished to. The council did not say that the Gentiles could not or must not practice the law of Moses, only that they need not do so for salvation. By wording the decision the way they did, the Brethren probably avoided a schism in the Church and no doubt also the ire that would have come from the Jews had the decision been stronger. There must have been many who would have preferred a stronger declaration, but the Brethren acted in the wisdom requisite for their situation.

Not long after the council adjourned, when Paul was on his second mission, he wanted Timothy, a Greek convert at Lystra, to accompany him. Because Timothy's mother was a Jew and his father a Greek, he had not been circumcised. Paul therefore circumcised him so that he would be more acceptable to the Jews among whom he would do missionary work. That may seem contradictory to Paul's standards, but it is fairly simple: the action was expedient because of Jewish tradition and culture, but it was not necessary for Timothy's salvation.

The effects of the moderate decision of the council were far-reaching and long-lasting. Ten years later, when Paul returned to Jerusalem at the end of his third mission among the Gentiles of Greece and Turkey (Galatia and Asia), he was greeted by the Brethren, who rejoiced at his great success among the Gentiles of the Roman Empire but cautioned him about preaching strong doctrine, especially about the law of Moses, in Jerusalem. Even a decade after the council, Jewish members of the Church in Judea were still observing the law of Moses. The Brethren

> said unto him, Thou seest, brother, how many thousands of Jews there are which believe; and they are all zealous of the law:

And they are informed of thee, that thou teachest all the Jews which are among the Gentiles to forsake Moses, saying that they ought not to circumcise their children, neither to walk after the customs.

What is it therefore? the multitude must needs come together: for they will hear that thou art come.

Do therefore this that we say to thee: We have four men which have a vow on them;

Them take, and purify thyself with them, and be at charges with them, that they may shave their heads: and all may know that those things, whereof they were informed concerning thee, are nothing; but that thou thyself also walkest orderly, and keepest the law.

As touching the Gentiles which believe, we have written and concluded that they observe no such thing, save only that they keep themselves from things offered to idols, and from blood, and from strangled, and from fornication.

Then Paul took the men, and the next day purifying himself with them entered into the temple, to signify the accomplishment of the days of purification, until that an offering should be offered for every one of them. (Acts 21:20–26)

There is no question that Peter and the other Brethren knew that the law of Moses was fulfilled. The doctrinal question was settled. The law was no longer a requirement for salvation now that Jesus had made the Atonement. Missionary work among the Gentile nations could go forth directly and without impediment. But there was a conflict between culture and doctrine. The Brethren were clear on the matter, but long-standing culture and tradition persisted among many Jewish members of the Church even after the doctrinal question had been settled. Latter-day revelation leaves no doubt that the law of Moses was fulfilled in Christ (see 3 Nephi 15:4–5; Moroni 8:8; D&C 74).

In like manner today there may be points about which the doctrinal foundation is clear but about which tradition or custom or the ways of the world are so strong that the Brethren hope, as did the New Testament leaders, that the Holy Ghost will eventually cause the adherents to forsake tradition, academic popularity, and peer pressure for the word of God. Perhaps the theory of organic evolution, some political and economic issues, the doctrine of election as pertaining to the Abrahamic covenant, and several other points are in this category requiring time to elapse and changes to occur before definitive pronouncements can be made beyond what is already in the revelations. At any rate, the book of Acts gives our present generation an informative model of how both members and non-members react when revelation confronts tradition and long-standing custom. Only living prophets could correctly handle the situation then. Only living prophets can do so now.

NOTES

1. See William Byron Forbush, *Fox's Book of Martyrs* (Philadelphia: Universal Book and Bible House, 1926), 1–5; M. R. James, *The Apocryphal New Testament* (Oxford: Clarendon Press, 1969), 14–15n, and such geographic areas as Persia and India as are listed in the index).
2. Joseph Smith, *Teachings of the Prophet Joseph Smith,* comp. Joseph Fielding Smith (Salt Lake City: Deseret Book, 1976), 199.

CHAPTER NINETEEN

WALKING IN NEWNESS OF LIFE: DOCTRINAL THEMES OF THE APOSTLE PAUL

ROBERT L. MILLET

It is given to but few to wield a more powerful influence over Christian history than to Saul of Tarsus, the persecutor who became a prophet, the Pharisee who became the Apostle to the Gentiles. The life and teachings of the Apostle Paul stand as bright reminders of the power of Christ to transform the souls of men and women, to remake the human heart, and to refocus one's misdirected zeal into the way of the Master. When the risen Lord appeared in vision to Ananias of Damascus and instructed him to send for the stricken and blinded Saul, Ananias answered: "Lord, I have heard by many of this man, how much evil he hath done to thy saints at Jerusalem: and here he hath authority from the chief priests to bind all that call on thy name." The response that followed bespeaks the Redeemer's insight into the wonders that would be done at Paul's hand: "Go thy way: for he is a chosen vessel unto me, to bear my name before the Gentiles, and kings, and the children of Israel" (Acts 9:11–15).

In this chapter we will consider briefly some of the more significant doctrinal messages from his epistles. Many of those are, in the language of Simon Peter, "things hard to be understood, which they that are unlearned and unstable wrest, as they do also the other scriptures, unto their own destruction" (2 Peter 3:16). I begin with the testimony that the message of Paul was a proclamation of the gospel—Jesus Christ and Him crucified—

Robert L. Millet is a professor of ancient scripture at Brigham Young University.

and that he was no more the originator of Christianity (as some foolishly suppose) than Abraham was the originator of the everlasting covenant. Further, as F. F. Bruce observed: "Paul himself is at pains to point out that the gospel which he preached was one and the same gospel as that preached by the other apostles—a striking claim, considering that Paul was neither a companion of Christ in the days of His flesh nor of the original apostles, and that he vigorously asserts his complete independence of these."[1] And yet Paul knew as Peter knew. He knew as Thomas knew. And what he knew—whether from the teachings of Stephen, from the other Apostles, from his own study of the Old Testament with new eyes, or by means of personal revelation—he taught. And he taught with a power, a persuasion, and a holy zeal known only to those who, like Alma and the sons of Mosiah, have gone from darkness to light and whose whole soul yearns to lead others to that same light.

"ALL HAVE SINNED"

One cannot fully appreciate the need for medicine until one is aware of a malady. One does not pant after the cooling draft until one has nearly died of thirst. In the same way, as President Ezra Taft Benson observed, people do not yearn for salvation in Christ until they know why they need Christ, which thing they cannot know until they understand and acknowledge the Fall and its effects upon all mankind.[2] The Atonement of Jesus Christ is inextricably and eternally tied to the Fall of Adam and Eve. To teach the Atonement without discussing the Fall is to teach the Atonement in the abstract, to lessen its impact, to mitigate its transforming power in the lives of men and women. Thus the Apostle Paul began at the beginning; he laid stress where it needed to be. Quoting the Psalmist, he affirmed: "There is none righteous, no, not one: there is none that understandeth, there is none that seeketh after God. They are all gone out of the way, they are together become unprofitable; there is none that doeth good, no, not one" (Romans 3:10–12; see also Psalms 14:1–3; 53:1–3).

Though we as Latter-day Saints do not subscribe to the belief held by many in the Christian world about the depravity of humankind, yet the burden of scripture, including the New Testament, is that there was a Fall and that it does take a measured toll on all humanity. Paul taught plainly that men and women must be extricated and redeemed from the Fall. Because our first parents partook of the forbidden fruit, death and sin entered the world. We are, as God taught Adam in the earliest ages, "conceived in sin," such that when children "begin to grow up, sin conceiveth in their hearts, and they taste the bitter, that they may know to prize the good" (Moses 6:55). In the words of Lehi, God revealed to the ancients that all persons "were lost, because of the transgression of their parents" (2 Nephi 2:21). Truly, "because of the fall our natures have become evil continually" (Ether 3:2).

We do not believe there is sin in the sexual act, so long as it is undertaken within the bonds of marriage. Nor do we subscribe to the belief in the inability of men and women even to choose good over evil. To say that we are conceived in sin is to say, first of all, that we are conceived into a world of sin. But, more significantly, it is to declare that conception is the vehicle, the means by which a fallen nature, what we know as mortality or what Paul calls "the flesh," is transmitted to all the posterity of Adam and Eve. The revelations declare that little children are innocent, not because they are that way by nature but rather because Christ's Atonement declares them to be so (see Moroni 8:8, 12, 22; D&C 29:46; 74:7). In short, "as in Adam, or by nature, they fall, even so the blood of Christ atoneth for their sins" (Mosiah 3:16). Thus all of us struggle not only for forgiveness for individual sins but also for relief and redemption from a fallen nature that yields to sin. That is to say, salvation in Christ consists not only in meeting and satisfying the demands of God's justice (which forbids uncleanness) but also in enjoying the renovating and cleansing powers of Christ's blood such that we begin to die as pertaining to unrighteousness and the ways of sin.

"All have sinned, and come short of the glory of God," Paul wrote to the Romans (Romans 3:23). In speaking of life before coming unto Christ, Paul further taught: "For when we were in the flesh, the motions of sins, which were not according to the law, did work in our members to bring forth fruit unto death. . . . For I know that in me, that is, in my flesh, dwelleth no good thing; for to will is present with me"—that is, to do what is right is in my heart—"but to perform that which is good I find not, only in Christ" (JST, Romans 7:5, 19). Herein lies the solution to the problem of the Fall: though all of us are subject to sin and to the pull of the flesh, there is hope for liberation through Jesus. The Son of God has "delivered us from the power of darkness" (Colossians 1:13). He truly "hath abolished death, and hath brought life and immortality to light through the gospel" (2 Timothy 1:10).

JUSTIFICATION BY FAITH

The scriptures are consistent in their declaration that "no unclean thing can enter into [God's] kingdom" (3 Nephi 27:19). In theory there are two ways by which men and women may inherit eternal life. The first is simply to live the law of God perfectly, to make no mistakes. To do so is to be justified—pronounced innocent, declared blameless—by works or by law. To say that another way, if we keep the commandments completely (including receiving the ordinances of salvation), never deviating from the strait and narrow path throughout our mortal lives, then we qualify for the blessings of the obedient. And yet we have just attended to the terrible truth that all are unclean as a result of sin. All of us have broken at least one of the laws of God and therefore disqualify ourselves for justification by law. Moral perfection may be a possibility, but it is certainly not a probability. Jesus alone trod that path. "Therefore," Paul observed, "by the deeds of the law"—meaning the law of Moses, as well as any other law of God—"there shall no flesh be justified in his sight" (Romans 3:20; see also 2 Nephi 2:5).

The second way to be justified is by faith, for the sinner to be pronounced clean or innocent through trusting in and relying upon the merits of Him who answered the ends of the law (see Romans 10:4; see also 2 Nephi 2:6–7). Jesus, who owed no personal debt to justice, is that Holy One who can now "claim of the Father his rights of mercy which he hath upon the children of men" (Moroni 7:27). Because we are guilty of transgression, if there had been no Atonement, no quantity of good deeds on our part, no nobility independent of divine intercession could make up for the loss. Truly, "since man had fallen he could not merit anything of himself" (Alma 22:14). Thus He who loved us first (see 1 John 4:10, 19) reaches out to the lost and fallen, to the disinherited, and proposes a marriage. The Infinite One joins with the finite, the Finished with the unfinished, the Whole with the partial, in short, the Perfect with the imperfect. Through covenant with Christ, and thus union with the Bridegroom, we place ourselves in a condition to become fully formed, whole, finished—to become perfect in Christ (see Moroni 10:32).

The means by which the Savior justifies us is wondrous indeed. It entails what might be called the great exchange. It is certainly true that Jesus seeks through His atoning sacrifice and through the medium of the Holy Spirit to change us, to transform us from fallen and helpless mortals into new creatures in Christ (see 2 Corinthians 5:17). But there is more. Jesus offers to exchange with us. In his epistle to the Philippians, Paul speaks of his eagerness to forsake the allurements of the world in order to obtain the riches of Christ. "I count all things but loss," he said, "for the excellency of the knowledge of Christ Jesus my Lord: for whom I have suffered the loss of all things, and do count them but dung, that I may win Christ"—and now note this important addition—"and be found in him, not having mine own righteousness, which is of the law, but that which is through the faith of Christ, the righteousness which is of God by faith" (Philippians 3:8–9). Paul's point is vital: justification comes by faith, by trusting in Christ's righteousness, in His merits, mercy, and grace (see Romans 10:1–4; see also 2 Nephi 2:3; Helaman 14:13; D&C 45:3–5).

Though our efforts to be righteous are necessary, they will forevermore be insufficient. Paul teaches a profound truth—that as we come unto Christ by the covenant of faith, our Lord's righteousness becomes our righteousness. He justifies us in the sense that He imputes—meaning that He reckons to our account—His goodness and takes our sin. This is the great exchange. To the Corinthians, Paul explained that "God was in Christ, reconciling the world unto himself, not imputing their trespasses unto them. . . . For he [God the Father] hath made him [Christ the Son] to be sin for us, who knew no sin; that we might be made the righteousness of God in him" (2 Corinthians 5:19, 21). As Paul explained elsewhere, Christ "hath redeemed us from the curse of the law, being made a curse for us" (Galatians 3:13; see also Hebrews 2:9). Sidney Sperry thus spoke of being justified as a matter not only of "acquittal" from guilt and sin but also of "being regarded as 'righteous' in a future Divine judgment."[3] Those who enter the gospel covenant and thereafter seek to do their duty and endure to the end the Lord "hold[s] guiltless" (3 Nephi 27:16; compare D&C 4:2). It is not that they are guiltless in the sense of never having done wrong; rather, the Holy One removes the blame and imputes—accounts or decrees to the repentant sinner, the one who comes unto Christ by covenant—His righteousness. "For as by one man's disobedience"—the Fall of Adam— "many were made sinners, so by the obedience of one [Jesus Christ] shall many be made righteous" (Romans 5:19).

One Protestant theologian, John MacArthur, has written: "Justification may be defined as an act of God whereby he imputes to a believing sinner the full and perfect righteousness of Christ, forgiving the sinner of all unrighteousness, declaring him or her perfectly righteous in God's sight, thus delivering the believer from all condemnation. . . . It is a forensic reality that takes place in the court of God."[4] MacArthur also explained: "Justification is a divine verdict of 'not guilty—fully righteous.' It is the reversal of God's attitude toward the sinner. Whereas He formerly condemned, He now vindicates. Although the sinner once lived under God's wrath, as a believer he or she is now under God's blessing. Justification is more than simple pardon; pardon alone would still leave the sinner without merit before God. So when God justifies He imputes divine righteousness to the sinner. . . . Justification elevates the believer to a realm of full acceptance and divine privilege in Jesus Christ." The harsh reality is that "the law demands perfection. But the only way to obtain perfect righteousness is by imputation—that is, being justified by faith."[5] "Therefore being justified by faith, we have peace with God through our Lord Jesus Christ: by whom also we have access by faith into this grace wherein we stand, and rejoice in hope of the glory of God" (Romans 5:1–2). Since all have sinned and come short of the glory of God, we are "justified only by his grace through the redemption that is in Christ Jesus," or in other words, "justified by faith alone without the deeds of the law" (JST, Romans 3:24, 28). The comforting message of the gospel is that Jesus the Messiah has, "according to his mercy," offered to save us "by the washing of regeneration, and renewing of the Holy Ghost; which he shed on us abundantly . . . ; that being justified by his grace, we should be made heirs according to the hope of eternal life" (Titus 3:5–7).

SALVATION BY GRACE

As we are all aware, the theological debate between whether we are saved by grace or by works has continued for centuries. In reality, it is a meaningless argument that radiates more heat than light. Perhaps because Latter-day Saints have been so hesitant to acknowledge any virtue in the argument that we are saved by grace alone, some of us have not taken the Apostle Paul seriously enough; sadly, we have too often robbed ourselves of sacred insights, understanding, and comfort to be found not only in the New Testament but also in the Book of Mormon.

Paul certainly understood that the works of righteousness are an important part of our salvation. He taught that God "will render to every man according to his deeds" (Romans 2:6). Of course we must receive the ordinances of salvation. Of course we must strive to live a life befitting that of our Christian covenant. Of course we must do all in our power to overcome sin, put off the natural man, and deny ourselves of all ungodliness.

These things evidence our part of the gospel covenant. They allow us, in fact, to remain in the covenant with Christ, even as we occasionally stumble and fall short of the ideal. The question is not whether good works are vital—they are. As we have already observed, they are not sufficient. The harder questions are: In whom do I trust? On whom do I rely? Is my reliance on Christ's works, or do I strive to save myself?

Paul asked: "What shall we say then that Abraham our father, as pertaining to the flesh, hath found? For if Abraham were justified by the law of works, he hath to glory in himself; but not of God. For what saith the Scripture? Abraham believed God, and it was counted unto him for righteousness. Now to him who is justified by the law of works, is the reward reckoned, not of grace, but of debt. But to him that seeketh not to be justified by the law of works, but believeth on him who justifieth not the ungodly, his faith is counted for righteousness" (JST, Romans 4:1–5). Abraham's faith—his willingness to believe the promises of God, to trust in Jehovah's power to accomplish what to him seemed impossible, and thus to sacrifice Isaac—was what gained him the approval of the Almighty. It is with us as it was with Abraham; if in fact we are saved by our deeds and our merits alone, then we might have something about which to boast; namely, that our own genius, our own resources, our own righteousness were what allowed us to bound into glory.

It isn't that Paul believed that only those who do not work receive eternal life but rather that those who labor, knowing their own fallibility and limitations, never trust in their own works. Paul taught what James taught—that true faith is always manifest in righteous works and that one who relies wholly on the merits of Christ, who has faith in Him, will evidence that faith through noble actions and Christian conduct (see James 2). To argue that we are saved by our works is to argue that Christ's atoning mission was unnecessary. "I do not frustrate the grace of God," Paul wrote, "for if righteousness come by the law, then Christ is dead in vain" (Galatians 2:21). John MacArthur has suggested that the word *grace* makes an acronym for a glorious concept—"God's Riches at Christ's Expense."[6]

"How else could salvation possibly come?" Elder Bruce R. McConkie asked. "Can man save himself? Can he resurrect himself? Can he create a celestial kingdom and decree his own admission thereto? Salvation must and does originate with God, and if man is to receive it, God must bestow it upon him, which bestowal is a manifestation of grace. . . . Salvation does not come by the works and performances of the law of Moses, nor by

'circumcision,' nor by 'the law of commandments contained in ordinances' . . . , nor does it come by any good works standing alone. No matter how righteous a man might be, no matter how great and extensive his
good works, he could not save himself. Salvation is in Christ and comes
through his atonement."[7]

New Creatures in Christ

Paul taught that to come unto Christ is to enter into a new realm of
existence, a spiritual realm. It is to forsake death and come unto life, to put
away evil and darkness and learn to walk in righteousness and light.
"Know ye not," Paul asked the Romans, "that so many of us as were baptized into Jesus Christ were baptized into his death? Therefore we are
buried with him by baptism into death: that like as Christ was raised up
from the dead by the glory of the Father, even so we also should walk in
newness of life. For if we have been planted together in the likeness of his
death, we shall be also in the likeness of his resurrection: knowing this,
that our old man is crucified with him, that the body of sin might be
destroyed, that henceforth we should not serve sin" (Romans 6:3–6).

The new life in Christ entails a new energy, a new dynamism, a new
source of strength and power. That power is Christ. So often people simply
go through the motions, do good and perform their duties but find little
satisfaction in doing so. One Christian writer offered this thought:

> There are few things quite so boring as being religious, but there
> is nothing quite so exciting as being a Christian!
>
> Most folks have never discovered the difference between the one
> and the other, so that there are those who sincerely try to live a life
> they do not have, substituting religion for God, Christianity for
> Christ, and their own noble endeavors for the energy, joy, and power
> of the Holy Spirit. In the absence of reality, they can only grasp at rit-
> ual, stubbornly defending the latter in the absence of the former, lest
> they be found with neither!
>
> They are lamps without oil, cars without gas, and pens without
> ink, baffled at their own impotence in the absence of all that alone
> can make man functional; for man was so engineered by God that
> the presence of the Creator within the creature is indispensable to
> His humanity. Christ gave Himself for us to give Himself to us! His
> presence puts God back into the man! He came that we might have
> life—God's life!

There are those who have a life they never live. They have come to Christ and thanked Him only for what He did, but do not live in the power of who He is. Between the Jesus who "was" and the Jesus who "will be" they live in a spiritual vacuum, trying with no little zeal to live for Christ a life that only He can live in and through them.[8]

The disciples of Jesus must strive to do what is right. They should do their duty in the Church and in the home, even when they are not eager to do so. They cannot just leave the work of the kingdom to others because they have not been changed and reborn. But that doesn't mean they must always remain that way. Each of us may change; we can change; we should change; and it is the Lord who will change us. Coming unto Christ entails more than being cleansed, as important as that is. It entails being filled. We speak often of the importance of being cleansed, or sanctified. It is to have the Holy Spirit, who is not only a revelator but a sanctifier, remove filth and dross from our souls. We refer to this process as a baptism by fire. To be cleansed is essential, but to stop there is to stop short of great blessings. Paul presents the idea of (in a sense) nailing ourselves to the cross of Christ—nailing our old selves, the old man of sin. He wrote: "I am crucified with Christ: nevertheless I live; yet not I, but Christ liveth in me: and the life which I now live in the flesh I live by the faith of the Son of God, who loved me, and gave himself for me" (Galatians 2:20).

This is a new life in Christ. To the Ephesian Saints, Paul wrote: "For by grace are ye saved through faith; and that not of yourselves: it is the gift of God: not of works, lest any man should boast. For we are his workmanship, created in Christ Jesus unto good works, which God hath before ordained that we should walk in them" (Ephesians 2:8–10). To the Hebrews, he said: "Now the God of peace, that brought again from the dead our Lord Jesus, that great shepherd of the sheep, through the blood of the everlasting covenant, make you perfect in every good work to do his will, working in you that which is wellpleasing in his sight, through Jesus Christ" (Hebrews 13:20–21). When we have been filled, the Spirit is with us and Christ comes to dwell in us through that Spirit. Then our works begin to be motivated by that Holy Spirit and they are no longer our works; they are His works.

The risen Lord said to the Nephites that certain things were required before a church would be truly His Church: it must have His name, and it must be built upon His gospel. If these two conditions are met, then the Father would show forth His own works in it (see 3 Nephi 27:5–10). How?

Through the body of Christ, through the members of the Church. The Father's Spirit motivates them to greater righteousness. It is not expected that we "go through the motions" all our lives. There can come a time when the Spirit changes our motives, desires, and yearnings, and we begin to do works the way God would do them, because He has now begun to live in us through that Spirit.

On one occasion Paul wrote: "Wherefore, my beloved, as ye have always obeyed, not as in my presence only, but now much more in my absence, work out your own salvation with fear and trembling." If we stop our reading there, and that's usually where we stop, we wonder about the phrase "work out your own salvation." How? There's not a person living on this earth who can work out his own salvation, if that entails doing so without divine assistance. There aren't enough home teaching visits; there aren't enough cakes and pies to be delivered to the neighbors; there aren't enough prayers to be uttered for a person to work out his own salvation. But Paul didn't stop there: "For it is God which worketh in you both to will and to do of his good pleasure" (Philippians 2:12–13). The works are the Lord's works through us, and thus we are doing not our works but His works.

Through the Atonement of Christ, we do more than enjoy a change of behavior; our nature is changed. "Therefore, if any man be in Christ, he is a new creature: old things are passed away; behold, all things are become new" (2 Corinthians 5:17). Isn't that what the angel taught King Benjamin—that the natural man is an enemy to God and will stay that way unless and until he yields himself to the enticings of the Holy Spirit? (see Mosiah 3:19). John Stott explained: "We may be quite sure that Christ-centredness and Christ-likeness will never be attained by our own unaided efforts. How can self drive out self? As well expect Satan to drive out Satan! For we are not interested in skin-deep holiness, in a merely external resemblance to Jesus Christ. We are not satisfied by a superficial modification of behaviour patterns. . . . No, what we long for is a deep inward change of character, resulting from a change of nature and leading to a radical change of conduct. In a word we want to be *like Christ,* and that thoroughly, profoundly, entirely. Nothing less than this will do."[9]

Elder Glenn L. Pace put it this way: "We should all be striving for a disposition to do no evil, but to do good continually. This isn't a resolve or a discipline; it is a disposition. We do things because we want to, not just because we know we should. . . . Sometimes we overlook the fact that a spiritual transformation or metamorphosis must take place within us. It comes about through grace and by the Spirit of God, although it does not come about until we have truly repented. . . . My conclusion is that we will not be saved by works if those works are not born of a disposition to do good, as opposed to an obligation to do good."[10] That, of course, is what President Ezra Taft Benson meant when he taught that although the world deals in externals, the Lord works from the inside out.[11]

Bob George, a Protestant writer, described the spiritual transformation this way:

> Being made into a new creation is like a caterpillar becoming a butterfly. Originally an earthbound crawling creature, a caterpillar weaves a cocoon and is totally immersed in it. Then a marvelous process takes place, called metamorphosis. Finally a totally new creature—a butterfly—emerges. Once ground-bound, the butterfly can now soar above the earth. It now can view life from the sky downward. In the same way, as a new creature in Christ you must begin to see yourself as God sees you.
>
> If you were to see a butterfly, it would never occur to you to say, "Hey, everybody! Come look at this good-looking converted worm!" Why not? After all, it *was* a worm. And it was "converted." No, now it is a new creature, and you don't think of it in terms of what it was. You see it as it is now—a butterfly.[12]

THE FRUIT OF THE SPIRIT

The Apostle Paul declared that one mark of true discipleship, one significant evidence of our growth into the new life in Christ, is the degree to which we enjoy the fruit of the Spirit. In three different books of scripture, the Lord discusses the gifts of the Spirit—such things as discernment, tongues, interpretation of tongues, administration, prophecy, healing, and so forth. In 1 Corinthians 12, Paul suggested that the gifts of the Spirit are intended to enhance, build up, and make perfect the body of Christ, meaning the Church. They are for the good of the Church and kingdom. In addition, Paul spoke of the fruit of the Spirit. In Galatians 5, he contrasted the works of the flesh with the fruit of the Spirit: "Now the works of the flesh are manifest, which are these; adultery, fornication, uncleanness, lasciviousness, idolatry, witchcraft, hatred, variance, emulations, wrath, strife, seditions, heresies, envyings, murders, drunkenness, revellings, and such like: of the which I tell you before, as I have also told you in time past, that they which do such things shall not inherit the kingdom of God" (Galatians 5:19–21).

There is a natural birth, and there is a spiritual birth. The natural birth comes with mortality, and the natural birth creates the natural man. The spiritual birth comes later. The natural birth has its own set of fruits, or works. Paul mentioned several of them. The spiritual man or woman brings forth his or her own fruits. "But the fruit of the Spirit is love, joy, peace, longsuffering, gentleness, goodness, faith, meekness, temperance: against such there is no law. And they that are Christ's have crucified the flesh with the affections and lusts. If we live in the Spirit, let us also walk in the Spirit" (Galatians 5:22–25).

Some of the gifts we know as the gifts of the Spirit may have begun to develop within us before we came here.[13] Many aptitudes, capacities, and talents may thus come quite naturally for us. For some, the gift of speaking or the gift of teaching comes naturally, and these are spiritual gifts. For others, discernment or wisdom is an integral part of their lives. But there are people who are wonderful speakers and poor Christians. There are people who do remarkable things in the classroom and hurtful things outside the classroom. Talk to their family, secretary, staff, or coworkers. The gifts of the Spirit are one thing, the fruit of the Spirit another. Patience, mercy, meekness, gentleness, longsuffering, and, of course, charity, or the pure love of Christ—these characterize men and women who have begun to live in Christ. Such persons are simply more Christlike. Elder Marion D. Hanks frequently asked a haunting question, one that strikes at the core of this matter of being Christlike. He would inquire, "If you were arrested and were to be tried for being a Christian, would there be enough evidence to convict you?"

The interesting thing about the fruit of the Spirit is that attitudes and actions do not seem to be situational. In other words, a person is not just very fruitful in the Spirit only while the sun shines, pleasant and kindly only when circumstances are positive. Rather, those who enjoy the fruit of the Spirit feel "love for those who do not love in return, joy in the midst of painful circumstances, peace when something you were counting on doesn't come through, patience when things aren't going fast enough for you, kindness toward those who treat you unkindly, goodness toward those who have been intentionally insensitive to you, faithfulness when friends have proved unfaithful, gentleness toward those who have handled you roughly, self-control in the midst of intense temptation."[14]

Not All Israel Are Israel

Once Christ came into his life, nothing was quite the same for Saul of Tarsus. The scriptures, our Old Testament, became a new book to him. He saw the life and ministry of Jesus Christ in and through all things, and he became a witness that all things bear testimony of the Redeemer (see Moses 6:63). Paul knew, for example, that the gathering of Israel was first and foremost a gathering to Christ and only secondarily a gathering to lands of inheritance. He taught that to be a true son or daughter of the covenant was to be fully Christian, to have accepted completely Jesus Christ, the mediator of God's new covenant with Israel. "They are not all Israel, which are of Israel," he pointed out. "Neither, because they are all children of Abraham, are they the seed" (JST, Romans 9:6–7). Descent from Abraham, Isaac, and Jacob was significant to the degree that one received the God of Abraham, Isaac, and Jacob. In Nephi's words, "As many of the Gentiles as will repent are the covenant people of the Lord; and as many of the Jews as will not repent shall be cast off; for the Lord covenanteth with none save it be with them that repent and believe in his Son, who is the Holy One of Israel" (2 Nephi 30:2).

In bearing witness of Christ, Paul drew upon the prophetic promise that through Abraham's seed all humanity would be blessed (see Genesis 12:1–3; 17:1–7; JST, Genesis 17:11–12). "Now to Abraham and his seed were the promises made. He saith not, And to seeds, as of many; but as of one, And to thy seed, which is Christ" (Galatians 3:16). Paul's point might be restated as follows: although it is certainly true that through Abraham's seed all nations would be blessed—meaning that through his endless posterity the blessings of the gospel, the priesthood, and eternal life would be dispensed to the world (see Abraham 2:8–11)—the ultimate fulfillment of the Abrahamic promise came through the One who was truly the Chosen Seed, Jesus of Nazareth, son of David and thus son of Abraham (see Matthew 1:1–16).

Paul also taught that many of the performances and ordinances of the ancients (animal sacrifice being the most obvious) had their fulfillment and thus ultimate meaning in Christ and His redemption. For example, circumcision was given originally as a token of God's covenant with Abraham, a commandment that male children were to be circumcised at eight days as a reminder that because of the Atonement little children are not accountable until they are eight years old (see JST, Genesis 17:11–12). "For he is not a Jew, which is one outwardly," he wrote, "neither is that circumcision, which is outward in the flesh: but he is a Jew, which is one inwardly; and circumcision is that of the heart, in the spirit" (Romans 2:28–29). Stated another way, "In Jesus Christ neither circumcision availeth any thing, nor uncircumcision; but faith which worketh by love" (Galatians 5:6). Truly, in Christ we "are circumcised with the circumcision made without hands, in putting off the body of the sins of the flesh by the circumcision of Christ: buried with him in baptism, wherein also [we] are risen with him through the faith of the operation of God, who hath raised him from the dead" (Colossians 2:11–12).

In short, Paul's message to those who took pride and license in their lineage was clear. He declared boldly that it is a blessed privilege to be a chosen people, to be heirs to the adoption, the glory, the covenants, and the promises (see Romans 9:4). But true heirship is to be secured through adoption into the family of the Lord Jesus Christ. "For there is no difference between the Jew and the Greek: for the same Lord over all is rich unto all that call upon him. For whosoever shall call upon the name of the Lord shall be saved" (Romans 10:12–13). "For ye are all the children of God by faith in Christ Jesus. For as many of you as have been baptized into Christ have put on Christ. There is neither Jew nor Greek, there is neither bond nor free, there is neither male nor female: for ye are all one in Christ Jesus. And if ye be Christ's, then are ye Abraham's seed, and heirs according to the promise" (Galatians 3:26–29; see also Colossians 3:11).

A NAME ABOVE ALL OTHERS

Paul affirmed that Jesus Christ transcends all things, is superior to the gods of the pagans, has preeminence over the mystical deities of the Gnostics, and is, under the Eternal Father, the One before whom all creatures bow in humble reverence. Paul wrote to the Ephesians that he did not cease to "give thanks for you, making mention of you in my prayers; that the God of our Lord Jesus Christ, the Father of glory, may give unto you the spirit of wisdom and revelation in the knowledge of him." The Apostle then added that the Father's power had been "wrought in Christ, when he raised him from the dead, and set him at his own right hand in the heavenly places, far above all principality, and power, and might, and dominion, and every name that is named, not only in this world, but also in that which is to come: and hath put all things under his feet, and gave him to be the head over all things to the church, which is his body, the fulness of him that filleth all in all" (Ephesians 1:16–17, 20–23).

Many of the ancients believed that names held power and that to know the name of a deity was to possess power with or over it. Paul let it be known that Christ was the name above all other names and that salvation, the greatest of all the gifts of God, was to be had only in and through that holy name. "Let this mind be in you," he pleaded with the Philippian Saints,

> Which was also in Christ Jesus:
> Who, being in the form of God, thought it not robbery to be equal with God:
> But made himself of no reputation, and took upon him the form of a servant, and was made in the likeness of men:
> And being found in fashion as a man, he humbled himself, and became obedient unto death, even the death of the cross.
> Wherefore God also hath highly exalted him, and given him a name which is above every name:
> That at the name of Jesus every knee should bow, of things in heaven, and things in earth, and things under the earth;
> And that every tongue should confess that Jesus Christ is Lord, to the glory of God the Father. (Philippians 2:5–11; compare Ephesians 3:15)

The united testimony of the Apostles and prophets is that God the Eternal Father has delivered us from the power of darkness and "translated us into the kingdom of his dear Son: In whom we have redemption through his blood, even the forgiveness of sins: Who is the image of the invisible God, the firstborn of every creature"—meaning, all creation—"for by him were all things created, that are in heaven, and that are in earth, visible and invisible, whether they be thrones, or dominions, or principalities, or powers: all things were created by him, and for him: and he is before all things, and by him all things consist. . . . For it pleased the Father that in him should all fulness dwell" (Colossians 1:13–17, 19; compare Hebrews 1:1–3). Thus in adoration and worship, Elder McConkie wrote:

> The name of Jesus—wondrous name—the name in which the truths of salvation are taught; the name in which the ordinances of

salvation are performed; the name in which miracles are wrought, in which the dead are raised and mountains moved;

The name of Jesus—wondrous name—the name by which worlds come rolling into existence; the name by which redemption comes; the name which brings victory over the grave and raises the faithful to eternal life;

The name of Jesus—wondrous name—the name by which revelation comes and angels minister; the name of him by whom all things are and into whose hands the Father hath committed all things; the name of him to whom every knee shall bow and every tongue confess in that great day when the God of Heaven makes this planet his celestial home.[15]

Conclusion

I love the Apostle Paul. I love his personality—his wit, his charm, his firmness, his unquestioned allegiance to the Christ who called him. I love his breadth, his vision, his flexibility, and his capacity to be "all things to all men" (1 Corinthians 9:22). And, most important, I love his doctrine— particularly as revealed in his epistles, the timely but timeless messages in that regulatory correspondence by which he set in order the branches of the Church. Jesus of Nazareth, Savior and King, was the Lord of his life and the burden of his message to the world.

As he closed his last epistle, Paul said: "I am now ready to be offered, and the time of my departure is at hand. I have fought a good fight, I have finished my course, I have kept the faith: henceforth there is laid up for me a crown of righteousness, which the Lord, the righteous judge, shall give me at that day: and not to me only, but unto all them also that love his appearing" (2 Timothy 4:6–8). The "chosen vessel" (Acts 9:15) ran the race of life and did all he had been commanded to do, namely, open the eyes of the people far and wide to the gospel of Jesus Christ and "turn them from darkness to light, and from the power of Satan unto God, that they [might] receive forgiveness of sins, and inheritance among them which are sanctified" (Acts 26:18). And surely his was a glorious reunion with the Master whose name he had declared and whose gospel he had defended. In Christ, Paul found a newness of life, and through Christ, Paul inherited the greatest of all the gifts of God—that life which is eternal and everlasting.

NOTES

1. F. F. Bruce, *The New Testament Documents: Are They Reliable?* (Grand Rapids, MI: Eerdmans, 1960), 79.

2. Ezra Taft Benson, *A Witness and a Warning* (Salt Lake City: Deseret Book, 1988), 33.

3. Sidney B. Sperry, *Paul's Life and Letters* (Salt Lake City: Bookcraft, 1955), 176.

4. John F. MacArthur, *The Gospel According to Jesus,* rev. ed. (Grand Rapids, MI: Zondervan, 1994), 197.

5. John F. MacArthur, *Faith Works: The Gospel According to the Apostles* (Dallas: Word Publishing, 1993), 89–90.

6. MacArthur, *Faith Works,* 57.

7. Bruce R. McConkie, *Doctrinal New Testament Commentary,* 3 vols. (Salt Lake City: Bookcraft, 1965–73), 2:499–500.

8. W. Ian Thomas, foreword to Bob George, *Classic Christianity* (Eugene, OR: Harvest House Publishers, 1989), n.p.

9. John Stott, *Life in Christ* (Wheaton, IL: Tyndale House, 1991), 109; emphasis in original.

10. Glenn L. Pace, *Spiritual Plateaus* (Salt Lake City: Deseret Book, 1991), 62–63.

11. Ezra Taft Benson, "Born of God," *Ensign,* November 1985, 6.

12. George, *Classic Christianity,* 78.

13. Bruce R. McConkie, *A New Witness for the Articles of Faith* (Salt Lake City: Deseret Book, 1985), 1, 31, 359.

14. Charles Stanley, *The Wonderful, Spirit-Filled Life* (Nashville: Thomas Nelson Publishers, 1992), 108.

15. Bruce R. McConkie, *The Promised Messiah* (Salt Lake City: Deseret Book, 1978), 300.

CHAPTER TWENTY

THE STUMBLING BLOCKS OF FIRST CORINTHIANS

MONTE S. NYMAN

The Church members in Corinth were having problems. Word had reached the Apostle Paul of various sins that were causing them to stumble in their progress toward eternal life. The epistle known as 1 Corinthians was a follow-up of a previous letter admonishing them concerning the conditions that existed among them. This previous letter has either been lost from the original New Testament or was never collected to become a part of that canon. Therefore we are left without knowledge of what Paul had previously advised. The letter we do have contains much worthwhile doctrine and counsel that if followed will also prevent members of the Church from likewise faltering along the path to exaltation in the kingdom of God.

The epistle is lengthy and includes a wide variety of subjects. This article is limited to those major problems within the middle chapters of the letter that Paul treats as stumbling blocks to the weak (see 1 Corinthians 8:9). Furthermore, since Paul addressed these problems, other stumbling blocks have surfaced in the interpretations of this letter, undoubtedly because of the loss of plain and precious truths from the original treatise. Thanks to the Prophet Joseph Smith, many of the misunderstandings of the present text have been clarified through his inspired work, now referred to as the Joseph Smith Translation.

Monte S. Nyman is a professor emeritus of ancient scripture at Brigham Young University.

THE STUMBLING BLOCK OF IMMORALITY

Following a careful accreditation of himself as an Apostle of the Lord Jesus Christ (see 1 Corinthians 4), Paul launched into the most notorious problem in the community of Corinth. "'To live like a Corinthian' was . . . a phrase used both in Greek and Latin to express immorality."[1] His counsel is full of doctrine and advice very fitting in our world, where similar moral problems abound.

The common problem of fornication had worsened in Corinth. At least one member was having an incestuous relationship with his father's wife. This grievous sin Paul recognized as beyond that of the Gentiles (see 1 Corinthians 5:1). He was further perplexed by the Church communities' apparent lack of concern and action over the matter (see 1 Corinthians 5:2). The Joseph Smith Translation renders Paul's decision on the matter as follows: "For verily, as absent in body but present in spirit, *I* have judged already *him who hath so done this deed,* as though I were present. In the name of our Lord Jesus Christ, when ye are gathered together, and *have* the Spirit, with the power of our Lord Jesus Christ, To deliver such a one unto Satan for the destruction of the flesh" (1 Corinthians 5:3–5).[2]

He was declaring that when a Church court was held, the Church leaders would judge the offender as Paul was then judging if the decision was made by the Spirit. Such gross immorality meant an automatic excommunication in that day as well as today. This action was necessary for any hope of salvation for the offender (see 1 Corinthians 5:5). Some sins are so serious that the kindest thing to do is to take away Church membership and let the person get a fresh start.

Paul gave some further admonitions to the Church members. He reminded them that his previous letter had given a similar warning against association with fornicators (see 1 Corinthians 5:9). Such association cannot be totally avoided. It is a commandment of God to associate with the world, but it is not necessary to allow such association in the Church. Of course, those who are excommunicated can repent and regain more pure association (see 1 Corinthians 5:10–13).

Other Sexual Sins

Other sins of immorality were also enumerated by Paul. Adulterers, sexual abusers of children,[3] and homosexuals shall not inherit the kingdom of God (see 1 Corinthians 6:9–10). Although some of the Corinthian Saints had been guilty of such sins prior to their baptism, they were now forgiven and were no longer free to indulge in such practices (see 1 Corinthians 6:11). Paul bore testimony that "all these things [immoralities] are not lawful for me, therefore I will not be brought under the power of any" (JST, 1 Corinthians 6:12). Just as Jesus taught that the truth would make people free (see John 8:32), so Paul was saying that observing the moral laws of God would keep people free from the bondage of sin. The prevalence of these types of sin in our world shows the universal relevance of Paul's admonitions today.

Paul then presented an argument for chastity: "The body is not for fornication, but for the Lord; and the Lord for the body" (1 Corinthians 6:13). In support of his argument, he reasoned that a relationship with a harlot makes the two of one body. Therefore, the whole body is impure. In contrast, the unity of the body with the Spirit makes the whole body pure (see 1 Corinthians 6:16–17). Every sin committed is against *the body of Christ;* but fornication, Paul declared, is a sin against the body. Why? Because the body is the temple of the Holy Ghost, and when one is immoral, the Spirit withdraws from the body (see JST, 1 Corinthians 6:18–19; see also 3:16–17). Since men are bought by the Atonement of Christ, all men are born with the Light of Christ. Those who sin lose that inherited gift. Furthermore, the members of the Church have the Holy Ghost conferred upon them as another gift. This gift also withdraws from an impure body.

Celibacy

Another stumbling block related to immorality is the question of celibacy. One justification for this incorrect doctrine comes from 1 Corinthians 7. As this chapter is recorded in the King James Version, it appears that Paul was opposed to marriage. Much theory and speculation have resulted from this corrupted text. Again, thanks to the Prophet Joseph, greater light is shed on Paul's views in the Joseph Smith Translation.

Paul's declaration that "it is good for man not to touch a woman" (1 Corinthians 7:1) is clarified in the Joseph Smith Translation as a statement by the Corinthian Saints in a letter previously written to Paul. He responded to the statement in reference to the subject being addressed— fornication. Marriage would be a great deterrent to the sin. This is not to be considered the major reason for marriage, as other scriptures would confirm, but the natural consequences of marriage would satisfy innate sexual desire in mankind. As a further precaution against adultery for those who are married, Paul advised the members to be considerate of each other in their sexual desires and aware of Satan's temptations during long abstinence. Paul wisely and carefully labeled these admonitions as his own opinion. In other words, he was speaking by way of reasoning and not by revelation.

UNBELIEVING SPOUSES

Paul next gave advice to the woman who was married to a husband who was not a Church member. He advised the woman not to leave her husband because she might be a positive influence towards his conversion. However, if the unbelieving husband chose to leave his wife, Paul advised her to let him go because she might not be able to convert him (see 1 Corinthians 7:13–16). The fourteenth verse may be misconstrued as suggesting that a good woman's conduct will somehow save her deviating husband who does not repent—an idea that could cause people to stumble. The Prophet Joseph Smith received a revelation clearing up such a possible misinterpretation:

> For the unbelieving husband is sanctified by the wife, and the unbelieving wife is sanctified by the husband; else were your children unclean, but now are they holy.
>
> Now, in the days of the apostles the law of circumcision was had among all the Jews who believed not the gospel of Jesus Christ.
>
> And it came to pass that there arose a great contention among the people concerning the law of circumcision, for the unbelieving husband was desirous that his children should be circumcised and become subject to the law of Moses, which law was fulfilled.
>
> And it came to pass that the children, being brought up in subjection to the law of Moses, gave heed to the traditions of their fathers and believed not the gospel of Christ, wherein they became unholy.
>
> Wherefore, for this cause the apostle wrote unto the church, giving unto them a commandment, not of the Lord, but of himself, that a believer should not be united to an unbeliever; except the law of Moses should be done away among them.
>
> That their children might remain without circumcision; and that the tradition might be done away, which saith that little children are unholy; for it was had among the Jews.
>
> But little children are holy, being sanctified through the atonement of Jesus Christ; and this is what the scriptures mean. (D&C 74)

Paul said that the salvation of the children is the important consideration. If the woman is able to keep her children in the faith while she is
married to an unbeliever, she should remain with him in hopes that her
influence might bring about his conversion. However, if the children are
going astray because of the influence of their father, it was Paul's opinion
that she should leave him for the sake of the children. Before those children were accountable, they were saved automatically by the Atonement,
but as they became accountable, their salvation was more important than
that of the husband, who was already an unbeliever. Such advice, although
not a revelation, would be applicable in today's world as well.

MISSIONS AND MARRIAGE

Next, Paul encouraged the Corinthians to fulfill their callings and to abide
in the Lord regardless of their marital status (see 1 Corinthians 7:20–25). Paul
encouraged them not to change their marital status so they would be able
to concentrate their efforts on their callings and do a better job (see 1
Corinthians 7:26–27). The Joseph Smith Translation makes this clear:

I suppose therefore that this is good for the present distress, I say, that it is good for a man so to be. (KJV, 1 Corinthians 7:26)	I suppose therefore that this is good for the present distress, *for a man so to remain that he may do greater good.* (JST, 1 Corinthians 7:26; emphasis added)

However, if they were married, they were not sinning, but Paul said the
newlyweds would be given no special considerations, "For I spare you not"
(JST, 1 Corinthians 7:28).

Having spoken in general concerning their callings, Paul now became
specific concerning those who are called as missionaries, as the Joseph
Smith Translation clarifies:

But this I say, brethren, the time is short: it remaineth, that both they that have wives be as though they had none; And they that weep, as though they wept not; and they that rejoice, as though they rejoiced not;	But *I speak unto you who are called unto the ministry. For* this I say, brethren, the time *that remaineth* is *but* short, *that ye shall be sent forth unto the ministry. Even* they *who* have wives, *shall* be as though they

and they that buy, as though they possessed not;

And they that use this world, as not abusing it: for the fashion of this world passeth away.

But I would have you without carefulness. He that is unmarried careth for the things that belong to the Lord, how he may please the Lord.

But he that is married careth for the things that are of the world, how he may please his wife. (KJV, 1 Corinthians 7:29–33)

had none; *for ye are called and chosen to do the Lord's work.*

And *it shall be with them who* weep, as though they wept not; and *them who* rejoice, as though they rejoiced not, and *them who* buy, as though they possessed not;

And *them who* use this world, as not *using it;* for the fashion of this world passeth away.

But *I would, brethren, that ye magnify your calling.* I would have you without carefulness. *For he who* is unmarried, careth for the things that belong to the Lord, how he may please the Lord; *therefore he prevaileth.*

But he *who* is married, careth for the things that are of the world, how he may please his wife; *therefore there is a difference, for he is hindered.* (JST, 1 Corinthians 7:29–33; emphasis added)

The mission calling was a full-time responsibility, and those who were married would be expected to devote themselves wholly to that labor as if they were not married, thus not becoming distracted from their work (see 1 Corinthians 7:35).

Paul conceded one exception to his advice concerning the missionaries' marrying. He who had espoused a virgin, or who was engaged, should fulfill the promise of marriage before he left if it were probable that she would be beyond childbearing age before his return (see JST, 1 Corinthians 7:36). Paul added that being unmarried was better yet.

So then he that giveth *her* in marriage doeth well; but he that giveth *her* not in marriage doeth better. (KJV, 1 Corinthians 7:38; emphasis added)

So then he that giveth *himself* in marriage doeth well; but he that giveth *himself* not in marriage doeth better. (JST, 1 Corinthians 7:38; emphasis added)

Paul gave a further reminder that the woman is bound to her husband as long as he is alive; following his death she may remarry but only if done in the manner of the Lord (see 1 Corinthians 7:39). In his judgment, which he felt was influenced by the Spirit, she would be happier if she waited until after his mission (see 1 Corinthians 7:40). Thus much enlightenment on Paul's views on marriage is shed through Joseph Smith's inspired work.

THE STUMBLING BLOCKS OF IDOL OFFERINGS

The Corinthian Saints had apparently asked if it were against the newly restored religion to buy and eat things that initially had been killed as sacrifice to gods of other religions. In a conference of the elders and Apostles previously held in Jerusalem, this question had been considered. The main concerns in Jerusalem seemed to be whether or not the surplus meat from these festive occasions had been properly bled (*orset;* see JST, Genesis 9:10), and over whether it had been sacrificed to other gods (see Acts 15:20, 29). Whether the question by the Corinthian Saints had been prompted by this decision or whether the decision of the Jerusalem conference was not known to them is not stated. However, Paul's reply gives some further reasoning on the decision of that conference. He gave three bits of counsel regarding the matter. Following a treatise on the danger of knowledge and the value of charity, or the love of God (see 1 Corinthians 8:1–3), Paul said that the "things which are in the world offered in sacrifice" are not affected because they were offered to a god that does not really exist since "there is none other God but one" (JST, 1 Corinthians 8:4).

Second, to those who have a true knowledge of God there is no problem. Eating meat is not against the law of God, but the danger lies in the possibility that some weak in the faith might assume that those members who eat the idol offerings are doing so as a religious act. This misinterpretation may cause the observer to be misled and worship falsely. Therefore, Paul concluded, it is wisdom that they do not follow any practice that may be a bad example to others (see 1 Corinthians 8:7–13).

Third, Paul gave instructions regarding being invited to a feast and being served meat that had possibly been sacrificed to idols. Paul advised the Saints to ask no questions but to go ahead and eat. However, if someone called it to the guests' attention, then Paul counseled them not to eat lest it be a stumbling block to the observer (see 1 Corinthians 10:27–33; note JST, v. 27). Today as the Church becomes more international, this advice will become more appropriate. Many Church members may wonder about the propriety of eating ritually prepared foods or other special religious products. The same three guidelines given by Paul would be applicable in such situations.

THE PLURALITY OF GODS

In answering the question of meat offered as sacrifices, Paul also offered the solution to another problem raised about the doctrines of the restored Church. The Church of Jesus Christ of Latter-day Saints is criticized for believing in a plurality of gods rather than in only one God. This criticism comes in various forms based on the critics' beliefs. The Christians who believe in the trinitarian God justify monotheism through the three-in-one concept. As Joseph Smith taught, the teachings of the New Testament are explicit about the three separate members of the Godhead. He referred to Paul's quoting of Psalm 82:6 as further evidence of the plurality of Gods (see 1 Corinthians 8:5) but also emphasized that there was "but one God—that is *pertaining to us*."[4] That one God is, of course, the Lord Jesus Christ, the administrator of this world by divine investiture of authority.[5] The usual interpretation of Paul's comments regarding the Psalm is that he was referring to the many pagan gods. Joseph Smith refuted this explanation:

> Mankind verily say that the Scriptures are with them. Search the Scriptures, for they testify of things that these apostates would gravely pronounce blasphemy. Paul, if Joseph Smith is a blasphemer, you are. I say there are Gods many and Lords many, but to us only one, and we are to be in subjection to that one, and no man can limit the bounds or the eternal existence of eternal time. Hath he beheld the eternal world, and is he authorized to say that there is only one God? He makes himself a fool if he thinks or says so, and there is an end of his career or progress in knowledge. He cannot obtain all knowledge, for he has sealed up the gate to it.[6]

The Bible is very clear on the subject of the Godhead when read under the influence of the Holy Ghost and in light of the Prophet Joseph's explanation. The philosophies of men as determined in uninspired councils have led the world to confusion.

THE APOSTLESHIP

Chapter 9 is Paul's defense of his privileges and responsibilities as an Apostle. Obviously, many of the Corinthian Saints had challenged his position (see 1 Corinthians 9:3). Is this not a stumbling block in our world as well? To those who would discredit some or all of the modern Apostles, a review of this chapter should rouse them to their senses.

Paul argued that he was free (from the bondage of the law) through the acceptance of Jesus Christ. He had seen the Lord personally (see 1 Corinthians 9:1–2). Are not latter-day Apostles special witnesses of Christ who are free from the sins of the world? Although the scriptures justified Paul and the other Apostles in being sustained monetarily for their work, Paul had not accepted such pay. Nonetheless, he had labored diligently to bring souls to salvation. What was his reward? His reward was gaining eternal salvation (see 1 Corinthians 9:4–19). Paul had become all things to all men in an attempt to save some and at the same time save himself (see 1 Corinthians 9:20–27). Do not current Apostles labor diligently, often under trying circumstances, to bring salvation to all who will listen? Through their service will they not assure, or have they not already assured, their salvation?

THE STUMBLING BLOCK OF TEMPTATION

The Apostle next warned his fellow Saints against the evils of temptation. He used the example of the Israelites, who were led by Christ in the wilderness yet yielded to sins such as idolatry, fornication, failure to recognize and worship Christ as their leader through the symbol of the serpent, and their murmuring, which allowed Satan to overcome them (see 1 Corinthians 10:1–11). These same styles of temptation are prevalent in the world today. The same formula given by Paul for avoiding these sins is applicable today. Paul said: "There hath no temptation taken you but such as is common to man: but God is faithful, who will not suffer you to be tempted above that ye are able; but will with the temptation also make a way to escape, that ye may be able to bear it" (1 Corinthians 10:13).

Modern rationalizations or excuses of being tempted beyond endurance are swept away by this scriptural injunction. The Book of Mormon gives a second witness of the validity of this formula (see Alma 13:28), and the Doctrine and Covenants adds a third (see D&C 64:20). However, man has agency and must choose to follow the Lord's "way of escape," or the formula is void and he will succumb to the devil's way.

THE STUMBLING BLOCK OF GENDER

In our own day, society has reared its ugly head in a manner apparently similar to that among the Corinthians in Paul's day. Although we have no specifics about the practices and philosophies being taught, the instructions in 1 Corinthians 11 imply that questions regarding the role of men and women had been asked, or problems had been drawn to Paul's attention (see 1 Corinthians 11:17–19). Basing the principles upon the customs of that day, Paul reminded the people of the eternal verities of the gospel plan. "The head of every man is Christ; and the head of the woman is the man; and the head of Christ is God" (1 Corinthians 11:3). This is not a dictatorship or even a democracy but a theocracy, an order of governing based on revelation and sustaining, or common consent. While the roles of men and women are separate, they are unified through Christ. "Neither is the man without the woman, neither the woman without the man, in the Lord" (1 Corinthians 11:11). The position of the Church in this regard was beautifully stated by President Joseph Fielding Smith:

> I think we all know that the blessings of the priesthood are not confined to men alone. These blessings are also poured out upon our wives and daughters and upon all the faithful women of the Church. These good sisters can prepare themselves, by keeping the commandments and by serving in the Church, for the blessings of the house of the Lord. The Lord offers to his daughters every spiritual gift and blessing that can be obtained by his sons, for neither is the man without the woman, nor the woman without the man in the Lord.[7]

We should learn the role of both man and woman and submit ourselves to the Lord in those separate roles. This will overcome false notions of society, of which President Spencer W. Kimball warned: "Some people are ignorant or vicious and apparently attempting to destroy the concept of masculinity and femininity. More and more girls dress, groom, and act like men. More and more men dress, groom, and act like women. The high purposes of life are damaged and destroyed by the growing unisex theory. God made man in his own image, male and female made he them. With relatively few accidents of nature, we are born male or female. The Lord knew best. Certainly, men and women who would change their sex status will answer to their Maker."[8]

THE STUMBLING BLOCK OF THE SACRAMENT

The law of Moses was a law of ordinances and performances practiced daily to remind the Israelites of Christ (see Mosiah 13:30). The sacrament was instituted to remember the greatness and love of our Savior in bringing about the Resurrection and the Atonement. The primary purpose of meeting together, in Paul's day and our own, is to worship the Lord through partaking of the sacrament. "When ye come together therefore into one place, *is it not to eat the Lord's supper?*" (JST, 1 Corinthians 11:20; emphasis added).

The Lord has given the same commandment today: "And now, behold, I give unto you a commandment, that when ye are assembled together ye shall instruct and edify each other, that ye may know how to act and direct my church, how to act upon the points of my law and commandments, which I have given. And thus ye shall become instructed in the law of my church, and be sanctified by that which ye have received, and ye shall bind yourselves to act in all holiness before me" (D&C 43:8–9).

We bind ourselves through the covenant made in partaking of the sacrament. Through partaking of the bread, we remember the body of Christ and His Resurrection (see 1 Corinthians 11:24; see also 3 Nephi 18:6–7). Through partaking of the water, we remember the blood of Gethsemane or the Atonement (see 1 Corinthians 11:27; see also 3 Nephi 18:10–11). To partake of the sacrament requires us to be worthy. Therefore, we must reflect or examine ourselves before partaking (see 1 Corinthians 11:27–28). To partake unworthily will cause us to stumble and bring about sickness, either physical or mental, and, as Paul said, may even bring death (sleep; see 1 Corinthians 11:29–30). Such is the order revealed to the Corinthians by Paul and verified in the Book of Mormon as a second witness (see 3 Nephi 18:28–32; Mormon 9:29). The sacrament is thus either a stepping-stone or a stumbling block.

CONCLUSION

The gospel is eternal. Although customs and traditions become linked to their practice in various locations, the truths and principles of salvation are the same. The devil is always opposing the Lord's plan for bringing to pass the immortality and eternal life of man (see Moses 1:39). These temptations of Satan were called stumbling blocks by Paul since they obstruct our progress on the path to eternal life. As indicated in the above analysis, these stumbling blocks seem almost as eternal as the gospel. There are certain things that Satan always tosses in our way. The sins are the same even if they are dressed charmingly in varied robes of deceit. However, the road signs given us by the Lord's Apostles to avoid the detours and chuck-holes are also eternal and will lead us through the rough places of the wilderness of Satan to the bosom of Christ.

NOTES

1. Benjamin Willard Robinson, *The Life of Paul* (Chicago: University of Chicago Press, 1928), 136.
2. Joseph Smith Translation quotations not available in the Latter-day Saint edition of the Bible are from Thomas A. Wayment, ed., *The Complete Joseph Smith Translation of the New Testament: A Side-by-Side Comparison with the King James Version* (Salt Lake City: Deseret Book, 2005).
3. As footnoted in the 1979 publication of the Bible by The Church of Jesus Christ of Latter-day Saints, the Greek word translated *effeminate* in the King James Version is *catamites*. A catamite is a sexually abused young boy. This is the basis for the idea that Paul chastised sexual abusers of children.
4. Joseph Smith, *Teachings of the Prophet Joseph Smith*, Joseph Fielding Smith, comp. (Salt Lake City: Deseret Book, 1976), 370. This paper will not fully treat the Trinitarian concept; however, the reader should carefully study this explanation given by Joseph Smith.
5. See "The Father and the Son: Doctrinal Exposition of the First Presidency and the Twelve," quoted in James E. Talmage, *Articles of Faith* (Salt Lake City: The Church of Jesus Christ of Latter-day Saints, 1949), appendix 2, section 11, 465–73.
6. Smith, *Teachings*, 371.
7. Joseph Fielding Smith, Conference Report, April 1970, 59; see also "Magnifying Our Callings in the Priesthood," *Improvement Era*, June 1970, 66.
8. Edward L. Kimball, *The Teachings of Spencer W. Kimball* (Salt Lake City: Bookcraft, 1982), 278.

CHAPTER TWENTY-ONE

LAW AND LIBERTY IN GALATIANS 5–6

GAYE STRATHEARN

Members of The Church of Jesus Christ of Latter-day Saints believe in agency, or the right to make choices. The scriptures and modern-day prophets have repeatedly taught us the central role of agency in the plan of salvation. The scriptures also teach us that agency in this life was guaranteed by the outcome of the war in heaven during the premortal life. That war was initiated when Satan rebelled against God "and sought to destroy the agency of man, which I, the Lord God, had given him" (Moses 4:3). The Doctrine and Covenants teaches us that a third of the hosts of heaven were lost in that war because they exercised their agency unwisely (see D&C 29:36). That agency, which was secured in the premortal life, is central to the plan of salvation and our mortal existence. In fact, President David O. McKay has said, "Next to the bestowal of life itself, the right to direct our lives is God's greatest gift to man."[1]

As important as the doctrine of agency is, we would do well to heed the caution of Elder Dallin H. Oaks. He taught that "few concepts have more potential to mislead us than the idea that choice, or agency, is an ultimate goal. For Latter-day Saints, this potential confusion is partly a product of the fact that moral agency—the right to choose—is a fundamental condition of mortal life. . . . The test in this postwar mortal estate is not to secure choice but to use it—to choose good instead of evil so that we can achieve our eternal goals." He then goes on to remind us that "in mortality, choice is a method, not a goal."[2] Thus Lehi taught his son Jacob that "men are

---

Gaye Strathearn is an assistant professor of ancient scripture at Brigham Young University.

free according to the flesh; and all things are given them which are expedient unto man. And they are free to choose liberty and eternal life, through the great Mediator of all men, or to choose captivity and death, according to the captivity and power of the devil" (2 Nephi 2:27; see also 2 Nephi 10:23). President Gordon B. Hinckley stressed, "This, my brethren and sisters, is our divine right—to choose. This is our divine obligation—to choose the right."[3] In other words, it is not enough that we have choice or liberty; what is really important is that we use that liberty to make the right choices in our lives. One of the difficulties of mortality, however, is learning how to successfully accomplish that obligation in a world of competing calls for allegiance.

These competing calls were certainly an issue for the early Christian Church, in which some members struggled to understand the concept of liberty in a Christian context. In other words, they struggled to understand what liberty they were afforded because of Christ and His Atonement and also how to use that liberty. Paul deals with this issue throughout his epistles,[4] but I would like to concentrate our discussion primarily on his teaching in Galatians, particularly chapters 5 and 6. In this epistle, Paul reacts to a group of Christian teachers who came to Galatia and taught, at least in part, that even Christian liberty was grounded in the law of Moses.[5] In the last two chapters, he identifies four important elements that help Saints of all ages to understand the nature of their liberty. These elements include the use of liberty in relation to the law, the Spirit, the principle of love, and the need to understand the relationship between our use of liberty and our need to follow the Brethren.

THE HISTORICAL SETTING FOR GALATIANS

One of the difficulties of understanding Paul's epistles is that they are like hearing only one-half of a telephone conversation. If we are to understand what Paul is saying, then we must re-create the other side of the conversation. In other words, we need to put Galatians 5–6 in its historical context. To do that, we need to understand the tensions of the early Church, including what Paul's opponents were teaching in Galatia that upset him and caused him to write this epistle.[6] In Acts, Luke tells us that after Paul and Barnabas returned from their successful first mission, "certain men which came down from Judæa" taught their Gentile converts, "Except ye be circumcised after the manner of Moses, ye cannot be saved." Luke then goes on to record that when Paul and Barnabas found out what was happening, there was "no small dissension and disputation with them" (Acts 15:1–2). Paul later claimed that the confrontation was not just about the law of Moses but that it was also centered on the issues of liberty and bondage. He told the Galatian Saints that these men "came in privily to spy out our liberty which we have in Christ Jesus, that they might bring us into bondage" (Galatians 2:4).

This dispute in Antioch eventually led to the convening of the Jerusalem Council, where Peter declared, "Now therefore why tempt ye God, to put a yoke upon the neck of the disciples [i.e., the Gentiles], which neither our fathers nor we were able to bear? But we believe that through the grace of the Lord Jesus Christ we shall be saved, even as they" (Acts 15:10–11; see also Acts 15:19–20; 28–29). Paul tells the Galatian Saints that it was also at this conference that the decision was made to have two missions: Paul and Barnabas would be responsible for the Gentile mission, while Peter would have stewardship for the Jewish mission (see Galatians 2:7–10). Yet even the decree of the Jerusalem Council did not put to rest the tensions between the two Christian groups.[7]

We find one of the most significant examples of this tension in Paul's epistle to the Galatians. When Paul originally arrived in Galatia, he taught the people the gospel of Jesus Christ (see Galatians 1:6–11). The letter suggests that he taught the gospel in a context of the fulfillment of the law of Moses.[8] It is difficult to pinpoint exactly who Paul's early converts in Galatia were;[9] most likely they were God-fearing Gentiles; that is, Gentiles who were attracted to the moral teachings of the law of Moses, attended the synagogue, and obeyed their kosher laws without ever fully converting.[10] Acts tells us that this group was an important source of converts for Paul during his early missions (see Acts 13:26; 16:14). Two textual clues suggest that the Galatian Saints were God-fearers. They were Gentiles because they once worshipped pagan gods (see Galatians 4:8–10) and they were not circumcised.[11] If the Galatians were Jews, the debate in chapter 5 over the value of circumcision for them would have been a moot point. But if his audience was Gentiles, why did Paul and his opponents feel the need to argue over the law of Moses and its relationship to the gospel? Surely that discussion would have been more at home with a Jewish audience, unless the Galatian Saints had been God-fearers who were already familiar with, and impressed by, the law and its teachings.

The identification of the Galatian Saints as God-fearers helps make sense of two issues. First, it explains why Paul would plead with the

Galatians to not be "entangled *again*" in the law (Galatians 5:1; emphasis added). The word *again* indicates that they had previously been "entangled" in the law. This would not have been the case for most Gentiles. Second, if the Galatians were God-fearers, then we can perhaps better understand why the Gentile and Jewish missions intersected in such a volatile way in Galatia even after the pronouncement of the Jerusalem Council.[12] Paul would have identified the Saints as Gentiles and therefore under his stewardship, whereas his opponents would have viewed them as part of the Jewish mission because they had previously committed themselves to the law of Moses. It seems that the best way to reconcile all of this data is if his audience was composed of God-fearing Gentiles.[13]

After Paul had taught the gospel to these Saints and left to continue his missionary journey, another group of Christian missionaries arrived on the scene and began teaching. Paul argues that their teaching is "another gospel" (Galatians 1:6), but then he immediately clarifies this statement by declaring that it is not really "another gospel" because its teachers "pervert the gospel of Christ" (Galatians 1:7). It appears that these teachers were still in Galatia when Paul wrote his letter and that what they were teaching was appealing to the Saints.[14] What we know about this "other gospel" is what we can glean from Paul's epistle because it seems that he is reacting to specific things that the new missionaries were teaching.

We know from the force of Paul's letter that the new missionaries, like the men in Acts 15, were teaching that the gospel must include the law of Moses and circumcision. From their perspective the law was the equivalent of provisions needed for the journey to salvation.[15] One scholar described their teaching in this way: although Christ's Atonement and Resurrection provided the gate for salvation, the law provided the provisions and directions once a person had entered the gate.[16] It also seems, given Paul's response, that they argued that the law is what enabled the Saints to exercise their Christian liberty. The law was not just a system of rules and regulations; it was a system that enabled its followers to be free from sin and tyranny.

Historically, there are examples where the people of the covenant sought for political and religious freedom through recommitting themselves to the law. For example, Ezra recommitted his people as they returned from the Babylonian exile so that they would never have to experience bondage again (see Ezra 9–10), Mattathias instituted the Maccabean revolt so that his people would have the freedom that comes from living the law (see 1 Maccabees 1–2), and the people of Qumran fled into the wilderness so that they would also have freedom to live the law as they understood it.[17] So we know that many looked to the law for freedom. Perhaps the new missionaries in Galatia shared similar feelings with groups such as these. They surely argued that liberty can never exist in an absence of law. If there is no law, then it is anarchy that prevails, not liberty! It also appears that they, like their counterparts in Rome, interpreted Paul's teachings about the law to actually be "an occasion to the flesh," or a license to sin (Galatians 5:13; see also Romans 3:8; 6:15). Nothing could be further from the intent of Paul's teachings. With this background established, we can now turn to Paul's teachings about Christian liberty.

Liberty and Law

It would be inaccurate to think that Paul's view of Christian liberty was independent of law. The force of his teachings in Galatians is specifically directed to those who claim that the law of Moses is the means of achieving liberty. Certainly he recognized the important part that the law of Moses had played in its time: it was a "schoolmaster to bring us unto Christ" (Galatians 3:24). Six hundred years before Paul, Nephi taught the same principle: "Behold, my soul delighteth in proving unto my people the truth of the coming of Christ; for, for this end hath the law of Moses been given; and all things which have been given of God from the beginning of the world, unto man, are the typifying of him" (2 Nephi 11:4). But even in its pure form, Abinadi taught that it was only "a law of performances and of ordinances, a law which they were to observe strictly from day to day, to keep them in remembrance of God and their duty towards him" (Mosiah 13:30). By the Christian period, the Pharisees had greatly expanded those laws to include a complex system of oral traditions, which acted as "fences around the law" to protect their sanctity (Talmud, *Aboth* 1.1). Although Peter judged it impossible to live under such a yoke (see Acts 15:10), Paul told the Galatian Saints that he had been "more exceedingly zealous" than his peers in living "the traditions of my fathers" (Galatians 1:14). He knew what it took to try to live that law.

So it seems that the question for some in Galatia was if they weren't to have the law of Moses to guide them in making right choices, how were they to achieve liberty? Paul understood that this whole idea of the law was to bring covenant Israel to a point where they were spiritually prepared to accept the higher law—a law that they had already rejected once at Mount Sinai. That's why he described the law as a schoolmaster.

Jeremiah had plainly taught that the time would come when the Lord would "make a new covenant with the house of Israel, and with the house of Judah," but this new covenant would be written "in their inward parts," and He would "write it in their hearts" (Jeremiah 31:31–33; see also 2 Corinthians 3:1–3). Paul recognized this new covenant as the new law—the "law of Christ" (Galatians 6:2; 1 Corinthians 9:21). This was not a law of performances and ordinances or, as one scholar noted, "a detailed code which has a ready-made answer for every circumstance."[18] Instead, the law of Christ, a higher law, centers on eternal principles (see Matthew 5:21–48).

As Richard Longenecker said: "Paul would have agreed with E. F. Scott's understanding of the ethical teaching of Jesus at this point: 'Instead of framing laws [Christ] stated principles, and made them so few and broad and simple that no one could overlook them. . . . It is true that he enounced a large number of precepts which appear to bear directly on given questions of conduct. . . . But when we look more closely into the precepts we find that they are not so much rules as illustrations. In every instance they involve a principle on which all the stress is laid; but it is applied to a concrete example, so that we may not only grasp it as a principle but judge for ourselves how it works.'"[19] Latter-day Saints are familiar with this concept because of the Prophet Joseph. When asked how he governed such a vast people, he replied, "It is very easy, for I teach the people correct principles and they govern themselves."[20]

The difficulty with this higher law is that while it provides us with a greater liberty to choose, it also comes at a much higher individual cost because it requires that we have a relationship with, and recognize, the promptings of the Spirit.

LIBERTY AND THE SPIRIT

Paul taught the Galatians that "if ye be led of the Spirit, ye are not under the law" (Galatians 5:18). Later, in his epistle to the Romans, Paul expanded this concept:

> There is therefore now no condemnation to them which are in Christ Jesus, who walk not after the flesh, but after the Spirit.
> For the law of the Spirit of life in Christ Jesus hath made me free from the law of sin and death.

For what the law could not do, in that it was weak through the
flesh, God sending his own Son in the likeness of sinful flesh, and
for sin, condemned sin in the flesh:

That the righteousness of the law might be fulfilled in us, *who walk
not after the flesh, but after the Spirit.* (Romans 8:1–4; emphasis added)

Paul makes it clear here that he is not just talking about the law of
Moses but any law that is imposed because of our fallen nature.
Righteousness is not a function of following law per se, but it is a function
of following the Spirit. President Ezra Taft Benson taught that "righteousness is the one indispensable ingredient to liberty."[21] With righteousness
comes liberty from the demands or consequences of the law. So Paul
taught the Corinthian Saints that "where the Spirit of the Lord is, there is
liberty" (2 Corinthians 3:17).

Why is the Spirit so critical to our Christian liberty under the law of
Christ? The simple answer is that it is the Spirit that guides us in applying
the principles Christ taught in our everyday life. But what does that mean
for Saints struggling to use their liberty to "choose the right"? Sometimes it
seems easier to make choices when there is a specific law to draw upon.
The onus is then upon God, parents, or the government to determine how
we should act rather than on us. Whereas in the time of Christ the law of
Moses had become a complex system of laws to judge actions by, the law
of Christ enabled individuals to use their Christian liberty through the
promptings of the Spirit. Remember that the Savior promised His disciples
that He would "not leave [them] comfortless" because He would send
them a Comforter who would "teach [them] all things, and bring all things
to [their] remembrance, whatsoever I have said unto you" (John 14:18,
26). In other words, Christ could teach principles because the Spirit would
help His followers both remember those principles and teach them how
to use them in any given situation.

There are two major advantages to a pedagogy that relies on the guidance of the Spirit. First, it recognizes that what is good for a people to do at
one time is not necessarily right for them to do under different circumstances.

The law of Moses exemplified that concept for Paul. For centuries it had
been "our schoolmaster to bring us unto Christ" (Galatians 3:24), and Paul
had once lived that law zealously. As a result, he had progressed in Judaism
further than many of his Jewish contemporaries (see Galatians 1:14). But
now Christ had come, and all of Paul's righteousness in living the law of

Moses was no longer applicable. "But now we are delivered from the law, that being dead wherein we were held; that we should serve in newness of spirit, and not in the oldness of the letter" (Romans 7:6).

One of the clearest applications of this principle in the scriptures is Nephi's experience with Laban when he found him "fallen to the earth . . . drunken with wine" (1 Nephi 4:7). All of his life, Nephi had been taught the commandment "Thou shalt not kill" (Exodus 20:13), but now the Spirit was telling him to do the exact opposite. No wonder he hesitated. But the law could not help Nephi make the right choice in this instance; only the Spirit could do that.

Second, relying on the Spirit enables people at different levels of spiritual progression to journey along the path to salvation. This leads Paul to tell the Galatians that all people, regardless of their background, are children of God. "For as many of you as have been baptized into Christ have put on Christ. There is neither Jew nor Greek, there is neither bond nor free, there is neither male nor female: for ye are all one in Christ Jesus" (Galatians 3:27–28). Paul considered himself to be one of the chiefest of sinners (see 1 Timothy 1:15) and "the least of the apostles that am not meet to be called an apostle because [he] persecuted the church of God" (1 Corinthians 15:9). Even so, he "press[ed] toward the mark for the prize of the high calling of God in Christ Jesus" (Philippians 3:14). How is it possible to hope for exaltation when a person is just at the beginning of a personal spiritual journey? The Spirit guides them. For new members, keeping the Sabbath day holy may mean attending Church and refraining from Sunday shopping. But as new members progress spiritually they come to realize that keeping the Sabbath holy also means much more.

Elder Oaks gave the following instruction to gospel teachers: "Teachers who are commanded to teach 'the principles of [the] gospel' and 'the doctrine of the kingdom' (D&C 88:77) should generally forgo teaching specific rules or applications." He continues, "Once a teacher has taught the doctrine and the associated principles from the scriptures and the living prophets, . . . specific applications or rules are generally the responsibility of individuals and families."[22] One of the benefits of such lessons is that members of the class can be uplifted and motivated regardless of where they are spiritually. Another benefit is that members, after being reminded of the principle, can then use their liberty to exercise what President Hinckley defined as their divine obligation: to "choose the right."

Note also that in Galatians 5:25 Paul makes a distinction between having access to the Spirit and walking in it. It is not enough to be confirmed a member of the Church and commanded to receive the Spirit. The law of Christ can only help us use our Christian liberty when we have paid the price to recognize the Spirit's promptings in our lives. Thus President Joseph F. Smith taught, "The only safe way for us to do, as individuals is to live so humbly, so righteously and so faithfully before God that we may possess his Spirit to that extent that we shall be able to judge righteously, and discern between truth and error, between right and wrong."[23] Likewise, President Wilford Woodruff taught that "there is nothing that we ought to labor more to obtain while in the flesh than the Spirit of God, the Holy Ghost, the Comforter, which we are entitled to receive by reason of our having obeyed the requirements of the Gospel. When you get acquainted with the Spirit, follow its dictates, no matter where it may lead you; and when you do that, it will become a principle of revelation in you." Then he bore his testimony and implored the Saints: "I know by experience the value of it. You . . . should live in such a manner as to be entitled to the operations of the Holy Ghost within you, and, as I have said, it will become a guide as well as a revelator to you, and never leave or fail you."[24] Paul says that the fruit of living by the Spirit is "love, joy, peace, long-suffering, gentleness, goodness, faith, meekness, [and] temperance" (Galatians 5:22–23). Note that he doesn't say that these are "the works of the Spirit" that people do when they follow the Spirit; rather, they are the rewards that come to those who follow the Spirit.[25]

LIBERTY AND LOVE

The third concept that Paul taught the Galatians was that love is an essential element in helping them to use their liberty to make right choices. "For, brethren, ye have been called unto liberty; only use not liberty for an occasion to the flesh, but by love serve one another. For all the law is fulfilled in one word, even in this; Thou shalt love thy neighbour as thyself" (Galatians 5:13–14). Here is the irony. This commandment was a part of the law of Moses that Paul's opponents were advocating (see Leviticus 19:18). But whereas those missionaries had emphasized the law through circumcision, Paul followed Christ's lead when he taught that this was the second great commandment after loving God with all of our heart, soul, and mind (see Matthew 22:37–40). I love what President Hinckley had to say on the importance of love: "Love is like the Polar Star. In a changing world, it is a constant. It is of the very essence of the gospel. It is the security of the home. It is the safeguard of community life. It is a beacon of hope in a world of distress."[26] When faced with a decision about how to use our liberty, one of the most important questions we can ask ourselves is "How will my decision affect the lives of others?" If we choose to serve others, then we will invariably choose to serve God. Thus King Benjamin taught that "when ye are in the service of your fellow beings ye are only in the service of your God" (Mosiah 2:17).

Perhaps for Paul the greatest evidence of our love for a neighbor was the decision to "restrict [our] personal liberty in matters which are of secondary importance for the sake of the Gospel."[27] This is a concept that Paul mentions in Galatians but develops most fully in 1 Corinthians. There he responds to a dispute over whether Christians should eat meat that was sacrificed at pagan temples. The ruling at the Jerusalem Council was that they should not (see Acts 15:19–20, 28–29). Even so, some of the Saints in Corinth argued that it didn't matter if they ate it because the idols weren't real gods. In one sense, Paul agreed with them: there is only one true God. But what really concerned Paul was the fact that in claiming their "right" to eat that meat these Saints had not considered the effect their actions might have on others. He counsels them:

> Take heed lest by any means this liberty of yours become a stumblingblock to them that are weak.
>
> For if any man see thee which hast knowledge sit at meat in the idol's temple, shall not the conscience of him which is weak be emboldened to eat those things which are offered to idols;
>
> And through thy knowledge shall the weak brother perish, for whom Christ died?
>
> But when ye sin so against the brethren, and wound their weak conscience, ye sin against Christ.
>
> Wherefore, if meat make my brother to offend, I will eat no flesh while the world standeth, lest I make my brother to offend. (1 Corinthians 8:9–13)

The issue here for Paul is not that he should become a vegetarian. The issue is that he would rather put aside his liberty to eat meat than risk a new member's salvation. Thus he implores the Corinthian Saints, and all Saints, that when we are faced with these types of situations, to "let no man seek his own, but every man another's wealth" (1 Corinthians 10:24). Then he concludes with the following exhortation:

> Conscience, I say, not thine own, but of the other: for why is my liberty judged of another man's conscience?
>
> For if I by grace be a partaker, why am I evil spoken of for that for which I give thanks?
>
> Whether therefore ye eat, or drink, or whatsoever ye do, do all to the glory of God.
>
> Give none offence, neither to the Jews, nor to the Gentiles, nor to the church of God:
>
> Even as I please all men in all things, not seeking mine own profit, but the profit of many, that they may be saved. (1 Corinthians 10:29–33)

Although Paul's message in 1 Corinthians 8 and 10 deals with the specific issue of eating meat, the real principle that Paul stresses is that we sometimes need to restrict our personal liberty so that another's salvation will not be put in jeopardy. In this way we see, as he told the Galatians, that the liberty Christ provided for us is governed by the commandment to "love our neighbour as ourselves" (Matthew 22:39).

LIBERTY AND FOLLOWING THE BRETHREN

Our final element in understanding Paul's teachings in these chapters is often overlooked. Granted, he only makes a passing reference to this element in one verse in Galatians, but I believe this verse is significant. The issue is whether a Saint can exercise liberty and still be in subjection to someone who has progressed further spiritually than they have. Is the use of terms such as *liberty* and *subjection* in the same sentence an oxymoron? Some have concluded from Paul's teachings on Christian liberty and Christ's principle-centered teaching that "not even an Apostle can tell you what you ought to do."[28] Some modern members have also struggled with this dilemma.[29] However, I believe that this conclusion misrepresents Paul. As an Apostle himself, Paul taught with authority. As one scholar has noted, "He also insisted that he could legitimately reprove, discipline, instruct, and even command."[30] Although he does not use the term *Apostle,* in Galatians 6:1 Paul teaches that those who are "spiritual," or who are further along in their spiritual progression, should "restore . . . in the spirit of meekness" a "man . . . overtaken in a fault." In Romans, Paul is even more explicit: "Let every person be subject to the governing authorities. For there is no authority except from God, and those that exist have been instituted by God. Therefore he who resists the authorities resists what God has appointed, and those who resist will incur judgment. For rulers are not a terror to good conduct, but to bad. Would you have no fear of him who is in authority? Then do what is good, and you will receive his approval, For he is God's servant for your good" (Revised Standard Version, Romans 13:1–4).

The principle Paul is trying to teach is that Christian liberty is advanced discipleship. The reality is that many of us have not yet progressed spiritually enough to a point where we are sufficiently schooled or confident in discerning the promptings of the Spirit. In such cases, we can turn to those who are further along in their spiritual progression. One of Paul's frequent pleas with the Saints is that they imitate him because he is imitating Christ (see 1 Corinthians 11:1; 2 Thessalonians 3:7).

Is there a lesson here for Latter-day Saints? I think so. President Boyd K. Packer taught that there is no contradiction between liberty and obedience:

> We are all free to choose. . . .
>
> Choice among my freedoms is my freedom to be obedient. I obey because I want to; I choose to.
>
> Some people are always suspicious that one is only obedient because he is compelled to be. They indict themselves with the very thought that one is only obedient because he is compelled to be. They feel that one would only obey through compulsion. They speak for themselves. I am free to be obedient, and I decided that—all by myself. I pondered on it; I reasoned it; I even experimented a little.
> . . .
> Obedience to God [or his servants; D&C 1:38] can be the very highest expression of independence.[31]

FREEDOM IN CHRIST

Paul's teachings on Christian liberty in Galatians came about because some members of the Church sought to undermine that liberty by holding on to the law of Moses. He implored them to "stand fast therefore in the liberty wherewith Christ hath made us free" (Galatians 5:1). Today modern Saints don't keep the law of Moses, but perhaps sometimes, either consciously or unwittingly, we bind ourselves to the things of the world. As we do so, we place ourselves in a comparable position to Paul's opponents in Galatia. President Brigham Young taught:

> This is the deciding point, the dividing line. They who love and serve God with all their hearts rejoice evermore, pray without ceasing, and in everything give thanks; but they who try to serve God and still cling to the spirit of the world, have got on two yokes—the yoke of Jesus and the yoke of the devil, and they will have plenty to do. They will have a warfare inside and outside, and the labor will be very galling, for they are directly in opposition one to the other. Cast off the yoke of the enemy, and put on the yoke of Christ, and you will say that his yoke is easy and his burden is light. This I know by experience.[32]

Christian liberty does not come from an absence of law; it comes from willingly yoking ourselves to Christ. The difficulty comes when we refuse to give up our other yokes, as did Paul's opponents in Galatia. The yoke that they clung to was the law of Moses.

In our day, our yoke, our law of Moses, is anything that prevents or impedes our total commitment to Christ and His gospel. How do we use the liberty that Christ has afforded us? Do we use it as an opportunity to follow the ways of the world or, as Paul said, "an occasion to the flesh" (Galatians 5:13), or do we use it to choose the right and further the work of God in our own lives and in the lives of those around us? If Paul were with us today he would also implore us to "stand fast . . . in the liberty wherewith Christ hath made us free, and be not entangled again with the yoke of bondage" (Galatians 5:1).

NOTES

1. David O. McKay, in Conference Report, October 1965, 8.
2. Dallin H. Oaks, "Weightier Matters," *Ensign,* January 2001, 13–14.
3. Gordon B. Hinckley, *Caesar, Circus, or Christ?* in *Brigham Young University Speeches of the Year* (Provo, October 26, 1965), 8.
4. For a detailed discussion of Paul's teachings on liberty, see Richard N. Longenecker, *Paul: Apostle of Liberty* (New York: Harper & Row, 1964).
5. Paul's epistle to the Galatians is clearly a reaction to what his opponents were teaching in Galatia in his absence. It seems to me, therefore, that the best way to understand Paul's pointed remarks on the nature of

Christian liberty in this epistle is to understand them as a reaction to what his opponents were teaching.

6. This is the only Pauline epistle where after his introduction he doesn't commend his readers for something. Instead, he immediately chastises them: "I marvel that ye are so soon removed from him that called you into the grace of Christ unto another gospel: which is not another; but there be some that trouble you, and would pervert the gospel of Christ" (Galatians 1:6–7).

7. It should be remembered that the decision of the Jerusalem Council affected Gentile converts only. They made no decision about whether Jews could or should continue living the law of Moses. By the first century after Christ, the law had become as much a part of cultural identity as it was a reflection of spiritual commitment. In Acts 21:20, James tells Paul: "Thou seest, brother, how many thousands of Jews there are which believe; and they are all zealous of the law." The Ebionites were a group of Christians who maintained their commitment to the law of Moses. We know that at the end of the first century after Christ there were still such groups because Ignatius denounces them in his letter to the Magnesians (8:1; 10:3).

8. Paul does not specifically mention that he taught the fulfillment of the law of Moses through Christ prior to his Galatian epistle, but the fact that the teachers from Judaea put such a heavy emphasis on it in their teachings suggests that it was in reaction to what Paul had originally taught (see the Savior's teachings in 3 Nephi 15:1–10; Matthew 5:17–48; and Stephen's teachings and the response they elicit in Acts 6:9–15).

9. Scholars have debated this point at great length. There are two main theories for the location of the Galatian church: the North Galatian hypothesis and the South Galatian hypothesis. The South Galatian hypothesis argues that the churches are located in the southern part of the Roman province. If this was the case, then these churches may have been the ones established by Paul during his first missionary journey (see Acts 13–14). We know from that first mission that there were synagogues in many of the cities that he visited and that many of his converts were Gentiles. The North Galatian hypothesis is that the churches were located among the ethnic Galatians in the north around Ankyra and Pessinus. In this area the churches probably consisted of people of Celtic descent, with the possibility of a mixture of "some Greek and a few oriental immigrants" (J. Louis Martyn, Galatians, volume 34A of the Anchor Bible [New York: Doubleday, 1997], 15–16), although there was a Jewish element in this area as well (see Hans Dieter Betz, *Galatians: A Commentary on Paul's Letter to the Churches in Galatia* [Philadelphia: Fortress Press, 1979], 4–5).

10. Emil Schürer, *The History of the Jewish People in the Age of Jesus Christ (175*

BC–AD 135), rev. and ed. Geza Vermes, Fergus Millar, and Martin Goodman, 3 vols. (Edinburgh: T&T Clark, 1986), 3:161–71.

11. The fact that in Galatians 5 Paul insists that circumcision was not an important issue strongly suggests that it was an important issue for his opponents. Richard Lloyd Anderson characterizes "the chief problem of Galatians" as "whether Gentile converts should be circumcised" (*Understanding Paul* [Salt Lake City: Deseret Book, 1983], 151).

12. "Paul can tolerate, and even recognize as God's doing, a *parallel,* Law-observant mission to the Jews, so long as that mission is and remains truly parallel, that is to say, so long as it does not infect the Gentile mission with the demand for Law-observance. Nothing would have been further from Paul's mind than to indicate that there was a Law observant mission to Gentiles, considered by at least some members of the church to be authorized by God" (J. Louis Martyn, "A Law-Observant Mission to Gentiles: The Background of Galatians," *Michigan Quarterly Review* 22, no. 1 [1983]: 223).

13. One argument against this reading is if one accepts the North Galatian hypothesis, then there were no Jews in that area for the Gentiles to come into contact with. However, archaeological discoveries have uncovered Jewish inscriptions in the north (see Betz, *Galatians,* 4–5).

14. Betz, *Galatians,* 8–9.

15. Perhaps these missionaries felt that Paul was acting like some members of the Church in the Americas just after the Savior was born. "And there were no contentions, save it were a few that began to preach, endeavoring to prove by the scriptures that it was no more expedient to observe the law of Moses. Now in this thing they did err, having not understood the scriptures" (3 Nephi 1:24).

16. Martyn, "A Law-Observant Mission to Gentiles," 235.

17. These actions were not just the result of oppressive acts that denied Jews the opportunity to practice their religion but also reflect the idea that freedom, true freedom, is found in living the law of Moses (see Longnecker, *Paul: Apostle of Liberty,* 156–58).

18. Longnecker, *Paul: Apostle of Liberty,* 191.

19. Longnecker, *Paul: Apostle of Liberty,* 192.

20. John Taylor, in *Journal of Discourses,* 26 vols. (London: Latter-day Saints' Book Depot, 1854–86), 10:57–58.

21. Ezra Taft Benson, *The Teachings of Ezra Taft Benson* (Salt Lake City: Bookcraft, 1988), 346.

22. Dallin H. Oaks, "Gospel Teaching," *Ensign,* November 1999, 79.

23. Joseph F. Smith, *Gospel Doctrine* (Salt Lake City: Deseret Book, 1986), 45.

24. Wilford Woodruff, *Collected Discourses Delivered by President Wilford Woodruff, His Two Counselors, the Twelve Apostles, and Others,* comp. and ed. Brian H. Stuy, 5 vols. (Sandy, UT: B. H. S. Publishing, 1991), 4:327.

25. Betz, *Galatians,* 286.

26. Gordon B. Hinckley, "Let Love Be the Lodestar of Your Life," *Ensign,* May 1989, 66.

27. Longenecker, *Paul: Apostle of Liberty,* 206.

28. Emil Brunner, *Divine Imperative,* trans. Olive Wyon (Philadelphia: Westminster Press, 1947), 118.

29. For one example, see L. Jackson Newell, "Scapegoats and Scarecrows in Our Town: When the Interests of Church and Community Collide," *Sunstone,* December 1993, 22–28.

30. Longenecker, *Paul: Apostle of Liberty,* 197–98.

31. Boyd K. Packer, "Obedience," in *BYU Speeches of the Year* (Provo, UT: Brigham Young University Press, 1971), 2–3.

32. Brigham Young, in *Journal of Discourses,* 16:123.

CHAPTER TWENTY-TWO

"AS THE BODY WITHOUT THE SPIRIT": JAMES'S EPISTLE ON FAITH AND WORKS

BRIAN M. HAUGLID

When Latter-day Saints emphasize the importance of exhibiting faith in Christ by works, they commonly refer to the second chapter of the Epistle of James. Surely this epistle is one of the most pragmatic of the twenty-seven books of the New Testament. James considers works to be the lifeblood principle of faith: "For as the body without the spirit is dead, so faith without works is dead also" (James 2:26). James consistently focuses on the *actions* of individuals—for example, the use of the tongue and the treatment of widows.

After I address the historical authenticity and authorship of the Epistle of James, I will analyze the Greek words for *faith* and *works* and discuss Elder James E. Talmage's teachings on these terms. I will then demonstrate that all the chapters in James's epistle, even while not specifically referring to the terms *faith* and *works*,[1] support James's primary injunction that we be "doers of the word, and not hearers only" (James 1:22).

HISTORICAL AUTHENTICITY AND AUTHORSHIP

Surprisingly, the Epistle of James was not readily accepted as part of the New Testament canon. Even though it was considered one of the Catholic epistles (that is, one written to a general rather than a specific audience),[2] the Epistle of James was not included in early Christian canons such as

Brian M. Hauglid is an associate professor of ancient scripture at Brigham Young University.

those by Marcion (d. 144),[3] Irenaeus (d. 202), Muratorian (d. ca. second century), and Eusebius (d. 340). It is not known for certain why this epistle was disputed; it may have been a question of authorship. Jerome (d. 420), speaking of James as the brother of the Lord, said: "He wrote only one Epistle, which is reckoned among the seven Catholic Epistles, and even this is claimed by some to have been published by some one else under his name, and gradually, as time went on, to have gained in authority."[4] However, from as early as the third century, both Origen (d. 254) and Eusebius refer to James as the author of the epistle.[5]

Although specific reasoning and evidence concerning the question of authorship no longer exist, these divergent views indicate that concerns arose over this issue. In any case, in AD 367, Athanasius included the Epistle of James in his authorized collection of the twenty-seven books of the New Testament, which became the officially accepted canon in AD 382. Inclusion of the Epistle of James was not questioned again until 1522 when Martin Luther, in his preface to the New Testament, called it "an epistle of straw."[6] "Because of what he saw to be James's rejection of the Pauline doctrine of justification by faith, Luther denied that the epistle had apostolic authority; and in his translation of the NT he relegated it from its canonical position to the end, together with his equally disliked Hebrews, Jude, and Revelation."[7] Despite the previous questions of authorship and Luther's concern with James's emphasis on works, James's teachings are generally highly valued by Christians.

FAITH (*PISTIS*) AND WORKS (*ERGON*)

Among the most quoted verses in the Epistle of James is the declaration that "faith without works is dead" (James 2:26). Throughout his epistle, James uses the Greek terms *pistis* for "faith" and *ergon* for "works." Identifying these Greek words and defining them helps us see that James's use of *pistis* and *ergon* varies from the generally accepted view in Christianity.

Faith is seen in two distinct ways in the modern Christian context: (1) "It is applied objectively to the body of truth ('the Christian faith') to be found in the Creeds, . . . Councils, . . . teachings of doctors and saints, and, above all, in the revelation contained in the Bible." (2) Subjectively, "it is the human response to Divine truth, inculcated in the Gospels as the childlike and trusting acceptance of the kingdom and its demands."[8] Christians view the subjective part of faith as a supernatural event wherein the "Christian can make an act of faith only in virtue of God's action in his soul," and this is possible "only in the context of the Christian revelation."[9] Latter-day Saints also recognize faith as a spiritual gift (see Moroni 10:11). However, an important difference emerges regarding the emphasis on obedient activity, which grows out of faith.

Christian faith in its subjective sense as a "childlike and trusting acceptance"[10] likely emerges from the Greek word *pistis,* which has both the sense of "trusting" and "worthy of trust."[11] However, "inasmuch as trust may be a duty, [*pistis*] can come to have the nuance 'obedient.'"[12] In fact, the Septuagint renders a common form of *pistis* from the Hebrew *amin,* which when referring to "God's requirement, order, or command . . . implies acknowledgment of the requirement and man's obedience."[13]

Even in later Judaism, "faithfulness is also obedience. Hence the Law and commandments are among the objects of faith. In the [rabbinic] writings to believe in God and to obey God are equivalent in meaning."[14] Faith as obedience is an idea found in the New Testament, particularly in Hebrews 11, which cites examples of many Old Testament prophets who exhibited their faith through obedience.[15] Although most modern Christian scholars now interpret *pistis* as the "saving faith which recognizes and appropriates God's saving work in Christ," with obedience being implied,[16] I believe James says it differently—for one to exercise faith in Christ, one must exhibit obedience to God through good works.

The Greek term *ergon* is translated as "works." Its fundamental meaning is to "denote action or active zeal in contrast to idleness."[17] In the Septuagint "many words which denote conduct in general are brought under the concept of work."[18] According to rabbinic Judaism, "he who has learned Torah and yet acts contrary to it blasphemes God. Christianity, however, demands a preaching of action, . . . and contradiction between word and act is a denial of Christ."[19] Many Pauline scholars view *ergon* in a "completely negative sense whenever it is a matter of human achievement."[20] James, on the other hand, emphasizes works within the context of faith in Christ, not as a negative but as a natural, positive outgrowth of faith: "Yea, a man may say, Thou hast faith [in Christ], and I have works: shew me thy faith [in Christ] without thy works, and I will shew thee my faith [in Christ] by my works" (James 2:18). James's epistle follows the meaning of *pistis* and *ergon* as defined by the Septuagint and rabbinic Judaism, connecting them to faith in Christ.

The Epistle of James clearly teaches that faith and works complement each other and belong together. In fact, it is impossible to separate them. In a way, faith is like water. We think of water most often in its liquid form, but when the temperature is substantially increased or decreased, the water changes to steam or ice. In comparison to each other, ice and steam may look different, but they are still essentially the same compound of elements. In the form of steam, water can serve to power engines. When it converts to ice, it can be used as a cooling agent or act as a solid layer over bodies of water on which heavy vehicles may drive. So it is with faith. Our service in the Church, our enduring of trials and tests, our obedience to commandments—these works are all expressions of our faith. Faith and works are of the same compound. They are inseparable. You cannot have one without the other. In other words, good works are to faith as steam and ice are to water. This is the essence of the Epistle of James.

TALMAGE ON FAITH AND WORKS

A review of Elder Talmage's understanding of faith and works helps Latter-day Saints better appreciate James's teachings. In 1899, Elder Talmage published the first edition of *A Study of the Articles of Faith.* This highly valued and well-known study represented the first formal analysis of each of the articles of faith by a Latter-day Saint scholar. Talmage's eloquent examination of faith, like James's, clearly distinguishes between faith and belief. He writes, "Belief, in one of its accepted senses, may consist in a merely intellectual assent, while faith implies such confidence as will impel to action."[21] Talmage defines belief, faith, and works (very much in harmony with the Hebrew and Greek definitions stated above) and emphasizes how both faith and works should be centered in Christ. "Belief is in a sense passive, an agreement or acceptance only; faith is active and positive, embracing such reliance and confidence as will lead to works. Faith in Christ comprises belief in Him, combined with trust in Him. One cannot have faith without belief; yet he may believe and still lack faith. Faith is vivified, vitalized, living belief."[22]

In a 1914 article titled "Prove Thy Faith by Thy Works,"[23] Elder Talmage demonstrates his concern that modern translations of the Bible view the terms *faith* and *belief* as synonyms:

> Belief is the mechanism, like a locomotive standing with tank empty and fire-box cold upon the track; faith is the fire and the resulting steam that gives it power and makes it work such miracles

as had never been dreamed of in days of yore. Faith is vitalized, energized, dynamic belief. . . . Strange, is it not, that there are yet those who hold that the use of the term belief in the Holy Scriptures means empty, intellectual, negative belief, and that alone? Because of the fact, already cited, that in early English the term belief was used as a synonym of faith, we find it occurring and recurring in our translation of the Scriptures given to us as the Holy Bible, when by the context it is absolutely plain, and, by derivation beyond all question, that living belief, or actual faith, was intended, and that the term meaning this did occur in the original.[24]

Elder Talmage further notes, "James, an Apostle of the Lord Jesus Christ, found it necessary to warn the people against belief as a saving principle if left to stand alone."[25] Elder Talmage demonstrates that the entire Epistle of James was written with the fundamental assumption that true faith in Christ will lead to good works.

TEXTUAL STUDY OF THE EPISTLE OF JAMES

In his epistle, James emphasizes the need to exercise faith and identifies appropriate works that grow out of true faith, such as prayer, visiting the sick and afflicted, controlling the tongue, and using the priesthood. He also shows that lack of faith is demonstrated through inappropriate works such as double-mindedness, deception, pride and riches, and sin in general. James wrote this epistle "to prevent the danger of separation (*diastasis*) between faith and works. . . . It is this coherence of faith and deeds that gives the unifying theme to the entire document and makes it a genuinely Christian writing."[26] James identifies various activities that the follower of Christ should pursue. Faith is the element that holds these disparate subjects together. James illustrates the active faith of believers with his instruction to follow the path to perfection, seek wisdom, and avoid the sins of pride. His use of the imperative tense throughout the text further evidences his concern that we put our discipleship into action.

Perfection

According to James, afflictions try faith, which then strengthens patience. "But let patience have her perfect work, that ye may be perfect and entire, wanting nothing" (James 1:4).[27] The word for perfection in the Greek (*telos*) refers to "fulfillment" or "completion" and "denotes that which has reached maturity or fulfilled the end contemplated."[28]

Perfection, then, in the Epistle of James is more akin to spiritual maturity rather than absolute sinlessness.

James clearly teaches that to gain perfection one must perfect faith through good works: "Thou believest that there is one God; thou doest well: the devils also believe, and tremble. But wilt thou know, O vain man, that faith without works is dead? Was not Abraham our father justified by works, when he had offered Isaac his son upon the altar? Seest thou how faith wrought with his works, and by works was faith made perfect?" (James 2:19–22). The phrase "the devils also believe, and tremble" indicates that passive belief is not enough: faith must impel the disciple to acts of righteousness. President Joseph F. Smith explains Satan and his followers' fatal flaw as a lack of pure intelligence: "There is a difference between knowledge and pure intelligence. Satan possesses knowledge, far more than we have, but he has not intelligence or he would render obedience to the principles of truth and right. I know men who have knowledge, who understand the principles of the Gospel, perhaps as well as you do, who are brilliant, but who lack the essential qualification of pure intelligence. They will not accept and render obedience thereto. Pure intelligence comprises not only knowledge, but also the power to properly apply that knowledge."[29]

President Smith would agree with James that faith (pure intelligence) and obedience (works) are inseparably connected.

Interestingly, a number of parallel verses can be identified between James's path of faith to perfection and the Savior's teachings in the Sermon on the Mount in Matthew. A comparison of the two shows that James's epistle reiterates the Savior's command that His disciples "let [their] light so shine before men, that they may see [their] good works and glorify [their] Father which is in heaven" (Matthew 5:16).

Matthew	James
Rejoice in trials (see 5:12).	"Count it all joy when ye fall into many afflictions" (JST, 1:2).
"Ask, and it shall be given you" (7:7).	"Ask of God, that giveth . . . liberally" (1:5).
"Be ye therefore perfect" (5:48).	"Be perfect and entire, wanting nothing" (1:4).

Matthew	James
"Judge not unrighteously, that ye be not judged" (JST, 7:1).	"For he shall have judgment without mercy, that hath shewed no mercy" (2:13).
"Let your communication be, Yea, yea; Nay, nay" (5:37).	"Let your yea be yea; and your nay, nay" (5:12).
"Blessed are the meek" (5:5).	"Shew . . . meekness of wisdom" (3:13).
"Lay not up for yourselves treasures upon earth" (6:19).	"Your riches are corrupted" (5:2).
"Whosoever is angry with his brother shall be in danger of his judgment" (JST, 5:24).	"The wrath of man worketh not the righteousness of God" (1:20).
"Not every one that saith unto me, Lord, Lord, . . . but he that doeth" (7:21).	"What doth it profit . . . though a man say he hath faith, and have not works?" (2:14).[30]

As Jesus does in the Sermon on the Mount, of which James likely was aware, James gives counsel on what the faithful should do to reach perfection or spiritual maturity. One powerful example James uses to illustrate the connection between spiritual maturity and faith is in the controlling of the tongue: "For in many things we offend all. If any man offend not in word, the same is a perfect man, and able also to bridle the whole body" (James 3:2). James characterizes the tongue as "a little member, and boasteth great things" (James 3:5), "a fire, a world of iniquity: . . . and setteth on fire the course of nature; and it is set on fire of hell" (James 3:6), "but the tongue can no man tame; it is an unruly evil, full of deadly poison" (James 3:8).

President N. Eldon Tanner was as blunt as James. He said: "The tongue is the most dangerous, destructive, and deadly weapon available to man. A vicious tongue can ruin the reputation and even the future of the one attacked. Insidious attacks against one's reputation, loathsome innuendoes, half-lies about an individual are as deadly as those insect parasites that kill the heart and life of a mighty oak. They are so stealthy and cowardly that one cannot guard against them. As someone has said, 'It is easier to dodge an elephant than a microbe.'"[31] Learning to control the tongue, according to one commentator, is "overcoming the tendency of the mouth 'to stay open when it were more profitably closed.'"[32]

To attain perfection, or completeness, according to the Epistle of James, the believer is expected to exhibit a living, vitalized faith. This faith is manifest by good works such as patience and control of the tongue.

Wisdom

James discusses two kinds of wisdom: the wisdom of the world and the wisdom of God: "Who is a wise man and endued with knowledge among you? let him shew out of a good conversation his works with meekness of wisdom. But if ye have bitter envying and strife in your hearts, glory not, and lie not against the truth. This wisdom descendeth not from above, but is earthy, sensual, devilish. . . . But the wisdom that is from above is first pure, then peaceable, gentle, and easy to be intreated, full of mercy and good fruits" (James 3:13–15, 17).

James inextricably ties wisdom to good works. Like true faith that leads to righteous works, true knowledge correctly applied is wisdom that will lead to appropriate action. Nowhere is this more poignantly portrayed than in the account of the First Vision. After reading James 1:5, "If any of you lack wisdom, let him ask of God, that giveth to all men liberally, and upbraideth not; and it shall be given him," Joseph Smith recorded:

> Never did any passage of scripture come with more power to the heart of man than this did at this time to mine. It seemed to enter with great force into every feeling of my heart. I reflected on it again and again, knowing that if any person needed wisdom from God, I did; *for how to act I did not know,* and unless I could get more *wisdom* than I then had, I would never know; for the teachers of religion of the different sects understood the same passages of scripture so differently as to destroy all confidence in settling the question by an appeal to the Bible. At length I came to the conclusion that I must either remain in darkness and confusion, *or else I must do as James directs, that is, ask of God.* (Joseph Smith–History 1:12–13; emphasis added)

Joseph Smith's willingness to act on his faith, "as James directs," produced consequences beyond what even the Prophet himself could understand at that time. The effects of Joseph's decision to apply James's directive continues to unfold in both collective and individual ways and will likely do so until the work is done. Joseph may have read many other verses that taught about faith, but it was this verse in James that most profoundly compelled him to go into the grove of trees and offer his prayer of faith. Elder Bruce R. McConkie expressed it well: "This single verse of scripture has had a greater and a more far reaching effect upon mankind than any other single sentence ever recorded by any prophet in any age. It might well be said that the crowning act of the ministry of James was not his martyrdom for the testimony of Jesus, but his recitation, as guided by the Holy Ghost, of these simple words which led to the opening of the heavens in modern times."[33]

Works of Pride

James exposes some common manifestations of pride that the spiritually alert should avoid. These sins of pride are opposite of the fruits or works that grow out of true faith. James identifies some of these vices as coveting, killing (see James 4:2), adultery (see James 4:3), and greed (see James 5:1–5). James clearly ties these acts to pride with the question, "Know ye not that the friendship of the world is enmity with God?" (James 4:4). President Ezra Taft Benson observed that the meaning of pride is enmity or hostility toward God or our neighbor.[34] Well aware that pride is the source of evil, James counsels: "God resisteth the proud, but giveth grace unto the humble. . . . Humble yourselves in the sight of the Lord, and he shall lift you up" (James 4:6, 10).

Whether encouraging one to attain perfection, to seek wisdom, or to abhor the sins of pride, the Epistle of James bases its approach on the application of faith. Its pragmatic themes build on the notion that "faith without works is dead" (James 2:26).

James's Use of the Imperative Tense

The imperative command found throughout the letter displays James's desire for our dynamic discipleship. The following are some examples of his imperatives:

Chapter 1
  "Be perfect and entire" (1:4).
  "Ask of God" (1:5).
  "Ask in faith" (1:6).
  "Rejoice in that he is exalted" (1:9).

"Be swift to hear, slow to speak, slow to wrath" (1:19).
"Lay apart all filthiness" (1:21).
"Receive with meekness" (1:21).
"Be ye doers of the word" (1:22).
"Visit the fatherless" (1:27).

Chapter 2
"Hearken, my beloved brethren" (2:5).
"Love thy neighbor" (2:8).
"Keep the whole law" (2:10).
"So speak ye" (2:12).
"Shew me thy faith" (2:18).

Chapter 3
"Shew out of a good conversation" (3:13).
"Lie not against the truth" (3:14).

Chapter 4
"Submit yourselves . . . to God" (4:7).
"Resist the devil" (4:7).
"Draw nigh to God" (4:8).
"Cleanse your hands" (4:8).
"Purify your hearts" (4:8).
"Be afflicted, and mourn, and weep" (4:9).
"Humble yourselves" (4:10).
"Speak not evil" (4:11).

Chapter 5
"Go to now" (5:1).
"Be patient" (5:7).
"Stablish your hearts" (5:8).
"Grudge not" (5:9).
"Swear not" (5:12).
"Confess your faults" (5:16).
"Pray one for another" (5:16).

Things of Lasting Value

James counseled: "Go to now, ye that say, To day or to morrow we will go into such a city, and continue there a year, and buy and sell, and get gain: Whereas ye know not what shall be on the morrow. For what is your life? It is even a vapour, that appeareth for a little time, and then vanisheth away. For that ye ought to say, If the Lord will, we shall live, and do this, or that" (James 4:13–15). These verses point out that the time we are given in this life will eventually pass like a vapor and that we should focus our attention on the things that are most worthy—things that bring us closer to God. In the same vein, the Nephite prophet Amulek said: "For behold, this life is the time for men to prepare to meet God; yea, behold the day of this life is the day for men to perform their labors" (Alma 34:32).

Although James's epistle may have raised questions in the minds of some earlier Christians, it is a blessing that his inspired message on faith and works was providentially preserved for later generations. The words *faith (pistis)* and *works (ergon)* were defined to demonstrate their strong connection to obedience and faith as a living belief. Elder Talmage's thoughts on faith and works helped to illuminate James's views. The concepts of faith and works throughout the Epistle were examined according to three of James's general themes: perfection, wisdom, and pride. Finally, James's use of the imperative tense was shown to demonstrate his desire to reinforce an active faith.

Like the instructions of James to couple our faith with good works, the Lord has given similar counsel today: "Wherefore, if ye believe me, ye will labor while it is called today" (D&C 64:25). The Epistle of James is an articulate expression of the interrelationship between faith and works for Christians of his day and ours: "For as the body without the spirit is dead, so faith without works is dead also" (James 2:26).

NOTES

1. The term *faith* is used sixteen times in the Epistle of James, thirteen times in chapter 2. *Works* occurs thirteen times, twelve times in chapter 2.

2. Traditionally there are seven Catholic epistles: James; 1 and 2 Peter; 1, 2, and 3 John; and Jude.

3. Marcion rejected the entire Old Testament and accepted only the Gospel of Luke and ten epistles of Paul.

4. As found in Bruce M. Metzger, *The Canon of the New Testament* (Oxford: Clarendon Press, 1997), 235.

5. Eusebius assumes James is the brother of Jesus (see David Noel Freedman, ed., *The Anchor Bible Dictionary*, 6 vols. [New York: Doubleday, 1992], 3:622–23).

6. Freedman, *Anchor Bible Dictionary*, 3:622.

7. Freedman, *Anchor Bible Dictionary*, 3:622. "It is sometimes suggested that James's argument is prior to Paul's and that Paul wrote in part to answer

it, but while Paul's argument on justification does not require James's to explain it, the strongly polemical tone of James's language indicates that he knows a position which he is concerned to refute: 'and not by faith alone'" (Freedman, *The Anchor Bible Dictionary,* 625). See section 2 on James and Paul in the entry "James, Epistle of."

8. F. L. Cross, ed., *The Oxford Dictionary of the Christian Church* (Oxford: Oxford University Press, 1985), 499.

9. Cross, *The Oxford Dictionary of the Christian Church,* 499.

10. Cross, *The Oxford Dictionary of the Christian Church,* 499.

11. Gerhard Friedrich, ed., *Theological Dictionary of the New Testament,* 10 vols. (Grand Rapids, MI: Eerdmans, 1968), 6:175.

12. Friedrick, *Theological Dictionary of the New Testament,* 6:175.

13. Friedrick, *Theological Dictionary of the New Testament,* 6:187. See also Deuteronomy 9:23; Psalm 119:66.

14. Friedrick, *Theological Dictionary of the New Testament,* 6:199.

15. Friedrick, *Theological Dictionary of the New Testament,* 6:205; see also Ether 12:7–22.

16. Friedrick, *Theological Dictionary of the New Testament,* 6:208.

17. Friedrick, *Theological Dictionary of the New Testament,* 2:635.

18. Friedrick, *Theological Dictionary of the New Testament,* 2:637.

19. Friedrick, *Theological Dictionary of the New Testament,* 2:651.

20. Friedrick, *Theological Dictionary of the New Testament,* 2:651.

21. James E. Talmage, *A Study of the Articles of Faith* (Salt Lake City: Deseret Book, 1983), 87.

22. Talmage, *A Study of the Articles of Faith,* 88; see also James E. Talmage, *The Vitality of Mormonism* (Boston: Gorham Press, 1919), 79.

23. James E. Talmage, "Prove Thy Faith by Thy Works," *Improvement Era,* August 1914, 940–47.

24. Talmage, "Prove Thy Faith," 941.

25. Talmage, "Prove Thy Faith," 942. Concerning the writings of Paul, Talmage writes, "The spirit of all of Paul's writings is to the effect that when he thus spoke of a saving faith he meant faith; he did not mean mere belief, but belief plus the works which that belief comprises and postulates, and such combination is faith" (943).

26. Ralph Martin, ed., *World Biblical Commentary* (Waco, TX: Word Books, 1988), lxxix.

27. "Note James' characteristic corroborations of a positive statement by a negative clause: *entire, lacking in nothing; God that giveth and upbraideth not; in faith, nothing doubting*" (Martin R. Vincent, *Word Studies in the New Testament,* 4 vols. [Grand Rapids, MI: Eerdmans, 1975], 1:725).

28. Vincent, *Word Studies in the New Testament,* 1:724.

29. Joseph F. Smith, *Gospel Doctrine* (Salt Lake City: Deseret Book, 1977), 58.

30. Adapted from the *World Biblical Commentary,* lxxv–lxxvi. Note other parallels this commentary cites.

31. N. Eldon Tanner, in Conference Report, April 1972, 57.

32. Martin, *World Biblical Commentary,* 109.

33. Bruce R. McConkie, *Doctrinal New Testament Commentary,* 3 vols. (Salt Lake City: Bookcraft, 1973), 3:246–47.

34. Ezra Taft Benson, in Conference Report, April 1989, 3.

CHAPTER TWENTY-THREE

PETER, THE CHIEF APOSTLE

ANDREW C. SKINNER

Of all the personages in the New Testament, none is more important to the Latter-day Saints, save Jesus only, than Peter—Simon bar Jona by name. There is no question that the Church of Jesus Christ is founded upon the "chief corner stone," Jesus Christ Himself (Ephesians 2:20). All that the Church *is* and *was* is rooted in the Master. But Peter was the "seer" and "stone" of the early Church, titles designated by the Savior according to the Joseph Smith Translation of the Bible (JST, John 1:42).

Though the Apostle Paul is sometimes regarded by the world as the architect of Christianity,[1] and we ourselves look to him for doctrinal understanding, Peter was the chief Apostle in the meridian dispensation and held the position equivalent to that of the President of the Church of Jesus Christ in our day. Peter was a great prophet, seer, and revelator. He, along with James and John, who together constituted "the First Presidency of the Church in their day,"[2] received the keys of the kingdom from the Savior, Moses, Elijah, and others on the Mount of Transfiguration (see Matthew 17:1–13). In June 1829, Peter, James, and John returned to earth as immortal beings and conferred upon Joseph Smith and Oliver Cowdery the Melchizedek Priesthood and its keys and ordained them to be Apostles of the dispensation of the fulness of times (see D&C 27:12–13). Truly, Peter was a man for all seasons of the Lord's kingdom. Our purpose is to look at his life and actions and their significance for us today.

PETER'S LIFE AT THE TIME OF HIS CALL

We do not know when Peter was born, only that he was an adult living in Capernaum at the time the scriptures first introduce him to us. John's

---

Andrew C. Skinner is director of the Neal A. Maxwell Institute for Religious Scholarship.

Gospel says that Bethsaida was "the city of Andrew and Peter" (John 1:44), meaning perhaps that this was the ancestral family home or that these brothers were born there. Peter was married, and we know that his mother-in-law was staying in his house at Capernaum at the time Jesus healed her of a fever (see Mark 1:29–31), though we do not know if she was a permanent occupant of Peter's home.

Peter's house itself has an interesting history of its own that tells something about Peter's open and hospitable personality. Apparently, it was also the home of Peter's brother, Andrew (see Mark 1:29). It seems to have become the headquarters of the Church in Galilee, where lots of people gathered, especially after Jesus was rejected for the first time in His hometown of Nazareth (see Luke 4:23–31), and Capernaum came to be known as His "own city" (Matthew 9:1). One scholar has opined that Jesus "probably chose it because his first converts, the fishermen Peter and Andrew, lived there."[3] Note the way Mark describes one of the many gatherings in Peter's home after Jesus had been rejected in Nazareth:

> And again he entered into Capernaum after some days; and it was noised that he was in the house.
>
> And straightway many were gathered together, insomuch that there was no room to receive them, no, not so much as about the door: and he preached the word unto them.
>
> And they come unto him, bringing one sick of the palsy, which was borne of four.
>
> And when they could not come nigh unto him for the press, they uncovered the roof where he was: and when they had broken it up, they let down the bed wherein the sick of the palsy lay.
>
> When Jesus saw their faith, he said unto the sick of the palsy, Son, thy sins be forgiven thee. . . .
>
> I say unto thee, Arise, and take up thy bed, and go thy way into thine house.
>
> And immediately he arose, took up the bed, and went forth before them all. (Mark 2:1–5, 11–12)

Archaeology supports this story in an interesting way. The drystone basalt walls of the excavated house which is purported to be, and almost certainly is, Peter's domicile could have supported only a light roof and, when viewed on site by anyone familiar with the text, automatically conjures up the episode of the curing of the paralytic. Much evidence shows that this house was singled out and venerated from the mid-first century after Christ. One specific room in the house complex bears plastered walls and a large number of graffiti scratched thereon, some mentioning Jesus as Lord and Christ. In the mid-first century, the house underwent a significant change in use, from normal family activity to a general gathering or meeting place, indicating that it became one of the first house-churches in the Holy Land.[4] Additionally, the synoptic Gospels portray Peter's house as being near the Capernaum synagogue, and archaeological excavations reveal that it was indeed situated near both the ancient synagogue of the town, which was situated on a slight rise just north of the house *and* the shores of the Sea of Galilee, immediately south of the house. New Testament passages indicate that Peter was a fisherman with his brother and was an owner of fishing vessels on the Sea of Galilee.

That Peter was married is an important doctrinal statement, for marriage was a vital, even indispensable, institution both in first-century Judaism and among the leaders of the very Church the Lord Himself established while He was on the earth. From a comment in one of Paul's letters to the Corinthian Saints we learn that Peter carried out his ministry and pursued his apostolic travels with his wife at his side. Speaking for himself and his companion Barnabas, Paul asks rhetorically in his letter, "Have we not power to lead about a sister, a wife, as well as other apostles, and as the brethren of the Lord, and Cephas?" (1 Corinthians 9:5). Though the King James Version is a bit convoluted here, Paul is literally asking, "Don't we have the right to take a believing wife along with us, as do the other apostles and the Lord's brothers and Cephas [the Aramaic form of Peter]?"[5]

It seems significant that Paul gives Peter's name separate mention, apart from the "other apostles" whom he cites in a general way. Perhaps Peter's association with his wife was especially prominent, or perhaps Paul is recognizing Peter's preeminent status and example.

PETER'S CALL

Undoubtedly, Peter was foreordained in the grand council of our premortal life to occupy the singular position he was called to fill by the very Savior who was also foreordained and whom Peter would come to love and value more than life itself. The Prophet Joseph Smith taught, "Every man who has a calling to minister to the inhabitants of the world was ordained to that very purpose in the Grand Council of heaven before this world was."[6] The accounts of the four Gospels indicate that Peter became a disciple of our Lord in the very early days of Jesus' ministry but that the call to service was administered in stages, and the full realization of the significance of that calling was understood in stages. Perhaps curious at first blush, his initial call was bound up with his name. But when fully understood, the episode becomes a powerful illustration of an eternal principle.

Peter's actual given name was probably the Hebrew or Aramaic *Shim'on,* anglicized as Simeon (see Acts 15:14), meaning "one that hears." More often than not he is called Simon or Simon Peter in the New Testament. It has been argued that the frequency of the name *Simon* and the rare use of *Simeon* indicates that *Simon* was an alternate original name, was in common use during Jesus' day, and hints at Peter's contact with Greek culture. Thus, he was not simply an Aramaic-speaking Jew unaffected by Hellenistic forces in Galilee but rather "a bilingual Jew who thereby had some providential preparation for later missionary preaching."[7] Peter's father was Jonah. Hence, when Peter was addressed formally he was called, in Aramaic, Simon Bar Jona, "Simon son of Jonah." This is important information because it helps us to understand the significance of the first recorded encounter between the future Apostle and Jesus.

> Again the next day after, John stood, and two of his disciples,
> And looking upon Jesus as he walked, he said; Behold the Lamb of God!
> And the two disciples heard him speak, and they followed Jesus.
> Then Jesus turned, and saw them following him, and saith unto them, What seek ye? They said unto him, Rabbi, (which is to say, being interpreted, Master;) Where dwellest thou?
> He saith unto them, Come and see. And they came and saw where he dwelt, and abode with him that day; for it was about the tenth hour.
> One of the two who heard John, and followed Jesus, was Andrew, Simon Peter's brother.
> He first findeth his own brother Simon, and saith unto him, We have found the Messias, which is, being interpreted, the Christ.
> And he brought him to Jesus. And when Jesus beheld him, he said, Thou art Simon, the son of Jona, thou shalt be called Cephas, which is, by interpretation, a seer, or a stone. And they were fishermen. And they straightway left all, and followed Jesus. (JST, John 1:35–42)[8]

Here we learn several interesting things, not the least of which is the superior reading of the Joseph Smith Translation over the King James Version. However, note in particular that this first call to discipleship includes the promise of a new name for *Shim'on bar-Yonah.* This was not simply the offhanded bestowal of a convenient nickname as some have supposed. Rather, it was the application of a sacred and ancient principle, which is still administered in our own day. Whenever a new or higher level of commitment is made to the Lord and administered by the Lord or His servants, those disciples who agree to live on a higher plane or commit to a higher covenant receive a new name, just as the scriptures of the Restoration teach (see Mosiah 5:9–12; D&C 130:11).

In this case, the new name, Aramaic *Kepha'* (anglicized as Cephas), is the equivalent of the Greek *Petros,* or Peter, meaning "stone." But Joseph Smith presents an expanded interpretation of the Savior's intention by describing the meaning as "a *seer* or a stone," thus implying that the new name is better understood as "seer stone." Simon's new name reflected something of his mature role as "seer stone" or revelatory anchor of God's earthly kingdom. In other words, just as a seer stone is an instrument of revelation, the Savior was outlining the future role of the chief Apostle by saying, in effect, Peter would be the instrument through whom revelation for the Church would come. An example of this may be seen in Peter's vision concerning Cornelius reported in Acts 10.

Also important to note is that Peter and John, the first of the specifically named disciples to be called, had been looking for the Messiah. Their commitment to Jesus of Nazareth as the Christ was not "out of the blue." They had been led to search for the Messiah by a mentor. That mentor, as implied in a few New Testament passages, was none other than John the Baptist, whose testimony occupies a good portion of the prologue or first chapter of the Gospel of John the Revelator. In other words, Peter was a disciple of John the Baptist *before* he became a disciple of the Savior. And probably so had most of those disciples who later became the members of the first Quorum of the Twelve Apostles in the meridian dispensation. This is implied in a statement attributed to Peter himself. During one of the first meetings of the Church held after the Savior's ascension, Peter explained to the congregation—about 120 in number—that another needed to be appointed to fill the vacancy in the Quorum of the Twelve left by Judas's death: "Wherefore of these men which have companied with us all the time that the Lord Jesus went in and out among us, beginning from the baptism of John, unto that same day that he was taken up from us, must one be ordained to be a witness with us of his resurrection" (Acts 1:21–22).

As indicated above, Peter was called to the ministry in a *series* of episodes, each of which progressively impressed on his mind a fuller understanding of both the nature of the call, as well as the nature of the Being extending it, *and* the need for Peter to live in complete harmony with his new calling, which was to become his vocation. Sometime after Peter's initial call from the Savior, Luke's record indicates that Peter was back fishing in the Sea of Galilee when the Savior again bade Peter to follow Him.

> And [Jesus] saw two ships standing by the lake: but the fishermen were gone out of them, and were washing their nets.
>
> And he entered into one of the ships, which was Simon's, and prayed him that he would thrust out a little from the land. And he sat down, and taught the people out of the ship.
>
> Now when he had left speaking, he said unto Simon, Launch out into the deep, and let down your nets for a draught.
>
> And Simon answering said unto him, Master, we have toiled all the night, and have taken nothing: nevertheless at thy word I will let down the net.
>
> And when they had this done, they inclosed a great multitude of fishes: and their net brake.
>
> And they beckoned unto their partners, which were in the other ship, that they should come and help them. And they came, and filled both the ships, so that they began to sink.
>
> When Simon Peter saw it, he fell down at Jesus' knees, saying, Depart from me; for I am a sinful man, O Lord.
>
> For he was astonished, and all that were with him, at the draught of the fishes which they had taken:
>
> And so was also James, and John, the sons of Zebedee, which were partners with Simon. And Jesus said unto Simon, Fear not; from henceforth thou shalt catch men.
>
> And when they had brought their ships to land, they forsook all, and followed him. (Luke 5:2–11)

Though Peter had had previous encounters with the Savior, this time he was so impressed and overcome by the dramatic miracle Jesus performed (perhaps precisely in order to get Peter's attention) that Peter not only recognized his own unworthiness in the face of such staggering power and towering righteousness but also forsook his fishing business with whole-hearted commitment. Commensurate with Peter's commitment on this occasion, Jesus in turn promised Peter and the sons of Zebedee that thenceforth they would do far more than harvest a few fish to satisfy only temporal desires—they would now "catch men," meaning they would have the ultimate power to perform a greater harvest of souls and bring them within the wide sweep of the gospel net. Hence, the object lesson of the increased catch of fish wrought by the Savior's power moments before would, at that instant, have conveyed a poignantly symbolic message, with the Savior saying, in effect, just as I increased the fish harvest manyfold, the greater miracle is the power I will now give to you to increase the soul harvest.

From this time onward, it appears that Peter and his associates fulfilled their commitment to Jesus and to the kingdom with total devotion. We do not see them returning to their old vocation of fishing until *after* the Savior's Crucifixion and Resurrection. During that period of transition the Apostles knew they were supposed to do something to lead the Church in the absence of their Master but seemed unsure of what exactly they were supposed to do because the Savior was not constantly and directly tutoring them anymore. (It will be remembered that this episode occasioned the Savior's renewed call yet again to Peter to feed His sheep as recorded in John 21.)

PETER'S APOSTOLIC ROLE

Thus, from the day of the Savior's call by the Sea of Galilee to the time Jesus was taken away from him, Peter followed the Savior, first as a full-time disciple, and then as a full-time Apostle, living with his Teacher, learning his Master's message and method of ministry, and performing delegated tasks. The Greek word for "disciple," *mathētēs,* is the equivalent of the Hebrew *talmid* and means "learner," or "pupil/student," hence "disciple." The rabbis taught that continual and intimate association with one's teacher was an integral part of the learning process. And so it was with the disciples of Jesus. However, unlike the disciples of the other great rabbis of intertestamental Judaism, who were encouraged to choose for themselves their own master or teacher, Peter and his associates who eventually became members of the Quorum of the Twelve were reminded that they had been chosen by the Master (see John 15:16).

Jesus chose the first members of the Quorum of the Twelve from among all the disciples by the same method by which we may be guided: personal revelation.

> And it came to pass in those days, that he went out into a mountain to pray, and continued all night in prayer to God.
>
> And when it was day, he called unto him his disciples: and of them he chose twelve, whom also he named apostles;
>
> Simon, (whom he also named Peter,) and Andrew his brother, James and John, Phillip and Bartholomew,
>
> Matthew and Thomas, James the son of Alphaeus, and Simon called Zelotes,
>
> And Judas the brother of James, and Judas Iscariot, which also was the traitor. (Luke 6:12–16)

Noteworthy in this passage, and also typical of others, is the mention of Peter's name first. Whenever the Quorum of the Twelve is discussed in the New Testament, Peter is *always* mentioned and is always the *first one* mentioned or named. In fact, Peter is often singled out even when the rest of the group is noted only in a general way. A few examples will suffice:

"Simon and they that were with him followed after him" (Mark 1:36);

"Peter and they that were with him said, Master, the multitude throng thee and press thee, and sayest thou, Who touched me?" (Luke 8:45);

"Peter and they that were with him were heavy with sleep" (Luke 9:32);

Even the angelic messenger in the sepulchre says to the women, "But go your way, tell his disciples and Peter that he goeth before you into Galilee" (Mark 16:7).

As these passages demonstrate, often Peter's name is given specifically, while the others "that were with him" remain anonymous. But that is not all. In the New Testament, Peter is usually found acting or speaking for the whole group of Apostles and disciples and is inferred to be the authorized spokesman for the group. For example:

At Caesarea Philippi, after a few comments had been proffered by various members of the Quorum as to what people were saying about Jesus' identity, Peter spoke out boldly, declaring his apostolic witness ultimately for the whole group, and affirmed Jesus' messiahship and divine sonship (see Matthew 16:13–16).

In Capernaum, after many had ceased from following the Savior owing to their offense at the Bread of Life discourse, Peter spoke for the entire group of Apostles in affirming to Jesus their commitment to remain with Him because they were sure that He was Christ, the Son of the living God (see John 6:66–69).

In Perea, after their encounter with the rich young ruler who went away sorrowing over his inability to give up his possessions, Peter spoke on behalf of the whole group to remind the Savior that they had forsaken all and followed Him (see Matthew 19:27).

Many other examples of Peter's recognized leadership of the disciples generally, and his preeminent position in the Quorum of the Twelve specifically, could be marshaled. But more important than amassing examples of his preeminence is to understand why Peter was singled out and that such prominence was not based on favoritism but on Peter's role among the Apostles as the senior member of the Quorum. The principle of seniority in the Quorum of the Twelve is critically important in the Lord's Church—not to the men themselves but to the Lord because of the implications such seniority has for determining who the next President of the Church will be.

Peter was the senior Apostle on earth and as such held the keys of the kingdom. President Harold B. Lee taught that "Peter, holding the keys of the kingdom, was as much the president of the High Priesthood in his day as Joseph Smith and his successors, to whom also these 'keys' were given in our day, are the presidents of the High Priesthood and the earthly heads of the Church and kingdom of God on the earth."[9] From Doctrine and Covenants 132:7 we learn that "there is never but one [man] on the earth at a time on whom this power and the keys of this priesthood are conferred." In other words, the keys of presidency over the whole Church "can be exercised in their fulness on the earth by only one man at a time; and that man in the period just after Jesus ascended into heaven was Peter."[10]

The man who holds the keys in their fulness at any one time on the earth is always the Lord's senior Apostle on earth. That is why seniority is so critical. Elder Russell M. Nelson provided an important insight into an episode from Peter's life which demonstrates the principle of seniority:

> Seniority is honored among ordained Apostles—even when entering or leaving a room. President Benson related to us this account:
>
> "Some [years] ago Elder Haight extended a special courtesy to President Romney while they were in the upper room in the temple. President Romney was lingering behind for some reason, and [Elder Haight] did not want to precede him out the door. When President

Romney signaled [for him] to go first, Elder Haight replied, 'No President, you go first.'

"President Romney replied with his humor, 'What's the matter, David? Are you afraid I'm going to steal something?'"

Such deference from a junior to a senior Apostle is recorded in the New Testament. When Simon Peter and John the Beloved ran to investigate the report that the body of their crucified Lord had been taken from the sepulcher, John, being younger and swifter, arrived first, yet he did not enter. He deferred to the senior Apostle, who entered the sepulcher first. (See John 20:2–6.) Seniority in the Apostleship has long been a means by which the Lord selects His presiding high priest.[11]

In this light, it seems significant that after His Resurrection, Jesus appeared to Peter singly and apart from all others (see Luke 24:34). And though Peter always maintained a reverent silence about the nature of the visitation, surely it had something to do with the fact that Peter was the President of the Church and held the keys in their fulness, and as such was the one being on earth commissioned to receive the mind and will of Deity in all matters.[12] In a sense, he was taking the place of Jesus as the head of the Church in mortality.

CAESAREA PHILIPPI AND THE PROMISE OF KEYS

Crucial for our understanding of Peter's role as President of the Church and holder of the keys of the kingdom are two pivotal events occurring only a week apart—both of them associated powerfully with the principle of revelation. In the fall season of the year, some six months before His Crucifixion, the Savior took His disciples to the northern reaches of the Holy Land—a beautiful area at the foot of Mount Hermon called Caesarea Philippi. There Peter, acting as spokesman for the group, testified with certitude that Jesus was both Messiah and Son of the living God. In turn, the Savior then promised the chief Apostle that he would be given the keys of the kingdom of God on earth; that is, the power to direct and administer the use of the priesthood on the earth, the power to seal and unseal all matters relative to eternal life. But the manner in which the Savior instructed Peter and the group surely ranks as one of the great, almost unparalleled, teaching moments in all of scripture. For the Master Teacher used not only a wordplay on the name "Peter" but also employed the surrounding geography (the bedrock base of Mount Hermon) as a grand visual aid to impress upon Peter and the others the fundamental principle underlying all that is done in the Lord's Church. Here are Jesus' words immediately following Peter's declaration of testimony:

> And Simon Peter answered and said, Thou art the Christ, the Son of the living God.
>
> And Jesus answered and said unto him, Blessed art thou, Simon Bar-jona: for flesh and blood hath not revealed it unto thee, but my Father which is in heaven.
>
> And I say also unto thee, That thou art Peter, and upon this rock I will build my church; and the gates of hell shall not prevail against it.
>
> And I will give unto thee the keys of the kingdom of heaven: and whatsoever thou shalt bind on earth shall be bound in heaven: and whatsoever thou shalt loose on earth shall be loosed in heaven. (Matthew 16:16–19)

Anyone who has stood at the bedrock base of Mount Hermon can almost picture the Savior riveting His gaze upon Peter and saying to the chief Apostle, "You are *Petros*" (meaning "stone" or "small rock" according to footnote Matthew 16:18a in the LDS edition of the King James Bible). Then, in the same breath, pointing to the bedrock face of the mountainside near where they stood, Jesus declared, "And upon this *petra* [meaning "bedrock"] I will build my church."

Through this very graphic, natural visual aid, the Savior's instruction, and hence His wordplay, becomes clear to us. Though critical to the Lord's true Church, it wasn't the chief Apostle himself who formed the foundation of the Church or the basis that underlies all that the Church does. True enough, Peter was, metaphorically speaking, a seer stone; he was to be the revelator for the Church, the person through whom came the mind and will of the Lord for the members of the Church. But pointing out Peter's role simply serves to underscore the basic principle upon which the Church was founded. The Church, including leaders, members, ordinances, and activities, was built upon the foundation of *revelation*, more specifically the personal revelation that Jesus is the Messiah, the actual Son of God, and the ultimate head of the Church.

Revelation (particularly the revelation that Jesus is the Christ) is the immovable base upon which the Church is built and the foundation upon which every person's testimony must be established, Apostle and layperson alike. Revelation is the foundation upon which Joseph Smith's faith and action were based. It is the principle underlying the First Vision. It is the principle which cannot be replaced by anything else. Possessed of his knowledge of Jesus' divine sonship and the revelatory experience by which that knowledge came, Peter could then serve as the vessel or instrument of revelation for the whole Church and the possessor and delegator of the keys and authority necessary to make Church ordinances and operations valid.

The Gospels of Matthew and Mark tell us that from this point on in His ministry the Savior began to teach His Apostles of His impending death and Resurrection. But Peter did not receive this idea warmly and attempted to rebuke the Savior, telling Him that death could not possibly be His lot (see Matthew 16:21–22). Likely Peter was still thinking of a Messiah in worldly terms—a political ruler and military conqueror on the order of King David or Solomon, who would restore Israel's grandeur and smash all enemies underfoot. Death at the hands of chief priests and scribes was not very messiahlike, let alone divine. Elder James E. Talmage says, "Peter saw mainly as men see, understanding but imperfectly the deeper purposes of God."[13] Peter still did not understand the nature of the true Messiah, and his outburst was an appeal to vanity, an encouragement for Jesus to demonstrate the overwhelming power of the kind Peter thought the true Messiah should possess.

Peter's remonstration evoked from Jesus a stern rebuke of his own. The Savior turned to the chief Apostle and uttered these famous words: "Get thee behind me, Satan: thou art an offence unto me: for thou savourest not the things that be of God, but those that be of men" (Matthew 16:23). Of this Elder Talmage says:

> In addressing Peter as "Satan," Jesus was obviously using a forceful figure of speech, and not a literal designation; for Satan is a distinct personage, Lucifer, that fallen, unembodied son of the morning; and certainly Peter was not he. In his remonstrance or "rebuke" addressed to Jesus, Peter was really counseling what Satan had before attempted to induce Christ to do, or tempting, as Satan himself had tempted. The command, "Get thee behind me, Satan," as directed to Peter, is rendered in English by some authorities "Get thee behind me, tempter." The essential meaning attached to both Hebrew and Greek originals for our word "Satan" is that of an adversary, or "one who places himself in another's way and thus opposes him." . . . The expression "Thou art an offense unto me" is admittedly a less literal

translation than "Thou art a stumbling-block unto me." The man whom Jesus had addressed as Peter—"the rock," was now likened to a stone in the path, over which the unwary might stumble.[14]

This is not the only instance of Peter being chastened by the Savior. There were others. But this episode provides a significant window of insight into Peter's personality, for it allows us to reflect on one of the truly admirable, even remarkable, qualities of Peter. Whenever he was corrected by his Master, he listened without argument, accepted the chastening, never became embittered, and demonstrated the kind of meekness that the greatest mortals on this earth have shown, including the very men Peter respected most (both Moses and Jesus were described as the meekest of men). Meekness is not weakness; certainly Peter was not weak. Meekness is teachableness in the face of correction or even provocation.

Speaking to a group of young people years ago, Elder Neal A. Maxwell provided a much needed reminder about this virtue of meekness possessed by the chief Apostle. He said: "Meekness, however, is more than self-restraint; it is the presentation of self in a posture of kindness and gentleness, reflecting certitude, strength, serenity, and a healthy self-esteem and self-control. . . . President Brigham Young, who was tested in many ways and on many occasions, was once tried in a way that required him to 'take it'—even from one he so much adored and admired. Brigham 'took it' because he was meek."[15] This not only describes Brigham Young but Simon Peter as well. He was chastened and he "took it" because it was administered by the perfect judge, and it was proper. However, a lesser man may not have reacted so well. In fact, was this Judas Iscariot's very problem?

THE MOUNT OF TRANSFIGURATION

Almost one week after Peter's historic declaration of testimony, the Savior's promise of forthcoming keys was fulfilled when Peter, James, and John accompanied their Master to a high mountain where they were transfigured in order to endure the presence of heavenly beings (Moses, Elijah, John the Baptist,[16] and probably others[17]). They heard the voice of God the Father bear witness of His Son in words reminiscent of Joseph Smith's First Vision, and they were shaken by it. "Then answered Peter, and said unto Jesus, Lord, it is good for us to be here: if thou wilt, let us make here three tabernacles; one for thee, and one for Moses, and one for Elias. While he yet spake, behold, a bright cloud overshadowed them: and behold a voice out of the cloud, which said, This is my beloved Son, in whom I am well pleased; hear ye him. And when the disciples heard it, they fell on their face, and were sore afraid" (Matthew 17:4–6).

We note again Peter's role as spokesman for the three Apostles and his offer to build tabernacles, indicating that the Feast of Succoth or Tabernacles was at hand. Several happenings marked this experience of the Apostles, and it is clear from Peter's mature reflection about the event, recorded sometime afterward, that it affected him deeply. Elder Bruce R. McConkie indicates that Peter and the other two Apostles apparently received their own endowments while on the mountain[18] and that Peter himself said something even more significant about his experience on the mount. From Peter's second epistle we read:

> Wherefore the rather, brethren, give diligence to make your call-ing and election sure: for if ye do these things, ye shall never fall: . . .
>
> For we have not followed cunningly devised fables, when we made known unto you the power and coming of our Lord Jesus Christ, but were eyewitnesses of his majesty.
>
> For he received from God the Father honour and glory, when there came such a voice to him from the excellent glory, This is my beloved Son, in whom I am well pleased.
>
> And this voice which came from heaven we heard, when we were with him in the holy mount.
>
> We have also a more sure word of prophecy; whereunto ye do well that ye take heed, as unto a light that shineth in a dark place, until the day dawn, and the day star arise in your hearts. (2 Peter 1:10, 16–19)

Elder McConkie seems to interpret Peter's language in light of Doctrine and Covenants 131:5, for he concludes that while Peter was on the Mount of Transfiguration he and his associates were sealed up to eternal life and this was made known to them by revelation. Doctrine and Covenants 131:5 states that "the more sure word of prophecy means a man's know-ing that he is sealed up unto eternal life, by revelation and the spirit of prophecy, through the power of the Holy Priesthood." Thus Elder McConkie wrote:

> Those members of the Church who devote themselves wholly to righteousness, living by every word that proceedeth forth from the mouth of God, make their *calling and election sure.* That is, they receive the more sure word of prophecy, which means that the Lord

seals their exaltation upon them while they are yet in this life. Peter summarized the course of righteousness which the saints must pursue to make their calling and election sure and then (referring to his experience on the Mount of Transfiguration with James and John) said that those three had received this more sure word of prophecy.[19]

The context of 2 Peter 1 lends some support to Elder McConkie's statement. Here Peter seems to be devoting an entire chapter to encouraging the Saints to make their "calling and election sure" (2 Peter 1:10) by discussing principles associated with this doctrine. This further leads Peter to discuss his own personal eyewitness experience of Christ's glory on the Mount of Transfiguration, which discussion he concludes by stating that he and the others with him received the more sure word of prophecy.

The Joseph Smith Translation of 2 Peter 1:19 provides another insight into Peter's thinking when it states, "We have therefore a more sure knowledge of the word of prophecy, to which word of prophecy ye do well that ye take heed." In other words, the heavenly voice gave the Apostles a more sure knowledge of the word of prophecy. They knew that the Old Testament prophecies were fulfilled regarding the Messiah; they had a surer sense of the accuracy of prophecies because they saw them actually fulfilled; they knew Jesus had the power to give eternal life.[20]

However one chooses to view Peter's experience on the Mount of Transfiguration as described in his second epistle, it seems absolutely clear that by the time 2 Peter 1 was written the chief Apostle knew a great deal about the doctrine of being sealed up to eternal life, undoubtedly through personal experience.

Peter also witnessed several other happenings of import on the Mount of Transfiguration, including a vision of the transfiguration of the earth. That is, he and his fellow Apostles saw the earth renewed and receive again its paradisiacal condition at the Second Coming and beginning of Christ's millennial reign. The Prophet Joseph Smith wrote: "Nevertheless, he that endureth in faith and doeth my will, the same shall overcome, and shall receive an inheritance upon the earth when the day of transfiguration shall come; when the earth shall be transfigured, even according to the pattern which was shown unto mine apostles upon the mount; of which account the fulness ye have not yet received" (D&C 63:20–21).

Peter's experience on the Mount of Transfiguration was monumental by any standard and may well have been the most significant event for the Church between the start of Christ's mortal ministry and His atoning sacrifice. It secured the keys of the kingdom to man on earth and taught the Lord's prophet about the reality of visions, heavenly beings, and the true relationship between Jesus and His Father, who is the true and living God.

WITNESS TO MIRACLES

It was Peter's special privilege to witness powerful miracles performed by Jesus, often in the company of few others. He was singled out, for instance, with James and John to see the Savior raise the daughter of Jairus from death back to life (see Mark 5:37–43). He was present on one occasion with the other disciples when the Savior fed five thousand with just a few morsels of food (see John 6:5–13, 68). He was in the boat when Jesus stilled the storm-tossed waves of the Sea of Galilee and then saw evil spirits cast out of someone of the Decapolis region (see Luke 8:22–33). He witnessed the Savior heal the blind, deaf, and crippled, and perform several other healings which demonstrated the Lord's compassion and power (see Luke 8:1; Mark 1:30–34). By the time the Lord's mortal ministry came to an end, the chief Apostle was no stranger to supernatural occurrences, for he was an eyewitness to marvelous manifestations of the powers of faith and priesthood. On one occasion, immediately following the feeding of the five thousand, Jesus sent the Apostles on ahead in a boat across the Sea of Galilee, while he went to "a mountain apart to pray" (Matthew 14:23) because the people wanted to "take him by force, to make him a king" (John 6:15). When night had fallen, and the wind on the sea became "boisterous," Jesus began walking on the water to go to the Apostles in their boat, sometime between 3:00 and 6:00 A.M., the time when fishermen on the Sea of Galilee are concluding their nightly fishing expeditions. The Apostles were naturally afraid, believing they were seeing a ghost. But Jesus identified Himself and encouraged His disciples to "be of good cheer" (Matthew 14:27). Certainly the Savior's power to perform mighty miracles was confirmed to Peter, and perhaps emboldened by a demonstration of that incomparable power, Peter requested of the Savior to bid him to come to Him. But once upon the water, and seeing the tumultuous wind and waves all around, Peter began to sink.

We glean from Peter's experience a significant lesson—one doubtlessly recounted many times in our New Testament classes: when Peter's focus was taken off the Savior and attracted to the surrounding conditions and great turbulence, he floundered. How like life for us! We must ever stay focused on the Savior. But if we flounder, as did Peter, we too may be lifted up by the Savior's outstretched hand of help (see Matthew 14:28–31).

But also we learn from this experience, as did Peter, another lesson: that faith and fear are incompatible (see Matthew 14:31). How many times do we take counsel from our fears and ultimately forfeit a glorious reward we might have received if we had pressed forward in faith? Perhaps this is why Oliver Cowdery was not allowed to continue his initial efforts at translating the Book of Mormon—distractions and fears overcame his capacity to receive revelation (see D&C 9:5).

I believe Peter learned much about himself as well as the Savior on this occasion. But I also wonder if this episode didn't come back into sharp remembrance for Peter on a future occasion when he came across another person years later at the entrance to the Jerusalem temple who was struggling—only with a physical infirmity. Luke describes the episode with poignancy.

> Now Peter and John went up together into the temple at the hour of prayer, being the ninth hour.
>
> And a certain man lame from his mother's womb was carried, whom they laid daily at the gate of the temple which is called Beautiful, to ask alms of them that entered into the temple;
>
> Who seeing Peter and John about to go into the temple asked an alms.
>
> And Peter, fastening his eyes upon him with John, said, Look on us.
>
> And he gave heed unto them, expecting to receive something of them.
>
> Then Peter said, Silver and gold have I none; but such as I have give I thee: In the name of Jesus Christ of Nazareth rise up and walk.
>
> And he took him by the right hand, and lifted him up: and immediately his feet and ankle bones received strength. (Acts 3:1–7)

The parallel can hardly be missed. The chief Apostle took the floundering man at the temple by the hand and lifted him out of his distress just as Jesus had lifted Peter out of his distress years earlier on the Sea of Galilee. This shows us just how much Peter was destined to become like his Master when he became the earthly head of the Church.

THE LAST SUPPER

Peter's prominent role among the Twelve during the planning of and participation in the Last Supper is reported by the four Gospels. Mark and Matthew indicate that as Passover approached, the disciples asked about preparing for the feast (see Mark 14:1; Matthew 26:17). Knowing how Peter usually acted as the spokesman for the group, one wonders if he wasn't the one asking the question for the disciples. Luke says Jesus sent Peter and John to prepare the Passover, giving them specific instructions on when to make ready the feast and giving them a prophetic sign on how they would find the preappointed place. "And he said unto them, Behold, when ye are entered into the city, there shall a man meet you, bearing a pitcher of water; follow him into the house where he entereth in. And ye shall say unto the goodman of the house, The Master saith unto thee, Where is the guestchamber, where I shall eat the passover with my disciples? And he shall shew you a large upper room furnished: there make ready" (Luke 22:10–12).

This instruction is interesting for at least two reasons. A man bearing a pitcher of water was an unmistakable sign since it was such an unusual sight. Also, it is obvious that the man whose house was to be used for the Passover or Seder meal that evening was himself a disciple of the Savior. Jesus tells Peter and John that the owner would know they were making the request on behalf of the Savior when they invoked the phrase, "The Master saith unto thee . . ." The owner of the house would not understand who "the Master" was unless he was a disciple.

As the actual Passover supper unfolded in the Upper Room, several significant events occurred that directly involved Peter. Jesus revealed His knowledge of a betrayer, and Peter was the one who prompted John to ask of Jesus the identity of the betrayer (see John 13:24). During the course of the evening, two great ordinances were instituted that have had lasting impact. One was the transformation of the Passover meal into the Sacrament of the Lord's Supper, and the other was the washing of the feet. As Jesus prepared to wash His disciples' feet, Peter objected—perhaps believing that such a menial task was beneath the dignity of his Master. However, the Savior both reproved and instructed the chief Apostle, teaching him that he would someday come to a knowledge of the true significance of the ordinance and thus appreciate why it was performed the way it was (see John 13:6–11).

Of tremendous significance during the Upper Room experience were the

Savior's instruction to His Apostles about their ultimate reaction to the evening's proceedings—"All ye shall be offended because of me this night"—and Peter's response, even protest, that "though all men shall be offended because of thee, yet will I never be offended" (Matthew 26:31–33). Jesus' pointed and specific rejoinder to Peter teaches profound lessons, especially the confidence Jesus had in Peter's faithfulness and the potential He knew Peter possessed. "And the Lord said, Simon, Simon, behold, Satan hath desired to have you, that he may sift you as wheat: But I have prayed for thee, that thy faith fail not: and when thou art converted, strengthen thy brethren" (Luke 22:31–32).

The thought that any prayer offered by the Savior would not come to pass nor that any prediction of His not be fulfilled is unthinkable. Peter's faith would not fail even though he had a deeper conversion yet to experience. The texts of all four Gospels indicate that even up to that point Peter still did not fully comprehend the earth-shaking events soon to overtake the Savior and the early Church. But again the Savior patiently tried to teach Peter of things that must come to pass. "Simon Peter said unto him, Lord, whither goest thou? Jesus answered him, Whither I go, thou canst not follow me now; but thou shalt follow me afterwards. Peter said unto him, Lord, why cannot I follow thee now? I will lay down my life for thy sake. Jesus answered him, Wilt thou lay down thy life for my sake? Verily, verily, I say unto thee, The cock shall not crow, till thou hast denied me thrice" (John 13:36–38). Peter was never one to shrink from danger, and we cannot doubt that at that moment and all the moments before and after that point Peter would have forfeited his life for his Master's.

PETER'S DENIAL

Of all the episodes associated with the life of Peter, perhaps the most famous and oft-repeated is his denial of the Lord when the latter was being arraigned before the high priest. The sequence leading up to this scene is important for helping us understand the nature of the denial. After the Last Supper concluded, events moved quickly as the Apostles followed Jesus to the Garden of Gethsemane. Again, Peter's prominent status was manifested as he and the sons of Zebedee, James and John, were given a special vantage point from which to witness the Savior's suffering—though fatigue and doubt ultimately prevented them from both receiving the blessings that could have been theirs and from providing the hand of support to their Master that He so desperately needed at that hour in the garden (see JST, Mark 14:36–38). Three times the Savior came to reprove their murmurings and their weariness. However, in all fairness to the Apostles, we need to remember that they had been awake for a long time and had just gone through a long and emotionally draining Passover experience with the Savior.

When the Savior finished praying the same prayer for the third time in Gethsemane, the Jerusalem temple police force appeared on the scene ready to arrest Jesus. What happened next is stunning, to be sure, but completely in harmony with everything we know about the boldness, fearlessness, and death-defying willingness of Peter to defend his Master. John's Gospel tells the story best.

> Then asked he them again, Whom seek ye? And they said, Jesus of Nazareth.
>
> Jesus answered, I have told you that I am he: if therefore ye seek me, let these go their way:
>
> That the saying might be fulfilled, which he spake, Of them which thou gavest me have I lost none.
>
> Then Simon Peter having a sword drew it, and smote the high priest's servant, and cut off his right ear. The servant's name was Malchus.
>
> Then said Jesus unto Peter, Put up thy sword into the sheath: the cup which my Father hath given me, shall I not drink it?
>
> Then the band and the captain and officers of the Jews took Jesus, and bound him. (John 18:7–12)

It must be remembered that Peter's selfless act of protection was done in the face of an armed mob who could have easily overwhelmed the chief Apostle. And it should be noted that Jesus rebuked Peter for trying to stop the arrest. It should also be noted that with the retelling of this episode John highlights a theme woven throughout the evening's happenings: Jesus was extremely protective of His Apostles.

Jesus was taken to the palace of the high priest, where He first appeared before the former high priest, Annas (father-in-law of the current high priest), then arraigned before Caiaphas and others. All the Gospels report Peter's denial, suggesting to us that this was truly a pivotal event. The details need not detain us here, how Peter stood outside of the high priest's house on that cool night and denied knowing Jesus after interrogation by two women and a man (see Matthew 26:69–75; Mark 14:66–72; Luke

22:56–62; John 18:17–27). What gives us great pause, however, is consideration of Peter's motivation. Why did he deny knowing his Master? The reasons usually given range from fear of personal harm, to weakness, to embarrassment, to pride, to indecision or some other reason centering on a flaw or weakness in Peter's character.

However, this seems to contradict everything else we know and have read about Peter in the New Testament, including his confession of the Savior's sonship at Caesarea Philippi and his single-minded resolve not to allow anyone to harm the Savior, especially evil men. In every instance where the impending arrest or death of Jesus had come to Peter's attention, he had been both quick and forceful to say that he would not let such a thing happen (see Matthew 16:21–23) and he would protect Jesus at all costs, even at the peril of his own life, which is what we saw happen in Gethsemane when the armed forces of the chief priests could not intimidate a chief Apostle who was ready to battle them all (see John 18:7–12). Now we are to believe that in the face of a challenge initially put forward by a slave girl, the most unimportant person imaginable in Jewish society, Peter denied even knowing Jesus for fear of being exposed as a follower? (The word *damsel* used in the KJV does not convey the true, lowly position of Peter's first interrogator.)

Years ago, President Spencer W. Kimball invited us to reevaluate our understanding of Peter's actions in a magnificent article entitled "Peter, My Brother." Here another chief Apostle, writing about his model and mentor, asks crucial and penetrating questions: Do we really know Peter's mind and heart? Are we sure? Do we understand the circumstances of Peter's denial as well as we think we do? President Kimball discusses the tremendous strength, power, faithfulness, and apostolic attributes of Peter, including his boldness, and then says:

> Much of the criticism of Simon Peter is centered in his denial of his acquaintance with the Master. This has been labeled "cowardice." Are we sure of his motive in that recorded denial? He had already given up his occupation and placed all worldly goods on the altar for the cause. . . .
>
> Is it conceivable that the omniscient Lord would give all these powers and keys to one who was a failure or unworthy? . . .
>
> If Peter was frightened in the court when he denied his association with the Lord, how brave he was hours earlier when he drew his sword against an overpowering enemy, the night mob. Later defying

the people and state and church officials, he boldly charged, "Him [the Christ] . . . ye have taken, and by wicked hands have crucified and slain." (Acts 2:23.) To the astounded populace at the healing of the cripple at the Gate Beautiful, he exclaimed, "Ye men of Israel . . . the God of our fathers, hath glorified his Son Jesus; whom ye delivered up, and denied him in the presence of Pilate. . . . ye denied the Holy One. . . . And killed the Prince of life, whom God hath raised from the dead; whereof we are witnesses." (Acts 3:12–15.)

Does this portray cowardice? Quite a bold assertion for a timid one. Remember that Peter never denied the divinity of Christ. He only denied his association or acquaintance with the Christ, which is quite a different matter. . . .

Is it possible that there might have been some other reason for Peter's triple denial? Could he have felt that circumstances justified expediency? When he bore a strong testimony in Caesarea Philippi, he had been told that "they should tell no man that he was Jesus the Christ." (Matthew 16:20.)[21]

To what then might we attribute Peter's denial? Simply, to Jesus Himself—to the Savior's request that Peter deny knowing the Savior, not deny the Savior's divinity but deny knowing the Savior. Why? To ensure Peter's safety as chief Apostle and to ensure the continuity and safety of the Quorum of the Twelve.

By the time of His arrest, Jesus had become very protective of His Apostles, and the safety of the Quorum had become a major concern for the Savior. In His great high priestly prayer, the Savior prayed for the safety of the Apostles. "I have given them thy word, and the world hath hated them, because they are not of the world, even as I am not of the world. I pray not that thou shouldest take them out of the world, but that thou shouldest keep them from the evil" (John 17:14–15). When He was arrested in the Garden, He said to the mob, "I have told you that I am he: if therefore ye seek me, let these go their way" (John 18:8). Jesus did not want and could not let anything happen to those who were ordained to take over the earthly leadership of the Church. Jesus had told Peter at the Last Supper that He had prayed that Peter's faith would not fail—and it did not. As President Kimball stated: "Peter was under fire; all the hosts of hell were against him. The die had been cast for the Savior's crucifixion. If Satan could destroy Simon now, what a victory he would score. Here was the greatest of all living men. Lucifer wanted to confuse him, frustrate him, limit his prestige, and totally destroy him. However, this was not to be, for he was chosen and ordained to a high purpose in heaven, as was Abraham."[22]

In sum, it is apparent that Jesus knew of Peter's fearlessness in defending Him. He had seen several manifestations of Peter's unswerving, almost reckless, commitment to prevent any physical harm from coming to the Savior. And this was something Jesus knew could get Peter into trouble if not tempered. It would put the chief Apostle in grave physical danger. Therefore, I believe that when Jesus told Peter he would deny Him thrice before the cock crowed twice, it was not a prediction; it was a command. This is, in fact, a possible reading of the synoptic texts, according to the grammatical rules of Koine Greek found in the New Testament. Matthew 26:34, 75; Mark 14:30, 72; and Luke 22:61 all use the same verb and verb form, *aparnēsē,* which can be read as an indicative future tense or as an imperative (command) tense.[23] We are grateful to a prophet of the stature of President Kimball for helping us to look at events in the New Testament differently.

Some might ask, "Why then did Peter weep bitterly after his denial?" I believe these were tears of frustration and sorrow in the realization that he was powerless to change the Lord's fate. He had done what needed to be done, but every impulse inside him was to act differently—to prevent the suffering of the Savior. This was a bitter pill for Peter to swallow. These were tears of frustration precisely because he was obedient but now also fully cognizant of the fact that he was going to lose his Messiah to the inevitability of death. In my view, Peter's denial adds to his stature—not detracts from it!

JUST BEFORE THE ASCENSION

No doubt Peter endured some awful moments during and just after the Savior's horrible Crucifixion, but the joy of seeing for himself his risen Lord again and knowing that all the messianic promises were truly fulfilled in the Being he had followed the previous three years surely must have made up for the anguish. After His Resurrection, the Savior appeared to Peter at the Sea of Galilee (called Tiberias in John 21:1) to reinforce the most important lessons of Peter's life. John tells us that this was the Savior's third postresurrection appearance to His disciples (see John 21:14). Peter and his associates may have been frustrated, struggling to find their niche during this challenging period of transition. For when Peter announced that he was going fishing, the others said they were going too (see John 21:3). What else was there to do besides return to their old profession now that things had changed so radically after the Resurrection and they were not sure exactly how to proceed with the work of the Lord?

After the group had fished all night and caught nothing, Jesus appeared on the shore, told them where to cast their nets, and watched them gather a miraculous harvest. When Peter realized it was Jesus, he became so eager to be reunited with his Master that he jumped into the water to hurry to shore. There he found that the Savior had fixed a fire and cooked breakfast for him and his associates. What a scene it must have been, and what emotions must have swelled within the disciples! They were cold and tired and hungry. They needed help, and once again there was the Savior to minister to their needs. We must be clear about this. The Savior of the universe had already performed an eternity's worth of service to them and all humankind through the infinite Atonement. He was God! And yet it was not beneath His dignity to care for their personal needs, to demonstrate His personal concern for their economic circumstances, to warm them and make them comfortable, and even to cook for them. In this atmosphere of total service and against the backdrop of His personal example of selfless concern for others, Jesus was able to teach Peter what he must do for the rest of his life—feed the Savior's sheep as the Savior had fed him that morning (see John 21:9–17). The rest of the New Testament from this point on shows us that the lesson was not lost on the chief Apostle.

A Mighty Church President

After the Savior's ascension, it is clear that Peter assumed the reins of Church leadership with the same boldness he executed his role as chief Apostle when Jesus was on the earth. He guided the selection of Judas Iscariot's replacement in the Quorum of the Twelve by teaching powerfully from the scriptures (see Acts 1:15–26). In fact, he taught from the scriptures on many occasions. He received a reconfirming witness from the Holy Ghost on the day of Pentecost regarding the divinity of the work and issued his clarion call to the pentecostal converts to be baptized and receive the gift of the Holy Ghost (see Acts 2). He was arrested, imprisoned, and threatened by the Sanhedrin for powerfully declaring his eyewitness testimony of the Savior's Resurrection without equivocation, as well as charging the Jewish leaders with the death of his Master without flinching (see Acts 3:12–26; 4:8–20).

When the Lord was ready to expand His Church, He revealed to Peter His plan to allow Gentiles to be admitted to the ranks of Church membership. And it was simultaneously to Cornelius that the Lord revealed His will that Cornelius send messengers to bring Simon Peter to Caesarea (see Acts 10). This helps us to remember that as the President of the Church and the holder of the keys of the kingdom, such monumental changes in the Church were mandated by the Lord to come through Peter and through no one else.

Peter continued to have marvelous manifestations after the Lord's ascension, as when the angel of the Lord came at night to release Peter from prison and protect him from the same fate that James, the brother of John, had suffered at the hands of Herod Agrippa I (see Acts 12). In fact, the first twelve chapters of Acts center on the actions of Peter, while chapters 13–28 highlight the ministry of Paul—the great Apostle to the Gentiles. But other books make it clear that Peter continued an active ministry to and was the revered leader of the Jewish segment of the Church while Paul was working with the Gentiles (see Galatians 2:8). During this time Paul had an open dispute with Peter over the Gentiles in the Church. Apparently, at one point after submitting to the influence of James, Peter withdrew from eating with the Gentiles, for which Paul "withstood him to the face" (Galatians 2:11). Yet, as Elder McConkie pointed out, even though Paul may have had a legitimate issue to raise, Peter was still the President of the Church and Paul was still his junior.[24]

CLOSE OF HIS MINISTRY

Toward the end of his life, Peter ended up in Rome. In one of his personal letters addressed to the Saints in the five major provinces of Asia Minor, he sends greetings from "Babylon," which is probably none other than the great capital city of the Roman Empire (see 1 Peter 5:13). The early Church historian Eusebius tells us that 1 Peter was written in Rome.[25] Even more interesting is the statement telling us of those who were with Peter at that time in his life, particularly Marcus (1 Peter 5:13)—likely the same who was the author of the Gospel of Mark and scribe for the chief Apostle. One can imagine the younger John Mark recording the teachings and reminiscences of Peter, copying down the eyewitness testimony of all the Lord said and did including the foundational doctrines learned. Surely it was from these experiences with Peter that Mark gleaned the necessary

information for his Gospel record as well as the content for the two sur-
viving letters sent by the chief Apostle.

Within Peter's two epistles is to be found an important and helpful survey of some of the major doctrines of the early Church of Jesus Christ,
including the sinlessness of Jesus; the redemptive power of His atoning
blood (see 1 Peter 1:18–20; 2:24–25; 3:18); the postmortal, spirit-prison
ministry of Christ (see 1 Peter 3:19–20; 4:6); baptism (see 1 Peter 3:21);
priesthood (see 1 Peter 2:9); and others. Some of the greatest contributions
towards helping the Saints (ancient and modern) understand, appreciate,
and withstand life's trials and tribulations come from Peter's two epistles.
These include such encouraging exhortations as the following:
- The Saints must remember that they are the elect according to the
  foreknowledge of God and are kept by the power of God (see 1 Peter
  1:2–5).
- The Saints should remember that adversity has eternal value (see
  l Peter 4:12–14).
- The Saints must endure in righteousness and bear afflictions patiently
  (see 1 Peter 2:19–20).
- The Saints will receive great blessings if they do not render evil for evil
  or railing for railing (see 1 Peter 3:9).
- The Saints should love and strengthen one another (see 1 Peter 1:22;
  3:8).
- The Saints should remember that mortality is temporary, but God's
  promises are eternal (see 1 Peter 1:24–25).
- Husbands and wives should strive to strengthen marriage and family
  bonds (see 1 Peter 3:1–7).
- The Saints should remember the reward of false prophets, false teachers, and false disciples (see 2 Peter 2:1–4, 9, 12–14, 20–21).
- The Saints can make their calling and election sure through faith and
  effort (see 2 Peter 1:4–12, 18–19).

In a very touching and uplifting section of his first letter, Peter teaches
us about the Savior's basic nature. Though "he was reviled [he] reviled not
again; when he suffered, he threatened not" (1 Peter 2:23). Because of the
Savior's meekness and patience in bearing His sufferings and "stripes"
without revenge, by His stripes are we healed (see 1 Peter 2:24). One has
little doubt that Peter saw in his Master the desirable pattern and much-
to-be-sought-after ideal for his own life. Thus, as Paul did in his second letter to Timothy, Peter stated in his own second letter that he shortly "must

put off this . . . tabernacle, even as our Lord Jesus Christ hath shewed me" (2 Peter 1:14). This is undoubtedly a reference to the resurrected Lord's prophecy of Peter's own crucifixion as recorded in John 21:18–19: "Verily, verily, I say unto thee, When thou wast young, thou girdedst thyself, and walkedst whither thou wouldest: but when thou shalt be old, thou shalt stretch forth thy hands, and another shall gird thee, and carry thee whither thou wouldest not. This spake he, signifying by what death he should glorify God. And when he had spoken this, he saith unto him, Follow me."

CONCLUSION

According to reputable tradition, recorded in the statements of various early authorities of the Christian Church, Peter's death fulfilled the prophesy of the Savior. The chief Apostle died in Rome—martyred in the last years of the reign of Emperor Nero (AD 67–68). In 1 Clement 5:4, it is said of Peter that he suffered not one or two but many trials, and having given his testimony, he went to the place which was his due. Ignatius, bishop of Antioch, refers to the deaths of Peter and Paul in Rome, as does Eusebius of Caesarea. Tertullian refers to three martyrdoms at Rome: Peter, Paul, and John. And, finally, Origen reported that Peter "at the end . . . came to Rome and was crucified head downwards."[26]

To the very end, Peter followed his Lord and Master in both word and deed. He acted like Him, taught like Him, was rejected like Him, and in the end, suffered the same kind of ignominious death like Him. Thus "Peter holds up the goal of becoming godlike in every sense of the term."[27]

Few men in history had the experiences that Peter had. Fewer still refined their understanding of the things of God and honed their spiritual sensitivity as did Peter. Even fewer served the Savior and the kingdom from start to finish with such unflagging courage and selfless dedication as did Peter. Only a handful of prophets have ever been commissioned to teach the gospel in more than one dispensation and restore their keys in this, the dispensation of the fulness of times (see D&C 7:7; 27:12; 128:20). Peter continues to be our model missionary. In giving instruction to elders of the Church in this dispensation, the Lord commanded them to do exactly as Peter of old: preach faith, repentance, baptism, and the gift of the Holy Ghost (see D&C 49:11–14). But Peter also made it clear that Christlike love is the ultimate measure of spiritual progression (see 1 Peter 1:22; 4:8; 2 Peter 1:7).

NOTES

1. This is the judgment of many historians. See, for example, John P. McKay and others, *A History of World Societies,* 2d ed. (Boston: Houghton Mifflin, 1988), 199.

2. Bruce R. McConkie, *Mormon Doctrine,* 2d ed. (Salt Lake City: Bookcraft, 1966), 571.

3. Jerome Murphy-O'Connor, *The Holy Land: An Archaeological Guide from Earliest Times to 1700,* 3d ed. (New York: Oxford University Press, 1992), 223.

4. Murphy-O'Connor, *Holy Land,* 225.

5. This is the actual NIV wording of this passage, which is closer to the modern colloquial meaning intended by the Greek text than the KJV demonstrates.

6. Joseph Smith, *Teachings of the Prophet Joseph Smith,* comp. Joseph Fielding Smith (Salt Lake City: Deseret Book, 1970), 365.

7. Floyd V. Filson, "Peter," in George A. Buttrick, ed., *The Interpreter's Dictionary of the Bible* (Nashville: Abingdon, 1962), 3:749.

8. In addition to the Joseph Smith Translation Appendix at the back of the LDS edition of the Bible, see Thomas A. Wayment, ed., *The Complete Joseph Smith Translation of the New Testament: A Side-by-Side Comparison with the King James Version* (Salt Lake City: Deseret Book, 2005).

9. Harold B. Lee, in Conference Report, October 1953, 25.

10. *The Life and Teachings of Jesus and His Apostles* (Salt Lake City: Church Educational System, 1979), 200.

11. Russell M. Nelson, in Conference Report, April 1993, 52.

12. Bruce R. McConkie, *Doctrinal New Testament Commentary,* 3 vols. (Salt Lake City: Bookcraft, 1965–73), 2:143.

13. James E. Talmage, *Jesus the Christ* (Salt Lake City: Deseret Book, 1962), 364.

14. Talmage, *Jesus the Christ,* 368.

15. Neal A. Maxwell, "Meekness—A Dimension of True Discipleship," *Ensign,* March 1983, 71.

16. Joseph Smith Translation, Mark 9:3.

17. McConkie, *Doctrinal New Testament Commentary,* 1:400.

18. McConkie, *Doctrinal New Testament Commentary,* 1:400.

19. McConkie, *Mormon Doctrine,* 109.

20. I am indebted to Richard D. Draper for articulating so well the concept being taught by Joseph Smith Translation, 2 Peter 1:19.

21. Spencer W. Kimball, "Peter, My Brother," in *Life and Teachings of Jesus and His Apostles,* 488–89.

22. Kimball, "Peter, My Brother," 489.

23. Luke 22:34 also uses *aparnese* (identical to all the other synoptic texts); however, the context seems to force a different sense. Yet when Luke repeats the verb form in verse 61 of the same chapter, he falls back to the same construction and sense that Matthew and Mark use. Personal communication with Richard D. Draper.

24. McConkie, *Doctrinal New Testament Commentary,* 2:463–64.

25. Eusebius, *Ecclesiastical History,* translated by Kirsopp Lake, 2 vols., Loeb Classical Library (Cambridge: Harvard University Press, 1992), 2.15.2.

26. Eusebius, *Ecclesiastical History,* 3.1.2. For an excellent summary of these sources see Filson, "Peter," in Buttrick, *Interpreter's Dictionary of the Bible,* 3:755.

27. Richard L. Anderson, "Peter's Letters: Progression for the Living and the Dead," *Ensign,* October 1991, 7.

CHAPTER TWENTY-FOUR

VISIONS OF CHRIST IN THE SPIRIT WORLD AND THE DEAD REDEEMED

M. CATHERINE THOMAS

A scene from Dante's *Inferno* will set the stage for this chaper. The poet Virgil brings Dante to the ledge of the abyss of hell:

> *Death-pale the Poet spoke: "Now let us go*
> *into the blind world waiting here below us.*
> *I will lead the way and you shall follow . . ."*
> *No tortured wailing rose to greet us here*
> *but sounds of sighing rose from every side,*
> *sending a tremor through the timeless air,*
> *a grief breathed out of untormented sadness,*
> *the passive state of those who dwelled apart,*
> *men, women, children—a dim and endless congress . . .*
> *I thought how many worthy souls there were*
> *suspended in that Limbo, and a weight*
> *closed on my heart for what the noblest suffer.*
> *"Instruct me, Master and most noble Sir,"*
> *I prayed him then, ". . . has any, by his own or another's merit,*
> *gone ever from this place to blessedness?"*[1]

Virgil answers that a Mighty One did come and took with Him the

---

M. Catherine Thomas is an assistant professor emeritus of ancient scripture at Brigham Young University.

ancient patriarchs and other righteous souls. But those who remained endured in hell without hope of deliverance.

Dante's theology of the plight of the unredeemed dead stands in sharp contrast to the belief of the early Christians and those who remembered the teachings of the Apostles. In the early Church, there was no more prominent and popular belief than the Descent to hell and the redemption of the dead. Ignatius (AD 35–107),[2] Polycarp (AD 69–155),[3] Justin Martyr (AD 100–165),[4] Irenaeus (AD 130–200),[5] Tertullian (AD 160–220),[6] and other early writers either explicitly mention or allude to the Descent, several linking the Descent to redemptive work for the dead.

It is important to note that *hell* is a translation of *sheol* in Hebrew and *hades* in Greek. Both terms refer to the place of departed spirits and not necessarily to that place where only the wicked go. Selwyn writes:

> The concept of Sheol or Hades as the abode of the dead generally, without ethical or other distinctions, was later differentiated to admit of distinct regions for the righteous and wicked respectively, as in *Enoch xxii.* As late as the *Psalms of Solomon* (cf. xiv. 6, xv. 11, xvi. 2) Hades was used for the place of punishment of the wicked, which is normally termed in N.T. Gehenna. The abode of the righteous, on the other hand, when a special term other than Hades is used, is spoken of as "Abraham's bosom" (Luke xvi. 23) or "Paradise" (Luke xxiii. 43).[7]

The ancients believed that the spirit world lay under the earth. Paul speaks of the Savior's Descent into the lower parts of the earth (see Ephesians 4:9).[8] Peter does not use a term for descent, rather, a form of the verb "to go." I will use the term *Descent* hereafter to mean the Savior's journey to the spirit world. (The common Latin term for the Descent is *descensus ad inferos.*)

In modern times the Descent is perhaps the most neglected piece of Christian theology. According to F. Loofs, a prominent biblical scholar:

> The Descensus belongs in fact to a group of primitive Christian conceptions which are inseparable from views then current, but now abandoned, and which accordingly can now be appraised only in a historical sense, i.e. as expressions of Christian beliefs which, while adequate enough for their time, have at length become obsolete. . . . The modern mind cannot bring to it more than interest; we cannot now accept it as part of our faith. . . . It were fitting, therefore, that

the Churches distinguished as Evangelical should omit the Article "descendit ad inferos" from their programmes of instruction in Christian doctrine and worship.[9]

Indeed, what shall the world do with the doctrine of the Descent? Richard L. Anderson includes in a discussion of baptism for the dead a conversation with the New Testament scholar Edgar Goodspeed. Dr. Goodspeed was asked, "Do you think it [baptism for the dead] should be practiced today?" He answered, "This is the reason why we do not practice it today. We do not know enough about it. If we did, we would practice it."[10]

My purpose will be to treat five major points on the Descent and the redemption of the dead as outlined in D&C 138—President Joseph F. Smith's "Vision of the Redemption of the Dead"—presenting supporting material from early Christian and Jewish writers to illustrate that the remarkable teachings pertaining to the redemption of the dead in section 138 represent truths accepted by the early Christians. I will comment little on D&C 138 itself but rather will use its major points relating to the Descent as outline for my presentation. These five points are: (1) some history, translation, and interpretation of the much-disputed passages in 1 Peter which section 138 includes, 3:19 and 4:6, focusing on the baptismal context of these passages; (2) early Christian and Jewish evidence bearing on the Savior's redemptive work in the Descent; (3) evidence of belief in a division of spirits in the spirit world and in the anticipation by the righteous of the Messiah's appearance to them; (4) evidence of the organization of the righteous to take the gospel to the wicked; and (5) evidence of vicarious work for the dead in early Christianity.

History of 1 Peter 3:18

The history of the interpretation of 1 Peter 3:18 (that Christ preached to the spirits in prison) and its context form a tangled jungle representing the confusion that came in the wake of the Apostasy. I will touch here only lightly on the creative means by which exegetists have through the centuries wrested this passage. For greater detail, the reader may consult several writers who have made thorough studies of the complicated network of factors, grammatical and exegetical, which the passages in 1 Peter embrace.[11] The difficulty does not actually lie in the passage but in the minds of the interpreters who find a conflict here with their own views of the afterlife and the impossibility of progress or redemption there. Nearly all the interpretations of 1 Peter 3:19 and 4:6 from ancient times to our own day are confined to these following alternatives: (1) The Lord preached the gospel to these spirits and offered them repentance. Under the influence of later theological ideas many commentators have been unwilling to admit this interpretation, maintaining (2) that Christ must have preached to them not hope but condemnation; or (3) that He preached only to those who were righteous; or (4) only to those who, though disobedient, repented in the hour of death; or (5) that He preached the gospel to those who had been just, and condemnation to those who had disobeyed.[12] The ancient Alexandrian school of theology accepted the plain interpretation of 1 Peter 3:19 that Christ preached the gospel of hope to the unbelievers in the spirit world. Later many commentators of the Middle Ages (as well as of modern times) did not find in this verse any allusion to the Descent at all. Where some did find a Descent, they interpreted it to mean deliverance of the Old Testament Saints only and the defeat of Satan in that event which came to be known as the Harrowing of Hell, where the belief that Christ had liberated any others than those holy persons became heretical.[13] Modern Catholic theology mostly tends to regard those who heard Jesus preaching in the spirit prison as sinners converted before they died.[14]

We should note here that mention of the Descent appears in many early Christian creeds, such as the famous Apostles' Creed (AD 390). But the earliest creed of which we have record is known as the Fourth Formula of Sirmium (a council of Western bishops) which came thirty-one years earlier in AD 359 and was a descendant of many former Christian creeds that did not contain anything about the Descent. I quote the section on the Descent from the Sirmium Creed: "And [Christ] descended to hell, and regulated things there, Whom the gatekeepers of hell saw and shuddered, and [he] rose again." After years of creed without mention of the Descent, why was the Descent inserted into this creed? J. N. D. Kelly points out that this Sirmium Creed was drafted by a Syrian, Mark of Arethusa, and that the Descent had a place very early in Eastern creed material.[15] He gives the Syrian *Didascalia* (a collection of miscellaneous precepts of professedly apostolic origin, c. AD 250) as an example. There it says: "[Christ] was crucified under Pontius Pilate and departed into peace, in order to preach to Abraham, Isaac, and Jacob and all the Saints concerning the ending of the world and the resurrection of the dead." Why the Descent was so long neglected in the Western creeds is not clear, but Kelly speculates that Mark of Arethusa, having credal materials before him that contained mention of the Descent, felt the interpolation in the Western creed was important to show the full scale of the Savior's work of redemption.[16] At about the same time, synods at Nike (AD 359) and at Constantinople (AD 360) published creeds with a Descent clause. Rufinus records (c. 404) that the Aquileian creed contained the Descent clause which he connected with 1 Peter 3:19, and he says that the Descent passage is included in that creed to explain "what Christ accomplished in the underworld."[17]

Even though many references to the Descent appear in early Christian literature, curiously, interpretations, reflections, or quotations of 1 Peter 3:19 are missing in the oldest Christian literature. No writer before Hippolytus (c. 200), Clement of Alexandria (AD 150–215), and Origen (AD 185–253) (who do indeed make clear connection between the Descent and 3:19) appears to allude to this verse.[18] The reason may lie in the difficulties mentioned in the connection of the Descent with redemption in 1 Peter 3:10.[19]

Translation, Interpretation, Baptismal Context of 1 Peter 3:18–21; 4:6

1 Peter 3:18–19. "For Christ also hath once suffered for sins, the just for the unjust, that he might bring us to God, being put to death in the flesh, but quickened by [the Greek may be rendered 'made alive in'] *the Spirit: by which also he went and preached unto the spirits in prison."*

Much debate has taken place over what condition "alive in the Spirit" implies. The King James Version gives "quickened by the Spirit" and capitalizes *Spirit,* implying the interpretation that He went in the power of the Holy Spirit or that this journey refers not to His descent but to His Resurrection and to a proclamation of His triumph over the powers of evil.[20] But it is more likely that the two datives, flesh and spirit, should be understood as antithetical, meaning that when Christ's flesh was dead, His spirit continued alive into the spirit world. Joseph Smith taught: "Now all those [who] die in the faith go to the prison of spirits to preach to the dead in body, but they are *alive in the spirit,* and those spirits preach to the spirits that they may live according to God in the spirit. And men do minister for them in the flesh, and angels bear the glad tidings to the spirits, and they are made happy by these means."[21] Origen understood this sense of the verse that Jesus went in His spirit: "We assert that Jesus not only converted no small number of persons while he was in the body . . . but also, that when he became a spirit, without the covering of the body, he dwelt among those spirits which were without bodily covering, converting such of them as were willing to Himself."[22] Hippolytus (c. 155–236) wrote, "The Only-begotten entered [the world of spirits] as Soul among souls."[23]

For Augustine (AD 354–430), Bede (AD 673–735), Aquinas (AD 1225–74), and others, the difficulties in accepting the plain sense of 1 Peter 3:19 were insuperable. Although at first Augustine accepted the literal view of 1 Peter 3:19,[24] he later proposed a new interpretation which was that Christ was *in* Noah when Noah preached repentance to the people of his time, and the spirits in prison were taken to mean "those who were then in the prison of sin," or "those who are now in the prison of Hades, but were then alive."[25]

Peter spoke of the Lord's visit to the spirits *in prison*. He did not mention paradise, where the righteous dwell who also benefit from the Savior's redemptive work. Doctrine and Covenants 138:50 reveals that "the dead had looked upon the long absence of their spirits from their bodies as a bondage." Even the righteous spirits viewed their existence in the spirit world as living in prison because of their separation from their bodies. Therefore, the term *prison* refers here to the entire spirit world.

1 Peter 3:20. "Which sometime were disobedient, when once the longsuffering of God waited in the days of Noah, while the ark was a preparing, wherein few, that is, eight souls were saved by water."

Why did Peter single out Noah's generation? One reason may be suggested in "Sanhedrin" (10.3) in the Mishnah: "The generation of the Flood have no share in the world to come, nor shall they stand in the judgment." This group was considered by the rabbis to epitomize the most wicked generation in the history of mankind. Therefore, Peter may have been using them as typical of the most wicked and says in effect that the Savior's mission to the spirit world embraced all spirits, even the most wicked. The Joseph Smith Translation adds three clarifying words to verse 20: "*Some of whom* were disobedient in the days of Noah," confirming the sense that Noah's generation was only part—perhaps the most wicked part—of the spirits who benefited from the Savior's mission. A few verses later, 1 Peter 4:6 implies that the gospel was preached to all the dead. Doctrine and Covenants 138:30–33 says the gospel was preached "even to all the spirits of men; . . . even unto all who would repent of their sins and receive the gospel. . . . To those who had died in their sins, without a knowledge of the truth, or in transgression, having rejected the prophets.

These were taught faith in God, repentance from sin, vicarious baptism for the remission of sins, the gift of the Holy Ghost by the laying on of hands."

What kind of redemption could those spirits hope for? The foundation of redemption is Resurrection, which, by virtue of the Savior's work, all who had had earthly bodies could anticipate. In addition, each could expect to be redeemed "through obedience to the ordinances of the house of God" and "receive a reward according to [his] works (D&C 138:58–59). In the book of Moses, the Lord spoke to Enoch about Noah's generation: "But behold, these which thine eyes are upon shall perish in the floods; and behold, I will shut them up; a prison have I prepared for them. And That [Christ] which I have chosen hath pled before my face. Wherefore, he suffereth for their sins; inasmuch as they will repent in the day that my Chosen shall return unto me, and until that day they shall be in torment" (Moses 7:38–39; see also Moses 7:57).

Doctrine and Covenants 138:59 teaches the fate of these spirits: "And after they have paid the penalty of their transgressions, and are washed clean, [they] shall receive a reward according to their works, for they are heirs of salvation." That is, Noah's generation, as well as all those who enter the spirit world unrepentant, experience a cleansing process in the spirit world in preparation for the Resurrection. Many of these spirits will receive a degree of redemption in the terrestrial or telestial kingdoms (see D&C 76:72–78; 88:99).

1 Peter 3:21. "The like figure whereunto even baptism doth also now save us (not putting away of the filth of the flesh, but the answer of a good conscience toward God,) by the resurrection of Jesus Christ."

I include here 1 Peter 3:21, which refers to the Flood being like baptism because it indicates that Peter's attention turned from the subject of those who received the preaching to the subject of baptism: "Which (water) saves you now as a type, namely baptism, which is not the removal of uncleanness of [from] the flesh, but a covenant before God of a right mind, through the resurrection of Jesus Christ" (my translation).[26] In some areas of the early Church,[27] candidates for baptism put off their clothes, entering the baptismal water naked; then, upon emerging from the water, they were clothed with a white garment. For this reason, Reicke perceived a possible allusion to a baptismal service in the language of this verse about putting off the uncleanness of the flesh.[28] Several scholars have observed that 1 Peter, which identifies itself as an epistle, has elements reminiscent of an actual baptismal service. First Peter 3:18–22 contains what looks like a basic creed embracing in a few words a summary of the Lord's ministry: He suffered for sin, died, went in the spirit and preached to spirits in prison (Peter inserted the figure of baptism here), and went to heaven at the right hand of God, having angels subject to Him. One significance of this creedal section is that Peter has put baptism in close proximity to the Savior's Descent, linking the two. A parallel text in 1 Timothy 3:16 says, "God was manifest in the flesh, justified in the Spirit, *seen of angels* [can refer to spirits], preached unto the Gentiles, believed on in the world, received up into glory" (emphasis added). Reicke comments, "The whole hymn in 1 Timothy 3:16 has . . . great similarity to 1 Peter 3:18–22. From this it is fairly clear that the appearance to the Angel world is a *motif* organically embodied in the Salvation drama."[29]

After study of pre-Nicene paschal and baptismal texts, F. L. Cross concluded that 1 Peter 1:3–4:11 has a baptismal setting and that the rite is understood to have taken place after Peter's words in 1:21, which are: "Who by him do believe in God, that raised him up from the dead, and gave him glory; that your faith and hope might be in God." At this point, the person was baptized. Here is the verse that follows the alleged baptism: "Seeing ye have purified your souls in obeying the truth through the Spirit unto unfeigned love of the brethren, see that ye love one another with a pure heart fervently: Being born again, not of corruptible seed, but of incorruptible."[30] However, whatever the original setting of the elements in 1 Peter, the significant point is, again, that baptism is seen by many scholars to be the main theme of Peter's letter, and thus the context for the Descent and the preaching to the spirits.

Early Christians associated the Lord's Passion and the Descent with baptism, Easter Eve being a popular time to receive baptism. Tertullian (AD 160–220) observed, "The Pascha offers the most solemn occasion for Baptism."[31] Of course, baptism by immersion is itself a figure of death, being a descent into a watery tomb preceding the deliverance from the water of spiritual rebirth. But again Peter's association of baptism with the Descent and the preaching to the spirits should be noted because the linking of these two ideas may constitute a cryptic reference to the offering of baptism to the dead and even to vicarious work for the dead.

1 Peter 4:6. "For this cause was the gospel preached also to them that are dead, that they might be judged according to men in the flesh, but live according to God in the spirit."

Again scholars debate what "them that are dead" means, some wishing to interpret the phrase as pertaining to the spiritually dead. Augustine, Cyril, Bede, Erasmus, Luther, and others took "the dead" to mean "those who were dead in trespasses and sins"—the spiritually dead or more especially the Gentiles[32]—since these fathers could not assent to the wicked in hell receiving the gospel. But Clement of Alexandria (AD 150–215) wrote, "If then He preached [the gospel to those in the flesh that they might not be condemned] unjustly, how is it conceivable that He did not for the same cause preach the gospel to those who had departed this life before His advent?"[33]

EVIDENCES IN JUDAISM AND EARLY CHRISTIANITY OF THE SAVIOR'S REDEMPTIVE WORK IN THE DESCENT

Foreshadowings of the redemptive nature of the Descent appear in the Old Testament (see Zechariah 9:11: "By the blood of the covenant I have brought forth the prisoners out of the pit wherein is no water"; see also Hosea 13:14). In Jewish literature, we read not only of the Descent but also of the Messiah's redemptive work in the spirit world. Several apparently Jewish texts, some based on Old Testament passages, contain descriptions of the Lord's work among the spirits of the dead. Justin[34] and Irenaeus[35] quote a passage which they claim was formerly found in the text of Jeremiah (once Irenaeus attributes it to Isaiah) but which they say had been excised by Jewish controversialists. This passage is called the Jeremiah Logion: "The Lord remembered His dead people of Israel who lay in their graves, and went down to preach to them His own salvation." One scholar observes:

> It is strange that no trace of this text is found in the LXX of Jeremias, if what Justin alleges is true, but it must now be admitted (in the light of the Qumran scrolls) that some tampering with controversial texts was practised by the Jews, for the Isaias scroll at 53:11 has a reading which favours the Christian argument (and which is found in the LXX), but this reading has disappeared from all later Hebrew mss. Moreover, the Greek Fragments of the OT found at Qumran present a type of text which is often in agreement with Justin.[36]

From rabbinic literature, which contained ideas likely contemporary with early Christianity, comes an account of the Lord's visit to the spirit world. The first of two passages from the *Bereshith Rabba* says of the Messiah's appearance at the gates of Gehinnom:

> But when they that are bound, that are in Gehinnom, saw the light of the Messiah, they rejoiced to receive him, saying, He will lead us forth from this darkness, as it is said, "I will redeem them from Hell, from death I will set them free" (Hosea 13:14); and so says Isaiah (35:10), "the ransomed of the Lord will return and come to Zion." By "Zion" is to be understood Paradise.[37]

And in another passage, "This is that which stands written, We shall rejoice and exult in Thee. When? When the captives climb up out of hell, with the Shechinah at their head."[38]

An early Christian hymn, dated about AD 100, contains additional insight into the early understanding of the Descent and the redemption of the dead:

> Sheol saw me and was shattered, and Death ejected me and many with me. . . . And I made a congregation of living among his dead . . . and those who had died ran towards Me and cried: "Son of God, have pity on us . . . and bring us out from the bonds of darkness, and open to us the door by which we shall come out to Thee. . . . Thou art our Savior." Then I heard their voice. . . . And I placed my name upon their head, because they are free and they are mine.[39]

A second passage from this hymn represents Christ as speaking:

> And I opened the doors which were closed . . . and nothing appeared closed to me, because I was the opening of everything. And I went towards all my bondsmen in order to loose them; that I might not leave anyone bound or binding. And I gave my knowledge generously, and my resurrection through my love . . . and transformed them through myself. Then they received my blessing and lived, and they were gathered to me and were saved; because they became my members and I was their head.[40]

The combination of Christ's placing His name on the heads of the dead, references to the Savior's liberating work, and the spirits' reception of Christ's blessing strongly suggest the giving of baptism to the spirits.

THE DIVISION OF SPIRITS IN THE SPIRIT WORLD; ANTICIPATION BY THE RIGHTEOUS OF THE MESSIAH'S APPEARANCE

In Doctrine and Covenants 138, President Joseph F. Smith recorded that the righteous were assembled in one place waiting for the appearance of the Lord (see vv. 11–19, 38–49). This division of spirits is supported by the apochryphal book of Enoch (dated by Charlesworth as second century before Christ to first century after Christ), which, though not Christian, contains a view of the spirit world current among the Jews of Jesus' time which apparently influenced such New Testament books as Jude and 2 Peter (chapter 2). Enoch, on a tour of the spirit world, asks the attending angel what the hollow places in the rock are. The angel answers:

> These beautiful [or "hollow"—the Greek words are similar] corners [are here] in order that the spirits of the souls of the dead should assemble into them. . . . They prepared these places in order to put them there until the day of their judgment. "For what reason is one separated from the other?" And he replied and said to me, "These three have been made in order that the spirits of the dead might be separated. And in the manner in which the souls of the righteous are separated by this spring of water with light upon it, in like manner, the sinners are set apart when they die." (22:8–10)

President Smith wrote, "I beheld that they were filled with joy and gladness, and were rejoicing together because the day of their deliverance was at hand" (D&C 138:15). The joy of the spirits is also supported by Enoch (69:27), "Then there came to them a great joy. And they blessed, glorified, and extolled [the Lord] on account of the fact that the name of that [Son of] Man was revealed to them."

A Jewish text dating about AD 100 describes the state of the spirits after death: "Did not the souls of the righteous in their chambers ask about these matters, saying, 'How long are we to remain here?' [The archangel said] in Hades the chambers of the souls are like the womb. For just as a woman who is in travail makes haste to escape the pangs of birth, so also do these places hasten to give back those things that were committed to them from the beginning" (4 Ezra 4:35, 42; see also Odes of Solomon 24:5).

The Gospel of Nicodemus, a Christian document dating from the time of Justin Martyr who shows familiarity with it, describes the Savior's advent in Hades:

We, then, were in Hades with all who have died since the beginning of the world. And at the hour of midnight there rose upon the
darkness there something like the light of the sun and shone, and
light fell upon us all, and we saw one another. And immediately our
father Abraham, along with the patriarchs and the prophets, was
filled with joy, and they said to one another: This shining comes
from a great light. The prophet Isaiah, who was present there, said:
This shining comes from the Father and the Son and the Holy Spirit.
This I prophesied when I was still living: . . . the people that sit in
darkness saw a great light.[41]

The Organization of the Righteous to Take the Gospel to the Wicked

Section 138 maintains that the Savior did not descend personally to the
wicked but organized the righteous and gave them authority to engage in
the preaching of the gospel to all the dead (see vv. 29–30). Later
Muhammadan theology also contains a trace of this doctrine, which says,
"The righteous ones, who have safely passed the bridge which crosses Hell
to Paradise, intercede for their brethren detained upon it. They are sent to
Hell to see if any there have faith, and to bring them. These are washed in
the Water of Life and admitted to Paradise."[42] In *Yalkut Shim'oni* (Jewish),
the godless are rescued from hell by the righteous dead and pass to eternal
life, while in the *Zohar*, the righteous or the patriarchs are said to descend
to hell to rescue sinners from the place of torment.[43]

The early Christian author Ignatius (AD 35–107) writes about the
Savior's visit to the prophets: "If these things be so, how then shall we be
able to live without him of whom even the prophets were disciples in the
Spirit and to whom they looked forward as their teacher? And for this reason he whom they waited for in righteousness, when he came, raised them
from the dead."[44]

Another early Christian document refers to the Lord's visit to the
righteous:

I have descended and have spoken with Abraham and Isaac and
Jacob, to your fathers the prophets, and have brought to them news
that they may come from the rest which is below into heaven, and
have given them the right hand of the baptism of life and forgiveness and pardon for all wickedness, as to you, so from now on also

to those who believe in me. But whoever believes in me and does not do my commandment receives, although he believes in my name, no benefit from it. He has run a course in vain. . . . O Lord, in every respect you have made us rejoice and have given us rest; for in faithfulness and truthfulness you have preached to our fathers and to the prophets, and even so to us and to every man. And he said to us, "Truly I say to you, you and all who believe and also they who yet will believe in him who sent me I will cause to rise up into heaven, to the place which the Father has prepared for the elect and most elect, (the Father) who will give the rest that he has promised, and eternal life."[45]

Rising "up into heaven" reminds us of a striking parallel in Doctrine and Covenants 138:51: "These the Lord taught, and gave them power to come forth, after his resurrection from the dead, to enter into his Father's kingdom, there to be crowned with immortality and eternal life."

Other early literature adds some interesting details to the idea of the righteous taking the gospel to the dead. Hippolytus writes, "John the Baptist died first, being dispatched by Herod, that he might prepare those in Hades for the gospel; he became the forerunner there, announcing even as he did on this earth, that the Savior was about to come to ransom the spirits of the saints from the hand of death."[46]

Again, in a sixth-century manuscript, Hippolytus distinguishes between those who saw the Savior and those who only heard His voice, the voice being figurative perhaps for hearing the gospel from His authorized servants:

Oh, Thou only-begotten Son among only-begotten sons, and All in all! Seeing that the multitude of Holy Souls was deep down and had been deprived of a Divine visit long enough, the Holy Spirit had previously said that they should be the object of a meeting with the Divine Soul, saying: "His form we have not seen, but His voice we have heard." For it behoved Him to go and preach also to those who were in Hell, namely those who had once been disobedient.[47]

One more example will illustrate the righteous spirits' taking the gospel to the wicked spirits and will also provide a transition to the topic of vicarious work for the dead. The Shepherd of Hermas (first century) was, according to the fourth-century Church historian Eusebius, considered by some valuable for instruction in the Church and was quoted by some of the most ancient writers.[48] Hermas saw in a vision that the Apostles took the gospel into the spirit world so that the dead might receive the seal of baptism:

> These apostles and teachers, who preached the name of the Son of God, having fallen asleep in the power and faith of the Son of God, preached also to those who had fallen asleep before them, and themselves gave to them the seal of the preaching [baptism]. They went down therefore with them into the water and came up again, but the latter went down alive and came up alive, while the former who had fallen asleep before, went down dead but came up alive. (Sim. 9.16.5)

Clement of Alexandria also cited this passage, commenting "that it was necessary for the apostles to be imitators of their Master on the other side as well as here, that they might convert the gentile dead as he did the Hebrew."[49] In another place, citing Hermas again, he wrote, "Christ visited, preached to, and baptized the just men of old, both gentiles and Jews, not only those who lived before the coming of the Lord, but also those who were before the coming of the Law, . . . such as Abel, Noah, or any such righteous man."[50] Clement's observation recalls D&C 138:40–41 and the description of all the righteous prophets, including Abel and Noah, who waited in that assembly for the Savior's advent.

VICARIOUS WORK FOR THE DEAD

The writer of Hermas obviously treated two kinds of death, spiritual and physical, but his poetic writing is not clear, and one might easily find in this passage only a description of Apostles giving baptism in the spirit world. But note the sentence, "The latter [the baptizers] *went down alive and came up alive,* while the former [those baptized] . . . went down dead but came up alive." The wording suggests that the former group—the baptizers—is physically alive and the latter—those baptized—physically dead, and therefore cryptically alludes to vicarious baptism for the dead.

Why is baptism for the dead only hinted at in early writings? It was likely a restricted part of the Savior's teaching. The New Testament contains many references to mysteries of the kingdom that were shared only in the Savior's most intimate circle.[51] Some of the early Fathers exhibit this same sense of secrecy about the special doctrines that the Savior taught, probably during the mysterious forty-day ministry (see Acts 1:3). With regard to secrecy, Clement of Alexandria says of himself, that he writes "in a studied disorder"[52] and has "here and there interspersed the dogmas which are the germs of true knowledge, so that the discovery of the sacred traditions may not be easy to any one of the uninitiated."[53] As a result of the secrecy, after the first century and the demise of the authority to administer baptism, the doctrine of vicarious baptism is hardly referred to, and then only with confusion, since those who knew the truth were probably not writing it down in any detail. Finally, no one could remember just what it was all about. However, traces linger in the literature. Epiphanius, bishop of Salamis (AD 347–403), wrote:

> From Asia and Gaul has reached us the account [tradition] of a certain practice, namely, that when any die without baptism among them, they baptize others in their place and in their name so that, rising in the resurrection, they will not have to pay the penalty of having failed to receive baptism, but rather will become subject to the authority of the Creator of the World. For this reason this tradition which has reached us is said to be the very thing to which the Apostle himself refers when he says, "If the dead rise not at all, what shall they do who are baptized for the dead?" Others interpret the saying finely, claiming that those who are on the point of death, if they are catechumens, are to be considered worthy, in view of the expectation of baptism which they had before their death. They point out that he who has died shall also rise again, and hence will stand in need of that forgiveness of sins that comes through baptism.[54]

Later writers thought that only the heretics had practiced baptism for the dead. Many heretics had. For example, the Marcionites would lay a catechumen (candidate for baptism) who had just died upon a bed and lay a living person under his bed. Then they would ask the corpse if he wished to receive baptism, and the living person would reply that he did wish to. Then the living person would be baptized for the dead one.[55]

It was a short step from baptism *for* the dead to baptism *of* the dead. Greek Canon 20 from the Council of Carthage in 419 (reporting a council in 379) reads, "It also seemed good that the Eucharist should not be given to the bodies of the dead. For it is written, 'Take, Eat,' but the bodies of the dead can neither 'take' nor 'eat.' Nor let ignorance of the presbyters baptize those who are dead."[56] Some of our Mormon literature has claimed that a

Council of Carthage banned baptism for the dead, but in fact it was the baptism of corpses that was banned.[57]

The idea that the living might do something efficacious for the dead was not new in Israel. In 2 Maccabees 12:42, we read:

> The noble Judas called on the people to keep themselves free from sin, for they had seen with their own eyes what had happened to the fallen because of their sin. He levied a contribution from each man, and sent the total of two thousand silver drachmas to Jerusalem for a sin-offering—a fit and proper act in which he took due account of the resurrection. For if he had not been expecting the fallen to rise again, it would have been foolish and superfluous to pray for the dead. But since he had in view the wonderful reward reserved for those who die a godly death, his purpose was a holy and pious one. And this was why he offered an atoning sacrifice to free the dead from their sin.

Montefiore quotes from fifth-century rabbinic literature on the redemption of man from hell:

> Hence we learn that the living can redeem the dead. Hence we have established the rite of holding a memorial service for the dead on the Day of Atonement . . . for God brings them out of Sheol and they are shot forth as an arrow from a bow. Straightway a man becomes tender and innocent as a kid. God purifies him as at the hour of his birth, sprinkling pure water on him from a bucket. Then man grows up and increases in happiness like a fish which draws happiness from the water. So is a man baptized every hour in rivers of balsam, milk, oil, honey: he eats of the tree of life continuously, which is planted in the division [*Mehizah*, term refers to the divisions in Paradise] of the righteous and his body reclines at the (banquet) table of every single saint and he lives for eternity.[58]

Vicarious work in fact underlies the whole of the gospel, since Jesus Christ performed proxy work by suffering for the sins of the world. Similarly, acting in his priesthood office, the priesthood holder acts by proxy, in the name of Jesus Christ, in doing the will of God on the earth. The doctrine of baptism for the dead marvelously illuminates the plan of exaltation: man develops into God by doing what God does; that is, by extending himself in behalf of souls living and dead. Christ did for us what we could not do for ourselves; in turn, we do for others what they cannot do, becoming, as Clement of Alexandria said (of the Apostles in the spirit world), "imitators of our Master."[59] Likewise, section 138 recorded that baptism for the dead made it possible for the righteous, "clothed with power and authority, . . . to go forth and carry the light of the gospel to them that were in darkness, even to all the spirits of men" (D&C 138:30), continuing, in the process, their own godly development.

It is clear then that abundant writings from the early Christian period, especially from the earliest Church writers, support the thesis that the early Church accepted the doctrine that the Son of God journeyed to the spirit world and there performed a work of enormous magnitude which, with His mortal ministry, offered redemption to the entire family of God. Section 138 is not new doctrine but a restoration of the knowledge that God had given the ancients.

NOTES

1. Dante Aligheiri, *The Inferno,* trans. John Ciardi (New York: New American Library, 1954), lines 15–60.
2. J. A. MacCulloch, *Harrowing of Hell* (Edinburgh: T&T Clark, 1930), observes that the earliest patristic references to the Descent occur in the Epistles of Ignatius and are made in such a way as to show that he is treating a well-known belief (83): *Magnes* c. 9; *Phila* c. 5. c. 9; *Trall* c. 9.
3. Polycarp, in his *Epistle to the Philippians* (1.2), implies the Descent by his citation of Peter's sermon in Acts 2:24 (MacCulloch, *Harrowing of Hell,* 84).
4. *Dialogue with Trypho,* c. 72.
5. *adv. Haer.* 4.27.2; Irenaeus says he heard this doctrine that Jesus "descended into the regions beneath the earth . . . preaching the remission of sin received by those who believe in Him" from "a certain presbyter, who had heard it from those who had seen the apostles, and from those who had been their disciples" (4.27.1–2).
6. *de Resur. Carnis,* 43, 44; *de Anima* 7, 55, 58; *adv. Marcionem,* 4.34.
7. Edward G. Selwyn, *The First Epistle of St. Peter* (London: Macmillan, 1958), 322n.
8. Although Brigham Young taught that the spirit world is organized upon the earth, perhaps when we see the spirit world, we will understand the use of the word *descent* (*Discourses of Brigham Young,* comp. John A. Widtsoe [Salt Lake City: Deseret Book, 1954], 376).
9. *Encyclopedia of Religion and Ethics,* ed. J. H. Hastings, 13 vols. (New York: Scribners, 1951), 4:654–63.

10. Richard L. Anderson, *Understanding Paul* (Salt Lake City: Deseret Book, 1983), 413.

11. Charles Bigg, *Critical and Exegetical Commentary on the Epistles of St. Peter and St. Jude* (Edinburgh: T&T Clark, 1902); William J. Dalton, *Christ's Proclamation to the Spirits: A Study of Peter 3:18–4:6* (Rome: Pontifical Biblical Institute, 1965); J. A. MacCulloch, *The Harrowing of Hell* (Edinburgh: T&T Clark, 1930); Hugh Nibley, *Baptism for the Dead in Ancient Times* (Provo, UT: FARMS, 1987); Bo Reicke, *The Disobedient Spirits and Christian Baptism* (New York: AMS Press, 1946); Edward G. Selwyn, *The First Epistle of St. Peter* (London: Macmillan, 1958).

12. Bigg, *Commentary,* 162.

13. Augustine, *de Haer.* 79; St. Gregory, *Ep.* 15; J. N. D. Kelly, *Early Christian Creeds* (New York: David McKay Company, 1972), 381.

14. Reicke, *Disobedient Spirits,* 14.

15. Kelly, *Creeds,* 379.

16. Kelly, *Creeds,* 383.

17. Kelly, *Creeds,* 378.

18. Reicke, *Disobedient Spirits,* 14.

19. Reicke, *Disobedient Spirits,* 16.

20. Samuel Fuller, *Defense of the Version of King James I, "The Spirits in Prison"* (New York: T. Whittaker, 1885).

21. Andrew F. Ehat and Lyndon W. Cook, *The Words of Joseph Smith* (Provo, UT: Religious Studies Center, Brigham Young University, 1980), 370; emphasis added.

22. *c. Cels.* 2.43.

23. *de Antichr,* c26.

24. *De Haeresibus,* 79.

25. *AdEvocUum, Ep.* 164.

26. Compare Mosiah 3:19, "natural" and "spiritual."

27. Probably the earliest reference to nudity in baptism is found in Hippolytus, *Apostolic Tradition* 21.3 (early third century) and possibly in the *Syria Didascalia* (c. 250), where nudity in baptism is strongly implied. The practice of nudity in baptism probably stems from the period when baptism became confused with other sacred ordinances. Several phrases from Paul were later interpreted to allude to the practice of nudity: Galatians 3:27, Colossians 3:9–10, Ephesians 4:22–24, and so on.

28. Reicke, *Disobedient Spirits,* 189–90.

29. Reicke, *Disobedient Spirits,* 234.

30. F. L. Cross, *1 Peter: A Paschal Liturgy* (London: n.p., 1954).

31. *De Baptismo,* 19.

32. Bigg, *Commentary,* 171.

33. *Stromata* 6.6.48.

34. *Dial.* 72.

35. In five places: *adv. Haer.* 3.22.1; 4.3.61; 4.50.1; 4.55.3; 5.31.1H.

36. J. H. Crehan, A *Catholic Dictionary of Theology* (Nelson, 1967), 163.

37. Most easily accessible in MacCulloch, *Harrowing of Hell,* 31; also *Encyclopedia of Religion and Ethics,* 4:653.

38. MacCulloch, *Harrowing of Hell,* 31.

39. Odes of Solomon 42:11–20, in J. H. Charlesworth, *The Odes of Solomon, The Syriac Texts* (Missoula, MT: Scholars Press, 1977).

40. Odes of Solomon 17:9–16.

41. Hennecke, Schneemelcher, and Wilson, *New Testament Apocrypha* (Philadelphia: Westminster Press, 1963), 1:471.

42. This reference is most easily available in MacCulloch, *Harrowing of Hell,* 32, and *Encyclopedia of Religion and Ethics,* 4:653.

43. MacCulloch, *Harrowing of Hell,* 31; *Encyclopedia of Ethics,* 4:653.

44. *Magn.* 9.2.

45. *Epistula Apostolorum* (c. AD 100–150), 27–28. Hennecke, Scneemulcher, Wilson, *New Testament Apocrypha,* 209–10.

46. *De Antichr.* c. 45; so Origen in two places, *In Luc. Hamil.* C.4. and *In Evang. John* 2.30.

47. Reicke, *Disobedient Spirits,* 24.

48. *HE* 3.3.6.

49. *Stromata,* 6.6.

50. *Stromata,* 2.9.

51. Matthew 13:11; Mark 4:11; 2 Corinthians 12:2–4; 1 Corinthians 2:6; see also Eus. *HE* 2.1.4 and Nibley, Part 1, *Baptism for the Dead in Ancient Times,* 1–5.

52. *Stromata,* 6.2.1.

53. *Stromata,* 7.110.4.

54. *Adv. Haeres.* 1.28.6.

55. John Chrysostome, *Homil. 40 in 1 Cor.*

56. Philip Schaff and Henry Wace, eds., *Nicene and Post-Nicene Fathers,* "The Seven Ecumenical Councils" (Grand Rapids, MI: Eerdmans), 14.451.

57. Joseph Fielding Smith, *Doctrines of Salvation,* 3 vols. (Salt Lake City: Bookcraft, 1955), 2:163.

58. Tanhuma, "Ha'asinu," I f. 339b. om C. G. Montefiore, *A Rabbinic Anthology* (New York: Schocken Books, 1974), 675.

59. *Stromata,* 6.6.

CHAPTER TWENTY-FIVE

THE APOCALYPTIC WITNESS OF THE MESSIAH

RICHARD D. DRAPER

The book of Revelation is not easy reading. As one New Testament authority observed, the book either finds a man mad or leaves him that way.[1]
I must admit that I can sympathize with that sentiment, even though it is
overstated. Anyone who has spent time trying to decode John's message
knows the difficulties involved in extracting its meaning. One major problem is that some passages can be understood on more than one level or in
more than one way. Consider the first line of the first verse: "The
Revelation of Jesus Christ." What does the phrase mean? Does the revelation belong to Jesus, or does the revelation disclose Him? The context suggests the first idea is correct. John expressly states that "God gave [it] unto
him, to shew unto his servants things which must shortly come to pass"
(Revelation 1:1). Still, as we look at the book's prophetic message, we cannot doubt that the great revelation emphasizes the work of the Savior in
its full cosmic scale. So, though Revelation belongs to Jesus, it is also the
revelation that discloses Him.

THE REVELATION OF THE SAVIOR IN THE FIRST VISION (REVELATION 1)

In the very first chapter of the book of Revelation, John records the
Savior's testimony of Himself: "I am Alpha and Omega, the beginning and
the ending, saith the Lord, which is, and which was, and which is to come,
the Almighty" (v. 8). That the Lord introduced Himself with these

Richard D. Draper is associate dean of Religious Education at Brigham Young
University.

elements suggests that they form the framework of what He wants to disclose about Himself. The Lord begins that disclosure by identifying Himself with the first and last letters of the Greek alphabet. In doing so He stresses His overarching role in the process of salvation. The Lord begins as "Alpha" by giving people the "light of Christ" (Moroni 7:19; see also D&C 88:7–13) by which they are able to discern and live the way of God. As they respond to their new understanding—by entering into and keeping covenants with Him—He is able to finish their perfection as "Omega" by bringing them to the Father (see Moroni 10:31–32; D&C 84:46–47). Thus, salvation begins and ends in Him.[2]

Jesus describes Himself further as "the Lord, who is, and who was, and who is to come" (JST, Revelation 1:8). The descriptive title is a paraphrase of the name of God given to Moses in Exodus 3:14–15 as translated in the Septuagint (the Hebrew Bible translated into Greek sometime between 300 and 100 BC).[3] The Greek phrase, as written by John, begins with *apo,* "from," which takes the genitive case but here is followed by three nominative phrases linked by the connective *kai,* "and." By keeping the form in the nominative, John emphasizes the idea that the Savior is always the subject. He holds the initiative. From the beginning, "He ordered all things according to the council of His own will."[4] Men do not force His hand. Everything they do, even in their rebellion, works according to His plan.[5] We can understand the phrase as an indeclinable noun, a rephrase of the tetragrammaton, *YHWH,* "he who is."[6] This rephrase of Jehovah's name reminds the reader that Jehovah is eternally existent. As He said to Moses, "Endless is my name; for I am without beginning of days or end of years; and is not this endless?" (Moses 1:3).[7]

The title "Endless" does more. It brings the Endless One onto the stage of history. He alone stands as the Lord of the past, the present, and the future. He "contemplated the whole of the events connected with the earth, pertaining to the plan of salvation, before it rolled into existence, or ever 'the morning stars sang together' for joy; the past, the present, and the future were and are, with Him, one eternal 'now.'"[8] Jesus, by virtue of His eternal existence, exercises power and fulfills His purposes throughout the course of history.

The last title the Lord uses to describe Himself is "the Almighty" (Revelation 1:8). The appellation emphasizes His power over and throughout history. The Greek word used here, *pantokrator,* is not a synonym for the omnipotent: those who have power to do all things. Rather, it designates one who holds together and regulates all things.[9] In this title, "Almighty," we see the central message of Revelation, which is reiterated in modern scripture: He "ascended up on high, as also he descended below all things, in that he comprehended all things, that he might be in all and through all things, the light of truth" (D&C 88:6). It is this "light which is in all things, which giveth life to all things, which is the law by which all things are governed" (D&C 88:13). Thus the Savior oversees the sun, the moon, and even the stars with all their world systems. He rules world history and determines humankind's destiny. As will be shown, nothing goes beyond the limits He sets. He is indeed God, the Almighty.

This auditory witness was the beginning of John's understanding of the nature of the Lord. Within moments the Savior parted the veil and appeared to His beloved disciple. With powerful imagery, John records his encounter with Christ, the Second Comforter. As the vision opened, the prophet saw in the midst of seven lampstands "one like unto the Son of man, clothed with a garment down to the foot, and girt about the paps with a golden girdle" (Revelation 1:12–13).[10] The phrase "Son of man," found in all the standard works, usually refers to the Savior, though in the Old Testament it is used to distinguish mortals from Gods—especially in the context of judgment (see Numbers 23:19; Psalm 8:4; Isaiah 51:12). The book of Moses gives another dimension to the title. There the name is capitalized, "Son of Man," making it a proper name or title. According to that passage, "in the language of Adam, Man of Holiness" is the name of God, "and the name of his Only Begotten is the Son of Man, even Jesus Christ, a righteous Judge" (Moses 6:57). In this context, the name designates Him who is the Son of the Man of Holiness.

John's culture gives the title a further dimension. The term can be found in a number of writings during the first century after Christ.[11] Though scholars are still unsure about its full meaning, the term designated a supernatural figure who was to act as the vice-regent of God at the close of the age.[12] It is noteworthy that Jesus first applied the term to Himself when His dual power to heal physical and spiritual illness proved His divinity (see Luke 5:18–26). The ancient definition of supernatural being and God's vice-regent seems to fit much of the profile of the Savior.[13] The implications of the title would have been obvious to John's readers.

The imagery John uses to describe the Lord reveals much. His appearance, along with the lampstands, ties the vision to the temple. The words John uses to describe the Lord's robes are the same as those used in the

Septuagint for the vestments of the high priest (see Exodus 28:4; 29:5; Daniel 10:5). The golden girdle, or clasp, worn at breast level, marked royalty.[14] Thus, the Lord presents Himself as both king and priest, offices associated with the temple and the fulness of the priesthood. The revelation foreshadows His standing at the head of the patriarchal order, presiding as Eternal Father, king, and priest.

John goes on to describe the Lord's countenance as that of the sun shining in its strength; His hair, "white like wool, as white as snow; and his eyes . . . as a flame of fire." Fire also surrounded His feet and legs, "as if they burned in a furnace" (Revelation 1:14–15). John's vision mirrors that of Joseph Smith and Oliver Cowdery. When they saw the Lord, "His eyes were as a flame of fire; the hair of his head was white like the pure snow; his countenance shone above the brightness of the sun; and his voice was as the sound of the rushing of great waters, even the voice of Jehovah" (D&C 110:3). Both visions emphasize the celestial, almost overwhelming glory associated with the Lord.[15]

There is a dramatic difference between the two visions, however. In John's, "a sharp two-edged sword" issues from the Lord's mouth (Revelation 1:16). The image is a bit startling, but like much in John's visions, the symbolism is meant not for the eye but for the mind. In other words, John means to teach us something through his imagery, not to have us draw it. The King James Version translates two Greek words as "sword": *machaira* and *rhomphaia*. Both terms refer to swords in general, but a *machaira* also described a butcher's knife and a surgeon's scalpel. The *rhomphaia*, the word John used, specifically designated a Thracian broadsword but was sometimes used to denote a lance or spear with a broad, double-edged head.[16]

The symbolism echoes Isaiah 11:4: "He shall smite the earth with the rod of his mouth" (the Septuagint replaces *rod* with *word*), and 49:2: "He hath made my mouth like a sharp sword." The sword makes an excellent symbol for the executive and judicial powers of the Lord: that which severs, cuts, opens, and reveals. It stands as a perfect symbol of the word of the Lord, which is "quick and powerful, . . . to the dividing asunder of the joints and marrow, soul and spirit; and is a discerner of the thoughts and intents of the heart" (D&C 33:1).

Before giving John his commission, the Lord revealed one more fact about Himself: "[I] have the keys of hell and of death" (Revelation 1:18). Many find that phrase surprising, feeling that Satan possesses those keys.

Revelation, however, has it right. Keys give access or control; they symbolize authority. The Greek word translated "hell" (*hades*) denoted, in its Christian context, the world of spirits where the rebellious await the Day of Judgment in torment. The Lord holds power over spirit prison as well as paradise. The wicked, consigned to hell, feel "a certain fearful looking for of judgment and fiery indignation, which shall devour the [Lord's] adversaries" (Hebrews 10:27). Alma testified that "this is the state of the souls of the wicked, yea, in darkness, and a state of awful, fearful looking for the fiery indignation of the wrath of God upon them" (Alma 40:14). The Lord's judgment places the wicked in torment so they will repent, be purged, and be prepared through the fire for a kingdom of glory and happiness.

The Lord's power over death and hell comes through the Atonement and the Resurrection. Peter testified that the Lord's descent into the spirit world made it possible for the souls in spirit prison to be taught the gospel that they might be judged with the same judgment as men in the flesh (see 1 Peter 3:18–20; 4:6). The Savior's descent was that of a conquering hero come to liberate the prisoners. His ministers declared "liberty to the captives who were bound, even unto all who would repent of their sins and receive the gospel" (D&C 138:31). It was, however, through the power of the Resurrection that the Lord fully demonstrated His complete authority. Indeed, one day, through the twin keys that belong to Him alone, all hell and every tomb will stand empty.

The Message of the First Vision

From the very first vision, Revelation shows Jesus not only as king and priest but as caretaker and director as well—a God immediate, intimate, and cognizant. "I know your doings," He assured the servants of the seven churches (see Revelation 2:2, 9, 13, 19; 3:1, 8, 15; the KJV "works" translates the Greek quite well, but "doings" is somewhat better).

John's Lord stood not outside history but at its very core. He was the mover and shaker. "I can stretch forth mine hands and hold all the creations which I have made; and mine eye can pierce them also," He assured Moses (Moses 7:36). He warned the seven churches to mend their ways or He would take away their candlesticks. The Lord reveals Himself as caring and compassionate, yet exacting and unyielding.

THE REVELATION OF THE SAVIOR IN THE SECOND VISION (REVELATION 5)

As a prelude to the second appearance of the Lord in Revelation, John was invited to see the celestial kingdom with God sitting upon His throne surrounded by cherubim and elders. In the Father's hand was a scroll. It was the book of destiny, for in it was recorded "the revealed will, mysteries, and the works of God; the hidden things of his economy concerning this earth during the seven thousand years of its continuance, or its temporal existence" (D&C 77:6). John understood that someone had to execute God's will. John also recognized a problem: the heavens could find no one worthy to do the job. Indeed, no one "was able to open the book, neither to look thereon" (Revelation 5:3). The earth stood in danger of not having the will of God executed because no one "was able." The Greek word (*dunamai*) suggests that no one had the power or ability in or of himself to do the task, not even the angels of heaven.

John's reaction was instant and heartfelt: "I wept much" (Revelation 5:4). His sorrow, however, was short-lived, for one of the elders assured him that "the Lion of the tribe of Juda, the Root of David, hath prevailed" and could, therefore, open the scroll (Revelation 5:5). Both titles come from Jewish messianism. The first echoes Genesis 49:9–10, in which Judah is called a "lion's whelp" and is promised that the scepter would not depart from him "until Shiloh [that is, the Messiah] come." The second title suggests Isaiah 11:1, which refers to the root of Jesse, the future ideal king of David's line, who was to usher in the millennial era of peace. Both combine to reveal the Savior as the true king of Israel, the sovereign of heaven and earth ready to bring in His millennial reign. John turned to look, but he did not see the majestic figure of a regal lion. Instead, he saw a lamb "in the midst of the throne" (JST, Revelation 4:4). The phrase gives the lamb a position nearest the throne, sharing, as it were, the central place. In this way, the Father symbolized a principal reality. The Lamb is the center of all things, preeminent over all His creations.

The Lamb, though living, bore the marks of a violent death. The Greek verb used to describe the wound, *sphazo,* meaning "slaughter," refers to the act of sacrificing. John could have had the paschal lamb in mind. If so, his imagery echoed the celebration of the Passover with its ritual slaughtering of a lamb. That would have reminded his Jewish readers of the ultimate victory and freedom from death they gained through Jehovah, the Lamb of God. This powerful symbol also emphasized a central biblical theme:

victory through sacrifice.[17] The Lamb prevails not by sovereign might but by sacrifice grounded in love (see John 16:33). He derives His worthiness by purchasing God's people with His own blood (see Ephesians 1:7; Titus 2:14). The metaphor of John the Seer emphasizes both the high value of those the Redeemer purchased, costing Him His blood and His life, and the universality of the Lord's action in redeeming all the faithful from death and hell.[18]

John described the Lamb as having seven eyes and seven horns. Again, the image created suggests symbolic interpretation rather than visual reconstruction. The eyes depict knowledge, the horns represent power, and the number seven suggests fulness or completeness.[19] Christ possesses with His Father the powers of omnipotence and omniscience; He has "the power of God, and the wisdom of God" (1 Corinthians 1:24). To these the Seer adds, through the symbolism of the "seven Spirits of God," the fulness of administrative authority. Each image shows the Lord's connection to earthly government, which He is about to assume in His redemptive role as "slain."

Through "the seven Spirits of God sent forth into all the earth" (Revelation 5:6), John represents the omnipresent nature of the Lamb. The Joseph Smith Translation provides an additional insight. There the Lamb has twelve horns and twelve eyes, "which are the twelve servants of God, sent forth into all the earth" (JST, Revelation 5:6). The text defines the nature of the power of the Lamb. Twelve symbolizes the priesthood, and the Joseph Smith Translation seems to be teaching that all priesthood centers in and flows from the Lamb. The Doctrine and Covenants notes that at one time "it was called *the Holy Priesthood, after the Order of the Son of God.* But out of respect or reverence to the name of the Supreme Being, to avoid the too frequent repetition of his name, they, the church, in ancient days, called that priesthood after Melchizedek, or the Melchizedek Priesthood" (D&C 107:3–4; italics in original). Further, "The Melchizedek Priesthood holds the right of presidency, and has power and authority over all the offices in the church in all ages of the world, to administer in spiritual things" (D&C 107:8). All this power centers in the Lamb and flows from Him to His leaders, especially His Apostles. By its authority the Savior acted to bring about the Atonement and continues to minister its saving power in the world. This is the central deed in the scroll of destiny, for all history pivots on this one act. It alone allowed for the complete fulfillment of the Father's will.

The Message of the Second Vision

The imagery in which God chose to clothe the revelation of His Son in this vision manifests the Redeemer's role as the slain or sacrificed Lamb. But though the wound is horrible, it does not dominate the metaphor. The Lamb's horns and the eyes stand out. The image draws the reader's mind to those elements that explain why the Lamb prevailed to open the scroll and why He could act when no one else "was found worthy to open and to read the book, neither to look thereon" (Revelation 5:4). Remember that John could clearly see the scroll from where he was standing, but he could not "look" on it. The Greek word John chose (*blepo*) suggests not just viewing but reading, understanding, or comprehending. This he could not do. It took more power and knowledge than he had to comprehend the will, economy, and mystery of God as it played out in the world's history. The Lamb possessed those powers. He received them, we must remember, because of the wound. It was the sacrifice that made the Lamb "worthy to open the book, and to loose the seals thereof" (Revelation 5:2). The imagery of the vision brings the reader's mind to an even higher understanding. The horns and eyes do indeed invest the Savior with the attributes of deity, but, more importantly, the whole image—the Lamb, the eyes, the horns, and especially the wound—force a new definition of omnipotence. Often used to describe God's power of unlimited coercion, John the Seer reveals its true nature as the power of infinite persuasion, the invincible strength of self-sacrificing love.[20]

THE REVELATION OF THE SAVIOR IN THE THIRD VISION (REVELATION 14)

As the next vision opened, John saw the Savior standing with 144,000 of the Saints of God. These represent those whom the Savior has sealed unto eternal life. We do not need to take the number literally. The Doctrine and Covenants states "that those who are sealed are high priests, ordained unto the holy order of God, to administer the everlasting gospel; for they are they who are ordained out of every nation, kindred, tongue, and people, by the angels to whom is given power over the nations of the earth, to bring as many as will come to the church of the Firstborn" (D&C 77:11). Note that this scripture does not specify a number. Instead, it says that they are high priests who have a special calling "to administer the everlasting gospel" and "to bring as many as will come to the church of the Firstborn."

Joseph Smith associated the 144,000 with the temple.[21] The symbolic meaning of the number supports this association. Twelve represents the priesthood. Biblical people squared numbers to amplify their symbolic meaning. Thus 144 suggests a fulness of priesthood authority. But the Lord was not satisfied with that. He gives the image a superlative quality by multiplying 144 by a thousand, representing completeness. In this way He shows the strength and breadth of the priesthood in the latter days, in this dispensation, which is, indeed, the dispensation of the fulness of times. During this period, complete priesthood authority will operate. It is little wonder that as the world spurns this authority, it will be condemned.

It is these people who have built the New Jerusalem and established the foundation of Zion. It is here, John understands, where the Lord will dwell before the great and dreadful day overtakes the rest of the earth. The presence of the Lord prepares the Saints against the judgments He is about to unleash on the rest of the world.

The momentum of John's vision up to this point has prepared the reader for the onset of a great battle, but, as usual, God throws in a twist. He does not disclose the figure standing on Mount Zion as a terrible warrior-king garbed in battle array but instead as a lamb, the symbol of meekness and peace. Further, harmony and joy reign over the entire scene. These people do not know worry or distress; they seem unconcerned about the war clouds gathering over the whole earth. The harmony of sweet music fills the region and reaches from earth to heaven, where it ignites a rhapsody expressing itself as a new song—new not only because it has never been sung before but because it could never have been sung before. It signals a total victory which only now becomes possible. For this reason, only the 144,000—representing the sealed, those who have won the battle—are able to sing it. The Doctrine and Covenants provides the setting for the song and its content. In it the Lord states:

For I, the Almighty, have laid my hands upon the nations, to scourge them for their wickedness.

And plagues shall go forth, and they shall not be taken from the earth until I have completed my work, which shall be cut short in righteousness—

Until all shall know me, who remain, even from the least unto the greatest, and shall be filled with the knowledge of the Lord, and shall see eye to eye, and shall lift up their voice, and with the voice together sing this new song, saying:

> The Lord hath brought again Zion;
> The Lord hath redeemed his people, Israel,
> According to the election of grace,
> Which was brought to pass by the faith
> And covenant of their fathers.
> The Lord hath redeemed his people;
> And Satan is bound and time is no longer.
> The Lord hath gathered all things in one.
> The Lord hath brought down Zion from above.
> The Lord hath brought up Zion from beneath.
> The earth hath travailed and brought forth her strength;
> And truth is established in her bowels;
> And the heavens have smiled upon her;
> And she is clothed with the glory of her God;
> For he stands in the midst of his people.
> Glory, and honor, and power, and might,
> Be ascribed to our God; for he is full of mercy,
> Justice, grace and truth, and peace,
> Forever and ever, Amen. (D&C 84:96–102)

In these verses, the Lord reveals the triumphant nature of the song. It celebrates the time when the plagues of judgment will cleanse the earth. Only the redeemed will remain. God and His Saints will win the day, and Zion will stand supreme.

Chapter 14 explains the underpinnings of the song, allowing us to understand why it can be sung. In the dramatic closing scene, John beholds "one like unto the Son of man" (v. 14) seated upon a white cloud. The imagery is taken from Daniel 7:13–14 and appears to be a reference to the resurrected Lord coming in the fulness of His power. On his head sits a golden wreath. The King James Version describes it as a "crown," but the Greek word *stephenos* does not refer to a diadem, the mark of civil rule, but rather to a wreath, a sign of the highest athletic achievement or of a great military victory. In His hand, He readies the sickle of judgment and begins to harvest the wheat fields. The day of judgment has fully come, "for the harvest of the earth is ripe" (v. 15). It is the ripeness that determines the timing of the reaping. The Lord expresses this idea in a parable of harvest: "But behold, in the last days, even now while the Lord is beginning to bring forth the word, and the blade is springing up and is yet tender—behold, verily I say unto you, the angels are crying unto the Lord day and night, who are ready and waiting to be sent forth to reap down the fields; but the Lord saith unto them, pluck not up the tares while the blade is yet tender (for verily your faith is weak), lest you destroy the wheat also. Therefore, let the wheat and the tares grow together until the harvest is fully ripe; then ye shall first gather out the wheat from among the tares, and after the gathering of the wheat, behold and lo, the tares are bound in bundles, and the field remaineth to be burned" (D&C 86:4–7).

The first harvest, the harvest of the Lord, is the gathering in of the wheat. That time is now, and the time is urgent. To His Saints, the Lord declared: "For verily, verily, I say unto you that ye are called to lift up your voices as with the sound of a trump, to declare my gospel unto a crooked and perverse generation. For behold, the field is white already to harvest; and it is the eleventh hour, and the last time that I shall call laborers into my vineyard" (D&C 33:2–3).

It is in this light that the Lord admonishes, "Whoso desireth to reap let him thrust in his sickle with his might, and reap while the day lasts, that he may treasure up for his soul everlasting salvation in the kingdom of God" (D&C 11:3). Now is the time when the wheat must be gathered in. Those who participate are the Lord's sickle. The Lord will reward the effort of His laborers with the security and peace of Zion.

Through the efforts of the laborers, the world will hear the gospel. But when the world openly rejects goodness and turns against God's people, then another sickle will begin to do its terrible work.[22] That will be the day when the voice of God will utter

> out of the heaven, saying: Hearken, O ye nations of the earth, and hear the words of that God, who made you.
>
> O, ye nations of the earth, how often would I have gathered you together as a hen gathereth her chickens under her wings, but ye would not!
>
> How oft have I called upon you by the mouth of my servants, and by the ministering of angels, and by mine own voice, and by the voice of thunderings, and by the voice of lightnings, and by the voice of tempests, and by the voice of earthquakes, and great hailstorms, and by the voice of famines and pestilences of every kind, and by the great sound of a trump, and by the voice of judgment, and by the voice of mercy all the day long, and by the voice of glory and honor and the riches of eternal life, and would have saved you with an everlasting salvation, but ye would not!

Behold, the day has come, when the cup of the wrath of mine
indignation is full. (D&C 43:23–26)

The period of the second sickle begins when all peaceful attempts to
redeem the world have failed. At that point, the warning of the Book of
Mormon may again find fulfillment: "For behold, there is a curse upon all
this land, that destruction shall come upon all those workers of darkness,
according to the power of God, when they are fully ripe" (Alma 37:28).
The warning applies not only to the Americas but also to the world at
large.

The harvest of ruin will be carried out not by the Lord but by an angel
of destruction. His target is not the fields but the vineyards.[23] He is to
"gather the clusters of the vine of the earth; for her grapes are fully ripe"
(Revelation 14:18). Further, he is to cast the fruit "into the great winepress
of the wrath of God" (Revelation 14:19). The destruction will be tremendous and bitter.

The Message of the Third Vision

In the third vision, the Father reveals His Son as the victor, the great
general who has met His foe and won. It is out of this victory that the
144,000 sing their song and celebrate both security and peace. But the celebration, in the context of Revelation, seems premature. The actual battle
has not commenced, and the enemy still stands strong, arrogant, and
undefeated. How then can the Saints celebrate with such surety? There are
two reasons: the first is grounded in their absolute faith in the ability of
the Lord to overcome. Part of this is based on the redemption He has
already won for them. Their absolute confidence echoes the same faith
they exhibited during the great War in Heaven when "they overcame him
[Satan] by the blood of the Lamb, and by the word of their testimony"
(Revelation 12:11). The second stems from the fact that the Lord is personally with them, directing affairs and attending to the Saints' needs and
assuring their safety. The Lord promised the Saints of America that here
"shall be a New Jerusalem. And the powers of heaven shall be in the midst
of this people; yea, even I will be in the midst of you" (3 Nephi 20:22). He
assured them further that His shall be "a land of peace, a city of refuge, a
place of safety for the saints of the Most High God; and the glory of the
Lord shall be there, and the terror of the Lord also shall be there, insomuch
that the wicked will not come unto it, and it shall be called Zion" (D&C
45:66–67). It is not the Saints who need to fear, but the enemy.

The Lord directs the work of the harvest from Zion. The 144,000 act as the sickle of the Lord moving among the nations to gather out all who will come to Zion. John emphasizes the Lord's saving ministry. Neither he nor any of his people work to destroy the world or its enemies. It was another angel whom John saw that "came out of the temple which is in heaven, he also having a sharp sickle" (Revelation 14:17). It is this one to whom the angel of the altar commands: "Thrust in thy sharp sickle, and gather the clusters of the vine of the earth; for her grapes are fully ripe" (Revelation 14:18). John's point seems to be that, at least at this juncture, the Lord does not come to destroy the earth or its people. He comes to save it. Revelation gives credit for destruction to the five angels of the Lord (the four in chapter 7 and the one in chapter 14) on one side and to Satan on the other. The actual work is done by the army described as horsemen with "breastplates of fire, and of jacinth, and brimstone" (Revelation 9:17) and led by one "whose name in the Hebrew tongue is Abaddon, but in the Greek tongue hath his name Apollyon," and in English, the Destroyer, or Perdition (see Revelation 9:11; D&C 76:26).[24] Out of the horsemen's mouths come fire and smoke and brimstone, and "by these three was the third part of men killed" (Revelation 9:18). So what does the Lord do at His coming? John understood perfectly. The Lord comes to "destroy them which destroy the earth" (Revelation 11:18).

The point is that the Savior does just what His name says: He saves. The paradox is that the Lord's destruction becomes His tool of salvation. He uses that tool, however, only when all others have failed. Still, it is a tool of salvation, and for that reason the angels can say, "Lord God Almighty, true and righteous are thy judgments" (Revelation 16:7). The Lord is perfectly prepared to allow His destroying angels and the beasts of Satan to have a certain destructive power over millions. Some may have trouble with this idea, but Revelation forces upon us a very realistic understanding about death. From the Lord's perspective, all must die. The question is only when and how. Ultimate destiny is not determined by the moment or manner of death: it is by the manner of life. Keep in mind that those who are destroyed are not annihilated. They have further existence. For the present, they refuse to play the game by God's rules. They have become mean and violent, and so they are thrown into the penalty box, so to speak, for unnecessary roughness while the game goes on. We must fight against the current idea that mortality is so infallibly precious that, as one scholar put it, "the death which robs us of it must be the ultimate tragedy." Such an idea, he says, "is precisely the idolatry that John is trying here to combat. We have already seen that John calls the enemies of the church 'the inhabitants of earth,' because they have made themselves utterly at home in this transient world order. If all men must die, and if at the end heaven and earth must vanish, along with those whose life is irremediably bounded by worldly horizons, then it is surely in accord with the mercy of God that he should send men from time to time forceful reminders of the insecurity of their tenure."[25]

Besides, John shows us clearly that the purpose of the plagues is to drive those who would not do so otherwise to repentance and thus into the protective arms of God. Those who will not repent must be accountable to the fire. What happens to those who refuse to repent leads us to God's next revelation of His Son.

THE REVELATION OF THE SAVIOR IN THE FOURTH VISION (REVELATION 19)

At the beginning of his heavenly revelations, John saw "a door . . . opened in heaven" through which he was able to see the throne of God (Revelation 4:1). Later "the temple of God was opened in heaven," such that the Seer could behold the ark of the testimony (Revelation 11:19). Then the whole temple opened so that the seven angels with the seven bowls could come out (see Revelation 15:5). Now John sees the entire expanse of heaven unfold to make way for the warrior-king and His army prepared to battle the hosts of darkness.[26] The rider, terrible in majesty upon His white horse, is the Savior, "called Faithful and True" (Revelation 19:11; compare D&C 45:74–75). These names of Christ, as Elder Bruce R. McConkie points out, "signify that he is the embodiment and personification of these godly attributes. Above all His fellows, he was obedient to the will of the Father and true to every trust imposed upon him."[27] John clearly states the rider's purpose: "In righteousness he doth judge and make war" (Revelation 19:11). War results from His just judgment. Evil must be put down even by force when necessary.

John sees the Lord coming with crowns upon His head. These are not wreaths but diadems, the symbol of political rule. The king comes to take back His domain. John deliberately contrasts the King with the dragon and the sea beast met in Revelation 12. Whereas the former two possess seven and ten diadems respectively, the warrior has "many" diadems (Revelation 19:12). The king's true royalty far surpasses the false sovereignty of Satan and his minion. He now rides as "KING OF KINGS, AND LORD OF LORDS" (Revelation 19:16)—and He has acquired His crowns since John last saw Him. Although John had seen Him in regal authority early in the revelation (see Revelation 3:21; compare 1:5), John mentions no diadem. Here they are prominently displayed. They signify that the "kingdoms of this world are become the kingdoms of our Lord, and of his Christ; and he shall reign for ever and ever" (Revelation 11:15).[28]

The rider bore a name "that no man knew, but he himself" (Revelation 19:12). Again Elder McConkie gives insight: "As with all glorified beings, our Lord has a new name in celestial exaltation, a name known to and comprehended by those only who know God in the sense that they have become as he is and have eternal life. See Rev. 2:12–17. Thus, Christ's 'new name' shall be written upon all those who are joint-heirs with him (Rev. 3:12), and shall signify that they have become even as he is."[29]

But the warrior does have a known name: "The Word of God" (Revelation 19:13). John calls Him by this same title at the beginning of his Gospel (see John 1:1–3). In Revelation the name emphasizes that He judges the kings of the world.[30] Among many ancient peoples, a word was not simply a lifeless sound but an active agent bringing into being the intent of the one who spoke.[31] The Savior is the active agent who executes the word (that is, the will) of God. That word is now judgment. Thus the rider's vestments are blood red, for the judgment is one of death (compare Isaiah 63:1–6). According to the Doctrine and Covenants, His appearance will cause consternation among the nations. Many will ask:

> Who is this that cometh down from God in heaven with dyed garments; yea, from the regions which are not known, clothed in his glorious apparel, traveling in the greatness of his strength?
>
> And he shall say: I am he who spake in righteousness, mighty to save. . . .
>
> And so great shall be the glory of his presence that the sun shall hide his face in shame, and the moon shall withhold its light, and the stars shall be hurled from their places.
>
> And his voice shall be heard: I have trodden the wine-press alone, and have brought judgment upon all people; and none were with me;
>
> And I have trampled them in my fury, and I did tread upon them in mine anger, and their blood have I sprinkled upon my garments,

and stained all my raiment; for this was the day of vengeance which was in my heart. (D&C 133:46–47, 49–51)

Clearly John depicts the moment of vengeance when the Lord will destroy all wickedness by the brightness of His coming (see D&C 5:19). But He does not come alone. With Him comes His army "upon white horses, clothed in fine linen, white and clean" (Revelation 19:14). Against these "the kings of the earth, and their armies, gathered together to make war" (Revelation 19:19), but they will be "slain with the sword of him that sat upon the horse, which sword proceeded out of his mouth: and all the fowls were filled with their flesh" (Revelation 19:21). At this moment, all nations will come under His authority, "and he shall rule them with a rod of iron" (Revelation 19:15).

The Message of the Fourth Vision

Revelation 19 gives us a clear view of the nature and purpose of the Second Coming. Unlike other accounts in which the glory and burning power of the Redeemer dominate, Revelation stresses the regal and martial authority of the Lord. He appears as the warrior-king at the head of His angelic host to take back His land from the dark lord and his legions. Actually, He does not need to take it back, for He has never lost it. His is more of a mopping-up exercise against those that have tried to take His world and failed.

Some may be concerned because the day of the Lord is filled with destruction. But it has its purpose. Nothing unclean (that is, unjustified) can enter into the Lord's presence and survive (see John 6:46; Moses 7:35). Christ is about to sweep the earth with His glory so that the millennial era may be established. Therefore, evil must come to an end. By the time the Lord comes, there will be very little evil left to put to an end. Throughout Revelation, we have seen the self-destructive nature of wickedness. God cannot allow such self-destruction to act as an impersonal nemesis: an independent, self-operating moral law sweeping away all in its path. To do so would allow the powers of evil to carry all the inhabitants of the earth down with them to utter ruin. God would be left with a hollow, Pyrrhic victory. Because God's victory must also be the Saints' victory, it must be won through righteous human agents exercising faith in God. Evil must be allowed to combine its forces against the Savior's people and then fall back in utter defeat through their faith and trust coupled with the glory of those who come with the Savior.[32]

Because His victory is theirs, they reign with Him. As John declared, "I saw thrones, and they [who] sat upon them, and judgment was given unto them" (Revelation 20:4). These "lived and reigned with Christ a thousand years" (Revelation 20:4). His coming, then, results in a world over which He will preside with the faithful and without opposition from the dragon. The result will be that His people "shall be priests of God and of Christ, and shall reign with him a thousand years" (Revelation 20:6).

WHAT REVELATION REVEALS ABOUT THE LORD

The book of Revelation contains, as John clearly stated in his introduction, the revelation of Jesus Christ. God the Father chose the imagery and focus of that revelation. Three images eclipse all others. The first is that of Christ as the divine Lamb executing the will of His omnipotent Father. Revelation underscores the work of the Savior as the executor of the Father's will. He is the active God in history. It is true that for much of earth's history the Lamb has chosen to act behind the scenes. That has made it easy for the natural man or woman to attribute the course of history to political, social, and other causes. The naturalistic view, however, will soon prove untenable. Already the great Jehovah is beginning to direct more openly the course of history and manifest more directly His control over the destiny of humankind. An iron curtain has crumbled, the gospel is preached across many lands, and worthy men of all nations can hold the priesthood. Before long, all will see that the Lamb does indeed execute the will of God, whose grasp none can escape.

Tied closely to the image of the Lamb is that of the Almighty God—the one who directs, controls, and orchestrates. John reveals the power of God on two levels. One is through the active voice, by which the prophet attributes direct authority and movement to the Lamb. The other is through the passive voice, by which indirect credit is given to the Lamb. To understand, consider the subtle hope lying behind one of the most frightening chapters—Revelation 9. John records a vision in which he saw "a star fall from heaven unto the earth: and to him was given the key of the bottomless pit" (Revelation 9:1). God chose a star to represent His rebellious son Satan and the pit to symbolize the source from which powers of hell will be unleashed upon the world in the last days.

Notice, though, that Satan did not possess the key to the pit in the abyss. He had to receive it from someone. Further, John sees that the destructive beasts, described as "locusts," will be "given power, as the scorpions of the earth have power. And it was commanded them that they should not hurt the grass of the earth, neither any green thing, neither any tree; but only those men which have not the seal of God in their foreheads" (Revelation 9:3–4). Something sets limits on these beasts. It gives them power, it tells them what and who they can and cannot hurt, and it dictates how long they shall act: "five months" (Revelation 9:5). Something even limits the angels of destruction. Their time is set for "an hour, and a day, and a month, and a year," and they can slay but "the third part of men" (Revelation 9:15).

John clearly reveals that something overmasters all that goes on, setting boundaries and establishing limits. What is the power behind history? It is Jehovah. Revelation gives more than a powerful testimony of the prophetic abilities of this God. It shows not only that He knew the end from the beginning and contemplated the whole of earth's history but also that He arranged and continuously orchestrates it. History has moved according to the script He has written, and all movements have stayed within the bounds He has set. He is indeed the Almighty.

The last image through which God reveals His Son is that of the warrior-king destroying evil with His victorious hosts and reigning with them for a thousand years. Along with the white horse of war, the myriad of diadems atop the king's head dominate the scene. In this way, God set the political aspect of the Lord's power center stage. The millennial era will see true theocracy established and flourishing in preparation for the time when this earth will enter the family of celestial planets. This is the time, as John saw, that "the holy city, new Jerusalem, [will come] down from God out of heaven, prepared as a bride adorned for her husband" (Revelation 21:2). Then "the tabernacle of God [will be] with men, and he will dwell with them, . . . and God himself shall be with them, and be their God" (Revelation 21:3).

It is Christ, the Lamb, the Almighty, the warrior-king, who shall bring all these things to pass. Little wonder that the angelic hosts will praise His name, singing "the song of Moses the servant of God, and the song of the Lamb, saying, Great and marvelous are thy works, Lord God Almighty; just and true are thy ways, thou King of saints. Who shall not fear thee, O Lord, and glorify thy name? for thou only art holy: for all nations shall come and worship before thee; for thy judgments are made manifest" (Revelation 15:3–4).

NOTES

1. Northrop Frye, "Typology: Apocalypse," in *The Revelation of St. John the Divine,* ed. Harold Bloom (New York: Chelsea House Publishers, 1988), 71.

2. Elohim also uses these same elements as disclosure points. See Revelation 2:6, wherein He uses the phrase to introduce the reward He will give the faithful. Both the Father and the Son act together to bring eternal life to humankind.

3. Compare Jeremiah 1:6; 14:13; and 32:17 in the Septuagint (LXX).

4. Joseph Smith, *Teachings of the Prophet Joseph Smith,* comp. Joseph Fielding Smith (Salt Lake City: Deseret Book, 1976), 220.

5. See Romans 9:15–18; John 10:18; Ezekiel 38:1–4, 14–22. One of the aspects of apocalyptic literature in general and Revelation in particular is predeterminism. Revelation testifies that all things move in concert toward a divinely predetermined end. Everything is inevitable; nothing is left to chance. The problem of human agency or free will within the context of God's omniscience never surfaces. But there is a tacit insistence that God's ultimate victory is worked out within the framework of human freedom.

6. Josephine Massyngberde Ford, *Revelation,* vol. 38 of *The Anchor Bible* (Garden City, NY: Doubleday, 1975), 376. The Song of the Doves at Dondona speaks of "Zeus who was, Zeus who is, Zeus who will be" (Pausanias, *Asinaria,* 10.12.10). At Sais the shrine of Minerva boasted, "I am that hath been and is and shall be" (Plutarch, *Moralia, De hide et Osiride,* 9). See Robert H. Mounce, *The Book of Revelation* (Grand Rapids, MI: Eerdmans, 1977), 68. For a technical study of the name/title, see R. H. Charles, *A Critical and Exegetical Commentary on the Revelation of St. John,* 2 vols. (Edinburgh: T. & T. Clark, 1920), 1:10.

7. Jesus may well have been speaking by divine investiture of authority as He uttered these words. In that case, it is Elohim who is "Endless" and "Eternal." Revelation 21:6 has Elohim declare that He is "Alpha and Omega, the beginning and the end." Such titles seem to apply to both Father and Son because the perspective of the Father is shared by the Son through the power of the Holy Spirit. According to *Lectures on Faith* 5:1, the Son possesses the same fulness with the Father and "having overcome, received a fulness of the glory of the Father, possessing the same mind with the Father." By sharing the same mind, the Savior can speak from the perspective of the "Endless" and the "Eternal" (see Larry E. Dahl and Charles D. Tate Jr., eds., *The Lectures on Faith in Historical Perspective,* Religious Studies Center Monograph Series [Provo, UT: BYU, Religious Studies Center, 1990], 84).

8. Smith, *Teachings of the Prophet Joseph Smith,* 220.

9. Bruce R. McConkie, *Doctrinal New Testament Commentary,* 3 vols. (Salt Lake City: Bookcraft, 1965–73), 3:439.

10. The phrase "like unto" seems to suggests that John did not actually see the Savior. Such is not the case. There are a number of scriptures where the phrase "like unto the Son of Man" refers to none other than the Savior (see Abraham 3:27; Revelation 14:14).

11. See James H. Charlesworth, ed., *The Messiah: Developments in Earliest Christianity and Judaism* (Minneapolis: Fortress Press, 1992); for the concept of Messianism in earliest Judaism, see 79–115; on the term "son of man," see 130–44.

12. For discussion, see M. D. Hooker, *The Son of Man in Mark* (London: SPCK, 1967), 81–93.

13. Luke spoke previously of the Lord's power (*dunamis*) to heal. Here Luke focuses on his authority (*exousia*) to do so.

14. See Septuagint Exodus 28:4, 5, which indicates that the girdle is connected with the attire of the high priest. His girdle was made of fine-twined linen and embroidered with needlework (see Septuagint Exodus 28:36), while the clasp or girdle that gathered together the long robe of the Lord was of gold. Josephus, however, notes that during his time the high priest's girdle was interwoven with gold (*Antiquities of the Jews*, 3.7.2). The golden clasp, or *porpe,* was worn by the king and his associates (1 Maccabees 10:89; 11:58) and so served as a mark of an important office. For further discussion, see Charles, *Commentary*, 1:28; and Mounce, *Book of Revelation*, 77–78.

15. Joseph Smith and Oliver Cowdery may have been echoing the words of Revelation with which they were both acquainted. Even so, those words best described what they experienced.

16. G. Kittel and others, eds., *Theological Dictionary of the New Testament*, trans. Geoffrey W. Bromily, 10 vols. (Grand Rapids, MI: Eerdmans, 1964), s.v. "*machaira*" and "*rhomphaia.*"

17. Mounce, *Revelation*, 144.

18. Elizabeth Schussler Fiorenza, *The Book of Revelation: Justice and Judgment* (Philadelphia: Fortress Press, 1985), 73.

19. The possession of seven eyes echoes Zechariah 4:10, in which they are symbols of God's omniscience. The horn is the Old Testament symbol for power (see Numbers 23:22; Deuteronomy 33:17; 1 Samuel 2:1; 1 Kings 22:11; Psalms 75:4; 89:17). Thus it was the mark of kingly dignity (see Psalms 112:9; 148:14; Zechariah 1:18; Daniel 7:7, 20; 8:3). In 1 Enoch 90.9, the Maccabees are stylized as "horned lambs" (see Charles, *Commentary*, 1:141–43).

20. G. B. Caird, *A Commentary on the Revelation of St. John the Divine* (Peabody, MA: Hendrickson Publishers, 1966), 75.

21. Joseph Smith, *History of The Church of Jesus Christ of Latter-day Saints*, ed. B. H. Roberts, 2d ed. rev., 7 vols. (Salt Lake City: The Church of Jesus Christ of Latter-day Saints, 1932–51), 6:365; Andrew F. Ehat and Lyndon

W. Cook, *The Words of the Prophet Joseph Smith* (Provo, UT: Religious Studies Center, Brigham Young University, 1980), 368.

22. Compare 2 Nephi 28:15–20 with Alma 37:30–31, which teaches that the world is fully ripe when it both rejects and fights against goodness.

23. The *drepanon* was an all-purpose blade used for pruning, cutting clusters of grapes, and harvesting grains. Its roughly foot-long curved blade made it easy to handle, with clean cutting power.

24. The Greek word, a feminine noun, is *apoleia,* which carries the meaning of something that destroys or brings to utter ruin.

25. Caird, *Revelation,* 113.

26. Exodus 15:3 describes Jehovah as a man of war. The idea persists in 2 Maccabees 3:22–30 and in the Qumran scrolls 1QM 12.10–11; 19.2–4.

27. McConkie, *Commentary,* 3:566.

28. Caird, *Revelation,* 241.

29. McConkie, *Commentary,* 3:567.

30. Mounce, *Revelation,* 345–46.

31. Mounce, *Revelation,* 345–46. See, for example, Genesis 1:3, 7, 9; Hebrews 4:12.

32. Caird, *Revelation,* 145.

CHAPTER TWENTY-SIX

NEW TESTAMENT PROPHECIES OF APOSTASY

KENT P. JACKSON

The Church of Jesus Christ of Latter-day Saints has proclaimed to the world consistently since its beginning that there was an apostasy of the Church founded by Jesus during His earthly ministry and led by His Apostles following His Ascension.[1] This is a fundamental belief of Mormonism; in fact, the Apostasy of early Christianity provides much of the very justification for the existence of the Latter-day Saint faith. If there had not been an apostasy, there would have been no need for a restoration. Latter-day Saint theology asserts that the Church of Jesus and His Apostles came to an end well within a century of its formation; the doctrines which its inspired leaders taught were corrupted and changed by others not of similar inspiration, the authority to act in God's name was taken from the earth, and the Christian systems that then remained did not enjoy divine endorsement. It was precisely the question of divine endorsement—in Joseph Smith's words, "which of all the sects was right" (Joseph Smith–History 1:17)—that led to the glorious event that ushered in the Restoration of the gospel, the appearance of the Father and the Son to the young Prophet. In response to Joseph's search for a true church, he was told to join none of them, "for they were all wrong," and all their creeds were "an abomination" in the sight of God (Joseph Smith–History 1:19).

The message of the Latter-day Saints is that following seventeen centuries of darkness since the days of the Apostles, the heavens were again

---

Kent P. Jackson is a professor of ancient scripture at Brigham Young University.

opened, divinely authored doctrines were revealed anew, the authority to speak and act in God's name was brought back to earth, and the Church of Jesus Christ was established by divine command.

PROPHECIES ABOUT APOSTASY

Possibly the best single witness of the Apostasy of New Testament Christianity is the New Testament itself. In it there are several statements made by Jesus and His Apostles about the future of their work. Though they labored with great zeal to bring souls to the Lord and establish the Church throughout the world, still their prophetic utterances concerning the end result of their efforts foretold tragedy. In short, they knew that the Church would fall into apostasy shortly after their time, and they bore candid testimony of that fact. In this study I will examine selected prophetic passages in which Jesus and His Apostles foretold the falling of the Church or events associated with it.

Matthew 24:5, 9–11. One of the most significant sermons of the Savior is that which is recorded in Matthew 24–25, the so-called Olivet Discourse. In response to questions of the Twelve regarding the destruction of the temple and the destruction of the world (see also Joseph Smith–Matthew 1:4, 21), Jesus prophesied of events that would transpire in the near and distant future. Matthew 24:9–11 records a prophecy of great importance concerning the future of the Church: "Then shall they deliver you up to be afflicted, and shall kill you: and ye shall be hated of all nations for my name's sake. And then shall many be offended, and shall betray one another, and shall hate one another. And many false prophets shall rise, and shall deceive many."[2]

The Joseph Smith–Matthew rendering of this passage places it clearly in the context of the last days of the early Church (see Joseph Smith–Matthew 1:4–21). A number of important statements are contained in these verses. Verse 9 foretells the fate of the Apostles themselves: affliction, hatred, and death for Christ's sake. The only scripturally attested fulfillment of the martyrdom prophecy is the death of James at the hands of Herod Agrippa I (see Acts 12:1–2), but early Christian tradition tells of similar fates for other Apostles.[3] Yet the killing of the Apostles was not the cause of the Apostasy. Other references clearly teach that Christianity died from an internal wound, the rejection of true doctrine by the members of the Church. Still, the death of those who alone held the authority to lead the Church could only mean the death of the Church itself.

Verse 10 provides a valuable prophecy of the rejection of truth by the Saints. Unfortunately, the King James translation obscures its intended meaning beyond recognition with the phrase "Then shall many be offended." In the New International Version (NIV), a highly recommendable recent translation, we read, "At that time many will turn away from the faith." From the Phillips Modern English Version: "Then comes the time when many will lose their faith." The Greek verb *skandalízō* in the passive voice as here (a third person plural, future tense), means, in a theological sense, "to give up one's faith" or "fall into sin." "Many," the Savior foretells, will do it at that day.

Verse 11 records an additional prophecy, namely, that many false prophets would arise and would "deceive *many*" (emphasis added). Recall that the historical context here is the last days of the apostolic era, when the Apostles would be afflicted, hated, and killed (see Matthew 24:9). Taking their places would be what the Savior calls "many false prophets" (Matthew 24:11). The related passage in verse 5, which Joseph Smith–Matthew places clearly in the early Christian period (see Joseph Smith–Matthew 1:6), is also significant: "For many shall come in my name, saying, I am Christ; and shall deceive many." Notice that there would be *many* false Christs, and, like the false prophets, they would deceive *many*. One can only lament the fact that the available sources, scriptural or nonscriptural, do not give us a complete history of the fulfillment of these words.

Acts 20:29–31. On his way from Greece to Jerusalem at the end of his third missionary journey, the Apostle Paul stopped at the city of Miletus and called for the elders of nearby Ephesus. On their arrival he gave an important address of which Luke records only excerpts (see Acts 20:18–35). The prophecy relevant to the future of the Church reads as follows: "For I know this, that after my departing shall grievous wolves enter in among you, not sparing the flock. Also of your own selves shall men arise, speaking perverse things, to draw away disciples after them. Therefore watch, and remember, that by the space of three years I ceased not to warn every one night and day with tears" (Acts 20:29–31).

Paul warned the elders of Asia that following his departure, forces would damage the Church from without and within. From without, "grievous wolves" would invade the Church and would not spare the flock. At this point in Paul's career, he had experienced years of trouble with Judaizers trying to gain influence among his converts. Perhaps it was similar infiltration of apostate forces that Paul foresaw. It should be recalled that the Judaizers, who had already had great success opposing Paul (for example, see Galatians 1:6), were members of the Church. In spite of the wolf metaphor, what is being alluded to here is undoubtedly not physical attack or external persecution. Instead, Paul is describing the entering of evil forces *into* the Church and their gaining power over the Saints. This is borne out as Paul continues by telling of those who were part of the Asian Church—and who were perhaps in Paul's audience at that very moment— who would, in an effort to draw away disciples to themselves, "distort the truth" (Acts 20:30, NIV).

Paul ends his tragic prophecy by testifying that for three years he had warned the Asian Saints constantly, "with tears" (Acts 20:31). Similarly, in his great prophecy of apostasy in 2 Thessalonians, which will be examined next, he also bore witness to the Saints that he had warned them well of the coming fall (see 2 Thessalonians 2:5).

2 Thessalonians 2:1–12. The Thessalonian letters are Paul's most eschatological in emphasis. In the first letter, Paul cleared up a doctrinal misunderstanding concerning the status of those who had died prior to the Second Coming of Jesus. In the second, he had to respond to a much greater doctrinal problem, the belief among the Thessalonian Saints that the "day of Christ" was "at hand" (2 Thessalonians 2:2). We do not know the details of the problem in Thessalonika, nor do we know its origin. The Greek verbal conjugation *enestēken,* translated as "at hand" in the King James Bible, has been rendered in a variety of ways in other translations. The basic meaning of the word is "is present," so perhaps the reading "has come" (RSV), or something similar to it as found in the majority of the versions, is more accurate than the ambiguous "at hand."[4] Whatever the exact misunderstanding of the Thessalonians may have been, Paul responded clearly that the day of Christ's coming would not take place until the "falling away" and the revelation of the "man of sin," "the son of perdition" (2 Thessalonians 2:3).

The King James words "falling away" are translated from the Greek noun *apostasía,* from which we get our word *apostasy,* which is equal in meaning to it. Whereas the term "falling away" may give the incorrect impression of a process of drifting or gradually losing ground, the original term means something much more drastic. Some modern translations use "the rebellion" (NIV, RSV), "rejection of God" (Phillips), or "the Great Revolt" (JB). The two Greek elements combined in *apostasía* are the verb *hístēmi,* "to stand," and *apo,* "away from"; the basic meaning of the word is "rebellion." Semantically, ancient sources use the term to describe political rebellion and revolution.[5] What Paul was describing in the future of Christianity was a rebellion against God and His position in the Church. And, as he wrote in the following verses, the rebellion would succeed. The chief feature of this time of rebellion would be the triumph of the "man of sin." Paul wrote: "Let no man deceive you by any means: for that day shall not come, except there come a falling away first, and that man of sin be revealed, the son of perdition; who opposeth and exalteth himself above all that is called God, or that is worshipped; so that he as God sitteth in the temple of God, shewing himself that he is God" (2 Thessalonians 2:3–4).

Latter-day Saint commentators generally equate the "man of sin" mentioned in these verses with Satan, an interpretation with which I certainly concur.[6] As part of the rebellion, as Paul noted, Satan would be made manifest. He would exalt himself over all that is called divine and would assume the place of God in the Church, supplanting God in that position. The metaphorical term "temple," referring to the Church, is used by Paul also in 1 Corinthians 3:16 and Ephesians 2:21.[7] Of historical and theological significance is the fact that in Paul's prophecy the Church survives. But God is not at its head, making that church—following the appearance in it of Satan—no longer the Church of God.

Paul's words correspond well with evidence that we have from other scriptures. When the Lord appeared to Joseph Smith in the spring of 1820, He told the young Prophet that all of the Christian churches of his day were "wrong" (Joseph Smith–History 1:19). The Book of Mormon prophet Nephi envisioned in the latter days following the Restoration only *two* churches: "the church of the Lamb of God" and "the church of the devil" (1 Nephi 14:10). Since whoever does not belong to "the church of the Lamb of God" belongs to "the church of the devil," as Nephi announced, *all* false religion and all wickedness would be classified as "the church of the devil" by Nephi's definition. Paul told us the same thing as he foretold the "man of sin" replacing God at the head of the Church in the era of the rebellion.

To say that apostate Christianity has at its head Satan sitting in the place of God is not to say that all that is in it is satanic. Indeed, Latter-day Saints should rejoice—as the heavens undoubtedly do—at the great works of righteousness and faith, and the leavening influence on the world, of those whose lives are touched in any degree by Christ. But it is only in The Church of Jesus Christ of Latter-day Saints, which the Lord himself has proclaimed to be "the only true and living church upon the face of the whole earth" (D&C 1:30), that "the power of God unto salvation" (Romans 1:16) is found. The Restoration of the fulness of the gospel, with its priesthood and other blessings, took place because it is only in *its* light that salvation in its true sense is possible to mankind. While these are absent as Satan sits enthroned in what was once the Lord's Church, Satan's goal of hindering God's children from returning to their Father's glory is realized. How appropriate, therefore, is Paul's description of him sitting in the place of God in the church of the *apostasía*.

In the next verse, Paul punctuated his prophecy by reminding the Saints that he had taught them of the Apostasy and the coming of Satan into the Church when he had been with them personally: "Remember ye not, that, when I was yet with you, I told you these things?" (2 Thessalonians 2:5). But his message did not stop there. Even at that time, said Paul, the "man of sin" was being restrained "from appearing before his appointed time" (2 Thessalonians 2:6, JB). "For the mystery of lawlessness [KJV, 'mystery of iniquity'] is already at work; only he who now restrains it will do so until he is out of the way. And then the lawless one will be revealed" (2 Thessalonians 2:7–8, RSV). In these verses, Paul stated that the overt manifestation of Satan in the Church was still in the future. Yet even then the "mystery of iniquity" was operating, waiting in the wings, as it were, for its chance to come to the fore. Paul wrote of some force which restrained the "man of sin" from making his appearance before his time. It is not altogether clear whether he is referring to the Lord, the collective power of the apostleship, or something or someone else as the obstacle to the day of the "man of sin." In any case, the message comes through clearly that Satan and his works were at that time already operational but were being held back until the divine power that restrained them would "be taken out of the way. And then shall that wicked one be revealed" (2 Thessalonians 2:7–8, JST).[8]

In verses 9–12, Paul told of Satan's deceptive power with his church and apostate priesthood. They would come with "power and signs and lying wonders, and with all deceivableness of unrighteousness." Those who would follow them are they who "received not the love of the truth," who "believe a lie," and who "believed not the truth, but had pleasure in unrighteousness." In short, Satan's work, accompanied by signs and miracles meant to counterfeit those of the Lord's true servants, would prosper because the Saints would reject the truth and believe falsehood.

Second Thessalonians 2:1–12 constitutes perhaps the most important prophecy in the New Testament concerning the Apostasy. Scholars of all perspectives generally agree that Paul is, in fact, expressing his belief in a rebellion against God that would precede the anticipated Second Advent of Jesus Christ.[9] What they do not agree on, of course, is what such a rebellion means and how it would manifest itself. Through the light of the restored gospel, Latter-day Saints can understand Paul's words in proper perspective.

1 Timothy 4:1–3. In Paul's first letter to Timothy, he prophesied concerning the departure of some of the Saints from the faith. "Now the Spirit speaketh expressly, that in the latter times some shall depart from the faith, giving heed to seducing spirits, and doctrines of devils; speaking lies in hypocrisy; having their conscience seared with a hot iron; forbidding to marry, and commanding to abstain from meats, which God hath created to be received with thanksgiving of them which believe and know the truth" (1 Timothy 4:1–3).

This prophecy has a number of features that make it of considerable interest. First of all, Paul specifically stated that his belief in the future defection was the result of revelation. In fact, not only did the Spirit speak these words to Paul, but it did so "expressly." The chronological note is also important. Paul used the term "latter times" (*hústeroi kairoí*) to denote the period in which the developments that he foretold would take place. In the ultimate sense, the period of time in which we now live can be called "the latter times" better than any other. As we learn through modern revelation, our day is the dispensation of the fulness of times—the preparatory era that precedes the Second Coming of the Savior. Yet Paul spoke using a different definition for "latter times." His focus was on the last days of the Christianity of his era, the "latter times" of the early Church.

A few decades after Paul foretold the departure of some from the faith in the "latter times," Jude announced to his readers that they were then in "the last time" (*éschatos chrónos;* see Jude 1:17–19). Similarly, John expressed to the readers of his first letter the certainty of the fact that they themselves were in "the last hour" (*eschátē hōrā;* see 1 John 2:18–19). Clearly John and Jude knew that they were not in the final era of the world, but their words reveal the fact that they knew that they were in the final days of the Christian Church. That was the period of time concerning which the Spirit spoke "expressly" to Paul. Paul's term "the last days" in 2 Timothy 3:1 (*eschatai hemerai*) should be understood in the same light.

As we have seen in other prophecies examined so far, the departure from the faith would be a defection from true principles of doctrine. Paul wrote that those who would depart would give heed to what he calls "seducing spirits" and "doctrines of devils." It must be emphasized that what Paul saw was not an abandonment of religion but a shifting of loyalties from "the faith" to a false faith. Accompanying this defection would be the manifestation of the negative character traits cited in verse 2 (see also 2 Timothy 3:2–4).

Verse 3 is interesting because it mentions two examples of the false ideas that the counterfeit religious system would foster: a prohibition against marriage and a prohibition against certain foods. Beyond that the Apostle gave no further details.

In his prophecy in 1 Timothy, Paul did not express any of the feelings of doom or urgency that are so obvious in the letters of his fellow Apostle John, written about thirty-five years later. Yet for Paul, the present danger was real enough that he admonished Timothy personally to reject strange ideas (see v. 7) and to remind "the brethren" of his warnings (v. 6).

2 Timothy 3:1–5, 13. In the prophecy in 2 Timothy 3, which parallels that of 1 Timothy 4, Paul told his beloved coworker that "perilous times" would come in the last days (v. 1). In this passage, he emphasized the spiritual depravity that would be characteristic of the world in that era. "This know also, that in the last days perilous times shall come. For men shall be lovers of their own selves, covetous, boasters, proud, blasphemers, disobedient to parents, unthankful, unholy, without natural affection, truce-breakers, false accusers, incontinent, fierce, despisers of those that are good, traitors, heady, highminded, lovers of pleasures more than lovers of God" (2 Timothy 3:1–4). Elder Bruce R. McConkie has referred to such things as "signs of the times,"[10] common to an age of the world in which the sanctifying power of the gospel is rejected and the Lord's Spirit is withdrawn.

Paul continued his sentence as follows: "having a form of godliness; but denying the power thereof" (2 Timothy 3:5). Latter-day Saints recognize these words as being among those spoken by the Lord to the Prophet Joseph Smith (see Joseph Smith–History 1:19). Paul's point within the context of his prophecy of the time of apostasy is that despite the inward corruption, the outward trappings of sanctity would remain. Yet the power of God would not be found there. It was in such a circumstance that the Lord spoke the same words to Joseph Smith in response to his question about which of the churches of his day was right.

As Paul continued his warning to Timothy of "perilous times" ahead, he spoke with increasing concern. In verse 13 we read, "But evil men and seducers shall wax worse and worse, deceiving, and being deceived." The fact that Paul knew that those "perilous times" were not far in the future is demonstrated by his personal plea to Timothy in verse 14: "But continue *thou* in the things which thou hast learned and hast been assured of, knowing of whom thou hast learned them" (emphasis added). Paul was confident of Timothy's unceasing faithfulness if he would but *continue* in the things that the Apostle had taught him and also in the words of the scriptures (see v. 15). For others of Timothy's generation there was more cause for concern.

2 Timothy 4:3–4. Paul's final prophecy of the abandonment of true religion is found in the last chapter of 2 Timothy. From the New International Version we read: "For the time will come when men will not put up with sound doctrine. Instead, to suit their own desires, they will gather around them a great number of teachers to say what their itching ears want to hear. They will turn their ears away from the truth and turn aside to myths" (2 Timothy 4:3–4). This passage paints a picture of rejection of the truth that is consistent in every detail with the other prophecies examined so far. In the verses that precede it, Paul charged Timothy strongly to "preach," "correct, rebuke and encourage" (NIV) the Saints. Verse 3 reveals that the reason for his urgency is the fact that he knew that a time was coming in which the Saints would no longer accept the truth. Paul's desire in this, his last preserved letter, was to hold off the onslaught of the inevitable rebellion. As has been noted already, what he foresaw was not an abandonment of religion. Much more serious than that, it was a willful rejection of true doctrine and its replacement by doctrines which were untrue but more to the liking of the hearers. Notice that the people involved, although unwilling to put up with correct teachings, desired teachings nonetheless. Having "itching ears," that is, a desire to hear religion, they would acquire teachers whose doctrines were acceptable to them. The final outcome of their actions would be the abandonment of truth and the acceptance of "fables."

2 Peter 2:1–3. Paul was not alone among the Apostles in prophesying doom for early Christianity. In 2 Peter, the chief Apostle foretold the introduction of false teachers into the Church. "But there were false prophets also among the people, even as there shall be false teachers among you, who privily shall bring in damnable heresies, even denying the Lord that bought them, and bring upon themselves swift destruction. And many shall follow their pernicious ways; by reason of whom the way of truth shall be evil spoken of" (2 Peter 2:1–2).

These false teachers, according to Peter, would "secretly introduce" (NIV) "damnable heresies." So successful would they be that as a result of their efforts, "the way of truth" would be blasphemed (future passive from *blasphēméō*).[11] Verse 3, quoted as follows from the New International Version, tells us more: "In their greed these teachers will exploit you with stories they have made up." This tells us something concerning their purpose: to exploit the members of the Church (KJV, "make merchandise of you"), and their method of doing so: by making up doctrine.

1 John 2:18; Jude 1:4, 17–18. There are a few passages in the New Testament that give evidence indirectly that an apostasy had been foretold. Of these, the most informative are found in 1 John 2:18 and Jude 1:4, 17–18. These verses actually speak of apostasy already present in the Church. While doing so they make mention of the fact that the Saints knew that it would come and had been warned appropriately. John wrote: "Little children, it is the last time: and as *ye have heard that antichrist shall come,* even now are there many antichrists; whereby we know that it is the last time" (1 John 2:18; emphasis added). What is important at this point is the fact that John reminded the Saints to whom he wrote that they had heard earlier that a time would come—called the "last time" (*eschátē hōrā*)— in which "antichrist" would come among the Church. They had been warned.

Similarly, Jude wrote: "Certain people have infiltrated among you, *and they are the ones you had a warning about,* in writing, long ago, when they were condemned for denying all religion, turning the grace of our God into immorality, and rejecting our only Master and Lord, Jesus Christ" (Jude 1:4, JB; emphasis added). This passage, which is much less clear in the King James Version and some other translations, tells that the readers had received written warning in the past of the coming of "godless men" (NIV) who would pervert the gospel and reject the Lord. After writing more about those predicted apostates and likening them to some of more ancient times, Jude continued: "But, dear friends, remember what the apostles of our Lord Jesus Christ foretold. They said to you, 'In the last times there will be scoffers who will follow their own ungodly desires.' These are the men who divide you, who follow mere natural instincts and do not have the Spirit" (Jude 17–19, NIV; emphasis added). The coming in the "last time" (*éschatos chrónos*) of those who would scoff at the true faith had been foretold, according to Jude, by "the apostles."

Revelation 13:1–9. The final prophecy to be examined is found in Revelation 13. Here we read John's vision of the victory of the forces of Satan over the Saints of the Lord. In chapter 12, John characterized the continual conflict between Satan and the works of God as the efforts of a red dragon—Satan—to destroy a woman and her children. In Revelation 12:17 we read, "And the dragon was wroth with the woman, and went to make war with the remnant of her seed, which keep the commandments of God, and have the testimony of Jesus Christ." This is part of an ongoing conflict that has existed since before man was placed on the earth, and it will continue until Satan suffers final defeat following the Millennium (see Revelation 20:10).

The episode from that conflict that is recorded in chapter 13 is directly relevant to the end of the early Christian Church. As the vision continued, John saw the appearance of a beast, "having seven heads and ten horns, and upon his horns ten crowns, and upon his heads the name of blasphemy" (Revelation 13:1). This beast was the agent of the dragon, Satan, from whom he had received "his power and his throne and great authority" (Revelation 13:2, NIV). In John's narrative, we find the beast blaspheming God, God's name, His dwelling place, and those who live in heaven (cf. *blasphēméō* in 2 Peter 2:2). John continued: "And it was given unto him to make war with the saints, *and to overcome them:* and power was given him over all kindreds, and tongues, and nations" (Revelation 13:7; emphasis added).

Without yielding to the temptation to attach rigid interpretations to John's metaphors, I feel that the information provided for us is sufficient to enable us to draw two confident conclusions about the beast, its identity, and its work. First of all, it is a deputy of Satan; it derives its power from him and does his work (see Revelation 13:2, 4). As God's work is "to bring to pass the immortality and eternal life of man" (Moses 1:39), Satan's and that of his beast is to do the opposite. The Prophet Joseph Smith said that the beast was "in the likeness of the kingdoms of the earth"

(Revelation 13:1, JST). "Kingdom" in a scriptural context can mean, of course, any kind of institution, movement, force, or power—religious, political, or otherwise. The second statement that we can make concerning the beast is that it accomplished what it was sent to do. Verse 7 records the tragic fact that it succeeded: it overcame the Saints.

In viewing John's beast in the light of its context in Revelation 13 and other prophetic statements concerning the fall of the Church, we can identify it as the institutions or forces of Satan that prevailed over early Christianity following the time of the Apostles. As for the nature of those forces, it should be remembered that the scriptures we have examined so far present in clear focus the prophetic vision of the Apostles: the cause of the Apostasy would be the rejection of the truth by the members of the Church. In this light, the beast seen by John that overcame the Saints might be interpreted best as being Christianity itself—not the Christianity of Jesus, Peter, John, and Paul, but the Christianity that overcame the Saints and Apostles and survived into the next generation.

CONCLUSION

The foregoing scriptural passages demonstrate that Jesus and His Apostles knew that the church that they headed would come to an end shortly after their generation. They bore a somber witness to that knowledge in the record that they left behind for later readers—the New Testament. All Christians who take seriously the apostolic testimony must reckon with the prophetic word of the inspired witnesses that the forces of false religion would prevail over those of the truth and that the church which was guided by the power of the apostleship in the first century would no longer exist in the second.

NOTES

1. See, for example, James E. Talmage, *The Great Apostasy* (Salt Lake City: Deseret Book, 1909); James E. Talmage, *Articles of Faith* (Salt Lake City: The Church of Jesus Christ of Latter-day Saints, 1913), 198–216. After the original publication of this article in 1983, I expanded on the theme in "Watch and Remember: The New Testament and the Great Apostasy," John M. Lundquist and Stephen D. Ricks, eds., in *By Study and Also By Faith: Essays in Honor of Hugh W. Nibley on the Occasion of His Eightieth Birthday, Vol. 1* (Salt Lake City: Deseret Book and FARMS, 1990), 81–117, a briefer version of which appeared earlier as "Early Signs of Apostasy," *Ensign,* December 1984, 8–16. My book *From Apostasy to Restoration* (Salt Lake City: Deseret Book, 1996), 8–18, summarizes the same thoughts and

puts the apostasy in the broader context of Early Christianity and the Restoration.

2. All biblical quotations are from the King James Version unless indicated otherwise by the following abbreviations: JB—Jerusalem Bible, JST—Joseph Smith Translation, NIV—New International Version, Phillips—Phillips Modern English Version, Reicke—Bo Reicke, *The Epistles of James, Peter, and Jude,* vol. 37 of the Anchor Bible series (Garden City, NY: Doubleday, 1964), RSV—Revised Standard Version.

3. John Foxe, *Book of Martyrs* (London: Seeley and Burnside, 1837), 1:27–32.

4. Albrecht Oepke, "Enistemi," *Theological Dictionary of the New Testament,* ed. G. Kittel (Grand Rapids, MI: Eerdmans, 1964), 2:543–44.

5. Heinrich Schlier, "Apostasia," *Theological Dictionary of the New Testament,* ed. G. Kittel, 10 vols. (Grand Rapids, MI: Eerdmans, 1964), 1:513–14; F. F. Bruce, *1 and 2 Thessalonians,* vol. 45 of the Word Biblical Commentary (Waco, TX: Word Books, 1982), 166.

6. See, for example, Bruce R. McConkie, *Doctrinal New Testament Commentary,* 3 vols. (Salt Lake City: Bookcraft, 1973), 3:63; Sidney B. Sperry, *Paul's Life and Letters* (Salt Lake City: Bookcraft, 1955), 103.

7. William F. Orr and James Arthur Walther, *1 Corinthians,* vol. 32 of the Anchor Bible series (Garden City, NY: Doubleday, 1976), 172–74.

8. Bruce, *1 and 2 Thessalonians,* 170–71; John W. Bailey, "2 Thessalonians, Exegesis," in *The Interpreter's Bible* (Nashville: Abingdon, 1955), 328.

9. See, for example, Bailey, "2 Thessalonians, Exegesis," 327.

10. Bruce R. McConkie, *The Millennial Messiah* (Salt Lake City: Deseret Book, 1982), 42.

11. Hermann W. Beyer, "Blasphemeo," in Kittel, *Theological Dictionary of the New Testament,* 1:621–25.

INDEX

and baptism, 361; evidences of redemptive work in, 362–63; hymn about, 363; brings liberation, 377
Destruction, 385–86, 388, 390
Diaspora, 238
Diatessaron, 78
Disciple(s): suffering of, 83, 97–98, 138; impressed by healing, 96; being true, 98, 104; and love, 159; abandon Christ, 180, 343–44; don't understand resurrection, 193–94, 200–201, 202; Christ appears to, 202–4; duties of, 275; meaning of word, 331
Discipleship, 307
Divorce, 3–4, 218–19
Doctrinal New Testament Commentary, 79
Doctrine, false, 71–72, 75, 403
Doctrine and Covenants, 11–12
Draper, Richard D., 155, 190–206, 373–93

Elias, 6–7, 111
Elijah, 123
Elijah, 192
Elisabeth, 99, 103, 110–11, 119
Elisha, 192
Enable, 169
Endless, 374, 391 n. 7
Enemies, 2–3
Enoch, 364
Ephesians, 232
Epiphanius, 368
Equity, 2
Ergon, 313–15
Eternal life: heirs of, 272; and work, 273; Christ gives, 282; sealed up to, 338–39, 380–81
Eunuch, 73
Eupolemus, 246
Europe, 256
Eusebius, 190, 228, 230, 246
Evil, 21, 388
Evolution, 18
Example, 290, 305–6

Excommunication, 285
Eyewitness(es): Peter as, 4–5; do not convince everyone, 7; as foundation of testimony, 99; of crucifixion, 198; Paul and, 213–17. *See also* Witness(es)
Eyring, Henry B., 152
Ezekiel, 40, 65

Fables, 402
Faith: as personal, 7; light of, 28; justification by, 47, 270–72; activates Atonement, 169; in God's love, 173; and works, 273, 313–19; as body of truth, 313; as response to truth, 313; as gift, 314; as obedience, 314; as active, 315; and belief, 315–16; incompatible with fear, 341
Fall of Adam: and Atonement, 63, 268–69; brought death, 135; mankind not punished for, 165–66
Faust, James E., 1–7
Fear, 160, 341
Feast of Tabernacles, 143
Featherstone, Vaughn J., 35 n. 16
Federalist, The, 20, 21
First Vision, 319
Fish, 330
Fitzmyer, Joseph A., 212–13
Flesh, 269, 277–78
Foreordination, 119
Forgiveness: in parable of prodigal son, 29; suffering for, 167; promise of, 169; and faith, 171; Paul on, 233
Fornication. *See* Immorality
Founding Fathers, 19–20
Four Gospels as One, The, 79
Fourth Formula of Sirmium, 357
Freedom, 21, 63, 297, 307–8. *See also* Agency; Liberty
Fruit(s), 159, 277–79, 304
Full, 151
Furnish, Victor, 242

Gabriel, 99, 109–10

of Luke; 183, in Gospel of John, 184–85; and meekness, 337

Jude, 403–4

Judgment: based on intent of heart, 1–2; of God, 30; accepting Christ at day of, 40; Book of Mormon explains, 64–66; final, 166; Christ speaks against, 224; in book of Revelation, 382–83, 387

Justice: and equity, 2; Christ satisfied, 62, 134, 168; and mercy, 72, 167; law of, 167–68

Justification: by law, 47, 49–50, 52, 270; by Holy Ghost, 47, 50, 54–56, 272; by blood, 47, 52, 54; by faith, 47, 270–72; simplicity of, 47–48; definition of, 48–50; need for, 51–52, 54; inheritance and, 53; ongoing, 55; Jesus Christ and, 55–56; contradictions about, 55–57

Justin, 362

Kadash, 48–49, 57

Keller, Roger R., 92–107

Kelly, J. N. D., 357–58

Kenyon, Frederic, 14

Keys, 334–37, 376–77

Kimball, Spencer W., 167, 293, 345–47

King Benjamin: on walking guiltless, 55; on Christ's suffering, 62, 70; on children of Christ, 156; on service, 305

Kingdom, 141, 145, 404–5

King James Version, 9

King of Kings: The New Testament Story of Christ, 80

Knowledge, 317

Laban, 303

Lamb, 378–79, 389

Largey, Dennis L., 59–76

Last days: Book of Mormon written for, 42, 72; harvest in, 382–84; of early Church, 400–401; as "perilous times," 401–2

Last Supper, 342–43

Latter-day Saints: and New Testament, vii; scriptures of, 9–10, 15, 80; as realists, 10; beliefs of, about Christ, 13–16; and personal revelation, 43; and Book of Mormon study, 59; and knowledge of Atonement, 62–63; scripture scholars among, 209; early, 256; and grace, 272; and agency, 296; spiritual progress of, 303, 307; and apostasy, 394–95

Law: letter of, 1, 4; spirit of, 1, 4; and justification, 47, 49–50, 52, 270; violating, 53; and sanctification, 56; ends of, 62; Christians obey, 85; blessings and, 167; commitment to, 299–300; higher, 301

Law of Moses: fulfilled in Christ, 4, 85, 258, 260–61; and lineage of priests, 111; dietary restrictions of, 222, 258; and circumcision, 260–61, 279–80, 287; lingers among Saints after Christ, 264–65; Gentiles follow, 298; as schoolmaster, 300–301; Paul's opponents cling to, 302–3, 308

Lazarus, 164

Leaders, 307

Learning, 248

Lee, Harold B., 333

Lehi, 63, 71

Lewis, C. S., 153, 158, 169–70

Liberty: using, to choose right, 297; and law, 300–301; and Spirit, 301–4; and love, 304–6; restricting own, 305–6; and following Brethren, 306–7; Paul on, 308. *See also* Agency; Freedom

Lieberman, S., 240

Light, of Christ, 286, 375

Lion, 378

Longnecker, Richard, 301

Loofs, F., 355–56

Love: for enemies, 2–3; as theme of Gospel of John, 150–61, 173;